PENGU

Ascen

As well as being a novelist, John Matthews is an experienced journalist, editor and publishing consultant, though after the success of *Past Imperfect*, which became an international bestseller, he has devoted most of his time to writing books. In 2004, *The Times* compiled a list of top ten all-time-best legal thrillers which included *Past Imperfect*. He lives in Surrey with his wife and son.

Praise for John Matthews and his books:

'Matthews certainly knows how to keep the reader hungry for the next revelation.' *Kirkus UK*

'Matthews maintains the suspense . . . an engrossing odyssey into the seamy side of a world that is so near, yet sometimes seems so far. Compulsive reading.' *The Times*

'Impressive . . . strong characterization and a relentless race against time to avert the worst carry the reader along the thick pages of this psychological and legal thriller with a difference.' *Time Out*

'One of the most compelling novels I've read . . . an ambitious and big novel which will keep you enthralled to its last page.' *Cork Examiner*

'Matthews delivers one of the best debut thrillers in years, brave, ambitious and remorselessly entertaining. *Past Imperfect* is a stormer.' *Dublin Evening Herald*

'Distinctively written . . . all the forceful energy of the best thrillers.' *Kirkus UK*

'A thumping great read and a terrific tale, terrifically told.'
Ireland on Sunday

Ascension Day:

'*Ascension Day* is like a narcotic, laced with danger, and totally addictive. Impossible to put down. This is what thrillers are meant to be. Jac McElroy is a character I want to read more of.' Jon Jordan, *Crime Spree Magazine*

'If John Grisham ever developed a sense of irony, or Scott Turow ever tried to write from the other side of the prison bars, they might come up with something like John Matthews's *Ascension Day*. This is a book that doesn't sacrifice style for suspense, or character for plot. The legal thriller has needed a jolt of electricity for a few years now and Matthews may just be the man to throw the switch.' Peter Blauner, author of *Slipping Into Darkness* and *The Intruder*

'*Ascension Day* is a fast-paced thriller set between New Orleans and an upstate Louisiana prison, and Matthews's strong descriptive prose brings the darkness at the heart of Libreville penitentiary alive. His chief protagonist, Jac McElroy, is particularly interesting with his Franco-Scottish heritage and his ever-changing relationship with prisoner Larry Durrant sets the main pulse for this race-against-time thriller . . . with the stakes and tension ratcheted up throughout the book.' Luke Croll, *Reviewing the Evidence*

'Lock the doors and turn off the phone. Once you start this compelling, thoughtful, edge-of-your-seat thriller, you won't have time for anything else. A riveting read that hits it just right – right on the knife-edge between psychological and action thriller.' Chris Mooney, Edgar-nominated author of *Remembering Sarah*

Ascension Day

JOHN MATTHEWS

PENGUIN BOOKS

PENGUIN BOOKS

Published by the Penguin Group
Penguin Books Ltd, 80 Strand, London WC2R ORL, England
Penguin Group (USA) Inc., 375 Hudson Street, New York, New York 10014, USA
Penguin Group (Canada), 90 Eglinton Avenue East, Suite 700, Toronto, Ontario, Canada M4P 2Y3
(a division of Pearson Penguin Canada Inc.)
Penguin Ireland, 25 St Stephen's Green, Dublin 2, Ireland
(a division of Penguin Books Ltd)
Penguin Group (Australia), 250 Camberwell Road, Camberwell, Victoria 3124, Australia
(a division of Pearson Australia Group Pty Ltd)
Penguin Books India Pvt Ltd, 11 Community Centre,
Panchsheel Park, New Delhi – 110 017, India
Penguin Group (NZ), 67 Apollo Drive, Rosedale, North Shore 0632, New Zealand
(a division of Pearson New Zealand Ltd)
Penguin Books (South Africa) (Pty) Ltd, 24 Sturdee Avenue,
Rosebank, Johannesburg 2196, South Africa

Penguin Books Ltd, Registered Offices: 80 Strand, London WC2R ORL, England

www.penguin.com

First published in Penguin Books 2007
1

Copyright © John Matthews, 2007
All rights reserved

The author and publishers are grateful to Crosstown Songs
for permission to reproduce lyrics from Fleetwood Mac/
Peter Green's 'Man of the World'

The moral right of the author has been asserted

Set in 11.75/14 pt Monotype Bembo
Typeset by Rowland Phototypesetting Ltd, Bury St Edmunds, Suffolk
Printed in England by Clays Ltd, St Ives plc

Except in the United States of America, this book is sold subject
to the condition that it shall not, by way of trade or otherwise, be lent,
re-sold, hired out, or otherwise circulated without the publisher's
prior consent in any form of binding or cover other than that in
which it is published and without a similar condition including this
condition being imposed on the subsequent purchaser

ISBN: 978-0-141-00485-3

I

October 2004. Libreville, Louisiana.

At first, Larry wasn't sure why the sound had awoken him.

He'd become familiar with all the usual night-time sounds: the clunk of the cell doors and the rattle of keys whenever anyone had to be let in or out unexpectedly after last shutdown; the steady, ominous clump of boots along the steel walkways with the regular cell patrols every hour, punctuated by the impromptu sliding back of two or three inspection hatches along the line; the mumble of the guards at the end and the occasional peal of laughter; the jibes and taunts of new prisoners or regulars who'd suddenly fallen from grace; the gentle sobbing of some of those same new inmates that might take up to a week to finally abate; and the klaxon blare of the Amtrak from Baton Rouge to Jackson seven miles away across the Bayou plain, a siren call to the prisoners from the world outside, elusive freedom – only one of eight attempted break-outs over the past thirty years had got even that far, and they'd all been rounded up within the week between New Orleans and Baton Rouge.

Over the past eleven long years, these sounds had been Lawrence Tyler Durrant's nightly companions. But this sound was different.

He could recognize the voices of two of the guards, but they were fighting not to be heard: little more than muted whispers along with the soft sliding back of the bolts on a cell door. Normally, their boot-steps would be heavy and purposeful, cell-door bolts would be slammed back like gunshots, whatever the time of night, and the prisoner's name shouted out, as if by some miracle the clamour of the guards' approach might not have awoken him along with everyone else on the cell-block row.

This time they didn't want anyone to hear them.

Larry kept his breathing low and shallow, trying to pick out more. But suddenly his heart was drumming fast and strong, threatening to drown everything out. And when he finally tuned in beyond his own heartbeat, everything was still and silent, as if they somehow knew he was listening in. Then a sudden flurry of shuffling footsteps from five or six cells along.

'*What*? . . . What the ffffmmm!'

Even from that muffled exclamation, before a hand was clamped across to completely strangle it, Larry clearly recognized the clipped Latino intonation: Rodriguez. 'Roddy', who'd managed to make him smile and laugh on even the darkest of days; a rare spark of light and life in this pit of gloom he'd called home for over a decade, and one of the closest friends he'd ever had, inside or out. He couldn't just close his mind and shut his eyes, as he had to so much over the years.

Maybe he could have turned away if he thought they were just going to give Roddy a beating, but he'd seen that look fired across the canteen earlier by Tally Shavell. It was only a fleeting stare, but in Libreville that was often all you got as warning. The last two on the end of that same look from Tally had both been killed; one with a shiv through the neck in the showers, the other garrotted with a guitar string. There was no reason to believe that with Roddy it would be any different, especially after the beating Tally had given him five months back. Tally didn't issue second warnings.

Larry looked towards his cell's makeshift altar with its array of photos for inspiration: his mother who'd died after a stroke in year five of his sentence, ten months after his appeal failed; his father who'd died when he was only fourteen, mercifully before he'd started to slip into bad ways; his wife, Francine, who hadn't visited him for the first five years and after that only infrequently, depending on her current-partner-situation, though they still hadn't divorced yet; his son, Joshua, now twelve, who, except for some recent e-mail contact, he'd seen at most half-a-dozen times over the years – occasional birthdays and at Christmas-time. The only one not represented from his family was his elder sister, who'd disowned him the day of his incarceration, told his mother – as if she didn't already have enough heartbreak that day – that as far as she was concerned 'he no longer exists'.

But swamping his family photos were religious prints: Dali's *Christ on the Cross*, Michelangelo's *Creation of Adam*, Da Vinci's *Last Supper*, Caravaggio's *St Francis*, Raphael's *Madonna and Child*.

When word had first got around that Larry had found religion, one of the other inmates, Sal Peretti, had his aunt, who still lived in her native Umbria, send a collection of prints and cards, eleven in all, from the gift shop at Perugia Cathedral, to complete the array on his makeshift altar.

Upon sight of the finished display, given a misty, eerie glow from fifteen interspersed candles, Roddy had commented simply, 'Christ!'

'Exactly.' Larry smiled back drolly.

Now Larry wasn't looking just at the altar for inspiration, but beyond – his eyes boring through to the hole they'd dug in the wall behind, along the ventilation shaft, then the twists and dog-legs through three hundred yards of ducting barely enough to squeeze through and two more walls before arriving at the vents by the boiler room; then the final sixty-foot waste-pipe slide to the Achalaya river. The passage that the five of them – himself, Roddy, BC, Sal Peretti and Theo Mellor – knew every inch of, had consumed every spare minute they could steal away over the past ten months.

That's where they'd be taking Roddy, for sure: the boiler room deep in the prison's bowels, where the clank and hiss of the boilers and pipes and two-foot thick walls would prevent even the loudest screams reaching the cells above.

Larry also knew that if he used their escape passage to get to the boiler room, it would be uncovered, their last hope gone and four of them condemned to die. Those were the odds at Libreville: twenty per cent reprieved, pardoned or commuted to life imprisonment, eighty per cent executed.

That was the choice right there: Roddy's life saved for four others lost, including his own. And with two or three attackers now with Roddy, what chance did he have in any case of being able to save him? Another muted mumble from Roddy, fading quickly with the rapid shuffle of footsteps along the outside walkway, gave him a sharp prompt. He had to decide quickly.

But Larry Durrant stayed staring at his makeshift altar, frozen with indecision. Just when he needed guidance the most, there was nothing.

'That's the original trial preparation file. That's the trial transcript and notes. Appeal preparation and appeal transcript and notes.' John Langfranc piled each file on the desk before him, some of them four inches thick, with an appropriate pause. 'Finally, any case notes since.' The last file was thinnest of all. 'Though to be honest, not much has happened over the last seven years. Lawrence Durrant has been all but forgotten. Until now.'

'Now that they're about to kill him,' Jac said, though his disdain could equally have been aimed at the mountain of paperwork he'd have to plough through over the coming days.

Langfranc raised an eyebrow and smiled smugly. 'First thing to get clear, Jac, is that the State of Louisiana never kills anyone. They execute, process, fulfil sentencing, lethally inject, expedite and terminate . . . but they never *kill*. If you're going to use a word like kill, you'll have to get used to putting *legally* in front. Presumably, that one word differentiates the State's actions from those of the people they're killing. Sorry, *processing*.'

'Why me?' Jac asked.

Fair question, thought Langfranc. He shrugged. 'Time for you to prove yourself, I guess.' No point in embellishing beyond that, trying to kid Jac that this might be a landmark glory case. They knew each other too well for that now, and with Jac only passing his criminal law bar exams ten months ago, he'd be aware that he was a long way from being handed the firm's prize cases. 'You and I both know that if there was a good angle left in all of this,' Langfranc waved one hand across the files, 'Beaton would have taken it himself.'

Clive Beaton, senior criminal trial lawyer at Payne, Beaton and Sawyer, New Orlean's second largest law firm, at which Langfranc was a junior partner. Strange title, 'junior', for someone fifty-two years old, Jac had always thought. In a way it further underlined Langfranc's frustration that he should have been made a senior partner earlier. Perhaps one reason why the two of them had bonded so well, the feeling that the firm's main head-pats and accolades had gone to others, often less deserving. Though in Jac's case that was mainly because he'd spent his first years wallowing in corporate and tax law before he'd turned to criminal law. The easy route after his initial years of practice in France; commercial law in Louisiana followed the French Napoleonic code, criminal law didn't.

Langfranc looked up as the clatter from the general office drifted in.

'I've re-scheduled Donneley for three-fifteen,' Penny Vance, his PA who Jac also shared as a secretary, said through the half-open door. 'That will give you a clear hour at Liberty Street. Oh, and Jem Payne has called for an update briefing on Borkowski before you head out this afternoon, so you might have to cut lunch short to make the time.'

The information brought a faint slouch, an extra ruffle to Langfranc's appearance. He always wore the best Versace or Missoni suits with slip-on Italian loafers to match, but with his wild, wavy, greying hair, to Jac he still looked somehow unkempt; as if there'd been a strong breeze on his way into work, and then the rush of the day simply kept him that way.

'Thanks.' Langfranc sighed as the door closed; only ten

minutes into the day and already everything was at full tilt. He brought his attention back to Jac and Durrant's files. 'It's a no-goer from the outset. Full confession. Every possible angle exhausted at the appeal. No new evidence since. Your only hope is to try and get our good – or bad – Lawrence Durrant pardoned. Throw all on the mercy of our good – or bad – Governor. The illustrious Piers Candaret. And to a lesser extent, the Board of Pardons.'

Jac's eyes narrowed. 'Candaret holds the whip hand?'

'Without a doubt. He nominates the Board to begin with, and while they're meant to sift through and review everything on his behalf – when it comes to big cases, he likes to have a hands-on, first look-see. And while he's also meant to accept their recommendations, in many cases he's gone his own way. So, you'll file simultaneously with both of them – but the buck stops with Candaret.'

'And that's all there's left to do – prepare a simple plea letter?'

'Well, there's a tad more to it than that. You're going to have to plough through most of this to get the tone right for the letter. Hit the right notes. Durrant's apparently very religious. Candaret is too, or at least he pushes Christian and family values at every photo opportunity. And by all claims, Durrant has been a model prisoner. Kept his nose clean. So those are probably good start points. We're talking about quite a long, considered clemency plea. Six or seven pages, maybe more – plus any relevant file attachments. It might only take a day to prepare the letter, but you could spend a good week in preparation.' As Langfranc fought to boost the case's merits, Jac's quizzical eyebrow merely arched higher. 'For God's sake, Jac, this is a big case. For Louisiana murder cases, they don't come bigger. So don't make light of it. And whatever might or might not be involved, also don't lose sight of what's at stake here. Good or bad or rotten to hell's core – a man's life.'

'I know. I know.' Jac held up one hand in submission and

bowed his head slightly. When Langfranc had first told him he'd be getting the case, he was excited: murder of the wife of Adelay Roche, one of Louisiana's wealthiest industrialists, the case had occupied more newspaper column inches than any other Louisiana case since the Garrison investigation into the JFK assassination. He'd immediately dived into the library on St Charles Street to leaf through clippings. But most of the attention had been at the time of the trial and the appeal. For the past seven years the newspapers, and the world out-side, had forgotten about Lawrence Tyler Durrant; though now no doubt there'd be a renewed flurry of media activity. 'I suppose I'm just disappointed to know that all the main angles have gone, all avenues for appeal already exhausted. All I'm left with is sweeping up the dust of the case.'

'The only shot at appeal was centred around Durrant's accident and his resultant memory lapses at the time. And all hopes on that front died seven years ago.' Langfranc shrugged. 'And as I said, if there were any angles left, Beaton would have taken the case himself. But it's still a big case, Jac. The biggest. Life or death for Larry Durrant and every local TV network and newspaper, and some beyond, covering which way it's going to swing. You might not be Beaton's golden boy, but the fact that he's even given you a high profile case like this – even if all that's left is a clemency plea – means that he's noticed you. You exist.'

'Therefore I am.'

Langfranc smiled back thinly. Jac McElroy had set his cap on criminal law with a determination that probably was largely lost on old man Beaton. At thirty-one, with six years practice under his belt, he could have just kept coasting along with corporate law, raking in the big bucks. Taken the easy route. But, no, he'd wanted to do criminal law, so that meant going back to square one and taking a fresh set of bar exams alongside a bunch of fresh-faced graduates while still juggling the remainder of his corporate caseload. So that meant he was either crazy, or it was a real vocation. From Jac's first ten

7

months of criminal case-handling, Langfranc hadn't yet made his mind up which.

Jac was thoughtful for a second. 'What's Candaret's track record on pardons and reprieves?'

'Pardons are rare, and will no doubt now be doubly difficult since the last but one guy pardoned, Aaron Harvey – also African-American, as it happens – killed again just six months back. With commuted to life there's far more chance, I think running somewhere between one in five or six. But that could be one of the first things to check – along with case histories. Get a feel for what might hit the right note with Candaret.'

'So, slim chances – but not impossible.'

Langfranc held one palm out. 'Better than that buffoon in Texas. Like his predecessor, he sends everyone for the chop. No exceptions. Thinks that's what the public wants, might make him potential White House material. And Florida's not much better. At least with Candaret there's *some* chance.'

Jac studied the files a second longer, then laid one hand firmly on top of them, exhaling wearily. 'Don't worry. Slim hopes or not, I'll give it my best shot. I won't let Larry Durrant down.'

But belying the brooding look that Jac gave the files, Langfranc caught a fleeting gleam in his eyes – challenge, defiance – that sounded a faint alarm bell. In Jac McElroy's first year with the firm, Langfranc had often found him sullen and contemplative, which as they'd got to know each other he'd learnt was due to the recent death of Jac's father – a Scotsman who twenty-odd years ago had taken his family to France to pursue his dream of running an artists' retreat. But Langfranc had also discovered that nothing lifted Jac out of that slump like a good challenge. Of only eleven criminal cases that Jac had so far handled solo – the most serious a grand-theft auto and representing a colourful local forger, Morvaun Jaspar – he'd turned four of them into major pro-ductions. 'And no grandstanding and glory-searching on this one. No screaming the client's innocence against impossible odds. That's not what Beaton wants, nor what the case calls for.'

'Rest easy, I'll be a good boy.' Jac stood up and hoisted the files under one arm, firing Langfranc a strained smile as he took on the extra weight. 'I'll do what I'm told and just sweep up the dust.'

Just a look.

There'd been a few derisory looks from Tally to Roddy during the first couple of years, but nothing too intense or worrying. Just a sly, conciliatory smile and shrug, 'Funny guy,' as the other inmates guffawed and belly-laughed at Roddy's latest quip.

None of the comments was aimed at Tally, and on occasion when the target was someone he didn't like, he'd join in laughing with everyone else. But gradually resentment grew in Tally at Roddy's constant flow of jokes and jibes, as if, as Roddy's popularity grew as a result, Tally felt that his power base was being threatened; or simply because humour undermined the mood of menace and fear which helped Tally operate more effectively.

But that was exactly why everyone loved Roddy: a rare, bright light in the stifling gloom, he lifted everyone's spirits, made them forget, even if for only part of the day, where they were. For Larry in particular, Roddy had been a godsend, a lifeline, arriving at Libreville only five months after Larry's mother died and his spirits were at their lowest.

Just a look. The first came when Roddy compared the grunts, snorts and hisses coming from the men in the muscle yard to the pigs at feeding time in Libreville's farm compound. Tally overheard, and took it as an insult of the muscle-yard men in general, and of him, as their leader, in particular. He warned Roddy that if he was loose with his mouth again, he'd be taught a lesson.

The second came when Peretti complained that his library

9

duties weren't giving him enough time either for farm duty or general exercise. He was finding it hard to keep in shape.

'Don' worry,' Roddy assured. 'You got the best end of the deal. Some of those guys on farm duty are worked till they drop. And as for the yard guys, they might be developin' their pecs and abs – but not much up here.' Roddy tapped his forehead. 'The only time they use a fuckin' tome is as a doorstop or to rest barbells either side o' their head.'

Roddy had made sure this time that Tally was out of earshot, but one of the other yard-men overheard, and duly reported.

Tally beat Roddy to within an inch of his life, using two of his favourite books: *Murder Machine* and *Hollywood Hulk Hogan*.

'So, we never read tomes, huh?' he taunted, misquoting selected lines from the books with each blow: ' "I don' min' killing people, I just don' like takin' 'em to pieces . . ." "But right there, that's my damn place and nobody can fuck wit' me . . ." ' The irony lost on Tally that if not his choice of reading, then certainly his quotes, simply supported the claims of illiteracy.

The books were heavier in weight than content or merit, cracking two of Roddy's ribs, bruising his shoulders and chest to the point of bleeding in three places, and breaking his nose and two finger joints where he'd put one arm up to protect himself. Tally warned that if it happened again, he'd be taken out.

That final look, just two days ago, had come when Arneck, BC, Peretti and Roddy had been discussing what had originally landed Tally in Libreville.

'Some scam involving computer clocks adjusting for Y2K, by all accounts,' Arneck offered. 'During the overnight downtime to make the switch, the interest on a score of bank and insurance accounts was routed to an outside account.'

'Not exactly what you'd expect from Tally,' Peretti said. 'White collar crime like that.'

BC huffed. ''Cept that's not what landed him here. 'Sfor cutting his partner's throat, when he tried to stiff Tally outta part o' the fuckin' take.'

'So, more like red collar crime,' Roddy quipped.

Everyone laughed, except Peretti, who was still slightly lost in thought and managed only a meek smile. Peretti shook his head.

'Still, not the sort of crime you'd expect Tally to get tied up with in the first place – Y2K scam like that.'

Roddy nodded, smiling drolly. 'Yeah, daresay the closest he's ever come to that is askin' Lay-lo whether he wants some KY too?'

The laughs were louder this time, and Peretti joined in as well. Lay-lo was the name given to Maurice Lavine, a soft, doe-eyed Creole African-Mexican drag-review dancer, who, when made up and wearing the right wig, could give J-Lo a run for her money. Lay-lo had earned a life sentence for poisoning a rival dancer who'd started to steal the limelight, and Tally quickly corralled him as his exclusive love interest.

But it was a touchy subject for Tally – never openly admitted. And for all of their liaisons, Tally had Lay-lo dress up in full regalia – J-Lo, Halle Berry, Beyonce, a different fantasy every time – so that Tally could hide away from the fact that he was having a gay relationship. Not good for his tough guy image. And so Tally also liked to kid himself that it was a closely guarded secret, even though most of the prison knew yet never dared openly talk about it.

Because of the nature of the conversation, they'd made sure that Tally or any of his goons weren't around – but then Tally walked into the canteen just as Roddy delivered his killer punchline. The guffaws and belly-laughs died as quickly as they'd started under Tally's stony stare.

Just a look, but in that moment everyone present knew that Roddy's days, more than anyone else on Libreville's death row, were numbered.

★

Larry regretted the decision as soon as he was a few yards into the ventilation shaft. It was pitch black. Peretti always came armed with the penlight for their digging sessions, from his shared library duty with Larry; with his poor eyesight, he used it for highlighting fine text or picking out titles in the darker corners of the library.

But even if Larry had the penlight now, he wasn't sure he would use it. They never dug at night, and the faint light might be picked out shining through where there were corridor grilles. Though the main reason they never dug at night, even if they could dummy up their beds and sidestep lock-up, was due to the noise; the hectic hubbub and clatter of daytime prison activity drowned out their digging and scratching.

Now it was deathly silent, and Larry was aware that his slightest movements seemed to bounce and echo along the steel shaft and sail free into the prison.

He closed his eyes and swallowed hard as he crawled forward another couple of feet. Anyone close to the shaft could surely hear him. They'd done this journey so many times now that he could picture practically every inch of the prison below him as he went. For another five or six yards, the shaft ran along the back of the cells in his row. Then it crossed a corridor, ran along its side for another eight yards, and dog-logged to run along the back of the cells in J-block.

Careful, *eeeassy does it*, he told himself as he crawled the first stretch at the back of the cells; though maybe if one of the other inmates did hear him, staring wide-eyed at the ceiling and unable to sleep, as he'd done for much of his first year, they wouldn't give him away. *Go on, man. Make it! Make it to freedom! Show some hope for all of us.*

He was doubly careful crossing the stretch running by the corridor, edging forward a few inches at a time. The slightest sound reaching the guards on duty, the alarm would be raised in a heartbeat.

Heartbeat. Pounding rapidly, deafeningly, so that he could hardly tell if his movement was making any noise or not.

Unconsciously, he'd been holding his breath, and as he came to the final yard of the corridor stretch, he started to ease it loose – then suddenly sucked it sharply back up again. And froze.

Footsteps. Boots on steel. Shuffling to a stop almost directly beneath him. Larry wondered if they'd heard him, were at that moment looking up, appraising. Trying to pinpoint exactly where they'd heard sounds coming from.

His chest ached with the effort of keeping his breath held, his heartbeat rapid as if it wanted to burst through. So loud that surely that alone could be heard by the guard below. Larry stayed deathly still.

Another set of footsteps, the muffled sound of voices. *Oh Jesus.* All he needed. They could be there half the night talking about the latest Saints game and sorting out the world.

Tally wouldn't waste time; Roddy's throat would be slit within the first minutes of reaching the boiler room.

The seconds dragged in time with the heavy pounding of his heart. Indecision now freezing his mind along with his body, afraid to move, breath held, for what seemed a lifetime – though was probably no more than ninety seconds – before the footsteps finally started moving away, the voices receding.

Larry scrambled hurriedly on, letting out his breath in a burst as soon as he was a couple of yards into the turn behind the cells and felt he was out of earshot of the guards.

Just what was awaiting him in the boiler room dawned on him. Tally wouldn't do something like this without back-up, never did. Two men, maybe three. Then the couple of guards who'd helped get Roddy out of his cell.

Larry had been good in his day, one of the best, but even then taking out four or five at once would have been a tall order. And unlike Tally and his crew, he didn't spend every day in the muscle yard training up. The hopelessness of what he was attempting weighed heavy on him, telling in the ache in his limbs as he dragged himself through the narrow shaft.

As he came to the junction with the main shaft rising up

13

from the boiler room, the warm air wafting through intensi-fied. He scrambled forward faster, more desperately, not sure whether it was to get away from the intense heat or to ensure that he got to Roddy in time. He'd given up caring whether he was making a noise or not, the thud of his elbows and knees against steel a repetitive, penetrating echo.

He stopped abruptly as he came to the grille by the upper part of the boiler room, hurriedly unscrewed its bolts, and yanked it aside. Still on his hands and knees he kept still, his breathing shallow, taking stock. No sounds or voices that he could pick out.

Though something else reached him in that moment that made him have doubts again: the soft lap and sway of the Achalaya river echoing up through the waste pipe a yard to his side, beckoning, taunting. *Elusive freedom*. Yet suddenly so tangible, real, that he felt he could reach out and touch it.

Probably his last and only chance. He'd long ago decided that he couldn't face another day inside, so a commute to life imprisonment held nothing for him. And his chances of a complete reprieve were practically nil – so his only real hope of freedom lay in what he could hear now with the gentle lapping of the Achalaya river. *Make the break and find out what was happening with Joshua, hold him in your arms again . . . stay back and save Roddy . . . make the break . . .*

Or head back to his cell and then all make the break to-gether in three weeks when the tide would be right, as they'd all originally planned. He wasn't going to be able to save Roddy in any case. One against four or five, he didn't stand a chance. Maybe he should . . .

His thoughts were broken. He could hear voices from the far end of the boiler room.

2

Lawrence Tyler Durrant, born 8 May 1962 in Knoxville, Tennessee, the second child (there's an elder sister) of Nathan Joseph and Myrie-Jane Durrant. The family moved to New Orleans when Durrant was eleven.

First arrested 19 August 1992, six months after the offence, made a full confession on his second interview, held without bail in Oakdale Detention Centre until trial, which ran through April and May 1993. Sentenced to death by lethal injection by Judge Thomas S. Colby on 26 May and bought to Libreville prison.

Jac lifted his head from the files and took a quick sip of coffee, grimacing as it trickled down. It was already cold; he'd been reading longer than he had realized.

Most of the information was in a five-page summary provided at the time of Durrant's appeal, but Jac found himself leafing back through the files each time he hit a key point – parents, siblings, wife and young child, past criminal form – to find out more.

No history of criminality in the family. Nathan Joseph had been a postal sorting worker for most of his life, then later managed a small chain of grocery stores, while Myrie-Jane worked in a local Ninth Ward café once the kids had grown up. The only other family member with any run-ins with the law, though once removed, was Lawrence's first cousin, Simon: juvenile shoplifting and one count of assault when he was nineteen.

Lawrence was a different matter. After five years of trying to make his name as a light-heavyweight boxer, interspersed with casual jobs, he became a serial house thief – though out of four previous arrests, New Orleans PD had only managed to make one conviction stick.

While his falling from grace as a boxer could have been viewed as the start of his criminality, his police file noted that there was 'suspicion of other robberies both before his boxing career and while he was still amateur, albeit that no arrests were made during these periods'. And little pattern of violence connected with the robberies, except on one occasion when he was disturbed and knocked a man unconscious with a couple of pistol-whip blows from behind.

But the NOPD argued that Durrant had simply been lucky enough not to have been seen on any of the past robberies. And on this occasion, Jessica Roche had seen him, and he was desperately afraid of going down for a second time. He'd had a taste of prison, a three-year stretch in Oakdale, and didn't want to return. Second offence, he'd have got a minimum of five years.

Jac rubbed the bridge of his nose. With Durrant's later self-educating and finding religion in prison, his life was certainly one of contrasts – boxer, thief, scholar, preacher – few of them sitting that comfortably together.

Jac went back to the beginning of the segment on Durrant's family. Second marriage to Francine Gleason (Durrant's first at the age of nineteen ended in divorce after only fifteen months) just three years before the Roche break-in, no record of other robberies in that period, or at least none that the NOPD had him down as a specific suspect for, and a baby son, Joshua, only three months old at the time. Not the best timing to re-offend.

But then that had been part of the motive, the prosecution had argued: the financial pressures of the new family and Durrant losing his job as an assistant in a sporting-goods store only six weeks previously. Then his return to heavy drinking and his car accident four months after the murder while out on one of his binges. Larry Durrant's life was a wreck of mishaps and falling from graces. Doing the right thing at the right time was far from his strongest suit.

Then the therapy sessions following the accident to treat his resultant partial amnesia – or 'selective amnesia' as the prosecution later termed it, 'to blank out the darkness of his actions that night with Jessica Roche' – and his confession coming out when . . .

Jac jumped, a sudden bang from next door sounding like a pistol-shot, before he realized it was a door slamming. A man's voice, shouting, came straight after.

'I told you. I don't like you working there any more.'

'And how am I meant to take care of Molly and pay for my courses?' The woman's voice higher-pitched, shriller. Defensive.

'I'm workin' again now, I could take care of you. And you got that *other* money.'

'Yeah, Gerry. And you know what that other money was for. You *know*! And how come you're still splashing it around?'

'Come on, babe – give me some credit. I told you what mine was for, too. But this time, I'm like an assistant bar-manager rather than just a barman . . . and the tips are big.'

Muted mumbling and rustling, as if he was in close, trying to hug and sweet-talk her. Then, after a moment, rising from the mumbling:

'Give it up, babe . . . give it up.' The words punctuated by what sounded like gentle kisses. 'For me. Is that too much to . . .'

'No . . . no!' Sharper, louder. Annoyance at his intimacy to try and sway her. 'It's not even open for . . . *what*? What are you doing? You're hurting me.'

'I just don't like other guys lookin' at you like that. It drives me, well . . . crazy, thinking about it.'

'Yeah, yeah. *Crazy*'s about right. Now let me go.' Brusquer rustling as she wrenched free, and then the slamming of another door.

But his voice followed her, and the argument continued in more muted, indistinct tones behind the closed door.

Jac had heard quite a few arguments coming from next

17

door over the past couple of months. He could hear them clearly when they were in the lounge or kitchen directly adjacent, the bedrooms less so, and the bathroom at the far end not at all.

He listened out for a moment more, but all that reached him was the low drone of traffic, like a muffled swarm of bees, passing on Highway 90 a few blocks away. These were the main disadvantages of his apartment block. At the low-cost end of housing in the Warehouse District, the minimal partition walls meant that you could hear your neighbours when their voices raised, as well as the traffic on the nearby main arteries heading out of the city.

Jac brought his attention back to the files, opening the police report with due veneration and turning over the photos that earlier he'd flipped firmly face-down. He hadn't wanted to look at them initially, in case they influenced his judgement of Larry Durrant before he started. He wanted to get a feel for the man first, then the crime. Get the sequence right.

One gun-shot to the stomach from eight to ten feet, according to ballistics, then the final shot to the head from close range, only a few inches. The photos of Jessica Roche's splayed body were painfully raw and would have had a strong impact on even the most hardened juror: one of her legs was crooked behind her at an impossible angle, her blood on the black-and-whites merging with where she'd soiled her dress, and one side of her face collapsed where her skull had shattered, stark horror in contrast to the beauty of her unblemished side.

Jac rubbed his forehead and reached for his coffee cup, before realizing that it was already empty. He could imagine the first shot being fired by somebody already on edge, suddenly disturbed. But that final shot seemed out of character for someone who'd never killed before, and that thought preyed on Jac's mind as he went through the rest of the police report.

He tried to piece together the sequence of events in his mind from Durrant's confession and the evidence presented at trial.

But still something didn't quite fit, and the same sequence kept replaying in his thoughts long after he'd given up trying to make conscious sense of it, along with the rest of the police report, and had gone to bed.

In the final re-runs, Jac was playing the role of Durrant, standing over Jessica Roche's sprawled body with the still-smoking gun, begging for clues as to why he'd killed her. 'Please tell me . . . if you know? Any small sign. *Anything*!'

But then suddenly the body beneath him became the girl from next door, her long auburn hair cascading either side of her naked body, and she was reaching up for him. 'Make love to me . . . *Fuck me*!'

Jac could feel the heat and sweat of her skin, her hazel eyes piercing straight through him before slowly closing in abandon. 'Oh lover, fuck me. Fuck me!'

And her gasps of pleasure felt all *so real*, Jac so wrapped up in it that he didn't hear Durrant's footsteps from behind, the shot slamming into the body beneath him changing it abruptly back to Jessica Roche – her blood sticky against his skin, replacing the sweat and passion – and Jac struggled to get away from her clutch as the head-shot came . . .

Jac awoke with a jolt – suddenly realizing that it was his neighbour's door slamming again, raised voices following straight after like a tidal wave.

'No, no . . . please, Gerry, please!'

'I ask you one small favour. Just one. But with you . . . *no*. No movement. No negotiation.'

'Please, Gerry, I'm begging you. Don't be like this.'

'That's your problem. You never listen to me. Most other people, I tell 'em once – that's it. But you . . .'

'No, Gerry, please . . . I'm begging you. If I'm bruised, I won't be able to work for a few days.'

'Maybe that's what I want. In fact, that would probably suit me just fine.'

'No, Gerry . . . *No*!' Desperate now, almost a scream. 'You'll wake Molly.'

Snorting derision. 'You make me sick. You use that girl like a shield. And your beauty. And your precious fucking work and your college course. And all I feel like doin' is putting a fist right through it, smashing it all . . .'

'No, Gerry, no!'

Jac heard a thud, together with a shriek from her, and was convinced she'd been hit.

He was now bolt upright in bed, his breathing rapid and fractured with the drama unfolding next door, wondering whether he should go and help her.

The sharp pistol-shot came a second later, and with the long silence following, Jac remained uncertain – his pulse galloping almost in time with his breathing – whether this time it *had* been a gunshot.

But after a moment he was relieved to hear from next door the sound of her gently weeping.

This was the heart of Libreville. Heart of darkness.

Its six oil boilers pumped and spewed hot vented air to the cells, corridors and general open areas, and hot water to the showers, kitchens and laundry area, which was adjacent.

Some air-conditioning units had been linked up to the venting eight years ago, but they were insufficient to cool the vast prison, and the temperature rarely dropped more than five degrees below the outside temperature, which hovered in the nineties for much of the summer.

The heat and stench of the prison became insufferable during those months – but in the boiler room and laundry it was insufferable at all times of year. A permanent hell.

It was supposed to be lit twenty-four hours a day by rows of emergency lights – but over half of them were out, either blown naturally and not yet replaced, or broken by inmates who'd wanted to make sure that a particular section remained dark so as to mask one activity or another: a sexual liaison, a drugs handover, a beating. A murder.

Despite the heat, Larry felt a cool tingle run down his

spine. He couldn't see anybody at first, only hear muffled voices and make out some indistinct, jostling shadows from the far corner. A couple of the shadows became longer, more defined, as they fell under the starker light from one of the emergency lights still in place.

The shadows his end, hopefully, were equally as heavy, but he had to ease himself down cautiously from the ventilation shaft ledge to the floor. The slightest sound, and the mumbling voices would suddenly halt and someone would break free from the shadows to head his way.

As his feet touched the ground, the voices were slightly louder; Larry was able to risk a few brisk steps to hide behind the nearest pillar. Then he froze again, swallowing back against his rapid heartbeat so that he could listen: was Roddy's voice there, or was he already too late?

'Always such a wise mouth, huh? Always the clown. D'yer think this is a funny place, then? Barrel o' laughs a day?' Tally's voice, rising from the earlier muted tones, gave the answer.

'Not particularly. But I reckon – why not try an' brighten the days some. I mean, if I can . . .'

The rest from Roddy was lost as one of the boilers fired up. Someone had turned on a hot tap or a thermostat had dropped somewhere in Libreville's labyrinths.

Whatever had been said, Tally didn't appear to like it. The sudden burst of air from Roddy as he was hit in the stomach almost mirrored the hurrrumph from the boiler.

'B'fore I slit your throat, I'm gonna beat you like y'never . . . *known . . . before.*'

Tally timed his blows to emphasize his last few words, and Larry used the sound-cover to shuffle quickly forward to the next pillar.

'I wantya t'feel this first. Each blow like the rotten, fuckin' jokes yer told . . . *day in . . . day out . . .*'

The sound of the blows landing, accompanied by Roddy's guttural groans, was sickening, and his coughing and retching straight after sounded as if it already carried blood.

Larry clenched his jaw as he risked a glimpse past the pillar. There were three of them with Tally: Dennis Marmont, one of the guards in head-guard Glenn Bateson's pocket – he should have guessed Bateson wouldn't risk being present personally – and Jay-T and Silass, two of Tally's main muscle men.

Jay-T worried Larry the most. The only true brother of the group – Tally was a Creole-African mix – at six-five, a full four inches over Larry, he was surprisingly fast for his size, and had good technique for someone who'd never been formally trained.

'*What's that*? I thought I saw something.'

Larry ducked quickly back into the shadows behind the pillar as Marmont's torch flicked on and shone his way.

A frozen few seconds with only the sound of the group's suppressed breathing before Tally said, 'Only a rat . . . or maybe you jus' seein' things among the shadows.'

'Fucking big rat, when I can see its shadow halfway up a pillar,' Marmont retorted, and Larry heard his footsteps start towards him.

But after a moment the steps became uncertain, then stopped completely.

'You check it out –' Larry saw the beam of the torch swing back and then towards him again – 'I'm only meant t'be here as a witness. To ensure fair play.' Faint chuckle from Marmont, but along with his faltering step, it betrayed his nervousness.

More footsteps. Larry stayed deathly still, struggling to make out whose they were above his pounding heart. He looked at the advancing shadow in Marmont's torchlight beam but, exaggerated and elongated, it told him little.

Marmont also started moving forward again, no doubt feeling braver now that someone else was a few steps ahead of him.

Larry held his breath, his whole body rigid as the footsteps approached.

He'd have to make his first punch count and jump Marmont almost in one – otherwise Marmont would have a clear shot with his night-stick or gun, and it would all be over. But if it was Jay-T or Tally, he'd be hard pushed to do much with just one punch. His breath fell fast and shallow, his flank pressed firm against the pillar shielding him as the footsteps moved closer.

And as the torch-beam came to within a few feet, bathing the area just to his side in light, suddenly he was a fresh-faced twenty-two-year-old contender again, facing his first big fight in Atlanta's Omni arena – the clapping and stomping of the crowd almost in time with his thudding heartbeat.

His mouth was dry, his skin bathed in sweat – as it had been then – as the adrenalin rush fired up every nerve-end and muscle.

But as the approaching footsteps and the torch-beam's angle passed the point of no return, and Larry lunged fully into its light with his first punch, he wasn't sure if it was the roar of approval of his first fights, or the groans and shouts of derision of his last – when only four years later he lay on the canvas for the last time.

Glory or demise? Like so much else in his life, the line between them had been slight, almost impossible to discern.

Jac was running late.

He was fifteen minutes later than planned getting into the office because he'd dozed off again for a while after his alarm sounded; he'd slept fitfully after being awoken in the middle of the night by the slamming doors and voices from next door, which, in turn, meant that he didn't have time to get Penny Vance to type up Langfranc's dictation notes on Libreville – he'd simply grabbed a hand-held cassette before rushing out again, and planned to listen to it on the journey.

He caught his train connection with only a minute to spare and it left on time – but then it was held up for twenty-five minutes while the Santa Fe railroad shunted a never-ending stream of freight trucks past them on a dual-track junction.

So now Jac found himself rushing to make up time, pushing his rented Ford Taurus for the most part past sixty on the country roads that made up the last forty-five miles between Baton Rouge and Libreville. Jac anxiously checked his watch as the flatlands and swamps of the Mississippi Delta flashed by.

'*Haveling runs a tight ship at Libreville. Everything by the book and strict routine. And God help anyone who upsets that routine.*' Faint chuckle from Langfranc on tape. '*So while you and timekeeping might often not be the best of buddies – try and be on time for all your meetings with him and Durrant. Get everything off on the right foot.*'

Jac edged his foot down. If he pushed it, he might be no more than five minutes late. He'd started playing Langfranc's dicta-tape on the train – until a man across the aisle started paying him and the tape too much attention. He'd saved the rest for the car journey.

'*But the upside of that is that Haveling will deliver everything you need – reports and recommendations on Durrant – strictly on time. No delays or hassle. And talking of God, Warden Haveling's even more devout than our dear Governor Candaret. Stories abound of him taking a bible with him into the execution chamber, and, if the condemned is stuck for an apt last passage to be read by the prison Pastor, Haveling will recommend a few. He even offers to hold the condemned's hand in the final moments – if they should so require.*' Langfranc paused markedly. '*Which I suppose raises more awkward questions about Haveling's character and state of mind than it should – but at least it supports that pushing Durrant's religious bent as hard as you can is without doubt the main ticket. And in Haveling's defence, he's a lot better than his predecessors. Claims of turning a blind eye to, or even supporting, institutionalized violence hung over most of them. Haveling's immediate predecessor was as straight as they come, but lacked the backbone to push through what he wanted. High levels of violence still continued. A year ago there was a New Orleans magazine piece on Haveling picturing him with a bible in one hand and night-stick in the other, which just about*

24

summed him up. *"Iron fist, with — he believes — God's backing and approval."*

'*There are still incidents of violence, but probably no more than most maximum-security penitentiaries. Certainly, things now are a far cry from the dark days of the seventies and eighties when there were regular pitched battles with Cleaver-style radicals and assorted psychos going at each other with machetes sneaked in from the fields. Inmates then regularly slept with steel breastplates to protect them from getting hacked to death in the night.*

'*Libreville was in fact originally a slave plantation dating back to the 1830s, and its name came from the West African port where most of the slaves were shipped from, with the change from plantation to penitentiary coming in the early 1900s when . . .*'

Jac's cell-phone rang. He looked at the display: his mother or younger sister. He stopped the tape and answered.

His mother, Catherine, quickly launched into a subject she'd broached at the weekend past when he'd visited.

'Have you given it much thought yet?' she pressed.

'A bit,' he lied. Even without the Durrant case, he wouldn't have given it much consideration. Arranged date; he thought that sort of thing had died out a century ago. 'But I haven't decided yet.'

'Well, let me know when you have. She came by the other day with her father to Aunt Camille's place, and she seems a very nice girl. And attractive, too.'

Jac sighed. 'Come on, Mum. This is more about pleasing Camille than you or, more importantly, me. One more step in her social-climbing ladder.'

'That's true. She's from a very good family, and no doubt that's what Camille saw first. But now having met the girl, it would be easy for you to forget that this is all about Camille. You could get on very well.' Catherine sighed. 'And it has been a while now since Madeleine.'

Madeleine. *Madeleine.* Thirty-seven months, to be precise, just before they'd left France. Perhaps his mum was right: if she was nice and they got on, what harm could it do? But most of all, he could hear the uncertainty, almost desperation, in his mother's voice. The need to do this to please Camille. And that part of him made him want to rebel, say no.

His mother and sister stayed in one of Camille's houses in Hammond at only half rent, and Camille also paid half of Jean-Marie's college fees. He paid the other half; his was the only family work-visa so far granted, and it was all he could afford while doing criminal law bar exams. Meanwhile his mum and sister lived partly in his aunt's pocket, part of the legacy left by his father's early death and disastrous state of affairs at the time – which his aunt took every opportunity to remind them of: 'What a mess Adam left. All of his wild dreaming. So lucky I was there to help all of you.'

Jac's aunt was the exact opposite of his father. Maybe that's why he rebelled and railed so against any of her suggestions: in part, it kept alive his father's spirit.

'Okay, I'll think seriously about it. But if I agree to it, I'm doing it for you or because I feel it's right – not for Camille.'

'That's very noble. But you need to please yourself first and second on this, Jac – not anybody else.'

'I know.' With a promise that he'd let her know that weekend when he came over, he rang off.

After the argument through the wall the night before, the only girl he'd given any thought to had been his next-door neighbour, starting to wonder what she might look like. He'd purposely listened out for her movements as he got ready that morning: she was still moving around inside when he left, but if he timed it right one morning, hopefully he'd get to see her on the corridor.

He shook his head, smiling. Obsessing over a girl just from a few sound-bites through a wall. His mother was right: he *had* been too long without a date.

Jac switched on Langfranc's tape again, and, as he approached Libreville, the details started to mirror what he saw through his car window.

'*Spread over 17,000 acres in total, with the closest towns Libreville,*

26

four miles away – which sprung up shortly after the plantation was founded – and St Tereseville, seventeen miles away. The term "plantation" hung on until the mid-sixties, when it was dropped because it smacked too much of the early slave days, and was replaced with "ranch" – possibly due to its sheer size, the fact that they rear their own cattle as well as farm, and have an annual rodeo. The term could easily evoke a laid-back High Chaparral-*style atmosphere – but don't be fooled. This is hard-graft, rock-breaking* Cool-Hand Luke *territory all the way.*'

Jac approached the main gate of Libreville. Fourteen feet high, matching the perimeter fence, with another three feet of rolled razor wire on top.

After announcing his meeting with Chief Warden Haveling and handing over his card, Jac checked his watch while the guard phoned through for confirmation. Four minutes late; not too bad. But from the sprawl of the place, it looked like it was going to take him another four or five to actually get to Haveling's office.

The guard returned, handed him back his card, and pointed along the shale road ahead.

'Ignore the first three buildings, two one side, one the other – all single storey – and after a lil' more than a mile, you'll see the main building. Can't miss it. Rises up four floors out o' nowhere. Visitors' parking on the right.'

'Thanks.'

'. . . *Three thousand eight hundred inmates – forty per cent increase since the late fifties, which led to three new blocks being built in the grounds. All high risk or death row prisoners are held in the main block, with time allowed out of holding cells for them just two hours a day, unless they have allocated duties or privileges – though that never includes field work. Their work assignments are again all within the main block, which is like a fortress.*'

Of the half-dozen or so workers that Jac passed that troubled to look his way, at best they were sullenly curious, at worst surly and menacing; no smiles. It was difficult for Jac to believe that these were the best of the bunch.

'*Sixty-one per cent African-American inmates, sixteen per cent mixed race, and twenty-three per cent white. And with the guards, that ratio is reversed. Only nineteen per cent are black or mixed race – though a marked improvement on twenty or thirty years ago. Take the clock back to the early sixties, and there wasn't a single black guard.*'

But as Jac entered deeper into the bowels of Libreville's main block, he began to appreciate the difference. Here, at best the stares were surly, at worst taunting and disturbingly intense; and there were a few smiles, though invariably leering and slanted, as if fuelled by madness, or challenging, as if viewing him as prey.

Jac felt that the stifling oppression and heat of the block – unless he was imagining it – seemed to be getting more intense as he progressed, pressing heavier on him with each guard check-point and heavy steel gate opened and bolted shut behind him. And as a few sexual taunts were thrown at him as he passed the cells – 'Like the way you walk, pretty boy', 'Sweet ass – I could fuck you right through that Armani' – he felt his face tingle and burn.

He was probably still flushed, agitated, his shirt sticking to his skin, as he was ushered into the contrasting coolness of Warden Haveling's wood-panelled office. But he knew immediately – unless Haveling had taken to appearing as surly as his prisoners or was far more upset by his tardiness than he'd envisaged – that something serious was wrong.

It was that time of day.

Leonard Truelle nursed the two fingers of Jim Beam between his hands with due reverence, as if warming his hands through the glass. Then, with a faint gleam of expectation in his eyes, brought it to his lips and felt its warmth and aroma trickle slowly down. He closed his eyes in appreciation. Pure nectar. With a part sigh, part murmur as he felt its after-burn, he set the glass slowly down.

The hand clamping over his came an inch before the

tumbler touched the table, and he flicked his eyes open again, startled.

'What *the* . . . oh, *oh* . . . it's you.'

'Now that's no way to greet a long-lost friend.'

'You startled me, that's all. Probably because it *has* been so long.' Nelson Malley, Nel-M, or just plain Nel. Almost five years now, but it wasn't a face he was ever likely to forget. There was a tinge of grey now in Malley's tight-knit curls, and it looked as if his mahogany skin tone was becoming greyer each time, as if someone had thrown potash in his face which hadn't completely washed off.

'Anyway, nice to see you again.' Nel-M gave Truelle's hand a couple more squeezes – though to Truelle they felt threatening rather than reassuring – and as Nel-M felt the trembling there, he smiled. 'Is that because of me? I'm touched. Or because you haven't kicked this stuff yet?' Nel-M flicked his hand towards the whisky tumbler as he lifted it away.

Truelle didn't want to let Nel-M inside his head, show weakness either way. 'Expecting Sharon Stone any minute, and, you know, first dates. Always nervous.' Truelle forced a weak smile. 'I might need some Dutch courage to actually get to fuck her.'

Nel-M smiled back, but his charcoal eyes fixed steadily on Truelle showed no hint of warmth; as always, icy and bottomless, as if they were independent monitors searching for weak points to signal what his next move should be. They cut Truelle to the core, ran a shiver up his spine.

This drink now was part of a ritual, every Tuesday and Friday night when he left work. One glass of Jim Beam slowly and reverently sipped – then home. Before when he'd been on the wagon, he'd always felt in danger that if he had just one drink, he wouldn't be able to stop. And on a couple of occasions, that was exactly how he'd started again. This was his way of proving that he was in control, could stop at just one drink – but he was damned if he was going to share his innermost secrets with Nelson Malley. He could feel Nel-M's eyes still on him as he looked down thoughtfully at his glass, and shrugged to ease his discomfort.

'Look, if you wanted something, why didn't you come by my office – like most normal people?'

'Normal people?' Nel-M raised one eyebrow and smiled slyly. 'Bit of a contradiction in terms in your line of work, isn't it? I wouldn't want to rob any of your patients of their precious fifty minutes or, God forbid, get seen walking in and confused with all those crazies. I got a reputation to uphold.' The smile broadened, then died just as quickly. 'But you've probably guessed the reason I'm here now. No doubt you've seen or read the news: Durrant's execution has been set. Only forty-seven days left now, and counting.'

'Yeah, I know. I've read it.' Truelle kept his eyes on his tumbler, didn't want to risk what Malley might see in them.

'And, well, we just wanted to make sure that you were still cool about everything. No last minute stabs of conscience.'

Truelle smiled drolly. '*We* – as in you and Addy Roche?'

'As in.'

'Yeah, I'm cool.' Truelle nodded, still staring at his glass. 'Resigned to' or 'numbed by' would probably have been more accurate expressions. He'd shed so many tears of conscience over Durrant that now there was nothing left. 'I got rid of all my demons years ago.'

Though looking at the tumbler now, he could almost still picture it being refilled time and time again, until he'd stagger from the bar in a daze. If he'd had a problem before Durrant, the aftermath was without doubt the main event. He'd drunk half the state dry before resorting to more AA meetings and colleagues' couches than he dared remember. But the problem was that he could never tell them what lay at the root of what was troubling him. *Never.*

'You're sure now that you're cool about it?' Nel-M pressed, laying his hand back on Truelle's. 'No recriminations?'

Truelle shook his head and looked back at Nel-M. 'I'm sure. No recriminations. Not any more.'

But Nel-M kept his hand there, squeezing bit by bit harder as he stared into Truelle's eyes, searching for doubt. He stopped short of a complete crush, and although he couldn't discern anything from Truelle's eyes — too lifeless, dulled by the years of drink — he could feel the tell-tale trembling back in his hand.

'Though nice to know you still have feelings for me,' Nel-M said, giving the hand one last pat before he lifted his away and, in the same motion — before Truelle could object — waved towards the barman.

'And another of the same for my friend here.'

Nel-M slapped some money on the counter and slapped Truelle on the shoulder. 'Remember — stay cool.' Then, with one last taunting smile, he headed out.

Truelle hardly acknowledged him, his eyes fixed on the second drink as if it was poison. He could feel the trembling in his hands reverberating now through his entire body. Of all the times he could do with a second drink, it was now. But he was damned if he was going to fall off of the wagon just for Nel-M. And the fact that Nel-M had bought the drink made it all the worse — it would be like supping with the devil.

He knocked back the last of his first drink, closing his eyes again as he felt it trickle down. In control. *Still in control.* Then, bringing the tumbler down with a firm slam on the bar counter, he walked out.

3

'The first guard, Glenn Bateson, suffered only minor bruising to the face and upper body.' Haveling opened his hands palm out. 'But the second, Dennis Marmont, fared much worse. Dislocated jaw and a life-threatening skull fracture . . . he's still in a coma at St Tereseville General. His injuries were too severe for us to deal with here at the infirmary.'

Jac had felt his stomach sink, along with any hopes of saving Durrant, as Haveling related the nightmarish drama of the previous night: Durrant along with another inmate, Hector Rodriguez, had made an escape attempt using a route they'd apparently been digging for several months. They were discovered by two guards, and a struggle ensued. Rodriguez's injuries, from the sound of it, were almost as bad as Marmont's, while Durrant had earned a fractured forearm and hairline rib crack. He'd already been released from the infirmary.

'The damnest thing is, they used the altar in Durrant's cell as the main cover for their escape route. It looked fixed to the ground, unable to be shifted – but if you pressed a couple of points near its base, some castors dropped down and it could be easily moved aside.' Haveling held his palms out again; openness or helplessness? 'Must have taken someone a fair time in the machine room to knock that up. They'd wheel it out and dig behind at will. Guard comes by, and they make out they're praying.'

'Pretty ingenious,' Jac said, smiling dryly.

Haveling's eyebrows furrowed, though quickly lifted, as if he'd had second thoughts on what he was about to say. 'Yes . . . I suppose so. In a perverse sort of way.'

The redness of Haveling's florid face contrasted with his wheat-blond hair. But he was one of those stout types that looked like he worked out; most of his fat had turned to muscle.

His office walls were lined with books, photos, memorabilia, and a row of four Louisiana State office commendations that Jac couldn't read from where he was. A couple of New Orleans Zephyr pennants framed two photos of Haveling with what Jac presumed were Zephyr players. The coolness of his office seemed at odds with the warmth of its redwood panelling; it was like a cosy, warm log-cabin, but felt as cold as the grave. Whereas in the cold steel of the prison outside, it was as hot and clammy as a Chinese laundry.

Jac felt the sweat from his walk through the prison cooling on his skin with the air-conditioning's efficiency. Or maybe it was the realization that the case was slipping from his grasp before he'd even started. He shook off a faint shiver.

'But what upset me most,' Haveling said, 'was being taken for a fool. I really believed Durrant when he told me how devout he'd become. Said he needed to formally pray at least three times a day.' This time his hands stayed cradled, protective; he wasn't going to leave himself open again. 'With the times death-rowers are allowed out of their cells, no way could he have made it to the chapel that often. So I bent the rules especially for Durrant. Thought it might also get some of the other death-rowers to pray more as well – with the altar being right there. So they were encouraged to go to Durrant's cell when the need arose – and, indeed, a fair few took up the offer. So you can imagine my upset at now discovering that it was all just a cover for an escape route. I feel that my good nature has been used, betrayed.'

'Yes, I can understand that.' Jac nodded sombrely, making sure to suppress even the hint of a smile. He could just imagine the private hoots and gloating from the prisoners at scamming Haveling like this: Haveling believing that they were seeking heaven, when in fact they had more immediate salvation in mind – *freedom*.

But Durrant had certainly done himself no favours. His

main hope of a plea had hinged on his religious bent and good character, and now there was no hope of getting a recommendation letter from Haveling to support that. There hardly seemed any point in Jac even asking.

'Have you had a chance to speak to Durrant or the other prisoner yet? Hear their account?'

'No, not yet. Rodriguez is still in no fit state, and Durrant only came out of the infirmary an hour or so ago. Durrant was blabbing to my assistant, Pete Folley, something about Rodriguez already being down in the boiler room. But, as I say, we just haven't had a chance to talk to him or Rodriguez.'

'I see.' Jac had taken a pad out at the outset of the meeting for procedures, dates or names; but all he'd written were a few cryptic notes on points that didn't quite sit right. He decided to probe with one, asking Haveling how it had developed into such an affray. 'Why didn't the guards just hold off the prisoners with their guns?'

Haveling sucked in his breath; mild impatience. 'Marmont was jumped immediately and lost his gun. And Bateson was halfway through drawing his when Durrant took his first swing with an iron bar. His second swing caved in half of Marmont's skull.' Haveling raised an eyebrow. 'Does that answer your question?'

'Yes, I . . . I suppose it does.' Jac looked down at his pad. He could hear a bell somewhere in the bowels of the prison, and part of it seemed to keep ringing in his head after it had stopped. He decided to save the remaining questions for now; until he'd spoken to Durrant, he wouldn't be able to gauge the best angle of attack. He asked Haveling if that might be possible. 'Now that I'm here, I can hear Durrant's account at the same time as talking to him about his plea petition – *if* you have no objections?'

Haveling shrugged. 'I suppose not. We'll do our own interview later in any case, if possible get Rodriguez's account too, and send you a transcript.' Haveling pressed a button on his desk.

As Jac followed Haveling's assistant, Pete Folley, back

through the heated, foetid corridors of Libreville, he found it hard to shake off a pervading sense of hopelessness. However revealing Durrant's account might be, now that Haveling's religious feathers had been ruffled, it was going to take a miracle to shift his stance to the stage where he'd assist with a plea recommendation letter. And without that, they were sunk.

Jac's steps echoed emptily through the corridors of Libreville prison as he went to meet Lawrence Durrant for the first time.

Jac had been ensconced with Durrant in Libreville's one-way glass interview room for almost twenty minutes before he saw the first glimmer of hope; the first moment he thought that Durrant was actually telling the truth.

The interview had started slowly, guardedly; Durrant was nonchalant, almost disinterested, and after a while Jac became tired of pressing and pushing, and slipped into similar mode. Partly defensive, but it also mirrored how he felt: he'd arrived fired-up and eager to get to grips more with Durrant and the murder of eleven years ago – not try and patch up some fiasco from the night before.

But as Durrant got into his account, his early manner faded and he became more animated. Watching Durrant's eyes as he described the onset of fighting, Jac realized in that moment that Durrant was telling the truth. Jac could see him reliving the events, his eyes flickering, winding through the scenes like a movie reel.

'You're saying that Bateson was never there?' Jac quizzed.

'No, just Marmont. And of course Tally and his two happy helpers – Jay-T and Silass.'

'Now I know that Marmont was hurt badly – but what sort of injuries did this Tally and his henchmen receive?'

'Jay-T was hurt worst, without a doubt. Lot of body hits, and bleeding real bad around his left eye. But Silass was out of it quickly, and Tally only came in at the end – so maybe just a few bruises for those two.'

To Larry, relating the events, it seemed strange taking twenty minutes to describe something that had probably taken no more than three minutes. From the point he'd stepped into the torch-beam, it all became a quick-frame blur: knocking Marmont's gun loose and a swift, low body-punch to Silass almost in one; his second punch hitting Marmont's jaw solidly and putting him to his knees as Jay-T moved in. The trading of blows with Jay-T was the hardest, and as Jay-T started to come off worse, Tally moved in – Larry only caught a glimpse of the iron bar as it swung, and brought one arm up defensively. He ducked the swing back, and its arc caught Marmont squarely on the head as he struggled to his feet. Larry lunged and gripped the bar just as it started to swing at him again, jabbing an elbow back hard and fast at Tally, twice to his ribs and once to his face, before finally wrestling the bar free – when the siren sounded followed by boot-steps rushing down to the boiler room. Roddy, forgotten in the fray, had staggered to the back of the room and pressed the alarm.

'So it was this Tally that swung the bar at Marmont?' Jac confirmed.

'Yeah, sure. Why?'

'Haveling's been told – presumably by Bateson – that it was you. And that it was Bateson who pressed the alarm, not Rodriguez.'

Larry huffed and smiled wryly. 'Makes sense,' he said, in a way that indicated it made anything but. 'As I say, Bateson wasn't even there. He only showed with a couple of guards when the alarm sounded.'

Jac glanced towards the red light on the table. As Haveling had promised, it had stayed off throughout: they had sound privacy, if not visual. All category 'A' prisoners had to remain under observation during interviews. Haveling and Folley were behind the one-way glass screen to their side, looking on, and a guard stood the other side of the door.

The first things that struck Jac about Durrant were the length of his arms and size of his hands. He was no more than a couple of inches beyond Jac's five-eleven – but his arms and hands seemed decidedly over-proportioned. He didn't have the gargantuan biceps of some of the muscle freaks Jac had seen on his way through, but his forearms were particularly thick, with a single tattoo – 'Francine' through a thorn-wrapped heart – on his unstrapped arm.

He had deeply hooded eyes with a slow blink, and his smile too was slow to rise – as if he was either sly or indolent – but at its extremity it became more open, and a light would lift his dull eyes. A light that perhaps the past eleven years had faded. His skin was mahogany with a dark grey rather than black undertone; as if the years inside had faded and dulled that too.

Jac spent a few more minutes clarifying Durrant's story, but towards the end Durrant said something that knocked him back a step – and for the first time he questioned why he was fighting Durrant's corner so hard. He hardly knew Durrant as yet – so was it just good lawyerly duty to fight a client's case to the best of ability, regardless; or because he just couldn't face heading straight back to the office and admitting that his first big case had collapsed before it had started?

'Stay here,' he said. 'I want to check some things out before we go further.'

The guard moved to just inside the door as Jac headed back through the prison with Haveling. For the first time Jac sensed some purpose, if not yet hope, rekindle with each strident, echoing step and sliding back of cell bolts to reveal the prisoners Durrant had named.

Haveling had pressed at the outset, 'What did Durrant say?', but Jac said that he wanted to check a few things first. 'We'll know soon enough if there's any substance in what he claims.'

Jay-T's left eye-socket was so swollen that it was almost closed, and there was a cut and heavy bruising to the right side of his face. But facial bruising was only slight on Silass and Tally, and Jac had to ask them to lift their shirts – Tally reluctant to do so until prompted by Haveling. Jac pointed out the heavier bruising to Haveling, making sure not to actually touch flesh. Tally looked ready to strike out.

As the heavy steel door was slid back on the cell block, Haveling asked, 'Now do you mind telling me what's going on?'

Jac related Durrant's account as they headed back towards the interview room, but saw the doubt grow steadily in Haveling's face.

'I'm sorry,' Haveling said finally, 'but it's just too far from Bateson's account for me to take on board seriously. And then how would you explain Bateson's injuries?'

'Easier to fake one set of injuries than two,' Jac offered, shrugging.

Haveling hardly paused for breath as he opened the door to the interview-observation room. 'And it would also mean me going against not only Bateson, one of my most trusted guards – but also the other two guards that first came on the scene when the alarm sounded. I think you can understand why I'd be loath to do that.'

'Yes, I can.' Jac looked down for a second. He had no ready answers, his only possible counters were the anomalies he'd noted earlier. 'I think you have to admit – knocking the gun loose from one guard makes a lot more sense than *two* of them being disarmed at the same time. Also – how did Rodriguez get into Durrant's cell at that time of night to be able to use the escape route?'

'He dummied up his bed, apparently.'

'This from Bateson too?'

'Yes, from Bateson.'

Now it was Jac's turn to appear doubtful. 'Is that easily done?'

'No, I suppose not, but . . .' Haveling shook his head, suddenly losing patience. 'Look, this is ridiculous. What you have to realize here, Mr McElroy,' Haveling nodded towards the glass and Durrant beyond, 'is that Durrant will obviously say anything to save his own neck.'

'No, no. That's where you're wrong.' Jac had planned to keep this one bit of information to himself, but he couldn't resist the opportunity to make the point. The final clincher that had convinced him Durrant was telling the truth. 'He said that he didn't know why I'd bothered coming here to try and help him. He said that he'd rather die than spend the rest of his time in here.'

'So, how was our good friend Truelle?'

'Not bad, not bad,' Nel-M said. 'After he got over the shock of seeing me.'

'So, no signs of him falling apart?'

'None that I could see, beyond the normal PMT – post-Malley tension.' Nel-M chuckled briefly. 'He claims that he exorcized the demons over Durrant years ago. And apparently he's also kicked the demon drink. Truelle was reluctant to tell me himself – but I checked back with the barman after he left: it appears he goes in there only twice a week and has just a single Jim Beam each time. And he left the extra drink I bought him.'

'Impressive. And the gambling?'

'Unless he's using a bookie or is into some private games we just don't know about – looks like he's clean there too.'

'Sound almost too good to be true. *Two* vices overcome.'

The voice at the other end was punctuated by laboured breathing from years of emphysema and, as a chortle was attempted, it lapsed into a small coughing fit.

Adelay Roche, Louisiana's second richest man, twenty-ninth nationally. He'd earned his main money in petro-chemicals and refining, and his detractors claimed that his emphysema was God's punishment for poisoning the lungs of millions of others; whereas his supporters said that it was brought on by the death of his beautiful young wife twelve years ago. As many years ago now as the age-gap between them.

VR, Vader-Raider, he was unaffectionately nicknamed, homage to his breathing problems and his fierce reputation for corporate raiding. On occasion, he'd ask people what the VR stood for, and, not wishing to upset him, they'd either claim that they didn't know or, with a tight smile, 'Perhaps "Very Rich".' Roche would nod knowingly. 'That's nice.' He'd long ago heard what the initials stood for, but couldn't resist watching them shuffle awkwardly around the issue.

'And what about Raoul Ferrer?' Roche enquired.

'I haven't caught up with him yet. I thought I should speak to you again first.'

'Yeah, I know. He could be more of a worry. Two money demands now. No knowing when we might get another.'

'True.' Nel-M didn't say any more, just let the steady cadence of Roche's breathing get there on its own.

'If that's going to be an ongoing situation, then we might have to nip it in the bud. Let me know how you read it once you've met with him.'

'Will do.' As much of a green light as he was going to get from Roche. He might have to nudge that situation along himself.

'Oh, and there's a new lawyer been handed Durrant's final plea at Payne, Beaton and Sawyer. Name of Jac McElroy. Doesn't have too much experience, from what I hear – so looks like end-of-the-line throwing-in-the-towel time. Otherwise they'd have given it to someone with a bit more weight. But warrants watching all the same.'

A small shudder would run through Jac's body at times; a small electrical surge buzzing through him for no reason, often in the dead of night and just when he was on the verge of sleep, snapping him back awake again.

The same chilling shudder that had run through him when his mother's voice had lifted from her weary, trembling body into the silent, expectant rooms of the sprawling Rochefort farmhouse they'd called home for the past nineteen years, to tell him that his father was dead. That had been daytime, hot and sunny, though the large house had never felt colder when that news, even though half-expected, dreaded for so long, finally came from the hospital.

And he'd felt that same shudder even more in the following months: at his father's funeral, when the bank foreclosed and the bailiffs came, with his mother's muffled sobbing through walls or half-closed doors, or after his father had appeared in a dream, smiling warmly, telling him everything was okay. *Lived before I died.* Or sometimes for no reason that he could fathom, as if telling him there was something he might have missed. Stay awake for another hour staring at the ceiling and you might just work out what it was. Some magical way of getting your family out of this mess. After all, you're the man of the house now.

The Rochefort artist's retreat had been his father's dream for many a year, long before he finally summoned up the courage to pack in his job at a small design and print company and transplant his family from a cold, grey Glasgow to the sun-dappled vineyards and wheat-fields of the Saintonge. And now the dream had died along with his father, as his father in his fading years knew all too well it would, many saying the money problems had in fact caused his illness: income dwindling, financial problems mounting and banks pressing in pace with the cancer eating him away; a race as to which would hit the tape first.

But it was difficult for Jac to get angry with his father for the financial fall-out after his death because, as his father's good friend Archie Teale had said, unlike most people he'd actually *lived* his dream, and Jac's abiding memory of that period was of an almost idyllic childhood: looking over his father's shoulder as he'd bring to life with his paintbrush a patchwork quilt of vines, lavender and sunflower fields spread before them; Jac sitting on the hillside by the L-shaped farm-house, the sun hot on his back, his father in the courtyard below sweeping one arm towards the same patchwork land-scape as he instructed a group of eight by their easels – his father living his dream and the rest of the family happily riding along in the wake of that glow; powder-white sand slipping egg-timer slow through Jac's fingers on an Isle de Ré beach, or chasing small fishes through its shallows, his father telling him if he ran fast enough and scooped down quick enough with his cupped hands, he might finally catch one. But, of course, he was never able to.

Those had been the overriding images in Jac's mind from those years, rather than remembering his father tired and wasting away, his mother weeping and the court's gavel and bailiffs' knocks that had marked their final days in France.

Jac saw his father as some fallen-through-no-fault-of-his-own hero, rather than the failure that others, particularly his aunt, had labelled him.

And so as the months passed the brief shudders in the dead of night became less frequent, then finally one day stopped, and Jac was able to sleep easy.

So when that brief shudder hit Jac again, snapping him awake in the dead of night after he'd visited Larry Durrant for the first time, it caught him unawares.

He stared up at the ceiling long and hard, wondering what it could be: that one vital detail or clue he'd missed reading Durrant's trial files? A hint at how to handle this fresh problem with the attempted break-out and the injured guards? But all that lifted from the muted streetlight orange-greys on his ceiling was the last image to hit him before he'd awoken: Durrant in his cell, lonely and afraid, sweat beads massed on his forehead with the crippling fear that he was about to die – the antithesis of the cool and distant, guarded front he'd shown to Jac – reaching out to say something, but the words never forming in his mouth.

But with the e-mail that was waiting on Jac's computer when he switched it on early the next morning, Jac wondered if it was some kind of strange premonition.

Only three lines, his blood ran cold as he read it, a nervous tingle running down his spine.

Looked like he might have a breakthrough with Durrant before he'd hardly started.

4

'Whadya call that, fuckhead? I could cue a better shot with my dick.'

'I didn't see you do so well with that last yellow.'

'That's 'cause there were two other fuckin' balls in the way, Stevie Wonder. This one, you had a clear shot.'

Nel-M had arranged to meet Raoul Ferrer in a bar in Algiers.

Ten years ago it was a no-go area day or night, but now, with a string of new bars and restaurants nestling in the shadows of the dockside warehouses, according to local city guides it was now inadvisable to walk around only *after* midnight.

They'd been perched up at the bar only a few minutes when the argument erupted at the pool table a couple of yards to their side. As the insults picked up steam and the two opponents moved closer, one of them raising his cue stick threateningly, Nel-M shifted from his bar stool.

'Let's get outta here.'

'No, no. Wait a minute,' Raoul said. 'This is just gettin' interesting.'

One thing Nel-M hadn't considered, looking at the warped leer on Raoul's face. The excitement of the fight.

'Look, I haven't come here to watch a bunch of goons fight. We got business to discuss.' Nel-M turned and took a pace away.

Raoul got up and lightly tugged at his arm. 'Come on, man. Won't take a minute to kick-off, by the looks of it.'

Nel-M noticed the man with the raised cue stick, a biker with wild red hair, flinch and fleetingly gaze their way. He hoped Raoul hadn't read anything into it.

'You wanna watch that wise mouth.' Red-hair waved the

cue stick more threateningly at his opponent. 'Otherwise one day someone will bust it wide open.'

'Yeah. Yeah.' His opponent stepped forward, taunting, challenging. 'Will probably be the best fuckin' shot you've had all night, too.'

They were running out of script. One more minute and Raoul would guess that something was wrong, that it was all staged.

'I'm outta here,' Nel-M said. 'You want to waste time watching these assholes, then do it on your own time, not mine.' He paced purposefully away, and by the time his hand reached for the door, Raoul had shuffled up quickly behind him. 'The sort of business we need to talk about can't be done here.'

'Okay, man. Okay. I understand. Business. *Business*.'

Nel-M waited until they were a good dozen paces from the bar before he spoke again. He took a deep breath of the warm night air and slowly let it out.

'You probably guessed why the meeting at this particular time. Larry Durrant's coming up for his big day, and Roche wants to know if there might be any more surprises waiting in the wings. You know, as in another big pay-off.'

'No, man. No. Of course not. That was a one-off deal, never to be repeated . . .'

'Except that there were *two* pay-offs.'

Raoul shrugged awkwardly. 'The second was only ten-G . . . just a top-up of the main pay-off. And only, ya know,' Raoul grimaced, ' 'cause I was in such a jam at the time. I'm okay now. Doin' fine. No troubles, no problems. I got a good deal runnin' now with Carmen, ya know.'

'Yeah, I know.' Carmen Malastra, Louisiana's leading rack-eteer. But at Raoul's pecking level in Malastra's empire, one call from Roche would easily smooth over any move they had to make against Raoul. Although that might all change once Raoul was a 'made' man. 'But what we wanna make sure is if that's *always* going to be the case. I mean, what happens if you hit hard times later, fall out with Carmen, or business goes bad? Or he changes your deal or territory, so you're just not pulling in the same?' Nel-M shrugged. 'You know, it happens. It happens all the time.'

'No, no. It won' happen. Don't worry.'

But there was a heavy pause before Raoul answered that told Nel-M that Raoul was far from sure.

'Maybe not now, this year, or next. But who knows what can happen in five or ten years.' Nel-M shrugged again. 'And if that was going to be the case . . . or even if there was a slim possibility that it *might* be the case, then Roche would prefer to make that payment now rather than later.' Nel-M shuffled to a stop and fixed Raoul with a stony gaze. 'Because once Durrant's gone for the chop, Roche doesn't want to hear mention of his name again, or anyone or anything to do with Durrant. Once the chapter closes in forty-five days time, it closes for good. Understand. So if there was ever again to be money involved, as Elvis once said – it's now or never.'

Nel-M watched Raoul look thoughtfully, agitatedly at his shoes for a second – snakeskin with a maroon leather band – pursing his lips as he mulled it over. It looked like he was going to need a bit more push.

'Roche has even thought of a figure for you. Forty grand. No arguments, no questions. But also, no come-backs or demands later. It's a one-shot deal.'

Raoul looked up and blew a soft whistle into the night air. 'Same as the first time, huh?'

'Yeah. Same as.' Nel-M held Raoul's gaze for an instant; snake-eyes, snake-shoes. He could tell that Raoul was close, teetering on the edge. Behind them a ship's horn sounded as it approached Algiers Point.

Raoul looked over his shoulder as a sudden babble of voices burst from a bar eighty yards up the road.

They were away from the main bar and restaurant area, but obviously still not far enough, thought Nel-M. And there was still a thread of uncertainty holding Raoul back.

'I've got the money right over there, in my car. Should you decide to take it.' Nel-M started pacing towards his car without looking back for Raoul's reaction.

After five yards they came alongside a large warehouse, and, as they turned the corner to follow the flank of the building, the atmosphere changed completely. It was darker, the street-lighting sparser, the bars and restaurants a hundred yards away completely hidden from view by the two-storey corrugated warehouse walls. At the end of the warehouse and before the next was a small patch of waste-ground used as a makeshift car lot for twenty or so cars. At this time of night only three cars were there, one of which was Nel-M's.

Nel-M knew that if he'd arranged to meet Raoul here initially, Raoul would have balked, or at least would have been suspicious and wary. That's why he'd decided on the bar and the staged fight.

'And you got the money right here, in your car?'

'Yep.' Nel-M could tell from the edge in Raoul's voice that he'd taken the bait. The smell and immediacy of the money was just too tempting. 'No point in delaying. One quick call to Roche for a final nod, and the money's yours. Done deal. So, what do you think?'

One final appraisal of his shoes, lips pursing, before Raoul looked up again. 'Okay, *okay*.' The words rode a hushed exhalation, as if he was accepting the money reluctantly.

Equally, Nel-M kept his voice low as he took out his cell-phone and started speaking to Roche, holding one hand up towards Raoul as he took a couple of steps away.

'So, you were right,' Roche said on the back of a tired sigh. 'He *did* want an extra payment.'

'Yeah, yeah. Looks like it.'

'Another forty grand, you say?'

'Yeah.'

'And do you think he'll come back for more again later?'

'Yeah, looks like it. At least, that's how *I* read it.'

Another tired sigh. 'I suppose we're going to have to take

the option you suggested, against my better judgement. Less possible problems later. Except, that is, for how we're going to square things with Malastra.'

'That too will be better dealt with now rather than later.'

'You mean once he becomes "made"?'

'Yeah.'

'*Okay.*' Roche exhaled as the silence lengthened. 'I understand you can't say too much your end.' One final weary sigh. 'Just take care of it the best way you see fit.'

'Will do.' Nel-M beamed widely as he looked back at Raoul. 'Great. He's given the okay.'

Raoul mirrored Nel-M's smile; but then it quickly faltered, sinking, as, in the same motion of Nel-M putting away his cell-phone, he saw him slide a gun out, a 9mm with silencer already attached.

Raoul held one hand up defensively, his eyes darting in panic. 'Roche said for you to gimme the money.'

Nel-M cocked an eyebrow. 'Now, let me think. When he said to "let you have it" – could I have got the wrong meaning?' Nel-M had wanted to kill Raoul from the outset He might as well squeeze every bit of juice from it. 'Maybe my poor grasp of English letting me down again? You know, us poor Southern "boys", they didn't let us near any books until much later in life.'

'You . . . you *can't* do this.' Raoul's eyes continued darting for possible options. Hoping that someone from the nearby bars might suddenly come around the corner, a verbal gem to stop Nel-M in his tracks; empty prayers on his breath falling into the night air. 'You wouldn't dare touch me. Carmen would tear your fuckin' heart out.'

'You're just small potatoes in Carmen's empire. And Roche could buy and sell Carmen ten times over. So in the scheme of things – you're *really* small.' Nel-M raised his gun and aimed. 'And about to disappear completely.'

Raoul moved his hand higher in response, and Nel-M's bullet took off Raoul's index fingertip before slamming into his left cheekbone, leaving a gaping hole as it deflected and exited just below his temple. The impact threw Raoul Ferrer back a full yard and left him partly on one side, his body twitching as blood pumped up through the hole in his cheek.

Just in case it was Raoul's nervous system and brain still intact, rather than death throes, Nel-M put the silencer barrel by Raoul's left eye and squeezed off a second shot. It certainly wasn't to put Raoul out of pain quickly.

'Let me get this straight,' John Langfranc said after the first couple of forkfuls of duck in black-olive sauce. 'Durrant not only attempts to escape – according to the guards' account – but seriously treads on Haveling's religious toes in the process. In arguing your client's case, you first of all question the integrity of Haveling's head guard; then, when that doesn't appear to be working – you practically blackmail Haveling?'

Jac shrugged awkwardly. 'Well, I wouldn't exactly call it blackmail. I just pointed out that since the question of Durrant and Rodriguez trying to escape looked in doubt – perhaps it was best not to announce that fact. For *all* concerned.'

'You asked Mr Holier-than-thou to bury it?'

'I didn't *ask* anything – just gently hinted.' Jac shrugged again, this time with a wry smile. 'But I'm sure it wasn't lost on Haveling that it wouldn't do him any favours either to make the escape attempt public. Almost a year digging without anyone noticing? Would bring up a lot of questions – not least why Durrant was allowed an altar in his cell in the first place. Haveling has raised a fair few eyebrows as it is over his religious fervour – the last thing he'd want is more focus on that.'

Langfranc winked and smiled as he pierced another forkful. 'You're either completely mad, or catching on fast, kiddo.'

The morning had been hectic and this was their first opportunity to discuss Jac's visit to Libreville. They were in Lilette's; not one of the local 'power' restaurants, just good contemporary local cuisine at reasonable prices. They rarely chose power restaurants unless they had particularly prestigious clients –

which was equally rare. They were invariably saved for Clive Beaton and Jeremiah Payne, or one of their favoured rising protégés.

Odds-on, therefore, that they'd avoid Clive Beaton and any potentially awkward questions – but then on walking in they'd spotted Dougy Sawyer in the corner, who they'd acknowledged with a quick smile. Too late, too obvious to head out and choose another restaurant. They should have remembered that this was also one of Sawyer's favourites when he had a heavy workload, for much the same reasons: he could bed down in the corner without interruption from other partners.

Sawyer was the only partner Langfranc had any real respect or time for, mainly because he'd risen up through work and application rather than influence and power-broking. As a result, Sawyer's knowledge of comparative-case-histories was second to none within the firm.

They saw Sawyer look up at them and the activity around at intervals – but for the most part his head remained buried in the file before him.

'When's Haveling letting you know?' Langfranc asked.

'Said he wouldn't get firm statements from the guards for a day or two, and he wants some time beyond that for consideration. So not till next Monday, Tuesday.'

'He's making you sweat the weekend?'

'Looks like it.' Jac inadvertently looked at his watch. Five more days gone of Larry Durrant's life.

Seeing Jac's pained expression, Langfranc reached a hand across and touched his arm. 'Don't beat yourself up so. If it goes the wrong way, you did your best.'

Jac nodded a doleful acceptance. *At least one person out there thinks Durrant's innocent*, he thought, but decided against mentioning the e-mail; not yet. Trying to glean more from what few words there were, he'd also started to rationalize: it could be anyone or anything; a hoax or prank, a friend or supporter of Durrant's, or even someone from his own family desperate to save his neck. He needed to find out more to know if it might have any substance.

Jac took a sip of water, grimacing as he swallowed. 'But if it's a no-go with Haveling, it just seems wrong having to throw in the towel so quickly – particularly since it's my first big case. Striking out before it's even started isn't exactly the best way to score points with Beaton.'

'I think it's the other way round. I don't think Beaton expected this to go anywhere. Otherwise, as I say, he'd have taken it himself or given it to one of his favourite ass-kissers, like Kyle Everett. I think Beaton would have been surprised if you *had* made any headway with it.'

'Well, at least I'm not disappointing him.' Jac smiled dryly, chewing at his food for a second. 'But I still can't shake off the feeling that I'm not only letting Durrant down, but everyone else. Also, the sense that I'm missing something vital.'

'Trust me, your first year at criminal law – there's probably a dozen things you're missing.' Langfranc raised his glass in mock salute. 'If you're missing only one, you're doing well.'

'Thanks.' Jac returned Langfranc's smile lamely. 'I feel so much better now knowing that I'm even more incompetent than I appreciated.'

'Anytime.' Langfranc raised his glass a fraction higher. 'I think most people would have thrown in the towel when their client said that he wanted to die.'

'So we should add foolhardy to the list?'

Langfranc, now in full flow, waved his glass. 'And add ambitious, ruthless, greedy and slick – great name for a law firm, don't you think? – and you'll be halfway to making a good criminal lawyer. No, seriously, I think you should . . . *Dougy*!' Langfranc's gaze shifted suddenly past Jac's shoulder.

Dougy Sawyer had decided to stop by their table on his way out. 'I . . . I was wondering if you've had a chance to speak to Mike Coultaine yet?'

It was Sawyer who'd recommended to Langfranc that whoever took on the Durrant case should speak to Coultaine.

'No, not yet,' Jac said. 'There's been some initial – '

'Jac thought he should find his feet first,' Langfranc cut in; the last thing Jac needed was news of problems with Durrant getting back to Beaton. 'Get through his initial interviews with Durrant before seeing Coultaine.'

'Well – you want to speak to Coultaine soon as you can,' Sawyer said. 'Except that now the hurricane season's winding down he's probably out on his boat fly-fishing every day. Harder to get hold of than when he was with the firm.' Sawyer smiled meekly, but there was a faint gleam in his eye, as if he too might like to escape and fly-fish the rest of his days away. Or because he considered it pure folly, reserved only for the mad or brave, like Mike Coultaine. 'I know that he was upset at losing the appeal. I think Durrant touched him deeper than any of us appreciated . . . along with a few other cases. Probably the reason that Mike retired so early. Still . . .' Sawyer half-turned, distracted, as a noisy group took up seats a couple of tables away.

'I . . . I'll get in touch with him some time next week,' Jac shouted above it all.

Sawyer exited with a half-wave and pained smile, and, after a brief lull, conversation turned to their respective plans for the weekend. Langfranc's sly smile returned as Jac related his mother's and aunt's efforts at match-making.

'Oh, to be young again,' Langfranc said theatrically. 'So, apart from a client that tried to escape, creamed two guards and says he wants to die, and now your aunt trying to marry you off to Louisiana's finest – life's just fine.'

'Yep . . . just fine.' For a moment the hubbub in the restaurant became the echoing shouts and taunts on the corridors of Libreville. His mouth was suddenly dry, a sour, copper tang as if once again he was sucking in the stale prison air, and he found it harder this time to push a smile – though he was sure Langfranc caught the shadow that crossed his eyes before he looked down to mask it.

But Langfranc said nothing then – saving any comment

until they were settling the bill and he saw the same shadow as Jac's cell-phone rang. His sister, no doubt with a pre-weekend briefing. Jac let it go into message service.

'Something else is troubling you, isn't it, Jac?'

'Yes . . . yes, it is.' Jac exhaled heavily. 'Haveling phoned me this morning to tell me that Marmont's condition had worsened. The hospital give him less than twenty per cent chance of pulling through. Haveling said that the next forty-eight hours would be the most telling – but that, obviously, if Marmont died, all bets were off.'

Jac found himself on edge over the following days, fearful each time the phone rang that it would be Haveling calling to say that Marmont had died.

Late afternoon, with the help of the company's IT man, he'd discovered more about the e-mail: signed up and sent from an internet café, Cybersurf on Prytania Street, and an anonymous, untraceable e-mail address: *durransave4@hotmail.com*. He phoned Cybersurf – it had been paid cash and they didn't recall who'd been on that computer then.

Just as the last people were leaving the office, Penny Vance calling out, 'Have a nice weekend', Jac finally sent the reply he'd been turning over in his mind the past twenty-four hours. Equally brief, but hopefully it might draw them out and give him what he needed; *if* anything came back.

His phone started ringing only minutes after he got back to his apartment, his hand hovering a second before he picked up; *Haveling*? But it was Jeff Coombs, his squash and tennis partner and one of the few friends he'd made in his three years in New Orleans. He begged off a squash game Jeff was trying to organize for early Saturday evening.

'Heading out to Hammond for the weekend to see Mum and Sis.'

'I understand. Duty calls. Maybe we'll get in a game in the week, Wednesday or Thursday night? I'll phone you then.'

Part of that duty now included pressure to get him married

off. He tried to relax in the shower, breathing long and slow with his eyes closed as he let the water run over his body, as if at the same time it was washing away the pressures of the week and some of the sticky heat and grime still there from Libreville.

Traffic was slow heading out of the city, probably because the weekend weather promised to be fine, and everyone had the same thing in mind: escape to the beaches or bayous. His phone rang again halfway along the Lake Pontchartrain Causeway: his mother, no doubt wondering where he was. He was twenty minutes later in leaving than he'd said, and the traffic had held him up still further. He let it go into message service.

The reason for the call he was confronted with as soon as he arrived.

'Aunt Camille has arranged dinner for us all, and you know how fastidious she is.' His mother looked anxiously at her watch. 'Already it looks like we're going to be ten minutes late. She'll give us hell.'

A twenty-minute run to the far side of Amite, they decided to all go in his car.

'If you'd called and told me, I'd have made sure to be on time,' Jac said as he made the turn back onto the highway.

'She didn't tell me until very late.'

But as he glanced across, his mother looked slightly away. Either she had been told late – probably because his aunt's last dinner invite he'd begged off with an excuse – or his mother had decided to delay telling him, for much the same reason. Either way, his lack of enthusiasm for his aunt's company was now out in the open. Official.

Aunt Camille's house was a sprawling Southern mansion complete with Doric columns on its front façade, straight out of *Gone With the Wind*. A servant with white tails and gloves greeted them and served them dinner. Perpetuation of the plantation-era image, except that he was white. Hired from an Atlanta-based agency that specialized in English servants, because she'd heard that they were the best.

That must have caused her weeks of mental anguish, thought

Jac: choosing between what was considered traditionally 'correct' and what was best.

To her friends and those wishing to be kind to her, Camille was a colourful eccentric, a character. To nearly everyone else, including Jac, she was an impossible snob and social aspirant.

Camille waited until the second course before broaching the subject. Everything with a purpose, but also very much in order. Arranged liaisons with the Blanquette de Veau.

'I suppose Catherine has talked to you about Jennifer, the Bromwells' daughter?'

'Yes . . . yes.' He caught his mother's eye fleetingly before, slightly flushed, she brought her concentration back to her plate. 'She mentioned that she was very nice.'

'Yes . . . *nice*.' Camille aired the word as if it had scant relevance in her world. 'She also happens to be the daughter of one of the richest men in the state, Tobias Bromwell. And I have to tell you, he was more than a little intrigued when I shared with him the noble line running through our family.'

'Ooooh . . . right.' As Jac let out the words with a tired exhalation, his eyes drifted to the coat of arms on the far wall. Soon after arriving in America, Camille had traced her family history back, she claimed, all the way to Louis XV. In fact, it had only been a distant cousin of Louis XV, a grand duke with an estate in Bourges. But she'd used that relentlessly as her ticket to every society gathering she could, as well as to attract her husband, one of Louisiana's leading property realtors, dead these past eight years. When she'd previously pressed home the importance of their royal lineage, they'd argued, Jac pointing out that the relevance of royalty to most French people, including himself, had probably been best demonstrated by what they did to Marie Antoinette. Camille, though, was hopelessly blinkered and, having gone that route herself, she no doubt saw it as the way forward for everyone else: the use of their royal lineage, however tenuous, to snag a wealthy partner; money meets respectability. But as he went to answer, he caught his mother looking across anxiously, hoping that he wouldn't make a scene. 'Yes . . . I can see how that might intrigue him.'

The sarcasm was lost on Camille. Her knife and fork hovered only a second above her plate before she continued. 'Of course, Jac. This isn't France, you know, where there's fallen royalty in practically every other hamlet. Here in America, such things are a rarity. You've got to make best use of it where you can.'

'Yes, I appreciate that better now.' Again, it went a mile above Aunt Camille's head, or didn't penetrate her rhino skin. But as Jac pushed a tight smile, he caught his mother suppressing a smirk at the corner of her mouth. He'd handled it the best way.

'So . . . good.' Camille placed her cutlery in line on her plate as she finished. 'I can take it then that you're keen to see Jennifer for a date?'

'Well, I don't know, I . . .' He was about to comment that he didn't want to rush into it, but caught again his mother's anxious look.

'You know, opportunities like this with girls like Jennifer don't come along every day,' Camille said. 'And if we snub her or dally around, the door will probably be closed straight in our faces – never to open again.'

Jac felt the pressure like a tight coil at the back of his neck. His aunt pushing, persuading, controlling, like she did with so much in her life – almost second nature now. And his mother subservient, living in her shadow, afraid to go against her. The way they'd lived practically since his father's death. Over three years now, but at times it felt like a lifetime – probably because so much had changed. Their life now bore no resemblance to their life before. Sun-glowed days at their Rochefort farmhouse or Isle de Ré beaches, his parents both carefree, relaxed, his mother smiling and laughing at his father's comments and quips. Not a care in the world. And his mother now: her eyes dull and haunted, shoulders slumped as if holding the weight of the world, chewing at her bottom lip as she panicked over what he might say next.

'I know, I . . . I . . .' Jac felt terribly torn: his mother urging him to acquiesce, anything for an easy life, his father telling him to fight back, don't stand for it any more, break the cycle now or you might never be able to.

Perhaps his aunt had been right on one front, even if her comment had been intended as just another snipe: '*Surely you can't be serious, doing criminal instead of corporate law? Corporate is where the money is, and you've already got your feet under the table. You don't want to end up a pipe-dreamer like your father. I mean, look where that got him.*'

At least with the money from corporate law, he'd have been able to free his mother and sister from Camille's clutch. And now, like his father, his life was becoming a series of diminishing options.

'I . . . I think I should . . .' A tingle ran up Jac's spine. The vital element he'd missed earlier with Durrant suddenly hit him. He delved into his pocket for his cell-phone, holding one hand up in apology as he dialled. 'One minute. Sorry . . . someone I remembered I have to call.'

As it rang, Aunt Camille contemplated him with rueful impatience, as if convinced the call was just a ruse, a diversionary tactic. His mother looked away awkwardly, her face flushed. On the third ring it went to an answerphone.

'You're through to the office of Thomas. J. Haveling, Chief Warden of Libreville prison. I'm either away from my office right now or unavailable, so please . . .'

Jac was about to ring off and try his assistant Pete Folley, but then had second thoughts: he didn't know how far Bateson's grapevine of influence went, whether Folley could be trusted. Any passing of information between them, and the game would be up.

He left a message asking Haveling to call him back urgently.

'So . . . what do you want me to tell Jennifer Bromwell?' Camille pressed.

'Sorry . . . just one more minute.' Haveling might not pick up the message for hours, or perhaps not until the next morning. Jac couldn't risk the wait; he needed to put something in motion immediately. Every second could be vital. He dialled out to John Langfranc, who thankfully was there and answered quickly.

Jac explained the problem, looking away from his aunt as she held one hand out in exasperation and lifted her eyes heavenward.

'The best guy I know for that sort of thing is a private eye and writ-server called Bob Stratton in Morgan City,' Langfranc commented. 'It could take him a couple of hours to get out to Libreville. And from the sound of it, you don't want to lose even that time. Worth a try though, in case you're stuck or he knows someone closer.'

Halfway through Jac scribbling a contact number on the back of a business card from his wallet, Camille silently mouthed, 'Well?' She whisked the air with her raised hand as she added voice. 'What do I tell her?'

'Thanks, John.' Jac sighed as he rang off. 'Okay. Okay. Tell her we're on for a date. But not this coming week. Too much to sort out. Next weekend.' What would it harm, one date, thought Jac. How bad could it be? At least the pressure was off for all concerned. His mother risked a faint smile, relieved that battle was done. But as he saw his aunt's fuller, more satisfied smile, basking in the glory of yet another triumph – once again he heard his father's voice telling him that he should have put up more of a stand, shouldn't have given in so quickly.

Perhaps in one way Aunt Camille was right. Like his father, he was a dreamer. Any chances of saving Lawrence Durrant's life were fast ebbing away before he'd even started. Jac dialled Bob Stratton's number. But with each extra ring with no answer, Jac felt any remaining hope slipping further away.

5

Larry Durrant could feel his mother's eyes on his right shoulder, all but burning a hole right through it. She'd always been there in the same position in the courtroom through those days of the trial, give or take a few seats either way. And Francine, too, had sat in a similar place – but they'd hardly ever been together at the same time because of them alternating on taking care of Joshua, except for the few times Franny's mother had helped out.

Franny's stare had been different: shifting, uncomfortable, not meeting his gaze directly for too long when on occasion he'd turned around, as if uncertain whether he was guilty or not. But his mother's stare had been direct, unflinching: either she believed in him no matter what, or was trying to see through to his very soul to understand what might have possessed this being that she'd brought into the world to kill that poor woman.

He'd had the first dream then: a shadowy figure holding the gun on Jessica Roche, firing just as he was screaming out for him not to. Unsure if it was someone else, or he was merely looking at himself, that shaky, unstable side of himself that he had little control over and might have actually done it. The evidence said he'd done it, his memory, such as it was, said that he'd done it, and then he'd said it himself in his confession. But suddenly that shadowy figure was there to say maybe . . . *just maybe*.

When he'd first had the dream, shaking his head from fitful sleep as he sat by a bailiff ready for the next day's court battle, his first thought was that it was a protective device for his psyche; creating another character who'd actually fired the gun, because part of his mind couldn't accept that he'd done something so horrific.

But as the court case continued, with his mother's eyes each day boring into his shoulder, he wondered if it was also partly for that; that if the shadowy figure in his dreams looked his way and he was able to see its face, he'd have been able to turn and call out to his mother that he'd seen who it was and it wasn't him! '*I didn't do it*!'

Yet the figure in his dreams never did turn his way, and so he was never able to rid himself of that penetrating stare and all the guilt, recrimination, anguish and lost hope that went with it.

And years later when he was still having the same dream, by then often mixed up with his mother staring at his back on those courtroom days – he was still never able to see its face. He was never able to phone his mother before she died, five years after the trial, as he'd hoped and prayed he'd be able to, and say, 'Ma, I don't think I did it.'

Bob Stratton was in his local bar watching his favourite football team, the New Orleans Saints, play the Arizona Cardinals, when his cell-phone rang.

He'd switched it off at the beginning of the game, but when the Saints were trailing 14–6 by the first quarter, his enthusiasm began to wane and, remembering the call he'd been waiting for hadn't come through yet, he switched it back on.

'Jim, is that you?' he shouted above the noise of the television.

'No, as I said, it's Jac McElroy,' Jac repeated a shade louder. 'John Langfranc gave me your number.'

'Oh, right. And what can I do for you, sir?'

Stratton nodded at intervals and watched Hambrick of the Cardinals rip through the Saints' defence with another run as Jac explained what he wanted.

'The problem is, I'm tied up with something right now,' Stratton said. 'Can it wait until tomorrow?'

'No, that's just the problem.' Jac told Stratton why there was such dire urgency. 'If this guard comes around before we have someone present to take his account – it could be too late.'

Stratton looked at his watch, then at the game on the TV. It didn't look like the Saints were going to pull this around, so maybe he should save himself the pain. He could listen to it on the radio on his way out there, and at least vent his frustration in private by banging the steering wheel when need be. The couple of times he'd slapped the bar counter and shouted abuse at the TV, a few heads had turned his way.

'It'll take me at least two hours to get out there. Any use to you?'

'Yes. Absolutely.' Jac filled in the rest of the details. 'Thanks, you're a life-saver.'

Aunt Camille was looking keenly at Jac as he hung up. Having watched him pace like a caged lion at the close of dinner as he tried to get hold of Stratton, her interest had been piqued.

'Important, by the looks of it?'

'Yes, yes. It's a murder case.' Jac couldn't resist it. In their last heated debate about his move to criminal law, she'd commented disdainfully: '*Starting from rung one like this, it'll be years before they hand you anything worthwhile, heavyweight.*'

Camille arched one eyebrow. 'Murder, you say. Any case we might know?'

Jac eased back. Eleven years on, Durrant was still a landmark trial, and in the run up to his execution was again grabbing major headlines. Camille would be bound to voice strong comment and, in responding, he'd risk breaching client confidentiality.

'No, no. Nothing important. Just an also-ran.'

'Oh, I see.' Camille nodded and smiled tightly. 'An also-ran case.'

Back to where she expected his legal career to be. Going nowhere fast.

The guards' regular card game took place in the watch room an hour after shut-down. Every lock and bolt had been secured, monitors checked, and residual hubbub and chatter from the inmates had by then faded out. All that lay ahead was a long, quiet night, so out came the cards.

Glenn Bateson presided, but not everyone was invited to join in. Bateson ran a strict game, minimum stake of $20 a hand, poker or thirteen-card canasta, and one of those who looked on with curiosity as voices and blood pressure rose with the heat of the game, but had never been invited to join in, was Miles Elden, or 'Scope' as he was nicknamed, because he was always scoping around, head turning and craning to every corner of the prison. Hardly ever stopped moving.

Scope was a regular visitor to the prison chapel, so Bateson always thought his religious principles would keep him away from the game – but now he was keen to have him join in. When he saw Scope pass the open door to the watch room and glance over, Bateson beckoned him over enthusiastically.

'Hey, why don't you join us?' Bateson beamed his widest smile.

'I don't know . . . I . . .' Scope hovered uncertainly by the door.

'Come on. It's not really gambling with thirteen-card canasta. More of a mind- and skill-game than chance. We'll show you how to play and give you a few trial hands with no stakes – then go in at just $10 a hand if and when you feel confident.'

Scope put up a bit more resistance, but it was clear that Bateson wasn't about to take no for an answer, and with a final welcoming smile and nod of encouragement he had a spare seat swiftly pulled up.

On the first night, Scope won $40, on the second $110,

and Bateson waited until the third night to put in the sting. Scope dropped $680 on two almost unbeatable hands.

'Don't worry. Hands like that, you're bound to make it back the next night,' Bateson assured.

Scope didn't. He dropped another $1,140 the following night.

Scope looked panic-stricken as he took Bateson to one side at the end of the game. 'That's a big chunk of my month's salary there. I was hoping you might cut me a bit of slack and let me pay, say, over the next few months?'

Bateson sucked in his breath. 'If it was just up to me, sure. I'd wait. But some of the other guys here, they got heavy commitments and maybe other dues from games they gotta settle. So it ain't so easy.' Bateson paused heavily, enjoying letting Scope stew for a moment more before becoming pensive. 'But maybe there's something else you could help me out with that could settle this.'

'You didn't have to agree to the date, if you didn't want to, you know,' Jean-Marie said. 'Certainly not just because of me and Mum.'

'I think I did, and you know it. Camille would have just kept on pushing, and you and mum would have got the worst of it. Thankfully, I only have to see her when I choose.'

They'd left Camille's an hour ago, and Jac's sister Jean-Marie had grabbed his ear as soon as their mother had gone to the kitchen to make coffee before he left.

Jean-Marie looked down thoughtfully for a second. Seventeen going on twenty-something, the past six years with their father's business collapse, the cancer which finally led to his death, then the upheaval and move to America to live partly in the shadow of their aunt's charity and favour, had made her world-weary beyond her years. Petite, quiet and studious, the extra age didn't show in her body or face, only in the sullen intensity in her eyes now and then; the same gaze she levelled now at Jac as she looked back up.

'I suppose you're right. She's a determined old dog, even if often she aims to be well meaning.'

Jac smiled. 'I think you give her too much credit. I think she enjoys turning the screws and watching people squirm. You should have just ended on "old dog" – just about hits the right note.'

Jean-Marie chuckled. 'Anyway, talking of "old dogs", you certainly could do a lot worse than a date with Jennifer Bromwell. She's quite cute, in fact – in a Britney Spears sort of way. "Hot" I think is the American term for it. Or is it "cool"? I forget now.'

Jac fired a doubtful grimace. His sister no doubt knew the right term long ago, but he rode along with the tease.

'Spoilt though, I suppose?'

'No, didn't seem it. I've only met her a couple of times when she came over to Camille's with her father – but she seemed quite normal and approachable. She spoke to me and Mum for a bit, and she was very friendly.'

'That's probably just because she thinks we're royalty.' Jac couldn't resist teasing back.

'No, I don't think so. I got the impression that for her that was all just a their-generation thing – Camille's and her dad's. Royalty and money. I don't think she gives a damn about either – came across as a bit of a hippy in that respect. Or maybe just a silly idealist.'

This time when Jean-Marie forced a smile, Jac couldn't tell whether she was teasing or not. The lessons for them with money had come harder than most.

Jac feigned a crestfallen look. 'Oh, that's a shame. I was hoping that with my royalty connections, I might get "lucky". If that's the American term?'

Jean-Marie leant forward and lightly punched him on the arm. Few of their teasing jousts did she ever win, but the contests were becoming tighter as she got older.

With the jolt, Jac instinctively stole another glance at his watch – the umpteenth time he'd done so since leaving Aunt

Camille's. *Why hadn't Stratton called yet?* He'd expected his call to say he'd arrived at the hospital over an hour ago now.

'Is it the same thing you were worried about earlier?' Jean-Marie asked. 'You know, the murder case you called about when we were at Camille's.'

'Yeah, the same.'

'And is it just an also-ran case, like you said?'

Jean-Marie knew him better than most, and from her tone he could tell that she'd read the earlier lie. No point in continuing it.

'No, it's quite a big case. But it's only a clemency plea, and looks bound to fail. That's why the senior partners have given it to me. So that when it goes down in flames, their reputations are well clear of any heat.'

'And, as Aunt Camille asked – is it a case that anyone might know?'

'Yes, it's the Lawrence Durrant case.' Jac said the words flatly, plainly, belying the gravity and intent they deserved. Perhaps because, by now, he'd become used to repeating them. Or due to the pervasive feeling that had swept over him as the evening progressed: a sense of guilt clinking glasses and chatting aimlessly while Durrant lay in his cell at Libre-ville, the clock fast ticking against him. Was that what it was going to be like for the forty-four days: guilt at every moment that breathed freedom and life, or was it just the sense of time being wasted that jarred?

'Oh, I see.' Equally flatly, plainly. Even within her own little world of studies, computer games, pop posters, starting to look at boys differently and coping with the transition from French to American culture – the increasing media barrage of the Durrant case had managed to penetrate.

'But for God's sake, don't tell anyone – not even Mum. If she's pushed by Camille, she'll find it hard to keep it under wraps.'

Jean-Marie hastily shook her head. 'Don't worry, I won't say anything. I promise. I'll . . .' She quickly side-tracked as she saw their mother walking back in with the coffee. 'I was just saying to Jac that he shouldn't worry about the date with Jennifer. She seems very nice.'

'Yes, she does – as I already told Jac.' Catherine set the coffee tray down. 'No need to worry at all.'

But from his mother's forced smile, Jac could tell that the thought of her son having to go on an arranged date because of the situation they were in was troubling her more than any of them.

Bob Stratton's journey out to St Tereseville was marked by stages in the Saints–Cardinals game on his car radio.

As he started on the Lake Pontchartrain Causeway, they'd managed to claw back three points with a field-goal. But only four miles in, as the first swirls of mist started to hit his windscreen, they fell back eight points from a touch-down that was converted. And as the mist became heavier, as if mirroring the cloud of doom fast descending over his team, they fell back another three points.

Stratton switched off when the next touch-down against came. It was becoming too painful, and no way were they going to be able to play their way out of this particular hole. Immediately the radio commentary died, he heard the sirens from behind and saw brake lights through the mist ahead.

He tapped his brakes and followed behind a slow crawling tail-back for three minutes before it ground to a complete halt.

More sirens – two police cars and an ambulance twenty seconds behind – screamed past him.

Obviously a collision ahead. Stratton looked at his watch. Could be a long one. He toyed with the idea of tuning back into the game, but the combination of the Saints' doomed performance and the traffic jam would probably be too much for his blood pressure.

He tuned into an easy-listening station, KMEZ, and started humming along to Glen Campbell's 'Wichita Lineman'.

★

Jac had heard the boyfriend's voice next door only two nights after the big argument, but for the last three nights she seemed to have been alone. Or at least he hadn't been able to discern any other voices from next door.

After the night of the argument – '*I just don't like other guys lookin' at you like that*' – Jac had become curious to see her, and he'd started working on a plan.

She probably headed for the stairs at the other end of the apartment complex – he never recalled hearing her pass his door after leaving. If it was at night, she'd put on the timed hallway lights, and if he left instantly and rushed towards the L-bend where the corridor turned towards the far stairway, he might catch a glimpse of her before she headed down. The corridor was carpeted, but if he kept his shoes off as an extra precaution, hopefully she wouldn't hear him approaching.

Having devised a plan, Jac found himself listening out more acutely for movement and voices from next door, trying to gauge when she would be leaving so that he could accurately time his own exit. The first occasion, by the time he'd heard her door shut, it was practically too late for him to bother running out. The second, the only other opportunity so far, by the time he'd reached the corner of the L, she'd already started down the stairs the far side. She didn't glance round in that fleeting second before disappearing from view, and he was no nearer knowing what she looked like.

When he'd first returned from his mother's, he hadn't heard any noises from next door. Just after midnight, she was either still out or already in bed.

But having still not heard from Stratton, Jac wasn't ready for bed yet. And, sitting there with the TV on low and not really paying attention to Bloomberg's financial forecasts and next day's weather, suddenly he heard movement from next door. Sounded like the bedroom – cupboard doors and drawers being opened and closed. There'd been the sound of another door opening and closing just before – but it hadn't been the front door. So probably she'd been in the bathroom, furthest away from him. Sounds from there barely reached him.

He moved closer to the wall, ear nestled against it and strained for the minutest sound from next door – a familiar position for many of the past few nights now – and for a moment a picture of her fresh from the bath or shower, hair still wet, hit him. But still he had no face to match to that misty image.

He stayed there listening longer than he realized, his legs starting to have a few cramp twinges, and for a while the sounds became more muted and indiscernible. Probably she was getting ready for bed.

And so when he heard more strident opening and closing of cupboard doors, and then suddenly the front door slamming, he was caught by surprise.

Shoes off and thrown brusquely aside, he managed to reach his own front door in just two strides. Out and running, breathless. He tried as best he could to suppress it so that she didn't hear him approaching like some rampant buffalo. Soft and swift strides too, stockinged feet on carpet.

He could hear the steady pad of her footsteps fifteen yards the other side of the corner, and prayed that it masked his own rapid stride.

And this time he did reach the corner before she headed down the stairs – just as his cell-phone rang.

She wheeled around, and he ducked back round the corner equally as sharply and hit the button to put the call into message service.

He could hear that she wasn't moving, was still rooted to the same spot, and could almost feel her eyes boring through the bit of corner wall shielding him. He kept perfectly still, struggling to swallow back the weight of his breathing from his brief madcap run. He feared for a moment that she was going to head back towards him. He looked at the number calling: Bob Stratton! He was desperate to get to it before Stratton rang off – but couldn't risk moving or making any sound.

She stayed in the same position a moment longer, un-decided, though to Jac it felt like a lifetime with his back pressed hard against the wall, breath held, staring helplessly at Stratton's number on his cell-phone as the vital seconds ticked by. Finally she turned and headed down the stairs.

He waited for her to get a few paces down before he raced back to his own apartment, and as soon as the door was shut he pressed to take the call.

'Hello, hello! Bob! Are you still there?'

'Yes, I . . . I was just leaving a message. I didn't think you were answering.'

'I was tied up for a moment. Sorry.' Jac fought to regain his breath. 'But I'm here now. So, tell me. How did it go?'

'I was held up on the Causeway due to an accident – that's why I haven't been able to call till now. I was late getting there. But no worries – Marmont is still spark out.' Stratton's tone dropped. 'The only thing was that one of Marmont's prison guard buddies was already there when I arrived. Some guy called Miles Elden.'

'Oh.' Jac felt a twinge of concern. Elden? The name didn't strike a chord. He had no idea if he was part of Bateson's clique or not. Could be just innocent.

'It was okay. I flashed my badge, and said no visitors unless first cleared with your office. Or, if anyone had a problem with that, the DA. He didn't look about to argue with the bluff, said he was simply looking in 'cause he was Marmont's best friend. And he left him a book to read for when he wakes up. Stephen King's *Pet Sematary*.' Stratton chuckled. 'Probably takes a while for books to reach the comatose reading lists.'

'At least we know one thing about this Elden: he's an opti-mist.' But Elden wasn't the only one praying that Marmont wouldn't die, Jac reminded himself.

Jac spent a moment confirming with Stratton how they were going to keep up the vigil on Marmont's bedside before ringing off, then once again he was with his back against the wall, eyes closed, trying to wind down from the evening. Only a glimpse, but she was gorgeous: a coffee-cream mixture of African and Caucasian, with a hint of something else from the faint slant at the corner of her eyes: Malaysian? Philippine? He let his breathing fall steadily as he tried to bring her clearly into focus again in his mind.

But the rush to see her and almost getting caught, like some pathetic voyeur, only served to remind him of the sorry state of his love life. How lonely and desperate he'd become. It was probably best that he was going on an arranged date. He could hardly be trusted any more to arrange anything for himself.

6

'Why do you want to die? Why is it you don't want me to try and save you?'

Jac went straight in with the key question. No point in beating around the bush. He might have got over most of the first hurdle with the attempted prison break, if Marmont survived, but unless he tackled this, they were all wasting their time. He could prepare the most marvellous clemency plea for the Governor's office, but Durrant had to agree to its contents and sign the plea petition.

Durrant shuffled uncomfortably, shrugged. He looked like he'd have preferred some delay, as if a question of such purport deserved reasonable preamble. He looked almost offended to be hit with it straightaway.

'I don't know. Tired, first and foremost. Tired of the appeals and empty promises, tired of waiting. Tired of false hope. Tired of *life*.' Durrant looked up with a steady gaze as he hit the last words, as if he'd only at that moment finally discovered what, most of all, he was tired of.

'You're tired, and so you want out. Is that about it?' Jac said it offhandedly, disdainfully, and Durrant's stare became icy. Jac fully expected some confrontation if he was to stand a chance of shifting Durrant's stance. It wasn't going to be easy.

'Yeah, that's about it.' Equally offhandedly, disdainfully.

Jac stood up and took a couple of paces away from the interview table before turning to look back again. 'That may be okay for you. But have you given a thought to those you're leaving behind. Your wife. Your son. How old is he now?' Jac remembered the age from Durrant's file, but he wanted Durrant to say it, be reminded.

'Twelve. Had his first birthday just a month before Christ-mas while I was held for the trial.'

Jac considered Durrant dolefully for a second. 'Maybe your wife will come to terms with you dying, has had a fair time to prepare herself. But do you really think your son will at that age?' And as he saw Durrant flinch and look away, he knew he'd struck a chord. The first chink in Durrant's armour, built-up hard these past eleven years.

Durrant knew he was being worked, but it was difficult to get angry. This new lawyer was young, still wet behind the ears, was probably not yet seasoned and world-weary enough to know that he was a hopeless case. But in a way that was also strangely gratifying. Most other lawyers wouldn't have bothered to put in the time at this stage, would already have been signalling the guards to be let out. '*Okay, so you want to die. I'll file accordingly: no clemency petition to be made.*' It was gratifying to know that someone still cared.

Durrant snorted derisively. 'You just don't understand. The first five years I was here, my wife and son didn't come to see me once. Too annoyed, too angry with what I'd done, she explained when she finally took the time to send me a letter. Then when the visits did eventually start, they were just token look-sees, at most once or twice a year: my birthday and sometimes just before Christmas as well. *Never* Christmas itself.' Durrant snorted again. 'She was always too busy with her *other* life and family outside.'

'*Her* family and relations?' Jac pressed to clarify. 'Because I didn't notice anything on the file about a divorce. You're still married?'

'Yeah, if you could call it that. Francine met someone new eighteen months after I was inside, and they started a relationship. Planned to marry too, if he'd been able to get his divorce papers through cleanly and on time from his ex. But by the time they looked ready to come through three years later, their relationship was already cooling off. When

71

they finally split was the first time Francine started visiting me here with Josh. Then just over two years ago, she meets a new guy, and after ten months with him, once again the visits stop. And again there's wedding plans. Next June, if I remember right, six months after I've gone. Suitable mourning and breathing space. Just wouldn't be right to mess up such plans with complications like, say, me stayin' alive.' This time the derisive smile became quickly lopsided and that cool stare was back again. 'So you see, Mr McElroy, my family deserted me long before I ever thought of deserting them.'

Jac took a long breath. It was going to be harder than he had realized. The only way he was going to prise Durrant from his death-wish was with a crowbar.

'So, you feel sorry for yourself because you think your family has deserted you. So now it's payback time: deserting them in the most dramatic way possible. No way they're ever going to forget that action – especially young Joshua.'

Durrant tensed as if he was about to get to his feet, but then his shoulders relaxed again. *Deserted*? Except, that is, for the regular e-mails of the past year – though now it had been almost two months since the last one. Had Francine found out and stopped Josh? Or maybe Frank, her new partner, had put his spoke in.

Durrant's wry, lopsided smile resurfaced. 'You don't get it, do you? This isn't about them, it's about me. Oh sure, they deserted me. But then that was no less than I deserved. And Francine, she's a good woman – still attractive, too. She deserves a good and full life out there.' Durrant shrugged. 'Who am I to deny that – especially after all I put her through. So it all comes back down to what *I* want and expect. Me.' Durrant tapped his chest. 'And, as I said, Mr McElroy, I'm tired. Tired of the appeals and promises. Tired of the false hope. Because, let's face it – you're not going to be able to get Governor Candaret to set me free with a full pardon. That just ain't going to happen. The best that you can hope for is a commute to life imprisonment – another twelve to fifteen years in here, maybe more. And so that makes my mind turn to what else I'm tired of. Tired of the heat and sweat of this hell-hole, tired of the guards clanking keys and stomping their boots along the walkways in the dead of night just to ensure we never get a full night's sleep. Tired of the weeping of prisoners when they first come in, or sometimes much later, when they finally break and can't stand it any more. Tired of the brutality of the guards and prisoners, mental and physical, constantly watching out for a shiv aimed for mine or Roddy's back. Tired of the corruption and drugs and stench of it all. And I don't just mean the stench of near-on four thousand caged and sweaty men, or the smell of their urine, or the smell of bleach that never quite manages to smother the sweat and urine. I'm talking about a stench of loneliness, fear and sheer hopelessness that don't just hit your nose and synapses – it reaches right down to grip your heart and soul like an icy claw. Leaves you completely empty. And hardly a day has passed over the past long years that I haven't prayed for a light to shine through the gloom and shift that emptiness. But the light that finally reached me, kept me going, wasn't for hope in *this* lifetime, Mr McElroy.'

Durrant fixed Jac with a steady gaze again, but this time the iciness had gone, his eyes little more than hollow orbs, weary and pitiful. 'You see, when they finally execute me, they're not really killing me. Because I died the day I came in here. When they finally do that deed, they'll be releasing me. I'll finally be going where I've wanted to be now for a long, long time. That'll be my freedom. My Ascension Day.'

'It all went well. Cleanly.'

'That's good to hear.'

'No possible comeback. Just like the others.'

'That's good to hear, too,' Roche said. 'Except for the one that didn't go so cleanly, started all this. We should never forget that.'

As if Roche was ever likely to allow him to, Nel-M thought, but said nothing. If he'd responded to every one of Roche's jibes and put-downs over the years – his way of compensating for the fact that he was only five-two, podgy, balding, lizard-eyed, and had emphysema, being the second richest man in the State wasn't enough – they'd have spent all their time arguing. But he was sure Roche kept him around not only for safety's sake – his darkest secrets held close under his wing – but so that he could keep reminding him of the main shadow that had hung over them the past long years. Meter out punishment like a slow-drip torture: a jibe or snide remark every three months, at most six months without one if he was lucky.

'Got a bit more background too on that lawyer you mentioned,' Nel-M deftly shifted the subject. 'Jacques McElroy. Lives in an apartment in the Warehouse District, mom lives out in Hammond with his younger sister. All of them fresh over from France just three years ago, shortly after his father's death – though they're originally from Scotland. And you were right about him being a greenhorn. Although he's thirty-one, he's been doing criminal law less than a year. His bag before that was corporate law, and French corporate law at that. Beaton couldn't have passed it lower down the rungs if he'd tried – which I think is an indication of what little weight the firm's attaching to this. They don't think he's got a chance of convincing Candaret to commute.'

'Pretty much what I heard initially. But it's good to get the detail and the confirmation.'

'But that's not the best part,' Nel-M continued. 'Apparently this McElroy's striking out before he's even started. It seems that Durrant and some buddies were trying for a prison break – which is gonna make any possible clemency from Candaret highly unlikely.'

Roche eased a muted chuckle. 'Always did have the knack of doing the wrong thing at the wrong time, our Mr Durrant.' He took a laboured fresh breath. 'Who was this from?'

'My prison contact, Bateson.' But with the mention of Bateson, Nel-M thought he'd better give Roche the full story. Unlikely that it would develop into anything; but if it did, Roche would question why he wasn't told earlier. 'The only small fly in the ointment is that this McElroy isn't accepting the prison break account for what it is – he's making out that Durrant was in fact trying to save the neck of a friend under attack.'

'Do you think he'll get anywhere with that?'

'No, don't think so. Guards' word against the prisoners – looks like a non-starter. But you never know.'

'No, you don't,' Roche agreed, his breathing suddenly heavier, more troubled. 'But one thing we do know is that this young lawyer, despite his inexperience, doesn't look like he's going to be the type to simply roll over and die at the first obstacle. And that's just what we don't need – some young Turk eager to make a name for himself.'

Nel-M left an appropriate pause. 'What do you want me to do with him?'

Roche's breathing was now rattling heavily at the other end, and Nel-M wasn't sure if he was mulling over the situation or having trouble catching his breath to form the words.

After a second, Nel-M prompted, 'I mean, do you just want me to warn him off at this stage, or, as you say, if he's so eager to make a name for himself – perhaps a few column inches arranged alongside Raoul Ferrer?'

Roche's breathing continued to rise and fall heavily for a moment, like a tide over rough shale, before he finally spoke again.

Ascension Day? So, Durrant's cell altar hadn't just been a cover for an escape route. His religious conviction was real. That might at least appease Haveling that his trust hadn't been *totally* abused; but then given Haveling's firebrand religious bent, that might actually work against getting his support. '*If*

Durrant truly believes that that's his calling – to be with God – then who are we to stand in his way?'

But it was one hell of a speech from Durrant. One that Jac couldn't immediately fathom out a way of countering. Jac was suddenly more conscious of the one-way mirrored screen, the guard the other side probably wondering what Durrant had said at such length that made his lawyer look so perplexed and lost for words. The sound link wouldn't be on: client confidentiality.

Jac had been scrambling from day one with Durrant – the attempted escape, Marmont in hospital, Durrant's apparent death-wish and appeasing Haveling – but now it was crunch time. It all ended here and now if he didn't think of something quickly. No point, though, in mentioning that mystery e-mail, at least not until he knew more: some anonymous crazy who thought he might be innocent? At best it would cruelly build up Durrant's hopes; at worst he'd simply sneer at Jac all the more, would underline just how desperately Jac was clutching at any last straw.

And he obviously wasn't going to get far simply trying to cajole and bully Durrant, push him in a corner. Eleven long years in Libreville had toughened his hide too much for that, and he'd used much of that time to educate himself. He was no longer the same man depicted in his initial arrest and trial folders. He was mentally tougher and far more astute. Maybe that was the key; or, at least, a useful conversational side-turn to diffuse things.

'Well, one compensation, I suppose: not all your time in here's been wasted,' Jac commented.

'In what way?' Durrant eyed him warily.

'The studying and literary degree you gained. Quite an achievement. Couldn't have been easy.'

No answer from Durrant, simply a wry smile of acknowledgement, as if he could see already where Jac was heading and wasn't about to be drawn in.

'Then helping run the prison library. Couldn't have been

easy either, and quite a challenge to organize,' Jac continued. 'Must have kept you busy.'

Still no answer from Durrant, only a gentle nod of the head and an impatient, weary gaze, as if to say, '*Tell me when you get to something important, won't you?*'

'The other inmates are going to miss you.' Still that impatient, steady gaze, so Jac clarified: 'You know, your organizational abilities in the library. How you've arranged everything now. No guarantee that whoever takes over from you will keep it the same. And, by the way, do you know who that will be?'

'Roddy,' Durrant said flatly, disinterestedly. 'Or maybe they'll stretch Peretti's duties.'

'Oh.' Roddy was Durrant's closest friend in Libreville, and, although Jac didn't know Peretti, obviously he handled the other two-hour shift of the four the library was open each day, barring Sundays. Durrant would probably have already talked to one or both of them about the continued smooth running of the library after he'd gone. Another dead-end. 'By the way, how did you get the nickname "Thes"?' Jac asked, eager to keep the conversation rolling.

'Short for Thesaurus.'

'Oh, right. Because of your literary expertise?'

'No, from crosswords.'

Durrant had retreated into a pattern of answers between nil and three words, seemed determined not to make things easy on Jac. He was going to have to work for it. 'From crosswords?'

'Yeah, 'cause if you think about it − apart from a few cryptics, most crosswords are built around alternative word choices. Another word for dumb: stupid. Another word for faltering: floundering. Like in a thesaurus.'

Some more words at least, but they were delivered with a tired, laboured tone, as if Durrant was enlightening an irksome, mentally challenged child. Jac couldn't help wondering whether stupid and floundering mirrored how Durrant felt about his lawyer at that moment.

Jac introduced a brisker tone. 'So did the reading and interest in literature come later, or about the same time as the crosswords?'

'Mostly later.'

Jac stayed silent, held a steady gaze on Durrant that made it clear he expected more. He was determined not to be taken for a fool, and probably the best way was to work Durrant equally as hard.

As the silence became uncomfortable and the muted clatter and murmur of the prison beyond reached them, Durrant looked at his shoes briefly before looking back up. 'Oh, sure, early on I was reading some light stuff now and then: Grisham, Patterson, Elmore Leonard. But then as I got deep into the crosswords and progressed from doing the local *Advocate* and *USA Today* to the *Washington Post* and *New York Times* cryptics – sometimes as many as three or four a day – my reading also became deeper and more involved: Steinbeck, Melville, Dostoyevsky, the Bible.'

Full circle back to Durrant's religion. And although he was finally starting to open up more, it was delivered begrudgingly, as if Durrant resented having to explain or saw little purpose to it. After all, he was going to die soon.

But for the first time Jac felt more in control of the situation, felt he'd pieced together enough to be able to fight back. He shook his head. 'You know, you're a real conundrum, Mr Durrant . . .'

'Conundrum . . . as in puzzle, enigma,' Durrant interjected.

Jac continued unabated. 'You've spent much of your time in here making your life more worthwhile: reading, organizing the library, getting a degree in literature, helping with the prison magazine. But then in the same breath, you tell me that everything here all around you is dire, worthless. So dire and worthless that you can't wait to die. And so keen on dying are you, so disinterested in continued life – that you and your prison pals have spent the last year planning to escape.' Jac leant forward over the interview table. 'You're well read, Mr Durrant, so you'll probably know your Plato: that a man is judged by his actions, not his words. And while you might tell me that you want to die and have thrown at me all sorts of reasoning to support that – your actions tell me otherwise. They tell me – correction, *shout* – that you want to live.'

Durrant's sly smile had started rising again – perceived challenge this time rather than annoyance – but halfway through it died with a flinch that brought something harder to his eyes. 'That's because you don't fully pay attention, Mr McElroy. What me and my buddies were aiming for was *freedom*. Not a continued clinging to what passes for life in this rat-hole – but full-blown freedom. And if you're offering me that – then I'd gladly grasp it with both hands, and say "Thank you." But you're not, and we both know damn well that that isn't even likely to happen. The best that you're offering is another ten to fifteen in here, and that being the case, I'd rather say "Thank you, but no thank you. I'll pass."' Durrant leant forward to emphasize his point. 'That being okay with you.'

'No, that's not okay with me,' Jac fired back. Durrant's face was only eighteen inches away, his heavy-hooded eyes drilling home his message, and he recoiled back slightly in surprise. 'I'm not offering an absolute by pleading to Candaret: freedom or even continued well-being in here for you. I'm even far from convinced that Candaret is going to offer *anything*. But what I am offering is *hope*. Hope that he might commute and that in a few years you might be eligible for release. Or that meanwhile something else might come out of the hat.' As close as Jac dared get to hinting at the e-mail. 'And for that alone, it's worth a try. Because even if you weren't well read, Mr Durrant, you'd remember from your Bible alone that when all the evils of the world were let loose from Pandora's Box – all that was left was hope.'

'Greek mythology again, as it happens. Hesiod's *Theogony*, if I remember right.'

'The point I'm trying to make,' Jac rolled on impatiently, 'is that you claim you've seen all manner of dark things in here over the years, all manner of evil – so maybe that hope at the end of the tunnel is somehow fitting. And that's what I'm offering. That's *all* I'm offering.' Jac held out one hand in a helpless gesture. 'But, fine, if you can look me straight in the eye and tell me there's nothing in life you want to hang on for, no possible hope around the corner in a few months or years – then I'll walk out of here now and not look back.'

Durrant's eyes had flickered uncertainly towards the end, as if Jac had hit a raw nerve; but it was only for a couple of seconds, as if what was troubling Durrant was too elusive, pushed quickly away.

'Sorry to disappoint you, Mr McElroy,' Durrant said at length, shaking his head. 'But there's nothing I'm hanging on for. And certainly not hope. I've been thinking things through for some while now – probably too long.'

'Then that makes you a somewhat unique human being, Larry Durrant. Unlike the rest of us. Because you'll also know from your reading that one of the most basic human desires is the need to know what happens next.' Jac kept his gaze steadily on Durrant. 'And do you mean to tell me that there's not a single thing left you want to live for or are curious about knowing what happens next?'

This time Durrant was quick to hide the flinch by looking down at the table, or maybe it was the intensity of Jac's gaze, possibly seeing things which Durrant was keen to shield. The private demons of eleven years in Libreville.

'Unique human being. Been called a few things in my time, but that's a new one.' Durrant smiled crookedly, but kept his eyes averted until he hit his last words. 'But the trouble with that theory, Mr McElroy, is that what happens next in here becomes somewhat predictable.'

Jac absorbed what he saw in Durrant's eyes for a moment before conceding that there was probably nowhere left for him to go. Whatever was niggling at Durrant in the background, in the end eleven years in Libreville had won out. Made him not wish to endure it a day longer.

'Well, I did my best,' Jac said, shuffling his papers back together from the table. 'But one thing I don't think you've thought about fully is Roddy. Seems to me that if you hadn't reached him when you did in the boiler room the other day – Tally would have had his way with him and he'd now be in a body bag. How long do you think he's going to last with you no longer there to watch his back? Three months, six?'

For the first time, Durrant reluctantly granted a more open smile. 'I've got to admit, you're good.'

'What you mean is, I'm not the hopeless, weak-assed rookie lawyer you thought I was when I first walked in here.'

'I wouldn't go that far.'

'More importantly, does that mean I might have finally convinced you to pitch for some hope with our dear Governor Candaret?'

'I wouldn't go that far, either. It might just mean that you're too young and foolish to know when to quit.'

'I think you've given me a pretty good object lesson on that score, Mr Durrant,' Jac said, putting the last of his papers in his case and snapping it shut.

'Yeah, I'm sorry if I went a bit hard on you.' Durrant grimaced. 'Because I know you've gone to some trouble on this.'

'Even sent a detective out to St Tereseville General in case Bateson and his cronies got to Marmont before he woke up. And a supposed friend of Marmont's, Elden, was already out there – though thankfully Marmont was still out. Even left him a book to read for when he woke up: Stephen King's *Pet Sematary*, if you will.'

Durrant smiled. 'Elden is okay. Not particularly one of Bateson's tight circle. But I appreciate it: if not directly for me, then for how Roddy will be dealt with after I'm gone.'

'That's okay.' Jac proffered his hand and Durrant took it

into a shake. 'I just wish you'd change your mind. Because I think Roddy's going to miss you – even if he does manage to survive in here with you gone. And your son. Twelve. Vulnerable age.' That uncertain flinch again, which if he'd been able to read, he might have been able to prise Durrant open more and convince him. But Durrant just nodded dolefully as Jac handed over his card. 'Call me, please, if you do have a change of heart.'

That look of uncertainty – that deep down there was something that Durrant wanted to live for – was the only hope Jac clung to as he paced back through the prison: 'Will call, won't call. Will call, won't call.' But with each echoing step and gate clanked shut behind him through the cavernous extremities of Libreville, that hope began to fade.

7

If nothing else, Dr Leonard Truelle was a creature of habit. He read the daily newspapers every morning in his favourite café on Iberville Street over coffee and croissants, except when he had outside assessments or clinical notes to review for patients that day, in which case he'd use his morning coffee break for that and delay catching up on the troubles of the world outside until he left work.

But on some occasions, like tonight, those assessment reviews also coincided with his Tuesday and Friday single drink rituals — so he'd then spread out with his papers at a corner table rather than sit up at the bar. But the order of reading, day or night, was always the same: first the majors, the *NYT, Washington Post* and *Chicago Tribune*, twelve to fifteen minutes on each, then finally the *Times-Picayune*, which held his attention for no more than six or eight minutes.

Truelle always felt more connected to the country at large than locally, possibly through having graduated from Cornell and spent his first eight years of practice in New York. He'd only gone to New Orleans when his mother became ill. She'd long since died, but through circumstance, the drink and a mess of other problems, he'd never managed to grasp a time when he was organized or brave enough to return.

He still felt, twenty years on from his last days of practice in the Big Apple, that he was in New Orleans through duty rather than choice. The only things he found solace in were the warmer climes and the seafood. The rest of it — the petty wrangling and corruption of city officials, the environmentalists fighting a losing battle against the oil refineries along the coast — constantly grated, and so he always gave the *Picayune* short shrift as he flicked through.

He was flicking through so rapidly, skimming half-blindly, that he could have easily missed the entry, tucked in the bottom left-hand corner of page fifteen: '*Raoul Ferrer, 36, financier and businessman, was found dead in an Algiers car lot in the early hours of Friday morning. Early police reports cite the cause as two gunshot wounds from a 9mm calibre weapon to the head. On occasion linked to the Malastra organization, Ferrer . . .*'

The noise and activity of the bar around him suddenly became more distant, muted. He wasn't sure if the barman, Benny, had heard him above the drone from the sudden blood-rush to his head as he called out for another drink.

But Benny was certainly looking his way, having paused mid-wipe of the bar counter as he saw Truelle suddenly transfixed by the paper as if he'd seen a ghost, one hand gripping tight to the page as he read and re-read, the other reaching absently to knock back in one the bourbon that he'd usually nurse for another half hour.

'Are you sure?' Benny asked, eyeing him with concern. Four months into the ritual, Benny felt that enough rapport existed between them for him to breach barman's protocol and ask why always only the one drink? From that point on, Benny had become a silent conspirator in keeping him clean.

'Yeah, Benny, never been surer. Bring it on.' He beckoned elaborately, but was careful not to meet Benny's eye. Shield the demons. Then, as he watched Benny pouring, 'In fact, bring over the whole bottle.' This time he looked even further aslant – somewhere between New York and New Orleans – to avoid Ben's withering gaze, only looking up with a tight smile as Benny came over and set the glass and bottle down.

'Your funeral,' Benny said resignedly. The tired tone of a barman who'd seen more than he dared count finally slip off the wagon.

Truelle knocked the drink down in two slugs as soon as Benny turned away. Poured, drank; poured, drank; poured, drank . . . but it did little to quell his panic or give him any clarity of thought. His head was still buzzing and his hands still shaking.

He pushed the bottle abruptly away, suddenly picturing the months ahead of trying to push away more and more bottles, but never quite succeeding . . . the lost hours and days and mental lapses, the patients neglected, the sickness and depression, friends patting his shoulder concernedly, 'Are you okay, Len?' . . . the steady downward spiral that he knew so well.

Truelle's eyes darted around the table. There was even a small article on Durrant on page nine of the *NYT*, obviously the first to hit the national press: '*Anti-capital punishment cam-paigners, both local and from out-of-state, are planning a vigil in front of Libreville's prison gates in the run-up to the execution . . .*'

Maybe that was it, Truelle thought. Surrounded by too many demons: the bottle, Durrant, Raoul Ferrer, the bar where Nel-M had paid him a visit just a week ago. He had to get out!

He pushed the table back, its legs grating roughly and turning a few heads from the bar. He felt himself sway uncer-tainly as he took the first few steps – he *had* been off the wagon a long while. In the good old days, he'd have put away a few stiff ones like that without hardly blinking. He waved briefly towards Benny as he passed, again careful not to meet his eye, or for that matter those at the bar who were now watching his exit with curious smiles.

'Tab it, Benny. I'll catch you next time.'

It was worse outside. A confusion of traffic noise, horns beeping, people rushing by and calling out – the height of the rush hour and happy hour on Chartres Street. All of it seemed amplified in his head along with the buzzing, and he felt himself swaying more – or was it the street and all the people around tilting? He bumped into a woman with her shopping bags, and reached out to steady himself on the man just behind – who pushed the arm brusquely away with a sneer. Another horn blaring, sharper, more immediate, the sudden flare of head-lamps making him realize he'd staggered into the road.

He jumped back and took a deep breath, trying to steady himself and his nerves. Maybe he was panicking for nothing. In Ferrer's line of work, it was only a matter of time before he was found in an empty car lot or ditch. But it was the timing in the run-up to Durrant's execution that made it ominous. Nel-M pays himself a visit to make sure that everything is 'cool' – then next on the list is Raoul Ferrer. This time, though, Nel-M had obviously decided that everything wasn't so cool.

The only way he could know for sure was by calling Nel-M. Nel-M probably wouldn't admit it outright, but he'd glean enough from the cadence and inflection of what was said. The trained psychiatrist's ear. But the call in itself might be the one thing to alert Nel-M that things might not be so cool with himself either, would make him next on the list.

Cool. It was a warm and sultry night, but Truelle felt ice-cold, his whole body starting to tremble and shiver. Rooted to the spot amongst the milling throng, his stance underlined how isolated he seemed at that moment, with nobody he felt he could turn to. Advising thousands through the years – but who had ever been there for him when he most needed it? And his burden had been far, far beyond that of any of those he'd had to sit patiently listening to through the years.

Perhaps it was time to tell Nel-M and Adelay Roche about his insurance policies. No point in them finding out after the event that killing him was the one thing that would throw everything into the open.

Jac was waiting in the ante-room to the Payne, Beaton and Sawyer boardroom along with seventeen other lawyers and paralegals for the company's regular Wednesday morning progress meeting, when the call came through on his cell-phone.

The ritual meetings were presided over by either Jeremiah Payne or Clive Beaton – Dougy Sawyer would take the role of company secretary, saying little but making furious notes throughout – and order of importance in the company was all but determined by time of arrival. Junior lawyers and paralegals were expected at 8.20 a.m. sharp, senior lawyers at 8.25, and, finally, the presiding partners at 8.30.

The message was patently clear: when the company gods arrived, woe betide any laggers that might hold up proceedings, even for a second.

The ten-minute wait for the juniors, though, was often insufferable. It was intended to give them more time to prepare their notes or get comments clearer in their minds – but more often than not it just gave them more time to dwell and become increasingly anxious.

Jac was no exception, particularly this morning. He'd been turning over and over in his mind just how much to show and tell about Durrant. If he told about the attempted prison break, Beaton might well axe the case; but then if Haveling decided finally to go with the guards' account of events, the whole thing would come out later. How was he going to cover for that? And he certainly couldn't reveal that Durrant wanted to die – didn't want a plea made on his behalf. For sure, Beaton would axe the whole case instantly.

His cell-phone ringing broke his train of thought. He looked at the number: same area code as Libreville prison, but it wasn't Haveling's direct number. *Durrant!*

Jac quickly answered. Perhaps Durrant had had a change of heart, and he wouldn't have to go through any subterfuge now at Beaton's meeting.

'Mr McElroy. It's about something you said the other day.'

'Yes.' Jac felt his hopes rise.

'About the book that Elden left at the hospital for Marmont.'

'*Pet Sematary*?' Jac subdued his voice to a mumble. He could feel a few eyes on him, particularly Kyle Everett. No calls during the meeting, obviously, but even those prior to it were frowned upon, might disturb the thoughts and note-making of others.

'Yeah. Well, thing is, Marmont has already read that book – several times. In fact, it's his favourite book, and he'll readily quote from it to anyone who's got the time and inclination to listen. Particularly the scene where the dog's brought back to life. Apparently, Marmont lost a much-loved pet dog years back, a Golden Retriever – and he's read and re-read that passage as if wishing the same might happen with his own dog.' Durrant sniggered lightly. 'Of course, on the way completely missing King's underlying message with what eventually happens with the dog.'

'I see.' Jac saw quickly where Durrant was heading. 'You mean there'd be absolutely no point in giving that book to Marmont – unless of course there was an ulterior motive. Such as, say, getting some sort of message to him?'

'Got it in one, Counsellor. Like I said the other day, you're brighter than I thought.'

'You're so kind. But you know, when I first took the call I was hoping it might have been about . . .' In his side vision, Jac could now see Clive Beaton and the other partners approaching the ante-room. He broke off from saying more.

After a second, Durrant prompted. 'About what, Mr McElroy?'

'You know, about . . .' After a peremptory survey of the room, Beaton's eagle eye settled on him. Jac nodded and held one hand up to indicate he'd be finished post haste. 'About what we were discussing the other day.'

'About me wanting to die, Mr McElroy . . . is that what you mean?'

'Yes, that's right . . . about that. I thought you might have had a change of heart.' After a quick aside to a colleague, Beaton's eyes were back on him, keenly. Jac felt himself flush and a tingle rise at the back of his neck. If he was feeling uncomfortable after just a quick glance, how on earth was he going to carry off the subterfuge throughout the entire meeting?

'Afraid of saying it, are we Mr McElroy?' Durrant's voice was jocular, taunting. 'Don't want to face it . . . so maybe if you don't even say it – you can push the spectre further away. Like it was a dirty word.'

'No, it's not that . . . it's . . .'

Durrant rolled straight over him. 'Well, I've done nothing but face death these past years, Mr McElroy, had precious little else worth thinking about – so it don't hold any fears for me any more. So that's why I'm not afraid to say it, use the word.'

'I understand.' All Jac could think of was getting off the line. Half the assembled group had already filed through to the boardroom, and Beaton's stare towards him was now penetrating, bordering on hostile.

'Yeah, you understand,' Durrant mocked. 'So you'll understand too that having thought about it for that long – it ain't exactly the sort of thing I'm going to change my mind about overnight.'

'No, really. I *do* understand. And I'll get somebody onto that book thing with Marmont straightaway. But if you'll excuse me now, I've got to go. I'm already late for a meeting.' Jac rang off and followed Beaton and the last few into the boardroom.

Probably sounded more flippant than he'd intended. *I've got a meeting to attend, so if you want to die – you just go right ahead.* But maybe it wasn't such a bad thing to mislead Durrant that he didn't care that much after all. If as a result Durrant dropped his defences, he might see a clearer way through.

Jac checked his e-mails as soon as he got out of the meeting. Still no reply as yet. He checked first thing every morning and kept half an eye on it through each day, but now four days had passed with nothing, it was starting to look more and more like a prank or hoax. Or a friend or relative of Durrant's that couldn't reveal themselves. If it was real, then why not say who they were or somehow back up their claim?

In the end, Jac hadn't said anything about the dramas with Durrant in the meeting; hopefully there'd be some clear resolve on both fronts over the coming days, and *then* he could say something.

Jac didn't want to call Stratton from inside the office, so told Penny Vance that he was going to grab a coffee. He hit the buttons of his cell-phone as his feet hit the pavement outside.

There'd been a heavy storm overnight, and with the sun burning off the last of the cloud and haze, humidity was high. Early November, but it was still in the seventies. Jac could feel his shirt sticking to his back after only a few paces.

Bob Stratton answered quickly, but there was a confusion of noise in the background from a busy shopping mall or store, and Jac had to raise his voice above the passing traffic as he explained about Marmont and *Pet Sematary*.

'So if you think it might be some sort of message, did Durrant give any hint as to what form it might take?' Stratton pressed. 'Do we know what we might be looking for?'

'No, that's it. All we know is that Marmont has these favourite scenes in the book due to his own dog dying years back, and that it's odd he should be given a book he's already read several times . . .'

'Especially when he's still in a coma.'

'That aside.' Jac joined Stratton briefly in a muted chuckle. 'We're assuming that if he doesn't wake up – whatever problem exists goes with him. It's only if and when he *does* come to . . . so perhaps there's a note with the book. Or maybe something inside the book itself. Outside of that, we're fishing.'

'And you want yours truly, the fisherman, to head out there and start reading Stephen King?'

'Yeah.' Jac stopped by the deli window, held back from going inside. He didn't want to add to the noise coming from Stratton's end. 'As soon as.'

'The only problem is, I'm not due out there until nine this evening – and I've got one of those days ahead of me. The earliest I could rearrange things to get out there is late afternoon: four or five.'

'Okay.' Jac recalled that Stratton had an arrangement running with a couple of shift nurses to block any visitors and phone him the minute there were signs of Marmont awakening. 'But could you meanwhile phone your friendly nurses and ask them to remove any cards and packages from Marmont's room for you to inspect when you arrive? He's not under any circumstances to see them.'

'Will do. And I'll phone as soon as I have news.'

Jac stepped inside the deli as he wished Stratton luck and rang off. With a busy mid-morning crowd and the steam from the espresso machine, it seemed even hotter than outside.

Shirt sticking to his back; the last time he recalled that was when he'd first walked through Libreville prison. Not just from nerves, but as the heat, stench and oppression – the staleness of thousands of caged hopes and emotions – sank through his skin. He felt as if he was still sticky and unclean hours later, even after showering as soon as he got home. That was how he felt after only minutes inside Libreville: Durrant had been there eleven years.

'Latte and a Danish, Mr Jac?'

'Yeah, Joe. Thanks.' His usual daily take-out.

For the first time Jac began to question his own motives. Probably Durrant had every right to want to die; he himself might well feel the same after all those years inside somewhere like Libreville. Was he hoping to save Durrant's life for Durrant's benefit, or merely for his own reputation, to stop his first significant case collapsing at the first hurdle?

Bob Stratton found the note straightaway, but it was brief, told him nothing:

Thought you might like to read again your favourite scene. Remember how the locks and light switches were tagged for your shift? Seek and ye shall find!

The only useful thing was that the note had been slotted as a bookmark in Marmont's favourite scene – the dog coming back to life. Stratton didn't need to hunt through to find it.

But there was nothing else on the pages, no underlining, circling or cryptic notes. Stratton flicked through the rest of the book and tipped it upside down in case there were other notes inside, but there was nothing.

He decided to grab a quick coffee from the canteen to clear his throat and his thoughts, and, while sipping, he studied the note again, hoping that something more might leap out at him.

The favourite scene was mentioned, so that was no secret – or perhaps they wanted in particular to bring Marmont's attention to it. But why mention tagging the locks and light switches? Why was that so important? *Seek and ye shall find*?

Stratton scanned and re-scanned the note in between sips. *Find what*? What on earth was there to find in just a three-line note? And why say *your* shift? Surely there were only two shifts: day and . . .

Stratton sat up with a jolt, almost spilling his coffee. *Night-shift*! If they'd put it like that, it might have given too strong a clue to an inquisitive third-party.

Stratton darted down the corridor and found one of his friendly nurses.

'Josie! Is there a cupboard or store-room that can be grabbed for a moment? Somewhere where it's dark.'

Josie raised an eyebrow and smiled slyly. 'Well, you sure know how to sweet-talk a girl.'

Stratton returned the smile, but a flush rose quickly from his collar. 'No, it's not that. I just need to be alone with this for a moment.' Stratton pointed to the book in his hand.

From the way Josie's eyebrow stayed arched quizzically as she led him along the corridor, he'd made the request seem no less odd.

Stratton found the first word on the second page of Marmont's favourite scene – highlighted silver-grey in the darkness – then two more on the next page, one on the next, two pages with nothing, then another word. Stratton flicked through almost thirty pages before the highlighted words petered out. He then went back to the beginning to put it all together, making notes on a pad as he went. When he'd finished, he flicked on the store-room light and read what he'd written:

Don't say anything about the fight until you've had a chance to speak to us. It's important we get our stories straight.

Stratton punched the air. 'Got 'em!'

'You look pleased with yourself,' Josie commented as he exited. 'I didn't know Stephen King had that type of scene in his books.'

Only a weak half-smile this time from Stratton. He was too busy concentrating on tapping out Jac McElroy's number on his cell-phone.

Jac took the call as he was walking along Camp Street, only a block away from his apartment. He'd got used to walking back and forth to work. Just over a mile, it was better than braving rush-hour traffic and paying all-day parking lot charges on St Charles Street. Only the firm's senior partners had reserved places in the back parking lot.

Jac beamed widely as Stratton told him the news from St Tereseville General. To those passing, they probably thought he'd just arranged a hot date. That was tomorrow night, and wouldn't raise much of a smile.

'That's great,' Jac said. 'Looks like we've got the guards' account roped and tied, even if Marmont *does* wake up.' Then, realizing that probably sounded flippant, 'Though obviously it would be better if he did – not least for Marmont himself.' In their brief association, he'd enjoyed Stratton's offbeat patter. Hopefully Stratton appreciated it being bounced back.

'If nothing else, so that he can read *Pet Sematary* for the hundredth time.'

'Might send him back into a coma again.'

Stratton's chuckle faded as they came onto the mechanics

of just where and when he'd be able to get a written report to Jac.

'I'm hoping to head back out to Libreville again this week-end,' Jac said. 'There's one final person I want to see who was involved in this. And, combined with your report, that should nail things once and for all with Haveling.'

As Jac swung open the door to his apartment block, the hall light was already on, so he didn't bother to push the timed switch.

Stratton said that he'd type up his report either when he got back that night or first thing in the morning. 'It'll be sitting here for you to pick up anytime after eleven tomorrow. Or, if you're not going to Libreville until Sunday – I've got time to messenger it over to you.'

'I've got a couple of calls to make first.' Jac had heard that Rodriguez was finally in a fit state to be interviewed, but aside from him verifying Durrant's account of the guards' assault, there was another vital reason to see him. 'I'll phone you back as soon as I know when I'm heading out there.'

Jac had just reached the top of the entrance stairs as he signed off and was slightly breathless, not just from walking and talking at the same time, but from the adrenalin rush of Stratton's news.

Only a second later the hallway light clicked off, plunging him into darkness.

Jac reached out and made contact with the wall to one side, feeling his way along. Three more paces to the corner of the corridor, then five or six feet the other side was the light switch. Surely he knew the positioning so off-by-heart now that he could locate it even in the pitch dark?

The fall of his own breathing seemed somehow heavier in the darkness – though suddenly he became aware of some other sound beyond it. He froze and held his breath, listening intently above his own rapid heartbeat. Someone else was there, only a few paces away. Moving stealthily towards him in the darkness.

8

Carmen Malastra was a Don from the old school: 'Moustache Petes', 'Don Corleones' and 'Dinosaurs' were amongst the many disparaging terms for them.

Malastra was keenly aware that, in order to survive, he should keep abreast of the times with at least one foot in the modern age: brutally wiping out anyone who got within a sniff of threatening his power base might not on its own be enough.

For years he'd resisted anything to do with modern electronics and computers: that was for his kids, correct that, *grandkids*, and whenever it played a part in his many business enterprises, well, that was what he employed geeks and nerds for.

Besides, at his age now, the wrong side of sixty, it wasn't seemly, gentlemanly, to be seen playing around on a computer next to some kid with a nose ring and half his hair dyed flame-orange. He was of a different era, an age where suaveness and 'style' still had meaning.

But as soon as that thought hit him, he realized he'd found the key to keeping one foot in the modern age. He took three two-month night courses without saying a word to anyone; his Capos and staff thought that he must have a private lady friend. Very private.

And when he'd finished the courses, he could talk Java, HotMetal, firewalls and Macromedia with the best of them, his liver-spotted hands flying across the keyboard. But the rest of him still remained very much old school: formal evening suits for dinners and functions, black in winter, white in summer, often with a cummerbund; Aqua di Selva doused liberally on his neck and mixed with olive oil to coat his swept-back grey hair.

The scent of pine and olive trees: it reminded him of playing in the woodlands and farm-fields of his native Calabria when he was a little boy.

The first thing he'd done with his new computer knowledge was go through his accounts, see if he could siphon even more cash out of reach of the IRS. That was when he discovered that some siphoning was already taking place, but heading the *other* way from his Bay Tree Casino.

Nel-M phoned in the middle of this dilemma, claiming the hit on Ferrer and apologizing for same.

'He was trying to stiff my Mr Roche outta some funds. Under normal circumstances, we'd of course have come to you first – let you deal with it your own way. But I got into an unfortunate argument with Ferrer, he went for his piece – and I was left with little choice.'

'I see. Unfortunate.' Malastra's attention was still mostly on his computer screen, trying to pick apart just how the scam had taken place and who was responsible.

'But as a mark of respect, we felt we should make a contribution. The same amount that Ferrer was demanding – forty thousand – seemed right.'

That got Malastra's attention. 'That's quite a sum Ferrer was after?'

'Yeah, it was.'

Silence. Nel-M obviously wasn't going to offer to explain, and Malastra wasn't going to be clumsy enough to ask.

'Thank you kindly for the offer – and I accept. It'll help fill the hole in what Ferrer was pulling in.' In reality, there'd be no hole; Ferrer had been replaced within two days. And Malastra was glad of the call: it got rid of the nagging worry that it might have been a rival and a turf war was looming. 'Give my regards to your fine Mr Roche.'

Two more days on and off at the computer and Malastra had put all the pieces together. Originally set up to skim money away from the IRS, involving exchanging cash for dummy receipts between the bar and chip-cashing booth, it looked like the Bay Tree's manager, George Jouliern, had been taking some off the top for himself.

Malastra picked up the phone and summoned one of his Capos, Tommy 'Bye-bye' Angellini.

Bye-bye eased his large frame into the proffered chair and waited patiently as Malastra went through his final deliberations on the computer.

Pushing fifty, Bye-bye's hair was dyed jet black; partly to hide the grey, but mostly in homage to his two idols, Elvis and Johnny Cash. With his bulk, he looked like Elvis in his final hamburger days.

Malastra looked up finally from his computer screen.

'George Jouliern. And soon.'

That was all that was said between the two men. Bye-bye nodded and left.

'I'm sorry if I startled you.'

'No, that's okay,' Jac said. The girl from next door! He felt his face still flushed from the adrenalin rush, or maybe it was her proximity. Viewed from a corridor's length away, she was a beauty, but up close she took his breath away. Her brown eyes seemed to sparkle and tease at the same time, and her body heat and perfume wrapped around him like a soft velvet shroud. His mouth was suddenly dry. 'I . . . I was just reaching for the light switch on the way to my apartment.' Jac pointed towards his door.

'Oh, right. You live there. We're neighbours and didn't even know it.' She smiled broadly and reached out a delicate hand. 'Alaysha Reyner. Pleased to meet you.'

Jac took the proffered hand and shook it lightly. 'Jac McElroy. Jack with no "k". Pleased to meet you too.'

They stood silently, awkwardly for a second, not sure who might speak next, *if* there was anything else to say – then she reached down to the bag she'd left on the floor as she'd pushed the light switch. But as she straightened, she looked at Jac again, as if as an afterthought.

'By the way – was that you I saw coming along the corridor the other day?' she asked. 'You suddenly disappeared from view.'

'Yes, I . . .' Jac was distracted as a door opened on the other side of the corridor, and Alaysha turned too: Mrs Orwin, pushing eighty and half-toothless, who made it her business to check any noise close by her door and strike up a conversation with the passer-by if she saw fit, appraised them briefly, forced a closed-mouth grimace so that she didn't frighten them too much, then as quickly closed the door back the few inches she'd opened it. The flushing in Jac's face had subsided slightly with the pause. 'I . . . I got a call on my cell-phone and had to head back to the apartment.'

'Oh, okay.' Alaysha appraised him with a wry smile. 'And here was me thinking that you were hiding from me.'

'As if,' Jac said, hoping that, despite his obvious embarrassment, she might take it as a compliment.

She studied him a second longer, as if unsure how to read his reaction. 'Well, must go now. Again, nice to meet you.'

'Yes, you too . . .' Then, as with a smile she turned away, Jac panicked that this might be the last time he'd see her for a while. He might not get this opportunity again. 'I was wondering if you might like to go . . .' But as she looked back, he felt himself melt again, along with any resolve, and thought better of it. 'No, it's okay . . . I . . . it doesn't matter.'

Alaysha studied him more intently this time, her eyes scanning from his shoes then back up to his face. Quite tall, light-brown hair, fairly handsome, though not pretty-boy so. But he had the most incredible blue-grey eyes, which somehow seemed sad, lost – she couldn't work out why she found them so appealing. And his accent: a faint hint of French along with something else? A coy smile tilted one side of her mouth. 'Were you just about to ask me out on a date?'

'No, I . . . I . . .' But under the intensity of her gaze, her coy smile becoming questioning, challenging, the pretence felt foolish. 'Well, yes . . . but I realize it could be awkward for you. You probably still have a boyfriend.'

Her mouth curled into a grimace, as if she'd encountered a bad taste. 'I haven't, as it turns out. He's history – even though very *recent* history.' Her face quickly brightened again as she gave him another once-over with her eyes. 'So, if you're asking – the answer is *yes*.'

'That's great.' Jac mellowed his rapidly rising smile so that he didn't come across as over-eager. 'Maybe we could go to Arnaud's . . . or Begue's.'

She seemed to only half take in the possible venues. 'But not tomorrow night, I'm working; and the same too most Fridays and Saturdays. Sundays or Mondays are the best . . . oh, except this Sunday I'm due to go to my mom's.'

Jac didn't want to leave it until the following weekend. 'This coming Monday, then. What, say, eight o'clock – give me time to get all the way over to your place.'

'Okay. You've got a date.' She smiled and nodded, putting one hand lightly on his shoulder in acknowledgement. Shaking hands suddenly seemed too formal, now that they were going on a date. Then her expression became slightly quizzical as what he'd said earlier suddenly dawned on her. 'You said *still* have a boyfriend. Have you maybe seen me coming in with Gerry sometime before, then?'

Again, with the steadiness of her gaze, any pretence felt out of place. Jac swallowed.

'No, it's not that. I heard him shouting at you a few nights back, and there was some banging and thudding that worried me. I'm sorry.' Jac wasn't sure whether he was apologizing for her having a boyfriend that shouted at her, or for listening in. 'That's why I tried to see you on the corridor the other day. To see whether he might have hurt you.'

Her eyes flickered as she took in what he said, rolling through varying emotions: pain of the memory, embarrassment that anyone had heard – but as her face softened and her eyes became slightly moist, it was clear the emotion that had finally won through.

She brought one hand up and lightly touched one of Jac's cheeks with the back of her fingertips. 'You're a sweet guy. Thanks. It's nice to know that you took the trouble to care.' She could have added: it was nice to know that *anyone* still cared.

But there was no point in burdening this Jac McElroy with the darker shades of her life. Frightening him off before they'd even started to get to know each other.

Jac's step was light as they said their goodbyes, 'Until Monday night,' and he walked into his apartment. No love-life to speak of since Madeleine, and suddenly he had two dates in as many days.

It looked like being a pivotal weekend for his career too; if he got nothing worthwhile from Rodriguez, he'd have little choice but to walk away from the Durrant case.

'So, they took you down to the boiler room,' Jac confirmed. 'Did you make any noise that might alert anyone? Did anyone else see you on the way down?'

'I made some noise at first when I realized what was goin' down – but one of 'em got a hand quickly over my mouth. And wit' the route they took, cutting down past the restrooms and laundry and only passin' a handful of cells with open fronts – I'm not sure just who mighta heard or saw me.' Rodriguez looked down thoughtfully for a second. 'Though, of course, with who showed up later – obviously *one* person did hear me.'

The tension mounted steadily in the small interview room as Rodriguez described the events on the night he was taken from his cell. Haveling, his assistant Pete Folley and a guard were ensconced behind the one-way glass screen, the red light on the base of the table microphone indicating that sound was going through to them.

When Rodriguez had entered the interview room, Jac saw

that he carried three books: *The Catcher in the Rye*, Steinbeck's *The Grapes of Wrath* and Dostoyevsky's *Crime and Punishment*. And beneath them, a hand-written letter and two editions of Libreville's quarterly magazine, *Libre-Voice*.

'I brought these,' Rodriguez offered, ''cause you said on the phone that you wanted support for why Larry, "Thes", should continue living.'

'That's true . . . I did.' Jac nodded towards the microphone. The red light wasn't on at that stage, Haveling and Folley were just getting settled behind the screen. 'But that's going to be for the second part of the interview. This first part, which will be monitored and recorded, is to establish what happened on the night of October twenty-fourth. The night you received your injuries.' The last thing Jac wanted to do was go into detail about Durrant's death-wish with Haveling listening in.

Rodriguez wasn't tall, no more than five-five, and was slightly built. Jac could see that he might have problems in Libreville without someone like Durrant to watch his back. And the evidence of that was strongly etched on his face with the welts and bruises still there, one of them a golf-ball-sized lump that half closed one eye. The sight of Rodriguez's injuries wasn't helped by the freckles across his nose and cheeks, some of them so large they looked almost like blotches, as if his Latino blood had had problems dispersing evenly through his skin.

But his liveliness of spirit was evident in his eyes: coal-black, constantly darting, assessing, sparkling with verve and cloaked humour — or, if you caught him on a bad day, malice. His only warning-off device.

Jac leant closer to the mike. 'And when they grabbed you in your cell, did you recognize them?'

'Not at first — it was too dark. But as they took me out into the corridor, I gotta better look.' Rodriguez glanced towards the mirrored-glass screen, as if appreciating that the information would have most impact to those behind it. 'The guard was Dennis Marmont. And the other two were inmates – Silass and Jay-T.'

'I see. And was there another guard with them at any time? A certain Glenn Bateson?'

'No . . . no, there wasn't. He only appeared at the last minute with 'nother two guards to break everything up. In fact, only one other person was present – Tally Shavell. He was already waitin' for me down in the boiler room. King Shit.' Rodriguez shook his head. 'Sorry, that's our other nickname for him.'

Before the meeting, Jac had spent twenty minutes in the annexe to Haveling's office going through Rodriguez's file. In Libreville for murdering a rival pimp for the heavy beating of one of his stable of girls, Rodriguez had taken a basic paralegal course, which had led to him being one of two inmates entrusted to help run the prison's 'communication and advice' centre, since a significant part of that would entail contact between inmates and their legal representatives. Jac could see Rodriguez's formal legalese phrasing take over as he explained events, but his more familiar prison jibe-talk wasn't far beneath the surface.

'Once you were down in the boiler room, what happened then?' Jac wanted more detail on the assault, not only for the impact of what they'd done to Rodriguez to sink home with Haveling – but because it was something difficult to lie about in minute, graphic detail.

As Rodriguez related the events, Jac could practically see him wince with the memory of each blow landing, the shadows in his eyes mirroring his fear in those desperate moments.

'And if Lawrence Durrant hadn't arrived when he did, what do you believe would have happened to you?' Jac asked.

'I believe they'da killed me – in fact, I'm sure that was their aim all along.'

Jac purposely left silence as breathing space to Rodriguez's closing comment, then leant closer to the microphone.

'Thank you, Mr Rodriguez. That concludes this part of the interview.' He fired a tight grimace towards the glass screen as he flicked off the red light. Hopefully it was enough to convince Haveling – especially with the coded note intended for Marmont that Jac had shown him.

The atmosphere in the interview room immediately eased with the red light off, both of them knowing that they were no longer being monitored, and as Jac's eyes fell again to the books, Rodriguez was there before him, explaining.

'If you look at the letter at the front, written by Larry eight years ago at the time of his appeal, then at the margin notes made in the books – you'll see what I'm gettin' at.'

Jac scanned the letter, then started flicking through the first pages of *The Catcher in the Rye*. It took a moment for Jac to realize what the notes were before confirming with Rodriguez.

'These are Larry Durrant's notes in the margin?' Jac rapidly flicked through the rest of the book. Some pages had no margin notes at all, some only one or two small entries – but in almost half the book the notes were extensive, often almost filling the available margin space. 'All of these suggested changes and corrections?'

'Yeah, that's right. He's been editin' *Catcher in the Rye*, for Christ's sake. A fuckin' 'merican classic.' Rodriguez picked up the other two books and quickly fanned their pages towards Jac. 'And the same with Steinbeck and Dostoyevsky. And going from that . . .' Rodriguez tapped the letter, then pointed back to the books . . . 'to that – you'll get some handle on just how much Larry Durrant has progressed while he's been in here. And on top we got all his good work an' contributions with the prison magazine.' Rodriguez pulled out one of the magazines and held it up. 'That's why he's worthwhile fightin' for. Why he's now a worthwhile citizen that shouldn't be allowed to die.' Rodriguez shook his head. 'He just ain't the same Larry Durrant he was when he first came in here.'

Jac looked again at the letter. Even though it was fairly basic and simple, with two or three spelling errors, it didn't smack of total illiteracy – although Jac took Rodriguez's point. There was a Grand Canyon gap between the letter and Durrant's editing notes and articles. A remarkable journey that could hopefully impress the State Governor as to Durrant's worthiness – *if* they got that far.

'Thanks for this. And believe me I'll put it all to good use to try and tip Governor Candaret's hand – but right now that's not the problem.' Jac grimaced tightly. 'The immediate hurdle is not whether we can convince the State not to execute Durrant – but whether or not he wants to live. Because he tells me flat out that he doesn't want to. He's tired, had enough, and doesn't even want me to put in a clemency plea on his behalf. He wants to die. His "Ascension Day", he calls it.'

'Oh, *that*.' From Rodriguez's tone, it wasn't clear whether 'that' referred to Durrant's admission of wanting to die, or his religion.

'He's shared this with you before? His wanting to die?'

'Yeah, a couple of times.' Rodriguez shrugged. 'But yer know – we all go through that in here from time to time. So down and weary of it all that we just want "out". And if we can't actually get out – then that becomes the alternative.' Rodriguez shook his head. 'But when it came t' the crunch – possible clemency on one hand and execution the other – I didn't think he'd actually go t'rough with it. That's sad to know. Sad and bad.' Rodriguez looked down morosely for a second, all the verve suddenly gone from his eyes. 'You tried pushin' him? Didn't just take it first-off that's what he wanted?'

'Yes, tried everything. Even that he needed to hang around to watch your back. That you wouldn't last long in here without him.'

'Nice to know that tactic was so effective.' Rodriguez smiled briefly. 'You know, on occasion when he got down and brought this subject up 'bout wantin' to die – I'd josh him, how could he? And miss out on all my good jokes over the next ten years? Even jus' making fun of Tally Shavell and takin' him down a notch or two was surely worth the ticket price of those extra years. And after that sly laugh of his, he'd pat me on the shoulder and say that I'd already brightened his days 'nough for a hundred years. He'd never forget me.' Rodriguez shook his head. '*Never forget me.* I should have caught on then that he was more serious 'bout it than I thought.'

Jac realized then that the association between them, at least from Rodriguez to Durrant, had been mostly jocular and bantering, with Rodriguez constantly trying to lift Durrant's mood whenever he was gloomy or down. It might have felt out of place for Rodriguez to suddenly step out of that mould and get serious, start probing Durrant whether he really wanted to die, or what had made him feel that way? Perhaps Rodriguez too, to keep his own psyche upbeat, wouldn't have wanted to hear the answers.

'That's the main reason I'm here now, Mr Rodriguez – apart from hearing your account of what happened that night in the boiler room with Shavell. To find out if there's anything you can think of that might convince Larry Durrant to want to continue living. *Anything*?'

Rodriguez looked uncomfortable. 'I don't know. Dealin' out his innermost thoughts and secrets where he might not want it – that's not what me and him are all 'bout. He's a very private guy. And, I mean, if he's already made his mind up – maybe we should respect that.' Rodriguez met Jac's eyes steadily for a second before casting them to one side, some darker shadows settling into them. 'Larry was in here five years 'fore I even got here, you know. And if things ain't bad 'nough here now – Libreville was a much more brutal, unforgivin' place then. The highest inmate murder rate of any prison nationwide. God knows what those years might have done to him – in here, man, yer know.' Rodriguez tapped his chest with his fist, then pointed to the books, forcing a smile. 'Also, it ain't as if he's the easiest guy to sway. Now he's got to the point of thinkin' he knows better than Salinger and Steinbeck – what the hell difference do you think you or I are gonna make?'

Jac looked down, conceding the point. He'd found much the same with Durrant, defiant and immovable. In their last meeting, he'd seen only one small chink of possible weakness.

'Durrant's son, Joshua?' Jac asked. 'What can you tell me about their association? When I mentioned the boy – it seemed to be the only thing to create some doubt in Durrant's mind. If only for a moment.'

Rodriguez looked even more uneasy. He raised a sharp eyebrow. 'Larry's family? Oooooh no. Definite no-go area. Larry guards them more jealously than any other secrets he might hold. I wouldn' dream of . . .'

'Look, Mr Rodriguez,' Jac cut in impatiently, looking at his watch. He'd done nothing but bash his head against a brick wall so far with Durrant, he was damned if he was going to do the same with Rodriguez. 'In forty-one days, Larry Durrant is going to die – if anyone in the State of Louisiana in fact needed reminding. And at that point, what his family means to him, or in turn him to them, is going to have little relevance – except in memory. So you'll perhaps excuse me if I appear not to have much time for your tip-toeing around prison protocol and what might or might not seem right between you and Larry Durrant.'

Rodriguez fired Jac a similar sly, challenging smile to Durrant's when he'd finally conceded the other day, '*You're good.*' But then his expression quickly sank back into doubt as he weighed up his position.

'Look, there was somethin' that happened recently with Larry's son, Joshua,' he said finally, looking up. He bit lightly at his bottom lip, as if still uncertain he was doing the right thing. 'But if I say anythin' – it wasn't from me, okay? I got 'nough injuries already, without having to put up with a neck brace for a few months.'

Jac smiled and nodded his assent.

'And I say that not just because of breakin' protocols between myself and Larry,' Rodriguez continued, 'but 'cause of the confidences I should keep as one of the main men in the communication room. On both counts I shouldn't be saying anythin' about this.'

Jac met the concern in Rodriguez's eyes with a more solemn gaze, and nodded again. 'I understand.'

Rodriguez shuffled slightly in his seat, as if he was still getting comfortable with what he was about to say. 'I don't know whether Larry has told you or not – but he's had very little contact with his son over the years. The first five years in here, Francine didn't visit, so no contact at all. Then when she did start finally visitin', at most once or twice a year – she only brought Joshua occasionally, maybe one in every three visits. So, eighteen months or two whole years would roll by without him seein' his son. As a result, he's only seen Josh a handful of times in all the years he's been in here. And when Francine did bring him, she'd make sure to keep the boy in the background. "*Say hello to your pa. Good. Now you sit back there like a good boy while we talk.*" Maybe only a handful of sentences, too, have therefore passed 'tween him and the boy.' Rodriguez shook his head. 'It's been one of Larry's greatest sources of guilt and regret, that boy.

'In particular because of the promise he made to Francine at the time.' Rodriguez paused as he levelled his gaze at Jac. 'When Josh was born, he promised Francine: "That's it! No more robberies." Then just three months down the line he's in the Roche home – which lands him in here. So, you see, he feels guilty for havin' broken that promise and deserted the boy through all these years. In fact, he sees most of this in here as punishment fo' that. Retribution and all that Bible stuff he got into later on. Maybe that was some kinda penance. Asking God's forgiveness not jus' for being a bad man and a

107

murderer – but for being a bad father and lettin' his family down.' Rodriguez took a fresh breath. 'But when Larry did have contact with Josh, I'd see the change in him. That weight o' guilt would lift from his shoulders and there was a fresh light in his eyes; as if, finally, he saw some hope. Hope, maybe, that with fresh contact, he could make good on havin' let the boy down and deserted him.' Rodriguez shrugged and gestured with one hand. 'But, like I say, his meetings with Joshua were rare, and so the same went for his hopes of makin' good – until just under a year ago.' This time Rodriguez's pause was heavier, as if purposely adding significance or waiting for the prompt.

'What happened then?' Jac asked.

'Well, yer know, I'd been handlin' things in the communication room for over eighteen months by then – so I was first to see them come through: e-mails from Joshua.' Rodriguez paused briefly again to let the information settle with Jac. 'The first month there were just two. Then they increased to once or sometimes twice a week, with Larry always makin' sure to answer 'em by the next day.' Rodriguez smiled. 'Man, Larry was alive through that period like I never saw him before. Then, suddenly, about seven weeks back, without warnin' they stopped. Nothin'. Nada.' Rodriguez's smile faded just as quickly. 'And Larry sank back into his gloomy pit. But probably even worse than before. Because now he'd been given a taste o' what things could be like with his son, only fo' it to be yanked away again. No more contact – and, as Larry sees it, no hope again.'

Jac rubbed his forehead as he considered the information. He could see now why Rodriguez was cautious about sharing it. It cut deep to the roots of Durrant's family and personal psyche.

'Any indication as to why the e-mails might have stopped?' Jac asked.

'No, only guesswork. Larry sent another half-dozen e-mails askin' for a reply or explanation before his pride – foolish or otherwise – made him give up. Got to the point where he felt he was beggin'.' Rodriguez shrugged. 'Maybe his mom or new stepfather cut in, stopped him sendin' more e-mails; or Joshua himself decided to stop – feared he was gettin' too close, 'specially when his father likely wouldn't be around much longer. Lot easier to take the loss of someone you're not *that* close to. Or his computer has broken down or his AOL account has been cancelled. In the end, we're fishin'.' Rodriguez grimaced. 'That's why things were planned earlier with the prison break. Larry didn't rate the chances of Candaret givin' him clemency, and, if he got out there – he could find out what'd happened with Joshua.'

'Right.' Jac nodded, glancing towards the glass screen. Even with the red light off, he felt uneasy at the mention of 'prison break'. It wasn't the best thread on which to hang Larry Durrant's life, he thought: the wants and reasoning of a twelve-year-old boy. But at this stage he was glad of any small mercies. 'So you think that if there was e-mail contact again from Joshua, or at least some reasonable explanation that would give him hope of future contact – that might make Durrant feel differently?'

Rodriguez shrugged. 'Again, only guesswork. But it's the best chance I can think of to raise Larry's spirits. Maybe make him wanna start livin' again.'

Asking a twelve-year-old boy to go through the emotional trauma of contact with his father while the shadow of execution hung over him, and no doubt with his mother and new partner strongly opposed to it for those same reasons – it wasn't going to be easy. But it looked like the best he was going to get.

Jac pushed a tight smile and nodded. 'Thanks for that . . . and for those, too.' He gestured towards the books. 'If we can convince Larry Durrant that there's still something worth living for, they might come in useful in convincing others he's worthwhile keeping alive.'

'S'okay.' Rodriguez nodded back with a light snort.

'Except that down here in the South, could be dangerous ground. Black man daring t'fool around with the classics – could send him for the chop straight-off for that alone.' Rodriguez smiled slyly. 'And thank God Larry never got 'round to editing the Bible. If he had, and Havelin' got wind of it – he'd make sure to switch on the poison-feed himself.'

Early the next morning, while sipping at coffee, Jac took the folded paper from his jacket pocket and spread it out on his dining table.

He'd looked at the printed e-mail and his reply already countless times, had unfolded and folded it back more often than he cared think about; but perhaps without the noise of the office buzzing around him, something might leap out that he hadn't picked up on before:

> I hear you're representing Larry Durrant. I know that he didn't
> do it. It wasn't him. I know, because I was there at the time.
> Don't let him die.

No name, initials or sign-off; just the e-mail address, *durran save4@hotmail.com*, and the time and date. Jac's eyes shifted to his reply:

> I need to know more to be able to do anything with this. Who
> you are? Or at least how and why you were there at the time?
> Also, why haven't you come forward before? I need to know
> more to help save Larry.

Only four lines, but Jac worried that already he'd said too much, frightened the sender off. Yet what else could he have said? He was just telling it how it was. On its own, the message meant nothing: he *couldn't* help Durrant with it unless he had more information.

But Jac knew that the other reason he was looking at it again now was because of something John Langfranc had said the other day. With still no reply, he'd finally told Langfranc about the e-mail and they'd brainstormed just who might have sent it – friend of Durrant's, relative, hoaxer, any of the new supporters he'd found since hitting the press again recently, or capital punishment opponents keen to throw a spanner in the works at the last moment – when Langfranc arched one eyebrow.

'Of course, one other possibility we haven't thought of: the murderer himself. That need to confess that criminologists are always talking about. Not to mention guilt – with Durrant getting close now to his final day.'

'No, surely not. I mean why would he –' Then suddenly Jac stopped himself as he thought about the e-mail's wording: *I was there at the time.* If it was just a hoaxer, then why not say simply that he knew or could tell them? Why be so bold and say that he was there at the time?

Those same words leapt out at Jac now, until everything else on the page evaporated and that was all that seemed to be there . . . *I was there at the time.*

9

For the first ten minutes they skirted around each other, keeping the conversation to safe, inconsequential ground: how long had he been in the States? How was he finding it? Relationships with his mother and aunt? But with that, he found himself choosing his words carefully. He knew that, at least from Aunt Camille's perspective, she considered the Bromwells to be quite close, and he didn't want to be too ungracious.

But as Jennifer Bromwell sensed his awkwardness, she reached across the table and lightly touched the back of his hand, their first physical contact.

'It's okay. I find her a big snob, too. Sometimes too much to take. So don't be afraid to speak your mind.'

And Jac, in turn, found her skewing her lip slightly when he asked about her father. He reciprocated by touching her hand back. 'Look, I don't even know him. But if I said he was a snob as well – would that make it any easier for you to talk about him?'

They laughed, and from there the conversation flowed easily: family, work, life, France – she'd visited twice, Paris for two days as part of a whirlwind European trip, and a holiday of two weeks spent between Cannes and Monte Carlo. Her work was in the PR and marketing department of a local fashion house.

They'd gone to Le Bon Temps Roule, his choice but under her guidance of liveliness and ambience before haute cuisine. 'I go to enough stuffy high-class joints with my parents.'

There was a funky jazz trio playing in the back room where they'd planned to go after eating, but all that reached them among the front dining tables was its steady bass beat and the occasional forceful vocals or saxophone burst.

At one point Jennifer paused again more thoughtfully, as if, despite his efforts to put her at ease, something still perturbed her.

'Look – about my father. My mother too, to a lesser extent. I feel I should say this now, before things get too far on, because if you found out later, you'd only be upset.' Jennifer glanced briefly towards the bar before looking back at him directly. 'All of this was my father's idea, with my mom, as always, meekly backing him up. And mainly because of my boyfriend – who they don't happen to approve of. Rock musician, you see, but just small gigs here and there. And, as my father likes to put it, not heading anywhere fast. Young lawyer with a blue-blood background looks a much better bet.' She shook her head briefly and reached out and lightly touched Jac's hand again. 'But now that I'm here, don't get me wrong – I'm glad I came. You're a really sweet guy.'

Jac resisted filling the gap with 'But?' – it would only make her feel more awkward, when it was obvious what the answer was: there wasn't any sexual spark between them, and wasn't going to be. He appreciated her boldness in speaking openly and, because it took the pressure off him, he felt the least he could do was return the gesture.

'Same here with me – with my Aunt Camille doing the pushing. Except in my case it was because I haven't had a serious relationship the past few years. Not since I split up with my girlfriend in France, Madeleine.'

'Oh, I'm sorry.'

Her hand reaching out and consoling again. Though Jac wasn't sure whether the 'sorry' was for his split from Madeleine, or because with him not having much of a love-life these past years, he might have expected more from this date now.

Jac shrugged. 'I don't do too badly. I get the occasional fresh date now and then.' He didn't want her to feel awkward for things not heading anywhere between them, but he stopped short of mentioning he had one of those fresh dates the night after next.

'Like this one.' She smiled. She started picking at the breaded prawn and calamares the waiter had just brought up. 'Lawyer and blue-blood was the bait used to get me here. So, what did Camille use with you?'

'Money.' No point in tip-toeing around it; blunt honesty had been the order of the day so far.

'Oh, that.' She said it with the disdain that comes only from those who've had big money for a while: so used to it that it invokes only boredom, and by now sufficiently well schooled to be wary of the associated problems and baggage that come with it.

Jac went on to explain the tragic chain of events that led to them leaving France – his father's financial collapse, illness and eventual death – and as a result being forced to live in Aunt Camille's grace and favour.

'What didn't help also was me choosing to switch from corporate to criminal law. Otherwise things might have been a bit easier financially, and I'd have got my mother and sister out from under Camille's wing by now.'

Jennifer sipped thoughtfully at her wine. 'Looks like you take after your father in that respect. You're not that bothered about money.'

'That's exactly what Camille says. That, like him, I'm foolish when it comes to money, a dreamer. As a result, I make bad choices.'

Jennifer shook her head. 'I wasn't criticizing. I meant it actually as a compliment. Kelvin, my boyfriend, is exactly the same. Just follows his dreams and where his nose might lead him, doesn't give a damn about money. That's what makes him so different, so refreshing. The problem I always found was that guys either came sniffing around me because of the money – put more effort into trying to impress my father than me – or they got intimidated by it and were frightened off.'

Jac studied her closely for the first time. More Belinda

Carlisle than Britney Spears, a touch of red in her blonde hair hinting at depth and fire beneath. And Jean-Marie had been right – he did like her, she was far from the spoilt rich brat he'd feared. Though 'cute' was without doubt too lightweight, didn't embrace her strong savvy streak. Jac wondered for a moment that if she didn't have a boyfriend and if he didn't have his thoughts filled with the girl next door – since setting the date, he'd kept running through mental scenarios of how it might go – whether anything might have developed between them.

But they were past that point now, and almost two hours later when they'd exchanged more likes and wants and stories about family and work and put half the world to rights – she was again reaching that hand across the table, this time to set in stone how their relationship would be in the future.

'Friends?'

He nodded and smiled. 'Yes, friends.'

She said that she'd like to see him again and he nodded.

'Yes, I'd like that too.' Though with the main reason for them continuing to see each other gone, he doubted that either of them would keep to it.

Although, two consolations, Jac thought: he'd had an enjoyable evening when he'd feared originally it might be a nightmare, and in part it would be like a dry-run for his date the night after next, would help ease his nerves.

But it wasn't, and it didn't.

Watching the reaction in Francine Durrant's eyes as Jac explained his dilemma with her husband was like viewing one of those old-fashioned, jolting-frame movies: pain, regret, fear, sadness, smiles and triumph – though the last were rarer, fleeting seconds, and always tinged with irony, as if they had no place amongst such an overriding swamp of regret and sadness. The past thirteen years of her life with Durrant condensed into a rapid succession of flicker-frames mirrored through her eyes.

The home she shared with her partner was a small wood-framed bungalow in a sector of the Upper Ninth Ward close to Bywater clinging to middle-classdom by its fingernails, with half-derelict project complexes and shotgun houses only three blocks away. Green-painted shutters and a mass of terracotta-potted-plants on its front veranda assisted that clinging; though perhaps it was just to brighten its façade and make it more homely.

Since the one photo Jac had seen of Francine in Durrant's file, taken at their wedding, she'd aged well. Maybe she'd gone up a dress size from an eight to a ten, with a few faint lines now around her eyes, and her wavy hair was tinged lighter and redder now, stronger contrast against her coffee-light-on-the-cream skin tone – but otherwise, little change; except perhaps that her open smile from then was now far tighter, more constrained. Although possibly that had more to do with his visit and the subject being discussed. Maybe as soon as he left, her old easy smile would return.

As he got to the part about the e-mails from their son, Joshua, her mouth became tighter still and she could hardly bear for him to see her reaction any more. She looked down and away, chewing at her bottom lip. When he finally finished, she was slow in looking back up at him.

'And who told you all of this? Larry himself?'

'No, he was pretty close-mouthed and defensive when I started asking about family. It came from his close prison buddy, Roddy Rodriguez.'

She smiled crookedly. 'Figures. He was pretty close-mouthed during our marriage, too. Rarely told me what he was up to.' The darker flicker-frames were quickly back again. 'Including that night he was at the Roche woman's house.'

Jac reached a hand towards her, but fell a few inches short of actual physical contact. 'I'm sorry, Mrs Durrant. I know how difficult this is for you. And if there was any other way of doing this without coming here to see you, believe me . . .'

'It's okay.' She forced the smile back after a second, but it was more laconic and bitter now. 'That was actually one of the biggest sources of argument between us, you know: Larry's reluctance to communicate openly – along with the drink, the drugs, the shooting pool and card nights when I suspected he was with other women and I would start phoning round his friends.' She shook her head. 'The "Stone Mountain" they used to call him when he was boxing. Not because he was particularly big, he was just light-heavyweight, or could take a lot of punches – but because he never said much. Never gave away what he was feeling inside.' She clamped one hand to her breast. 'And maybe that's okay when you're preparing for a boxing match and want to appear like a lump of stone, immovable, to your opponent – but let me tell you, Mr McElroy, it's pretty hard to take day in, day out in a marriage.'

'I know. I understand,' Jac said, although he had little idea. He was keen to get her back on track. Not just because the more maudlin she became, wallowing in her husband's failings, the harder it might be to gain her cooperation – but because of time: twenty-five, thirty minutes before her partner came home, she'd said. Unless he could keep her away from Memory Lane, he'd never get what he wanted in time. He took a fresh breath. 'It isn't my intention to get young Joshua into trouble here – but did you know about the e-mails he was sending to his father in prison?'

She cast her eyes down for a second, as if weighing up the implications of her answer. 'Yes. Yes, I did. Or rather my partner did – he was first to discover them on the computer and told me.'

'And was it you that stopped Joshua sending more e-mails, or did he decide to stop of his own accord?'

She forced a pained smile. 'More of a mutual decision, really. Between me, my partner Frank and Joshua.'

'I see.' Jac could just imagine what say Joshua had on the issue with the combined weight of his mother and stepfather ganged up against him.

'I know what you're thinking,' Francine said, catching his look. 'And at times there's been issues between Frank and Joshua – particularly where Larry was thought to have had an influence. But this is one occasion where I was right behind Frank. We might try at times to treat Josh like the little man of the house, but he's still only twelve, Mr McElroy.' She met his eyes challengingly for a moment before looking down. 'E-mails back and forth, back and forth . . . right up until . . . *until*.' Her voice cracked slightly and she bit at her lip as she looked up again. 'How long is it now that my Larry has left? Thirty-six, thirty-seven days? Just enough time for Josh to get close again to his father, huh? *Real* close. Close enough for him to really feel and know just what's happening to him. Can you imagine how that's going to crush the boy? The first time he's really got close to his father, and the next minute . . .' Francine snapped her fingers. 'He's gone. Is that what you want, Mr McElroy?'

'No, no.' Jac shook his head. 'That's what we're trying to avoid. That's the whole point of this clemency plea now. To hopefully get the Governor to commute the sentence.'

'And what if you don't succeed, Mr McElroy? And we let young Josh get sucked into this in the hope of keeping his father alive – only for it to fail. And, job well done, he gets close enough to give his father real hope to want to live again. That closeness and hope, that's all going to get to the boy, too.' Francine grimaced tautly. 'Make him do this, and the loss of his father is going to hit him like a freight train.'

'It's going to hit the boy hard anyway, Mrs Durrant.'

She snorted. 'Yeah, but it's going to be ten times harder if we get Josh close and build up his hopes that his father might actually live.'

When Jac had phoned Francine Durrant earlier, she'd initially refused to see him, saying that she had a new man and new life now. '*And that old life always drags us back, makes our new life more difficult to get on with. Even more so from my new partner's point of view – he won't stand for it for a minute.*' He'd had to push hard to get the meeting, tell her about her husband's death-wish and its apparent link to lack of contact with Joshua. '*So while I understand your resentment, if it goes as far as actually wanting to see Larry die – then, fine, don't see me.*' Hearing Francine Durrant's heavy sigh, her conscience wrestling with the demons that had no doubt already ripped her apart during these past eleven years – Jac had felt guilty using the sledgehammer approach. But now, he realized, it might take more of the same to finally shift her stance.

'I take your point, Mrs Durrant. It's not ideal to have Josh get close at this juncture. But then probably *anything* he does at this stage is going to be far from ideal. If he cuts himself off from his father and has little contact – do you think he's going to feel any better?' Jac's eyes searched hers for a moment before she looked down. Possible concession. 'Probably not. In fact, he might even feel worse – knowing that he purposely kept his distance and had no contact in those vital final weeks of his father's life.'

'I appreciate that, too.' Francine closed her eyes for a second. 'But the way we looked at it, that option was the lesser of two evils.'

'The lesser of two evils?' Jac repeated with a questioning tone. 'Is that what it's come down to now between your son and his father? And what if your son finds out at some later stage that his lack of contact in those final weeks was the main reason his father didn't want a clemency plea made on his behalf?'

Francine closed her eyes for a moment again, chewing at her lip. 'He won't find out. He'll *never* know.' When she opened her eyes again, she kept them slightly averted. She didn't want Jac to see what lay there.

'He'll never know?' Jac's repetition had now become faintly mocking. 'There's going to be a fair bit of media coverage of this, maybe even some books, too. It's pretty rare that a prisoner doesn't want clemency put in on his behalf, in fact *wants* to die. Gary Gilmore was the last, if I remember right. That generated countless articles and books, people were still debating it years later. And one of the key questions raised is always *why* they wanted to die. You think all of that's going to happen without your son ever finding out?'

'It'll only be the first year or so, I can keep it hidden from him for that time.' Francine fought for conviction to mask the desperation of the comment. She took a fresh breath. 'Besides, as you say, and I also know from bitter past experience – Larry is always so close-mouthed. No way is he going to admit that his wanting to die is down to his son not making contact. He's going to say just what he told you: that he's simply sick of facing more time in prison, and this is his going to God. His "Ascension Day".'

Give her credit, she was standing her ground well. Jac nodded and held a palm out.

'That's as may be. But there's always people like Roddy Rodriguez keen to speak out.' Jac knew that he was on more uncertain ground here. It had been hard to prise from Rodriguez the family backdrop to Durrant's death-wish. It was unlikely he'd speak so openly to journalists. 'And even if that wasn't the case – *you'd* always know. Something that might prey on your mind every time you look at Joshua.'

But as Francine looked at him directly and Jac saw the fiery spark there, he knew that he'd stepped too far.

'Don't you dare lay that on me. I've done nothing *but* think of Larry practically every time I've looked at the boy these past eleven years – so another ten or twenty isn't going to make much difference. And it's not just that his father's been locked away practically since he was born that I'm reminded of when I look at Joshua. All those taunts and jibes at school he's had to shoulder. You know what I'm reminded of most when I look at him?'

Jac shook his head and quietly mouthed, 'No', his voice suddenly choked of any strength.

'What I'm reminded of most is the promise that Larry made when Joshua was born: that he wouldn't – cross his heart and hope to die – do any more robberies. He couldn't face doing time again and spending even a minute away from the boy. Especially now we were both depending on him so heavily. And just three months later, he's in the Roche house – and, who knows, maybe even other robberies in between. Maybe he never stopped. Did you happen to know that too, Mr McElroy, about the solemn promise Larry made to his family?'

'Yes. Yes, I did.' Jac looked down slightly, as if he was somehow ashamed of sharing that knowledge.

'And did Larry himself tell you about that?'

'No. It was Rodriguez again.'

Some of the fire eased and the sly smile was back. 'At least he's consistent. The Stone Mountain remains close-mouthed till the end. He might have found God, but he's certainly not found his tongue.'

'I know how you must feel, Mrs Durrant. And you've got every right to feel angry for what he did, and the consequences that you and Joshua have had to endure.' Jac felt immediately at a loss for just how to fight back. All he could think of was placating so that at least she was more receptive when he finally found the right words. He glanced quickly at his watch: only six or eight minutes before her partner was due back. 'But the thing is, I . . .' Jac broke off as she looked sharply over her shoulder, and he too picked up on a faint shuffling in the hallway in that instant. She'd packed Joshua off to his room when Jac first arrived with the strict instruction not to disturb them. Either the boy had come out of his room or her partner was home early.

'Joshua, is that you there?' she called out.

They heard more shuffling that sounded as if someone was moving further away along the hallway. Then, 'Yes . . . I was just getting a drink from the kitchen.'

'Okay. Well, you head back to your room now. Leave us private like I said.'

She waited patiently until she heard his footsteps fully

recede and his bedroom door click shut again. But as she looked back at Jac, her face was slightly flushed, and he could imagine what she was thinking: how long had the boy been close by in the hallway, and had he overheard any of their conversation?

The momentary break had allowed Jac's thoughts to gel as he recalled Rodriguez's words: '*In fact, he sees most of this in here as punishment for having broken that solemn promise. Retribution and all that Bible stuff he got into later on.*'

Jac shook his head. 'As I was about to comment, Mrs Durrant, I find it ironic that you should mention that promise. Because that's one of the main reasons Rodriguez puts forward for Larry wanting to die: guilt over having let you and Josh down.'

'Oh. I see.' She let the words out on a heavy breath.

Jac could see that she'd taken the information badly. One of the main arguments behind her not helping now completely turned around as a cry for help: her husband wanting to die because of guilt over the promise he'd made to her and Joshua, and now she was ensuring he succeeded in that by cutting off further contact with his son.

'Rodriguez said that when the e-mails started coming through from Joshua, he saw the change in your husband. Some hope and light in him that just hadn't been there before.'

'Rodriguez again?' Francine nodded, but now the comment had lost any of its bite and was more of a knowing confirmation than a question.

'Yes. Hope that maybe with that contact, your husband would be able to face the years ahead. And not just because it felt good to have continuing contact with the boy and gave him some future purpose – but because Larry saw the e-mails as some sort of proof that his son had forgiven him for breaking his promise and letting him down. Deserting him through all those years.'

Francine visibly shuddered as she put one hand up to her mouth and closed her eyes for a second. Jac noticed as she opened them again the tears welling, and she held the same hand out as if to shield them as she shook her head.

'Please, Mr McElroy . . . don't say any more. Believe me, I've got the picture.' She wiped at her eyes with the back of one hand. 'And if I could help, I would. But I'm afraid, Mr McElroy. Frank's a good man, and I don't want to lose him over this.'

Jac held one hand out. 'But surely if you explained to him the situation, as difficult as it might be, in the end he'd understand.'

She shrugged. 'Maybe he would, maybe he wouldn't. Worst thing is, I'd probably never know – not, that is, until he just upped one morning and left. Said that he couldn't "cope" with me and Josh any more. Because that's what happened with my last partner.' She shook her head wearily. 'And I just can't afford to have that happen again now with Frank.'

'I see.'

'Maybe you do, maybe you don't.' She shrugged again and smiled tightly. 'Do you know what I earn, Mr McElroy?'

'*What*?' Jac was caught off-guard, bemused as to what that had to do with anything.

'Barely thirty bucks a day at the shoe shop where I work. Mainly because I leave at four most days to collect Josh from school. And I only got that job because the shop's owner was friend of a friend. "Lucky" to get the job with such kindly hours I was told at the time, and don't I know it – or, if I ever get close to forgetting, when things aren't going so smoothly, I'll get reminded of it by the manager. Well, apart from the fact that Frank's a good man and been good to me and Josh, without him we just couldn't manage on my wage. And it seems at times as if I'm just hanging on to that job by the skin of my teeth. "Taken on" is the expression often used. "Lucky to get taken on."' Francine shook her head and fixed her eyes levelly on Jac. 'And it's pretty much the same expression used when a man "takes on" a woman of my age with a child in tow. Particularly one still married to the father of that child – let alone that he might be on Death Row for murder.'

'I see. I understand.' And for the first time since arriving, as much as it went directly against what he was there for, he did see and understand.

'I'm sorry, Mr McElroy. But you can see the dilemma I'm facing. If I went against Frank over this and got young Josh to . . .' Her voice trailed off as, with a jolt, she looked towards the clock on the far wall. The mention of Frank reminded her that she'd got more carried away with explaining than she'd realized. Frank was due back at any minute. 'I . . . I think we'll have to leave things there, Mr McElroy.'

He fired a tight but understanding smile as he got to his feet, then handed her his card as they walked towards the front door. 'If you should happen to have a change of heart, please call me. *Please.*'

Jac clasped her hand gently and felt it shaking slightly. But she hardly looked at the card in her hand, or at him – her eyes were busy darting between the front door and a side window which gave a partial view towards the road.

They said a hasty goodbye and Jac gave a small wave towards Francine Durrant just before he got into his car, who was still looking through a six-inch gap in the front door. She was obviously anxious for Jac to be clear of the house before Frank got there, so that she didn't have to explain anything. But at least Jac now had a better understanding of her fears. As pitiful as it might be, she was simply clinging to the remnants of life left after her husband's long years in prison: a badly paid job and what she saw as her last chance at a relationship.

When he was a block away from Francine Durrant's house, he checked his cell-phone and saw that Haveling had called, but hadn't left a message. Good news or bad? Marmont's condition improved, or Marmont dead? Haveling rejecting or accepting Durrant's account?

Jac pulled over to the side of the road and eased out a slow, tired breath as he dialled Haveling's number. But it hardly mattered any more, he reminded himself: if he couldn't shift Francine Durrant's stance, the whole case was dead anyway.

10

Nel-M had spent the last few hours watching an apartment.

He'd seen Jac McElroy head into the building at 6.18 p.m., but it was almost two hours before he saw McElroy leave again – with a girl.

That was strange. Nel-M hadn't seen the girl go into the building and, from the information he'd so far gained, McElroy was meant to be single, wasn't shacked-up with anyone.

Well, he'd soon know what the score was. They looked dressed for a night out, but still Nel-M left it ten minutes before going into the building, in case they forgotten something they needed to go back for.

Straightforward bar and tumbler lock, Nel-M had it opened with a pick and credit card in just fifty seconds. He went round the whole apartment first to get his bearings before starting to go through drawers and wardrobes. He paused in thought as he finished, then gave all the side tables and shelves one last scan.

Not a single bra, panty or stocking in any of the drawers, and no make-up or women's perfume to be found anywhere. So, for sure, she wasn't living here with McElroy. Maybe she *had* sneaked in the building without him noticing. Nel-M shook his head. This one was a twenty-four carat babe. He'd have spotted her in a crowd at a hundred paces, even if he was half-comatose.

Strange, too, that there wasn't a single photo of her anywhere. Either she was a very recent event, or McElroy wasn't that serious about her.

Nel-M sat back in a nearby armchair and eased out a long breath. There was something else niggling at the back of his mind about the girl, but he just couldn't put his finger on it.

He glanced at his watch, timing for when they'd probably be back.

Much of the conversation from Jac's side was the same as two nights ago with Jennifer Bromwell, but practically everything else was different.

They'd gone to a more formal restaurant, Begue's, and the waiter was over-attentive, kept asking if everything was to Monsieur and Madame's liking or there was anything else that they desired. '*Yes, Monsieur would like to be left alone without interruption for ten minutes so that at least he is given a chance of impressing the girl of his dreams.*'

Dreams? That was half the problem right there. In the same way that Jennifer Bromwell complained of boyfriends being intimidated by her father's money, he found himself intimidated by Alaysha Reyner's beauty. His mouth felt constantly dry and he kept sipping repeatedly at his water, and he could tell from her facial expressions that he wasn't hitting the right notes.

Maybe because it had been so long since Madeleine, and he was coming across as too anxious, over-eager. Or because part of his thoughts was still tied up with Durrant: Haveling had phoned to say that Marmont was off the critical list, one bit of positive news, at least; but he'd found himself dwelling more and more on his meeting with Francine Durrant. Something perhaps he'd missed, some way of convincing her to get Joshua to make contact again with his father? Or, if there was to be no more contact, any other way of shifting Larry's stance?

The thoughts spun through Jac's mind as he took his shower, the water running for so long that he shook off a shiver, along with his unresolved thoughts, as he finally got out. And the same thoughts were plaguing him again now as he focused back on Alaysha Reyner across the candle-lit table, and forced his best smile.

There'd even been, as with Jennifer Bromwell two nights

back, a confession from Alaysha when she thought the moment was right.

'I wanted to put this on the table straightaway – because a lot of guys don't handle it too well, including my ex.' She grimaced wryly, glancing to the side to make sure their over-attentive waiter wasn't within earshot. 'And so I think it's only fair that you should know straight-off: I work as a lap-dancer.'

'Oh, I see.'

But even that part he'd got wrong. He'd kept his reaction bland so as not to give away that he already suspected: '*I just don't like other guys lookin' at you like that.*' But from her eyes searching his, he could tell that she'd expected something more, and it had probably come across that he *was* shocked or offended, and had opted for a bland reaction to mask it.

'It's mainly to keep my little girl, Molly. She's only four now. Her father and I were never married and, besides, he headed for the hills within six months of her birth. And not a penny in maintenance since . . . so it's just been down to me. I've been interested in interior décor for a while, just bits here and there for friends, but I decided in the end to take a course . . . and that meant extra money. So I thought – I've got maybe four or five good years left in me before . . .'

As she fought to explain, he felt he had to stop her. He reached a hand across the table. 'Really, you don't need to justify it to me. I'm not shocked or put out by it. All those years in France – most of the girls wore the same as the average lap-dancer on the beaches every day. I'd have to be a real hypocrite to be shocked by that.' He smiled coyly and shook his head. 'But I didn't want to smile and be *too* positive about it – otherwise you might think I'm a real lech.'

Her return smile rose uncertainly as she squeezed his hand back. 'Thanks. I appreciate it.'

A couple of favour points gained. Perhaps, if lucky, he was scoring four out of ten now.

Maybe, the thought hit him, he could tell Larry he knew

about the e-mails from Joshua, say that he was sure they'd start again later. Convince Larry to hang on. But then that would also mean giving away that he'd heard it from Rodriguez, when he'd promised Rodriguez that he wouldn't betray that confidence.

'Something bothering you?'

Jac brought his attention sharply back. 'Sorry. Problems with a case I'm handling. One of those impossible Catch-22's you get hit with every now and then.'

'Oh?'

Jac hadn't intended to say anything originally, but now it seemed odd holding back, and at least it removed the spectre that what was troubling him might have been due to her. He kept Durrant's name out of it in deference to client confidentiality, it was all just *this* prisoner throughout. 'As you can see, a pretty bitter history on both sides, him and his wife, and ironically much of it revolving around his son and those same broken promises that are weighing him down so.'

Alaysha's face clouded briefly. She forced a smile and ran one fingertip halfway round the rim of her wine glass. 'So if there was contact again from his son, you think that might change his stance?' Alaysha questioned. 'Solve the problem?'

'Yeah. High chances. But it doesn't look like there's any way of that happening.'

She gave a pained, understanding smile, but then as she fell silent and thoughtful, the noise of the restaurant around crashing in for a moment, Jac feared he'd said too much. Spoilt whatever remaining chances he had by burdening her with his work problems. Though as she started to open up with some of her own problems, he realized that she'd just been thinking about what or what not to share, or whether to say anything at all. And as for the first time the tension between them eased, he knew that it had been the right thing to do. For the first hour or so, they'd just been politely fencing with each other; now they were getting to the core of what shaped and drove them.

As Alaysha Reyner talked, the stark differences to Jennifer Bromwell's life became apparent. Where Jennifer had been financially cosseted, Alaysha's background had been one of dire poverty, the family arriving from Port of Spain when she was only seven and her father got a job with a local New Orleans trawling fleet. Things eased financially for a while, but when her mother felt she couldn't take any more of her husband's erratic behaviour and periodic beatings, they parted and Alaysha's father quickly disappeared to avoid maintenance payments. They were on their own and in dire straits again, with a vengeance. And that had practically been the pattern since. Alaysha had gone out to work rather than go on to university, mainly so that she could earn to provide for her mother and younger brother.

But at least, unlike Jennifer Bromwell, there hadn't been any parental interference in her lovelife. She'd been able to make her own bad choices without any help from them. After Molly's father had headed for the hills when Molly was only six months old, there'd been a couple of brief disastrous relationships, but Gerry – now an assistant bar manager at the Golden Bay Casino in Biloxi – had been her first serious boyfriend since then. Things had been okay for the first year or so, but then he'd become increasingly paranoid about her work.

'He hasn't hit me yet – just a lot of pushing and shoving. But give him time, I know he would – and I'm not waiting around for that to happen.' She played thoughtfully again with the rim of her wine glass. 'Seems to me like I'm continuing my mother's cycle: hopelessly drawn to guys who either can't put bread on the table, or are handy with their fists. Or both.'

Words would have been wrong at that moment, empty promises, which probably Alaysha Reyner had heard far too many of in her life – so Jac just reached out and gently squeezed her hand in reassurance. To their side an arched window looked onto a resplendent tropical courtyard, New Orleans' finest milling through it to the luxury hotel beyond;

sharp contrast to the life Alaysha had just described. Though with part of what she'd said, *bread on the table*, Jac had felt a stab of conscience. Given that same choice, career or family, unlike him it appeared she'd put family first every time.

'You're obviously very close to your mom.' Jac tightly smiled his understanding. 'Do you take after her?'

'A little, I suppose. But I probably look more like my father, as much as I might not feel comfortable with that.' She glanced down fleetingly before looking at Jac more directly. 'I think that was part of the problem right there. He knew he was good-looking, so thought that gave him the right to push women around, treat them bad. Felt that they'd always come running back for more.' She sniggered uncomfortably. 'And in a way, he was right – at least where my mom was concerned.'

'She's far better off without him, by the sound of it. As tough as it might have been.' Jac touched her hand again, hoping he'd read it right; after all, she'd had to sacrifice there, too: her mother's happiness put before her losing her father while she was young. 'You both are.'

'Suppose so.' Alaysha smiled and shrugged, as if freeing the weight momentarily hanging there. Though the other weight hanging over her would be more difficult to shift, she reflected, wondering whether she'd *ever* know him well enough to tell him that. And looking across at Jac, she realized in that moment what had attracted her about those blue-grey eyes when they'd first met; the sadness and loss in them made him look soft, vulnerable. Understanding. Most vitally, given her and her mother's history with men, he didn't look like a man who would ever hit her. 'Let's just hope that I don't take after him in temperament.'

'If you do – I'll remember to wear my body protector next time.'

Alaysha's smile widened and she lifted her glass to clink with Jac's raised glass. More points scored.

Enough, as the evening wound to a close and she kissed

him lightly on the cheek by his apartment door, for her to want to see him again.

'Do you like Creole food?' she asked, to which he nodded.

'Put it this way – since being in New Orleans I've developed more of a taste for it. It's been either that, or starve.'

She chuckled lightly. 'Okay. Maybe I can invite you round for some home cooking later in the week.'

Jac squeezed her hand in thanks and returned the kiss – both cheeks this time, French style. 'I look forward to it.'

Enough for another dinner date, though not enough to be able to share her bed that night.

Though when forty minutes later she phoned and asked, 'Are you still up?' – he thought for one hopeful moment she might have had a change of heart.

'Yes, yes, I am. Not in bed quite yet.'

'Because that problem you mentioned earlier. I thought of how you might be able to get around it. If you're interested?'

The second Jac picked up his phone, the tape activated and the sound-man, Vic Farrelia, leant closer as he listened.

Nel-M had left the apartment almost two hours before McElroy returned, having finished his search and planted the bug, and within half an hour he had Farrelia set up in a small room on Perdido Street six blocks away.

And when just after midnight, Farrelia phoned and related the first call to come over the line, Nel-M nodded thoughtfully. From this moment on, Jac McElroy's life was never going to be the same again.

11

The first time that Adelay Roche called, Clive Beaton got his secretary to lie and say that he was tied up until late morning, so that he could prepare himself before returning the call.

There were so many worrying no-go paths the conversation could take that he began to doubt the wisdom of talking to Roche at all – but his mounting curiosity finally won the day.

Roche quickly sought to quell Beaton's worries.

'I know you're probably thinking that we shouldn't be speaking, given the delicacy of things at this juncture. But, you know, we've been skirting around each other for eleven years for the very same reason – and now that everything is finally drawing to a close, I felt I should make contact.' Roche drew a fresh breath. 'In particular because what I'm calling about has nothing to do with the Durrant case.'

Beaton felt a weight ease from his chest as Roche explained how he'd been watching for the past couple of years the activities of one of the firm's associates, Ralph Miers, an expert in tax law.

'Seems to me he's one of the few guys in the State to also wear a strong hat on environmental issues. I saw what he did for Gulf-West petroleum, and, let me tell you – I was impressed.'

Beaton was happy just listening – it meant that he didn't have to defend any of the no-go conversation areas he'd run through – as Roche went on to explain that Miers looked like just the man he needed.

'I've been stalling on changes to my refinery at Houma for nigh on four years now – but if I can please the greens and environmentalists and at the same time get the right tax breaks for making the plant environmentally friendly, I'm all for it.' Roche chuckled, which quickly became a heavy wheeze. 'That is, assuming I'm correct in my judgement that your man Miers is right for the job and can get the government to pay indirectly for every penny of those changes, and hopefully more.'

'I'm sure he is,' Beaton said with a spark of conviction to hopefully lift it beyond stock response, as his thoughts automatically turned to the potential value of such an account.

'So I thought I should touch base now that the curtain is about to finally come down on the Durrant episode.'

'And I'm glad you did. I really appreciate it.' Beaton measured his words carefully: warmth and sincerity to hopefully lure Roche into the fold, but due deference and legal correctness for the firm's current client, Durrant. 'But it would probably be incorrect of us – perhaps even tempting fate – to second guess just what Governor Candaret might do with Durrant's plea for clemency.'

Roche chuckled again. 'I might have agreed with you – if it wasn't for the stunt that Durrant just pulled with his attempted prison break.'

'His wha–?' Beaton stopped himself sharply. Stock reaction had for a second overridden one of the prime legal commandments: never give away that you don't know *everything* about your client.

'You mean you didn't know?' Roche pressed.

'Of course I knew.' Beaton recovered quickly, beating back the resurging tide of his nerves and apprehension: he should have realized that Roche wouldn't have called without a sting in the tail. 'It's just that I was caught off guard as to how *you* knew. Especially since we're still in the midst of how to handle the situation.'

'I see.' Roche had to admit, Beaton was good, his thirty-five years of keen-edged law practice shining through. But the split-second falter had been enough to tell Roche that Beaton hadn't known. For whatever reason, his rookie lawyer had decided to keep Durrant's attempted break-out under

133

wraps. He could all but feel the seething anger in Beaton's undertone: he couldn't wait to get off the line and get his hands around McElroy's neck. 'Well, let's speak again when *you* feel the dust has settled enough on the Durrant case for it to be right for us to do so.'

Jac had just returned with a cup of water from the water-cooler when he saw the fresh e-mail on his computer. And as he clicked and saw who it was from, *durransave4@hotmail*, he jolted sharply, almost spilling it. After six days with no reply, he'd all but given up on another e-mail from his mystery sender.

His hands shook on the keyboard as he opened it.

Sent at 11.16:22. One minute, forty seconds ago. Would they still be sitting there to do something else, or have left immediately?

Jac clicked on the track-back software, its screen overlapping the e-mail so that he couldn't read it. Jac's fingers tapped anxiously on his desk as it traced and started displaying. Then he double-clicked IT-number find, and forty seconds later it popped up on screen:

Internet-ional on Peniston Street. An internet café. He or she was moving around.

Jac's heart was beating double-time, his finger tapping almost in time with it as he called 411 and waited to get routed through.

Please still be there : . . please . . .

Jac became aware of Langfranc looking at him through his office glass-screen, Langfranc's expression weighted with concern as he spoke on his own phone. Jac yanked his attention back as a girl answered.

'Internet-ional. May I help you?'

Jac introduced himself and explained what he wanted. 'Computer number fourteen. Message sent just over three minutes ago. Are they still there?' Jac held his breath in anticipation.

'I'm not sure. One minute . . .' Her voice trailed off and Jac heard her speaking with a colleague.

Jac looked again towards Langfranc, but this time Langfranc looked slightly away as Jac met his eye, as if he felt suddenly awkward or embarrassed. Jac closed the track-back screen so that he could see all of the e-mail.

The girl's voice returned: 'Yeah . . . computer number fourteen. Looks like he's still there.'

Jac leapt up. 'Okay . . . *okay*!' He hooked his jacket from the back of his chair. 'I'm heading down to you right now! Should be with you in no more than ten or twelve.'

The e-mail was now displaying, random phrases leaping out at him . . . *I'd have incriminated myself . . . know what I saw . . . Larry Durrant didn't kill Jessica Roche . . .*

Langfranc, seeing Jac about to leave in a rush, suddenly seemed equally panicked, ending his call abruptly and swinging his door open as Jac was only two paces away from his desk.

'Jac. *Jac*! That was Beaton just then – going on about something you've held back from him about the Durrant case. He wants to see you in his office right now.'

'I can't . . . I *can't* deal with this now.' Jac took a step further away, eyes shifting frantically. 'Something's broken on the Durrant case that just won't wait. I've got to sort it out now!'

'Beaton sounded pissed as hell – you're taking your life in your hands fobbing him off like this, Jac.' Langfranc's face flushed as he forced a tight-lipped grimace. 'But, okay, it's your neck. How long?'

'Thirty, forty minutes. Hour tops.' Jac took another couple of steps away, all that filled his mind at that second an image of Durrant's mystery e-mailer leaving his internet café computer.

'Okay, I'll tell him. But your story had better be good when you get back, Jac – otherwise it's probably kiss-your-ass-goodbye-time here. I've hardly ever heard Beaton that angry.'

Jac's stomach dipped at the possibility. He returned Lang-franc's grimace and held one hand up, thanks, *hold my job for me till I get back, if you can*, and sprinted out, a silent prayer on his breath that he'd make it in time.

Jac ran to the corner of Thalia and Chestnut Streets so that he had the benefit of cabs from both directions, and hailed one in less than a minute.

He said that he was late for a meeting, and the driver, seeing in his mirror the anxiety on Jac's face and the sweat on his brow, put his foot down. 'Might be able shave off a minute or so, if we're lucky.'

The air-rush through the half-open taxi window buffeted Jac's face as they picked up speed along Magazine Street, older two-storey antebellum buildings with quaint railed-terraces giving way to taller, newer, flat-fronted shops and offices; the transition from old to new as New Orleans became less Colonial-French and more like any other American city.

'Internet-ional on Peniston, you say?' The taxi driver con-firmed over one shoulder.

'Yeah.' Though as he said it, Jac was suddenly hit with something he should have covered while he'd been on the phone to them before.

Jac took out his cell-phone and punched in Internet-ional's number. But as he pressed to dial, another voice was suddenly there, crashing in. His heart leapt for a second, fearful that it was Beaton deciding to give him a roasting over the phone, or fire him – but it was Morvaun Jaspar, the forger he'd got cleared a couple of months back.

'*Jac*! Got a problem. Big problem!'

'I can't do this now, Morvaun. I've got someone I've got to call right now. Urgently!'

'This too, Jac. This too! The local blues have just pulled me in, and it's bullshit . . . absolute bullshit. They're tryin' to nail me for everyone they find with a forged document . . . or looks like one. And no doubt all 'cause we pulled the rug

136

out from 'em last time. It's a complete sham shake-down, and I ain't about to –'

'Morvaun – I can't handle this now!' Jac could imagine his mystery e-mailer getting up from his seat and leaving as they spoke; and if he didn't get back to the people at Internet-ional before that happened, he might not even get a description. 'I really *have* got someone I've got to call. Right now! Let's talk again later.'

'I can't call back later, Jac. This is my *one* allowed call. You gotta get down here – otherwise I'm here for the duration.'

'Okay . . . *okay*. Where are you now?'

'Fifth District station-house.'

'I'll get there as soon as I can. About –' Jac cradled his forehead as he remembered that he was meant to be back, *sharp*, to see Beaton. But he couldn't just leave Morvaun hanging for what might be almost two hours. He'd have to call Langfranc to pass the message to Beaton that his out-of-office meeting got more involved, was going to take longer. Jac sighed heavily. 'About forty minutes or so.'

'Your office is only fifteen minutes from here, Jac, can't you –'

'I'm halfway across town right now, Morvaun – trying to sort something else out. But I promise I'll get there as soon as. *Hold on!*'

'Yeah, okay . . . hear you loud 'n' clear Jac. Not much else f'me to do.'

The instant Morvaun rang off, Jac re-dialled Internet-ional.

'Jac McElroy again. I called a couple of minutes back. Is he *still* there – computer number fourteen?' Jac's breath froze in his throat in the two-second wait for the girl to look and answer.

'Yeah. I can still see him.'

'Okay . . . *okay*.' Jac exhaled heavily. 'Can you try and get a good look at him?'

'I . . . I can't see him that well from here. He's turned away from me, looking at his computer.'

'Right. What's your name, by the way?' *Personalize* to get closer, Jac thought.

'Uuuh . . . Tracy.' Hesitant, as if worried what he might do with the information.

'Okay, Tracy, I don't know how easy it is because I'm not there – but if you could shift more to a side-view . . . without, that is, being too obvious, making him suspicious. Just in case he leaves before I get down there myself to see him.' Jac looked up as they crossed Washington Avenue. Only a dozen or so blocks now to Peniston: four or five minutes at most. Hold on. *Hold on.*

'Oh . . . okay.' But Tracy still sounded uncertain.

'And if he does start to leave before I get there – maybe try and hold him up a bit, if you can. Keep him there.'

Only the sound of Tracy's breath falling for a second. 'That might be more difficult.'

'I know. *I know.* But maybe tell him that there's a free coffee today for customers . . . I'll cover for it when I get there.'

'I . . . I suppose I could . . . oh . . . *oh* . . .'

Hearing her sudden intake of breath, Jac asked sharply, 'What *is it?*'

'He . . . he's looking round, starting to get up.'

Jac felt his stomach tighten; but then he'd suspected all along that whoever it was wouldn't hang around long. His voice lowered, a conspiratorial hush. 'Okay, Tracy . . . try what I suggested.'

'I'll *try.* I'll do my . . .' Jac could hear her breath falling shorter, sharper as she broke off for a second. Then, a faint tremor in her undertone – or perhaps it was just Jac picking up on it because he knew she was nervous: 'Sir . . . there's a free coffee for customers today I forgot to tell you about earlier.'

Aline Street flashed by. Only four blocks to go now.

At Internet-ional, the man, African-American, late-thirties, in a maroon Hilfiger jacket, paused for a second, looked

138

tempted. But some noise from the street outside reached him then, strains of a brass band playing a block or so away, and he glanced distractedly over his shoulder for a second. And as he turned back, Tracy saw something shift in his eyes, flicking between her and the phone. Picked up a bad vibe, or just acknowledgement that he was interrupting her?

'Thanks for the offer.' He pushed a terse smile. 'But I gotta rush. Someone to see.'

Tracy watched helplessly as he scurried out; though maybe, like he said, he *was* in a rush. She let out a long sigh as she brought the receiver back.

'I'm sorry . . . tried my best. But he's gone.'

'I know. *I know*.' Jac had heard it all his end, closing his eyes as the sinking in his stomach spread, made every part of him feel empty, cruelly cheated. Though as he opened them again and saw the next cross street flash by, a spark of hope resurged. 'But you got a good look at him?'

'Yeah, sure did.' Tracy's tone brightened; one thing to have gone right.

Only two blocks away now, if Jac got a good description maybe he'd still be able to pick him out as they turned into the street – but at that moment the taxi slowed, then braked sharply. Jac looked ahead: four cars backed up at the next intersection as a procession of sixty or seventy people, some with banners, marched and sashayed by in rhythm to a small brass band leading.

Jac exhaled heavily, feeling his stomach dip again. He wouldn't make it now.

'That's okay,' he said resignedly. 'I'll be there in just a couple of minutes. Give me all the details then.'

Mr Mystery-e-mailer would be long gone by the time he got there; and if he'd now been spooked, that would probably be the end of any more contact.

Jac looked up towards the procession as it finally passed and the taxi crossed the junction. In his few years in New Orleans he'd discovered that bands were broken out for anything and everything – weddings, funerals, gay marches, dog's birthday – though from the banners this looked like a save some bay or other environmental protest.

Jac suddenly became aware of a man in the crowd looking back at him, smiling and waving. Probably just somebody random, catching Jac's eye as he'd looked towards them. But in that moment it became Jac's mystery e-mailer, teasing, taunting: you won't find me. *You won't find me.*

'Black guy, broad. Bit of bulk on . . . but not fat.'

'And height?'

'Five-ten, maybe six foot.'

'Age?'

'Mid to late thirties, maybe forty.'

'Anything that stood out? Beard? Moustache? Prominent scar or birth-mark?'

'No, clean shaven. But, oh . . . he had this gap between his front teeth when he smiled.'

'And what he was he wearing?'

'Hilfiger jacket, sort of dark-red, and jeans. And a baseball cap, dark-blue or black.'

Jac paused at that point, looking back at his notes for anything he might have missed. At the outset he'd ascertained from Tracy, an early-twenties short-cropped-blonde-with-a-lime-green-stripe and more nose rings than a Krishna, that it had been paid cash, as he'd suspected: no trace back. Now the description wasn't giving him that much either. Could fit twenty to thirty per cent of African-American males in that age band. But as Jac puckered his mouth, Tracy commented, 'But, hey, you can check all that for yourself.' She eased a sly smile as she looked up above the entrance. 'We should have him on video.'

Jac followed her eyes towards the camera there and, uncertainly, as if taking a second to believe his luck, mirrored her smile.

*

The atmosphere in the interview room was laden, tense.

Morvaun Jaspar looked tired, worn-down by the questioning and psychological games the two policemen had rained down on him over the two hours he'd been held. Pretty much the same Mutt and Jeff, black and white game as before. Jac knew the black officer, Jim Holbrook, from last time – the supposedly friendly voice in Morvaun's ear: 'Hey, come on bro', make it easy on yourself.' But the white lieutenant, Pyrford, Jac hadn't seen before. Rakish with heavily receding red-brown hair, a toothpick that he seemed reluctant to take out of the corner of his mouth, and a look of disdain down his nose at Morvaun that spoke volumes. Jac could imagine that ten years ago he'd have been addressing Morvaun, and probably his partner too, as 'boy'.

Jac had no doubt looked troubled and on edge as soon as he walked into the interview room, which had set the mood for what followed. He'd watched only a few seconds of the video with Tracy, just to make sure maroon-Hilfiger-jacket was there and it was the right segment, then had requested a copy to look at in more detail later. No time right then. He'd phoned Langfranc on his way over to Morvaun to tell him he'd be delayed, Langfranc warning that it could be one delay too many '. . . *the one that might just tip the balance on Beaton preparing your dismissal letter*', but Jac had become equally concerned about something else, asking Langfranc if there was any indication as to just what he was meant to have held back on.

'*No, no clue at all.*'

'*Or perhaps where Beaton might have got his information from?*'

'*No clue there either, I'm afraid, Jac. All I know is he's madder than hell, and says he wants it all straight from the hip from you – right now in his office.*'

What had suddenly hit Jac, started to panic him, was that he had no idea just *which* of his withheld secrets Beaton knew about: the alleged prison-break attempt or Durrant's death-wish? He was facing a firestorm back at the office with

Beaton, but with no idea from which direction the fire was coming. And if he picked the wrong one, Beaton would then know about *both*: full house!

Morvaun had acknowledged him with a numb smile as he walked in. He was wearing a bright crimson jacket with a silvery wave trim on each cuff. Quite conservative by his standards.

Morvaun liked to think of himself as a tough cookie, but he was no longer young, and beneath the veneer of bluff and bravado he'd built up over the years, Jac could clearly see – as he had done halfway through their first case together – his fear and frailty; fear that if he got anything more than a four- or five-year term, he might not make it through.

'I hope you two had the good sense not to ask my client any more questions after he informed you he had counsel on his way,' Jac said as he put down his briefcase. Stamp his authority on the meeting early.

'Of course, goes without saying,' Pyrford said with a dry smile, jiggling the toothpick in the corner of his mouth. 'We just kept it conversational after that. Mild weather for the time of year, and what a fine head of hair he still has for a man of his age.'

Holbrook looked down at the floor, and Jac swore he could almost hear a groan riding on his sigh.

'Never let it be said that you'd indulge in pointless questions or comments,' Jac said, peering sharply at Pyrford's shiny, wisp-haired crown. 'Let's get to the bottom line, shall we?' Jac continued curtly. 'Is my client being charged? And, if so, what's the evidence against him?'

'Not yet.' Pyrford was put out of stride by the directness, flushing slightly; he injected more authority into his voice. 'But we got a woman in custody, Alvira Jardine, a Haitian national with forged papers – passport and driver's licence – and they've got your client's trademark all over them.'

'Has Ms Jardine named Mr Jaspar as having forged them for her?'

'No, she hasn't, though we –' Pyrford fought to regain his step, the control he'd had over the meeting only minutes ago, but Jac rolled straight on.

'And apart from my client's "trademark" – what other evidence is there that might link him to this?' Jac's tone was acid and impatient; he had no intention of making it easy on them. One look at Morvaun told him how much he'd been railroaded over the past two hours.

'Well, we . . .' Increasingly flustered, Pyrford looked back towards Holbrook for support; but Holbrook did a wide-eyed, 'don't include me on where you might be heading'. 'We've done our own comparisons with Mr Jaspar's past work, and from that alone had more than good reason to bring him in now. But I'm not at liberty to discuss that, or the other evidence we have, until we've got the full analysis back from the lab. I'm confident, though, that will back up our findings to date – and then, believe me, your client's really going to feel our breath down his neck.'

'Not to put too fine a point on it,' Jac said cuttingly, 'wouldn't that have been the best time to haul my client in – *when* you've got your lab conclusions. Rather than bringing him in on this fine afternoon just to comment on what a good head of hair he has for a man of his age.' He smiled wanly.

Pyrford's jaw tightened. He glared at Jac for a second before answering. 'Don't worry – he'll be the first to know.'

'When?'

'Couple of days, tops.'

'Fine.' Jac picked up his briefcase and nodded to Morvaun. 'Look forward to it.'

'Me too, Counsellor,' Pyrford said, his stare icy. 'Me too.'

'Thanks, Jac,' Morvaun said as they headed down the corridor. He gave a lopsided smile. 'But less of the two white-boys-ego-posturing next time, if you could. If things turn sour, it's my po' black ass they take it out on.'

'I'll try,' Jac said, returning the smile. They went through the station-house doors and out onto the street. 'But if there's no connection with you on this one, Morvaun, stop worrying. They're not going to be able to pin it on you. I'll make sure of that.' The confident tone of a lawyer who, having cleared his client for a crime he *did* commit, thought one he hadn't should be a walkover.

'Like I said, Jac, I'm clean on this one. Never even heard o' Mrs Jardine before. They're just tryin' for a fix – most likely 'cause they couldn't nail me last time.'

'And they won't this time, either.' Jac smiled tightly and laid one hand reassuringly on Morvaun's shoulder as they parted. 'Don't worry.'

Watching Morvaun Jaspar head off along North Claiborne Avenue, shoulders slightly sunken, Jac wondered whether it was simply the gait of an old man worn down by the two hours of questioning, or if there was something Morvaun wasn't telling him.

Though as Jac turned and looked out for a cab, he probably appeared little different: the spark of fresh hope from the video in his briefcase not enough to lift his spirits from the nightmare showdown he was facing back at the office with Beaton.

12

'I thought I should let you know – I read what happened to Raoul Ferrer.'

'Yeah, you and half of New Orleans that read beyond the first page of the local rags,' Nel-M said with a huffed breath. 'And your point is?'

It had taken Truelle three full days to work up the courage to make the call. He'd turned over which path the conversation might take so many times in his mind that his concentration had started lapsing during sessions at work and he'd had to ask patients to repeat themselves. He thought he'd better make the call before it drove him and his patients mad – or 'madder' to be more precise with both of them – or ditch the idea completely. The final bit of Dutch courage was provided by an extra-curricular visit to Ben's bar, but he was still uncertain about the wisdom of making the call after the first shot, his hands still shaking. He ordered another – but then eyed it hesitantly. He'd need all his wits about him tangling words with Nel-M. He could feel the warmth of the drink in his hand drawing him in. Maybe he should just knock it back and forget the idea of making the call, stay here in the warm cocoon of the bar and order another, and another, and . . . He slammed the drink back down on the table and pushed it at arm's length as if it were poison, getting quickly to his feet and heading out before his resolve went completely.

He made the call to Nel-M when he was a block away from the bar – but now with just a few testy words from Nel-M, his nerves were back with a vengeance, his hand shaking on his cell-phone. He wished now that he had downed that second shot.

'My . . . my point is, the timing. You visit me one day to

make sure I'm okay with everything going down now with Durrant – then the next day Raoul Ferrer is dead.'

'Coincidence. In Ferrer's line of work, he's just one step away from a bullet every day. In fact, annoying little snake-eyed creep that he is – or *was* – I'm amazed he lasted so long.'

'Are you trying to tell me that you didn't kill Raoul Ferrer?'

'I'm not trying to tell you anything – it's you that's made the call, doctor. But if you're any good at analysing what your patients' say, you might have gathered from my last comment about Ferrer catching a bullet from anywhere that, yes, that's exactly what I'm getting at.'

Nel-M's tone was teasing, taunting. Truelle purposely kept his tone flat, matter-of-fact, didn't want to give Nel-M the satisfaction of knowing that he'd risen to the bait.

'You can say it whichever way you like – that doesn't mean I have to believe it.'

'Oh, is that what you're saying to your patients these days? You can tell me you're Batman as many ways as you like – but that doesn't mean I have to believe it? I thought you guys had more subtle ways of putting things, like: as much as you might have liked to take such an action yourself, the actual taking of it is too shocking and burdensome for your conscious mind to cope with – so your subconscious then develops various alternative scenarios.'

Truelle bit at his lip. Nel-M was playing with him. He should never have made the call, should have known that he wouldn't get a straight answer. But he just couldn't resist the snipe back.

'Yes, you're right – we do have more subtle ways of putting things. I just dumbed it down especially for you.'

'Ooohh, my, my. We are feeling frisky today.' Nel-M's voice suddenly dropped, becoming more menacing. 'But then if you truly believe that I did waste Ferrer – maybe that's not the wisest thing to be saying to me.'

'Ain't that the truth.' Truelle said it flatly. It was probably the *only* bit of truth to pass between them in the past couple of minutes, and he still had strong doubts that the call in itself was the wisest move. He took a fresh breath. 'Let's cut to the chase and the main reason for my call now. *If* you were responsible for Ferrer, and *if* you and Roche have got it into your minds to do the same with me – then think again. I took the precaution way back of preparing a couple of insurance policies. Everything surrounding us and the Durrant affair, chapter and verse. All in sealed envelopes – only to be opened in the event of my death.' Truelle paused to let the revelation sink home. 'So, you see, you and Roche have a great vested interest in keeping me alive. In fact, those envelopes get opened whichever way I happen to go – even in an unsuspicious, unrelated accident. So if there's been any talk of me being "taken care of" then, literally speaking, that's exactly what should be happening – if you've got any time to spare. Making sure the road's clear before I cross, or there's no banana skins in my way . . . or I haven't had one too many drinks before I get into my car.'

As Truelle got into his stride of taunting Nel-M in similar mode, giving as good as he got, he felt his nerves ease for the first time since he'd got on the phone. He couldn't resist a lightly mocking chuckle as he hit the last words – but it died quickly in his throat.

'We know all about your little insurance policies. Have done for some while now.'

'*What*?' Truelle quickly forced another chuckle to cover his surprise, but feared it had come across as quavering and uncertain. Surely Nel-M was bluffing? They might have guessed he'd somehow covered his back, but they wouldn't know any of the details. He took a long breath to calm his voice, sound more certain of his ground. 'I can read you like I read practically every one of my patients. You know nothing.'

'Don't kid yourself, Leonard. We know everything, every little move. You see, we've been listening, have been for some time now.' Nel-M paused, smiling slyly as he heard Truelle swallow hard and his breathing become more rapid. Either Truelle was walking fast, or the comment had hit the mark.

'You've been *what*?'

'You heard, man. *Listening*. You know – what you're meant to do every day with your patients. When I get off the phone from you now, I can go to a little room where a man will replay everything we've just discussed. And that's been the way for many a year now. We got more tapes with labels on them than the *Friends* re-runs library. Every little detail. Most of it painfully boring – but, hey, some of it, pure magic.' Nel-M's jocular, taunting tone was back. 'Especially where you've tried to outwit us and we've been listening in, knowing that you've failed before you've even started.'

'You're bluffing,' Truelle said, but his voice was suddenly hoarse, lacking any conviction. The blood was pounding so heavily through his head that when a large truck rolled past close by, the sounds merged; one thunderous, vibrating roar that seemed to fill the street.

'You just keep telling yourself that, Leonard. Our little man in his room is laughing himself stupid right now as we speak.'

Nel-M started laughing then, and it too became a roar that merged with the noise of the passing truck – until Truelle cut it short by ending the call.

And left there in the silence of the street as the noise of the truck faded into the distance, at least now Truelle had his answer: he shouldn't have made the call. His legs felt weak and unsteady, and there was a sudden wave of acid bile in his stomach that made him want to retch. Though when he shuffled to the kerb and leant over, nothing came up.

As he straightened and noticed a man passing on the opposite pavement looking over at him, he was reminded of past times when this had happened. He felt like shouting out, 'I haven't been drinking!' But of the two, sick with fear or from drink, he knew now which he preferred.

He looked pensively back along the street towards Ben's bar, wondering whether the drink he'd left on the table might not have been cleared away yet.

*

A faint tremble ran through Jac's body as he walked back into his apartment after work that evening; a combination of what he'd seen on the video tape from Internet-ional an hour before he left the office – the first undisturbed moment he'd been able to grab on the video player in the boardroom annexe – and his earlier confrontation with Beaton.

'*You see, Mr Beaton, the reason that I didn't say anything to you, or indeed anyone, was that Warden Haveling specifically asked me not to. Not, that is, until he'd had time to deliberate more on a certain situation with Lawrence Durrant.*'

'*You're talking in riddles, McElroy. I wanted to see you because I discovered you've been withholding information from me – and you're still doing that now.*'

'*I'm sorry, Mr Beaton . . . but, as you can see, it's awkward with my hands tied like this by client confidentiality.*'

Before the meeting, Jac had quizzed Langfranc again; but there wasn't even a hint as to which withheld secret Beaton knew about. So Jac hoped that if he fumbled around vaguely in the opening minutes, Beaton might let it slip – but there'd been several anxious, scrambling moments before he finally did, Beaton eyeing him as if he was some sort of alien bug as Jac explained about the differing accounts between the prison guards and Durrant giving Haveling pause for thought, and, in turn, Haveling asking Jac to maintain secrecy until he'd decided which account had the most validity.

As soon as Jac was inside his apartment, he slotted the video tape in his machine, his jaw setting tighter as it played; then stopped, rewound and played the segment again. Then one final play, this time stopping it at intervals and moving closer to the screen to gauge angles and clarity.

Beaton had made it clear though that he was far from happy, '*You've stretched confidentiality by the thinnest of threads here, McElroy. One more incident like this, just one . . .*' his parting words settling as a dull ache of tension at the back of Jac's neck as he'd returned to his desk; no doubt left in his mind what would happen if Beaton ever found out about Durrant's death-wish, let alone their planned e-mail ruse.

And Jac felt that same ache now. He went across to the side cabinet and poured himself a brandy, closing his eyes as he felt the first mouthful trickle down. It looked like Mr Mystery had been well aware of the camera's position – had kept his head tilted down, peak of his baseball-cap obscuring his face on the way in *and* out – and had chosen a computer with his back to it throughout. There were only a few seconds with a part profile from cheekbone to chin, and only a split-second with slightly more, from bottom of one eye to chin – but it was so fleeting and indistinct that it could still be anyone: Busta Rhymes, 50 Cent, Martin Lawrence – take your pick.

Jac took another quick slug, trying to focus on what he *did* have: a video that could fit three hundred thousand male African-Americans in New Orleans, a description that at most would narrow that down by half, an untraceable e-mail address, and a sender that might well have been spooked and so wouldn't make contact again.

But in that moment, as Jac turned it all over in his mind once more, the images on tape, Tracy's description and Langfranc's earlier comment all coalesced, and another unease suddenly gripped Jac's stomach. While, yes, it could well be a hoaxer or one of Durrant's friends, from all of that it could also be, as Langfranc suggested, the murderer himself.

Jac noticed his hands start to shake as he opened out the earlier e-mail and read it again:

> I couldn't give my name or come forward before, because I'd have incriminated myself. And that still stands now. But I <u>was</u> there, and I know what I saw. Larry Durrant didn't kill Jessica Roche.

Jac bit at his lip. Recalling something else criminologists said – that often those guilty gave a clue to what they'd done by only telling half the truth – along with *I was there*, another phrase now leapt out at him . . . *I'd have incriminated myself.*

*

'Hi. Bell-South. My name's Leonard Truelle and I made an earlier call requesting an engineer's visit to check my line.'

'Telephone number and zip-code?'

Nel-M gave them, and waited anxiously while the girl checked the details on the computer. As agreed with Roche, he'd left it twenty-four hours from his conversation with Truelle before making the call. But if there was no request made, he'd have to back-track quickly and say that he'd instructed his secretary but she obviously hadn't made the request yet. '*Staff these days!*' Then make the same call twenty-four hours later. Nel-M felt the tension ease from his chest as the girl started speaking again.

'Yes. Here it is. Appointment for an engineer to call at four-thirty p.m. at the number you gave me. And another one here under the same name the following morning, but a different number and address.'

'Yes, that one's for my office,' Nel-M said. 'But the problem is, I didn't have my diary with me at the time I made the appointments, and I fear those times might now be a problem. You said four-thirty tomorrow for my home visit , and what time was it for my office?'

'Eleven the following morning, Thursday.'

Nel-M sighed. 'I feared as much. Something's cropped up, and I just don't think I'm going to be able to make those now.'

'Do you want me to re-schedule them for you?'

'No, no. It's okay. If you cancel them for now, I'll phone in and book them again when I've got my schedule a bit clearer. As it is, I might have been worrying for nothing with the checks I wanted made.'

'That's been done for you now, sir. Those engineer visits have been cancelled – and we look forward to your contact again when you're ready. Thank you for calling Bell-South.'

Nel-M phoned Roche straightaway.

'He's taken the bait. But not just with his home-line – he's having his office checked as well.'

'You really did light a fire under him.'

'I think it was that bit about a man in a little room listening in for the past few years.'

'Well, that's *exactly* what's going to be happening from here on in.' Roche's chuckle rode a laboured wheeze. 'Nothing like a touch of irony to brighten the day.'

Tally Shavell counted down the last of forty push-ups on his cell floor, then, with a sharp sucking in of his breath, changed from flat palms to closed fists on the cell floor for a further twenty.

As he finished, his breathing hardly faltering from the exertion, he straightened up and admired himself.

Nothing larger than small shaving mirrors were allowed at Libreville; not only because of the danger of all that jagged glass if they were broken, but because vanity was frowned upon by Haveling. But pictures and paintings were allowed, again *with* Haveling's approval, and as long as they had Perspex rather than glass covering.

So Tally had chosen a five-foot high poster print of *Othello* from a production at Chicago's Shakespeare Theater. The poster depicted Othello looking towards a light high in the wings to which he was making an impassioned, hand-outstretched, plea. The light picked out only his face, part of one shoulder, and his outstretched hand. Everything else – the rest of his body and the surrounding stage scenery – was blacked out.

Tally knew that with its strong cultural and 'black roots' tag, Haveling wouldn't dare give it the thumbs-down. But it wasn't the image itself or its message that had attracted Tally, it was its blackness. He could see his reflection in the darkness surrounding Othello's lit face.

And perhaps, in an ironic way, he felt it also mirrored how he saw himself at Libreville: operating in the darker shadows beyond what everyone saw on the surface.

He took a deep breath and pumped up his torso and biceps. He wasn't as dark as the actor in *Othello*: his father's Acadian

Indian/Creole French blood had tempered his mother's African lineage to make his skin tone a dark bronze with grey undertone. It showed up well against the darkness of the poster, his skin shining and glistening with the sweat from his press-ups.

He tensed more, until the veins stood up proud and blue-grey on his skin, then kept his left arm rigid as he reached with his right hand for the syringe on the table to one side.

He found the vein without hardly looking and slowly and firmly squeezed it home.

'Ice' or 'chalk', it was favoured by those in the prison who wanted a sharper, adrenalin-pumped high – which included most of his crew – rather than become a zombie from crack or heroin.

Tally had his hand in the supply chain of nearly everything at Libreville, and most 'chalk' or 'ice' was supplied in tablet form or in crystals for smoking, though Tally preferred it intravenously: he liked to feel that hit after only seconds, preferably while he was still looking at his reflection and could see it practically coursing like a lit fuse through his bulging veins before exploding at the back of his brain.

His head jolted back as it hit, and every nerve end tensed of its own accord. He felt like that scene in *Highlander*, electrical surges connecting his body to the sky and half the universe beyond, lifting him off his feet. And he savoured the sensation, knowing that's how he'd feel when he made his next move against Rodriguez.

He knew that he couldn't leave it long. People were starting to talk: 'Can't even finish off a midget Mexican these days.' He knew that each day he left Rodriguez alive he risked letting slip his power grip over Libreville; and, as if echoing that thought, he felt the effects of the methamphetamine start to slide away from his body. He stared back at his image through the blackness, his widely dilated pupils settling back as he focused and started to plan where and when.

13

As they took up their seats in the canteen, BC nudged Rodriguez and looked towards the end of the table. 'Hey, don' forget. New kid on the block.'

'Yeah, yeah.' Rodriguez studied the boy. Barely in his twenties, brush-cut black hair, wide-eyed and bewildered from arriving at Libreville just the day before. Rodriguez hardly felt in the mood for it with everything with Larry still hanging by a thread; if McElroy got no joy over Josh's e-mails to Larry, that was probably it: throw-in-the-towel time.

But it had become standard routine, his greeting of new inmates to the cell-block. His audience now expected it of him, looked forward to it. One of the high points to break the dour, stifling routine. Rodriguez headed towards the end of the table, Theo Mellor sitting next to the new inmate promptly getting up and swapping places with him. Everyone knew their part in playing it out.

'Hey, howya doin'?' Rodriguez held out a hand in greeting which the boy uncertainly took to shake. 'Roddy . . . Roddy Rodriguez. I'm the communications guy here, yer know, for any letters and e-mails you wanna send to family and friends. An' it also falls down to me to give you a quick introduction to who's who here. An' you are?'

'Billy. Billy Hillier.' Still uncertain, a faint smile threatening to break through.

'Well, Billy, the first thing you're gonna have to know is everyone's names roun' here. Get their names wrong, and they'll likely slit your throat before you even started what you were gonna say to 'em.' Hillier went deathly white, and Rodriguez left it a few seconds before easing a smile and nudging him. 'Just joshin'.' Rodriguez glanced briefly back along the table, all eyes now on them expectantly, some already allowing themselves a small grin; they knew what was coming, and this one looked like he was going to make a good mark. 'And to make it more confusin', everyone round here's got nicknames. So the trick is to fix somethin' in your mind that'll help you remember them. Now let's start with a few easy ones: Sal Peretti along there, his first name's Salvatore – and maybe you'll remember Sal by the bit of salt in his hair. Well, more than a bit by now. And Gill Arneck up there, we just call him "Neck" – though that's as much 'cause he ain't got much neck, his fat head just sits straight on his shoulders.' The smiles broadened along the table, a couple of chuckles. 'And myself, Roddy . . .' Rodriguez held one hand out for Hillier to fill the gap.

'Uh . . . uh, short for Rodriguez?'

Rodriguez shook his head, knitting his brow. 'Now, you see, that's where you can easily go wrong here. Sometimes the nicknames are obvious, sometimes not so obvious. T'give you a clue, I used to be a pimp.' Rodriguez raised an eyebrow, but Hillier remained blank, none the wiser 'An' a few of the girls used to pay me a compliment.' Rodriguez glanced down so that there was no remaining doubt, but still it took a moment for Hillier to catch on.

'Oh, right . . . *right*.' Hillier smiled hesitantly.

'Yeah.' Rodriguez shrugged off the accolade with a coy smile. 'It was either that or Woody. Or Stallion.' More smiles and chuckles from around the table. 'Now let's get to the guys you gotta be *real* careful about gettin' their nicknames right. You see that guy two tables away over there. Guy with a mean look, shoulders like a line-back and skin colour somewhere between coffee and death?' Rodriguez nodded towards Tally Shavell rather than pointed. Then as Hillier looked over. '*Hey*, don't look too hard. He might think you're tryin' to read the tattoos on his eyeballs. Gets him real upset.'

Hillier looked swiftly away, then, as around the table a few chuckles broke out, he smiled crookedly. 'You're kidding, *right*?'

'Yeah, right.' Deadpan, Rodriguez shaking his head in wonderment. 'But let's see how you do with his nickname. His name's Shavell and he runs most of the rackets in here – and his nickname comes from the figures he's always addin' up to share out the take. Any ideas?'

'I don't know.' Hillier shrugged. 'Einstein.'

'Einstein was a fuckin' nuclear physicist, not a bean-countin' prison-fixer.' The chuckling heavier now, Peretti laughing so hard that he was holding his stomach. Rodriguez lifted his eyes heavenward for strength; though equally it was in thanks for sending him such a live one. 'It's "Tally", from tallying up all those figures. And that guard up the end there wit' the dark, lank hair, his name's Sam Morovitz – but what's your guess for his nickname?'

This time, though, Hillier just puckered his lips and shook his head.

' "More-zits",' Rodriguez said after a moment, holding out one hand. 'Sorta subtle word-play to fit his tenderized-hamburger face. Or maybe not so subtle: more "in your face".' Rodriguez eased a brief, sly smile. 'He's jus' one of many lapdogs of head-guard Bateson – the main guy you gotta keep clear of here. "Bate-Boy". I'll point him out later. And the guard we call "The Dark One", Torvald Engelson – he's actually one o' the good guys.' Rodriguez shrugged. 'Like I said, sometimes it's confusin'.'

Rodriguez took a fresh breath and nodded along the table. 'Now our good friend here that looks like Tyson's mentally challenged brother. Let's do it the other way roun'. I'll give you his nickname – BC, letter B, letter C – then by lookin' at him see if you can work out how he got it?'

Hillier pulled a face, shaking his head after a second. 'Uh . . . it's difficult.'

'Look at the flat shape o' the head . . . that Neanderthal look.'

'That *what*?'

The smiles and chuckles rising as much in anticipation this time. It was going even better than usual.

'You know . . . as in prehistoric. Like a caveman.'

Hillier chewed his bottom lip for a second. 'I know,' he said, stabbing a finger at Rodriguez. He thought he'd nailed it this time. 'BC. Like in that film . . . *Million Years BC*.'

'No, that's not it.' Rodriguez shook his head. 'But to give you another clue – his surname's Crosby.'

Hillier pondered for a moment, studying the table for inspiration before looking up again hopefully. '*Okay*. It's his initials. He's a Bob . . . or a Billy, like me.'

'No, not it either. Though again, not a bad guess.' Rodriguez left another pause, relishing along with everyone else Hillier's bafflement before giving the final clue. 'You don't see it on him now, but when BC showed us some of his ol' photos, he had more chains roun' his neck and rings on his fingers than Mr T.' Hillier's eyebrows still furrowed, the chuckles starting to rise again around the table. 'You know, *bling*. Bling Crosby. Then it became just BC.'

The group around the table had heard the punchline a score of times, but still it sent them into raptures of laughter, becoming heavier as Hillier's expression remained puzzled and Rodriguez had to prompt.

'Bling Crosby . . . you know, as in Bing Crosby.'

But Hillier's eyebrows just knitted heavier, and as he said, '*Who*?' the laughter became thunderous, Peretti bent over double as if he was in pain.

Rodriguez fired his audience a deadpan Jack Benny look. He should have realized that Bing Crosby to the rap generation was like Paul Robeson to his. Long-gone, no longer relevant.

Rodriguez was glad he'd done the routine, despite his concerns about the timing. It had certainly gone down well with his audience, and maybe at a time like this, with the shadow of Larry's death edging closer, they needed their spirits lifting all the more. Even Larry was appreciative, nodding his way with a smile, eyes bright and the shadows that haunted them gone for a moment, as if to say, 'Thanks. That might be the last time I'll be able to enjoy that.'

Roddy, prison clown. That's what he did best, Rodriguez thought wistfully, sneak-thieved some smiles and laughter from the doom and gloom where he could. And if he couldn't do that, then he wasn't good for much else. But as the laughter died, the grey walls and the dour routine settled back around them like a cloak, with only the faint clatter of their cutlery to punctuate the silence.

Jac had just come out of the shower and had started to get dressed when the phone rang. He thought for a minute it might be Alaysha asking him to bring something over, such as oregano, if he had any, or that dinner was taking longer to prepare than she'd anticipated, or, more worrying, cancelling completely. But it was Jennifer Bromwell.

'You know I said I didn't think we should date again . . . or, rather, we both more or less came to that conclusion. Well, I've been thinking . . . and maybe it is a good idea if we did.'

Jac paused halfway through buttoning his shirt. 'But I thought you had a boyfriend. The rock musician that your father wasn't keen on.'

'What, Kelvin? Oh sure, I'm still with him.' Jennifer chuckled lightly as she realized he'd grabbed the wrong end of the stick. 'I didn't mean *date*, date. I meant pretend to continue seeing each other as if we were dating.'

'Oh, right. I see.' Although he still had little idea.

'The way I see it – my dad and mom don't want me to continue seeing Kelvin, so every time I go out with him, I get grief. And they're already pressing for when I'm next meant to be seeing you – because when they asked how our date went, I said great, fine. Not only because that's what they wanted to hear, but because – the love and romance bit aside – that's *exactly* how I think the date went: great! And I thought that was pretty much how you felt about it, too.'

'Yes, I did,' Jac said automatically. He still wasn't fully up to speed on where she was heading, and he had half an eye on the clock. He'd left it tight as it was to get dressed on time, and, as if to remind him, next door he could hear the soft clatter of pans and opening and shutting of kitchen cupboard doors. The final minutes of preparation and setting the table.

'So, the thing is, I can see that I'm going to continue to get grief from my parents every time I date Kelvin . . . and you've got a similar problem with your Aunt Camille.'

'True,' Jac agreed. He'd only had one call so far from Camille asking how it went, but since he'd said much the same as Jennifer – '*Great, fine, nice girl*' – no doubt the enquiries would soon increase in intensity. His excuse that they hadn't yet set the next date because of his heavy workload was only going to buy him so much time.

'And if it wasn't me, she'd only try to set you up with someone else that she considered "suitable". So I thought if we made out that we were continuing to date, that would take all the pressure off – for *both* of us. I could keep seeing Kelvin whenever I was meant to be seeing you, and you, well . . . at least you wouldn't have Camille pushing every buck-toothed rich-kid in the State in front of you.'

'That'd be fine, I can see the sense in that,' Jac said, sighing gently as he prepared to let her down. 'Only problem is, I'm starting to see someone else.'

'My, my, Jac McElroy, you don't waste much time. We only just started courtin', and already you're cheatin' on me.' Jennifer feigned a heavy Southern Belle accent which lapsed into a chuckle.

'I know, I know. Just came up, out of the blue.' But with the thought of Alaysha so close to that of Aunt Camille, his mind fast-forwarded to the possible nightmare conversation: '*Thanks for the offer of Louisiana's finest and most eligible, but*

I've decided in the end to date a lap-dancer. Family? Struggling down-at-heel immigrants originally from Port-of-Spain. Father a wife-beater, deserted the family early, mother on welfare. Oh, and she's already got a child by another man who didn't have the courtesy to marry her and headed down the same route as her father: lashing out and leaving early. That's why she's lap-dancing – to support the child.' That would go down with Camille like an Islamic terrorist at a bar-mitzvah. She'd probably oust his mother and sister from her house that same night. 'Though . . . wait a minute. Perhaps this *could* work out – as you say, to *both* our advantages.' If Camille thought that he was going out with Jennifer Bromwell, at least she wouldn't ask any awkward questions. 'But I don't have the time right now to go through all the details . . . I'm already running late for a dinner appointment. So can I phone you when I get in from work tomorrow and we'll work out the timing for the first date? Make sure we get our respective stories straight.'

'Great. Look forward to it, Jac.'

And having just agreed to dating another woman, he finished getting ready for dinner with Alaysha Reyner.

Dinner was typical Creole: shrimp remoulade, chicken and smoked sausage jambalaya and catfish étouffée.

Alaysha was wearing jeans with a black semi-transparent gauze top that showed her bra. But it was an elaborate dress bra – black with silver stitching and studs – that was meant to be seen. Molly was staying with her grandmother that night, Alaysha explained as they sat down, noticing Jac's eyes stray and take in the room for a second. Almost a mirror image of his apartment, except that the décor was ten steps above: a lot of salmon and soft pastels, it somehow seemed larger yet at the same time warmer, more inviting.

With the way that her wavy dark hair tilted and swayed as they ate, her smiles and laughter at intervals as the small talk gathered pace, her lip-gloss making her lips look moist, inviting, and those warm brown eyes with green flecks that seemed to make him melt every time they settled on him – the effect was dazzling. As before, Jac found her beauty intimidating, his mouth suddenly dry with nervous anticipation of what might happen between them.

And on top of that he had the tension – a writhing, tightening ball in the pit of his stomach – of what he now had to broach with Alaysha.

After the let-down with the video tape, Haveling's call the day before had given him fresh hope that he might be on a roll again. Good news on two fronts: Dennis Marmont had finally come to in hospital, and while Haveling had decided not to fully accept one account over the other, guards' or prisoners', that mid-ground stance had at least meant that nothing would go on Durrant's file about an attempted prison break, and he'd overall provide a *'fair and sturdy reference to support his clemency petition'*.

Jac headed to Libreville to see Rodriguez straight after, because it wasn't the sort of thing they could discuss on the phone – *faking e-mails from Josh Durrant* – but Rodriguez wasn't able to help, communications were monitored too closely. 'Monitorin' guard would pick up straight-off that the message came from inside.' The only thing he could help with was to smooth the way for it incoming, *if* someone else was able to send it from the outside. 'I could also send the last few e-mails from Josh t'make sure the flavour was got right.'

But as Rodriguez looked across sharply with an arched eyebrow, and Jac realized that Rodriguez was suggesting that *he* send it – Jac explained that he couldn't. He felt uncomfortable enough even being involved with the deception, let alone actually sending e-mails himself. 'If something like this was traced back directly to me, I'd be struck off the bar before I could draw breath. I'd never be able to practise law again.'

They'd sat in awkward silence for a moment before Rodriguez commented with a shrug, 'Somehow don't sit right us all givin' up for no other reason than all our hands are tied. Mine, 'cause I can't send the message, yours, 'cause o' your career . . . and Franny Durrant 'cause she's afraid of losin' her new partner. And meanwhile we all just sit back and let Larry die.'

Jac had nodded numbly, eyes closing for a second as he felt Rodriguez's words settle like a ten-ton weight on his shoulders, *why couldn't Rodriguez just stick to comedy?* – when it suddenly struck him who might be able to send it. 'The person, in fact, who first suggested the idea.'

'What? Some lawyer buddy who, unlike you, don' mind playin' dirty?'

'No. It's a lap-dancer I just met.'

Rodriguez beamed widely. 'Now you're talkin'. Slip a C-note into their G-strings and those girls will do just 'bout anything. No, seriously. If you jus' met her – d'yer think she'll play ball on this?'

'Only one way to find out.'

'Yeah.' Rodriguez nodded with a wry smile. 'But one word of advice, if I may. You're meant to fuck 'em before you let them too much into your private life. Otherwise you risk fallin' into that awkward mid-territory of "just friends".'

Just friends. Jac had immediately discounted Langfranc or his sister – too close – and while Alaysha would keep it at arm's length from himself, and yes, it had been *her* suggestion – it was still a hell of a favour to ask of someone you'd just met.

Jac swallowed hard as he looked across the table at Alaysha. And the last impression he wanted to give now was that that favour was even close to the main purpose of the date – so he'd decided to wait before broaching the subject. Besides, from the way that at moments her eyes clouded and she'd look to one side, he got the feeling that she too had something on her mind. He decided to let her go first – but equally she was slow getting round to whatever was troubling her, as if it was awkward or she feared it was too sensitive for an early date.

'It's amazing we've lived next door to each other all this time without ever seeing each other,' she commented.

'Yeah.' Jac shrugged. 'I've had a hectic time the last year

or so with fresh bar exams. And a lot of weekends I head out to see my mum and sister in Hammond.'

Alaysha nodded thoughtfully. 'And is it your mom that's originally French?'

'Yes. My dad's Scottish.' Jac explained that his mother's parents hailed from near Bordeaux, but because of their anti-Vichy stance they left France during the Second World War and settled in Scotland – which is where she had met Adam, Jac's father. 'That's why when my father hankered after opening an artists' retreat, he chose the Bordeaux area. It would be like a return to roots for my mum. And that's where we lived from when I was eight years old up until just three years ago, when my father . . .' Jac's voice trailed off. Enough *death* hanging over him with Durrant.

Alaysha smiled tightly, as if in understanding, but the silence settled deeper as the seconds passed, a faint tension creeping into it.

'How's the jambalaya?' Alaysha asked, breaking it.

'Just how I like it.' He held up a forefinger and thumb pinched together in an O. 'Even though I've only had it a couple of times before.'

'Give you some grits and gumbos, and you'll almost be a native.' She smiled again, and Jac raised his wine glass in acknowledgement, returning her smile.

The small talk was running thin – but still she looked briefly again to one side before making the final resolve to say something.

'This "prisoner" you mentioned the problems with? Is it by any chance Lawrence Durrant?'

She held her gaze on him unflinchingly, and he had the same feeling as when he'd first met her. As if she could somehow see through to his very soul. And lying to her at this stage wouldn't exactly help him when he got around to asking his favour.

'Yes . . . yes it is,' he said on the back of a resigned exhalation. 'What made you suspicious . . . think that it might be him?'

'Oh. Intuition. Clemency appeal and "wanting to die" all but narrowed it down to a possibility of one.'

'Yeah, but how did you work it out from there?' He ducked as she smiled and threw her balled-up paper napkin at him, his brow creasing as he straightened. 'Really – was it that transparent?'

'Pretty much. There hasn't been an execution in Louisiana for over a year, and the only one I can see scheduled any time soon is that of Lawrence Durrant. At least from what I see in the news.'

'I'll have to be more careful in future not to mention death or clemency. Just saying "the prisoner" obviously isn't enough to protect my client's identity.'

'Looks like it.' She mirrored his thoughtfulness for a second before introducing a more upbeat tone. 'But, hey, one hell of a case to land. You must be excited?'

It would have been so easy to play the big shot and score points by saying that he'd got the case because he was such a high-flyer at Payne, Beaton and Sawyer. But, as with everything else so far with her, he had the feeling she'd see straight through it. It wouldn't get him anywhere.

'Not really.' Jac shrugged. 'The firm only gave me the case rather than keeping it for one of the senior partners because it's such a no-hoper. All the juicy stuff was apparently exhausted at appeal. All I'm left with is sweeping up the dust – but looks like I've broken my broom after the first couple of strokes. I'm striking out before I've hardly started.'

Alaysha's eyebrows knitted. 'But that suggestion I made the other day – I thought that was meant to have helped shift the deadlock?'

Jac nodded. 'It would have, except that Durrant's prison buddy, Rodriguez, can't do it. Everything in and out of the communication room is strictly monitored – so there'd be no way of him getting away with it.'

'Oh, I see.'

As Alaysha's eyes settled back on him, Jac felt a stab of

conscience. Still it felt wrong asking her to do it. Too early. *'You're meant to fuck 'em before you let them too much into your private life.'* Maybe *that* was the trade-off: any chance of a relationship with Alaysha gone to save Larry Durrant's life.

Jac swallowed, shook his head. 'I can't do it, either . . . it breaks every possible rule of lawyer–client trust.' Jac repeated much the same he had to Rodriguez about being struck off the bar in a heartbeat if he was found out. 'The only possibility I hit upon while with Rodriguez was that someone else do it. Someone not directly linked with Durrant . . .'

Jac was watching Alaysha's expression closely throughout, but it took her a second to realize that he was asking her if she could do it. The faint jolt to her body and clouding in her eyes was late in registering. She looked down fleetingly before looking back at him directly.

'That's a pretty big favour to ask?'

'I know. And I'd understand if you felt you couldn't help.'

'No . . . I didn't mean it like that. Okay, yeah, it was my idea – but asking me to be hands-on and actually do it. That's another level entirely. It means that . . . that you must trust me.'

In turn, it took Jac a second to realize that she felt strangely flattered rather than outraged. He smiled tightly and cast his eyes down, as if in coy acceptance. He didn't want to dilute the sentiment by saying he couldn't think of anyone else because in his few years in New Orleans he hadn't made that many close friends; or, as Roddy had put it, 'crooked lawyer buddies'.

'And is this your last hope of getting Durrant to want to live, as you see it?' she asked.

'Pretty much. If this doesn't work, I'd have to admit to being stuck for what next to do.'

She looked down briefly again, as if searching for invisible inspiration in her jambalaya.

'Okay, *okay*. I'll do it,' she said finally, exhaling as if she was easing a weight off her chest.

Jac eyed her cautiously. 'Are you sure you're okay with this?'

'Yes, I'm sure.' Her initially hesitant smile became fuller, more confident. 'In fact I'm glad to be able to help.'

Jac nodded gently as he saw Alaysha's last reservations slip away. He wondered whether to tell her about his mystery e-mailer – reciprocation for helping out with something so momentous, showing her even more trust – but in the end decided against it. There probably wasn't much advice she could offer and, besides, he'd already over-stretched client confidentiality.

They were silent for a moment, only the clinking of their cutlery and a Clara Moreno album playing softly in the background.

Jac saw something in Alaysha's eyes then, a warmth and soulfulness that went deeper, hit another level he hadn't been aware of before, as if she'd purposely shielded it from him till that moment. Though he had no idea what it meant until almost an hour later, as she was clearing away and leant in towards him and started kissing him.

They were tentative at first, as if she was testing the water before diving fully in. But after that, it was almost two minutes before she pulled back for air again, looking at him thoughtfully as she traced the moistness she'd left on his top lip with one fingertip.

'Now that I've agreed to do a big favour for you . . . well, looks like I might need one in return. It involves my boyfriend . . .'

Jac was quick to give his agreement to what she asked, probably far quicker than he'd have been without the heat of her closeness firing him on – because much of what she was suggesting helped close the door on the chapter with her boyfriend and left the way clear for himself.

And as he nodded and their bond of clandestine mutual favours was sealed with more rapid, fervent kisses and Alaysha started unbuttoning his shirt before leaning back to slide her own top over her head – that look returned again to her eyes, and Jac knew then what it was.

It signalled the moment that she'd first decided she was going to sleep with him, straight after she'd agreed to help him with his last-ditch duplicitous bid to try and save Larry Durrant's life.

Their love-making felt like a dream, happening so quickly, fervently, breathlessly, that the images were little different when they replayed in Jac's dream later that same night; tinged with the same hazy glow of the streetlight filtering into Alaysha's bedroom.

Her coffee-cream skin, bathed in orange light, her hazel-brown eyes drawing him in like a welcoming blanket of autumn leaves, the beads of sweat massing on her top lip and, when he looked down, spread across her entire body like fine raindrops; and her breath, hot and urgent in his ear, urging him on.

'Oh, fuck me . . . fuck me, Jac. *Fuck me!*'

But beyond her body heat and him frantically keeping rhythm with her, he started to hear the bed banging – though he could never remember that at the time. And he realized it was someone knocking at her apartment door, her boyfriend's voice.

'Who have you got with you? What are you doing in there?'

Then suddenly there was the banging of a door behind him, then another – the same banging he'd heard on that first night through the apartment wall – successive doors slamming like pistol shots as her boyfriend moved inexorably towards them.

But as the bedroom door burst open, it was Larry Durrant standing there, gun in hand, as in his previous dream. Yet this time, as the bullet hit and suddenly it was Jessica Roche beneath him, he didn't pull back, repulsed, but clung on, eyes searching for clues he might have missed last time . . .

something . . . *something* . . . her blood hot and clammy against his skin, mingling with his sweat.

'No, no, no . . . *No*!

Larry shouting from the doorway was little more than a silhouette, the stark light behind that of the corridor at Libreville, his desperate cries echoing through its cavernous grey depths. His face, fearful and beaded with sweat, became suddenly quizzical, pleading.

'Don't tell anyone what just happened here . . . *please*, Mr McElroy. Perhaps we can hide the body somewhere so that nobody will know. Maybe then I'll get to hear from my little boy again . . . I haven't heard from him in a while . . .'

Jac awoke with a jolt as the thunder crashed only a second after the lightning flash. His heart was beating wildly and his body was bathed in sweat, as if he *had* only seconds ago been making love to Alaysha.

Jac swallowed, trying to get his heartbeat settled again. He wondered if he was getting into a repetitive dream-cycle again, as in the year after his father died: the settings were usually familiar, their farmhouse, Isle de Ré beaches, but in many of them he was having fresh conversations with his father, as if he was still alive; and he'd start to panic that if he said the wrong thing, his father would then realize he was dead.

The storm outside growled and rumbled. It had been hot with the humidity sky-high before Jac went to sleep, pressure-cooking its way steadily upward through much of the day. The sort of weather that made you sweat just buttering toast, let alone making love. If it was uncomfortable here, it would be unbearable at Libreville, hot and foetid at the best of times. And for a second he had a mental snapshot of Durrant laying on his prison bed listening to the same storm, thinking about the days ahead until his execution and the many things he'd now never get to do . . . *like holding his son in his arms again*. Or maybe he was sleeping easy, like a baby. After all, he was finally going where he wanted. His Ascension Day.

He was still uneasy about misleading Durrant over his son's e-mails; though at least he was able to console himself that the end – keeping Durrant alive – justified the means. But what was starting to unsettle him more was misleading Durrant that his clemency would buy time to prove his innocence and finally gain him freedom. Jac hadn't even given a second thought to that, because, from what he'd seen in the police and trial files, such a quest seemed hopeless, impossible.

So while he might hopefully get Durrant clemency now, at best it would be a commute to life imprisonment. In the end all he'd be doing was sentencing Larry Durrant to another ten to fifteen in that foetid, oppressive hell-hole. And, thinking about that now, maybe Durrant had been right all along. Given that choice, maybe death would be preferable.

14

Death. Everyone at Libreville thought about it. Those on Death Row perhaps more than they should: even if their execution might be five or ten years away, with any number of possible lifelines in between – appeals and clemency pleas, State Governors offering across the board pardons upon retirement from office, as had happened once before – death was still there in some dark corner of their minds where they pushed everything they didn't want to face, gnawing steadily away.

But with an impending execution among their number, only thirty-six days away, it was that much harder to push away and not think about. Larry Durrant's approaching death hung over all of them. Sudden, stark reminder that it could be them next. And maybe not so long away as they thought.

Death reached out its icy hand to every corner of the prison, trickled down cell walls along with the ingrained grime and sweat, the smeared blood and faeces, brought a chill to the air and to inmates' spines, even when it was touching 90°. And if Death Row was the nucleus of that at Libreville, the queen bee's hive, it didn't lack for supporting drones.

Eighty-two per cent of inmates incarcerated at Libreville would die there: of pneumonia, heart failure, cancer, tumours, drugs overdoses, AIDS, murdered by fellow prisoners, or simply of old age. So there was a prison hospice, a chapel for prayers for the dead and a graveyard. Libreville seemed reluctant to let go of its inmates, even in death. And while most prisoners' families would choose to take the body home for burial – their only chance to get loved ones back – many had been so long forgotten by their families that burial at Libreville remained the only option.

Of that amount, the executioner would grim-reap less than two per cent. But that small number by far overshadowed all other deaths, because it underscored the reason they were all there. You commit murder, we kill you. When we're good and ready.

And the passage of time, while helping inmates push the spectre of death away in their minds, also made it like a slow-drip torture; death might be trickling down their cell walls *slowly*, but that ensured its omnipresence. Paradoxically, of all of them Larry Durrant was probably the least worried, because he'd resigned himself to death long ago. But others on Death Row watched with foreboding that passage of approaching death as the days wound down to Larry Durrant's execution, wondering when it might next reach out to claim them.

There were spaces though in the prison where you could escape: places that breathed life, transported you to the world outside in your mind, or simply numbed you, made you forget where you were.

For Rodriguez, the prison radio and communication room, all that contact with the outside world made it easy to transport himself, if only for a few moments here and there, to where that contact came from; or when he was playing songs, closing his eyes and imagining he was a DJ at some far-flung station – TKLM, Tahiti – or remembering where he'd been and what he'd been doing when he'd first heard that song. For Larry, it was the library and his books that would let him drift to other places in his mind.

And for other inmates it might be working the ranch, the annual rodeo or the muscle yard. Rodriguez had never been much for muscle training and category A prisoners weren't allowed to work the open ranch, so the only common area where he found a quiet corner was the showers. Not for the reason they were favoured by many inmates – scoping for prison bitches – but because, with his head back, eyes closed and the water running down his body, he could escape.

He could be anywhere: under a waterfall on some South Pacific isle, waiting for one of his stable of fine women to join him under its spray, or maybe at home when he was younger and his mom calling out if he was going to be long because dinner was ready.

It washed away the sweat and grime, the invisible aura of stale and trapped humanity, of oppression and *death*, that seemed to cling to the skin like a sticky blanket within hours.

Wash it away. *Wash it away.*

Rodriguez scrubbed hard. Then, when he felt he'd washed the prison away, he tilted his head back and closed his eyes, letting himself drift with the spray hitting his face and running down his body. *Pacific waterfalls, fine women soaping his body, at home and about to put on his best threads for a Saturday night out.*

And he'd been more successful in his reverie this time, Rodriguez thought, because he'd even managed to tune out the clamour and echo of the other voices in the showers.

The hand clamping suddenly over his mouth snapped his eyes sharply open.

Two striplights his end of the showers had been switched off and the five guys showering in his section and the guard by the showers' open entrance had suddenly gone.

Probably the other people showering and the guards further along out of sight were still there, but as Rodriguez writhed and tried to call out to get their attention, he made no more than a muted whimper. The hand across his mouth was clamped too firmly.

Rodriguez couldn't see who was holding him − the arm too across his chest was clamped tight − only feel his breath against the back of his neck. The only person he could see, in that instant sliding into the side of his vision a few paces away, was Tally Shavell: a towel around his waist, upper body glistening, muscles tensed like steel chords, the veins in his neck taut as he grimaced malevolently.

'Sorry. Didn't bring no reading matter wi' me this time.'

The open razor at towel level in Shavell's right hand was flicked out silently, imperceptibly, as he stepped closer.

And Rodriguez knew in that moment that death had come for him sooner than he had thought.

'Should be no problem handling two addresses. I got a friend, Mo, who does much the same as me. I've only got one Bell uniform, but I can head over to his place after I've finished and hand it to him.'

'Are you sure it will fit?' Nel-M quipped.

'Very funny,' Barry responded dryly. 'But if it looks like there's a problem, I can always stitch up the back for him.'

Barry Lassitter had become Barry-L, then simply 'Barrel', since he'd been three hundred pounds for more years than he cared to remember. But he was one of the best ex-Bell men that Nel-M knew and, from the name he'd given his company, 'Warpspeed Communications', he obviously didn't mind the world knowing that he was an ardent 'Trekkie'. Nel-M would have put in the bug himself if it wasn't for the fact that Truelle would recognize him; also, he needed someone who could do it in one minute flat rather than five or six.

'Nothing like a good stitch up,' Nel-M commented. 'Also, make sure there's no tell-tale egg or ketchup stains down the front that might give the game away that it's the same uniform.'

Barrel huffed and muttered a response that Nel-M didn't hear.

'And let me know as soon as they're both in place and we're live.'

Larry had just gone through the gate at the end of his cell block to head down to the showers when he was approached by one of the guards, Dan Warrell.

'You're wanted up in the library.'

'Am I back on duty there, then?'

Warrell shrugged. 'Don't know about that. All I know is the guy up there, Perinni –'

'Peretti.'

'Yeah. Well, he's apparently stuck with something. Needs a hand.'

'Okay,' Larry nodded. He wasn't suspicious. Warrell didn't have any allegiances with Bateson, was very much his own man. If you had a grievance and wanted it dealt with fairly and evenly, Warrell or Torvald Engelson were the best to go to.

'I'll see your way up there.' Warrell led the way up the two flights of steel steps, then along forty yards of corridor, half of it flanked by cells.

Warrell took out his security card as they approached the gate. Beyond lay store rooms, a guards' watch room and canteen, and the library.

Peretti was at the far end of the library and looked surprised to see Larry, though pleasantly so.

'Back to give me a hand then?' He smiled crookedly. 'Couldn't trust me to be on my own too long in case I screwed everything up?'

'But you said you wanted a help out with something?' Larry pressed, one eyebrow arching.

'Not me. Naah.' Peretti shook his head.

Larry turned to Warrell, his eyes narrowing. 'I thought you said I was wanted here?'

'Yeah. That was what I was told.'

'*Who* told you?'

With the intensity of Larry's glare and his cutting tone, Warrell flinched slightly. 'Uh . . . Bateson. Glenn Bateson.'

Jesus.

Larry ran ahead of Warrell, realizing he needed him as he came up to the gate.

'Get me back through this. And *quick*.'

Under Larry's icy glare, Warrell's hand shook uncertainly as he slid in his card. He wasn't about to argue or question.

Back along the corridor, down the two flights of stairs, leaping them three and four steps at a time, Larry was already breathless as he hit the passage by his cell block at full pelt. One more flight down to the shower stalls, and another thirty yards of passage before the security gate by the showers.

Breath ragged, heart pounding, Larry saw that there were five or six men by the gate to the showers, being handed towels and waiting for that same number to come out so that they could go through; the normal routine.

But what was not normal, Larry quickly picked out, were the lights out at the far end and no guard looking into that section.

'Man in distress at the far end!' Larry shouted, pushing through the men waiting.

The guard by the gate, Fisk, in thick with Bateson, blocked his way defiantly. 'What are you talking about?'

'I said man in distress at the far end!' Larry raised his voice to screaming pitch. His only hope was rousing the attention of the three guards by the early sections, and hoping to God they weren't all in on it with Bateson. '*Man in distress!*'

One of the guards looked uncertainly towards the rear cubicles then back at the gate, confused.

Larry saw the alarm button a yard to one side, and, remembering Rodriguez in the boiler-room, leapt across and hit it.

The jangling bell finally galvanized the guard into action, Larry keeping up his mantra, 'Man in distress . . . *man in distress*', as the guard darted towards the rear cubicles. Though Larry feared that it was already too late.

15

'Bye-bye' had got his nickname because fellow Malastra capos and soldiers had noticed that it was usually the last thing he said before he wasted someone with his favoured Cougar 9mm; and, as Malastra's main trigger-man, it was something he said often.

Though with the name apparently came some unintentional humour: often when he called out 'Bye-bye' in parting, others would flinch or lift one arm up, worried that any second his Cougar would be pointing and firing.

But it was difficult for George Jouliern to laugh about it now, because pretty soon those words would probably be the last thing he'd hear.

They were in an old warehouse, musty and humid, and Jouliern looked morosely at the blue plastic sheet, usually used as a damp membrane in construction, spread beneath him. Eight yards away a furnace, probably lit over two hours ago, glowed red from its aperture.

Jouliern sat in the middle of the blue sheet, his hands tied behind his back, but his ankles free. Bye-bye held his Cougar on him steadily from three paces away and, at points when Bye-bye had leant over or turned, Jouliern had noticed the sheathed machete and knife tucked in the back of his belt.

Jouliern knew the routine well enough. He'd be shot with the Cougar, his body chopped into pieces, the whole mess then wrapped in the blue plastic and thrown into the furnace. Within forty minutes there'd be absolutely no trace of him. Jouliern's stomach sank at the thought of it.

He looked up, trying to inject a hopeful tone into his voice. 'You kill me – you're not going to find out who else was in on it with me. You think I did the whole thing alone?'

Bye-bye smiled tightly. 'You know there's no deals on something like this. You know the score, George.'

'I know.' Jouliern's tone sank back as he arched an eyebrow. 'So, you're saying you don't want to know who else was involved?'

'I didn't say that.' Bye-bye contemplated his shoes for a second. 'Look, if you tell me who else was in with you – the best I can offer is to make it quick and clean. Painless.'

Now it was Jouliern's turn to look down, contemplating. But when he looked up again, his stare was icy.

'Fuck you . . . that's what I say.' Then, twisting himself as he rose up without warning, he lunged head-first towards Bye-bye, his voice rising to a scream. 'FUCK YOU! . . . FUCK Y–'

Bye-bye took him down with two shots before he'd moved a yard. Didn't even get time to deliver his favourite words.

'That was good,' Malastra commented when Bye-bye returned and explained what had happened. 'So he got his quick and painless death *without* having to give us any names?'

Bye-bye shuffled uncomfortably. 'Happened so quick, boss.'

Malastra held his stare on him a moment longer. All RAM and no hard-drive; but the advantage was that by the time of Bye-bye's next cheeseburger, he'd have forgotten all about killing George Jouliern. He'd sleep easy that night.

'Okay.' Malastra waved him away, his gaze shifting back to his computer screen.

His eyes narrowed as the first image of the Bay Tree Casino floor came up on the screen. He'd have to find out who else Jouliern had been involved with by tracing who he'd met over the past year, and what might have passed between them – particularly any envelopes.

'*And one of the key questions raised is always* why *they wanted to die. You think all of that's going to happen without your son ever finding out?*'

'*It'll only be the first year or so, I can keep it hidden from him for that time. Besides, as you say, and I also know from bitter past experience – Larry is always so close-mouthed. No way is he going to admit that his wanting to die is down to his son not making contact. He's going to say just what he told you: that he's simply sick of facing more time in prison, and this is his going to God. His "Ascension Day".*'

As much as Joshua Durrant tried to shake the conversation he had overheard loose from his head over the following days, it kept re-playing.

He tapped fast and furiously at the keyboard: *FrankG1427, FrankG4217, FrankG7412* . . .

Frank was a good enough guy, and that wasn't Joshua simply sharing his mother's standpoint because he'd been good to them; Joshua liked him because Frank gave him quality time when needed and accepted him as if he was his own. But there were times when Frank's reasoning ran thin, and more often than not it involved Josh's father.

Joshua had accepted at the time his mom's and Frank's reasoning over the e-mails, and the last thing he'd want to do is upset them or cause any problems. But now with what he'd overheard, *his father wanting to die unless he sent more e-mails* – that smashed through every possible rulebook, was something he couldn't bear for a second being responsible for. And what Frank and his mom didn't know wouldn't hurt them.

FG2417, FLG2417, FLG7412, FG7412, FG1427, FG4217 . . .

'Are you okay there, Josh?' his mom's voice trailed from the kitchen.

His hands paused on the keyboard, heart thumping in his chest. 'Yes, fine, Mom.'

'It's nice to see you getting down to your homework so early . . . but you do seem to be putting in a lot on this project.'

'I . . . I've got to finish by the end of the week – I'm already late with it.'

Frank had password-blocked all internet access. Josh had fed in over a hundred possible keywords in the half hour before Frank got in the night before – mostly around Frank's name, initials and birth-date – without success, and now he was on Frank's lucky numbers. Hopefully his mom wasn't getting suspicious. He looked at intervals over his shoulder as he resumed tapping. The computer was in a small recess in the hallway – but even if she came out from the kitchen, she probably wouldn't know the difference between his searching for entry keywords and his school project work. Just in case, to one side he had a project page with the Civil War and Paul Revere to click on and cover.

He tried another batch of combinations and glanced anxiously at his watch. Another six or seven minutes, then he'd have to quit until the next night. But as he continued, he started to sense the futility: he might have thousands more possibilities to work through, and even if he hit gold, while he could delete the e-mails sent, how on earth was he going to cover-up the replies? Unless they arrived in the half an hour before Frank got home, he was sunk.

His hands slowed on the keyboard. He'd give it his best shot that night, but if there was still no breakthrough, tomorrow he'd approach Danny Thorne, one of his closest school-friends. And, the resolve made, his hands picked up speed again on the keyboard, becoming suddenly a furious race against time to find the password, because he knew now this would probably be his last opportunity . . . *FrankLG4217, FrankLG2417, FrankLG7412* . . .

Or maybe it was his and his mom's initials or the first three letters of their names – combined with Frank's lucky numbers.

Joshua continued working through the combinations, and was over halfway through when the screen-door suddenly slamming made him jump. He'd got so engrossed that he hadn't even heard Frank's car pull up. His heart beating wildly, his hand trembling and suddenly clammy on the mouse, he quickly clicked off the password page and clicked on Paul Revere.

The document leapt to the forefront just a second before the door swung open and Frank stepped into the hallway.

'Like Fort Knox. Four heavy dead bolts on the door as I was let in. And, as you suspected, motion alarms in the main lounge and the hallway.'

At his end of the line, Nel-M nodded thoughtfully as Barry Lassitter ran through his visit to Truelle's apartment. The main factors that had stopped Nel-M simply breaking in and planting the bug himself.

'He hovered for a bit, watching me, but he had a coffee in his hand – so I nodded to it, "smells nice". He offered me one, and I finished up while he was back in the kitchen.'

'And he took the bait that his phone had been bugged?'

'Yeah. Held it up for him to see. Exact duplicate of what I'd just wired in while he was making my coffee.'

'Good going. Let me know when the other one's done.'

Lassitter's return call came at 11.43 the next morning. 'Just got the nod from Mo. Everything went fine at his office, too. No hitches.'

'Thanks.' Nel-M hardly paused for breath before calling Vic Farrelia. 'That's a go now for lines two and three as well.' Then he called Adelay Roche. 'My man just phoned. Truelle's just been done too – home *and* office. So we're live on all fronts.'

'That's good to hear,' Roche commented. 'Now we might be able to better decide just who needs to be dead.'

When Joshua broached the subject with Danny Thorne of using his home computer, Danny was wary. 'It's not to go porn-surfing, is it?'

'No, no. Nothing like that.' Out of his three closest friends at Elbrooke High, he'd chosen Danny because he was the only one to have his own, non-parentally controlled internet access. He'd worked before at Danny's house on school projects, so no eyebrows would be raised by him going over there for an hour or two after school. But from the concern on Danny's face, he was suddenly reminded that Danny was probably also his most cautious, conservative friend. 'It's to send some e-mails to my father.'

'Oh.' From Danny's heavy exhalation, it was unclear whether that was actually worse than porn-surfing. 'Why can't you send the e-mails from home? You were sending some before – I remember you telling me.'

'My mom would still let me like a shot. But Frank's stepped in – put his foot down.' He could see the clouds of doubt forming rapidly in Danny's eyes. 'Please, Danny . . . you've got to help me out here. If there was any other way, you know I wouldn't be asking.'

'Okay . . . *okay*. Let me think on it a bit, I'll let you know tomorrow.'

By the next day, Joshua had spent another frantic half hour keyword searching without success before Frank got home, so was even more desperate. But Danny's doubts and concerns seemed to have increased.

'I'm worried about my parents finding out, and from there you know it's only a heartbeat before yours find out, too.'

'*How* will they find out?'

'Get real. You know they speak sometimes on the phone, and they'll get talking even more if you're round my place once or twice a week. Reminding you what time dinner's ready . . . or Josh has forgot this or that. And I know my dad checks my e-mails now and then. He'd kill me if he found out I was trading e-mails in and out of Libreville when I shouldn't.'

They were in the corridor just after a lesson, and as their voices raised, they'd started to get the attention of some of the other students filing out.

'Come on, Danny. I'm real stuck here . . . can't you at least . . .'

But Danny was already sidling away as Joshua reached one hand out imploringly, and then they were both distracted by one of the onlookers, Ellis Calpar, who'd stopped to pay more attention to their conversation.

'That's the problem wit' those oreole's,' Ellis called out, moving a step closer. 'When it comes t' the crunch – the white, tight-assed, be ever-so-careful anal side always wins t'rough.'

Danny was mixed race, and as his friend headed away along the corridor, Joshua fired him a tight grimace that made it clear he wasn't keen on the barb either. But then you expected no less from Ellis Calpar.

'Libreville? That's where your ol' man is, isn't it? Not much time lef' now, from what I see on the news. So what's the beef with you and Danny? I thought yo' two were always like that.' Ellis interlocked two fingers.

At first, Joshua wasn't going to say anything. But Ellis's tone was weighted with understanding more than teasing, and he recalled one time when one of Ellis's crew had started to give him a tough time and Ellis had stepped in. '*Go easy on him, man. His ol' man's at Libreville. For murder!*' The crew member had jolted back a pace as if hit with an electric shock. To Ellis and his buddies, having a father in prison for murder was a mark of respect rather than one of ridicule.

As Joshua explained, Ellis's eyes lit up like a Christmas tree. He put a welcoming arm over Joshua's shoulder.

'Look no further – you have just foun' your Libreville e-mail sender. Not me personally – I don't have a computer. But one o' my crew, Friggy, does. That's our main message centre.'

Joshua felt immediately uncomfortable. He'd never got involved with Ellis before, let alone with something as personal as this.

'It's okay, Ellis . . . you don't have to trouble yourself none. I'm sure I can find another way round this.'

'No sweat t'all, man . . . would be a real pleasure passin'

e-mails in and out of Libreville to your ol' man.' Ellis smiled slyly. 'And the fact that your mom and new dad are against it and yo' not meant t'do it, makes it all the mo' fun.' Ellis gave Joshua's shoulder one last pat as he broke away and went ahead of him along the corridor. 'I'll talk to Friggy and let you know the timin'. Later, man.'

But as Joshua watched Ellis get swallowed up among the other students filling the corridor, he couldn't resist a sense of foreboding. He might have solved his e-mail problem, but how was he going to explain away to his mom and Frank spending time after school with Ellis Calpar and his crew? For sure they'd fear he was getting primed for future auto-theft or crack dealing.

16

Before contacting Rodriguez, Jac wanted to check again with Alaysha that she was still okay with taking part in the Durrant e-mail ruse, in case it had just been the heat of the moment or the wine talking the night before. It wasn't the sort of call he could make from the office – so he phoned just before he left for work.

She was still on for it – he'd never truly doubted – and for the first time he got some insight into her rationale. Though she brought a tingle to his cheek when she talked about the night before, and he could still feel a warm pang inside at the thought of her as he signed off and called Rodriguez.

'We're on for those e-mails,' Jac said as Rodriguez came on the line.

'The lap-dancer you mentioned the other day?'

'The same.'

'What did you have to do to her to get her to agree?' Rodriguez jibed.

'Well, you know – it's a dirty job, but someone's got to do it.' A handful of conversations with Rodriguez, and already Jac was sounding like one of his cell-block buddies.

Rodriguez chuckled, but it died quickly. He shook off a faint shiver as he thought about his close escape that morning. The shouting and alarm ringing had come as Tally was only a step away, already raising the razor. He'd have no doubt had time to slit his throat, but getting away cleanly was starting to look like a problem. Tally brandished the razor in warning – 'Your guardian angel again, by the looks of it. But he ain't gonna be around much longer' – then quickly palmed the razor and slipped away as the guard approached. Rodriguez decided against saying anything to McElroy. There probably wasn't much McElroy could do, and he had enough on his plate trying to save Larry without worrying about two of them.

'The only thing is – I gotta get back on communication-room duty to receive it,' Rodriguez said. 'Also to send out those last few sample e-mails from JD. Haveling mighta half-believed our account, but most of our privileges are still cut.'

'You didn't mention this before.'

'No need. Before it didn't look likely we were gonna be able to get any e-mails to Larry, now it does.'

Jac sighed. 'Okay. I'll phone Haveling, see what I can do.'

'Do you know someone who might be good for that?'

'I do, as it happens. And just down the road from me right here in Morgan City.' Bob Stratton scrolled down his Excel address list. 'Yeah, here it is. Dan Souchelle.'

The thought had suddenly struck Jac while shifting some files from his desk first thing that morning, recalling that in one of them, a shoplifting case, the police had requested image enhancement on the key security camera pictures. Jac wrote down the number, thanked Stratton, and dialled it straight after he'd hung up.

Souchelle confirmed that he could do the job and promised a forty-eight hour turnaround.

'Any chance of quicker?'

'Sorry. We're backed up like crazy right now, having trouble even keeping to that at times. But I'll make sure this one doesn't run over.'

Jac said he'd get the video tape over to him straightaway. Then seconds after he'd put the phone down from Fedex to arrange the messenger, it rang again; less than half an hour at his desk and already his fifth call: Lieutenant Pyrford.

Jac felt his pulse twitch in his jaw as Pyrford, in smug, sing-song tones, informed him that Morvaun Jaspar's next police interview was later that morning.

'Eleven-thirty. Be there or be square. Not that I care either way.'

'I'll be there.' Jac slammed the phone down sharply enough to hopefully make Pyrford jump the other end.

Fourteen minutes later the Fedex messenger arrived, and, as he left with the tape, Jac eased out a tired breath, closing his eyes for a second. Two days. But at least there was a fresh glimmer of hope again with his anonymous e-mailer. A chance rather than no chance.

Pyrford's call had unsettled him. Pyrford had no doubt made the appointment tight to give Jac little time to prepare himself, and it wasn't the best time for it to be happening, right in the middle of organizing the e-mail to Larry Durrant. And there had been that nagging glitch in Morvaun's demeanour that made Jac worry Morvaun was holding something back from him. Some big surprise that the police would suddenly spring. But it wasn't just that, Jac realized; it was something else not so easily quantified.

Jac had immediately warmed to Morvaun Jaspar when they first met. Sixty-seven, sharp as a razor, the product of an African-American father and Irish/French/African-American mother, he had wavy, black hair and an easy, full smile showing one gold tooth five from the back on the top row. 'All mine,' he'd proudly proclaim to anyone, interested or not, 'except this one.' His dress was often wild and eccentric, somewhere between Mr Bo-Jangles and Vivienne Westwood.

Morvaun had been a serial forger for over twenty years. Before that he'd been the make-up man for a local theatre group, but when it disbanded, the only work he could find was piece-meal with a brief flurry at Carnival time. Morvaun took a side-step into forging to supplement his income. Where before he was dealing with skin, hair and flesh tones, now he was dealing with paper, photos and document stamps. The core aim of both was the same: to create an illusion.

And sometimes there was crossover between the two, which had provided Jac with the vital key to getting Morvaun off the last charge.

Morvaun's last lawyer had retired, and when he approached

the firm, Beaton swiftly passed it down the rungs to Jac. Possibly because it was too lightweight, possibly because – like Durrant – he saw it as hopeless. But Jac quickly saw some hope in Morvaun Jaspar's case, mainly because this time there'd been no forged documents involved.

Antonio Amador, a Mexican national, had used the documentation of his brother, Enrique, who'd gained American citizenship six years previously. All Morvaun had done was make Antonio look like Enrique.

One drawback to their scheme was that Antonio wouldn't be able to use the documentation to work, otherwise it would look like Enrique had two jobs. But that hardly mattered since Antonio's main aim was to move freely back and forth across the Mexican border running cocaine. Apprehended one day during a routine search, Antonio promptly gave Morvaun's name in a plea bargain.

But Jac argued in court that no forging of documents had taken place, and since all Mr Jaspar had done was make Antonio look like his brother – unless he'd informed Mr Jaspar in advance that it was to perpetrate some criminal activity – Mr Jaspar himself had committed no crime. 'Given the circumstances, it's unlikely that Antonio Amador would have shared that information with Mr Jaspar.'

The judge agreed and directed the jury accordingly. It *was* unlikely, and on its own it was no crime to make one person look like another. Hollywood did it all the time.

Some chuckles from the courtroom floor, and a beaming hug of thanks for Jac from Morvaun when, forty minutes later, the jury acquitted him. But the police and the prosecuting attorney were far from pleased.

'Good result, Jac. Good result,' Langfranc congratulated him on his return. 'But you want to watch out you're not pushing your luck too far. The police might now target Jaspar, go all the harder on him.'

Pushing your luck. As soon as Langfranc said it, Jac realized that the Morvaun Jaspar case, along with a few others, embodied how he saw himself as a lawyer. Beaton would hand him these hopeless cases that nobody else wanted, and because he was eager to prove them all wrong and not fail, he'd go that extra mile, or two. *Push his luck.*

Perhaps it went deeper than that. Trying desperately to prove that in no way was he continuing his father's cycle, a scream back at the world and Aunt Camille: '*He was never a failure, and nor am I.*'

Jac realized that his main strength was also his Achilles heel, and began to worry that one day Langfranc would be right, that he'd push his luck too far.

Busying himself with preparation for Morvaun's police interview, Jac felt his chest tighten with anxiety as it approached eleven, his mouth suddenly dry. With still no answer back from Haveling, Jac wondered if finally his luck was about to run out.

'*No, I told you, Jac. I'm happy to help out and send the e-mail.*'

'*No morning-after second thoughts?*'

'*None. But if you're fishing for reasons why someone you just met would help out with something momentous like this. Well, you know, it's not often we get a chance to change things in this life — I mean, really make a difference. And helping to save a man's life must surely come close to the top of that poll. If this works, I can look at Durrant's face in future newscasts and think smugly to myself: "Hey, I actually helped save that man's life. I made a difference for once."*'

'*I can understand that.*'

'*But how about you after last night? No morning-after second thoughts?*'

'*None. Because, you know, it's not often we get a chance to really make a difference with things in this life.*'

A chuckle. '*So the spicy dish went down okay, and I'm not talking here about the jambalaya?*'

'*A treat. Except that it left my legs a bit weak heading back to my place.*'

'*Well, at least you didn't have far to go. If you couldn't make it a dozen paces, then I was rougher on you than I thought.*'

Nel-M waved one hand, indicating for Vic Farrelia to wind forward to the next conversation. They'd already played the tape once, this was just a highlights re-run.

So, that explained why he hadn't seen the girl going into McElroy's building that night, or why there was no trace of her belongings in his apartment: she was his neighbour! And with the earlier call from that other girl, it certainly looked like McElroy's love life was more complicated than most.

As the tape came to McElroy's conversation with Rod-riguez '*. . . I gotta get back on communication-room duty to receive it. Also to send out those last few sample e-mails from JD . . .*' Nel-M suddenly sat forward, the final pieces of the puzzle falling into place.

On that first taped call, McElroy's new girlfriend had suggested someone else sending an e-mail; now she was doing it herself! But still he was no closer to knowing why an e-mail from Josh Durrant held such a crucial key to keeping his father alive.

A bloodless coup. All over in less than twenty minutes. Jac shouldn't have worried.

From the outset, it was clear that the police evidence was slim, and while with a good deal of posturing and dark innuendo Lieutenant Pyrford tried to make more of it than it was, the crunch came when he passed across Alvira Jardine's forged passport.

'Do you recognize it now?'

'No, I don't,' Morvaun said indignantly, his glasses perched on the end of his nose as he inspected it. 'And you should be ashamed of yo'selves tryin' to link a piece of shit like this with my handicraft. An eight-year-ol' could do a better job.' Morvaun pointed out its many flaws and failings as Pyrford's jaw twitched. 'If you'd taken the trouble to study in detail any o' my —'

Jac stopped Morvaun there, before he incriminated himself on any past cases.

More congratulations from Langfranc. 'Luck's still holding with Jaspar, by the looks of it.'

But it did little to make Jac feel good, quell the uneasy feeling that some day soon it must surely run out. And that each time he got away unscathed merely increased the chances of a fall.

Jac finally got a call back from Haveling just before lunch, forty minutes after his return from the Fifth District station-house, agreeing to let Rodriguez back into his seat in the communication room later that same day, 'Sometime between three-thirty and four.'

Jac left his office immediately to call Alaysha from his cell-phone. She had to pick up Molly around that time, so she'd drop into a nearby internet café.

'There's one a couple of blocks away on Palmyra Street . . . Netwave. I've used it a few times before. Probably four-thirty by the time I get there.'

'That's fine.' Aside from haste, Jac didn't mention the other reason he was keen on the suggestion: it pushed things still further away from any connection with him. He explained that her initial e-mail to Rodriguez should be as if Josh Durrant wanted the last few e-mails to his father, mistakenly deleted, sent back to him to check on something. 'That way hopefully nothing will seem untoward with the monitoring guard when Rodriguez sends those samples out to you as a guide. Then send back the main e-mail when you're ready.'

'It'll probably be twenty minutes to half an hour after the samples arrive before I send it . . . I want to make sure to get this right. I'll go to their café section with Molly or maybe round the corner for a while in between.' Alaysha explained that Netwave had dedicated e-mail numbers for each computer to save people the time of setting up personal accounts. So tell Rodriguez not to send anything meanwhile – because I'll probably send that final e-mail from another machine.'

'Okay, will do.' Jac tucked his head deeper into his shoulder as the passing traffic got louder. 'And, once again, Alaysha . . . thanks for helping. Good luck.'

Then he phoned Rodriguez, and, after the usual long pause of getting routed through to the phone at the end of the cell block, kept his instructions ambiguous.

'We're on for four-thirty. One e-mail incoming with the address for the samples we discussed to go out to. And then the main return twenty minutes or so later.'

'Okay. Good going, Counsellor. Catch yer later.'

'Sorry to trouble you, Mrs Durrant. My name's Jim Whitman from the Prisoners' Liaison Committee. It's just a general survey, but I wondered if I might ask a few questions about what contact you and your son have had with your husband, Lawrence Durrant, while he's been incarcerated at Libreville prison.'

'Well . . . I suppose so.'

Nel-M could tell that she was hesitant, guarded, so he kept the first few questions very general – type and regularity of contact – without homing in on either her son or e-mails.

'And when was your last prison visit?'

'Nine, ten months ago now.'

'Any other contact since?'

'Just one phone call, about six or seven weeks after that visit. And the rest has been my son, Joshua, sending e-mails.'

'Regular e-mail contact?'

'Well, I suppose you could say . . . twenty or more e-mails over the past year. But that's stopped now too for a while.'

'How long ago did that stop?'

'Oh, a couple of months back, I suppose.'

'Any particular reason for it stopping?'

By the pause and heavy intake of breath from the other end, Nel-M knew that he'd stepped too far.

'Look . . . if this has got something to do with my husband's lawyer calling the other day, trying to persuade me by coming at me from another direction – you're wasting your time.'

'Lawyer? I'm sorry, Mrs Durrant, you've lost me. We work completely independently – we don't know anything about your husband's lawyer visiting, nor indeed have any contact with him.'

'I'm sorry.'

'No need to be. But you've intrigued me now, Mrs Durrant: why was your husband's lawyer visiting? And if you don't mind me saying, you sound somewhat troubled by it.'

Nel-M felt a tingle of anticipation as he realized he was poised on a knife's edge. She'd either open up or step back completely, in which case he'd get nothing and be left wondering.

But with another long breath, she started to relate Jac McElroy's recent visit, falteringly at first, but gaining momentum with her rising indignation, while Nel-M made a couple of cryptic notes at his end, a slow smile creasing his face as the final pieces of the puzzle fell into place. He'd struck gold big time and couldn't wait to get off the line to share his treasure with Roche.

'Believe me, Mrs Durrant, you or your son don't have to make any contact with your husband that you don't want to,' Nel-M assured. 'And his lawyer has no right to try and persuade you to do so, regardless of the reasons.'

'I . . . I suppose I shouldn't be too hard on him.' She mellowed as she became reflective. 'He's only doing his job, I suppose. I mean it's not his fault that Larry's suddenly decided he wants to throw in the towel.'

'No, I suppose not. Except these lawyers don't give much pause for thought on whether they should be too hard on us when they present their bills.'

Francine Durrant joined him in a brief chuckle before asking, 'And who did you say you were again?'

'Jim Whitman, Prisoners' Liaison Committee. And I thank you kindly for your time today, Mrs Durrant. You've been most helpful.'

*

'Are yo' done there yet, Friggy?'

'Just signing in now . . . aaaand we're there. All systems live and running.'

'Okay, man . . . *okay*. Make room for Josh. Let 'im do his stuff.'

As uncomfortable as Joshua Durrant felt because of the neighbourhood and company he was in – and what he was about to do – he had to admit, they were going out of their way to make him feel at ease. Ellis Calpar and his crew treating him like royalty? It felt totally alien, reminded him he was on unfamiliar ground and so added to his anxiety – but even so he could easily get used to it.

The neighbourhood was on the bad side of St Claude close to the rail-yards, though the house itself looked decent enough and a good size. The computer was in the garage, but there was no car there, only a couple of mountain bikes and a ton of junk: TVs, stereos, ghetto-blasters, microwaves, car radios, cell-phones. There were at least two of each item, but with the predominance of car radios and cell-phones – more than a dozen in each case – Joshua caught on that it wasn't because Friggy's father was an electrical repair man. This was probably stolen gear.

Aside from Friggy, there were two others from Calpar's regular crew; along with all the junk, about all the garage could take.

Friggy leant over and with a couple of taps got the e-mail box up for him.

Joshua sat staring at it for a second then, with a quick look over his shoulder, brought his hands up to the keyboard.

'Step back everyone, give 'im some space,' Ellis ordered. 'This is mean' t'be private, remember.'

Joshua took a final deep breath to compose himself. This was one of those important moments, like exams or making sure he was nice to his mom's new boyfriend, or when you got passed the basketball just before the hoop and the whole school was watching. It had to be the right tone and straight from the heart, but without giving away that he knew his father wanted to die. Only one chance to get it right.

Rodriguez hissed 'Yessss!' under his breath and went to make a clenched fist salute as the e-mail came through – but not too high in case Nielsen, the monitoring guard with his eyes fixed to his computer screen at the end of the room, paid him too much attention.

But his fist hardly got above chest height as he thought about its timing. Then he read it again and looked at the e-mail address.

'Oh *shiiiiii-*' The clenched fist was abruptly dropped. He looked towards the eight phones on the far wall separated by glass side-screens at head height, and nodded towards Nielsen. 'Quick call to make. Okay?'

Nielsen mumbled something indiscernible without hardly looking up and gave a begrudging nod.

It took Alaysha Reyner only eight minutes to get the e-mail from Joshua Durrant half right.

But from that point on it was slower going. Despite three more drafts and numerous small changes, it was still no more than seventy per cent there. One hundred per cent right was starting to look elusive.

She'd hopefully got the overall tone and phraseology right from Joshua's last few e-mails, but then she reminded herself that there'd been a long gap from the last e-mail, and also Durrant was now that much closer to his execution date. After a brief explanation and apology for the lack of contact, it should without doubt be weightier and more emotional than the past e-mails. After all, this might be one of the last times Joshua Durrant would have contact with his father.

Alaysha dabbed at a stray tear as she became deeper immersed in the e-mail and what it represented.

Molly at her side was looking concerned. 'Are you okay, Mommy?'

'Yes, I'm okay, honey. I'm fine.' She gave Molly a reassuring hug.

Though now, Alaysha started to worry that she might have overcooked it. Too much emotion, not enough . . . she continued juggling to try and get the balance right.

Jac found himself looking more and more at his watch as the afternoon progressed.

All of it happening out there in cyberspace between the city and Libreville prison, and now, having set it all in motion, the realization that he no longer had control over it. Everything hanging in the balance, Durrant's life, Jac's career too if it went wrong, and to make matters worse, he'd suddenly found himself facing a flurry of work to assist John Langfranc with a trial preparation.

Jac didn't want to let Langfranc down, but he was finding it increasingly hard to focus as it approached four-thirty. Langfranc, understanding as ever, had only asked once, 'How's it going?', but he couldn't help noticing Langfranc's look when he'd returned after disappearing without warning for twenty minutes to make his calls outside to set everything in motion.

The minutes dragged even more excruciatingly as four-thirty passed. Jac rubbed at his chest. Tension was knotted so tight there that it felt like indigestion.

He took a deep breath to try and ease it, pushed again to immerse himself in Langfranc's case, if nothing else as a distraction; and at some stage he was partly successful, his note-making on a pad at last beginning to flow – because when his cell-phone rang at 4.47 p.m. with Rodriguez's call, it made him jump slightly.

'We got that e-mail through . . . or should I say, *an* e-mail from Josh. But there's somethin' that worries me about it . . .'

Jac felt such a rush of elation and ebbing of tension at Rodriguez's first words that he only half-absorbed what followed.

'Whoa . . . whoa. Back up a minute. What is it *exactly* that worries you about it?'

'Like I said . . . first thing is that it arrived only fourteen minutes after I sent the samples, whereas I thought it'd be twenty minutes or so. Second thing is it said a couple o' things that didn't relate at all to those earlier samples . . . unless, that is, she's into makin' really big, not to mention *brave*, leaps o'magination. And third – and main – thing is it didn't come from the same e-mail address where I sent 'em, or anythin' like it.'

'How different are they?'

Rodriguez read them out, and Jac had to agree, it definitely wasn't from the same IP address and its personalization, *friggy22*, bore no relation to Alaysha's name or what they were doing that day.

'Are you thinking what I'm thinking?' Jac voiced. 'Even though we didn't think he could . . .'

'Yeah, that's what I thought immediately I saw it: the main man himself.'

Jac left his sentence unfinished in case of prying ears, and no doubt for the same reason Rodriguez said 'man' instead of 'boy', in case it was too obvious. But they were both clearly leaning the same way: that somehow, against the odds, Joshua Durrant himself had sent it.

'*Jesus!*' As the knock-on implication hit Jac, it brought him to his feet. 'That means if she still . . . I'd better get hold of her before . . .' He was still trapped in a cycle of unfinished sentences.

'Exactly my thoughts, Counsellor. We'd be in an overkill situation. That's why I called you straight off. You got some pretty fast shoe-shufflin' to do.'

'Yeah.' Instantly Jac cut off, he called Alaysha's cell-phone, but it went straight into her service provider's message service. She'd obviously switched it off so that she wasn't disturbed while preparing the e-mail.

'Alaysha. If you pick this up in time, something unexpected has cropped up . . . so for God's sake don't send that e-mail. And phone me as soon as you get this message.'

He dialled 411 to get the number for Netwave, and took the option of being put straight through. Jac looked anxiously at his watch: already three minutes over by her shortest estimate, six or seven to go by her longest.

But as he started explaining what he wanted, he noticed John Langfranc looking over at him again. Jac quickly averted his eyes to his desk, as if in concentration. He'd no doubt cut a picture of perfect panic the past few minutes.

'. . . can't miss her. Mixed race, real beauty. Somewhere between Beyoncé and Mariah Carey. And she's with a young girl.'

'I'm sorry, sir. The computers are all upstairs, and most people head straight up there, so often I don't get a good look at them.'

'She said she'd be there now . . . and it's really important that I get hold of her. Could you go up and see if she's there for me?'

'I . . . uh, it's pretty irregular, sir . . . and real difficult right now: I'm on my own here, and there's already people backing up waiting on their lattes. I just can't break away at this moment.'

Lattes? 'She said she'd be having coffee for a while.' As Jac spoke, he tapped out a quick message to Alaysha's last e-mail address. She said she'd shift to another computer, but it was worth a try. 'Maybe she's still with you in the café?'

'Mmmmm, no. Sorry. Nobody here right now fitting that description.'

'Then she must be upstairs.' He was getting desperate. '*Please*, I'm begging you. It's absolutely vital that I get hold of her – a matter of life and death.'

'I'm sure it is, sir. But if I break off right now and my manager finds out, it'll be *my* death.' His voice drifted for a second as he addressed someone in the background. 'Yes, I know . . . I *know*. Coming right up.' He sighed heavily as he came back to Jac. 'Look, give me a couple of minutes to serve these two people – then I'll go up. That's the best I can offer.'

'*Okay*. Thanks.' Jac in turn eased his own sigh of relief.

But hanging on the line, listening to the background clatter and hiss of the espresso machine as the seconds ticked by, Jac felt his nerves too begin to bubble and steam. If Alaysha had already sent the e-mail, they were sunk; with the one just arrived, the monitoring guard would know immediately it was false. The last chance of saving Durrant gone, and no doubt the death-knell for Jac's legal career too if it was connected back to him.

Jac looked up with a jolt as John Langfranc broke into his thoughts.

'Something wrong?'

Jac put one hand over the mouthpiece, shrugging with a tight-lipped grimace. 'I'm trying desperately to hunt down a lap-dancer.'

Langfranc raised an eyebrow. 'Can't you wait until after work to see them, like the rest of us?'

Jac forced a conciliatory smile. 'This one unfortunately is just about to do something that she shouldn't.'

Langfranc kept the eyebrow arched. 'I thought that's exactly what they were paid to do every day: things they shouldn't.'

Jac's smile was weaker this time. Still the empty background clatter on the phone: the rest of the world going on as normal, oblivious. Probably it was already too late, and all these obstacles were for a reason: he was being given the message not to be so foolhardy and push things, just let Durrant go where he wanted to. Be with his God.

Jac sighed and closed his eyes briefly in submission before looking up again at Langfranc. 'Sorry, John. I haven't been much use to you so far this afternoon. But as soon as I've got this sorted out, I'll –' Jac broke off, holding one hand towards Langfranc.

Alaysha's voice.

17

'*Yep . . . Nice to catch up after so long. But one of the reasons for my call now, Tom — you know that envelope I sent you to safe-keep all those years back.*'

'*Only to be opened in the event of your death? Have to say, Leonard, thought it was pretty morbid at the time.*'

'*The same . . . the same. Well, I need you to send it back to me. You don't need to safeguard it any more . . .*'

The second call was in much the same vein, but as it came to Truelle's third call, all made within minutes of each other, Roche sat forward, paying more attention.

'You already got a note of that address?' he quizzed Nel-M. 'Know who it is?'

'Old colleague of his from New York, now lives upstate in Binghamton.'

'Not that much imagination. His lawyer and a cousin for the first insurance policies, now he trades for an old work colleague and . . .' Roche let the sentence hang as the tape rolled on to Truelle's fourth call.

But Nel-M felt immediately more uncomfortable. The fourth, made two hours later — possibly because of some small time zone difference — was far vaguer. He had little clue where it might be.

'*Yeah, sure, buddy . . . no problem. Just send it to the same mailbox number.*'

'*Thanks, Chris. I appreciate it. How's the weather right now in the frozen north?*'

'*Not too bad, actually. Not that cold — hard weather hasn't hit yet — and real pretty. Autumn gold on the trees everywhere you look. When you get so as you start feeling sicker than your clients, you*' *should head up here and pay me a visit, get some fresh air for a change. Christmas is particularly nice . . .'*

Nel-M let it play to the end, watching Roche's face cloud.

'Is that it?' Roche quizzed. 'No address, town or even a country? Just a mailbox – which we don't even have the number of – and Chris?'

''Fraid so. All we know from "frozen north" is that it's either close to the Canadian border or, more likely, Canada itself. Or maybe Alaska.'

'Well, that really narrows it down.' Roche waved one arm effusively. 'Do you want to head up there with your snow shoes and start looking? Or should we call on America's finest, who've been searching for Bin Laden for the last few fucking years?'

Nel-M nodded in resignation, his face flushing. Roche rarely swore. 'We just have to hope for a break. Hope that they speak again and we get more detail.'

Roche raised an eyebrow. 'But as you and I well know, that might not happen. In fact, probably won't. Truelle will just send his envelope, and they might not speak again for six months or a year. Maybe longer. And we don't have that sort of time. We've only got thirty-four days.'

'I know. I know.' Nel-M closed his eyes for a second in submission. 'I'll think on how I can push things on. Like I did with the lawyer.'

'I grant you,' Roche shrugged, raising one hand, 'you did well there.' This was how he liked Nel-M: the puppy dog seeking approval, rather than posturing and cocksure, kidding himself he had anything like equal say on their best next move. And for the same reason, *control*, Roche loved what Nel-M had just laid in his grasp: the option of destroying Jac McElroy's career at the drop of a hat. But the last thing he wanted to do was let Nel-M know that. 'Although we still have to worry that if we get rid of McElroy, Clive Beaton might simply put someone else in his place. And someone that might be more able and competent.'

'Yeah, but surely once Durrant gets to know the e-mail is false,' Nel-M pressed, 'it's going to be game-on again with him wanting to die. And the clemency bid and all the lawyers with it then go straight out the window.'

'True. And it's nice to know that Durrant's finally got the message of what everyone wants from him.' Roche smiled thinly, but it faded just as quickly. 'However, the problem is that in achieving that we'd also show our full hand. And apart from the legal lines crossed in taping McElroy, not to mention phoning Francine Durrant and posing as a prison liaison officer – some awkward questions might arise of just why we were doing all of that. So, if it's okay with you, I'd like to give it just a tad more thought before deciding the best way to proceed.'

Nel-M felt stung by the meeting with Roche.

He'd gone there with such high hopes: the situation with Truelle's insurance policies eighty per cent there, and the whole caboodle about Durrant's apparent death-wish and the fake e-mails uncovered. What the fuck more did Roche want?

Nel-M popped back a blue pill from his glove compartment and pointed his car towards the French Quarter. He felt he had to take his frustrations out somewhere, and right now Misha seemed as good a bet as any.

Nel-M had been married once, a disastrous three years when he was only twenty-three. No children – though his wife blamed her two miscarriages on their arguments and his verbal abuse. He had never hit her.

Since then he'd taken solace at a number of cat houses in the city – the age gap between the girls and himself becoming ever wider. Though in the last few years he'd managed to narrow it down to a handful of regular favourites, of whom Misha at Madame B's was top of the list. A bubbly, curvy, African-French mix with wild red hair and nipples like mahogany door stops.

'Not your normal Friday night, then?' Madame B greeted him.

'No.' Nel-M kept things short and sweet as he paid and was led to a bedroom by Misha.

He couldn't wait to get down to business, couldn't wait to be inside her, even cutting short halfway through their normal ritual of her slowly undressing him and kneeling before him, allowing only a half-dozen languorous slides between her lips before throwing her back on the bed and entering her.

As she felt the urgency of his thrusts, Misha commented, 'Someone lit a fire on your tail tonight.'

'Damn right. Damn right.' And as he felt her responding, felt that her gasps were somehow stronger than before, he remembered from a couple of past visits that she enjoyed mild asphyxiation, that it seemed to heighten the sensations even more. He raised one hand to her throat, gently pressing.

'Oh . . . Ohhh. Yes . . . *yesss!*' Misha closed her eyes in abandon, hissing through clenched teeth as her breath became shorter.

Though at some stage it became Roche in his grip, and he started pressing harder, *harder – Want to give it a tad more thought, do you?* – oblivious to the fact that Misha's gasps of pleasure had suddenly turned to ones of panic. Her eyes were wide and pleading, and she started beating at Nel-M's shoulders and arms.

But Nel-M had already shut his eyes, lost in reverie that it was Roche beneath him, the tortured breathing convincing him all the more that it was him. *Or maybe you'd like to put on your snow shoes and search up there yourself? With your stump legs and emphysema, you'd be lucky to get five miles from the fucking Canadian border.* Squeezing harder, *harder*, a tingle of pleasure rising as he felt the last life ebbing from Roche, the beating at his arms becoming weaker.

The breathing was just short, strangled bursts now, almost non-existent. Nel-M kept up the pressure, felt one hand now clutching at his hair in desperation, the other . . .

Nel-M's eyes opened sharply with the sting of the fingernails digging in and raking down his back — suddenly snapped back to reality of who was beneath him, saw Misha's eyes stark and bulging with fear, her face starting to turn blue . . . but he was too close, felt his orgasm snaking up the back of his legs, and so he held her there for his last few thrusts, only letting go as he came, his ragged, tortured breathing finally matching hers.

Misha rolled quickly away, coughing and spluttering for her first full breaths. It sounded for a moment as if she was going to vomit, and when she'd finally got her breathing back to near normal, she glared at him.

'What's wrong wit' you? You half-killed me there.'

'Sorry. Bad day at work.' Nel-M forced a lame smile.

'Yeah, well. Next time you have a bad day — don't come seeing me. In fact, bad day or not — don't come seeing me again. Yer hear?'

Nel-M nodded dolefully. Frustrations all around, and so when he got back to his apartment, he was pleased to hear the message from Vic Farrelia, particularly when he phoned back and gained more detail.

Nel-M drove straight over to hear the latest tape offering from McElroy's phone line, his trademark sly smile firmly back in place as it finished. Roche wouldn't be able to delay any longer in making a move against McElroy.

'Freedom . . . oh, freedom. That's just some people talking.' Mike Coultaine looked wistfully across the City Marina and the Mississippi river beyond from the back deck of his cabin cruiser. 'So that's what Durrant's after these days? He doesn't ask much.'

'It wasn't a straight-out request.' Jac filled in the background with Durrant's initial death-wish. 'Although now I've finally convinced him to put in a plea — he has little interest in that possibly extended life still behind bars. It only has appeal to him if he might gain freedom — either now or in the near future. So, as part of putting in clemency, I promised.'

'Oooh, *promised*. That's something a lawyer should never do.' Coultaine's teasing smile faded as he looked at Jac directly. 'But if Candaret turns down that appeal – which he probably will given recent history – we're talking *now* rather than near future. How long left?'

'Thirty-two days.'

Coultaine looked out pensively across the marina again.

Three days, and everything had changed.

Alaysha had come on the line exuberant that she'd finally got the tone right with the e-mail; so when Jac had told her, no need now to send it, Joshua Durrant had already sent one, she'd immediately felt deflated. 'You've got no idea how long I sweated over that, Jac McElroy. No idea.' And then in protest didn't speak to him for twenty-four hours before finally softening. Durrant too let him stew; and when after two days he still hadn't heard anything, he put in a call to Rodriguez.

'I tell you, Counsellor, he was like cat's-got-the-cream with that e-mail from Josh. But you know what Larry's like – proud, stubborn – so it don't surprise me he hasn't called you. I think it's gonna be down to you givin' him a little nudge.'

Nudge quickly became push with Jac informing Durrant that this was absolutely his last visit to try and convince him to put in for clemency. 'When I walk away from here now, that's it. So if there's anything, *anything* that might make you want to continue clinging to life, now's the time to speak up.' It was as far as he dared go; he couldn't risk Durrant catching on that he knew about Joshua's e-mail.

But still Durrant was guarded, closed-handed. 'Before we get into that – how you getting on with gaining me freedom from this rat-hole? Made any moves yet?'

'I've already spoken to Mike Coultaine, your original lawyer,' Jac had lied. 'Got more background from the trial and appeal. But you're going to have to help me too. Give me some good reasons why you think you might be innocent. Something to fight with.'

Durrant flinched at the 'think you might be', a sudden reminder that he couldn't know for sure, and his face clouded as he fought to explain, though maybe it was the darkness of the images still haunting him as much as lack of clarity. Jac made brief notes and nodded knowingly at some points, as if they might be significant – and perhaps they would be when he finally got to speak to Coultaine.

Jac looked back over his notes as he finished, shaking his head. 'I want to help, Lawrence, I really do. But all of this is going to take time – time which we just don't have. And there's another reason why we need that extra time . . .' Jac had pondered long and hard whether to tell Durrant about the anonymous e-mails, had finally decided that he had to at some point; now it might be just the thing to tip the balance.

Durrant was lost in thought for a moment. A long moment. A wry smile finally surfaced, though uncertainly, as if the revelation had painted an extra confusing layer to his thoughts that would take him a while to filter anything through clearly. 'Nice to know someone else out there is thinking about me. Thought you were the only one.'

He asked a few questions for clarification. Jac stressed that while it could be a hoaxer or could be genuine, again, it would no doubt take time to find out which. 'Time which we don't have right now.'

Durrant looked down thoughtfully at that point, was slow in looking back up again. 'Okay, Counsellor. There is something that's given me some "hope", as you call it. So, bring on whatever paperwork you have to – I'll sign it.'

Secretive as ever, Durrant didn't elaborate on what might have given him fresh hope, but equally Jac didn't pursue it, was eager to tie up the details before Durrant changed his mind. But as Jac shook Durrant's hand in parting, Durrant reached up and gripped his forearm tight.

'Promise me, Counsellor – on a Bible if that's what it takes for you to *really* mean it – after I've signed these papers, you won't just forget about me and leave me here to rot. You'll do all you can to get me out.'

'I promise.' Jac felt the strength in Durrant's grip, saw the fiery intent in his eyes.

'Because there's somebody I've been apart from already far too long. And I don't want to spend the next ten to fifteen with us only being able to clasp fingertips through the holes in a glass screen.'

Jac had phoned Mike Coultaine when he got back to his apartment, but still now he found himself swallowing back a lump in his throat as he thought about the promise he'd made and what it signified to Durrant, Coultaine's gaze across the marina telling him just how distant and out of reach making good on that promise might be.

'You can actually see Adelay Roche's yacht from here,' Coultaine said, pointing. 'That gin palace on the end of the second quay.'

'I see.' Jac wondered if that's why Coultaine had arranged to meet him here; at the same time give him a feel for the victim's family.

'Never moves far. Roche either has parties on board so that everyone in the marina can see him – or at most it goes no more than a few miles offshore. Always still in sight of the refineries that paid for it.' Coultaine smiled tightly. 'Makes this thing look like a bathtub.'

Jac cast a quick eye around Coultaine's boat. 32ft Bayliner, more than big enough for Coultaine's favourite pastime of sports fishing. He seemed to have slipped fully into the lifestyle too: blue deck shoes, khaki shorts and denim shirt, with his greying brown hair tied back in a ponytail. A far cry from his cropped-haired, pinstripe-suited days defending Durrant.

'You know, at one point in the appeal, I really thought we were getting somewhere.' Coultaine looked keenly at Jac for a moment before his gaze drifted again across the marina and the river beyond; inspiration for distant thoughts, the steady timeless surge of the Mississippi pushing them on. 'Truelle the pyschiatrist's testimony, and everything surrounding Durrant's initial confession, was starting to look shaky. I mean, he still had gaps in his memory about so many other things after his car accident – so how could anyone be sure that his recall about what happened that night was accurate? But his depth of detail of the events that night with Jessica Roche – things that only the killer could possibly have known – killed it, if you'll excuse the expression.' Coultaine forced an awkward smile. 'That and the DNA evidence.'

Jac nodded. Before meeting Coultaine, he'd gone through the trial bundle again to get the sequence clear in his mind: the police working a general suspect list which didn't include Durrant, his car accident four months after the murder and his resultant partial amnesia and 'recovered memory' sessions with Truelle in which details of the murder emerged; then the final damning DNA evidence. 'Pretty conclusive from what I saw in the trial papers.'

'Yep. Four blood spots on one of Durrant's jackets with a hundred per cent match with Jessica Roche's DNA, found at his house straight after his confession. And on top, witness identification – even though it was from a hundred yards away at night.' Coultaine shrugged. 'So however much we might have cast doubt on Durrant's confession due to the fractured state of his memory at the time – we were never able to shift from the jury's or the appeal judge's mind the fact that Durrant must have been there.' Coultaine looked at Jac with his head lowered, eyes lifted – the look a judge might give above his pince-nez. 'And if you don't mind me saying, I think you'll find exactly the same. But if you want to give it a shot because of the promise you've made to Durrant, or whatever – I'll gladly give you some names and pointers.'

'Thanks, that'd be helpful.' Though Jac wasn't sure what he was thanking him for; it looked a hopeless quest. Jac started making notes as Coultaine related the key points and contact names, his memory at times stretched as it leapt the eleven-year gap.

'Lieutenant Patrick, "Pat", Coyne . . . that's it. He headed the investigation. He's probably long retired by now, he was over fifty at the time. But he had a bright-eyed assistant – Frier or Friar – something like that. Good chance he'd still be around. Truelle you've already got, and we had a psychiatrist countering for defence whose name for the moment escapes me. I'll have to phone you later with that.' As Coultaine finished, he asked, 'What's Durrant given you that might help fight his corner?'

'He said that he can't imagine he'd have broken the promise to his wife not to re-offend, especially with their son just born.'

'That old turkey.'

'And he has doubts about the jacket with Jessica Roche's bloodstains. Says almost certainly he'd have worn one of two other jackets for a "job". Oh, and the gun used – he's pretty sure it wasn't one of his. Doesn't recall it at all.'

'The jacket he's mentioned before, except then he just "wasn't sure". But the gun's something new. At the time, he simply didn't recognize it – but then he didn't have recall of *any* gun he'd had with him on past robberies. So at least his memory appears to be freeing up some. Makes a change. Most people's memories fade with the years. His seems to be getting clearer.' Coultaine grimaced. 'But it's still all supposition: Larry thinks this, Larry believes that. If Durrant's memory reached the stage where he could actually remember where he was that fateful night apart from at the Roche residence – drinking, playing pool, seeing a mistress, whatever . . . because all his wife remembers was that he was "out" – then you'd be getting somewhere.'

Jac nodded pensively. 'Anything you remember from the investigation whereby there might have been another eye-witness that never came forward?'

'No, not that I recall. But that's something you could ask

Coyne or his side-kick when you speak to them. I suppose it's possible that if someone else was seen, say by the woman walking her dog, but never came forward – it might not have featured in the police report if they decided it wasn't relevant. But it's unlikely.' Coultaine shrugged, then looked at Jac more keenly. 'Why do you ask?'

I was there at the time. Jac passed across the best of the three photos from the twelve enhancements Souchelle had sent him; and as Coultaine examined them, at moments turning them as if for a better angle, Jac explained about the e-mails, his close call with catching up with the sender at Internet-ional, and the thought processes he'd run through with Langfranc.

Coultaine pursed his lips, shaking his head after a moment. 'No, can't think of anything from the police reports that might fit in with that.' He handed the photos back. 'And can't say the face rings any bells either, from what little I can see there.'

'I know. Best I could get.' Jac sighed, his disappointment when the photos first arrived mirrored in Coultaine's face in that moment. A hundred per cent improvement from the cam shots, but still far from enough for identification; not even worth trying for an 'Anyone recognize this man?' posting with local newspapers.

Coultaine was lost in thought for a moment, his gaze drifting again across the river. 'For what it's worth, I'd throw my bet in with you and John Langfranc there: hoaxer, friend or anti-capital punishment campaigner without doubt look the prime suspects. But the murderer himself, there's a thought.' Coultaine raised a brow. 'Have you told Durrant yet?'

'Yeah, but just the other day. I stressed that it could well be a hoaxer, so as not to falsely build up his hopes. And for the same reason, I didn't show Durrant the photos or mention the possibility that it could be the murderer. Thought that might be just too confusing for him at this stage; not to mention cruel, if they didn't finally come forward.'

'Yeah.' Coultaine nodded, grimacing tautly. 'Confusing and cruel – pretty apt words given that Durrant's starting to have doubts as to whether he actually committed the murder. And still can't clearly recall half his life from that time.'

A heavier mood suddenly hung over them, a cooler breeze for a moment drifting in off the Mississippi, as if in sympathy. Though Jac couldn't tell whether the same thoughts had gripped Coultaine in that instant: Durrant confused, memory fractured, and as the days wound rapidly down towards his execution and his doubts grew about his guilt, a bolt comes out of the blue from someone claiming that he didn't do it; though, cruellest fate of all, even if they *were* real, they might well not reveal themselves in time to save his life.

Coultaine introduced a fresh tone. 'But, you know, with Durrant now remembering more – that could well be the key. He'd started to recall more even by the time of the appeal. I checked out a couple of pool buddies then he'd suddenly recalled that might have been able to give him an alibi.' Coultaine held up one palm. 'Didn't head anywhere in the end – but now, who knows? If you could find that one person to corroborate that he *was* somewhere else that night – then you'd have struck gold. You'd have something solid to counter the DNA evidence.'

'True.' Jac cast his eyes down for a second before looking up absently at half a dozen geese flurrying briefly in mid-river before taking flight again. *DNA*. Whatever else he might come up with, they were always going to be facing that final stone wall.

'But, hey, DNA these days,' Coultaine said as he caught Jac's expression, 'million miles from where it was then – practically its first days. Now with a bit more analysis and tweaking here and there, you could easily get lucky and be able to cast doubt on the original findings. And that's probably all you'd need to do – cast doubt.'

But Jac knew that Coultaine was saying it mainly to lift his spirits; it was far more likely that it would simply cement the original conclusion. He was kidding himself if he thought he might be able to prove Durrant's innocence. And worst thing was that Durrant had so little recall of the events of eleven years ago, he was kidding himself too. Had no idea if he was innocent or not.

Nel-M was having one last coffee before heading over to Roche's with the latest tape offering when Vic Farrelia rang.

'Another call just came in. Same guy as the other day.'

'Coultaine?'

'Yeah, Coultaine.'

Nel-M checked his watch. 'Okay, I'll be right over.' He downed one final gulp, put his foot down hard for the two miles to Farrelia's stake-out on Perdido Street, and signalled Farrelia to hit 'play' as soon as he walked into the room.

'Got that name of the defence psychiatrists for you: Ormdern. Gregory Ormdern. And Coyne's assistant's name is Friele. Dave Friele.'

'Thanks. I appreciate it.'

'But if I were you, I'd see Truelle first. Get the sequence right for how it was then: prosecution case . . . then counter arguments.'

'He in fact was top of my list. Because it seems to me that everything kick-started with the taped admission in Truelle's session . . .'

Nel-M signalled for Farrelia to stop the tape. He didn't want to be late, he'd play the rest at Roche's. More than enough to hang McElroy already, he thought, banging his hand against the steering wheel on his way over, clenching and unclenching his fists on his knees as he patiently sat through Roche listening to what he'd already heard on the two calls, as if he couldn't wait to unfurl them and get them around McElroy's neck.

'I daresay, though, it's not going to be easy, jolting eleven-year-old memories. Because, like I said the other day, while Durrant's memory might have improved and filled in some of the gaps, others will have faded.'

'I know. But I promised . . . which you said a lawyer should never do. Looks like I'm about to find out why.' Uneasy laugh from McElroy. *'I'm finding myself torn on this. I don't want to*

give in too easily, throw in the towel before I've started just because it looks too daunting and hopeless to try and prove Durrant's innocence. And on the other hand, I don't want to mislead him and falsely build up his hopes. He deserves better than that.'

'Well, I'm sure Larry Durrant's happy to know he still has friends out there batting on his behalf. And I say that for my part, too. I wish I could have done more for him at the time, so it's nice to see that he appears to be in good hands.'

'Thanks.'

'Oh, and for whatever it might help – I'll do a support letter to go along with the clemency plea: character reference, Durrant making good with his self-education, that type of thing, along with the questionable ethics of executing someone who still doesn't have possession of the faculties to know if they're guilty or innocent . . . maybe the first time that's happened. You want to check the records on that, spin it out for even more mileage if you can. When are you putting it in?'

'Day after tomorrow. Straight after Durrant has signed it.'

'I'll make sure to get the letter over to you by then.'

Roche waved a hand for Nel-M to stop the tape.

Silence. Stone silence.

They were in Roche's 'Terrace Room', an oversized conservatory replete with white wicker furniture, palm trees and a white cockatoo in a six-foot-high Moroccan-style white cage in one corner. To complete the image, Roche was wearing a white robe with his initials emblazoned in red on one breast pocket. The initials were the only splash of red in the room.

Though it was probably the most tasteful room in the house, Nel-M reminded himself. The rest was oppressively Baroque, with gilded statues of angels and cherubs everywhere, red velvet curtains on every window, and red and gold silk draped over practically every outstretched limb – or other protruding appendage – of the angels and cherubs. Nel-M hated it with a vengeance. It reminded him of a cross between a funeral parlour and a 1920s whorehouse.

The only sounds were the gentle hum of the pool filter beyond the glass and the occasional caw of the cockatoo; though that too seemed to have fallen silent with the stopping of the tape.

'Last thing we want is McElroy seeing Truelle,' Roche commented.

Exactly my sentiment, thought Nel-M, but all he said was 'Yeah.'

'Probably wouldn't find out anything, but it's the sort of thing that might just hit the final panic button with Truelle. Just what we don't need right now.'

Another 'Yeah,' Nel-M contemplating Roche coolly, evenly. After the other day, he wasn't going to put his head in the noose and try and push Roche this way or that, only to be shot down in flames again. So he'd decided to say little or nothing, just let Roche get there on his own.

'And we certainly don't want Durrant getting frisky, starting to remember things he shouldn't.'

'Certainly don't.' He'd noticed Roche flinch at that juncture on the tape: '. . . *while Durrant's memory might have improved and filled in some of the gaps . . .*'

Roche was anxious now as it hit him for the first time that he wasn't getting much feedback. He looked at Nel-M expectantly, as if hoping he'd elaborate, but Nel-M just kept the same cool stare straight through Roche. *You're on your own this time, fuckhead.*

'And . . . uh, well . . . looks like we can't hold back any longer from taking action.'

'Looks like it.' Nel-M relished Roche's discomfort as he noticed some sweatbeads break out above his top lip.

'Though it appears we're spoilt for choice there.' Small chuckle from Roche that fought for bravado, but failed. His breathing suddenly became more laboured. 'Destroy his career, or, as you so aptly put it, a few column inches alongside Raoul Ferrer.'

Nel-M didn't say anything, simply shrugged.

One hand of Roche's clutched at his thigh as he struggled with the decision, faint sweatbeads now on his forehead too. 'Which route do you think we should go?' he pressed.

'You know I always leave those sort of decisions to you.' Nel-M smiled tightly, refusing to be drawn. This time he didn't need to say anything; the tapes had done it all for him. Hardly any options left now for Roche.

The atmosphere was heavy, palpable, Nel-M suddenly aware of something he hadn't noticed before: gently playing in the background, like the soft, nondescript piped music in an elevator, an instrumental version of 'Fernando's Hideaway'.

'Weighing up not just the best option, but one which will ensure no possible links back.'

'Obviously.' Nel-M shrugged.

Roche's hand rose briefly to rub at his temple before returning to his lap, a small nervous tic appearing at the corner of his mouth. His breathing rattled faintly as it rose and fell.

'And of course, the best timing . . .'

Another shrug from Nel-M.

Roche's mouth dry, his fat pink tongue snaking out to moisten it, his hand clenched back on his knee starting to tremble slightly.

But Nel-M just held the same stare steadily on Roche, wallowing in every small nuance of his discomfort, while on his own knee he started to drum a steady rhythm with his fingers as he waited impatiently on Roche's final pearls of wisdom.

18

As Frank Sinatra invited Libreville's inmates to come fly with him and try some exotic booze in far Bombay, Rodriguez might have swayed to it if he hadn't heard it a hundred times before.

Now with all privileges returned, Rodriguez also had his daily ninety-minutes back on the prison radio, alternating between a 7 a.m. and a 6 p.m. slot with another prisoner, Tyrone Sommer – or Tired-Drone Insomnia, as he'd been nicknamed – an ex-part-time DJ from a small station in Shreveport who played far too much country music for the inmates' liking. Sad and lamenting at the best of times – the crops have all failed, my wife's done left me and my dog just died – it was noticed that the prison suicide rate was far higher during and just after Sommer's slots.

Rodriguez's sessions were decidedly more upbeat: Latin, reggae, calypso, rock, Latin-jazz, with Carlos Santana his all-time favourite. But over sixty per cent of their respective programmes and playlists were controlled by Haveling: prison activity announcements for the day and evening – which had been the original purpose of setting up the radio slots – followed by 'uplifting' religious music, then, interspersed with their own playlist choices, Haveling's favourite music: swing, songs from musicals and Bacharach.

Within Rodriguez's and Sommer's respective playlist choices, Haveling also wielded a heavy guiding hand: no heavy rock, nothing too aggressive and rousing, which left only Santana's lighter instrumental tracks; and nothing which might have sexual, violent or drugs connotations – which discounted most of the rest of rock music.

With swing, songs from musicals and Bacharach, Rodriguez

had a far freer hand – yet even there Haveling had presented them with a list of preferred tunes he wanted playing X-number of times a week, of which Sinatra's 'Come Fly with Me' was one. And when Rodriguez had studied the list in more detail one day – 'Fly Me to the Moon', 'Girl from Ipanema', 'Somewhere over the Rainbow', 'Bali Hai', 'Do You Know the Way to San Jose', 'Beyond the Sea' (Bobby Darin's 'Mack the Knife' was banned) – he couldn't help noticing that many of them had overt themes of freedom or far-away places, places that most of the Libreville inmates would never get to see.

Perhaps they were indeed Haveling's favourite tunes, or perhaps he was slyly rubbing salt in the wounds of their incarceration; like most things with Haveling, you never knew. But you stepped outside of Haveling's recommended playlist at your peril.

'He even stopped me playin' "Moon River" for fuck's sake,' Rodriguez once complained to Larry. 'Thought the line "I'll be crossing you in style tonight" might give people the idea of escapin' across the river.'

It was great to have all privileges back, but now that he and Larry were again in general circulation, the risks from Tally and his crew were far greater. The initial guarded, warning looks had now become icy and openly hostile, as if saying, 'You got lucky a couple of times. But that ain't gonna be the case for much longer.' On one occasion, Tally had even tapped his watch to make the message clear. Tally had been thwarted, made to look a fool, and that was something Rodriguez could barely remember happening before, let alone *twice*. Libreville's corridors and shower rooms – or even open areas with the right distractions, like the canteen or TV room – were going to be far more dangerous places from here on in. He and Larry were going to have to be extra-vigilant watching their backs.

Rodriguez leant forward to the mike as Sinatra came to an end.

'And that's Ol' Blue Eyes there, croonin' about places

that'll be all too familiar to all you well-heeled jet-setters here at Libreville. Just lay back on your bunk and fly, fly away. But now it's time for a touch of my main man, Carlos Santana.' Rodriguez reached for the record and cued it. 'Samba . . . Pa . . . ti. Played today for a very special lady. And not to be confused with *Samba Party*, a Swedish film which was tradin' at some high prices a few months back.'

As risqué as Rodriguez dared get, he sat back and closed his eyes, letting the softly soaring guitar and mellow background bongo suffuse through him. He was ten days late playing the tune, but then he'd been in the infirmary at the time. Better late than never, he thought, wiping a gentle tear from the corner of one eye.

While Carlos Santana's guitar sailed and cried through the concrete caverns of Libreville prison, Larry Durrant sat up on his bed.

He knew what the tune meant to Rodriguez. He'd played it at his mother's funeral – along with her own favourite, 'Besame Mucho' – four years ago now, late fall, not far from this date, and every year since on the same day. Rodriguez had also played the tune various other times over the prison radio, but with the mention of 'for a very special lady', Larry knew that today was significant.

Rodriguez had taken his mother's death hard. Coming just fifteen months after his incarceration, he'd partly blamed himself. Larry could imagine Rodriguez in the radio room now, tears streaming silently down his cheeks. Then, as soon as it finished playing, he'd be back to his lively, bubbly self again, lifting everyone's spirits, if not his own.

Larry wondered what Francine and Josh would play at his own funeral: Marvin Gaye's 'What's Going on', Sly Stone's 'Family Affair'? Both songs a decade ahead of his teens, and so long past now, he doubted that Franny even remembered his favourite tunes any more.

Although he had no idea what Josh's tastes in music were

either – maybe something he could broach in future e-mails. But the thought had already mugged him deep inside without warning, *too long apart*, and a single tear rolled down one cheek at the lost years.

Nobody rushing to work that morning paid much attention to the man in a lightweight grey suit entering the car park on St Charles Street and exiting ten minutes later. He appeared just one of many hurrying to work having parked their cars.

Except the man didn't head towards an office, he went fifty yards along the street to the nearest kiosk to make a call.

'It's all done.'

'Great. And what's the best point?'

'Eight to eleven miles in. But I wouldn't leave it beyond that.'

'Okay, got it. Eight to eleven.' Nel-M clicked off and dialled straight out again.

With another anxious check of his watch, Jac started reading through draft five – six? he'd lost count – of Durrant's clemency plea. *Please*, no more changes. *No time*! And Coultaine's support letter, which had arrived forty minutes earlier by messenger, he'd managed to give only a light skim, though the postscript had leapt out at him:

Thought you might find the enclosed of interest, found it amongst my old papers. It'll save you asking Truelle for a copy. Remember, everything started with this.

Jac twirled the cassette tape briefly in one hand before bringing his attention back to Durrant's plea on his computer screen, but found his eyes drifting back to the tape at intervals.

Finally, the distraction too much, halfway through reading what he hoped was the final, definitive version, he leapt up, grabbed a cassette player from a nearby shelf, slotted the tape in, and resumed reading again as soon as he pressed play.

'*Session fourteen. Seventeenth of August, nineteen-ninety-two. Subject: Lawrence Tyler Durrant . . .*'

One of Truelle's sessions with Durrant. There was a minute's preamble, settling Durrant down before Truelle hit any real topic: Durrant's heavy drinking the night of the accident.

'*You mentioned feeling guilty about that. Was that because of what resulted — the accident — or the drinking itself?*'

'*Mainly the drinking . . . because I'd promised Franny, yer know, to stop.*'

'*And do you remember drinking other times after you'd promised to stop . . . or was it just this one time?*'

'*There were a fair few other times I recall — all around that same time. I was goin' through a real bad cycle, man . . . didn't know what I was doing half the time.*'

'*And why was that? Or didn't you know that, either?*'

'*Oh, I knew all right . . . knew all too well. That's why I tried to bury it . . . burn it from my mind with as much rum and whisky as I could lay my hands on. But however hard I tried, it stayed with me. I jus' couldn't shake it.*'

'*Shake what, Lawrence?*'

'*More guilt . . . that's what.*' Durrant's breathing suddenly more laboured. '*More guilt because that wasn't the only promise I'd broken to Franny.*'

'*Guilt over what, Lawrence? What other promise?*'

'*I . . . I . . . It's difficult.*' Durrant's breathing hissing hard.

'*I know. But perhaps if you unburden whatever it is . . . you'll be able to break the cycle.*'

Listening to Durrant's fractured and uncertain breathing, Jac realized that this was one of the sessions where Truelle had used hypnosis to draw out his buried memory. As Durrant struggled with the decision — whether to take the leap or step back — Jac felt as if he was suddenly there with him in the moment, suspended.

He snapped out of it quickly, *no time now*, stopping the tape and reading the last few paragraphs of the plea. Okay,

okay. Plea, Coultaine's letter, and get there fifteen minutes early to read Haveling's support letter. He slid the papers into his briefcase, grabbed the tape recorder, and, with a quick wave to John Langfranc who mouthed 'Good luck' through his glass screen, skipped down the stairs two at a time.

There was a small hold-up along Esplanade Avenue, but as soon as he was clear of the main downtown traffic, twenty yards after making the turn into Claiborne Avenue, Jac hit play again on the recorder now on his passenger seat.

'*It . . . it was another robbery, that's why I felt guilty. And not just 'cause I'd promised Franny I wouldn't rob again, but because it went wrong . . . terribly wrong.*'

'*In which way did it go wrong?*'

'*There was somebody there when I broke in . . . a woman. Shouldn't . . . shouldn't have happened.*' Durrant's breathing erratic again. '*I . . . I'd checked for a few nights b'forehand . . . and there was no car either in the drive . . . or lights on that I could see. She . . . she wasn't mean'a be there.*'

'*And where was this house?*'

'*. . . Garden District.*'

'*Do you remember the road?*'

'*Coliseum Street. But I don' remember the number exactly . . . Four hundred and something.*'

'*That's okay, Lawrence. Relax . . . take it easy. And, in your own time, tell me what happened there.*'

Jac became aware of Truelle's tactic: getting background detail, district, road, because they were easier for Durrant to relate, got him talking more freely. Truelle had obviously worried that if he asked straight out 'What happened with the woman?', Durrant might lapse into rapid-breathing catatonia, and that would be all he'd get. Even now with a more general, soft-edged approach, there was a long pause, only the sound of Durrant's uneven breathing coming over on the tape.

Jac turned the volume up as he hit the start of the Lake Pontchartrain Causeway; with the increased tyre-noise on the rougher road surface, he couldn't hear whether Durrant had started speaking again or not.

'*As . . . as I said, there were no lights on at the front, or the side – which is where I broke in. Maybe if I'd gone round the back, I'd have seen a light on . . . or maybe she'd gone to bed early and there'd a been no light on there either.*'

'*So you broke in at the side,*' Truelle confirmed as Durrant paused again heavily, as if each time he side-tracked it took a moment to get the sequence clear again in his mind.

'*Yeah. Removed a glass pane and wired through on the frame so as not to break the alarm circuit. Two minutes, and I was in. Took a quick tour t'see where the best stuff was, and found a safe in the library that I reckoned I could break by drilling the lock without too much trouble. And I was just preparin' for that when I heard something behind me, and she . . . she was suddenly there. Like . . . like out of nowhere. Not there one minute . . . then the next . . .*'

Jac's hands gripped tight at the steering wheel, feeling Durrant's tension coming across in waves, as if he was right there alongside him as Jessica Roche confronted him, the police photos filling in the details of the room in his mind. He was suddenly reminded of Coultaine's words: *depth of detail . . . things that only the killer could possibly have known.*

Durrant's breathing was again erratic as he struggled with the images; or perhaps in anticipation of what he did next. '*"What are you doing?" she barked. She was pushy, had me rattled, and strange thing is . . . I don't even remember takin' out the gun, but suddenly it was there between us . . . her eyes wide, staring at it . . .*' A heavy swallow, Durrant fighting to get his breathing under control. '*You know, even then I didn't plan to . . . to . . .*'

The pause was even longer this time, and it looked for a moment as if Truelle had lost Durrant completely, his final actions too traumatic to voice, or perhaps part of him in denial that he'd actually done it. Jac tapped two fingers on his steering wheel, counting off the seconds, the sun creeping out from behind a cloud stinging his eyes as it reflected off the water. Jac slipped on his sunglasses and half-opened one window, feeling the warm Bayou breeze tease his hair. But memories of Isle de Ré seemed distant today as he felt himself immersing deeper into the shadows of the Roche residence of twelve years ago.

'*Plan to what, Larry?*' Truelle prompted as the silence prolonged. '*What happened then?*'

Jac tapped out another fifteen seconds with his fingers before Durrant's voice finally returned.

'*It . . . it all felt unreal, distant . . . like it was happenin' to someone else and I was just looking on. But in . . . instead of stepping back, she stepped forward . . . and I . . . I panicked . . . did the wrong thing . . . I didn't mean to . . . and . . . and she was laying there then, blood everywhere, looking at me with wide eyes. And she was in pain . . . real pain . . . a pitiful, throaty groanin' that went right through me. So I . . . I . . .*'

Even though Jac knew what happened next, he found his own breathing rapid and short in anticipation, almost matching Durrant's, and his hands gripped tight to the steering wheel started to shake. A sign to his right displayed the ten-mile Causeway mark.

'*I didn't want to . . . but she was in pain . . . the blood bubbling up from her mouth . . . her wide eyes almost pleadin' with me . . .*'

Long silence again. Ragged, uneven breathing.

'*What happened then, Lawrence? What did you do?*' Truelle's prompt quicker this time; the edge-of-the-seat listener, impatient for what happened next, in that heated moment holding sway over the trained psychiatrist.

'*She wasn't meant to be there . . . wasn't meant to be . . . I . . . I . . .*'

And Jac, impatient too, fast-forwarded in his mind to the close-up police photos of Jessica Roche, both shots fired, stomach and head, sepia-grey blood pools radiating from each.

Whether the image momentarily distracted Jac, or he glanced fleetingly at the tape recorder in expectation of Durrant's next words, the only warning was a reflected glint striking his eye – something suddenly different in the vista of roadway and sun-dappled lake spread each side.

A truck overtaking, its chrome bumper catching the sun as it veered lazily from its lane towards him, suddenly swung sharply across his front wing, pushing him towards the side-barrier.

Jac swerved, stock reaction, hitting his brakes hard as the barrier loomed before him. But they did nothing, *nothing* . . . and in panic he swung the wheel back, but not enough: he hit the barrier at a thirty-degree angle at almost the same speed, feeling himself shunted sharply forward and the airbag exploding against him, along with something else, sharper, harder, against one leg.

Momentary darkness, then the sun and lake seemed to be fighting through a hazy-grey mist. And, as the mist became darker, denser, Jac realized with mounting panic that his car was in the lake and sinking, feeling the first water swill against his thigh as it poured in through the half-open window.

Sinking . . . *sinking* . . . Jac felt as if he was in a washing-machine tumbler, the water swirling in relentlessly, the car swaying, tilting – then as it finally hit the bottom of the lake, a cloud of mud was thrown up, cutting visibility to almost nil. How far was he down: thirty feet, fifty?

Jac frantically tried the door, but it wouldn't budge with the pressure outside. His heart raced, his breath falling short, the water already up to his waist. Maybe the window, but it wasn't open enough to get through. He fumbled for the switch in the gloom, found it, pressed it – but after a second it fizzled out with a spark and the window stopped moving. Two-thirds down, maybe enough.

Jac squeezed his head and shoulders into the gap, but the surge of water rushing in was too heavy, impossible to push against. No choice but to wait until the pressure equalized, he pulled back and hoisted up until his head was against the car roof. Water up to his shoulders now, breathing in the last foot of air.

Trying to time it right, the air-gap ten-inches, eight . . .
praying that he wasn't too far down to make it to the surface,
six . . . and fighting to keep his breathing even – ragged and
frantic as it kept time with his racing pulse – so that he had
maximum air in his lungs when . . . *four* . . .

Jac made the break then, got his head and shoulders quickly
through, his chest . . . but as he tried to snake his waist
through, he felt something snagging on one leg, holding him
back. His seat belt or maybe part of the air-bag.

He wriggled hard, desperate to free it, knowing that he
was using vital air with each second lost. And as Jac frantically
jerked and tugged to get free, the images of Jessica Roche
were again there with him, the sepia-grey of the police photos
merging with the murky waters surrounding him, clogging
his nose, his mouth, suffocating his last breaths. Maybe
because they were the last images in his mind before his car
hit the barrier; or because he now shared Jessica Roche's
emotions in those final seconds as Durrant's gun barrel pressed
against her temple. Hoping against hope that she might survive, but knowing in her sinking heart that it was already
too late.

19

18 February 1992.

Silence. The thrum of the city pushed away and cushioned by the resplendent mansions of the Garden District, each sprawling edifice with its cosseted oleander-, juniper-, bamboo- and magnolia-rich grounds a punctuation space of tranquillity separated from its neighbour; on and on until the city itself and its hubbub seemed distant, remote. Almost another world.

Jessica Roche was wrapped in the spacious cocoon of that silence, the only sound coming from the house itself: the TV on low with a *Cheers* re-run, a grandfather clock ticking in the hallway, the faint hum and churn of the dishwasher in the kitchen – their maid Rosella had packed it and wiped all surfaces clean when she'd left for the day fifty minutes ago – the sharpest sound the turning of magazine pages as Jessica Roche flicked through a recent *Elle Décor*.

She glanced fleetingly at her watch. Over two hours gone, they'd be well into the desserts, brandies and after-dinner speeches by now. 'One of those boring business functions, all of the talk will be about trends and quotas and how to improve tanker facilities at Port Arthur. You wouldn't enjoy it.'

But at the back of her mind she'd begun to wonder if Adelay was purposely keeping her away from business functions because of their recent argument. It had all been behind closed doors, nothing overt that anyone else would have been aware of, even Rosella.

Maybe this was his way of punishing her, shutting her out in the cold for a while. Leave the trophy wife at home to cool off, realize her 'place'. Or perhaps, keeping her away from business functions, a more direct message: don't get involved in my business matters and things that don't concern you.

In sober reflection, possibly she had been too volatile, rash, taken things a step too far – or at least threatened to. But then, as so often, he'd been so annoyingly offhand and condescending. *Trophy Wife*. At the time, it had seemed the only way for him to pay her any notice, take her seriously; otherwise, he'd have just rolled straight over her.

She stroked her stomach gently with one hand as she felt it twitch and tighten. Hopefully finally some activity there, rather than just unease. Dr Thallerey, her obstetrician, had said that the next month or so would be the most telling for the treatment.

Perhaps she should back-step with Adelay and try and calm the waters over the next few days. The last thing she wanted – *they* wanted – was any upset that might affect the success of the treatment. After all, they finally had something to look forward to, some hope where before . . .

She froze, a tingle running up her spine. A sound out of place among the other faint noises of the house. A door opening, maybe a window. Somewhere towards the other side of the house.

She held her breath, listening more intently. *Soft rustling, scratching? Faint pad of steps towards her, or were they heading along the corridor?* Hard to pick out clearly as a gust of wind outside rustled the oleander bush close by the drawing-room window.

The door to the hallway was ajar just a few inches. She got up and moved closer to it, trying to hone her hearing to the sounds beyond; fearful now of actually opening it. If somebody was there, the first thing she should be doing is shutting it sharply, locking it, and lunging for the phone to dial 911.

Something there, but very soft, not . . . she back-stepped sharply, her heart in her throat, as the door started swinging wider open. Although by only a few inches – their grey Persian cat scurrying quickly through.

She reached down and scooped it up. 'Majestic! It's only you.' She hugged it close, feeling her heart still racing against its soft fur. She looked along the corridor to the rec-room with its basket; obviously the door hadn't been left sufficiently open, as it usually was, and it'd had to scratch and paw the door wider open. 'But stop sneaking around so will you, you gave me . . .'

The phone rang in the library. Adelay's business line; she'd better get it. He'd told her before going out that he was expecting an important call, and had specifically requested that she pass on his number at the function rather than let it go to answer-phone. No point in upsetting him even more. Majestic was abruptly dropped again as she went across the hallway to answer it.

Everything had gone smoothly. Breaking in the side-window and wire-crossing the alarm had taken no more than a few minutes, but then had come the trickiest part: edging three doors down the corridor without being heard.

He glided silently, feet floating an inch above the floor, each step hardly connecting before lifting and gliding again. He was sure he'd made no sound – but then the hackles suddenly rose on his neck as he passed the last but one door and saw the cat staring back at him from the near darkness. Hackles raised, back hunched, as if it wasn't sure whether to lunge forward or shrink back.

He swiftly reached out and closed the door, all but the last inch; the sound of it touching home would carry.

He glided silently on, breath held, gently opened the library door and, again, left it open only an inch as he headed towards the leather seat at its far end, sat down and waited.

Four or five minutes until the call came through, he checked from his watch. They'd left more than enough leeway.

But it felt like a lifetime waiting in the silence of the big house, his own heartbeat almost in time with a ticking-clock in the hallway and, beyond that, the muted sound of pages turning. And when after a few minutes there were some stronger, closer sounds – it made him sit up sharply. Rustling, *scratching*. The cat was trying to paw its way out of the room!

Movement now too from across the hallway, her getting up to investigate. He slid the silenced .38 from his jacket. He might not even have to wait for the phone call.

A suspended moment, then the sound of the cat scampering across the hallway and her voice riding a sharp intake of breath.

'Majestic! It's only you. But stop sneaking around so will you, you gave me . . .'

The phone ringing only a few feet to his side sounded obscenely loud. He took his own intake of breath in anticipation and pointed his gun towards the door.

Lieutenant Coyne of NOPD's Sixth District didn't arrive on the scene until 2.44 a.m., over two hours after the first squad car arrived.

There were a few reasons for that. First, there'd been a reported 'major' incident on Magazine Street. Started as a simple fender-bender, but the Saturday night specials had quickly come out and first radio reports were that 'World War Three' had erupted. Two shop windows were smashed, a passer-by hit in the leg from the stray bullets, and, amazingly, one of the combatants took four bullets and still survived. Second, he didn't like to arrive on crime scenes too early, felt that it took a while for all the confusion and emotions to settle down and anything clear start to emerge. But in this case there was a third reason: when it came to big-shot or celebrity incidents, Coyne had often found the participants high-handed and difficult; and as shots went, they hardly came any bigger than Adelay Roche.

Hopefully Roche would have vented his worst – whether blubbering or barking that they should be out there chasing his wife's murderer rather than tramping his best shag-pile – on his assistant, DS Dave Friele, who he'd sent there within minutes of the radio alert coming through, while he stayed to finish things up on Magazine Street.

'Tell me,' was all he said to Friele as he slipped under the yellow tape across the front doorway.

'Homicide. Two .38 calibre wounds, one to the stomach, the other to the head – close range. Victim: Jessica Anne Roche, age thirty-two, married, no children.' Friele glanced at his notepad only once. 'Her husband, Adelay Roche, was first to discover her.'

'At what time?'

'Twelve twenty-six. Or, at least, that's the time logged for his 911 call.'

'And what estimated time for the shooting?'

'At least two hours beforehand, maybe more. Medics found no trace of warmth from her body, and rigor had already set in. Though obviously we'll know more from the full autopsy.'

'Obviously. But for now, it doesn't look like Mr Roche simply shot his wife, then waited half an hour before calling 911?'

'No, doesn't look like it.'

'And where *was* the illustrious Mr Roche tonight?'

'At a business dinner function.'

'Okay. First thing to check: time he arrived at the dinner, time he left . . .' They'd been edging down the hallway as Friele gave the details, and as the main drawing-room came into view with Adelay Roche at its far end, Coyne turned back to Friele. 'How's he been?' he asked, lowering his voice. 'Been ranting why aren't you out there on his wife's killer's trail rather than asking him stupid questions? Telling you that you're useless?'

'No. He's been pretty subdued as it happens. Still in shock, I suppose.'

Coyne looked thoughtfully at Roche. It wasn't a cold night, but he had a blanket draped over his shoulders while a uniformed officer spoke to him, getting fill-in details: neighbours' names, numbers he could be reached on, other relatives of his wife that would need to be informed. '. . . And would you like us to do that for you, sir?' Roche looked frail and shaken, answered stiltedly. *Real shock, or an act?*

Coyne smiled tightly as he turned back to Friele. 'Obviously that'll come when he gets to know you better. What else?'

'Sign of break-in at the side of the house – a window-pane removed and alarm wired through – which appears to support the MO of an intruder who was subsequently disturbed by Jessica Roche. Although the actual shooting took place in the library.'

By the pause, Coyne knew that it was meant to be significant. 'Any reason for that?'

'The safe's there. It looks like maybe he was casing it when he was disturbed.'

'But hadn't started to break it?'

'No.' Friele's gaze shifted to the open doorway two doors down on the opposite side, the muted sounds of somebody making dictaphone notes drifting through.

'Okay. Let's take a look at her.' Coyne had specifically asked that the body not be moved until he arrived.

Despite the many corpses Coyne had viewed through the years, it never got easier. One side of Jessica Roche's face, closest to where the bullet had exited, had half collapsed, her teeth and gums on that side exposed all the more and stained reddy-brown in a rictus grimace. The blood pools by her stomach and head had already congealed to a sticky brown film, the latter carrying faintly glistening fragments of skull and white brain matter. The smell of body waste was strong and pervasive, one disadvantage of the two-hour wait, and hit high in his synapses like an ammonia burst, making him dizzy for a second. He pulled the cover back over the body and straightened up.

He looked towards the forensics officer speaking into a palm-held recorder, now examining dusted patches on the desk; the safe and window-frame had already been done.

'Any joy on prints?'

The officer shook his head. 'Not by the looks of it. Probably wearing gloves. No tell-tale clusters on the window where he broke in, at least.'

'And ballistics?' Coyne addressed Friele. 'We got the two bullets?'

'They found one – the head shot.' Friele pointed. 'Deflected through and was found a foot away, embedded in the carpet. The stomach shot looks like it's still inside her, will have to be retrieved at autopsy.'

Coyne was halfway through a scan of the room, looking for anything significant or out of place, when some excitable voices and movement from the hallway broke his attention.

A patrolman slightly ahead of his side-kick leant into the library doorway. 'Lieutenant. Looks like we might have a witness. A woman a hundred yards down the street was out walking her dog, and saw a man leaving the Roches' house about the time of the shooting.'

Coyne followed the patrolman back along the hallway, and looked towards the woman standing by the three patrol cars beyond the taped-off front gate, their flashing lights reflecting starkly on her face. She'd obviously seen the squad car lights and drifted along to investigate.

'She get a good look at him?' Coyne asked.

'Not sure, sir. We thought it best to leave her for you to question.'

Coyne had interviewed the eyewitness, but her description was far from conclusive: African-American, stocky build, six foot to six-two, maybe more, thirty-plus, maybe forty, wearing a dark-blue or black jacket, maybe dark-grey or brown.

'The 'maybes' had concerned Coyne: her core description was vague enough, could fit ten per cent of African-American adult males, without stretching the boundaries further. And with sixty per cent of New Orleans African-American, they were a million miles from a 'workable suspect list', as Sixth District chief, Captain Vincent Campanelli, had demanded on day one of the investigation.

Pat Coyne looked thoughtfully towards his neatly tended garden beyond the small back verandah, as if it might give him clearer focus on the events of twelve years ago. Strange, he thought: often he could recall the events of that time clearer than things that had happened only months ago.

'Would she recognize him again, I asked . . . not sure, she said. I took that as a "No", but thought: if we narrowed down the list of possible suspects and got a few faces in front of her – we just might get lucky. So we started working things from the other end – putting together a list of house burglars with that MO.'

'Was Larry Durrant one of those on that list?'

'No. No, he wasn't. Mainly because his past MO hadn't been violent. We were looking at a particularly brutal killing "in the course of" here. Somebody who could kill without raising much sweat. We had half-a-dozen suspects who'd shot and wounded or beaten their targets half to death in past robberies, two that we suspected of killing but had never managed to nail – and two more who'd tied up and tortured their robbery victims. We were spoilt for choice without looking at the likes of Larry Durrant.'

'So were you surprised when his confession came in?'

'Purely on a MO level, yeah.' Coyne shrugged. 'But then everything else tied in: not only the jacket with the DNA match, but his descriptions of the murder itself. Things that only the killer could possibly have known – particularly the head shot.'

'Why was that?'

Coyne shrugged with a palm out. 'Okay, first off it was the one thing that might not fit in with a robbery-gone-wrong theory, more hit-man territory. But that's also why we held it back from any official releases, press or otherwise – so that we could filter out any false confessions. All we released was that Jessica Roche had been shot twice, apparently while disturbing an intruder. Most people would assume: sudden surprise, blam-blam from five paces, and out. And that's pretty much what came in.' Coyne smiled ingenuously. 'Celebrity murder like that, we actually expected more

– but there were six confessions in all. Three were white, one was way off the mark of the eyewitness description, and of course the other two we grilled like all hell. They got all manner of things wrong with internal descriptions of the house, but most tellingly neither of them mentioned the close-up head shot. The only one to describe that was Larry Durrant.'

Coyne was silent for a second, the only sound from a couple of bees hovering by a nearby azalea bush. The muted sounds of the city beyond like a more distant swarm.

'But we're getting a touch ahead of ourselves here,' he continued. 'Hand in hand with us narrowing down the general suspect list, we also took a closer look at Adelay Roche. My superior, Captain Campanelli, wasn't at all comfortable with that – felt we'd get all kinds of backlash from Roche. Word had it that he was pretty buddy–buddy with the Assistant Commissioner at the time. But it's standard procedure, you know, looking close to home. And Roche wasn't giving us any grief at that stage – which also struck me as somewhat strange, not running completely true to form.'

Coyne took a fresh breath. 'But after months of digging into Adelay Roche's background, we found nothing. No possible link to him killing his own wife, and, most importantly, no motive: no other woman, no arguments, no pressures or problems that anyone was aware of, and no big insurance policy on her – not that he'd need the cash. In fact everyone we spoke to said they seemed very much in love. And to cap it all, they were hopeful of soon having their first child. Mrs Roche was undergoing fertility treatment, with high chances of success, according to her doctor. Perhaps if her doctor had said that the fertility treatment hadn't gone well and there was no possible hope of future children . . . then we might have had the seed of something. Or lack of seed, in this case. The Henry the Eighth motive, I think it's known as.'

Coyne smiled dryly, but noticed that his visitor mirrored it only half-heartedly, as if the subject was too weighty for humour. Or perhaps because of what he'd mentioned when they first sat down to start talking.

'But even if I had gone to Campanelli with that, he'd no doubt have told me that I was being too much of a cynical prick – as often was his wont to do – and I was stretching things too far. Then just as the dust was settling on the Adelay Roche front, he did run more true to form and start screaming why weren't we making more progress in finding his wife's killer. Maybe it took him a while to get over the initial shock and become obnoxious again, who knows? Then just two weeks later, Durrant's confession landed in our laps.'

'And did you feel comfortable with it, you know – given your concerns about Durrant's MO?'

Coyne held out one palm. 'I had *some* reservations. But listening to Durrant's voice on tape, there was only one possible conclusion: he *had* to have been there. So either he was the killer, or a fly on the wall at the time. And when the DNA evidence came in, that sealed it.'

Coyne's visitor looked faintly crestfallen at that moment, perturbed. It took him a second to decide where to head next.

'And the eyewitness?'

'Incidental by that stage. All she was able to do was provide a general fit for Durrant's appearance, not an exact ID. Early on, we'd narrowed down our list of hard-hitting robbers to three possibles and put them in a line-up with five others, including two police officers. She was split between three of them – two suspects and a police officer. Which I suppose from a hundred yards away at night, is understandable. So we didn't want to push our luck with Durrant, otherwise the defence could have had a field day. But, by then, we didn't need to.'

His visitor glanced absently towards the garden for a second before bringing his attention back. 'And were there any other witnesses or others on the scene at the time that weren't mentioned in the police report? Perhaps, say, because they didn't come forward?'

'No, the lady with the dog was the only one. Or, at least, if anyone else was there, they weren't seen by her or any of the Roches' neighbours we questioned.' Coyne raised an eyebrow, was about to ask *why*, when his visitor leant forward and passed across three photos.

'This is someone in touch recently by e-mail, claiming that he was *there* at the time and so knows Durrant's innocent. Probably a hoaxer, or maybe even a friend of Durrant's – but you never know. Strike any chords?'

Coyne studied them, grimacing tightly after a moment. 'Can't say that they do – even if there was more to pull a match from here.' Coyne shrugged as he handed the photos back. 'But, like I say, doesn't become a factor here: nothing to match to. No other sightings. If there had been, they'd have been in the report.'

His visitor nodded, his gaze towards the garden this time seeming to stop in mid-space – as if something was hanging there he couldn't quite bring into focus – before he looked back at Coyne.

'Thanks for that, Mr Coyne. You've been most helpful.' He switched off the tape recorder and put the photos back in his briefcase.

'Perhaps my assistant, Dave Friele, will remember more,' Coyne said. 'He's still with the department, though now he's moved to Central – Eighth District. But that's about all of importance I can think of now, what with the passage of the years . . . Mr . . . Mr Langford.'

'Langfranc,' his visitor corrected. 'John Langfranc. It was meant to be my colleague, Jac McElroy, making this call today. But, as I say . . . with his accident . . . I . . . I've had to take things over from him.'

'Yes, I'm sorry to hear about that, Mr Langfranc.' Coyne grimaced tightly as he stood to show Langfranc out. 'But feel free to call me if there's anything else you need clarification on.'

20

'. . . *Shall I tell you about my life . . . they say I'm a man of the world . . . I've flown across every time . . . I've seen lots of pretty girls . . .*'

Rodriguez had phoned Jac's office and been put through to John Langfranc. 'We wanted to play somethin' for him here on the prison radio. Felt, yer know . . . that's the least we could do. Do you happen to know his favourite tune?'

Langfranc didn't, but he had a number for Jac's mother and sister. He'd phone them and ask, and phone Rodriguez straight back. Langfranc hadn't wanted to give their number to an inmate or get them involved in whatever prison relationships Jac might have forged.

Langfranc phoned back minutes later, having just spoken with Jean-Marie. There were four choices: Sting's 'Roxanne', Simply Red's 'Holding Back the Years', Oasis's 'Wonderwall' or Fleetwood Mac's 'Man of the World'.

'The last apparently because it was also his father's favourite song.'

Rodriguez could only find 'Roxanne' and 'Man of the World' in the prison record collection, and given his own rap-sheet history and Haveling's likely reaction to him playing a song about a hooker, there was only one choice left.

'. . . *Played today for Jac McElroy . . . one of those who took the time and trouble to care – because, God knows there's few enough o' them left these days – and paid the price for it . . .*'

More maudlin a song than Rodriguez would have liked, maybe more 'tired-drone' territory, but the words weren't too bad a fit, perhaps even would have described part of his own life . . . and he loved that guitar work, reminded him of his main man Carlos S . . .

With everything that had happened with Jac McElroy, Larry's emotions were already raw and close to the surface. He lay with his back flat on his bed listening to the song as it played, staring up at the grey ceiling. It had in fact been his suggestion to Rodriguez that they play something for McElroy.

He'd already prayed for him, even though he no longer had an altar: just a four by three foot upright board where his altar used to be, covering the fresh cement laid behind. But he'd used the board to pin-up the photos from his altar that meant something to him. Only five of the religious photos sent by Peretti's aunt from Perugia Cathedral, though, made the transfer, the majority were of Larry's family: his mother, father, Franny, Joshua. Most of all, Joshua.

Joshua a year ago, the most recent photo, standing with his mother at the side of a brown Buick, probably Frank's; Joshua blowing out the candles at his eighth birthday party; Joshua at five or six in front of Orlando's SeaWorld, again with his mom – Larry aware that often the person who'd snapped the photos had taken his place in their lives; Joshua at three years old, looking up from playing on the floor with some toys.

But the only photos to have any life and movement in them were the two taken shortly after Joshua's birth: one a week after Francine had come out of hospital, lovingly cradling Joshua in her arms; the other with himself holding Joshua aloft towards the camera, beaming proudly: 'Look, unbelievable, isn't it: he's mine, *all mine*.'

From just those two photos, Larry was able to roll out in his mind everything else that had happened around that time: when the birth was announced in the hospital, his mother bought a cigar and a small bottle of champagne from a nearby liquor store, a 'Benjamin' – she didn't want to encourage him to drink too much, she'd defended when he'd remarked about its size – barely gave them half a glass each to toast with. Rocking Joshua in his arms at every opportunity he got, staring down at his cradle at night in wonderment sometimes for as much as an hour, feeling Josh's tiny fingers and the gentle fall of his breath against the back of one hand; staying awake sometimes for hours and checking regularly, fearful as he listened out that that gentle breathing might have suddenly stopped; and when Joshua did wake up in the middle of the night, crying, Larry swaying him softly in his arms and humming a Viennese waltz to get him back to sleep – Francine laughing as on one occasion she found him slumped in a chair asleep with Joshua still in his arms, the humming having lulled both of them to sleep . . .

The images playing clearly on his cell's grey ceiling, where he'd played most of them through the years.

And then nothing. Nothing but static, frozen pictures. His whole life with Joshua condensed into just a few months, then nothing after that. Larry tried as best he could to shift those other images, give them some movement in his imagination – but he'd never managed to bring any life to them as they scrolled across the grey ceiling.

Only in his dreams sometimes could he imagine talking or playing ball or mock-sparring with Joshua as he was in those photos when he was older, hugging him now and then – and then he'd awake to the cold reality of his cell, a slow tear already at the corner of one eye, even before he faced again the cold, static photos and the tears began to flow more freely. All those lost years. *Gone.* Gone for ever.

He'd stare at the photos wide-eyed, as if trying to immerse himself in their world, his body not moving, only his breath slowly rising and falling as the tears streamed down his face. Immobile, static. Frozen. As if somehow if they were both in the same pose, frozen, he would feel closer to Joshua in that moment.

Static. And that's probably just how he in turn had seemed through the years to young Joshua. *The Stone Mountain.* A pitiful grey figure frozen inside his prison cell, with little colour or movement or life that Joshua could attach to it.

In all the years, he'd never told Joshua how much he loved him, Francine neither. Oh sure, he'd told his precious God how much he loved them, many a time . . . but in all their visits or his letters or e-mails with Joshua, he'd never said it directly. Just talked about day-to-day stuff. How are you? How are things at school? Basketball team, huh . . . New computer, that's nice . . . What are you reading these days? . . . Given a few tips where he could.

Arm's length. Holding at bay his deeper feelings. As if afraid that if he opened up, the dam would burst on the tidal wave of emotions he'd bottled up through the long years. Hold it back . . . hold back. Be strong . . . *be strong*.

And he'd been the same when Jac McElroy had visited: played his cards close to his chest, kept everything tight inside, guarded, given McElroy a hard time. Sure, McElroy had mainly just been doing his job, but as Roddy had said, he was one of the few that had actually taken the trouble to care, had stuck his neck out and gone that extra mile for him. And now . . . *and now* . . .

The tears welled heavily in Larry's eyes. Roddy hadn't told him which song he'd be playing, but as he heard the softly lamenting guitar riff and opening words, he found the tears impossible to bite back any longer. Was that how it would forever be set in stone for his – probably short – time on this earth? His epitaph? Never able to tell people how he truly felt . . . only his God. Holding back . . . *holding* . . .

And as Peter Green's soulful cry – '*I just wish I had never been born*' – cut through the cold concrete caverns of Libreville prison, finally the dam did burst: he cried for the lost years, cried for all the things that now he might not get the chance to say, cried for having let Franny and Josh down – deserting them just when they needed him most – cried for breaking his mother's heart, cried for Jessica Roche's long-gone soul . . . and now for Jac McElroy too. How many more? Maybe best that he was going soon . . . He cried and cried until it became a pitiful sobbing that racked his entire body.

Sudden rapping on the side wall, three sharp knocks, startled him.

'You okay in there, Larry?' Theo Mellor's voice from the next cell. 'You okay, man?'

'Yeah. Yeah.' He clawed back some composure, wiped some of the tears away with the back of one hand. 'Bad song choice, that's all. Real bad song choice.'

21

Grey. Everything grey.

Clogging his nose, his mouth, trickling down and burning his lungs.

At most, twenty-five seconds before he finally wrenched his leg free, but it felt like a lifetime, sapping him of strength and vital time to get to the top to burst free for air.

Then he was rising up, up . . . his lungs searing and aching with the pressure and about to explode. Faint, distant light now touched the grey . . . how much further? Twenty feet, thirty?

His lungs finally gave just over halfway up, the water bursting down his gullet – and as the sunlight hitting the lake surface cut through the last of the grey, making him squint, his consciousness in turn started to dim, dragging him back into grey again. Then finally black.

He recalled briefly some voices, though had no idea how long after.

'I thought I saw him move a little.'

'Nah . . . he's not moving. He's dead.'

And he thought: I'm not dead. I can hear you. And he could also feel a soft breeze from the lake hitting one cheek just before hands started pressing hard at his stomach, pumping.

But the second voice was right, he realized, must have seen that he was a hopeless case, because once again the grey started dragging him back down, back towards the black.

There was a strange dream at some stage later; a dream that tried to fool him that maybe he'd made it and was still alive. His last subconscious bid not to accept that he'd actually died.

He was lying in a bed – whether at home or a hospital, he couldn't tell, because everything was whited out and indistinct. And Alaysha was leaning over and hugging and kissing him.

'Oh, Jac . . . *Jac*. You had us all so worried.'

The softness and warmth and perfume of her felt so good it made him ache and want to cry. And his mother and Jean-Marie were also there – got to meet and talk to Alaysha for the first time. John Langfranc, too, and even his occasional squash partner, Jeff Coombs . . . all of them smiling, nodding, talking . . . telling him how good it was to see him.

It was like that closing scene in *A Wonderful Life*, where half the town turn out to greet Jimmy Stewart and tell him how good it is to see him alive. Except that in this case, Jac knew that he was dead, because he could see his father hanging in the shadows at the back of the room; and then the grey was there again, dragging him back down . . .

Clogging his nose, his mouth . . . deeper into the blackness . . . away from the light at the top of the lake . . .

'Jac . . . *Jac*!'

Alaysha kissing him again, but this time he pushed her away . . . no . . . *no*! I've already had that dream. Don't tease me like this!

'Jac . . . *Jac*. Wake up . . . *wake up*!'

Struggling against her as she shook him harder . . . but unable to resist the blackness this time, feeling himself dragged deeper and deeper into it . . . the water again rushing into his mouth, black and thick with mud . . . filling his gullet, his lungs, stifling, *suffocating* . . .

'No . . . no . . . *no*!'

His scream was still reverberating in the room as he sat up, his body soaked with sweat. He was trembling violently and felt suddenly cold.

Eyes blinking, adjusting, looking around to get his bearings. Salmon pink and beige. Alaysha's bedroom.

She leant over and kissed him once more, one hand lingering on his shoulder as she pulled back, eyeing him concernedly.

'Bad dream again?'

'Yes . . . *yes*.' He eased a tired sigh and smiled crookedly. 'Unless I'm dead and this is the dream.'

Then, as he shook the last of the nightmare away, everything that had happened in the ten days he'd been away from the world flooded back in.

He was seen surfacing from the lake by the occupants of two cars passing on the Causeway, and was pulled from the water within minutes by one of them brave enough to take the plunge.

Four more cars stopped as the drama unfolded, and thankfully one of their drivers had basic First Aid experience – going through the resuscitation process for the first time with a real-life case.

A lot of water was coughed up, apparently, shallow breathing resumed and a weak pulse was finally felt, but Jac was still unconscious, and remained so – despite medics giving him oxygen and a shot of adrenalin in his drip feed on the way to the hospital – for the next nine hours.

There was some residual water on his lungs, which was duly drained, one badly bruised and cut leg was stitched and strapped and a scan of his brain carried out – no signs of problems there – and when Jac finally awoke, he felt as right as rain and was in good spirits, as if nothing had happened, and his visitors, who'd so far been kept at bay waiting anxiously between the coffee room and corridor outside were finally allowed in to see him.

His mum, Jean-Marie, Alaysha, John Langfranc, Jeff Coombs – just as in the dream, except for his father, and not all at the same time.

His assigned consultant talked about releasing him in only a couple of days. 'Just need to run a few more tests, some fresh strapping on that leg and let you rest a bit more – then you should be fine to go home.'

But the night before he was due to leave hospital, his

temperature rocketed to 102°F. Further tests ensued, this time considerably more frantic.

A lung infection was discovered, presumably from the lake water, but it had already entered his bloodstream. Septicaemia had set in.

The greyness was again dragging Jac back towards the black void, as for the next four days Jac hovered close to death.

Alaysha stayed with Jac's mother and Jean-Marie in the corridor outside his room for most of that time, didn't go to work and had her mom take care of Molly. Jac's mother found a church two blocks away where she lit a candle for him and prayed. There were prayers too from Larry Durrant inside Libreville, and Rodriguez had even played a song for him over the prison radio.

All of which Jac was brought up to date on when he finally emerged from the grey abyss, bringing a wry – albeit weak – smile to his face.

Four more days for more tests and for him to regain his strength, he was told.

But the first thing Jac thought about then was Durrant: six days already lost, now another four on top! *Twenty-one days left till Durrant's execution.*

John Langfranc had already reassured him about the clemency petition.

'Don't worry. I got everything necessary off your computer, put all the file attachments with it, and went out to Libreville and got Durrant to sign it. It's gone off already – copies to both Candaret and the Board of Pardons.'

When Jac voiced his concern about the extra four-day wait, Langfranc again offered to help.

'I can interview Coyne or Friele and put it on tape for you – at least get *something* rolling on that front. Hopefully you'll be able to pick up the ball from there.'

Jac had played the tape countless times during his last days in the hospital, as well as gone through again his earlier notes and the original trial and appeal files. So, that head shot and Durrant's past MO had initially struck Coyne as out of place.

But everything else from Coyne – the eyewitness, Durrant's descriptions of the house and the murder further bolstered by that final head shot being held back from all press releases, the blood spots on his jacket matched to Jessica Roche's DNA – piled irrevocably against Durrant.

Jac felt weak, his strength sapped. Not just from the accident and his illness, but with what he now faced with Durrant. He'd just fought his way out of one grey abyss, yet just how he was going to fight his way through this daunting ocean of proof against Durrant, he didn't know.

'I know this isn't the best time to bring this up,' Alaysha said. 'But you know that warning letter we talked about having sent to Gerry?' She sighed and rested her hands in her lap. 'I think it would be a good idea to now send it.'

When Alaysha had first mentioned likely problems with her ex, Jac had suggested sending an initial warning letter on the firm's letter-heading; then, if that didn't work, they'd go the whole hog and get a restraining order.

'I know you said he'd been phoning you.' Jac arched an eyebrow. 'But has he been round here at your door, too?'

Alaysha closed her eyes for a second and eased out a sigh of submission. 'Yes. *Yes* . . . he has. I didn't want to say anything before while you were ill.'

Jac nodded pensively. 'Was it bad?'

'No, I . . . I . . .' Alaysha's eyes flickered briefly shut again. '*Yes* . . . it was. He came round a couple of days before you came out of hospital, banging and shouting, and I told him to stop: Molly was home and he was frightening her. He kept shouting a while more, then finally calmed, saying he had a jacket of mine I'd left at his place a few weeks back. He'd come to give it back. I checked through the spy-hole, and, sure enough, I could see it in his hand – so I said, okay, but I was leaving the door on the chain. He wasn't coming in.

He seemed fine with that, just nodded numbly, as if all the fight had gone out of him. "Okay, babe, *okay* . . . I understand," he says.' Alaysha shook her head, her eyes shutting heavier this time as the memory of what happened played against the back of her eyelids. She bit at her bottom lip as she opened her eyes again, as if still fearful of what they might see. 'Then as soon . . . *as soon* . . .'

Jac reached out and gently touched her arm, consoling. 'That's okay . . . don't worry. I'll . . . I'll get the letter sent off as soon as I get to the office.'

'Thanks, Jac. I appreciate it.' She swallowed hard, shaking off the last of the images. 'You know, I thought he was going to rip the chain right off the door. I . . . I don't know how I managed to shut it again.' She glanced back briefly towards the door again, as if it still might suddenly burst open. Then she looked down uncertainly; something was still troubling her.

'What *is it*?' Jac asked.

'Unfortunately it . . . it didn't end there.'

Jac's concern gripped like a stomach cramp. His hand, laid lightly on her arm, pressed gently. 'What happened, Alaysha . . . what happened?'

'He came by the club the night after, making a scene.' The shadows in her eyes shifted hesitantly as she forced a tight smile. 'But, thankfully, the security at the club's good. They made quick work of getting rid of him.'

'Thankfully.' Jac felt his jaw tighten. But what was going to happen when next time he tried and there was no security or a chained door between them? 'I suppose if all else fails, there's always one way of handling Gerry.' Jac held a fist up.

'Oh?' Alaysha eyed him curiously.

'Young kid doesn't last long on the streets of Glasgow without learning to use these. And my father always kept a boxing bag at our Rochefort farmhouse – said that it was one of the best ways to keep fit.'

Alaysha gave another quick, tight smile, unsure whether

Jac was serious or if it was just bravado to make her feel more secure.

Jac wasn't sure either. He'd spent the first night out of the hospital at her place, for various reasons: he had no fresh food at his place, he was still weak, and Alaysha commented with a sly smile that she wanted to 'nurse him a bit'.

Their relationship had changed markedly while he'd been in the hospital, without much actually happening between them. Not only because he'd seen how much she seemed to care about him, belying the short time they'd been involved – but so had his mother and Jean-Marie, from witnessing Alaysha's vigil at the hospital and talking with her there. He'd begged both of them not to say anything about Alaysha to Aunt Camille. 'She probably thinks I'm still going out with Jennifer Bromwell, courtesy of Jennifer's parents. It's a long story – I'll tell you later.' But he decided to wait a while before telling them that Alaysha lap-danced. From what she'd told them, they appeared to think she did interior decorating and 'some modelling'.

He'd also finally met Molly. Almost as if Alaysha kept Molly away at her mom's while any new boyfriends visited, until they'd passed the initial acid test. Alaysha had brought Molly with her on her last visit to the hospital and introduced them, and Molly was there at Alaysha's when Jac first came out: 'Are you okay now?' she enquired. He couldn't help smiling, her soft, high tone attempting to be adult and grave. 'Yes, fine . . . *fine.*' He put one hand lightly on Molly's shoulder as he knelt down to her height. 'And you?' Fine too, she said; then he spent the next half hour on his knees as she led him through the fantasy world of her dolls and informed him who hadn't been fine recently amongst them.

Alaysha touched his cheek with the back of one hand. 'It's so good to have you back, Jac . . . *so good.*'

'For me too.' He closed his eyes at her touch. He could feel them getting closer, and wanted so much for it to work. But he'd seen those shadows in her eyes when she'd described

247

Gerry trying to break her door down and visiting the club. Just what baptism of fire might their relationship have to endure to finally be rid of him?

Alaysha stroked her fingers gently across Jac's cheek and back through his hair before taking her hand away. There was something else Gerry had said while at her door that had sent a chill through her, but that was the last thing she'd want to tell Jac about. After all, that was the whole point of this lawyer's letter now: hopefully finally closing the book on her past life with Gerry and what she'd done with him.

She swallowed, took a fresh breath. 'When are you supposed to be hearing from the police?'

'Tomorrow or the latest the day after, they said.' Shadows in *his* eyes: knowing finally if his car, dragged up from Lake Pontchartrain, had been tampered with. He put one arm around Alaysha and gave her a reassuring hug. 'And when Gerry gets this letter – let's just hope he gets the message and leaves you be.'

'Let's hope so.'

But Jac could see from her tight smile that she was as unconvinced as him.

Rodriguez felt in fine form this morning.

Jac McElroy had made it, the sun was breaking through a thin cloud cover, and the air was clear and crisp. Rodriguez inhaled deeply as he sauntered across the exercise yard. One of the first times the air had been crisp for a long while – Rodriguez liked this time of year. The temperature inside the prison was bearable for once, and hopefully would remain so for the next few months.

Rodriguez fired a quick fake-cap acknowledgement to BC and Larry lifting weights on the far side of the yard. BC was by far the keenest muscle-freak in their little circle, in the yard practically every day. Larry, Theo Mellor and Gill Arneck trained-up at most twice a week, and himself and Peretti, never.

'Hey, you wanna try this som' time, Roddy,' BC called out as he approached. 'Your arms are startin' to look like strands of spaghetti.'

'Nah. Might give myself an injury.' Roddy made a mock grab at his crotch. 'Would ruin my wild sex life here.'

BC shook his head and smiled. 'You know, Roddy, at times you're such a pussy.'

'Yeah, well.' Roddy shrugged amiably. 'Like they say – you are what you eat.'

BC and Larry laughed out loud, bringing a glare from Tally Shavell, six yards away at the other end of the muscle yard with Jay-T and another crew brother – the separation between them obvious, nobody else daring to go into that electrified no man's land.

Rodriguez gave them a guarded sideways glance, and signalled to Larry with a small nod of his head that he wanted to talk: they should move further away from Tally and his crew. They sidled five yards away so that even BC would have trouble overhearing them, but Rodriguez kept his voice low in case.

'Just got an e-mail in from Jac.' Having almost lost his life trying to help Larry, suddenly he was 'Jac' instead of Mr McElroy; one of them. 'As you know, his side-kick Langfranc filed last week with the BOP and Candaret, and part of that, Jac reminded me, was talkin' about your literary expertise. He'd like to send a couple o' the books you edited to back that up, if that's okay?'

'*Edit's* a bit strong a term. All I did was make some comments in the margin and change some words where I felt the same one had been used too much.' Larry shrugged. 'But sure, that's okay.'

'He expects Candaret to finally spill forth in about two weeks. But apparently the Board of Pardons will haul your ass in front of 'em four or five days before that. So they'll be the first you'll hear from.'

Larry arched an eyebrow. 'What the hell will they expect

from me? Show I'm a literary buff by quoting from Poe and Shakespeare?'

'Yeah . . . yeah. "Justice . . . *justice*! Where for art thou, justice?"' Rodriguez's smile faded quickly as he looked levelly at Larry. 'No, I think it's mainly to fin' out if you're a reasonable, balanced guy. Reformed character and all that shit. So don't be your normal indolent, uncooperative self. Okay?'

'I'll try.' Larry smiled lazily.

22

I desperately need you to tell me more to be able to do anything with your communication. As it stands, it could be from anyone: a hoaxer, a friend of Durrant's . . . I can't even begin to put it in front of the DA or Governor. If you can't give your name for some reason, then we can talk about protection and anonymity. You can also feel safe in initially sharing that information with me under client discretion. If you are serious about helping Larry Durrant, then please come forward. And at the same time I'll do everything I possibly can to help you.

Jac gave the e-mail one last read through, then pressed SEND.

He'd felt increasingly uneasy just leaving everything on that final, flawed note with his mystery e-mailer: very likely spooked and so no further contact. And when the night before he'd shared his thoughts with Alaysha, finally told her the whole saga, she'd urged him on.

'Don't just give up with him there, Jac. Keep pushing, send him more e-mails, try and draw him out. If he *is* real, he must have a conscience to have made contact in the first place. Remember that, try and play on that.'

Jac had nodded a slow acceptance, her words in that moment seeming *so* right. But now, having sent the e-mail, he wondered whether it wasn't just a desperate need to keep things rolling positively on at least *one* front.

Four calls he'd put in to Truelle's office, leaving messages, before he finally got a call back. Now there was a further forty-two hour delay – early the day after tomorrow – before he'd actually be able to see him.

'Sorry. That's the earliest, I'm afraid. I'm up to my neck with things – that's why the delay in getting back to you.'

And Dr Thallerey, Jessica Roche's old obstetrician, was away at a medical convention in Houston till the end of the week.

'He doesn't like to be disturbed at these things, so we have strict instructions not to do so unless it's an absolute medical emergency. Does it fall into that category, sir?'

'No . . . no. It's okay, I'll contact him when he gets back.'

Jac felt the clock ticking down against Durrant like a tight coil at the back of his neck.

Superficially he looked fine after his accident, except for a slight limp in his right leg. A thigh gash had taken fourteen stitches and his calf muscles had been heavily bruised, probably from when he wrenched his leg free. The doctor said that within a week it should have healed enough for the limp to subside; but what was going on inside Jac's head was another matter.

Now that the clemency plea had been filed, he was back assisting John Langfranc with other cases and was meant to spend no more than four man-hours a week on the Durrant case, for what Beaton described as 'residual maintenance'. But Jac found it hard to concentrate on the fresh files before him, and more than a few times he'd noticed John Langfranc look up at him through his glass screen: a searching appraisal that hadn't yet fully verged into concern; *yet*.

Sometimes, when Jac tried to focus, the words would swim and merge and become little more than a blur; a grey blur that seemed to draw him in, becoming deeper, darker as he sank through it . . . and suddenly he'd back in the lake again, lungs bursting, *choking for air* . . .

Jac's line buzzing broke his thoughts.

'Lieutenant Wallace for you,' Penny Vance called across the office.

'Thanks.' Jac swallowed and took a fresh breath, noticing John Langfranc look through his glass screen as he picked up: the police mechanic's report on his car dragged up from Lake Pontchartrain! Jac's brow knitted as he tried to disentangle

Wallace's description of brake fluid pressures and condition of joint threads. 'What exactly does all of that mean?'

Wallace took a fresh breath. 'It means that the findings are inconclusive. But if we had to put money on something – it'd be on it being caused by a fault or wear and tear rather than on tampering. Otherwise the thread on the brake fluid joint would have been clean and in perfect condition. It wasn't – the thread had shorn off.'

'I see.' Jac knew that he should have been relieved, but that emotion still felt out of reach, along with any clarity on Wallace's account. All he felt was numb.

'Perhaps the joint simply got weakened with time and wear and tear – then with the sudden jolt of you braking hard, it sheared off.'

'But what about that truck alongside swinging in? And the fact that he didn't stop?'

'I know. But it might have been a driver simply distracted or falling asleep, rather than purposeful. And once he'd straightened up, he'd have been past you by then. Might well not have seen what happened to you.'

'Yeah. Possibility, I suppose.' Jac sighed resignedly. Might, might, might. He wasn't convinced. Langfranc came out of his office as Jac thanked Wallace and signed off.

'Accident,' Jac said, looking towards Langfranc. 'Doesn't look like brake tampering. At least, that's what he's putting the money on.'

'Well, that's a relief.'

'Yeah.' Jac nodded dolefully. 'That's a relief.'

Schlish . . . schlap . . . schlish . . . schlap . . . schlish . . . schlap . . .
The monotony of the windscreen wipers was starting to wear on Dr Thallerey, might have got close to sending him to sleep, if he hadn't stopped just forty minutes back for a strong fresh coffee and popped a Ritalin straight after.

He'd decided to drive, because since 9/11 he just couldn't abide airports any more. One-and-half to two hours before check in, with invariably more delays on top. By the time he'd sat for three hours bored mindless at an airport, he could be halfway there in his car.

He tried to keep to 55 mph, but invariably he'd edge up to sixty on clear, flat stretches. Two hours more, and he'd be home.

Schlish . . . schlap . . . schlish . . . schlap . . .

Thallerey peered through the intermittent film of water on his windscreen at the murky road ahead. A quarter moon was there somewhere, drifting in and out of heavy cloud cover. His squint suddenly widened, hands gripping tighter to the wheel, as out of nowhere – not there in one sweep of the wipers, there in the next – red tail lights loomed ahead and he had to brake sharply.

Thallerey's speedo plummeted. He glanced at it as it bottomed out: twenty-two miles an hour! *Ridiculous!* He edged out. A large double-trailer truck, he'd need a clear, straight stretch to get past it.

They followed a long, slow bend, seeming to take for ever, and as they straightened out Thallerey peered through the gloom at a clear stretch illuminated in his headlamps, no curves for at least a couple of hundred yards. He swung out and floored it.

Forty . . . *fifty* . . . he should be past it soon. Longer than he thought . . . a lot longer. It struck him that he wasn't making much progress past it; the truck had at the same time picked up speed. He pushed the pedal harder – fifty-five . . . sixty . . . the curve in the road still a good hundred yards away.

Yet still he gained only a few yards, appeared to be in much the same position alongside it, just past the coupling for the rear trailer – which meant that it must now be doing the same speed. *Sixty.* Deciding that he wasn't going to make it past, Thallerey eased off the pedal and braked to cut back in – when a sudden blast of lights flooded him from behind.

Headlamps full beam, now a top searchlight switched on

as well. Looked like a big four-wheeler, but hard to make out fully beyond the glare. It had obviously swung out to overtake following him, and was now showing full lights as if to say: *go on, go on . . . get past it!*

He hesitated for a second whether to go for it, but then saw that the bend in the road was only forty yards ahead. He beeped his horn and hit his brakes again to pull back in behind the truck. But the truck also seemed to slow alongside him, and now the lights behind were even closer, only yards from his back bumper.

He felt his chest tighten, beads of sweat starting to break on his forehead. They had him jammed in! He braked and beeped his horn twice again – but still no give. The truck in turn also slowed, and the four-wheeler beeped back: still jammed tight behind, its headlamps flooding his car.

Then, as if the driver had a sudden change of thought, the four-wheeler pulled sharply back and tucked in behind the trailer-truck. In that split second Thallerey was disorientated – his car still seemed to be floodlit – wrenching his eyes from his rear-view mirror to the road ahead as it hit him just why the four-wheeler had cut back in so quickly: an oncoming trailer-truck suddenly, startlingly clear in the upward sweep of his wipers, bearing down on him. *Fast.*

At least he'd now also be able to tuck in behind the truck, he reckoned, braking hard. But again it braked to hold him there; and there was one difference between his braking and the truck's, perhaps because in his panic he'd braked that much harder: his wheels locked and his car started to slew on the wet road.

His last hope, as he squinted against the dazzling white of the oncoming headlamps and every nerve-end tightened and froze the breath in his throat, was that the oncoming truck, seeing him blocking the road, would brake and stop in time.

But it didn't. It just kept going at the same speed, shunting the front of his car straight through him.

*

'Yeah, okay babe. *Yeah*. Another one.'

Nel-M tucked a twenty-dollar bill into the girl's thigh garter as elegantly, defying her near-nudity – garters, stockings and cobalt blue high-heels were all she wore – she lifted her leg alongside his chair.

Coffee skin with a touch of au-lait, eyes almost matching – pale toffee with green flecks – full lips, a teasing slant at the corner of her eyes, chestnut brown hair in ringlets breaking on the curve of her breasts, and a bubble-butt to die for. Up close she was even better than viewed from a hundred yards through a car windscreen, Nel-M considered. Far better. Especially with her clothes off.

Nel-M had remembered why the girl struck a chord, where he'd seen her before: Mike 'Miko' Ortega's 'Pinkies' club.

Miko managed four lap-dancing clubs on behalf of Carmen Malastra: three in New Orleans and one in Baton Rouge, of which Pinkies was his latest addition. Miko and Nel-M went back twenty years, to the days when they both worked together providing club security muscle, and he'd called in on Miko not long after Pinkies first opened.

Three years ago now, the girl hadn't been there then. But Nel-M had reason to visit again eleven months back when Roche wanted to put the squeeze on a planning officer obstructing his application for a new refinery. They had discovered that he was an on and off visitor to Pinkies, and a few steamy photographs landing in his wife's lap would be none too handy. The only problem was that no photography was allowed inside the club; unless, that is, you first cleared it with Miko and slipped him a G sweetener.

That was when Nel-M had first seen the girl.

Nel-M swallowed, his mouth suddenly dry, as she bent down inches from him, parting her legs and looking back at him for a second before swinging round and, from a half-squat, her breasts only inches from his lap, slowly rose again, swaying as she went.

'Love Hangover' played, more his generation. He would

like to have recalled dancing to it, but more likely than not he and his wife would have been shouting at each other above it in some disco or other, or Miko and him would have been in a club side-alley pounding some drunk they'd just ejected in time with its beat.

'Okay?' the girl mouthed, mostly lost in the music, turning it into a wet pout as she half closed her eyes in abandon.

Oh God, she was good. Nel-M nodded back with a satiated smile, in turn half-closing his own eyes as he felt a wave of sensations he'd rather not have – especially with what he might soon have to do to her – wash over him.

Halfway through her first dance for him, he'd asked her name just to make sure.

She'd leant over so that she was heard above the music, her mouth close to his ear.

'Alaysha.'

Sounded like the gentle swish of surf on a tropical beach, thought Nel-M, hot breath on his ear and her closeness sending a tingle through his body.

No question, it would be a shame to have to kill her

He paid her for one more dance, then went over to the bar to talk to Miko.

'Any chance with her for an old fool like me, do you reckon?' Nel-M said it jovially, as if he was only half-serious.

'Nah. Missed the boat there. She just hitched with a new guy. Though you might have stood a chance while she was still going out with the last crazy guy.'

'Crazy?'

'Yeah. Real schizo. Pushing her around an' all sorts.' Miko shook his head. 'Even came by the club here just last week, making a scene.'

'Oh?'

Miko didn't take well to people making a scene in his club, let alone boyfriends of his dancers, so he'd made sure to find out all he could about Alaysha's ex from a couple of the other girls.

Nel-M made out that he was only mildly interested, but he committed the key details firmly to memory: Gerry Strelloff. Assistant Bar Manager. Golden Bay Casino. Biloxi.

Nel-M checked his watch.

'Staying long tonight?' Miko enquired.

'No, gotta move soon. Maybe just one more dance.'

But he never got to it. Alaysha was tied up with another client, and he was deliberating whether to ask another girl for a dance – maybe best that he didn't get *too* close to Alaysha – when the call he was expecting came through.

He escaped the noise of the club to take it, waving a quick goodbye to Miko.

'All done,' the voice at the other end confirmed.

'But sure this time?' Nel-M pressed. 'A hundred per cent sure?'

'Yeah. The impact cut him in half. They're still scraping bits of him into plastic bags.'

'And clean too, I hope? If you'll excuse the oxymoron.'

'Absolutely. Three firm witnesses: the two truck drivers and yours truly in the Bronco, all saying the same thing: he swung out without warning, didn't give the oncoming truck a chance of stopping.'

23

'*. . . And her eyes . . . her eyes.*'

'*What about her eyes, Lawrence?*'

'*She looked up at me then, just before I . . . I . . .*' Durrant swallowing hard, his breathing uneven on the tape. '*And, uh . . . the damnest thing was, I couldn't tell if she was angry with me, or was saying thank you for putting her out of her pain. But it stayed with me, you know, that look . . . I found it hard to shift from my mind as I ran out.*'

As Durrant described fleeing and seeing a woman a hundred yards away walking her dog, Jac realized that absolutely everything on tape matched the physical evidence of Jessica Roche's murder: the shot to the head, the telephone ringing, the witness. The only odd thing was that Durrant never actually described pulling the trigger either time; the gun was there and the blood and pain was described, but Durrant had skipped over the instant of actually pulling the trigger, as if it was too traumatic for him to fully face.

'That's it,' Truelle commented, stopping the tape. 'I brought Durrant back out at that point and the session ended.'

Jac brought his focus back to Truelle across the desk.

'*. . . I'm sorry. Dr Thallerey died last night in a car accident. We're still all in shock here from the news . . .*'

Jac wished now that he hadn't made the call; at least, not just before his meeting with Truelle. He'd had half an hour spare before leaving to see Truelle, and he remembered that Dr Thallerey was due back from Houston the night before. The news sapped him of all strength, left his legs weak. Worst of all, it numbed his thoughts. And so he'd asked Truelle to play the remainder of the crucial tape with Durrant at the Roche residence. 'After Durrant's made the first shot. I've

259

already heard up to that point.' While it played he'd get some breathing space to hopefully clear his thoughts.

Truelle had heavily thinning sandy brown hair, and looked worn, tired, with heavy bags under his eyes, as if he'd taken much of the woe of his patients on board personally. The word 'seedy' might have sprung to mind, except that he had a faint tan and his dress was quite dapper, with a navy polo-neck and burgundy corduroy jacket with leather elbow patches that screamed academia or doctor.

Jac sensed an edginess beneath Truelle's tight, ingratiating smile and professional patina, though perhaps no more than warranted by the adversarial nature of their meeting: Truelle had spoken for the prosecution and Jac represented defence.

But as the tape had played, rather than Jac's thoughts about Thallerey's accident settling, they'd gained momentum: surely too much of a coincidence, his and Thallerey's accidents so close together? But why on earth was Dr Thallerey seen as a threat? And by whom? After all, he was only Jessica Roche's obstetrician.

Jac swallowed, cleared his throat. 'And that was the four-teenth session with Durrant?'

'Yes.'

'And how many sessions with hypnosis had there been by then?'

Truelle considered for a second. 'That was the sixth, I believe. Fifth or sixth. We had eight or nine conventional sessions before deciding to try hypnosis in order to dig deeper.'

'Presumably because you didn't feel you were getting that far with conventional sessions?'

'Exactly.' Truelle's hands on his desktop, fingertips pressed together in a cradle, parted for a second. 'Don't get me wrong. There was *some* progress conventionally. But I just felt that if he proved a good subject, we'd make progress ten-times faster with hypnosis.' The hands opened and closed again. 'He was, and we did.'

'I see.' Jac looked briefly at the notes he'd made earlier. 'How often were the sessions?'

'Twice a week, normally. Every Monday and Thursday. Except for a couple of weeks where I could only see him once because I had such a busy appointment book.'

Jac nodded. He doubted that under normal circumstances Truelle would have recalled the days that far back; but having to repeat the same thing at both the trial and appeal three years later, it had no doubt become ingrained. Jac nodded towards the tape recorder.

'And this session, number fourteen, was the last you had with Durrant? You contacted the police straight after?'

Truelle shuffled slightly in his seat. 'Not immediately after. I wanted a short while to think over the implications, ethics of confidentiality in particular.' Truelle forced a tight smile. 'So first thing I did was cancel Durrant's next session to give me some time to consider. But when I checked, confidentiality didn't stretch as far as a murder confession. In fact, if I'd withheld the information – I could have been implicated as an accessory.' Truelle opened and closed the cradle again. Trapped within it. 'So in the end I had little choice. But, for that reason, there was a two-day delay from Durrant making the confession to my contacting the police.'

Jac rubbed his forehead. If it wasn't for his earlier notes, he'd have had trouble continuing. But he found it hard to push his focus beyond them, as he'd planned when he first made them: thoughts about Thallerey kept bouncing back, crowding out all else. *If both crashes weren't just accidents, how had whoever was responsible made the connection between him and Thallerey?* Thallerey's name had only come up when John Langfranc interviewed Coyne. And as far as Jac could remember, he himself hadn't mentioned planning to visit Thallerey to anyone; in fact, he'd only phoned once to Thallerey's office just before he went back into work that first day back.

'So, fourteen sessions over two months?' Jac confirmed. 'All recorded and with diary entries to match?'

261

'Yes, that's right.' Truelle took the tape out of the recorder, and Jac caught the heavy scent of cologne, along with something else. *Peppermint*? 'The trial judge ordered that I keep everything relating to Durrant until all possible appeals and pleas were exhausted. Which I suppose would include this plea now.' Truelle's smile this time was more hesitant, his cheeks slightly flushed. Reminder perhaps of Durrant's life hanging in the balance with what they were discussing. Truelle cleared his throat. 'Is there anything at this stage that might have given you cause for concern regarding the evidence against Durrant?'

'No. Not particularly.' Jac contemplated Truelle coolly. From the transcripts, Truelle had been given a hammering at trial and appeal over both the reliability of hypnosis and the ethics of revealing the tape. Despite any residual concern Truelle might have for Durrant, he was obviously more concerned that his reputation might again be brought into question. 'Except, that is, whether it's right to execute a man whose mind is still only half-clear regarding what he was doing around that time.'

'Yes, I can appreciate that.' Truelle swallowed, his flush becoming deeper. 'But apart from that, nothing particularly untoward?'

'No. Nothing untoward.' From Truelle's expression, it was obvious he'd had *some* stabs of conscience about Durrant over the years. Jac eased back. After the grilling at both trials, little point in putting him through it again now; especially if he might later need his co-operation in answering more questions. Jac shrugged. 'Durrant has some doubts in his own mind about his guilt, mainly because of some promises he made to his family at the time. But that on its own isn't really sufficient to –'

Telephone! The thought hit Jac in that instant like a thunderbolt.

He'd called Thallerey from his home telephone that first morning, and been told at the time that he was away till later in the week at a medical convention. That's how they'd made the link and knew that he was keen to see Thallerey, plus also found out where Thallerey was! The other call he'd made at that same time had been to Truelle.

Truelle, the desk, and the room beyond suddenly seemed more distant, Jac's ears ringing with the sudden blood-rush to his head. Truelle was eyeing him curiously.

Jac blinked slowly as he fought to regain some clarity.

'I'm sorry. I . . . I know this might seem a strange question. But has there been any interference with your phones recently – either here or at your home? Someone perhaps listening in?'

'No, I . . . I don't believe so.'

Slight hesitation from Truelle. Fazed by the sudden change of direction, or something else at the back of his mind? Jac pressed him again. 'Or anything that's happened with your car recently that might have looked like an accident on the face of it, or come close to it? Or any other incident where you feel your life might have been put in danger?'

'Why? In what way?'

As crazy as Jac knew he risked sounding, he felt he had to say something. If they'd monitored and targeted himself, they might well have done the same with others; which meant Truelle could be next. With a fresh breath, he explained about his recent encounter with a truck, his brakes failing and his car plunging into Lake Pontchartrain.

'I was lucky to escape alive,' Jac said. Truelle's face had clouded, his hands now clenched tight together. Jac shrugged, as if to make light of it. 'The police say that it was an accident, natural failure – though I have strong doubts. And with the call I made just before coming here, in which I learnt that Dr Thallerey died last night, also in a car accident – I now believe I was right to have those doubts.'

Truelle looked perplexed, struggling to make sense of what Jac was saying, and, as he asked who Dr Thallerey was and got Jac's answer, he in turn blinked slowly, heavily. No doubt thinking along similar lines: why on earth would anyone kill Jessica Roche's old obstetrician?

'I . . . I don't see,' Truelle said, gesturing once more with his hands.

'Me neither, as to why.' Jac shrugged. 'All I know is that I phoned to arrange to see Dr Thallerey – then the next day he was dead. And the other person I phoned that same morning was yourself, Dr Truelle.'

Jac saw it hit Truelle then, saw him flinch; but it was almost as if it was a blow he'd been half-prepared for. He looked anxious more than surprised.

'And you . . . you think that I might be next?' Truelle's voice was tremulous, his attempt at a weak smile lopsided.

'Of course, it might all be just coincidence.' Jac grimaced tautly. 'But it would have been remiss of me not to say anything. Though obviously I'll know more once I've –'

Jac stopped himself then, struck as to just why Truelle might not have at the same time been targeted. Or at least *one* good reason why.

And suddenly some of Truelle's words, rather than politely enquiring, became more ominous: '. . . *anything at this stage that might have given you cause for concern? . . . But apart from that, nothing particularly untoward?* Truelle had been fishing for what Jac might know!

Jac's pulse throbbed tight at his temples. He had to get out of here now, couldn't risk saying any more; though with his lips suddenly dry and his tongue sticking to the roof of his mouth, it felt as if he'd hardly be able to.

Jac checked his watch and mumbled an excuse about an urgent appointment he'd suddenly remembered he'd forgotten to rearrange, and, with a hasty goodbye and 'Thanks for the information on Durrant's sessions', he left the office of a somewhat bemused Leonard Truelle.

In on it with them.

The thought haunted Jac over the following days.

He called Bob Stratton from a pay-phone and asked if he knew anyone good to make a sound-bug sweep of his apartment.

'If it's just a basic check and sweep, I can do it myself. But if it looks like it's going to get complicated, I gotta couple of names.' Stratton arranged to come round his place at six o'clock that evening, straight after work. 'But let's first sit in my car parked in front and map out a game plan. We don't want your snoopers – *if* you've got them – to know what we're up to.'

Stratton's car instructions took only a few minutes. Jac followed them as he went ahead of Stratton back into his apartment, put on a CD and turned it up loud.

Bruce Hornsby had been top of the CD stack, and the first track was 'The Way It Is'. Its heavy piano cadence filled the room as Stratton moved silently and deftly around, swaying a small metal probe from side to side. Stratton kept his eyes glued to its monitor needle as he went.

The atmosphere was tense, the heavy music jarring on Jac's nerves as he watched Stratton expectantly; no talking throughout, some intermittent hand signals from Stratton only giving Jac half a guide as to what had been found. Stratton finished his sweep just as Hornsby's second track was starting. He motioned Jac out to the corridor to deliver his verdict.

'All clear on your open spaces – lounge and bedrooms – which means we don't really need to be standing here like two CIA spooks. But you were right about–' Stratton broke off as Mrs Orwin's door opened across the corridor. Though his '*You want something?*' stare had obviously been honed to perfection over the years; Jac had never seen her door shut so quickly. 'As I was saying – you were right about the phone bug. But it's connection activated – switches on only as you pick up. It's not picking up anything else you're saying in the apartment.'

Jac nodded thoughtfully. He'd noticed Stratton keep his

finger on the cradle button as he'd lifted the receiver and carefully inspected.

'So. Just the phone?' Confirming it as if it was a lesser issue, that he'd somehow got off lightly, belied how Jac felt. A shiver ran up his spine as he thought about the many conversations he'd had that had been listened in to: his mum and Jean-Marie, John Langfranc, Alaysha, and then Rodriguez, Coultaine and his calls to arrange to see Truelle and Thallerey that had finally targeted him to be killed. 'Okay. *Okay.*' Jac eased a burdened sigh. 'How do we get rid of it?'

'We don't,' Stratton said, shrugging. 'Not, that is, without them knowing.'

Jac's eyebrows knitted. With the impact the bug had so far had on his life, he couldn't bear the thought of it being around a second longer. Stratton gestured towards the apartment; he didn't want to explain on the corridor. They went back into the apartment and Jac turned down Bruce Hornsby.

'Think about it, Jac,' Stratton said. 'If you're right in your assumption – whoever's bugging you has already tried to kill you because they're afraid of what you might find out. If we remove the bug, they're gonna panic even more – thinking you're up to all sorts they don't know about.' Stratton shrugged as he viewed Jac's discomfort. 'Fear of the unknown. Odds are they'll try again to get rid of you.'

'But how will leaving it in help? Especially given the sort of conversations I'm having right now on the Durrant case?'

'Because you can use it for a handy bit of disinformation.' Stratton smiled slyly as he saw the first spark of realization hit Jac. 'You make sure that all vital calls on the Durrant case are made on your cell-phone, and you warn all potential incoming callers of the same: *nothing* surrounding the Durrant case to ever come in on your land-line here.' He nodded towards the phone. 'Then, to complete the picture, having primed a few key people on your cell-phone – you call on your land-line here and tell them that you're not going to be doing anything further on the Durrant case. You've looked at every possible angle, but it appears hopeless trying to prove his innocence. The whole thing now rests with Governor Candaret as to whether he gets clemency or not.'

Jac mirrored Stratton's smile. 'So they think I've given up, and meanwhile I've got free rein without having to worry about watching my back?'

'Yeah. And you can even play things up some more if you want. You set up a call to your phone here, someone claiming they've got vital information on the Durrant case. You're officially off it, you say – but if it's that vital, okay. You'll meet them. They then give you the name of some hotel in Rio or Montevideo and a time for the meet. Meanwhile you sit back here with your feet up and raise a glass, knowing that you've sent them on a wild goose chase halfway across the world.'

As uncomfortable as Jac felt leaving the bug in place, the thought of being able to mislead whoever it was, get some of his own back, was irresistible. Jac arched a sharp eyebrow.

'You've done this before?'

'Yeah.' Stratton smiled wanly. 'Just a few times.'

While Jac had been right about the phone bug, he wouldn't know whether his other suspicion – Truelle being involved somehow – was right until some days had passed. Which brought a smile to Alaysha's face when he explained the rationale behind his thinking.

'Let me get this straight,' Alaysha said, taking the first sip of the red Bordeaux Jac had just poured for her. 'If over the coming days Truelle is killed or, as happened with you, there's an attempt on his life – then he's probably one of the good guys. But if he remains alive, then most likely he's one of the bad guys. Is that about it?'

'Yes. More or less.' Jac shrugged awkwardly. 'Unless there's some other reason why, unlike myself and Thallerey, he can't be targeted.'

Alaysha's mouth skewed, half quizzical, half humorous.

'Sounds like one of those old witchcraft trials. If she sinks and drowns, then she's okay. If she floats and lives, then she must be a witch. You're not exactly going to be able to phone him after the event and congratulate him on passing the test. "Hey, you're okay after all. Let's go for a drink and talk some more."'

Jac held one hand out, smiling dryly. 'Unless, that is, like me he survives the attempt.'

'Yeah, yeah,' Alaysha agreed gleefully, taking another sip of wine. 'Durrant case survivors club. Maybe you can have tags printed, and hold a little convention.'

'I couldn't have done more with Truelle.' Jac introduced a more sober tone. 'I told him what happened with me, and warned him he could be next.'

'Well, that's really going to brighten the coming days for him.'

The darker, heavier side of their light banter hit them both at the same time. Alaysha's expression fell sharply and she reached out and gently stroked Jac's cheek with the palm of one hand.

'Oh, Jac. *Jac*. Have you thought seriously about giving up, throwing in this whole thing with Durrant? I mean, you're only Durrant's lawyer, for God's sake – not his keeper and protector. And certainly not at the risk of your own life.'

'Yeah.' He nodded slowly. 'I thought about it a lot. Especially in those last days recovering in the hospital.' Jac took a sip of his own wine as he focused his thoughts, his eyes staying on the glass for a second, as if the greyness of the lake might somehow lay beyond the red. 'Sure, I was scared out of my wits thinking about how close I came to death. And now I have the knowledge that it probably wasn't an accident, along with the worry that they might try again. But against that, and not just because I promised to try and help, I can't shift Durrant from my mind: cut off from his family for eleven years, his life ruined, and *his* death, now only seventeen days away – unless by some miracle he *does* get clemency – a certainty. And everyone else has given up on him as a lost cause, deserted him; apart from young Joshua.' Something tugged at the back of Jac's mind about Durrant that harked back to his own father's death; but he just couldn't bring whatever it was to the forefront. He shook his head. 'I can't desert him as well. Especially not now.'

'What makes *now* so different to before?'

'Because however much the evidence against Durrant appears overwhelming, what happened with me and now Dr Thallerey convinces me of one thing: there's something crucial I'm missing, something these people are keen for me not to find out. If only I could discover what.'

Alaysha shook her head. 'But it's not just *what*, Jac, you have no idea *who* – who is trying to kill you.'

'True. That would certainly help. Know thy enemy. I'll make a note to ask them when they next make contact.' Then held one hand up in apology as he became more serious. 'I know what you're saying, Alaysha. But, like I said, it would be wrong to give up on Durrant right now. Just when I've seen the first strong sign that he might be innocent.'

Alaysha looked at him levelly, sombrely. 'Even though it might end up costing you your life, Jac?'

Jac could see the brewing storm-clouds in her eyes, weighted emotions struggling for balance: one part of her admiring what he was doing in trying to save Durrant's life, the other questioning the terrible risk he was taking. He couldn't tell which one held sway.

'I know. I know.' Jac closed his eyes for a second in submission, as if accepting some of that weight and concern. She'd already almost lost him once; understandable that she wouldn't want to go through that again. 'But hopefully this little ploy of Bob Stratton's will take their eye off of me, take most of the heat and danger away.'

As Alaysha looked down for a second in muted acceptance, she noticed that her hands were trembling. All this talk of danger and lives threatened had got to her; though not just because of Jac's plight. She'd read the small entry in the *Times-Picayune* just the day before: he was noted only as 'missing', but now with his family receiving no contact for two weeks, the police were beginning to fear the worst. Her mind had gone into a white-hot spin, wondering when the knock might come at her own door and she'd be next to go 'missing'. Butterflies of unease writhed in her stomach, made her feel queasy. She gripped her hand tighter on her wine glass to kill the trembling as she raised it and looked up again at Jac.

'Hopefully,' she said, and took another sip.

But Jac could see that his attempt at reassurance had done little to shift her concern. The storm-clouds still lingered in her eyes.

'So, Gary did more lines this week. How many?'

'Three.'

'And did you show your parents?'

'Not at first. But I think they . . . they kinda guessed. So in the end I did show them what he did.'

'And were they upset?'

'A little, of course. But at least now they don't blame me any more. They seem to accept that it's Gary doing them – not me.'

Truelle nodded pensively. One of his most intriguing cases. Fourteen-year-old boy, Brad Fieschek, recommended by Social Services due to self-mutilation. Discovered by his parents three months back, although it had probably being going on for some time before that, the marks were thin knife or razor cuts on his arms and sometimes wrists. 'Lines' had quickly become his comfort-zone term for them, Truelle discovered; possibly to soften the impact in his mind, because some of the cuts had been so deep that when made on his wrists his parents were convinced that it was a suicide attempt.

But from there, the case became deeper and darker still, because Brad claimed a secondary character, Gary, was making the 'lines'. Perhaps again to push away what was happening to him – but the worry now was that schizophrenia was developing. And that this secondary character might become increasingly violent: the self-mutilation would get worse.

It was a case that required all of his attention, all his skills; and so he should have known better than to schedule his meeting with Jac McElroy for earlier that day.

Truelle noticed his hand starting to shake again, and pressed his pen firmer on his pad to steady it.

He'd broken the golden rule when – with the excuse to his secretary that he was grabbing a coffee from the deli – he'd had a quick shot of bourbon before his appointment with McElroy. It steadied his hands slightly, but he kept them clasped as much as possible during the meeting to mask any remaining tell-tale signs.

He popped back a few peppermints to kill any smell on his breath, then sprayed himself with some cologne from his office cabinet just to make sure.

But the shaking in his hands was back after talking to McElroy, with a vengeance.

Phones bugged, an attempt on McElroy's life, Jessica Roche's obstetrician killed . . .

He managed somehow to brave it through the one remaining patient session before lunch, then dived out to the nearest bar. What he'd intended as just one more shot quickly became two, then three. The bourbon did little to quell his churning thoughts, but at least took most of the tremble out of his hands.

He looked at them again now: still not too heavy a tremble, not too noticeable. He focused past them to his notepad and took a fresh breath.

'And, as I suggested last time – have you asked Gary to stop?'

'No. No, I haven't.'

'Why not?'

'Because . . . because, I'm afraid.' Brad's eyes flickered uncertainly. 'I'm afraid that'll make him angry, will just make it worse. He'll give me more lines.'

Looked like he'd taken out those phone bugs and changed his insurance policies just in time. If he hadn't, he'd have probably gone the same way as Thallerey by now . . .

'I can understand that. But you know – as we also discussed last time – if you don't confront Gary, he'll just become bolder. It could become worse anyway.'

'I know. But, like I said – I'm afraid. I just don't know what to do.'

Confront them? Know what to do? Afraid.

Truelle's hands were starting to shake harder. He clenched them tightly. Maybe it should be him lying on the couch. Maybe he could get one of his old colleagues from New York to pull him apart, guide him through what to do. Pull him apart before he fell apart.

He swallowed, took a fresh breath. 'But sometimes, Brad, however hard it might seem at the time – we have to confront our worst fears.'

'I know.'

'Otherwise they just become stronger.'

'I know, Doc . . . I know.' Brad bit at his bottom lip, close to tears. 'But sometimes it's difficult.'

'I *know*.' Truelle in that moment felt as if he wanted to join Brad in bursting into tears. He dabbed at some sweat beads on his forehead with the back of one hand. 'And, uh . . . have you been able to find out why Gary is doing this? Why he's giving you the lines?'

Brad looked quizzically at Truelle, his eyebrows furrowing. 'Yes. We discussed that at my last session.'

'Of course, *of course*.' Truelle covered quickly, reminding himself. 'What I meant was – have you been able to probe more about that with Gary? You were never really satisfied with what he said – because you thought that you *were* pleasing your parents with what you did.'

'I could try, but I don't think he'd tell me. It's like . . . like his little secret, his main hold over me, knowing better than me what might please my parents . . .'

Truelle knew that he should have stopped the session there. He was far too distracted.

As McElroy had been. Maybe it had been due to Thallerey's death – but then what had McElroy suddenly thought of to make him cut everything short and head off in such a rush? And why on earth had they killed Thallerey? How could he possibly have presented a threat?

Truelle pressed his hands firmer against his notepad as the shaking ran deeper. But this time the pad simply started shaking as well.

Oh God, help me. Help me!

Truelle battled his way through the remaining twenty minutes of the session, keeping his comments concise and simple so that he didn't make any more mistakes.

But when he finally ushered Brad out, his secretary Cynthia, seeing Truelle pale and shaky, enquired, 'Has it got worse?'

It took Truelle a second to detach from his own thoughts and realize that she was talking about the boy, not him.

'No, no. Much the same as before with Brad.' He shook his head. 'It's just a small fever that seems to have hit me. Cancel and rearrange my last two sessions today, would you?'

He headed back into his office without waiting for a response, went into the adjoining washroom and splashed water on his face as he leant over the sink.

Straightening up, his head was still burning as if about to explode, his eyes pin-pricks unable to fully focus on his reflection. And his hands shaking worse than ever.

Maybe he should head out and get another drink or two to steady them again. But he knew that if he did, it would end up as four or five, and by the next day he'd be on half a bottle; a day or two after that, a full bottle.

And so he stayed in the same position, hands gripped tight

273

to the edge of the sink, as if it were the last planks of a sinking ship that he dared not let go of.

'Does Durrant know yet that you can't do any more?'

'Not yet. I'm heading out there tomorrow to tell him.'

Nel-M had already heard the taped calls once at Farrelia's, so wound through to the main highlights. McElroy on the phone to Mike Coultaine.

'So that's it now? Last time you'll be seeing him?'

'Apart from sitting in with him for the BOP hearing, or if there's something else needed connected with the clemency plea. But that's going to be the only focus now. From hereon in, it all rests with whether or not Candaret feels generous-hearted.'

Coultaine consoled that at least he'd given it a shot before they signed off. Nel-M wound forward to McElroy's following call to Pat Coyne.

'. . . I know that my colleague John Langfranc said that I'd probably be following up on some details. That won't now be happening – I've decided there's nowhere left to go with it. Apart from the DNA, I just can't get my mind past Durrant describing that final shot to the head – particularly since you held that back from all releases.'

'I understand. Me neither, and I've had twelve long years to think it over.'

'But thanks for your time and the information you gave.'

Nel-M wound forward to the next call, this time incoming and left on McElroy's answer-phone.

'Jac. Jennifer. Jennifer Bromwell. I heard all about your accident. Your sister, Jean-Marie, kept me up to date. I didn't visit the hospital, because, well, I . . . I understood your girlfriend was there much of the time. But I hear from Jean-Marie that you're fine now . . . so this is to wish you well, and also to ask – and I'd understand perfectly if you didn't think you were well enough yet for it – about one of those dates we discussed. I sneaked off to see Kelvin a couple of nights back – but there's something coming up in a few nights that'll be hard for me to find an excuse for. So, if you thought you could oblige . . . call me.'

Nel-M stopped the tape and smiled thinly. Hardly got his pulse back, and McElroy's convoluted love-life was full-on again: screwing his lap-dancing neighbour while playing charades with this second girl.

Shame though it wasn't about to get more complicated, thought Nel-M. He'd already started to bring the lap-dancer's ex-boyfriend, Gerry Strelloff, into play; only a few words spoken on his anonymous call, but effective. And as much as Roche would be pleased to hear that McElroy had finally thrown in the towel with Durrant, Nel-M couldn't help feel disappointed that they wouldn't now be taking things to the next stage; his plan for McElroy had without doubt been his best yet. Nel-M picked up the phone.

As it rang, he tapped a finger slowly at its side. Something nagged at the back of his mind about McElroy's recent calls, but the thought hadn't sufficiently formed to be worth mentioning to Roche. He simply told it how it appeared: didn't look like McElroy was going to be giving them any more grief.

24

'Try . . . try and remember.'

Durrant looked at Jac levelly. 'You think I haven't tried, time and over again these past long years, to remember more – fill the gaps? Haven't had too much else worth thinking about.' Durrant shook his head, smiling crookedly. 'You think it's all going to magically come back to me just because you're pushing?'

'I know.' Jac closed his eyes for a second in acceptance. 'But this could be our last shot at this, Larry. Our very last shot.'

'Don't you think I know that too?' Durrant arched an eyebrow sharply. 'Believe me, I'm trying . . . raking and going over everything I've ever recalled these past years. *Every* damn thing.'

They were on the same side now, pulling in the same direction, but it would have been easy to believe from their often heated exchange of the past half hour that they weren't. Still stuck in the same mould of Jac pushing hard and Durrant resisting; except that this time it was Durrant's lack of memory providing the resistance. Trying to push beyond the shadows that shrouded his life of twelve years ago, the effort creasing and raising sweat on his brow.

The room they were in was hot and claustrophobic. No windows. No one-way mirror with guards looking on. No faint murmur or sounds of the prison beyond – the surrounding walls were sixteen inches of thick concrete.

Jac had requested privacy from Haveling and had got it in spades. They'd been allocated one of Libreville's 'Quiet Rooms'. Originally constructed for prisoners who'd gone mad so that their ranting and screaming didn't disturb anyone, prisoners or guards, they'd hardly been used since the opening of a dedicated sanatorium wing twelve years ago.

Back in those dark days, inmates would be leather-strapped to beds and chairs bolted to the floor. Now the room was completely bare, and a small table and two chairs had been brought in. Jac and Durrant sat facing each other.

Their voices echoed faintly in the bare concrete room, the silence when they weren't talking so absolute that when the door spy-hatch had been slid back eight minutes ago – the only guard check so far – it had sounded like a rifle shot, making them jump. On the table between them were Jac's hand held recorder, its cassette slowly turning, and his notepad.

Jac took a fresh breath. 'Okay, let's see what we've got.' He flicked back a page in his notes, then to the front again. 'These regular pool games were usually Tuesday, Thursday or Satur-day nights – with no particular pattern as to which night?'

'That's right. It was usually *one* of those nights – at most two in the week, but not too often.' Durrant grimaced. 'Some of the guys didn't want to get flak from staying out half the week.'

'You say *some* of the guys. Did that not include you?'

'From what I remember, I was better after Josh was born.' Durrant shrugged lamely. 'But I was still drifting off some nights to other bars.' Durrant caught Jac's look. 'Don't ask –'cause I hardly remembered then, let alone now. The only one that I ended up recalling, probably from reading Coleridge, was the "Ain't Showin' Mariner" – along Marais Street, if I remember right.' Durrant smiled briefly, the rest of what he was reaching for sinking back quickly into shadow. 'Probably changed hands a dozen times since.'

Jac made a brief note before looking up again. 'Anywhere else you can think of?

'There was a regular poker game I used to go to. But that was always on a Friday, *if* it was on. Sometimes we'd miss a week.'

'Or *anyone* else that you could have been with that night?'

Durrant thought briefly. 'Not that I can think of. And that's not just because it might have slipped from my memory after the accident. I just don't think there *was* anyone I was seeing then – at least not regularly.'

'So – no other women then?'

Durrant smiled slyly. 'I know that was what Franny thought some nights I was out. But no – it was just me and my pool buddies. Or me and a hand of cards. Or me and a bottle. Or, if Truelle's tape and the evidence is right –' Durrant's expression darkened – 'me and more house break-ins. Ain't no damsel suddenly going to come out of the wings to save my ass.'

'Okay.' Jac held Durrant's gaze for a second before nodding his acceptance. 'Going back to these pool games at the Bayou Brew. If you can't remember which night your game might have been the week of Jessica Roche's murder – could anyone else there?'

Durrant shook his head slowly. 'Doubt it. When I was arrested, already six months had passed. Even if I *had* remembered the game then as a possible alibi and the police had talked to the people there – they'd have had problems remembering by then. When I did finally recall the pool games and one of my playing buddies – Nat Hadley – we're talking three years later, just before the appeal. Coultaine spoke to him on the phone, but he couldn't remember which night it was that week. Now, twelve years on – forget it.'

Thursday night, that was the crucial night. Jac had circled it on his notepad. If Durrant had been playing pool then and had stayed until 10.30, 11 p.m., then he couldn't have been halfway across town killing Jessica Roche.

'What about the other two in the game?'

'Bill Saunders and Ted Levereaux.' Durrant blinked slowly. 'I couldn't remember either of them back then. Still can't picture them fully even now – their names were given to Coultaine by Hadley. Coultaine spoke to Saunders, but he

278

couldn't recall which night it was either, and Levereaux he wasn't able to contact. He'd moved to St Louis, then apparently on again from the last number given.'

Jac nodded pensively. He could try to locate Levereaux, it was an unusual enough name that it shouldn't be that difficult to track down, and perhaps go back also to the other two to try and jog their memories. But, as Durrant had pointed out, what were the chances of anyone remembering after twelve years?

There'd have been other people there, though, Jac reminded himself: bar staff, waitresses, perhaps people on set shifts that would have a better chance of remembering which night it might have been. Jac asked, 'Did Coultaine try any of the bar staff at the Bayou Brew?'

'No, he never got into that.' Durrant shrugged. 'But again we're facing that twelve-year gap. Staff all long-gone, bar changed hands, or maybe even isn't there any longer.'

But as Durrant's shoulders slumped, Jac found himself more fired-up. Work rosters, payslips giving working times, maybe even someone who kept a diary? Jac shared his thoughts with Durrant. 'We've only got to find *one* person who used to keep some sort of written record, and we've struck gold. We're not relying on twelve-year-old memories any more.'

'Yeah, suppose so,' Durrant agreed, half hopeful, half sneer. 'Don't have much else worth trying.' Then, sudden afterthought, he shrugged and smiled wanly. 'That is, *if* they've still got those records or diaries after twelve years.'

Jac nodded soberly, rubbing one temple.

Something vital and elemental had changed between himself and Durrant since their last meeting. Before, Durrant had been indolent, uncooperative. Now he was helpful, cooperative and finally appreciative of what Jac was doing. There'd been a maudlin moment when Jac started the interview and Durrant looked across at him meaningfully, his eyes moistening.

'I went hard on you last time, and I'm sorry for that. It

wasn't called for. You put your neck out for me, and there's not many would do that. But with me being such an ass, you might have got the impression I don't appreciate what you're doing – but that ain't so. I do.' Durrant twisted his mouth as if something still didn't quite sit comfortably. Only total honesty would do. 'Or rather, maybe I didn't last time – but *now* I do. You're all right.'

But there was still something holding Durrant back, and often he was still defeatist; though where before he'd been couldn't-care-less and relaxed, now he was tense and anxious. Perhaps it was that death was now that much closer, only fifteen days away, and it was finally hitting him.

Given that, and the fact that everything tried before had failed, Jac could hardly blame Durrant for looking on the down-side. With contact again from Josh, no doubt he did now want to live, cling to *hope*, as Jac had earlier sold him so hard on; but, worn down by the trial, the failed appeal, the long years of imprisonment, abandoned by his family for much of it, and throughout it all not even sure whether he had committed the murder or not – he'd probably given up long ago on just how that might be achieved. *Distant dream*.

A handful of old pool-buddies and the bar they used to play at now his only remaining hope.

Jac spent a while filling in details, those that Durrant could remember, then stopped the tape.

Faint rustling, shuffling.

Alaysha went to the door and looked through the spy-hole. Nobody there. She cupped one hand over her far ear to mask the sounds of Molly watching *Rugrats* in the lounge. No sounds now, either.

Second time in the past half hour she thought she'd heard something. Probably just people passing on the corridor or Mrs Orwin shuffling around and being nosy, rather than anyone hanging around outside.

She'd been anxious and on edge ever since Gerry had called

at her door, particularly with what he'd shouted through the forced gap. She'd countered quickly that he couldn't say anything because he'd be implicated too.

'That's the beauty of it, babe. I was just a go-between, made an introduction. All that was ever passed to me in envelopes at the bar were receipts. It's the courier they'll be looking for – and that's you, babe. That's you.'

Then when she'd read the news clipping the other day, her nervousness had leapt to a new level. Maybe Gerry had already said something, and they'd started targeting those involved. Maybe the knock would come at her door at any minute and . . .

She tried to put it out of her mind, concentrate on what she should prepare for dinner for herself and Molly. But opening the fridge and kitchen cupboard doors, she found herself staring blankly at their contents, unable to focus on anything. And when the bell did ring a couple of minutes later, it made her jump.

A voice, partly muffled by the TV, came through the door 'It's okay Alaysha . . . it's Jac.'

Molly was quickly on her feet confirming it as Alaysha passed her to answer the door. 'It's Jac, Mommy . . . it's Jac.'

'I know. I know.' Alaysha felt the weight ease from her chest. Probably the sound a moment ago had been Jac going into his apartment; or perhaps he'd disturbed whoever was in the corridor, *if* there was anyone. She slid back the top lock and turned the door handle as she unhooked the chain with her other hand.

Then, as she caught the shape of who was there, before he'd even looked up fully beyond the baseball cap peak partly obscuring his face – she went to ram it shut again.

She broke two fingernails clawing the chain back on, but she couldn't get the door closed the last inch. Gerry's weight was quickly against the other side, pushing hard.

'So that *is* his fucking name! *Jac*! Your new boyfriend.'

'Don't know what you're talking about.' Stock reaction,

breathless from the exertion of pushing against the door, her mind scrambling for how he might have found out.

'Yes, you do. And you sounded real pleased to hear it was him. Never answered the door that quick to me – even when we were at our hottest.'

'What are you doing here, Gerry? You got my lawyers' letter?'

'Yeah, I got your smarmy fuckin' lawyers' letter.'

He thrust harder against the door as he said it, and she couldn't hold it back any longer. It burst hard against the chain, rattling.

'Is that Gerry, Mommy? Wh . . . why's he being like that?'

Alaysha looked back at Molly a few paces away, pulling anxiously at a few strands of hair, trying to be adult to cope with the situation.

Alaysha's anger surged, fuelling a white-hot adrenalin burst. She barged the door back an inch, felt the satisfaction of a grunt from Gerry as he took the impact.

'I won't have it, Gerry. I won't have you coming round here terrifying Molly. We're getting a court restraining order, yer hear? You come round here again – next stop for you is a jail cell!'

'Yeah.' Challenging, sliding into a mocking chuckle. 'You do that, and you're dead, babe. You're –'

Gerry broke off as Mrs Orwin's door opened behind him. And, as he half-turned with the distraction, Alaysha managed to shove the door closed the last inch and flip back the latch.

There were a few words spoken between Mrs Orwin and Gerry that Alaysha couldn't make out clearly beyond her ragged breathing and pounding heart. Last time Gerry called, Mrs Orwin had been late in opening her door; no doubt because she'd been watching some soap at 200 decibels.

Alaysha swallowed, holding her breath for a second, listening. Silence for a second, then a light tapping at her door. Gerry or Mrs Orwin? Alaysha looked through the spy-hole. Gerry was silently mouthing something which she couldn't make out; obviously he didn't want to audibly threaten Alaysha with Mrs Orwin still looking on through the gap in her door. But shielded from Mrs Orwin's view by his body, the signal he made with one hand was unmistakeable: a gun pointing, his thumb flicking down like the hammer striking.

Gerry brought his face closer as he mouthed a kiss goodbye, his features warped all the more by the fish-eye of the spy-hole.

Jac looked at the rain on the café window as he took the first sips of his coffee. Large splatters spaced a second apart – which had been enough to bring him in from the street – teasing, warning of the deluge to come. And when it did arrive a minute later, the patter building like the drumming of impatient fingers before finally bursting loose, Jac could hardly see the street beyond for the water running down the glass; everything became a blurred pastel grey.

'Yo' okay there, Jac? Maybe wanna 'nother Po' boy?'

'No, I'm okay, Henny. Thanks.'

Then, as Henny saw him look thoughtfully back through the window. 'Don' worry. Mack'll sho'. He's slow an' sometimes annoyin' as hell. But he ain' forgetful. Not yet, at leas'.'

Jac nodded and smiled again. 'No problem. I'm here early because of the rain.'

Momma Henshaw, more affectionately Henny, or sometimes Momma Henpeck, because of the café she'd run for the past twenty-five years, The Red Rooster. A regular Ninth Ward landmark, according to some of the locals Jac had spoken to, 'An' she one of yo' best hopes fo' information on anythin' and everythin' from 'roun here. 'Specially from years back.'

Jac's enquiries hadn't been getting far. The Bayou Brew was now Jay-Jay Cool's. The new owner, Jay Cole, had been there three years and knew only the name of the guy he'd bought it from, not any of its history before that. 'And I think he only had the place two years – so I ain't sure how far back his recall would go, either. But I can give you his name and number.'

Jac took them, and phoned on his cell-phone minutes later. Miraculously, given his luck so far, it was answered on the second ring: but he too only remembered the name of the owner in turn before him, Rob Harlenson – who Jac had already discovered died two years ago from Bill Saunders, the only one of Durrant's old pool-buddies he'd so far tracked down. He didn't know the old staff or the head barman, hadn't kept any of them on when he took over.

Jac was particularly interested in Mack Elliott, the old head barman from the Bayou Brew. With Harlenson dead, Elliott might be the only one to know about past staff records and rosters: just who might have been working the night Jessica Roche was killed, and whether that could possibly have been Durrant and his buddies' pool night. Saunders didn't know where he might find Elliott.

Jac looked at the other two names on his pad: Nat Hadley and Ted Levereaux. He'd phoned Hadley yesterday and was told by his wife that he worked night shifts. Jac had left his cell-phone number, but no call back as yet. The trail with Levereaux petered out at his last known address in St Louis; and, while it might be an unusual name, a search in all states south from Missouri to Louisiana had alone brought up one hundred and twelve, seventeen with initials E or T. Jac had phoned nine of the seventeen E & Ts before it got too close to midnight to be calling any more; and, if the phone was in Levereaux's wife's name, he'd have to trawl through all hundred and twelve.

Jac felt worn down by it all: the endless phone calls, delays, dead-ends, the head-shakes as he'd asked about Mack Elliott or any of the old staff at the Bayou Brew. And, as Durrant rightly pointed out, even if and when he did track them down, what on earth were they going to remember after twelve years? Jac had a sinking, desolate feeling that he'd still be tramping the streets of the Ninth Ward and making phone calls that went nowhere as they strapped Durrant down for his injection.

Only thirteen days left now.

And as Henny had seen Jac's hand shaking lifting his coffee cup, his gaze through the window weary and lost, she'd asked if he was okay.

The light was sinking fast through the window of The Red Rooster, as if mirroring Jac's mood. He was only able to get to the Ninth Ward at lunchtimes and after work, as dusk was falling; now, second night there, the rain and clouds had smothered the remaining light even quicker.

The only brief spark of hope had appeared earlier, towards the end of his lunchtime visit when, sixth or seventh head-shake on Mack Elliott or the old Bayou Brew, someone finally pointed him towards Henny's café. But Henny had already seen him through the window asking questions in the street, with one of her old regulars, Izzy, lifting a bony finger her way, and so she had one hand on her hip to greet Jac as he walked in.

'What's a white bo' like you doin' askin' questions roun' the Ninth Ward? Yo' a cop, or y'jus' got a death-wish?'

'No, I'm a lawyer.'

Henny arched one eyebrow extravagantly. 'Oooh. Yo' *have* gotta death-wish.'

Jac explained about Durrant and trying to track down Mack Elliott or any of the old Bayou Brew staff.

Henny nodded thoughtfully, taking the hand from her hip and gesturing to a table. 'Tryin' to save Larry Durrant's neck, put a differen' complexion on it. But yo' still wanna be careful askin' questions roun' the Ninth – whit' bo' in a nice suit an' all. Yo' might not be able to spit alla dat out befo' someone takes yo' head off with a shotgun.'

Henny gave Jac a potted guide to the Ninth Ward. Safe around the main jazz clubs on St Claude Avenue, but venture a couple of blocks either way and it was a dangerous no-man's land, particularly at night and particularly if you were white.

Almost exclusively African-American, the birthplace of Louis Armstrong, Fats Domino and a long list of jazz greats through the years, on one side the Ninth Ward had a rich and proud cultural heritage; but on the other, its gritty underbelly was still dirt poor, and a place that half the city's muggers, robbers and drug dealers called home. The police never ventured too deep into the lower Ninth at night unless they were two or three strong, hands close by their guns in readiness.

'. . . And if yo' were fool 'nough to drift 's far as Tricou or Dalery on the north side, presumin' yo' was still alive by dat point . . . you might 's'well jus' phone the funeral parlo' befo' yo' get dere. Tell 'em where t'pick up yo' body.'

Jac smiled. Looked like he'd survived so far through ignorance and luck, with Henny's café now at least one safe haven. And, most importantly, she did know Mack Elliott and where to get hold of him, and had phoned him to arrange a meeting at her café.

Duck Gumbo, Dirty Rice, Boiled Crawfish, Beef P'Boy . . . Henny's was noted for its grass-roots Creole cuisine, her reputation stretching far beyond the Ninth Ward. No-frills but homely with red plastic tablecloths, a gospel version of 'Praise You' played in the background, one that Jac hadn't heard before; the sort of place where you'd expect Aretha Franklin to suddenly stand up from a table and burst into song, or the Blues Brothers start doing somersaults through. Instead, Mack Elliott walked in, tall, rangy, slightly hunched over with age, or perhaps through constantly reaching down to greet people.

Henny called over to Jac that it was him, otherwise he wouldn't have known. And as Jac stood to shake Mack's hand, whether just hopeful thinking or the setting sun dipping below the cloud layer, he thought he saw fresh light hanging over Mack Elliott's shoulder.

But what Jac didn't notice as they sat back down and started talking was the dark maroon Pontiac Bonneville parked thirty yards back on the opposite side of the street. Nel-M sat inside, obscured by the fading light and the water running down his windscreen. He'd only started following Jac again earlier that day, but already he was beginning to wonder.

Alaysha couldn't stay there any longer.

Every small sound: movement on the corridor, Mrs Orwin or someone else further along opening their door, the faint hum of the refrigerator, the muted sounds of neighbours from the floor above – twisted her nerves another notch tighter, made her worry that Gerry might head back to try and get in again. Or someone else threatening far worse.

She couldn't shift that last image of Gerry from her head. The gun pointing, the trigger hammer going down.

It would be okay if Jac was there. Feel him hugging her tight, stroking her hair, consoling. They'd sink themselves deep into a bottle of good Chateauneuf . . . *but still she wouldn't be able to tell him everything*.

She'd been listening out, but still no sounds of him opening his door or moving around. Where *was* he?

She felt alone, vulnerable, unprotected . . . *unprotected*!

As soon as the thought hit her, she turned to Molly. 'Come on, Molly, we're going over to your granma's.'

Halfway over to Carrollton in the taxi, Molly asked, 'Am I staying at Granma's tonight?'

'No, no. I'm just picking something up there.' Then, remembering that with all the fuss she'd forgotten to cook dinner. 'And we'll get a pizza on the way back.'

'Yeah . . . yeah! Pizza! Pizza!'

Alaysha pulled Molly in close, her smile fading back to taut anxiety, unseen by Molly, as she nestled one cheek against her daughter's hair.

Alaysha wondered if her mother still had the gun. An old Colt .38 she'd got hold of when she'd finally kicked out Alaysha's father, fearful that he'd return any day to give her an even worse beating.

Same too now with Gerry, she'd explain. But again, she

wouldn't be able to tell her mother *everything*. That would have to stay her secret. Just her and Gerry's.

Jac's own breathing within the hood.

All he could hear. All he could feel: his own hot breath bouncing back at him, stewing his pounding head all the more.

And the occasional prod with the gun in his back. 'Move mo'fucker. *Move!* This way . . . yeah. What's wrong – yo' blind or somethin'.'

Brief chuckle; but one, from what Jac had seen of the two edgy, bug-eyed teenagers before the hoods were put on him and Mack Elliott, that could easily end with an impatient gunshot for stepping the wrong way or saying the wrong thing, or because the kids' last few hours on their Gameboys had been frustrating.

Jac was beginning to think this wasn't such a good idea.

As Jac had half-expected, Mack Elliott hadn't been able to recall which night Durrant's pool game was the week of Jessica Roche's murder. 'Long time ago now . . . *long time.*'

'I know. But I wondered if you might have kept a diary or anything with old work rosters that could give a clue?'

'No. 'Fraid not.' Then, seconds later, his sullen thoughtfulness lifted. 'Might be a chance of yo' striking lucky, though. Might jus' be a chance.'

Mack explained that there were two eight-hour shifts at the Bayou Brew, with a barman and waitress for each one, and himself and the owner, Rob Harlenson, alternately running the bar. And one of the barmen, Lenny Rillet, used to keep a diary.

'. . . Though not fo' the best of reasons.' Mack looked down at that moment, thoughtful, troubled, as he weighed something up. 'Probably the best shot you're gonna get at it, though. C'mon. You'll be safe wi' me.'

Mack explained as they headed deeper into the Ninth Ward. Lenny Rillet used to keep a diary because he was dealing drugs from behind the bar. Small stuff then, packets of marijuana and speed, for which he'd enter times, names, weights and payments in his diary in code.

'Harlenson was already suspicious, found one o' the diaries one day, and finally got rid of Lenny. But that was way after Larry Durrant wen' down. And I know Lenny used to hang on to those diaries, 'cause in each one he'd have new names an' contact numbers. Business resource, yo' might call it . . .'specially with how things turned out later wi' Lenny.'

Rillet had either left drug-dealing for a while, or stayed so small time that nobody noticed. But then suddenly five years ago, he'd burst back on the scene big time, and now was one of the Ninth Ward's main crack dealers.

'Only a couple o' blocks away now. We'll be there soon.'

Jac felt his anxiety mount as they sank deeper into the shadows of the Ninth Ward; now four blocks from Henny's, the efforts at revival with restorations or newer community blocks started to fray, giving way to rows of older houses, many of them dilapidated or derelict. The light was sparser too, with many of the streetlamps smashed, the shadows in between heavier, more worrying. A wino suddenly appeared from one dark patch, making them jump – though Mack commented that he was probably playing look-out for someone; then, only twenty yards on, two sets of eyes emerged from the darkness of a car on bricks, watching them warily as they passed.

'Don' worry, you'll be safe wi' me . . . Now he's one of the Ninth's main crack dealers . . . You might s'well jus' phone the funeral parlo' befo' yo' get dere.'

Late fifties, Mack Elliott was already slightly out of breath; though maybe that was partly anxiety, too, Jac thought, because suddenly he wasn't so sure how safe they'd be. Certainly the nods and smiles of acknowledgement Mack gave to the few people they passed were now tighter, more hesitant.

And as they came to the row of eight half-derelict shotgun houses that Lenny Rillet apparently called home, and Mack announced himself as an 'old frien" of Rillet's and the hoods were slipped on them by two armed teenagers, Jac's foreboding settled deeper.

Shotgun houses were four or five rooms stacked back to back with no corridor; so called, because if you fired a shotgun at the front, the bullet would pass through every room.

In the last minute of their approach, Mack had explained that Rillet would move from room to room: he could be in the second room of the fourth house, or third room back on the sixth. Nobody ever knew. And all visitors were hooded and spun round several times to disorientate them before being led through. There were two or three armed teenage 'clockers' out front, half a dozen or more inside, plus two or three older, more experienced guards. Few people knew what Rillet looked like, and the chances of getting to him before catching a bullet were remote. 'That's how he's managed to stay alive s'far.'

And now the smells as they were led through: stale musk, urine, faeces, vomit, a pungent burning, like rubber mixed with rope, and a faint chemical smell that Jac couldn't place.

And now sounds: muted mumbling, coughing, a few groans, a sudden wild cackle subsiding to a chuckle. And every few steps, Jac could feel debris or rubbish around his feet, or maybe it was clothing and people. Something brushed past one ankle: a hand reaching out, or a rat?

Jac felt himself descend deeper into hell with each step. His head was burning inside the hood, his pulse pounding at his temples, his mouth dry. Each step had taken them further into the shadows and into danger, away from the light and safety; now, within only fifteen minutes, Henny's café seemed a lifetime away. *I'll be okay*, Jac told himself. Mack had promised, 'You'll be safe with me.'

But as he heard Rillet's tone greeting Mack, and the argument that ensued between them, Jac felt that last vestige of hope slip away. He knew then that they were about to die.

*

'Why yo' bring someone here, Mack?'

'He . . . he's the lawyer tryin' to save Larry Durrant. That's why I brought 'im to see you.'

'Uhhmmm. Larry Durrant? You think that's gonna score points wi' me. You an' I – we ain't eyeballed each other in what? Six, seven years? So fo' sure you don' score no points there, Mack.'

'He's tryin' to get some information on Larry's movements at the Brew from twelve years back. I couldn't help with that. And I thought yo' might be able to.'

'An' even when we used to see each other, we din' 'xactly swim in the same waters . . . if yo' know what I mean.'

It was like two disparate conversations, with neither party listening to the other: Mack desperately pleading his case of Durrant and the Bayou Brew of twelve years ago, while Rillet was making it clear that their past association cut no ice and Mack had made a big mistake in coming there.

Mack took a fresh breath, introduced a more hopeful tone. 'Thing is, Lenny, I thought to myself, while yo' might not remember that far back – you always kep' those diaries.'

As soon as the words left Mack's mouth, it became chillingly clear that it was a step in the wrong direction: sealed rather than saved their fates.

'Ooohh. Those diaries? Yeah. Funny thing that, 'cause, ya know – I always suspected it was you that told Harlenson 'bout them. Got my ass fired from the Brew.'

'Wasn't me, Lenny . . . *Promise*. Harlenson was already suspicious, and he foun' that diary that day all by hi'self – without no help from me. I didn' say nothin' to him.'

The desperation in Mack's voice was heavy, clinging by his fingertips to what little ledge was left.

Silence. Rillet let Mack's words hang in the air, savouring his discomfort.

'Yo' know, Mack. That's where all your figurin' has gone sadly wrong. Since you and I were on noddin' terms, I changed mo' than yo' can imagine. I've had guys killed here

291

simply 'cause I didn' like the tones o' their voices. Didn' think they gave me 'nough respect. Or 'cause I thought a splash o' red on the walls would bring the graffiti more to life.' Resigned, derisory snigger. 'So wi' the heavy doubt I got 'bout what you jus' tol' me – what makes yo' think now's gonna be any differen'?'

Silence again. Heavy, cloying.

And then, breaking it after a second, sounding deafeningly loud, the slide on a gun being snapped back.

'*Please* . . . Lenny. Don' do it. I'm not here for myself. I'm here tryin' to save Larry Durrant's ass. Nothin' more.'

Silence again. Longer than before.

Jac found that his breath was held, his body starting to shake, legs weakening as he anticipated the gunshot at any second.

'That's the beauty of the hoods. You can't see m' face. Don' know if I'm smilin', scowlin', makin' the signal to fire – or wavin' my boyz' gun arms away.' A purposeful pause, Rillet wallowing in their fear; a conductor's baton poise that could fall either way. 'An even if I am smilin' or wavin' them away right now – that could all quickly change.'

Jac jumped with Rillet's sudden clap; only a foot behind himself and Mack, it was no doubt intended to resemble a gunshot. Jac was hit with the realization that Rillet had probably done this before, many times; and that he relished the feeling of power it gave him over his victims. And, riding aboard that, the hope, however slim, that it was just that, a game, and Rillet wouldn't have them killed.

Silence again, Rillet milking the tension for every ounce. Jac's breathing rapid and shallow within the hood, his pulse double-beat, wondering whether next to expect a bullet or his hopes confirmed that it was just a game.

There was a bang then, but it was too distant for a gunshot: a door swinging open and banging back in one of the adjacent rooms, then a frantic rustling as someone ran through the debris and prone bodies, and a breathless, urgent voice:

'Someone out fron' . . . Come on der' tail!'

'Yo' brought someone here, Mack!' Rillet screamed.

'No . . . *no*! We're alone. Didn' bring nobody,' Mack quavered, struggling for conviction.

'You fuckin' brought someone here! Snoopin'. An' that somethin' I definitely ain't got no movemen' on . . .'

And as quickly as Jac felt hope enter his grasp, it was slipping away again.

As Nel-M saw them turn into Tricou Street, he thought twice about following them. He didn't want to end up getting car-jacked or his nice paintwork spray-painted or shot at by some punks.

A car just didn't look right on the north part of Tricou unless it was rusted, graffiti'd, standing on bricks and stripped, or pumped with bullet holes.

Two bars visited, questions on the street, then The Red Rooster café; now heading out with some black guy who looked like a retired basketball coach.

Nel-M knew that the Ninth was Larry Durrant's old stomping ground, but then the same held true for seventy per cent of New Orleans' black criminals. Nel-M was trying to get to the point where he knew what McElroy was pursuing in the Ninth: something to do with Durrant, or a new client?

When he saw them enter the warren of dilapidated crack houses ahead, he thought that he had his answer: new client. But then from what he'd heard, the guy operating on Tricou, Lenny Rillet, was meant to be a heavy hitter. And McElroy was way down the feeding chain at his firm, didn't normally get that calibre of client. Anything more complex than a straightforward plea petition, and he wouldn't have been let within a mile of the Durrant case.

Nel-M decided to keep watching, see what might transpire or where McElroy might head next that would make all the pieces finally slot into place.

Nel-M saw the fifteen-year-old clocker come out and give the street a quick up and down once-over; but, sixty yards down on the opposite side, it didn't seem he'd taken much notice of Nel-M's presence.

The clocker, though, at the same time as heading in to alert Rillet, also signalled his buddy towards the back of the shotgun houses.

A routine they'd played out several times before, the second clocker headed along the back yards of the neighbouring houses, and slipped out again onto the road forty yards behind Nel-M's car.

Nel-M didn't see him at first. He only picked up a shadowy flicker of movement when the clocker had already scampered twenty yards closer; and, as Nel-M focused intently on his rear-view mirror to be sure of what he thought he'd seen, there was movement too from ahead with the first clocker starting to head his way.

'Ohh . . . *shiiiiii* . . .' Nel-M hit his ignition, slammed into drive, and swung out, flooring it.

A shot came from behind, thudding into metal somewhere on his trunk, and now the clocker ahead was moving into aiming stance.

An ignoble epitaph that would be: killed by two clockers barely in puberty. Nel-M headed straight for the clocker ahead, ducking down at the same time. He heard the shot zing past, saw the kid start squaring for a second shot – but Nel-M was bearing down fast, less than ten yards away. The kid hesitated for an instant, then, realizing that Nel-M's car would hit him halfway through firing, he leapt out of the way as Nel-M flashed past.

Nel-M kept low, heard two more shots: one missed, but the other hit his back window, shattering it into a thousand ice-pellets.

Breath held, Nel-M did a quick self-check for injuries: pain, blood, flesh or clothing fragments where they shouldn't be? *Nothing*. He eased out again and swung off hard at the next cross street.

*

Nel-M was already fifty yards past the crack house as Rillet came out with Mack Elliott and Jac. They had their hoods yanked off, which Jac could now see were white pillow cases. Rillet stood behind them, looking clownish and ridiculous – though nobody would dare tell him that – in a George Bush mask. Dubbya meets the Ku-Klux Klan in front of a crack house.

'Yo' know that car o' that man?' Rillet asked.

Mack answered first. 'No. Never seen him befo'. An' don' know the car.'

'Me neither,' Jac echoed. 'Don't recognize the car or the man.' Even at first sight, the man inside had been little more than an indistinct shadow. Now he was a good seventy yards away.

Silence again, the George Bush mask giving nothing away. No sign of whether Rillet accepted their claims or not.

But watching the fading brake lights of the Pontiac Bonneville as it turned off of Tricou Street, Jac was suddenly struck with an idea. *If* he lived to implement it.

25

Soon after Alaysha had put Molly to bed, she took the gun out of her drawer and held it in her hand, turning it slowly, getting the feel of it, flicking the safety catch on and off. A Colt Cobra .38, it felt heavy in her grip, alien, but at the same time reassuring.

Her mother had been anxious about her taking it, getting her to swear on the Madonna and promise that she wouldn't use it. 'Unless your life is in danger because Gerry has a gun too.'

'No, I told you Mom. It's just to frighten him off. He's not going to come calling with a gun.'

Not him. But the other knock she feared at her door was another matter. They'd have a gun pointed through the gap before the chain was barely off.

She swallowed hard, felt her hand trembling against the weapon in her grip. Sudden concern that if and when it came to it, she wouldn't have the resolve to actually pull the trigger. She gripped the gun in both hands and stood up, bracing herself in aiming stance, and, after a second, felt the trembling subside; not completely, but enough to squeeze off a shot without missing wildly.

Alaysha went to put the gun back in the drawer, but then at the last second decided it wasn't a good idea to have it anywhere within Molly's reach. She opened her wardrobe and put it on a high shelf, tucked under a few of her clothes.

'Is that Jac McElroy?'
    'Yes. Yes, it is.'
    'I understand that you're handling the Larry Durrant case?'
    'That's right.'

'Because I've got some information that I think you'll find interesting.'

'Who *is* this?'

'That's not important. But if you want some information that'll help crack the case, you might want to talk to me.'

'That's very true, I would. So, tell me. What it is you know?'

'No, not over the phone. It's too sensitive. We should meet.'

'Whoever told you that I was handling the Durrant case, should also have told you that I'm not that active on it right now. The plea petition's already in, so now we're just waiting on its outcome.' Jac sighed heavily. 'But, okay, now you've intrigued me – let's meet.'

They arranged to meet at 12.45 p.m. the next day at a coffee bar on Camp Street. Jac could walk round the corner at lunch-time from work. The man said that he'd be wearing a light-blue jacket and carrying a salmon-pink folder under one arm. It was all spy vs spy stuff, but the next day, sitting by the café window sipping at a latte, Jac wasn't looking out for the man. He knew already that he wouldn't show.

The idea had come from Stratton's suggestion about a fake call on his land line to send his snoopers on a wild goose chase, combined with Alaysha's comment from the other night: '*But it's not just* what, *Jac, you have no idea* who – *just who is trying to kill you.* The final catalyst had been seeing the Pontiac Bonneville speeding away from Rillet's crack house the other night.

If Jac's fake caller claimed to have something juicy on the Durrant case, without doubt his snoopers would make sure to be there watching. Bob Stratton, in turn, would then watch them, note their registration number and take photos. More spy stuff, but at least Jac would hopefully, finally, discover who wasn't keen on him digging too deep into the Durrant case.

★

The next few days went by in a whirlwind.

As Stratton suggested, Jac waited in the café twenty-five minutes past the appointment time before finally leaving. Stratton said that he'd wait no more than fifteen minutes; by then he should have been able to observe all he needed and take more than enough photos. Jac spoke briefly with Stratton on his cell-phone shortly after leaving the café.

'It *was* a dark maroon Pontiac Bonneville, as you suspected,' Stratton confirmed. 'I got the registration, should have the results back on that tomorrow. And enough photos of the guy in it to fill a wall: black, mid-forties, salt and pepper hair. Tall, well built, but not heavy or stocky. Wiry-muscly, if you know what I mean.'

That night, Jac had another bogus date with Jennifer Bromwell. She was dropped off by her father Tobias, a squat bear of a man who beamed broadly and shook hands with Jac through the open window of his Mercedes S600. Perhaps he suspected something and feared she might be meeting Kelvin, or wanted to check Jac out in person. Blue-blood lawyer, okay, but did he have one eye, one leg or half his face tattooed?

Jac felt slightly guilty at the subterfuge, now having met Mr Bromwell. He sat with Jennifer for fifteen minutes in a bar, talking about the club where Kelvin was gigging that night and his own accident, so sorry about that, she said as she gingerly touched his forehead, as if afraid he might still be delicate enough to crumble, and then for the umpteenth time she thanked him for doing this just before heading off to see Kelvin. Jac headed back to his apartment to hit the phones.

Six more T. or E. Levereaux to go.

Two numbers rang consistently with no answer, and another was on answerphone the three times he'd tried; he'd left a message on his second call.

The same routine every time: 'I'm trying to locate a Ted Levereaux that used to live in New Orleans and worked at the Bayou Brew bar in the Ninth Ward between nineteen-ninety and ninety-four.'

And variations on the same answers each time: We've never lived anywhere but St Louis. Never worked in a bar. My husband's an Edward, always known as Eddy. I was only thirteen in ninety, couldn't work anywhere, let alone a bar. Or just, sorry, got the wrong person.

Jac felt numbed, worn down by it all, the questions, and now the answers too, starting to become mechanical.

And so when a teen boy's voice said, 'One minute – I'll get my pa', Jac took a second to snap his concentration back. He checked on his pad to see which number it was: one of the two that before had rung with no answer.

'Ted Levereaux.'

Jac felt immediately more anxious, a faint edge and tremor now in his voice, when, with the number of times he'd been through the same introduction, it should have come across as plain and matter-of-fact.

'God in a bucket, Bayou Brew – that takes me back a ways,' Levereaux exclaimed. Then, realizing he perhaps should have done it the other way round – question before commitment – a wariness crept into his voice as he asked, 'And why, pray, might you be enquirin' . . . Mr McElvey, was it?'

'McElroy. Jac McElroy.' And Jac went into the rest of his prepared speech that he'd rarely had a chance to use: Larry Durrant. Jessica Roche's murder. Possible alibi from the regular pool games he used to have. 'If you could remember which night they might have played the week of her murder?'

'*Jeez*. Hardly remember which nights I was there myself, now. You spoke to any of the others worked there then?' As Jac went through the names and outlined what he'd gained so far, Levereaux commented, 'Didn't know Harlenson had died, and my goodness . . . good ol' Mack, he still aroun'? Still livin' in the Ninth, you say?' Levereaux went off at a tangent for a moment about how nice it would be to see Mack again and catch up, before bringing his focus back. 'I'm sorry, Mr McElroy. Don' think I can be much help to yer. Too far back.'

'I wondered if you could try one thing for me. Try, if you can, to remember where you were when you heard Jessica Roche had been shot. I mean, was Durrant's pool game of that week before or *after* you heard the news? Because, if you remember the news coming straight after the pool game the night before – there's a high chance they coincided.'

Put the person in the moment. Jac had read somewhere that they'd remember more. It wasn't quite the same as everyone recalling where they were when Kennedy was shot. But for New Orleans, Jessica Roche's murder had been big news, so the chances were reasonable. He'd done the same with Mack Elliott, Nat Hadley and Bill Saunders. Elliott and Saunders had said straightaway that it didn't help, they still couldn't recall anything – but Hadley had said he'd call him back in twenty-four hours when he'd had a chance to think it over.

'Yeah, yeah. Know what you mean,' Levereaux said, and lapsed into thought.

Muted sound of a TV in the background, a woman's voice talking above it for a moment. Snapshot of life at 9.17 p.m. in St Louis; another to add to the brief sound-bite snapshots Jac had gained across half the South the past few nights.

'Sorry. Still can' place much from that far back. Not straight off, anyhow.'

'Do you maybe want to think on it a bit?' Jac prompted. 'Call me back?'

'Yeah, yeah. Okay,' Levereaux said after a brief pause.

Jac left his number and Levereaux promised to call back the next night.

Jac eased out his breath as he hung up and looked at his notepad on the table.

Four names with lines through them, two names blank, two with question marks; now three, as Jac put a question mark by Levereaux's name.

Jac had felt each line he'd had to put through a name like

a hammer-blow to his chest. And he wondered if that's why he'd opted so quickly to delay Levereaux rather than pushing him there and then? One more bit of hope left, however slim, rather than another strike against.

But that was how Jac had come to measure everything over the past days: strikes against, another chance gone of being able to save Larry Durrant, balanced against hope remaining.

Another strike against came the following day when Nat Hadley phoned him just before lunch to say that, sorry, he just couldn't fix in his mind which night the pool game had been in relationship to Jessica Roche's murder.

Then another name added to Jac's notepad and as quickly crossed off again when at lunch-time he'd gone out again to the Ninth Ward to see the new owner of what used to be the 'Ain't Showin' Mariner', now a short-order and burger restaurant. Jac was wary of visiting the Ninth at night after the incident with Rillet, but at least the timing had been fortuitous because the proprietor had the previous owner's number and had been able to raise him straightaway on his phone.

But, taking the first bites of a prawn and sliced avocado on rye back on home ground on Felicity Street, a part of Jac wondered whether he wouldn't have preferred some delay again: two more strikes against in just an hour gave him the uneasy feeling that the few names left on his pad would go the same way, leads evaporating in no time, and then there'd be no hope remaining; nothing left but to sit back and count the days until Durrant died.

Maybe he was kidding himself either way – whether slowly treading water or a quick free-fall, the result would be the same: every name on his pad would end up with a line through it. Coultaine had followed part of the same route at appeal only three years after the murder, and could hardly get anyone to remember anything then. What chance was there, as Larry had aired doubtfully, after twelve years?

As he finished the last few bites, Jac's cell-phone rang. Bob Stratton with news on the Pontiac registration.

'Traces back to a holding company of no other than Adelay Roche himself. And the guy driving is one Nelson Timothy Malley, forty-six years of age, down as Head of Security at Roche's Houma refinery. I'll get the photos messengered over to you this afternoon.'

A chill ran through Jac with the information. 'Answers not only who's been following me, but who apart from Larry Durrant might have killed Jessica Roche.' Jac swilled back a residue of chewed rye with a gulp of orange juice, but suddenly found it harder swallowing. 'Looks like the police should have kept doing what they normally do: looking closer to home.'

'That's *one* interpretation, Jac. But don't get too carried away. The other is that Roche simply wants to know your every move: is convinced that Durrant killed his wife and wants to ensure you don't get him freed at the last moment on some technicality or rabbit out the hat. Guys as powerful as Roche, seen many a time where they wouldn't even leave it just to the police, would take justice into their own hands.'

'So steam-rollering over yours truly in the middle wouldn't present much of a problem?'

'True.' Stratton chuckled lightly. 'Though there's another interpretation there, too: we can't say for sure that they tried to kill you; all we *do* know is that they've been nosin' and had your phone bugged. The police might have been right on that score: maybe it *was* just an accident.'

Now it was Jac's turn to say 'True', but with no laugh attached. He could still feel the cold darkness of the lake shiver through him. Attaching blame, giving it a home, maybe he'd be able to rid himself of it. Or perhaps it meant that he'd keep shivering, because they were still hanging over him like a shadow, listening in on his phone, silently watching, waiting for the next time to try and kill him.

That shiver ran deeper still when, three hours later, the

envelope arrived at Jac's office and he looked at the photos inside. Another for the gallery of Jessica Roche's possible murderers: Larry Durrant, the mystery e-mailer, now Roche's henchman: Nelson Malley.

At least it was one bit of positive news after the two rapid name-strikes of earlier, one more shade filled in. *Know thy enemy*.

Though as quickly countered, the pendulum again swinging the other way, when Ted Levereaux phoned early evening, not long after he returned from work, and told him, sorry, in the end he couldn't remember anything either. 'Racked my brain every which way . . . but nothin'. Nothin'.'

Another strike against.

Jac felt weary, tired, his nerves shot from the rollercoaster ride of the past days.

His hand shook as he crossed out Levereaux's name and looked at the two names remaining: Lenny Rillet and Lorraine Gilliam, the waitress that worked the other shift to Rillet.

Rillet said that he'd phone *if* he managed to find his old diaries. He'd told Jac and Mack Elliott in parting to say a prayer in thanks to Larry, because that was the *only* reason he was letting them go. 'Always felt a sorta kinship with Larry, even more so when he wen' inside. So I'm curious to see how this one plays out . . . if you're gonna be able to save his ass or not.' But Jac doubted that Rillet would phone. What, you want to not get shot *and* get a phone call? Lorraine Gilliam's phone simply didn't answer, and Mack Elliott wasn't hopeful that she'd remember anything: 'Dizzy blonde, if yo' know what I mean – 'xcept she was a red-head. Had trouble even recallin' half the drinks orders in the distance just from the tables to the bar.'

Jac felt lonely, cold and deflated that night. Lonely and cold because Alaysha wasn't there, had taken Molly to her mom's for dinner and to stay the night while she worked: her regular four-night-a-week ritual. And deflated from the day's let-downs and the scant remaining options.

He could have done with sharing his woes with Alaysha, felt her hugging and reassuring him; and, in turn, he'd have reassured her about Gerry, told her that the restraining order arriving in the asshole's lap the next day would surely stop him in his tracks. Hopefully soothe the lines on her brow and the quiver he'd seen on her lips when he'd come back from Rillet's and she'd told him about Gerry's second visit.

Jac reached for the brandy bottle to warm himself and lift his spirits, but stopped short after two heavy measures, tucking the bottle back in the cabinet. He knew that if he kept it close, he'd probably half finish it.

But it was enough, with the hectic, wearying day, to slide him into a doze not long after dinner; and so when his cell-phone rang at some stage later – Jac didn't know how long, he'd lost track of time – it took him a moment to orientate himself.

Lenny Rillet's voice, coarse and throaty, as if he'd just woken from the dark tomb that was his crack house.

'That be the same Jac McElroy pinchin' his ass that he still alive?' Sharp, rattling chuckle from Rillet. ' 'Cause I thought you'd like t'be the first to know – I foun' those diaries.'

Leonard Truelle was only twenty yards into the dusk light of the side-street, heading towards his car, when the blow came to his lower back, feeling like someone had hit him with a sledgehammer, his legs buckling as the pain shot up his spine and lanced like an ice-pick through his skull.

Then another blow quickly after, sending his pain sensors into overload as the breath left his body in a strangled groan and he fell to his knees. Something was slipped over his head then, some sort of fabric, the smell of cotton pleasant, welcoming; but the darkness he was plunged into, suddenly not being able to see anything, was decidedly unwelcome, *frightening*.

Aware now of sound and movement for the first time, rustling, shuffling – they seemed to have come out of nowhere behind him and he hadn't heard any approach – one person, no, *two*, he realized, as he felt himself being lifted and carried. But still no voices, nothing said between themselves or to him, which somehow made it all the more terrifying.

No more than eight or ten paces before a car door was opened and he was thrown brusquely into the back – Truelle trying to recall which cars he'd seen close by as it started up and pulled out. He could feel mucus on his chin, or maybe he'd vomited without realizing it, and the pain in his back had now spread like burning oil to his stomach, razor shards shooting up his spine as his body lurched with two sharp turns, one after the other. A long flat stretch for a while, a half mile or more, and a voice finally came from the front.

'You know, you should never have had those phone bugs cleared, otherwise we wouldn't have to do this now.'

Nel-M. As much as Nel-M's voice made Truelle's skin crawl each time, he felt an odd sense of relief hearing it now: a face put to one of his abductors at least. Two faceless abductors would have been more ominous, worrying. *Better the devil you know.*

'We've become concerned about what you might have been saying. Because we simply don't know any more. And that makes us worry perhaps more than we should.' Nel-M had got part of the idea when he'd looked in his car mirror the other night and seen the hood being taken off McElroy. The other part had been from an interview with Truelle in a psychiatric journal that Roche had got hold of, in which Truelle had talked about drawing out patient's fears and phobias, with a brief aside about his own fear of heights. 'Do you like dancing, Leonard?'

'*What*? What the hell are yoouuu – ' A cough rose from the back of Truelle's throat and became a brief coughing fit that he thought for a second would lapse into retching.

'Nasty cough you got there, Leonard. Maybe some fresh air would help . . . like somewhere up high. *Way* up high.' Nel-M smiled to himself as the silence settled deeper; he could almost hear the wheels in Truelle's mind turning in time with the thrum of the wheels on the road.

'Where . . . *where* are we going?' Hesitant, tremulous, as if afraid of hearing the answer.

Silence. Nel-M purposely let it lengthen, let the unknown, the uncertainties multiply in Truelle's mind as he motioned Vic Farrelia into the next turn, and then, two hundred yards along, pointed out a good parking spot. No words between them, as had been agreed at the outset: this was stretching Farrelia's call of duty, and so he wanted to remain as anonymous as possible.

They bundled Truelle out from the back, a dozen or so paces counted by Truelle before the sound of a door opening, closing, four more paces and then another door, mechanical, sliding. An elevator.

Nel-M didn't speak again until the elevator started rising.

'Like I said, Leonard . . . somewhere up high. Way up where you and I can get a good view of the city. A *real* good view.'

But Nel-M knew that Truelle was only half-listening, he was timing and counting in his mind just how far the elevator was rising.

Eighteen floors, Nel-M could have told him, but wasn't going to; the elevator wasn't that fast, in Truelle's mind it probably seemed more.

Out of the elevator, along and through a door, then up the steps to the roof and over to its far side. They stood Truelle up, but Nel-M kept one arm around him, bracing. Again, Nel-M didn't speak throughout, and he waited a moment now, wanted the air wafting up from eighteen floors below to hit Truelle's senses.

Nel-M took a deep breath. 'Real nice up here. And fine view . . . fine view, indeed. You can see the whole city.' He knew that his words combined with the heavier breeze on the rooftop had painted enough of a picture for Truelle inside the darkness of the hood. He could feel Truelle's body trembling in his grip. 'But you know, we don't have to do this now . . . we don't have to go *dancing*. If only you just told us where you've got those insurance policies held.'

'*What* . . . dancing?' Truelle's mind was scrambled. All he could think about was Nel-M's last words. That view. 'I . . . I can't tell you. You'd just kill me then.'

'Possibility that I would, I suppose.' Nel-M was silent for a moment, thoughtful. 'But you know, Leonard, if you'd seen some of the things I have in my lifetime, you'd know that there's actually worse things than death. Like pain. And dancing.'

There it was again, thought Truelle: dancing? Had Nel-M gone completely mad, was looking to book a session on his couch? He was still trying to work it out as with an, 'Okay . . . Huuuup,' from Nel-M, he felt himself being lifted bodily. He thought for one horrible moment – the intake of breath rising sharply in his throat, making him dizzy as it hit his brain – that he was being thrown straight over the edge. But then he felt something firm again under his feet, and Nel-M close, his breath hot against the cloth covering his face; strangely comforting, given how he'd have normally felt about that.

'Now you're going to have to keep real close, Leonard, and hold real tight – like we're dancing,' Nel-M said. 'Because this ledge – it ain't that wide.'

Oh God. Oh God. And suddenly it all made sense to Truelle, and he clung onto Nel-M as if his life depended on it; because now he knew with certainty that it actually did.

Nel-M could have found buildings higher, thirty floors or more, but this was the only one he knew with such a wide ledge running around, just over two foot. Enough for them to move around on, as long as they kept in close. At each corner and in the middle of each side were large Roman urns with squat fan palms. Probably the main reason for the width of the ledge. But there was still a good thirty feet between each urn for their dance run, Nel-M observed.

Nel-M started moving then, swinging Truelle out for a

second to feel the drop – heard him gasp and felt the trembling in his body run deeper – then swung him sharply back in again.

'So, shall we try again . . . where have you left those insurance policies?'

'I . . . I can't. It's . . . it's my only pro . . . protection.' Truelle was trembling so hard, he had trouble forming the words, his mind half gone. All he could think of was where he was putting his feet and that drop only inches away.

Nel-M reached deeper behind Truelle's back as they moved, two steps forward, two steps back, gently swaying. 'Now, where was it I punched you? There . . . *there*, I think.'

Truelle felt the pain rocket through his brain. Nel-M eased off for a second, then dug even harder with two fingers into Truelle's kidney, heard him groan as the shudder ran through his body, his legs buckling. Nel-M held him upright.

'Now, don't you go giving up on me, Leonard. Just as we're starting to get into the rhythm.' Nel-M smiled. The only thing missing from making this little scenario a hundred-and-ten per cent perfect, rather than just a hundred per cent: with the hood, Truelle couldn't see him gloating, his eyes dancing; see how much Nel-M was enjoying it. 'See what I mean about pain being worse than death, Leonard. Keep that up for a while, and you'd be begging me to kill you. But we'd have to be in a dark basement somewhere for that, where half the neighbourhood couldn't hear your screams. And I'm a real softy for mood, atmosphere. Much better up here with the city spread below us, *dancing*.' Nel-M leant in closer, his mouth only inches from Truelle's ear, his smile widening as he swore he could all but feel the shudder of revulsion run through Truelle's body with his next words. 'Don't you think, Lenny, *baby*?'

Nel-M started moving again, more fluidly, dramatically, swaying and leaning Truelle even further over the drop at times.

Truelle exclaimed breathlessly, 'Please . . . *please* don't do this.'

'You're not crapping out on our romantic date already, are you, Lenny? You know, I used to know this chick down at a club on Toulouse Street. Half pure Congo-African, half Spanish Creole . . . and boy, could she tango.' Nel-M started moving again. 'Man, we'd swing up and down so hard and fast we'd clear half the dance floor.' More elaborate swaying and swinging now, relishing Truelle's gasps as he hung him over the drop at almost a ninety-degree angle at points. 'Not like you. All stiff and formal, stumbling on your step. Something worryin' you, Lenny?' Nel-M chuckled.

'*Please* . . . I'm begging you.'

'Wanna die yet, Lenny? Think that's suddenly more appealing?' Nel-M chuckled again, lower, more menacing. 'Or have you worked out yet which you prefer: dancing or *pain*?'

On the last word, Nel-M dug his fingers again into Truelle's bruised kidney, felt his body jolt as the pain shot through it.

Truelle spluttered breathlessly, 'I can't . . . I *can't* tell you.'

Nel-M wondered whether to give Truelle a few more swaying steps, probably his first taste ever of real rhythm, then just drop him over the edge. *Last Tango in New Orleans*. But the fall-out might not be containable, and there were other things he wanted to know.

'Okay. *Okay.* If we can't do that – then tell me what happened when McElroy came to see you? He's making out that he stopped doing anything on the Durrant case soon after he saw you. But I've got my doubts. Strong doubts. So, what did he say to you, Lenny?'

'Not much, really.'

'I mean, did he tell you that he was going to stop digging? Was going to leave everything just with the Governor's plea?'

'No – he didn't say that. But . . . but also, there didn't seem much he knew.'

'And *you* didn't tell him anything, did you, Lenny?'

'No . . . *no.* Of course not.'

They started moving again then, but slowly, less flamboyantly. But Truelle was still petrified, fearful that with the slightest false half-step, he'd fall over the edge.

'So, what *did* happen in that meeting, Lenny?'

'Not that much. Not that I can think of.'

That didn't seem to please Nel-M. The step increased, the swaying bolder. 'Think, Lenny. *Think*. It's important.'

'Well, he . . . he seemed concerned about hearing that Doctor Thallerey, Jessica Roche's obstetrician, had died in a car accident. And an accident too that he'd had himself . . . thought they might be linked.'

'You see . . . you *see*. You can do it when you try.' The swaying subsided a little. 'What else?'

'I don't know . . . not much else, really.'

The step and swaying picked up again. 'Think harder, Lenny. Like I say, it's important.'

'He . . . he left in such a rush. That's why there wasn't . . . wasn't much else.' Truelle was having trouble talking and concentrating on his step at the same time. 'He nev . . . never told me what had troubled him so just before he left.'

The step steadied again. 'Okay. I buy that. Anything else?'

'With . . . with what had happened with himself and Thallerey, almost like . . . like a warning I might be next.'

'You might be, Leonard.' Another quick looping sway with Truelle held dramatically over the drop before quickly righting again. Nel-M's gloat slid into a brief chuckle. 'You might be.'

'And he . . .' Truelle suddenly stopped himself, worried that this part might bring back questions about his insurance policies.

'What else, Lenny?' The swaying step increased once more. 'Don't hold back on me now.'

'He . . .' Truelle's left foot slipped over the edge then, Nel-M quickly pulling him back up tight. But the pain lanced through him again as Nel-M's hand pressed harder into his back. Truelle took a second to regain his composure and breath. 'He . . . he asked me if my telephones might have been bugged. Said he was worried that *his* might have been . . .'

Now it was Nel-M's turn to hyper-ventilate, and he almost let Truelle loose from his grip with the jolt that went through him – or maybe it was as much shoving him away in anger, taking his frustration out on the nearest thing – as everything hit him in a rush: McElroy saying that he'd dropped the case and then the sudden lack of any meaningful calls on his home phone, except one; the one where he'd followed McElroy and nobody had showed up. Not only had McElroy thrown them a curve ball over his bugged phone-line, he'd also no doubt had yours truly followed the other day. Now knew more about himself and Roche than he dared think about.

But one consolation, he thought: he'd get to play out his plan B with McElroy. Roche would now jump for it quicker than . . . well, quicker than a 'Psychiatrist falls off the edge.' One last pause as he pondered whimsically what a shame it was that he wouldn't now be reading that headline tomorrow, then with one hand he helped Truelle down from the ledge.

'And thank you kindly for the dance, Mr Truelle. It's been most . . . most enlightening.'

26

Torch- and candle-light outside the prison gates.

If Jac didn't know that there wasn't long left now until Durrant's execution, he'd have become aware from the people holding vigil outside Libreville.

Only a small group now, eight or nine, but in the final few days those numbers would swell – local protesters and an increasing number of anti-capital punishment supporters, mostly from out of state – to probably a hundred strong by the end.

Jac had received the news that the Board of Pardons hearing would be in only two days' time. It wasn't the sort of news he wanted to give Durrant over the phone, it warranted face-to-face, and after the news from Rillet there were a few things he wanted to ask Larry directly.

There was also something he needed to pick up after work before heading out to Libreville, so the last of the dusk light was fast fading as Jac hit the Pontchartrain Causeway, a shiver still running through him each time he crossed it.

Ghosts. Even the corridors at Libreville now held them for Jac. Memories of when he'd first headed along their grey, footstep-echoing lengths, shirt sticking to his back, nerves bubbling wildly, to see Larry Durrant for the first time.

Felt like a lifetime ago now. Because now it seemed like they were long-lost old friends, Larry hugging him in greeting before they took up seats each side of the table in the 'Quiet Room'. Larry's expression darkened as Jac told him about the BOP hearing in two days' time.

'What do you think are the chances?'

'We've put in a strong plea, no denying: good character, strong religious values, your self-educating, and, of course, the key issue of executing someone who even now doesn't have all their memory faculties. I even sent in a couple of case examples to back that up. But against that we've got the thorny problem of Aaron Harvey re-offending. Killing again. There's a lot of political pressure on Candaret because of that. And so . . .' Seeing Durrant hanging on his words with fresh light, hope, in his eyes, Jac side-stepped, moderated what he'd initially planned to say. 'So it's all in the balance, Larry. All in the balance.'

Larry nodded thoughtfully, and Jac felt a stab of guilt to his chest. Having told himself that he couldn't and wouldn't fool Larry, in the end he'd weakened and done just that: the odds were far worse than fifty-fifty. From what he'd seen in the press and talking with John Langfranc, the political pressure on Candaret was so intense that the chances were probably no better than two or three per cent.

But having spent the past weeks giving Larry something to cling to, filling him with hope, Jac couldn't just come along now and tell him that there was little or no hope. Kill the faint light in Durrant's eyes he'd only just put there.

Jac introduced a fresh tone. 'But there's been movement too on other fronts.' He told Larry about Mack Elliott and Rillet and his conversations of the past few days. He didn't mention the crack house or being worried for their lives at one point, because Larry hardly remembered Rillet in any case; a reminder to Jac of how little Larry recalled from his past, how far he might be stretching for what he wanted now. 'And miracle of miracles, Rillet did manage to dig up his diary from that week.'

'*Oh*? That's great.'

Jac held one hand up, calming, as that hopeful light came back into Larry's eyes. 'It's only given us half the picture, unfortunately. He wasn't working the night of Jessica Roche's murder – so he can't tell us anything about then. But the good news is that the pool game wasn't one of the nights he *was* working that week. Otherwise we'd have struck out straightaway.' One trait Jac had gained from his father: look on the bright side. When Jac had first heard that Rillet hadn't worked that key night, he'd felt immediately deflated, especially after the lines he'd put through name after name over the last few days. But then he'd shaken himself out of it, started to look at the other options. 'So, of course, that means with the pool game taking place on one of those nights remaining, it could well have coincided with the night Jessica Roche was murdered. Out of those nights you used to play – Tuesday, Thursday or Saturday – Rillet was there Saturday, and it wasn't then. So that leaves just the Tuesday and the Thursday, the night she was murdered. We've managed to narrow it down to just *two* nights.' Jac held Durrant's gaze for a second. 'That's the other reason I've come here now, Larry. To hopefully try and fill in that final gap. I've asked everyone else, but not you.'

'Okay, fine.' Durrant nodded, something in his eyes lifting, as if only then did it fully dawn on him where Jac was heading. 'Fire away.'

Jac gave the background to how he'd handled things with Hadley, Saunders, Levereaux and Mack Elliott: *putting them in the moment.* 'So, I'm going to ask you the same as them: do you remember where and when you first heard Jessica Roche had been murdered?'

But as quickly as that light had come into Larry Durrant's eyes, it receded. 'I don't know. It's difficult.'

'I know.' Jac smiled tightly. 'But try. *Try.* It's important.'

Larry nodded, applying more thought, his eyes darkening with concentration. 'I'm not sure, but . . . but early evening news, I think.'

'Early evening? Not daytime news or in a newspaper?'

Durrant shook his head. 'No, don't think so. I wasn't working, but I was out in the daytime a lot . . . looking for work. So I think that's the first time I'd have seen it.'

'*Think*? Don't you actually remember where and when you saw it, Larry?' An edge now in Jac's voice.

314

'Don't know.' Durrant looked down again, that uncertainty, the shadows worming deeper. 'That's how I seem to remember it . . . evening news.'

'Evening news. Okay. *Okay*. And what do you remember feeling when you saw that news?'

'*Feeling?*' Durrant shook his head, his tone incredulous. 'I'm still working on where and when, and now you want me to tell you what I was feeling. And why's that so important?'

'Because, Larry, if you'd just killed Jessica Roche, you'd have been scouring the newspapers from first light, or at least made sure to catch a news bulletin a bit before early evening. That's why. And when you did first hear that news, a stone would have sunk through your stomach.'

'Oh, right.' Durrant exhaled dramatically, forcing a tight smile. 'Since you put it like that.' He applied more thought for a moment, faint shadows drifting behind his eyes again; then, as if as an afterthought, 'What did the others recall?'

'I've still got a couple more leads to hear from,' Jac lied. He didn't want to tell Durrant that there was only *one* lead remaining, and that it was a scatterbrained waitress who hardly remembered your drink order minutes later; let alone what, where and when from twelve years ago.

Larry nodded, 'Okay', blinking slowly as he sank back again into thought. But the shadows in his eyes just seemed to settle deeper, and after a moment he squinted and shook his head, as if he'd tried to read a distant number plate on a dark night, but the car had driven off at the crucial moment. He smiled wryly. 'You know, when I first lay on Truelle's couch, I couldn't even remember my son's middle name or his birthday. My mother's name had gone too, and what my father looked like and how old I was when he died . . . and *everything* about Francine's mother – though at first Franny thought I was just doin' that on purpose – all completely lost, out of reach.' Larry's lopsided smile quickly faded. 'I'm grateful just to have been able to get that back, Jac – let alone remembering what I was *feeling* twelve years ago.'

'I know. I know.' Jac nodded sombrely. 'But it's just that you said you'd started to remember more.'

'Yeah.' Larry held one palm out in tame concession. 'Like a bit of where and when and a couple of old buddies' names. But I think that what I was actually *feeling* then is gonna be stretching things. Maybe always will be.'

'Okay. Where and when.' Jac grabbed for what he could. 'Let's concentrate on that. See if you can remember when that week's pool game was in relation to you hearing about Jessica Roche's murder. I mean, was it just the day after? Or did there seem to be more of a gap?'

'I don't know. Day after . . . *day after*?' Larry's eyes and thoughts drifting again. 'Maybe something there . . . but . . .'

Jac sat forward, desperately afraid that whatever thin thread Durrant had grasped might be lost again. 'Try, Larry, *please* . . .'

Durrant nodded, blinking slowly. 'If only I could remember whether Bill Saunders was there that week. You see, if it was a Tuesday . . . I recall that often Bill wouldn't show then, because he had to take his little girl to some sort of dance practice. So we'd get someone else from the bar to fill in. So that would then leave just that crucial Thursday night.'

Jac nodded eagerly. 'Yes, *yes*. It would.' The night Jessica Roche was murdered. He fell quickly silent again so as not to break Durrant's concentration.

Larry was squinting at that distant number plate again; for a second it looked like he might have fixed on it, but then it was as if the tail-lights had in turn moved further away. He peered harder to try and compensate, but it was no good; it was lost again. Jac noticed Larry's hands and arms trembling then, as though the effort of remembering had set off a gentle quake in his body.

Larry shook his head finally. 'I'm sorry, Jac. Maybe led you on some there, too, with the "where and when". I *can't* remember whether Bill was there that week. Overall, I can recall only a handful of pool games, and maybe a handful of incidents too from those games. But ask me now which incidents were from which games, or which week or month – or even year – they were, I'd be lost. Never mind when one particular game was in relation to Jessica Roche's murder.'

Jac nodded, closing his eyes for a second in acceptance, and could almost feel the shuddering in Durrant's body pass through him. Seeing Durrant's eyes dark and haunted, grappling for segments of his life that were out of reach and probably now would for ever remain so, Jac felt like running down the corridor to Haveling or getting on the phone to Governor Candaret, screaming: You can't kill him! Look at him. *Look at him*!

Jac took a fresh breath. 'One other thing. On that tape you made for Truelle – do you recall anyone else being around, apart from that woman walking her dog as you ran away, but perhaps forgot to mention?' Jac said 'on the tape' because, outside of that, he doubted Durrant would recall anything.

Durrant pondered for a second. 'No. *Why*?'

'No particular reason.' Jac shrugged. *I was there at the time.* Although he'd told Durrant about the e-mails, he'd held back the sender's claim of actually being there. One more thing Durrant would now never know. 'Or perhaps even just the sense that someone else was there, either in the house or outside, looking on, that you didn't mention to Truelle?'

'No.' Larry's eyebrows knitted heavily, and Jac thought that was simply because he found the question odd. But the shadows returned to his eyes then, dragged him away again to that place where he found it hard to picture anything clearly. 'Though it's strange you should ask that – because I've had this dream a few times where it's someone else pulling the trigger on Jessica Roche, not me. I'm there just looking on.'

'Oh? And do you get to see a face in those dreams? Do you see who it is?'

'Nah.' Larry shrugged, smiling hesitantly. 'You know what it's like with dreams: a tease. When I first had it, it was all tied-in with my mother staring at me in the courtroom. Man, I could feel her eyes like they were boring a hole right through my shoulder. I could feel all her shame and disappointment at me in that stare. And, I thought: if I could just see his face, see that it wasn't me – I could turn and shout that out to her in the courtroom: "It wasn't me, Ma . . . it wasn't me. I saw him. *I saw him!*" ' Larry's last words echoed starkly in the bare concrete room, and again a faint shiver ran through Jac. Larry smiled tightly, the shadows, the lost hope, drifting away again from his eyes. 'But, you know, it was just a damn fool dream. And, in any case, he never did turn my way in the dreams; always stayed just a hazy shadow turned away from me, pointing the gun.' Larry gave a half-snort, half-snigger, as if, with that, tossing the image from his mind. 'But maybe it was just my mind self-protecting, throwing up all this because part of me couldn't accept that I'd done it.' Another brief, derisive snort. 'Though I was way away then from the likes of Truelle and any psychiatrist's couch. That's just me self-analysing.'

Jac swallowed hard. Didn't say anything, *couldn't* say anything, as he felt the guilt weigh him down. Here he was shielding truths or only dealing half-truths with Durrant, while meanwhile Larry was baring his soul to the bone. Almost a complete reversal of their first meeting together. But at least it perhaps answered why, on the key tape from Truelle, Larry never actually described pulling the trigger; even then, his mind was self-protecting, pushing away that he'd done it. Or, the other explanation: he *hadn't* done it.

Hadn't done it? Jac wondered whether he should mention Roche's henchman, Nelson Malley, trailing him the other day and the photos they'd gained. But, like the mystery e-mailer, it would just torment Durrant all the more, putting substance and a face to someone else who *might* have been the murderer when they were still a million miles from proving that. The cruellest fate of all, knowing that someone else might well have done what you were about to be executed for, yet with nothing left to stop it. Jac bit at his lip; another secret buried.

There was a gentle thrum in the background, maybe the prison boilers – but Jac could feel its rhythm coursing through him now, along with the dull pounding of his heart, like a distant drumbeat driving him on after all the madness and fallen hurdles of the past days, as if saying, you can't give up now. *You can't.* You've gone too far. But Jac felt tired, worn down from it all, and now the few options left appeared even more remote; as hazy and out of reach as the images in Larry Durrant's fractured mind from twelve years ago.

As the silence became uneasy, Jac said, 'But, while I'm here . . .' And with a fresh, expectant breath, he reached into his briefcase. He'd picked everything up before heading out to the prison, and now probably needed more than ever: clear the air of stale half-truths and half-memories hanging over them. Jac pulled out the two bottles and balloon glasses with a magician's flourish. '*Voila*! Choose your poison: twelve-year-old malt whisky, or twenty-year-old cognac. Symbols of my two past cultures.'

Larry beamed, shaking his head. '*Jeezus* . . . you're a man of many surprises, Jac McElroy. Most people would try and sneak in a file or a gun. You turn up with two bottles of liquor.' Larry applied brief thought and pointed to the cognac. 'I hear that's the new black yuppie drink of choice. Been out of touch for twelve years – might as well be in vogue now.'

'And I'll join you in that.' Jac poured the two glasses and passed Larry's across. He wanted to feel as close to and in harmony with Durrant as possible; at this moment of all moments.

Jac watched, as with eyes half-closed, Larry took the first sip. Jac remembered as a child going out on a hot day in the woods around the Rochefort farmhouse and getting lost. He'd been gone almost six hours in the hot sun without a drink, and his lips were dry and blistered as he lifted the glass his mother handed him. He remembered still vividly that feeling when the water first touched his lips and trickled down, and knew that it was akin to what Larry Durrant was feeling now.

The first real drink after twelve years. And mellow, twenty-year-old cognac. Pure nectar.

They drank in silence for a moment. A long moment, Larry alternating between closing his eyes as the cognac trickled down and its warmth hit his stomach, as if it was just another dream and not really happening, and smacking his lips, relishing its taste. 'Man, that's good . . . that's *sooooo* good.' Larry leant forward after a moment, peering at the label. 'What's this stuff called?'

'Frapin. It's one of the best.'

'Man oooohhh man . . . I can taste that for myself. Even if you hadn't told me.' Larry took another sip, closing his eyes for a second in reverie, then sank back into silence again, smiling.

Jac smiled back. Twelve years without a drink, and suddenly Larry was acting like a connoisseur.

This was one of those moments when they were meant to be silent; after all, they'd done nothing but rake over the coals of old ghosts and old memories the past forty minutes, said everything that needed to be said. But as Larry's eyes narrowed after a moment, it looked like there was something else on his mind. He took another slug, as if clearing his throat for the words; or perhaps, now they were drinking, that final bit of Dutch courage, licence to become more maudlin.

'One thing I never did work out about you, Jac. Why you went out on such a limb for me? I mean, it got to the point where your life was in danger, man. Maybe still is.'

'My girlfriend asked just the same the other day.'

'Don't blame her.' Larry smiled crookedly. 'She likes you, maybe she's keen on keeping your ass around a while longer.'

Jac mirrored the smile, took another sip of cognac. 'I think the first thing was, big case, and wanting to prove myself. But a lot of that was also wrapped up with what happened with my father. He died young, well, not exactly old: he was only fifty-four when he died.'

Larry slanted one eyebrow. 'So, you got a thing about people dying young? Is that what you're telling me?'

Jac shrugged. 'No, well, I suppose that's a pretty natural instinct for a lot of people. But it had more to do with the circumstances surrounding his death.' Jac explained about his father's business collapse and disastrous financial situation when he died, with a lot of people, including Jac's rich aunt, as a result labelling him a failure. 'So when anyone gets close to suggesting that I too might fail on something, it's like a red rag to a bull. I'll go to all sorts of lengths to prove them wrong. It's almost like I'm batting too on my father's behalf, setting the record straight on how people remember him.' Jac took another slug. 'That's how they were painting this case originally at Payne, Beaton and Sawyer: little hope, bound to fail. That's why they gave it to a young blood like me, rather than one of the senior partners. But what they didn't know was, because of that fear of failure, how hard I'd fight it.'

'Looks like I got the right man, then.' Larry raised his glass, smiling tightly, his expression faintly quizzical as he thought about the skewed logic of what Jac had just said. 'I think.'

A bit more truth, Jac thought, but again he still held back. He'd come here intending to be brutally honest, lay every possible card on the table, because it might be his very last chance. But once he was actually in front of Durrant, his resolve had melted and he'd only told half the truth. The real reason he'd gone out on such a limb for Durrant had hit him in the dead of night the day after Alaysha had asked him, awoken him in a cold, shivering sweat. At the same time it was strangely calming, settling: at least now I know. *Now I know.* And there'd been a moment now, a natural conversational lead-on, when he could have said it. *Dying young? Lived before he died.* But as he looked at Durrant, saw the eleven years of pain and loneliness in his eyes, he'd once again baulked; felt it might be too harsh for Durrant to take with only days left now until his execution.

Jac shrugged. 'Or maybe it's just that I don't agree with the state killing people. Anti-capitalist punishment thing.' Jac took a quick slug, grimacing. 'Almost required thinking for a European.'

Larry nodded thoughtfully. 'Yeah, I know. You don't have it over there.'

Jac nodded back. Easy to forget at times that Durrant wasn't just another homey, how well read he was. 'There hasn't been anyone executed in over thirty years in most of Europe. And it doesn't seem to have affected the murder rate. Still a quarter of that in the States.'

'Pretty much the same here. States with no death penalty don't have higher murder rates. In fact, in most cases, lower.'

Jac lifted his glass towards Larry. 'In a way, you're proof of that.' Jac made sure not to say 'living'. 'Wasn't too long ago that I asked you which might be preferable, death or another ten or fifteen in here, and . . . *well*, we both know what you said.' Death possibly so near now that Jac found himself tip-toeing around the word. 'Often a long sentence is as much a deterrent.'

Larry nodded again, this time more slowly, his eyes shifting uncertainly, as if, if asked the same question now, he wasn't sure any more what he'd answer. 'You miss your father, don't you?' he said after a moment.

'Yeah.' Jac looked down at the table and the bottle as his eyes moistened. 'And hardly a day goes by that I don't think about him.'

'I understand.' Larry contemplated Jac steadily, warmly. 'Same here too with my mother.' Then he closed his eyes for a second, though this time in acceptance rather than savouring the cognac. They drank in silence a moment more, and something crossed Larry's eyes then, something darker, more worrying. His eyes went between his glass, the bottle and Jac, as if he was struggling to fully fathom what it was, and the rest hit him in a rush then: Jac pushing so hard for a possible breakthrough, the drink, the maudlin, philosophical conversation. He nodded at his glass and blinked slowly. 'Don't think I don't appreciate this, Jac. 'Cause I do. I *really* do. But this is a dying man's drink, isn't it? You don't see much hope left, do you?'

'No, *no . . .* of course not. Like I said, there's still some leads left, we've got a strong plea in with Candaret . . . and we'll kick the BOP's ass like you wouldn't believe the day after next. And I'm sure that . . .' Jac stopped himself then, felt himself sag under Larry's steady, withering gaze, under that weight of half-truths he'd fed Larry since walking in the room; sag quickly becoming crumble as, with a heavy exhalation, he met Larry's gaze more directly, calmly. 'Sorry, Larry . . . *sorry.* It's not looking that good. I'm going to do my best with the BOP and Candaret, *and* with the few leads remaining . . . but it would be wrong of me to kid you . . .'

Larry nodded, and suddenly Jac didn't need to say any more, as if Larry had understood perfectly well all along. Had seen through the subterfuge right from the start.

Jac's eyes watered, the tears hitting him then without warning. Perhaps because of Larry's quiet acceptance, or his last words, *dying man's drink,* the sudden realization that this might be one of the last times he'd see Larry and there probably wasn't much more he could do for him.

Larry leant forward, putting one hand on Jac's shoulder, gently shaking. 'It's okay . . . *okay.* You did your best.'

But that physical contact made it all the worse, the tears flowing more freely. And then they were on their feet, hugging, Larry patting Jac's back, consoling, 'You couldn't do more, Jac . . . couldn't do more. Don't beat yourself up so.' Then, after a pause, Larry saying he'd be fine and don't worry about him; and Jac, biting back the tears, saying that he wasn't giving up on him and there was still a lot to do. Still strong hope. Both of them knowing in that moment that what they were saying was more wishful thinking than truth, and Jac thinking it was strange that they were standing now in this tableau, because in his mind driving to the prison, if the emotions *had* become too much, it had been Larry tearful and Jac consoling. 'And thanks for the cognac, Jac,' Larry said as, with a last few back-pats, they parted and sat back down. 'It's made my day . . . my *year*.'

They sat drinking in silence again, like two old friends who knew each other so well that often words weren't needed, the warmth of the shared drink and their companionship enough. And when Jac looked in Larry's eyes, he could see that the shadows had gone, no longer haunted by chasing distant, out-of-reach memories. He was calm again. At peace.

27

'Are you sure?'

'As sure as can be,' Nel-M said. That laboured, unsettling breathing from the other end. Darth Vader watching porno. 'I don't know what other explanation there can be for him leaving his phone bug in after telling Truelle he was sure it was bugged. Then all that crap with him saying he's dropped the case and that false lead the other day. McElroy's been playing us for mugs.'

Breathing heavier, more perturbed, as if it was a Geiger counter for Roche's thoughts. 'Looks like you could well be right. Did you notice anyone following you the other day?'

'No. But then I wasn't particularly looking out for them, because I didn't know then what I know now from Truelle. I think it might be time to –'

'I *know*. I know what it might be time to do,' Roche cut in. He swallowed, struggling to get his breathing back under control. 'Let me think on this a while. I'll phone you back.'

Roche's call came thirty-five minutes later, but in that time Nel-M was calm, relaxed – making a pot of fresh coffee, whistling softly to himself, watching some breakfast TV – because he knew already what the answer would be. He wondered what Roche had done in that same time: played some Vivaldi or Wagner, or sat silently with only the sound of his own breathing rising and falling, looking at his cherubs and red brocade, his swimming pool surrounded by Roman statues – the precious gilded world he'd made for himself – contemplating just how fragile it all might be.

'Okay. Do it. But make sure it's clean. No messy loose ends.'

'It'll be soooo clean, you'll be able to eat your dinner off it.'

An hour later Nel-M was inside McElroy's apartment, latex

gloves on his hands as he delicately lifted what he'd need from countertops and doors, and searched through cupboards and drawers for any vital papers Jac might have hidden. Nothing. He went over to the phone and removed the bug, then listened out for a moment: no sounds from next door, she'd probably gone shopping.

Nel-M decided to search there too, in case, knowing that he'd been targeted, McElroy had decided to hide anything at his girlfriend's apartment. And only minutes into his search, running one hand along a high wardrobe shelf, he found the gun.

Nel-M took it down, turning it slowly, deliberately, examining. An out of issue Colt, but looked in perfect working order. His plan was shaping up better by the minute.

Jac could feel even stronger the thrumming of the prison boilers almost in time with his pounding heart as he walked away from seeing Durrant, with the steady clip of his footsteps keeping rhythm too; the same distinctive but strangely hollow sound – as if echoing the lost hope of all Libreville's prisoners – he recalled from his first day going to see Durrant, now joining that dull, driving drumbeat: you can't give up now. *You can't.*

And he could still feel that drumbeat as he drove away, though now it was only his heart, its beat harder and faster as he drove back across the darkness of Lake Pontchartrain, remembering. His breath held for a moment, expectant, as if waiting for that first gulp of air again as he hit the surface. But it wasn't the image of himself fighting up through its murky depths that reached him this time, but Larry Durrant: struggling to pick out the images of twelve years ago from its shadowy greyness, but them never hitting the light of the surface. Never becoming clear.

And staring out across the dark expanse of lake, the thought hit Jac in that instant: '*It's there somewhere. It's there. Only you can't see it.*'

He drove the rest of the way back to New Orleans with only that one thought on his mind, and, as soon as he was inside his apartment, went over to his father's painting on the far wall of the dining room, leaning close to it, feeling the texture of its oil brushstrokes.

Their Rochefort farmhouse, a patchwork of vineyards and wheat and sunflower fields sloping up towards a more prominent pine-covered hillside as backdrop.

His father had painted it their first year in Rochefort, when Jac had been only nine. And when his father had first finished it, he asked Jac:

'What do you see?'

'Our farmhouse.'

'Yes, but what else?'

Jac had studied the painting more closely, looking for perhaps himself or his mother as a small dot hidden in the fields or the hillside like one of those 'Where's Waldo' puzzles. But he couldn't see anything, and shook his head after a moment.

'Look deeper into the painting,' his father prompted 'It's there somewhere. It's *there*. Only you can't see it.'

And after a while, Jac could finally see it: a vague, shadowy outline of what looked like their farmhouse in a slightly different position.

His father explained that he'd started laying down the outline of the farmhouse, then suddenly decided it would be better from another angle, the backdrop and depth of shadow and light more dramatic.

'But rather than waste the canvas, I decided to paint over it. It's something the Old Masters used to do all the time – because canvases were even more expensive then. Lean in close to many an Old Master, and you'll be surprised what you see buried in the background.'

And from then on, Jac had always looked. Whether at the Louvre or a local gallery, while everyone else was yards away, trying to appreciate the overall impact of the painting, he'd be only inches from it, trying to see what might lie beneath the surface.

Jac looked at his watch: 11.46 p.m. Late, but he didn't want to delay. He dialled out on his cell-phone. Mike Coultaine's throaty voice answered after three rings.

'That psychiatrist for the defence, Greg Ormdern, is he still practising?' Jac asked.

'I believe so.'

'Any good?'

'At the time, one of the best. Which is why I used to use him as an expert witness. Why?'

Jac explained his thinking to Coultaine: if Truelle had been able to unearth from Durrant's mind his actions that dark night with Jessica Roche, then perhaps Greg Ormdern would be able to fill in the gaps. 'Uncover the rest from that time. The things we still don't know.'

With the last call, Nel-M contemplated, the most important thing had been brevity:

'You wanna know who your girlfriend's new boyfriend is? Who's fucking her now? His name's Jac. Jac with no k.'

Hanging up before Strelloff had half a chance to think or ask who was calling. But this time he'd have to go into more detail.

He sat for almost an hour outside McElroy's apartment – in a rented grey Chevrolet Impala, because McElroy would now recognize his Pontiac – timing and planning.

Eight o'clock, McElroy said that he'd be over to eat at her place. He still used his home phone for day-to-day non-Durrant related calls because, as Nel-M hardly needed reminding – that's all they'd got the past six days on tape.

Nel-M left it half an hour for them to get their appetizers out of the way, then took out his cell-phone to order their main course.

Gerry Strelloff was slightly out of breath as he answered, as if he'd run from another room to pick up, or was on his way somewhere.

'Your friend again. You know that lawyer's letter and restraining order you just got?'

'*What*? Who is this?'

'That doesn't matter.' Nel-M knew they'd been sent from scuttlebutt at 'Pinkies', with Alaysha confiding in a couple of friends. 'Just take it that I'm someone who's got your interests at heart, and wants you to know what a fool you're being played for. Because that boyfriend I mentioned the other day – Jac McElroy – he's a lawyer working for the same firm that sent the letter and arranged the restraining order.'

'You're joking?' Incredulous, still slightly breathless.

'No fucking joke about it, man. And they organized it all just to get you off the scene – so he could get in there like the slimy jack-rabbit he is and take your place.'

'*Shit*! I don't believe it . . . I'll fucking –'

'But that's not the best part.' The touch paper lit – Nel-M could hear the bubbling acid-anger in Strelloff's voice – hopefully this final bucket of petrol would get the flames sky high. 'He lives right next door to her. Probably even heard you screwing her through the walls, and thought – I want somma that So that's where he is now, *right now* – you safely roped and tied by a restraining order while he's in *your* place in her bed . . . fucking her stupid.'

'What? He's there now . . . *this minute*?'

'Yeah . . . this fucking minute, as we speak. Probably already at the point where she's screaming his name out loud . . . Jac . . . Jac! *Oh . . . oh . . . Jac!*' Nel-M chuckled. 'You hurry, maybe you'll get there just in time for the money shot.'

Nel-M hung up and looked at his watch. Twenty-five minutes for Strelloff to get over from his place in Chalmette. Correct that, seventeen or eighteen with the speed he'd be driving.

'When my father died, I had trouble coming to terms with it. As a lot of people do with something like that.' Jac waved one hand above his wine glass towards Alaysha. 'But more than that, I felt he'd been cheated: he was only fifty-four, had many good years left, he'd been a good person with a kind heart, brought his family up well . . . so why him, God? Why him?'

Alaysha simply nodded, didn't speak. She could tell that this was a difficult, heartfelt subject for Jac to broach, so had suddenly stopped clearing their plates from the dinner she'd prepared, not wanting to make *any* noise at that moment. She could see Jac struggling with his thoughts, shadows alternating in his eyes like fast-drifting clouds as he tried to sift them into order.

'The main problem was, they didn't discover it was cancer until late. Because of my father's business problems, their first thought was that it was ulcers rather than stomach cancer. By the time they got to it, it had probably been there for three or four years. It had worked its way too deep, had reached his pancreas. There wasn't a lot they could do.' Jac shrugged, but Alaysha could see that it was like trying to flip off a ten-ton weight. His shoulders moved, but the burden stayed there. 'And shortly after my father had the prognosis, knew that there wasn't much hope left, his old friend from Glasgow, Archie Teale, came down to see him. Archie had kept contact with my father and visited a fair few times over the years, but we weren't sure this time whether my mother had phoned him, or it was some invisible thread between old, close friends to tell Archie that something was wrong with my father. Certainly my father wouldn't have phoned Archie to spill his woes, not his style – but the subject did soon get round to that.'

Jac smiled tightly. 'Though even when it did, typical of my father, he wasn't worried about himself, but more about how his family would cope with him gone. Particularly because of the financial situation, with things not going so well.' Jac held one palm out. 'Archie had been an accountant most of his life, and perhaps my father thought he might have some useful financial advice. Archie gave a few tips there, perhaps delayed the inevitable a year or two more, but it was his moral advice, his advice on *life* that I'm sure my father – and certainly I – remembered most. Because it appeared that Archie had visited at that juncture for a reason of his own.'

Jac took a sip of wine, a heavy sip, and Alaysha could tell that he was getting to the difficult part. His eyes were slightly glassy, moist, but there was a faint light in them too, as if there was some sort of warped joy amongst the pain of his father's death.

'Archie had just had a heart attack, and had been diagnosed by his doctor with congestive heart disease. He might last a year or two, he might last six or seven – but the thing was, like my father, he wasn't going to make old bones. I remember vividly the two of them sitting on the back terrace at Rochefort, with Archie raising a glass and smiling dryly. "It's going to be a race between you and I, Adam, to see who goes first." But what stood out most in my mind was what Archie said a bit later, after the coffees had turned to whiskies and they'd finished most of a bottle between them and reminisced and put half the world to rights. Archie leant forward at one point, gripping my father's arm across the table as my father became more maudlin, lamenting about the mess he'd made of things. "Don't you ever think that way! *Ever*! Because that's the one difference between what's happening to you and to me, Adam – you've *lived* before you died!"

'And as my father's eyebrows knitted, over another half-tumblerful of scotch each, Archie explained: he himself had been careful all his life, counted his pennies, but in the end, what good had that done him? He reminded my father that each time he'd come down to see him, they'd gone out to the marina at Arcachon and looked at the sail boats there. That had been Archie's dream: retire, get a place not far from my father's, and spend the rest of his days sailing. Now, even with his retirement pulled forward to fifty-five, it looked touch-and-go whether he'd make it. And even if he did, how many years sailing would he have? Maybe only a year or two, three if he was lucky. Whereas, he said to my father – you've *lived* your life, done what you want from age thirty and bollocks to the rest. Given your wife and son and little girl a damn good life at the same time. Watched them grow good and straight and tall amongst the sunshine and vines. "So don't you ever regret any of that, Adam. Because, unlike me, you've *lived* your life. You've lived before you died."'

Jac bit at his bottom lip, the tears closer then, Alaysha saw; but he seemed eager to continue, as if afraid that he might break down before he got it all out.

'Archie lasted only a year after my father.' Jac closed his eyes for a second, shaking his head. 'But when you asked the other day, what made me fight so hard on Durrant's behalf – not long after, that's what finally hit me, those words: "lived before you died". . . ' Jac shrugged, grimacing tautly. 'Because if you think about Larry Durrant's life, such as it is: his boxing career going down in flames before it hardly started, turning to petty crime to supplement his income; then just when he's newly married and got a son on the way – just when his life looks like it might be back on track for once – he lands himself on Libreville's Death Row. And on top a car accident that's scrambled his brain, so that he can't even remember half his life from back then – can't say with any certainty whether he actually committed the murder or not.' Jac's voice had risen with anger and exasperation, and he took a quick breath, calming himself again. 'If you think about all of that – if the term "not living before you died" fitted anyone, it fits Larry Durrant. And the fact that he might be innocent makes it all the harder to take. Almost unbearable.'

'I know. *I know.*' Alaysha reached out and gently touched one of Jac's hands on the table. With the talk about his father, the pain and loss she'd seen in his eyes when they first met she now better understood. But then an awkward silence fell, a pregnant pause that felt as if perhaps she should fill it with her own story. And the signals were all there – *illness, sacrifice and risk-taking for family* – of what that story should be.

Alaysha swallowed hard, wondering if the time was finally right to tell Jac. If she didn't, it would become like an ever-growing boulder between them, get in the way, weigh them down. But then Jac started speaking again.

'That thought, that realization, had hit me before I saw Durrant the other day. But when he asked me the same question as you — what had made me go out on such a limb for him — and I looked at him: life to date pretty well worthless and in ruins, last eleven years spent in hell without a single touch of warmth and closeness from his family, hardly even *knowing* what that was like from his own son, and only days left now until his execution — the fact that he'd probably now *never* get the chance to make good on all of that — I just couldn't come flat out and tell him the truth.' Jac shook his head, his eyes moistening again. 'Tell him that I'd done it all because his life so far had been so worthless. That I couldn't bear the thought of him not being able to live some before he died.'

Jac's eyes closed for a second in submission, or perhaps to blot out the images of Durrant in his cell, a single tear rolling down one of his cheeks which he wiped away hastily, and Alaysha had never felt closer to him than in that moment — now that he'd bared his soul. All the warmth, softness and vulnerability she'd never known in the men so far in her life — and probably looked for all the more as a result. But with what Jac had now added to the pot, *holding back secrets*, his emotions raw and close to the surface with the guilt of it, she felt her bottom lip trembling, the lump in her throat now almost impossible to swallow past.

'Jac . . . there's something—' Alaysha broke off, looking past Jac's shoulder. Faint noise outside on the corridor.

Jac didn't seem to have picked up on it — but then she *had* become more tuned in to sounds outside her door these past days — in fact he hardly seemed to have noticed either that she'd started to say something as he continued.

'. . . So I did what people often do when they're hiding

something: I brought a couple of props along for distraction.'

'That was a nice touch though, Jac. And by the sound of it, much appreciated.' Jac had told her about sneaking in the bottles, and Durrant the cognac connoisseur, at the start of dinner. She looked briefly past his shoulder again. Nothing there now. Probably just someone passing on the corridor. She reached across the table to his hand again, gently pressed. 'The thing is Jac, I –'

Her doorbell rang.

Then, seconds later, a high-pitched voice, sounded like a young boy.

'I'm looking for Jac McElroy . . . Got a message to pass to Jac McElroy.'

They exchanged glances for a second before Alaysha went to the door and, sure enough, about a foot below the spy-hole was a young boy holding out a folded piece of paper. Stories abounded of attacks from young gang-boyz, but this lad was too young, no more than twelve, and besides, this wasn't the neighbourhood for that. Probably it was just what it appeared.

'Message for Jac McElroy,' he repeated.

Alaysha flipped back the latch, unhooked the chain, and had barely got the door a few inches open when it was barged hard into her, swinging wide as she was flung back. She pushed back against the door, reflex reaction, but Gerry was already through it, eyes wild and glaring, as the kid scampered off along the corridor.

Jac was only a couple of paces behind Alaysha. His eyes locked with Gerry's in recognition, through the red mist of Gerry's rage.

'You must be . . .' Gerry swung his punch on his last word, and Jac, only managing to get his arms up in partial defence, caught it as a glancing blow on his left cheekbone, knocking him back half a step.

But he had his guard up better for Gerry's next punches, one blocked fully and the other deflected into his shoulder. They clinched and started to grapple, with Alaysha now raining punches on Gerry's shoulder and back, screaming, 'No . . . No! . . . Stop!—' before, wide-eyed, as if she'd suddenly remembered something, she ran into the bedroom.

Alaysha swung the wardrobe door wide and ran one hand along the top shelf for the gun. *What*? She ran it back and forth a couple more times, not believing that it wasn't there. She raised up and looked just to make sure, then, breathless now, frantic, quickly searched in the drawer, in case unconsciously she'd put it back there. *Nothing*.

Heavier tussling now from her hallway, a low groan. She ran back, relieved to see that the groan was from Gerry, not Jac.

It had taken Jac a moment to focus and realize just how wild and misjudged Gerry's punches were in his surging anger. He found the next two easy to dodge, and the one following no trouble to block and swing beneath it a solid punch to Gerry's stomach. Gerry buckled, and Jac got in another good one, this time square to Gerry's face, knocking him back against the wall by the door.

Jac seized the advantage, bringing his left hand tight to Gerry's throat, pinning him back against the wall, his right fist cocked only inches from Gerry's face. He felt Gerry's body move, saw one arm rising up again, and pressed harder against his throat, tensing his cocked arm – but Gerry just wiped the bit of blood from beneath his nose with the back of one hand.

'It ain't the end of this, my friend . . . by a long fucking way.'

'It is for now,' Jac said flatly, pushing Gerry back through the door. 'And if you come round here again bothering Alaysha, I'll–' Jac broke off, noticing for the first time Mrs Orwin looking through the gap in her door, eyes wide as she watched Jac, hand gripped around Gerry's throat, frogmarch him into the corridor. She hastily closed her door as Jac looked her way.

'You'll what, Mr – get a restraining order so I can fuck the girlfriend – McElroy?' Gerry taunted, smiling. 'You'll *what?*'

Jac glared back long and hard. Finally, 'You're not worth it!' And, with one hard push against Gerry's throat – Gerry falling back a step and almost stumbling over – Jac turned and slammed the door behind him.

A moment's breathless pause with his back against the door, taking stock, letting the adrenalin rush settle, with Alaysha's eyes on him somewhere between relief, apology and surprised admiration that he'd actually been able to see Gerry off – then a bang against the door, a punch or kick, and Gerry's voice again:

'Your new girlfriend . . . I'll bet you one thing. I'll bet you she hasn't told you what we did together. Our dirty, sordid little secret. Because . . . *well*, because, clean-collar lawyer like you – you're just too goody-two-shoes to know that kinda shit.'

Another punch or kick of frustration against the door, then silence.

Jac kept his gaze steadily, expectantly on Alaysha, and Alaysha held the look back, both of them knowing in that moment that as soon as they were sure Gerry had gone, the question would come. And Alaysha, perversely, for the first time wished that Gerry wouldn't go, so that she wouldn't have to answer.

But at that moment came another voice on the corridor, muffled, indistinct, with a brief, surprised exclamation from Gerry halfway through – then a gunshot.

Nel-M had finger-tapped against his steering-wheel while waiting on Gerry Strelloff. After a while the sound felt stark, uncomfortable in the silence, so he started pushing buttons on the radio to find some music. Classic soul, jazz and Latin samba were his favourites, and he finally settled on Dave Brubeck's 'Take Five' on an easy listening jazz channel. Two songs later, though, it was playing Louis Armstrong's 'Wonderful World', less conducive to finger-tapping or his

336

mood at that moment, so he stabbed some buttons again, after a moment finding Stevie Wonder's 'Superstition'.

As Gerry Strelloff swung his car in, Nel-M checked his watch: nineteen minutes. Not bad. He watched Gerry run into the building, then exit again only twenty seconds later, looking up and down the street as if he'd forgotten something. His eyes settled on a young black boy thirty yards along, and Nel-M watched as he talked for a minute with the boy, the boy nodding finally as Gerry handed over a piece of paper and a ten-dollar bill from his wallet. The boy went into the building, Gerry waiting anxiously for thirty seconds or so, pacing up and down, before heading in after him.

Nel-M, too, was starting to get anxious; he didn't like sudden changes, and if the boy stayed in there, it was going to kill his entire plan. As Stevie Wonder wailed about thirteen-month-old babies, broken looking glasses and seven years of bad luck, Nel-M's finger-tapping stopped, his hand gripping tight to the steering wheel.

It felt like a lifetime that the boy was in the building, but was probably less than a minute. Nel-M eased out his breath in relief as he saw the boy run out. He slipped on his latex gloves and got out of the car. The gun was already in his pocket, and he gave it a reassuring pat halfway towards the building entrance.

The boy had by then disappeared into the first turning forty yards away, but still Nel-M gave a quick each-way glance to make sure nobody was paying him too much attention as he went into the building.

Everything was in full swing by the time he got to the top of the stairs. He held back out of sight, a foot from the corner where the corridor turned towards the girl's door thirty feet along. Faint scuffling, raised voices, footsteps now . . . a door closing, but he didn't think it was the girl's; he could hear Gerry Strelloff's voice, taunting:

'. . . Mr – get a restraining order so I can fuck the girlfriend – McElroy. You'll *what*?'

Silence, so heavy that in that second Nel-M held his breath, fearing that if he even swallowed, they might hear him.

'You're not worth it!'

More scuffling, and then a door slamming hard. This time it probably was the girl's.

Second's pause, then a thud, followed by Gerry's voice again. Some dirty secret McElroy apparently didn't know about – perhaps her and Gerry were into bondage – then, with a half-grunt, half-frustrated-sigh, another kick against the door from Gerry.

Nel-M tensed, putting his right hand into his gun pocket. This was his cue. And, as he heard Gerry's first steps away from the door, he emerged from around the corner, a smile rising in greeting.

'Hey, man . . . that's not the way you do it.' Voice low, hushed, as if he was sharing a confidence with Gerry that he didn't want anyone else to hear.

'*What*? . . . Who the *hell?*–'

'Don't you recognize the voice, Gerry . . . *your friend*? And, like I say, that's not the way you do it . . .' His voice little more than a whisper now as he walked past a bemused Gerry Strelloff, until he was between him and the door. Then he turned, taking the gun out in the same motion. 'This is the way you –'

He fired only inches from Gerry's face, dropped the gun instantly, and ran for the corner and the stairs, leaping them three and four steps at a time.

28

As Jac opened the door, he heard the last couple of frantic steps on the stairs and the entrance door slamming. He ran a couple of steps past Gerry's body, then halted: Gerry might still be alive, surely he should be tending to him first, seeing what could be done? And with the moment's indecision, he knew that the assailant was by then long gone. He moved a step closer to Gerry's body, inspecting. A lot of blood, but any sign of breathing? He knelt down, feeling for a pulse among the blood; and if the full horror hadn't hit him then, he'd have known by Alaysha's gasps and screams.

'Oh God . . . *oh God* . . . No!' She brought one hand up to her mouth, as if to stop hyperventilating.

No pulse that Jac could feel, though he was no expert, but then he noticed the portions of skull amongst the blood, one section almost three inches round, seeing then too the glistening brain matter – and he straightened up quickly, taking a deep breath as he felt his stomach turn, the bile starting to rise.

He looked up sharply, like a cat caught in headlamps, as Mrs Orwin's door opened across the hallway. Her eyes darted rapidly, going over the scene a couple of times – the body on the floor, Jac, the blood all around – as if the first time she didn't believe what she saw. Then she started shouting.

'You've shot him! You've *shot* him!'

'No . . . *No!*' Jac implored, reaching a bloodied hand towards her. 'It was another man who came by on the corridor . . . Shot him and ran off.'

'You've . . . I . . . *I* . . .' Mrs Orwin started shaking heavily, and as Jac moved a step towards her, still with the same hand held out imploringly, she hastily closed her door.

Jac shook his head in disbelief, but as he looked back at Alaysha, her eyes were transfixed on the gun. 'What is it?'

'I . . . I think I recognize that gun. I think it . . . it's mine.'

'What do you mean, you think it's *yours*? I didn't even know you had a gun.'

'I didn't . . . but I . . .' Alaysha swallowed, trying to get her frantic breathing under control. 'I picked it up from my mom's the other day . . . be . . . because of Gerry coming round.' As she was met with Jac's questioning, penetrating stare, she shook her head. 'I was frightened, Jac, *okay* . . . he had me and Molly terrified! *Terrified*.'

'And what else is there you haven't told me, Alaysha? All that crap from Gerry about dirty secrets that –' Jac stopped, it all hitting him in that second: the killer breaking into her apartment to get the gun, her fingerprints still on it, Mrs Orwin as an eyewitness. The perfection of the set-up.

'I was trying to tell you, Jac.'

But Jac wasn't paying attention, his mind still reeling. *Mrs Orwin probably already on the phone to the police* . . . 'We've got to get rid of this gun, Alaysha.'

'*What*?'

'Your fingerprints are no doubt on it . . . and it's traceable right back to you through your mom. Have you got a . . . ? Never mind.' He could see that Alaysha was practically in a trance, frozen, biting at the back of one knuckle, so he ran past her into the apartment, grabbed a napkin from the table and, seeing the bag he'd brought the wine in still folded on a side-table, picked that up as well and ran back out. He lifted the gun with the napkin, wrapping it around once, and tossed it in the bag, shaking Alaysha gently by one shoulder as he stood. 'It's a set-up, Alaysha . . . a *set-up*. Don't you see?'

'But, why . . . I . . .' And in that moment, finally, she did see. Perhaps this was the other way they dealt with these things, rather than her disappearing and turning up in the river months later. A frame-up that got her locked up with the key thrown away. She nodded hastily, 'Yeah, *yeah* . . .

okay', patting his chest in acceptance as she said it, but also a parting, *take care*, gesture.

He grimaced back tightly, and was about to lean in for a parting kiss on one cheek, but he could imagine the alert being put out as Mrs Orwin spoke, there might even be a squad car just a block away. And whether just dutifully filling that gap in his imagination, he swore he could hear distant sirens in that moment. In the end he just gripped Alaysha's shoulder once more in reassurance, and ran off, leaping the steps three and four at a time, as Gerry's killer had done only a minute before.

The sirens seemed louder, closer, almost filling the air, as Jac's feet hit the pavement outside.

He didn't know whether they were for him, they could have been heading to something else nearby, but he instinctively headed away from them. He took the second turning off eighty yards along – felt the first would be too obvious – running flat-out all the way.

The sirens still closing in, seeming to echo all around him now.

He paused ten yards into the turn-off, taking stock, his breath already falling short. They were coming from two directions now, creating the echo. Hardly mattered which way he ran. If he kept straight on, he'd be heading towards the French Quarter where there was usually stronger police presence, especially at night.

But he had to keep moving, the urgency of the sirens pressing in on him, screaming, *get away, run. And keep running*. He decided to take the next turn-off on the left. The closest siren seemed to be coming from the right.

As Jac made the turn, the night-time activity of the street was busier, some groups of people milling between the bars and restaurants there, a dozen or so sitting at the pavement tables by one bar. As Jac noticed a few eyes on him starkly, questioningly, he thought it was purely because he was running and was now out of breath, frantic; but as a woman he passed sucked in breath sharply, taking half a step back, Jac took in his appearance for the first time as he looked down.

His bloodied hand, from feeling for Gerry's pulse, had brushed against his shirt at some point, and some of it was also smeared on the bag in his hand. While nobody might guess it was a gun in the bag, it could as easily be a body part he'd just removed.

The siren closest by stopped. Jac could feel his heart still pounding hard, but at least the constriction eased a bit.

He had to get rid of the bloodied bag with the gun. Perhaps a restaurant row somewhere with bins out back in an alley? Like the street he was on now.

He scanned frantically back and forth as he cleared the corner, saw what looked like a service alley ten yards to the right, and darted towards it. He paused, his eyes taking a moment to adjust to its darkness and shadows. A couple of small bins halfway down, then a delivery truck parked in tight behind. There might be some larger bins beyond it, but Jac couldn't tell from where he was. He ran towards the bins and the truck.

But what Jac hadn't noticed as he was surveying the alley was the patrol car gliding silently along behind him. They'd seen him run towards the alley, but perhaps wouldn't have paid him too much attention if he hadn't started running again.

They stopped by its entrance, and the officer in the passenger seat shone his torchlight down, calling out as its beam hit Jac's back.

'Hey . . . *hey*, there!'

Jac turned sharply, his shock slow to register because it took him a second, squinting against the glare, to make out the police car and patrolman shouting from its window. But he could tell from the look on the patrolman's face that the image he cut – blood on his shirt, the bloodied bag in his hand – hit home quicker. He turned and ran.

'Hold it! *Stop!*'

Jac glanced back as the shout came. But the patrolman hadn't got out of the car and didn't have his gun aimed through the window. And, by then, Jac prayed that he was too far away for a decent shot.

The patrol car swung back, turning, its headlamps bathing the alley for a moment; then, as if deciding that it might be too tight a squeeze past the delivery truck, it pulled off again with a screech of tyres, siren winding up.

Jac knew that they were going to try and race him around the block, head him off, and he put on an extra spurt, his chest aching now with the effort, legs weakening.

Again, the siren seemed to echo and spin around him, so he couldn't tell whether they were still behind him in the parallel street, running alongside, or just ahead.

He burst out of the alley at full pelt, eyes darting for the next alley on the opposite side: thirty yards along. He cut across at an angle after eight strides, just in front of a green Dodge Neon which was forced to brake sharply, and got to the mouth of the alley as the police car made the turn, its siren spilling onto the street – Jac unsure whether they'd seen him take the alley or not.

The siren came closer, *closer*, filling all of Jac's senses above his pounding heart and ragged breath.

The police car slowed, the patrolmen inside craning their necks – and then Jac had his answer as it screeched and swung in after him, its headlamps washing the walls and fencing of the narrow alley.

But he was only ten yards from its end by then, and it had to slow halfway down to negotiate past some bins and a badly parked motorbike.

Jac heard a faint bang behind him, sounded like one of the bins falling, but he'd turned off by then, frantically scanning for the next alley – twelve yards away on the opposite side – though as he took his first strides towards it, he had second thoughts: *too obvious*, just where they'd expect him to go.

343

He changed tack to the alley twenty-five yards along on the same side, effectively doubling back on himself, hoping and praying that he made it to the turn before they hit the street and saw him.

They flew out with their spinning siren scream just as he made the turn, Jac again unsure whether they'd seen him . . . a silent prayer into the night air as he listened to the direction of their siren above his pounding step.

And as he heard the siren fade slightly, heading away from him, his gasping breath fell heavier with an added burst of relief.

His step eased a fraction at the same time, unsure what to do next. He should put more distance between himself and the siren, but already he felt exhausted, his legs like jelly, the ache in his chest so heavy that he felt as if a knife had been plunged into it. And the more he ran on with the bloodied bag in his hand, the more attention he drew, perhaps running into another squad car . . . he *had* to get rid of it before he went much further.

The sound of the siren had paused, not moving away any more, as if they were edging down the alley opposite very slowly, or perhaps they'd already stopped, realizing he wasn't there, and were about to head back.

Jac picked up pace again, and it was then that he noticed the boarding sheet to one side, a rusted chain looped through a hole in it, and the gap between it and the next seven-foot-high boarding sheet. Could he squeeze through it?

The siren. Same distance away or moving closer? He had to decide quickly.

The gap appeared too narrow, but the board looked like it might have some give. And as Jac became surer that the siren was moving closer again, he barged against it, pressing hard.

He got a shoulder and part of one thigh through, but couldn't get further. He pushed again, got a few more inches in, but not enough. *Closer.* If he didn't hurry, he'd still be there, stuck half-in, half-out, as the squad car rolled by the alley.

With a heavy, grunting shove, he finally felt something

give, the chain biting deeper into the rotting board, and he slipped through.

Long weeds and grass. Rubbish strewn between. *Closer.* Jac pushed the board back so that it was adjacent with the adjoining board, didn't look like there'd ever been a gap, and eased out his breath. A dark, derelict building seven yards behind, an old warehouse or shop. Looked like it had been sealed off for development, then abandoned.

The siren stopped then, but a moment later there was the sound of radio static on the night air. If they weren't actually by the entrance of the alley, then they were very close. Jac held his breath.

The sound of another siren. Moving closer, louder. It cut off when it was only half a block away, then seconds later there was the sound of another engine idling and more radio static on the air, voices conferring.

Jac closed his eyes. *Oh God.* They'd called in support to close the net.

The voices more urgent for a moment, one of them calling out, 'Yeah, *yeah* . . . sure.' Then a car door closing and an engine revving stronger. Jac not sure at first what it all meant, until he saw headlamp lights point up the alley, then the sound of the patrol-car engine edging closer, echoing slightly as it bounced off the sides of the narrow alley.

It was moving slowly, *ever so slowly*, and Jac became aware of another light at that moment, shifting back and forth along each side: the patrolman obviously hanging his torch out the window, every inch of the alley being scoured and checked.

Jac sucked in his breath as they came closer – only six or seven yards away now – but in that instant he also became aware of movement and rustling in the grass, something brushing against one leg. His first thought, with all the rubbish around, was rats, but he daren't move. His whole body in that instant frozen, breath held, swallowing back even to try and calm the pounding of his heart in case they heard it as they edged alongside.

The rustling moved away from his leg, but Jac was worried that even that faint sound might be heard by them, and they'd stop to investigate – his eyes wide as the torchlight hit the board at his side. It moved gradually away in a steady sweep, then suddenly returned, lingering longer this time.

The sound of the engine idling and the radio static now seemed deafeningly loud, as if Jac was actually inside the car with them, and the torch-beam stayed on the boarding for a full eight seconds – though to Jac it felt far longer – before finally shifting.

The car, though, didn't start edging forward again immediately, as if the driver was more uncertain about the boarding – then its engine rattle slowly, *too slowly*, receded along with the fading torch-beam. Jac didn't finally ease out his breath again until it was a good thirty yards past and he was sure that they'd gone, that one of them suddenly wasn't going to pace back to investigate.

The sound of radio static stayed in the background for a while longer, between anything from half a block to two blocks away it sounded to Jac, with a fresh siren joining them at one point – before it all finally faded away.

Yet still Jac stayed where he was, breathless, body winding down, listening to the sounds of the night for almost ten minutes more – until he was sure that the police had cleared from the area and no more sirens were coming for him. Then he started thinking about what to do next.

He looked at the bag in his hand, then the wild grass and earth at his feet. It wasn't ideal, he'd have preferred an absolute guarantee of disappearance, but there was still a high chance that it would never be found here. And if he ran on with it, more eyes raised, more risk.

Jac looked around briefly, then started clawing at the earth with his hands.

But what Jac hadn't noticed was the man at a third floor window, who had seen him crouched in the rough grass and wondered if he might have anything to do with the sirens

he'd heard below a few minutes ago. And as he watched Jac
dig and bury the bag, thought he might have his answer.

Nel-M was late getting to the phone, slightly out of breath.

Glenn Bateson, a harrowed edge to his voice. 'I tried you
earlier.'

'I just got back in,' Nel-M said. He'd spent half the evening
waiting, tapping his fingers anxiously on his steering wheel
while McElroy and the girl ate. So after phoning Roche to
tell him it was all done, he felt he'd earned a celebratory meal
and dived straight into a plate of crawfish and crab claws at
Deanie's, bib up to his neck, smiling and raising a glass of
chilled Chablis to the air as he imagined McElroy at that
moment being grilled by the police, or perhaps already in
lock-up and making his one call to one of his buddies to save
his sorry ass. And he'd started to feel mellow, relaxed for one
of the first times in weeks. The sense that now, finally, it was
the end of everything with McElroy and Durrant. But with
the edge in Bateson's voice, he could feel the first bubbles of
anxiety returning. 'What is it?'

'You wouldn't believe it.'

'Yes, I would – just fucking tell me.'

'McElroy. He's arranged for a psychiatrist to come and see
Durrant. Some guy called Ormdern.'

'When for?'

'Two days time, straight after the BOP hearing, then
another session the day after. McElroy will be there as well,
presumably to –'

'No, he won't.'

'What do you mean – no he won't? I just picked this up
fresh and hot from Haveling's diary, and –'

'Can't say it plainer than that, my friend. McElroy *won't*
be there. And if you want to know why – I suggest you keep
an eye on local news channels between now and tomorrow
morning.' Nel-M sniggered, but he could still feel a tightness
in his chest where Bateson's word *psychiatrist* had hit him, as

if part of his crawfish hadn't digested and had decided to burn a hole through his ribs. Almost certainly everything with the psychiatrist would now be axed too, but it was an uncomfortable reminder of how close they'd come. More brownie points scored with Roche when he told him, more back-pats for his timely ingenuity. 'Or, if I were you – you know those special occasions when prisoners are allowed to watch TV? Like the World Series or President's inauguration, or last episode of *Seinfeld* or *Friends*? And you get them all in one room looking at an oversized screen? Why don't you arrange that now for the local news – then just watch Larry Durrant's face when the piece about Jac McElroy comes on.'

'What have you been up to?

Nel-M had never liked Bateson, and while he'd invited the question, Bateson's folksy, slyly gleeful tone made his skin crawl. *I'm not one of your good ol' boys, asshole!* he felt like screaming. But he immediately slipped into similar sly mode for his response.

'Now, that would be telling.'

Jac went to a cash machine on Gravier Street and took out $300 to add to the fifty in his wallet, then started thinking about how to get a change of shirt. He knew he'd be hard pushed to find any shops open, his only hope was probably the French Quarter, so he'd drifted that way, trying to keep in the shadows of the buildings. A police car had passed him on the way, but he'd just kept walking normally, one hand by the stain on his shirt, as if he was scratching his stomach. The car just kept drifting past, didn't pay him any attention.

Then, as he approached the corner of Bourbon and Iberville and saw a Lenny Kravitz look-a-like handing out promotional cards for a new club, he was struck with an idea.

Jac took one of the cards, 'Thanks,' nodding towards Lenny K's chest. 'And have you maybe got some club T-shirts to sell, like the one you're wearing?'

'Nah. Just paid me to hand out these here cards.'

'Maybe at the club itself?'

'Doubt it. I think these were jus' printed up for the bar-staff.'

'Shame. They're nice, jazzy design.' Jac smiled tightly. 'How about you selling me that one? Fifty bucks?'

Lenny K smiled incredulously. 'Man, I got another hour out here wit' these. An' how am I gonna explain away losing my shirt?'

'Shrunk in the wash, amorous stalker ripped it off.' Jac shrugged, smiling again. Despite the protests, there was a hint of temptation; though maybe, with the connected hassle, $50 for a ten-dollar T-shirt still wasn't enough. 'A hundred bucks.'

Lenny K looked each way, as if concerned who might be viewing the transaction, and part of his eye-shuffling also took in the stain on Jac's shirt; one last cloud of doubt before he finally nodded, 'Okay, man, let's do it', pulling back into the shadow of a shop doorway as he pulled off his shirt and held it out.

Jac peeled five twenties from his wallet and they made the exchange, and, as soon as he was round the corner, he ducked into another shop doorway to change into the T-shirt. He bundled his old shirt in his hand and threw it in a bin halfway along North Rampart Street, then headed towards the phone kiosk fifty yards along to call John Langfranc.

Jac checked his watch: 9.32 p.m. Just under fifty minutes since the shooting.

Langfranc answered quickly, and equally Jac started speaking rapidly, at one point garbling and running ahead of himself with pent-up tension as he struggled to explain.

'Whoa, whoa, back up a bit,' Langfranc said. 'So, *God's sake*, I can get this clear in my mind.' He took a heavy breath. 'Somebody comes by and shoots dead your girlfriend's ex, straight after you've just shut the door on him after an argument? And rather than run off with the gun, he drops it right there . . . and he's gone before you open the door again to see what's happened? Have I got it straight so far?'

'Yeah, *yeah*. That's right. As I opened the door, I just heard his last few footsteps on the stairs.'

'But then you picked up the gun and ran off with it? That's the bit I don't get. Why was that again, Jac?'

Jac sighed, his frayed nerves riding on it wearily. 'This is the client-confidential part, John, *okay*? Because as for the official line – I think we should make out that the killer ran off with the gun, as would normally happen, or just no mention of it at all.'

'Goes without saying, Jac. Without saying.' Langfranc sounded mildly offended to even be asked.

'The thing is, Alaysha recognized the gun. It's *hers,* or rather her mother's – but it was at Alaysha's apartment at the time. That's why I ran off and dumped the gun – because I was sure it would have her prints on it. It looks like whoever did this must have broken into her apartment earlier and got the gun, and then –' Jac was speaking rapidly again, slightly breathless as he fought to explain, and as he heard a police siren close by, his breath froze in his throat, the siren's passage counted in tight pulse beats in his neck before his breath finally eased as it drifted past, heading away from him. ' – then he uses it on her boyfriend, and the set-up's complete.'

'I hear what you're saying, Jac, but it's not good. Not good. I know you and so I know that you're telling the truth. But listening to this now wearing the hats of a couple of hard-boiled homicide cops – who don't know you and on top have heard it all before – it sounds like a story, Jac. And not even a good one at that.'

'There's a witness, too.'

From Jac's downbeat tone, Langfranc knew already that it was bad news. 'And don't tell me – they didn't see the shooter, either?'

'No. Old woman across the hallway. Opened her door a minute after the shot was fired – shooter long gone and just me and Alaysha standing by the body. Started screaming, "You've shot him! You've shot him!" '

Low groan from Langfranc and a throaty, doom-laden 'Terrific.'

'I need your help, John. That's why I called now.'

'Help, *yeah*. Miracles take longer.'

'I need someone I know to represent Alaysha. I need to know what's happening, which direction everything might go.'

'I can understand that.' Langfranc was quiet for a second. 'But this isn't just protectiveness for your girlfriend, is it Jac? Something else is worrying you about this.'

'Yeah.' Deflated sigh. The seed of doubt had been there from the moment he'd realized it was Alaysha's gun, rankling deeper as he'd ducked between the shadows of the night-time streets during the past forty-five minutes. 'The question that's bothered me is why frame Alaysha? With everything else that's been going on, I thought I'd have been the main target for something like that. So if they've gone to the trouble of lifting her gun from her apartment, what else might be waiting in the wings? Some hefty Accomplice to Murder rap, perhaps, from other evidence they've planted? That's why I need to know the lay of the land, John, before coming forward.'

'I can see that. There wasn't a *Times-Picayune* photographer there to snap you as you left the apartment block with the gun, was there?'

'No.' Jac chuckled, and Langfranc joined him a second later, as if making sure first that Jac was ready to see the light side. Though Langfranc's chuckle quickly died when Jac told him that he was spotted by a patrol car a few blocks away. 'And I ran.' Jac sighed heavily. 'It was dark, though, and I was probably too far away for a good ID.'

'Let's hope so.' Langfranc took a fresh breath as he focused on the remaining options; what few were left after Jac's catalogue of horrors and errors. 'Did the old girl across the hall see the gun?'

'No, don't think so.'

'Okay. Hopefully then we'll get away with the story of the killer running off with it. Or, as you say, just don't mention the gun – because that's what the cops will naturally assume. Hopefully, too, the story will wash that you ran off in pursuit of the shooter. As for why you're still AWOL, I'll think of something in the meantime.' Langfranc sucked in his breath. 'All will depend, though, on what Alaysha might have already told them. How long will the cops have been with her now?'

'Half an hour, maybe more.'

'I'd better get there. Couple of good detectives could pull her apart in that time, have her head reeling. Did you prime any sort of story with her?'

'No. No time. But she's bright – she'll know not to mention the gun, particularly with it being hers.'

'Let's hope so. Because if she mentions the killer dropping that gun on the hall floor – we're buried before we've started. And you also have to pray that the cops don't find that gun.'

'Don't worry – where I've hidden it, they're not going to find it. At least, not in a hurry.'

'Remember. You didn't tell me that.'

'I didn't tell you that.'

29

The first to arrive on the scene, six minutes after Mrs Orwin's call, were two patrolmen from the Eighth District, who immediately radioed in for what else they'd need: forensics, homicide and a meat wagon. They knocked on Mrs Orwin's door first because she'd made the call but, with their talking and the harsh static from their communicators, Alaysha's door opened seconds after, and, quickly sensing some unease between the two parties, the officers took one each for questioning – Mrs Orwin hastily ushering her officer in and closing her door behind him.

Two more patrolmen arrived minutes later and, having conferred with their colleagues, one yellow-taped the downstairs entrance before joining his side-kick in roaming and checking for tell-tale clues, though at all times two yards clear of the body; the hallowed forensics-only zone.

Questioning was basic at that point, setting the general scene, which was all dutifully relayed to Lieutenant Jerome Derminget, a bloodhound-eyed homicide detective with wavy, unkempt salt-and-pepper hair, when he arrived on the scene eighteen minutes later.

Derminget looked like the type that Alaysha would have liked under different circumstances. While his eyes looked tired, as if he read police reports or books late into the night, at the same time they appeared warm, understanding. Though that part also unsettled Alaysha; they looked like they might easily strip away her defences, get to the truth.

Derminget spent the first ten minutes questioning Mrs Orwin, and had been little more than that time with Alaysha when his station house called to inform him that they had Miss Reyner's lawyer on the line, a certain John Langfranc,

'And he insists on being present for any official questioning of his client.'

Derminget skewed his mouth. He didn't like the sound of the girl's story one bit: the shooter that nobody else had seen, appearing magically and firing just seconds after them closing the door, at the end of a big argument to boot; an eyewitness that saw both the argument and then her and her boyfriend over the body, and, to cap it all, her boyfriend, having apparently run off in pursuit of the killer, for some inexplicable reason hadn't yet returned. It sounded like a fairy story, but Derminget had so far only been filling in background, hadn't yet got to the harder-assed questions that might put her account to the acid-test. And the involvement of a lawyer so early rang instant alarm-bells, stank of barricades being quickly, desperately put up. If he didn't get to those questions before her lawyer showed, her story would probably for ever get stuck in la-la land. He saw his escape route in *official*.

'Tell our lawyer friend that we're still on the scene, and so we're not even sure at this stage if there will be any *official* questioning of Miss Reyner. But if that is to take place, that'll be at the station house later tonight; about which, of course, he'll be duly informed beforehand.'

'One minute.' The female duty officer broke off and he could hear other voices in the background – obviously they had the lawyer on another line – before her voice came back. 'He says he's a friend and so he'd like to be there in any case, for moral support. He's on his way.'

'Okay. *Okay.*' Fuck it. *Fuck it!* Derminget had drifted into the hallway as he'd taken the call and kept his voice low so that the girl wouldn't overhear. He gave his best smile and soft-eyed look as he turned back in through the doorway. 'Now, where were we?' Maybe only ten or twelve minutes before her lawyer arrived, he'd better make the most of it.

Two hours. That's when Jac had arranged to speak with Langfranc again when hopefully he'd be back from seeing

Alaysha and the police. Another phone booth call, Langfranc advised, 'Because we don't want anything possibly later being traced to your cell-phone.'

After the change of shirt, Jac had instinctively headed away from the French Quarter – less people, less police. But as another police car drifted by him on Baronne Street, he felt immediately uncomfortable, vulnerable. They didn't see him or even slow as they passed, but he was struck with the feeling that he was the only person there to draw their eye, and if one of them had looked his way, he'd have frozen or panicked in that gaze, the look in his own eyes instantly giving the game away.

He turned back towards the French Quarter. He felt in no mood to be around people, let alone crowds, but they'd at least offer some cover, distraction; to any passing police, he'd be harder to pick out amongst a milling throng.

He drifted along with the tourists and local out-on-the-towners on Bourbon Street, then turned into Bienville Street and found a bar after forty yards that looked busy and noisy enough to hopefully get lost in.

Jac ordered a Coors at the bar, then found a table deep towards the back where he was hardly visible from the street, let alone noticeable.

As Jac took the first sips of beer, he pictured again hearing the gun going off, those last footsteps on the stairs as he opened the door, Gerry's body on the floor with part of his skull blown away, Mrs Orwin screaming, *You've shot him! You've* shot *him!* Fourth or fifth time he'd run the sequence through for anything he might have missed, along now with how Alaysha might be coping with the police, how she'd explain the same sequence of events. Would Langfranc have arrived yet to be able to draw their fire?

Jac sipped anxiously at his beer. His running off wouldn't have helped – more possible suspicion and less back-up, Alaysha left to fend on her own – but with Alaysha's gun still there, it would have been far worse. Alaysha would instantly have been prime suspect with himself as accomplice. Only with the weapon gone did they have a chance of getting away with the story that someone else had shot Gerry.

Between the crowd at the bar and milling by the entrance, Jac caught glimpses of the street outside as he drank, and over the next half hour he saw a couple of police cars passing: the normal French Quarter patrols, he wasn't unduly worried. But when a police car stopped almost directly opposite and a patrolman got out and headed across the road, Jac's nerves immediately tensed, his grip on his beer bottle tightening. He watched like a hawk through the revellers – past two twenty-somethings hugging and back-slapping like they hadn't seen each other in years, past a girl half doubling over and cackling like a witch at the joke of one of her two friends – as the policeman went slightly to one side, a door or two away.

Jac didn't take his eyes off the entrance or fully ease his breath until two minutes later when he saw the policeman head away again; suddenly conscious of a few people at the bar looking his way curiously, Jac only then aware how hard his eyes had been burning through them, a trickle of sweat on his brow, his hand starting to shake on his beer bottle.

And in turn, with those stares, Jac suddenly realized how alone he was, separate from them all. A day ago, even a few *hours* ago, he'd have enjoyed the ambience, smiled at the bonhomie around him, felt the beer chill and mellow him, finger-tapped to the beat of the music: Lynyrd Skynyrd's 'Sweet Home Alabama' was playing, and people had started to sway and foot-tap, one couple even attempting a close-clinches jive. But Jac felt cut off from it all, as if he was a world away, the throbbing beat simply fuelling the pounding of his heart and pulse, a nerve jumping in time with it just below his earlobe – one solid, deafening drumbeat that screamed, get out, *get out! . . . you don't belong here . . .*

Jac quickly knocked back the rest of his beer and stood up, started making his way back through the heaving, milling mass. The bar had become a lot busier in the past half hour, and Jac had to push and sidle his way through, the atmosphere suddenly hot, oppressive, the feeling that they were all closing in on him – *we saw the way you looked at that policeman, and we're going to keep you here until they come back for you* – Jac knocking the arm of a satin-shirted young guy with a pony-tail and almost spilling his drink as he leant back into Jac. '*Sorry . . . sorry . . .*' Jac sweating now, heart pounding, breath short as he burst through the last of the bar crowd and back out onto the street.

But the throbbing, swirling echo of the music and people still seemed to churn through Jac's head as he paced along Bienville Street, crossing Bourbon this time . . . a police siren a block away suddenly screaming along with it so that he felt in that instant dizzy, his legs weak; the feeling that he might have to start fleeing again, but now had no strength left.

The siren faded after a moment, and he eased out his breath again, raising his hand to a cab as he saw it crossing on Dauphine Street.

'Yeah? Where to?'

Jac had to think for a second. His mum's place would now probably be too risky. 'Mid-City, on the way to the airport. One of the motels around Tulane Avenue.' He could make his call to John Langfranc from there and, as one of the city's most faceless, transient-client hotel areas, it would hopefully be ideal for laying low for a while.

As they turned onto Canal Street, the driver asked, 'You know which one?'

'No. Haven't booked one yet. Got any recommendations?'

As the driver threw up the pros and cons of a couple of motels he knew there, Jac was hardly listening, the throbbing beat, voices and sirens still ringing in his head, get away . . . *get away* . . . and even when the taxi driver had stopped speaking and a motel had been decided upon, it was still there for a while, until finally – Jac closing his eyes and taking slow, even breaths in the back of the taxi as the city receded behind him – it was just the sound of his own heartbeat and thrum of the taxi wheels on the road.

Steady rhythmic beat. Though now it was more from Jac's fingers drumming by the phone than his heartbeat. The only sound – apart from the traffic passing a block away on Tulane Avenue, heavily muted through the thick glazing of his second-floor motel window – as Jac made his call to John Langfranc.

When Jac had first called, after the agreed two hours, there'd been no answer – then successively after five minutes, eight minutes, twelve minutes. Still no answer, his finger-tapping by the phone heavier and more impatient each time. Now again after another three minutes. It answered late, at the start of the fifth ring, Langfranc slightly breathless.

'I just got back in this second,' he said to Jac's *where the hell had he been?*

'I've been going crazy here . . . didn't know what to think,' Jac said. 'What might be happening.'

'I know . . . *I know.* It got a lot more complicated while I was there, unfortunately. You see, the thing is –'

'How was Alaysha?' Jac was only half paying attention to Langfranc; his emotions so pent-up that all he could think of were the questions that had burned through his mind the past two hours. 'How did she cope with the police questioning?'

'She coped fine, Jac. But –'

'And had she said the right things before you got there, so that you were able to cover the bases okay?'

'Yes, she'd covered well, hadn't . . . but . . . but they found the gun, Jac.' Langfranc blurted it out mid-sentence, as if afraid that if he got stuck in question-answer mode, he might never get the words out. Langfranc let his breath out heavily. 'That's our main problem now.'

'But *how*? I hid it over half a mile away, and I –'

'You were seen burying it, Jac. A neighbour a couple of doors away, apparently.'

358

'Oh God. *God*.' Jac felt as if a trapdoor had opened beneath him, but it was Alaysha he saw tumbling into the abyss, her reaching one hand up desperately. Her gun. Her prints on it. He shuddered, his voice shaky, quavering. 'How on earth is Alaysha bearing up with that news? I . . . I should be with her now.' He realized something else too in that second. 'And now I've made things far worse for her . . . trying to get rid of the gun. Made her look guiltier still.'

'Jac, the problem is, it's –'

'*Jeezus* . . . I've made a right pig's ear of everything, I've –'

Jac was wrapped up in his own thoughts again, only half listening as Langfranc tried to broach the subject delicately, gently, soften the blow; but, in the end, as if the only way to get the words across, they came out sharply, a hatchet swipe:

'*Jac*! They're not Alaysha's prints they've found on that gun – they're *yours*!'

Jac felt the words hit, but they didn't sink home, as if Langfranc had said them to someone else. Then, hesitantly, 'That's . . . *that's* not possible. I . . . I never touched the gun with my hands.'

'The prints are there, Jac . . . they're *there*. No question.'

And as it did finally sink in, Jac felt himself falling again, as if Langfranc's words had held him in mid-air for a moment, suspended in disbelief, and now that the totality of the set-up dawned on him, he was in freefall again: Alaysha's gun, *his* fingerprints on it – he should have deduced earlier that if they'd gone to the trouble of lifting it from her apartment, that's what they'd do; after all, a part of him had questioned all along that *he* was meant to be the main target. The letter and restraining order, the argument, Mrs Orwin seeing him over the body, '*You've shot him! You've* shot *him!*' And now, as if he wasn't roped and tied enough, him fleeing and trying to dispose of the gun. He'd provided the final ribbon on top himself.

'Uuuhhh.' All Jac could manage; a half-grunt, half-wheeze as he felt all the air shunted out of him with the terrible

359

realization. After a moment, 'You . . . you know it's all a set-up, don't you?' But Jac's tone carried strong hesitancy, doubt, as if with the sheer weight of evidence, even John Langfranc might have trouble believing it.

'Yeah, I know.' Though there was a slight pause, and the tone was that of reluctant concession. 'But, like I said before, Jac – that's only because I know you. With everyone else, it's going to be tough. With the way everything's stacked against you – a real mountain climb to try and convince them.'

'What can we do?' Yet even as Jac said it, with the hopelessness of the situation, it sounded rhetorical; Langfranc was a lawyer, not Houdini.

Langfranc took a fresh breath. 'The first thing is – you've got to give yourself up to the police, Jac. Give them your side of things to back up Alaysha's account. That's the start point.'

But as Langfranc said it, Jac's first thought was Durrant. After all, Durrant's fate had been the main purpose of the set-up: to get him off the scene. 'Will I get bail?'

'I don't know, Jac. I'll try, obviously. But running off with the gun and hiding it hasn't helped. And your work-visa situation, too, is going to make it tricky – the fact that you're not an American citizen. DA will protest like all hell that you could flee.'

Jac had worked with Langfranc long enough to read a 'No'; Langfranc just didn't want to come flat out and say it. Like everything else so far and no doubt from here on in, he'd be let down softly, in stages.

Only eleven days left now until Durrant's execution. 'I just can't leave Durrant hanging now, John. Not when I'm so close.'

'*Durrant?*' Langfranc's voice was incredulous, cracking slightly. 'You won't be able to do anything to help him now, Jac. You'll be lucky to save yourself from sharing the cell right next to him, way things stand now.'

'I *can't* come in, if I'm not going to get bail – don't you see? He'll be dead before half this is sorted out – *if* it ever is.'

360

'It's not just the bail, Jac.' Langfranc's voice was stretched; the tone Jac had heard him adopt with difficult clients. 'Beaton's going to drop you from the firm quicker than a hot potato soon as he gets wind of all this. You won't be able to represent Durrant in any case.'

Jac heard Langfranc, but another part of his brain quickly rejected it; the part in denial, still stuck on everything he had planned before it had happened. 'There's the BOP hearing tomorrow, and I've got that psychiatrist, Ormdern, visiting Durrant a few hours after. I've got to be there for those. And, don't you see – that's why they've done this now. They've heard about Ormdern's visit, and are worried that I might be getting too close.'

'You *can't* be there, Jac. I can't say it plainer than that.' Tired, worn tone; shifted deftly from 'difficult clients' to 'insane'. 'And who the hell are *they*?'

'Roche and his henchman, guy called Nelson Malley. Remember, I told you the other day about him following me – the photos that Bob Stratton took?'

'Yeah, yeah. I remember now.' Langfranc rubbed his forehead. The Durrant case had gone through so many hurdles that, with his own heavy caseload, at times Langfranc found it difficult to keep track.

Jac continued, 'I'm convinced they're behind this now. And, in turn, I'm more convinced than ever that they somehow set Larry Durrant up. That's the link between the two, right there, don't you see? The perfect set-up.'

Part of Jac's thinking came across as totally rational, Langfranc considered; the other part now firing on odd cylinders at wild tangents, totally irrational.

'Perhaps that's something you could share with Lieutenant Derminget when you see him,' Langfranc said, still trying desperately to reel Jac in. Appeal to the rational side. 'Feed him everything you've got. Hopefully save your neck and Durrant's at the same time.'

Silence from Jac for a moment, as if he was seriously

contemplating it, before exhaling tiredly. 'No, *no* . . . it wouldn't work. There's still too much for me to piece together – and this Lieutenant Whatever is not going to do all that for me. And I can't do it while I'm locked up. I need to be out there.'

Langfranc lost his last shred of patience then. 'Jac, *Jac!* You're just not thinking straight! Any minute now there's going to be an all-points out for you, and you won't even be able to go to your local seven-eleven without being arrested – let alone walk into a maximum security penitentiary to see Durrant. So how the hell are you going to be able to help him then?'

'I don't know, I . . . I . . .' Jac could feel the options – practically feel the cell walls – closing in on him as Langfranc spoke. 'I need time to think. Get my head clear.'

'That's the other problem, Jac – we don't have much time.'

'How long?'

'Derminget originally gave me an hour to talk you in, Jac. But then when the lab came back with the news that it was *your* prints on the gun, all bets were suddenly off, and –'

'*How long?*'

'He cut it to half an hour, Jac.' Langfranc sighed heavily. 'And I've used fifteen minutes of that getting back home. He phoned about the prints as I was pulling up outside. And, of course, the six or eight minutes we've now been talking. He's expecting me to literally call right back after talking to you – he wants to know whether you're coming in, or whether he's got to set the dogs loose. Put out an APB and feed your photo to local news stations and newspapers.'

'*Photo?*' Barely a gasp. A cramp in his chest made it suddenly hard to breathe.

'Yeah. They dug one out when they searched your apartment.'

Jac closed his eyes, the continuing freefall now making him feel dizzy, as if he'd lost all orientation of where he was. *Closing in.* Spending that very night in a cell? It seemed ludicrous, unreal. Though at least from visiting Durrant, he thought sourly, he now knew what that might be like; and the many more nights that would no doubt follow. An icy chill ran down Jac's spine, though his skin felt hot, clammy, the motel room walls suddenly pressing in; the same hot-flushed claustrophobia that had gripped him when he'd first walked Libreville's corridors. And now only minutes to make up his mind. Jac swallowed hard, his throat suddenly tight, his voice strained.

'I . . . I hear what you're saying, John, loud and clear. But I just can't be locked up for the next eleven days – can't you see that? Isn't there some sort of deal that can be cut?'

'*Deal*, Jac?' Langfranc exclaimed, breathless disbelief. 'I was lucky to get even this from Derminget – the chance to be able to talk to you first. If he'd got his way, he'd have–'

'One minute, John,' Jac cut in as a knock came on his door. Holding the receiver away, he called out, 'Yes, what is it?'

'Sorry to trouble you, Mr . . . Mr Teale.' Desk clerk. Jac had paid cash and signed in as Archie Teale. 'But I was wondering if you could tell me if you want a paper tomorrow morning, or coffee or tea brought up – because your door-handle card's not here.'

'I'll mark it and put it out later,' Jac shouted. Jac brought the receiver back to continue with John Langfranc, but he could tell that the desk clerk was still there, as if waiting on something else. And, as Jac listened more intently, the hairs rose on the back of his neck as he heard other muted, mum-bling voices in the background. Jac kept his voice low to Langfranc: 'Are you sure this detective said he'd wait until you'd spoken to him?'

'Sure as can be, Jac.' But at the back of Langfranc's mind something niggled uneasily from Derminget's mention of hopefully catching a late news bulletin, '*If McElroy wasn't going to come in.*' '*Why*? What's happening?'

'I'm not sure, I –'

A heavier rapping came then, a booming voice in its wake.

'Police, Mr Teale. NOPD. We need to clarify something with you, sir.'

Jac's stomach leapt into his throat. He found it hard to swallow, his voice croaky as he shouted, 'One minute!' Then, to Langfranc, an under-the-breath hiss, 'This doesn't look to me like he's waiting!'

'*Shiiit*! Swear on my life, Jac – he promised. But look, now that they're there – just stay calm, do what they say. Don't do anything rash. And don't say too much.' Langfranc's words urged calm, but his staccato delivery screamed panic. 'Before you've even drawn breath at the station house, I'll be right there to cover the bases.'

Jac's whole body started to shake, and he only half-heard Langfranc's words beyond a sudden buzzing in his head. *Closing in.* His eyes darted frantically between the door and the window.

'I'm sorry, John, I –'

The door ram hit then, seeming to make the whole room shudder, and Jac dropped the phone and leapt back a yard with the jolt, as if the ram had hit him directly.

Langfranc at his end heard the sudden bang and clatter as the receiver hit the table. 'Jac! . . . *Jac*!'

Jac ran to the window, opened it, looked out. A thin ledge just below the window and further along a flat roof a floor below. But could he cling to the ledge for that seven feet to then be able to make the jump down? And could he make that ten foot jump?

The second ram strike came then, splitting some of the wood on the door frame. Jac slid out the window onto the narrow ledge, swaying nervously after a couple of steps and drawing blood from his fingernails as he clung desperately to the building, fearing with the sudden dizzying blood-rush to his head that he was going to fall. He took a long breath and opened his eyes again, starting to edge along the narrow ledge more rapidly, knowing the room door would burst open any second.

At his end, John Langfranc heard two more door ram hits before the last of the frame splintered and the door flew off and thudded to the floor. The room was suddenly filled with confused voices and rapid, trampling footsteps, before one voice cut through the rest: '*Here* . . . over here!' Then after a moment another voice, more urgent, shouting: 'Hey . . . *hey*! *Stop*!'

Then, seconds later, the sound of a gunshot.

30

Sirens filling the night. But this time Jac knew with certainty they were coming for him, not someone else or a nearby fire.

He'd been about to jump straight down from the side of the flat roof when he saw the two police cars only twenty yards to his left by the entrance. One with a patrolman inside, the other unmanned. Jac ran to the right to slip down the end of the flat roof, out of sight of the cars, when a flashlight beam from his room swung across and settled on him, and the shout came, 'Hey . . . *hey*! *Stop*!'

Jac looked up only briefly before taking the last two strides to the side to scramble down.

The shot came as he'd got half his body over, kicking up the roof asphalt two feet away, a fleck of it flying up and hitting him on one cheek – Jac jolting back for an instant as he thought he might have been hit. And with that jolt, the last strength went from his arms, and he fell down the remaining five feet.

Jac half-rolled to break his fall, scrambling into a run before he'd fully straightened. He headed further to the right away from the police cars, across twelve yards of motel car lot – another shout from the police behind, only half registering above his ragged breathing and the blood-rush like heavy surf through his head – then he was into the road, turning right again, putting more distance between himself and the police cars.

More motels. Small apartment blocks interspersed. Further ahead, wooden-boarded houses and bungalows, some with front verandahs.

Jac heard the siren winding up as he was only eighty yards along, then the second siren a few breathless strides later. He glanced desperately over one shoulder as the first car swung onto the road, roof light spinning.

Jac became frantic. The street was too open, wide, himself too visible as he ran along. The police car would see him the instant its headlamps hit him.

And he became aware only then of the cool dampness on one cheek, wiping at the blood there with the back of one hand as his eyes darted wildly for options. The sirens were deafening, smashing the night-time stillness of the street.

A turning on the left twenty-five yards ahead. Would he reach it in time before the squad car caught up? Probably, but it would clearly see him take it, would swing into the turn and catch up with him not long past it.

As Jac came alongside the first bungalows, someone pulled a curtain back to see what all the commotion was. Jac's eyes honed in on a gap between the houses. No gate. The police car had already covered half the distance towards him. No time to dwell on it, no other immediate options. Jac cut across their front yard, heading for the gap.

Old bicycle, dustbins. Some planks that Jac almost stumbled over. A couple of large bushes that Jac sped past, branches whipping back against him – and then he was in a more open lawn area, a fence twenty feet away: six-feet high. Siren closer now, almost alongside. He picked up his stumbling pace and leapt at the fence hard, levering up and scrambling down the other side.

A dog barking almost immediately his feet landed. Low and throaty, menacing. A big dog. Jac's heart froze, fearing it was there with him in the yard – but then, with another volley of barks, its front paws hit the fence a yard to his side with a bang. Jac jumped back a step, reflex response, relief quickly overlaying the shock as he ran on.

Sirens paused in the same spot now, taking stock of where he'd gone, a faint flicker of a searchlight spilling over the fence he'd just jumped.

Jac picked up pace. A clearer lawn area, he'd covered most

of it by the time he heard the sirens moving on again, starting to circle round the block. A side gate, but only waist high. Jac leapt it easily. But as he burst into the front yard, breath heaving, a couple of black teenagers stood by an old Trans Am in the driveway, surprise freezing them for a second as Jac, six yards to their side, sped past, the shout of 'Hey, man!' from one of them carrying surprise as much as indignation: wasn't often you saw a white man running from the police in this neighbourhood.

Jac headed deeper into the street away from the sirens, some sort of plan finally forming in his mind. He glanced anxiously over one shoulder, looking to see when the police cars would reach the turning, though he could have told simply by listening: the tone of the sirens suddenly became starker, clearer as they pulled alongside the opening, flashlight sweeping from a side window.

Jac knew that they'd pick him out easily – he was less than fifty yards into the road – but he kept running in the same straight line.

Jac heard the tyre-screech as they swung into the road, the stronger revving of engines. But still Jac kept on straight, knowing that soon they'd catch up with him – legs pounding flat out, until . . . *until* . . . with one last frantic glance over his shoulder, Jac saw they were already twenty yards into the road. Past the point of no return.

Jac cut off sharply at a tangent again, towards another bungalow on the far side, smiling to himself as he heard the squad cars brake sharply, tyres squealing as they negotiated rapid three-point-turns.

But Jac didn't run through to the back yard of the bungalow this time, he crouched down by its side gate out of sight, listening to the sirens receding – his frantic heartbeat counting off the seconds until it was safe for him to emerge again. In that instant Jac noticed a Hispanic-looking man eyeing him with concern from a neighbouring window, then suddenly shifting from it, as if about to come out.

Jac eased up – the police car tail lights were just turning off – then ran out again, legs pumping wildly. It was vital he gained as much distance as possible before they realized he wasn't in the next street. Already seventy yards into the road, hopefully at least a hundred before they caught on and turned back.

Jac listened to the sirens. Still seemed to be the same distance away in the next road. A light rain hit Jac's face then, and he tilted his head, welcoming it. Felt it cooling his blood-boiled head, felt some of it touch his dry lips.

Some brighter lights Jac could make out now just beyond the end of the road, misty and blurred with the rain. Jac squinted, the lights finally falling into focus: the Toni Morrison Interchange, where Carrollton Avenue and Interstate 10 met, a tangled web of highways and overpasses. And, where the first highway crossed, a barrier that Jac could see at the end of his road where it formed a T. If he could make it to the barrier, the squad car wouldn't be able to follow him.

Jac looked towards the end of the road. Eighty or so yards. Touch and go whether he'd make it to the end by then. Jac's legs felt weak, his chest cramped and aching. He wasn't going to be able to keep up the same pace much longer.

Sudden change in the tone of the sirens. It sounded like they were turning, starting to head his way. Jac pumped harder, pushing himself. The sirens drifted away for a second as they headed back up to the top of the adjacent road, then turned, starting to move closer again.

Jac pushed every muscle to the limit, felt them screaming for release. Sixty . . . fifty-five yards from the end by the time he heard the sirens spilling out openly as they came alongside the road. Jac glanced back to make sure, saw the spinning glare.

But they seemed to hang there for a second, as if unsure whether he was in the road, and Jac kept tight in by the front fences so that he wasn't too obvious as the flashlight swayed from side to side, probing. The flashlight finally picked him up, and they turned into the road – but by then he'd gained another dozen yards or so.

Jac pushed even harder, but the more he demanded from every muscle and sinew, the more they seemed to ache and shudder, beg for meltdown into welcome release. It felt like he'd hardly be able to make it ten yards, let alone forty . . . thirty-five . . . *thirty* . . .

The sirens pressed in closer, filling the air. Jac glanced back as the first set of headlamps reached him: sixty-five, seventy yards behind. Still almost twenty yards to the barrier.

Oh God. *God.* The sirens deafening, seeming to fill every space in Jac's head as the squad cars bore down, as if they were about to run him over as the barrier loomed ahead.

But they had to slow down, the front car screeching broadside as Jac reached the barrier and leapt it.

'Stop . . . *Stop!*'

A frozen second as Jac glanced back from the few yards of waste ground before the highway edge, already checking for gaps in the traffic to dart across. Car door swung wide, a patrolman tensed in aiming stance, his figure part-silhouette in the spinning glare of the roof lights.

Yet Jac saw hesitation too in the patrolman's eyes, worried that any stray shot would hit the traffic passing behind; and as Jac saw a small gap in the traffic, he turned and ran through the first clear lane, brief pause for a four-wheeler passing in the far lane, then on, jumping the central barrier – Jac only half paying attention to another shout of '*Stop!*' More desperate now, but less audible with the traffic noise in between.

And so Jac was startled, falling back a step, when a shot sounded – only realizing that it was a warning shot as he looked back and saw the patrolman lowering his gun from the air to point straight at him.

A moment's nervous Mexican standoff, Jac praying that he wouldn't risk a shot with the traffic passing in between – though maybe he would if there was a long, clear break – but then a large truck flashed between them, breaking the spell.

Jac darted into the next lane, letting one car pass, but then had to pause for a second, feigning like a matador as the next car approached faster than he'd timed, another car alongside in the fast lane swinging wide of Jac at the last second, blaring its horn.

Jac scurried across the last lane and leapt the side barrier. Rows of concrete and steel stanchions ahead, supporting the motorway above. Heavier shadows between them.

Jac weaved between the stanchions, trying to make best use of the shadows to lose himself as quickly as possible from view, glancing in between at the patrolmen across the highway· the one who'd fired was peering hard, trying to follow where he'd gone, his partner now on the radio, the second car pulling away, possibly to swing onto the highway further along.

Jac hoped by then he'd be long gone. Another busy four-laner thirty yards away, a ramp to one side swinging up to one of the highways above, another ramp on the far side of the stanchions. A choice of escape routes for once.

But in that moment, above the dull drone and swish of traffic from above, Jac thought he could hear other sirens: three or four, maybe more. He looked around frantically, caught a glimpse of two squad cars in the distance on the highway he'd just crossed, heading fast his way. But the directions of the sirens on the tangle of roads above were harder to place.

Jac ran for the closest ramp; he needed to get out of sight quickly from the highway behind.

More sirens. It sounded as if half the city's police were hunting him down. Jac had given up on judging direction; they seemed to swirl and echo from all around as he started up the ramp.

Another sound also reached him then, a shudder running through him as he paused mid-step to make sure: the rapid thud–thud of a helicopter winging through the night sky. Jac looked up, but couldn't see its lights yet; whether because of the clouds, the partial cover of the overhead highway, or it was still too far away, he wasn't sure.

But he knew with certainty that it would be upon him any second. Jac's eyes darted desperately: if he continued up the ramp, he'd be more visible from above, but if he headed back down, the two police cars bearing down on the highway behind would see him.

Sweat beads massed on his forehead, mixing with the rain-drops, chest heaving as he gasped like a dying frog into the night air. He felt completely worn, exhausted, the sirens echoing and spinning in his head making him feel dizzy, unsteady; his legs trembling so hard that they felt about to buckle at any second. It would have been so easy, welcome surrender, just to lift his hands to the helicopter searchlight or first police car to arrive – he couldn't go on much further in any case – but instead, as the lights of a car heading up the ramp hit him, he lifted one hand to that, trying to flag it down. It went past.

Sirens moving closer, one on the highway above now sounding no more than fifty yards away. Jac flagged more frantically. A camper van and a car not far behind went past too, the car beeping as Jac took a step in front of it.

Jac could now see the helicopter searchlight as it broke through the clouds: about sixty yards to his right, moving methodically forward with tight sweeps. And the closest siren above now sounded only twenty yards away.

It started raining more heavily then, and Jac mouthed one last silent prayer into the sodden, misty night air as the scream of the sirens and the thud-thud of the helicopter closed in all around him, becoming all-consuming. And as the next two cars on the ramp also swept past him without stopping – the beam of the helicopter searchlight now circling in to within thirty yards – Jac felt any remaining hope slip away.

31

May 1992.

At first, Adelay Roche wasn't too concerned about the direction of the police investigation. The account of a robbery gone wrong seemed to have been accepted, the crime-scene evidence supported that, and so Lieutenant Coyne was trawling for suspects almost exclusively in that area: house robbers with violent past form.

But every now and then there'd be a quick aside, a question thrown in out of the blue amongst the standard question line – as if slipped in like that the lieutenant thought he might not notice – that made Roche start to worry that Coyne was having increasing doubts about the robbery-gone-wrong theory. Was starting to fish closer to home.

The eyewitness had thankfully been distant enough to not be too precise; though perhaps if they got Nel-M in a line-up, it would be a different matter. And over that final shot to the head Roche had vented more than a few choice words at Nel-M.

Roche was convinced it was the one detail that didn't sit comfortably with Coyne. And if he kept digging, he might unearth more inconsistencies, things he wasn't happy with.

Roche phoned to check how much Coyne might have been raking around in the background; after all, it might just be his own empty paranoia.

Pretty much the same routine each time: 'Lieutenant Coyne said that he'd be in touch with you about my wife's investigation. I wondered if he's made contact yet?' The concerned husband checking on police progress; he'd started to get more on Coyne's back, so his following-up wouldn't look unusual. 'Oh right . . . *right*.'

Roche was alarmed at the extent of Coyne's background calls. He'd been busy. Very busy. Coyne obviously hadn't found anything yet, otherwise he'd have been on his doorstep with handcuffs and a caution; but as the asides and questions started to become more frequent, Roche worried that soon Coyne might stumble on something.

They needed to get Coyne back on track with the robbery-gone-wrong theory, stop his focus shifting, and soon after Roche struck on the idea of putting someone else in the frame; sufficiently roped and tied that Coyne would stop looking elsewhere. The only thing he could think of that with certainty would head Coyne off at the pass. Stop everything dead.

House robbers and the city's low-lives were more Nel-M's territory, and within a week he'd put together a potential list for Roche.

Larry Durrant was initially way down the list, mainly because his past form hadn't been that violent, the most serious a pistol-whipping 'in the course of'. But the details about his car accident and selective amnesia moved him higher. His scheduled recovered memory sessions with a psychiatrist, Leonard Truelle, higher still. By the time they'd dug down and uncovered Truelle's drinking and gambling problems, and his heavy book-debt to a street loan shark, Raoul Ferrer, Durrant was top of the list.

There was only one thing left to find out: whether Truelle, with the bait set how they planned, would go for it?

The first news bulletin complete with Jac's photo went out on a local TV station, WWL, at 11.45 p.m.

Derminget asked if they could delay to another bulletin in half an hour or an hour, but was told that was the last news bulletin of the day.

'It's either then, or wait until seven-thirty a.m. tomorrow.'

Immediacy, Derminget was convinced, was the main key to McElroy's lawyer being able to talk him in. A bulletin the next morning lacked immediate threat, gave McElroy too long to dwell on it.

So Derminget decided to mislead Langfranc that, along with the APB, he'd hold fire with the news bulletin for half an hour – though he did keep to his promise about the APB. One out of two, at least, and at first the late-night bulletin would probably only draw the attention of a few bleary-eyed bar-flies – it would take more than half an hour in any case for any worthwhile calls to come in.

But the desk clerk at the Palmetto motel recognized the photo straightaway and dialled 911 while the tail-end of the bulletin was still on screen: '. . .*a lawyer with local firm, Payne, Beaton and Sawyer, Mr McElroy has been in the news recently for* other *reasons: his plea petition handling of Libreville death row inmate, Lawrence Durrant, whose execution is scheduled for ten days time.*'

Derminget was notified of the call only minutes after putting the phone down from his last-shot warning call to Langfranc. Derminget paused only fleetingly before giving the nod to dispatch the closest squad cars. If McElroy's reaction to Langfranc's warning call was to flee, he'd never forgive himself – or more to the point, Captain Broughlan, head of the station house, would never forgive him – for letting the opportunity to grab McElroy slip from his grasp.

Two squad cars arrived at the Palmetto motel within only eight minutes. Impressive. But that was the last thing to go right.

Captain Broughlan scanned down the catalogue of disasters filed in Derminget's report at first light the next morning, the sharp glint in his eyes only softened by a teasing leer of disbelief as he finished and looked across at Derminget.

'So, you had half the Eighth and First tight on his ass, a chopper too – and he disappeared right under your noses?' Broughlan threw up invisible dust with one hand. 'Thin air.'

'Yeah.'

'And no sign of him since? Nothing from any other calls in?'

'No, none that have panned out.' Derminget nodded dolefully. His bloodhound eyes, quite sexy to women when he eyed them broodingly across a late-night cocktail bar, now morose and defeated, looked pathetic. 'He obviously got in a car passing on the interchange.'

'Obviously.' Broughlan smiled tightly. 'Busy that time of night?'

'Busy enough. We're not going to be able to narrow down to anything useful from nearby cams. Our only hope is that whoever picked him up will catch a later news bulletin and phone in. There's a lot of coverage right now.'

'Yeah, Jem, lot of coverage,' Broughlan echoed, his tone suddenly harder, warier. 'And the reason for that is it's a big event. Would have been anyways with a lawyer on the run for murder – but the fact that it's Larry Durrant's lawyer, with only days now till his execution, has shot the story into the stratosphere.' Broughlan held his palms out. 'So, as you say, a lot of coverage to help us succeed – but also a lot of eyes watching if we don't.' Broughlan tilted his swivel chair back a fraction, but his eyes stayed keenly, sharply on Derminget. 'And with half of New Orleans watching on the outcome – we can't afford to fail, Jem. That's simply not an option. Find Jac McElroy, and find him quick.'

Clive Beaton didn't see the 11.45 p.m. bulletin, but he received a call minutes later from Jeremiah Payne relating the bombshell news.

The minute he put down the phone from Payne, he called John Langfranc at home.

Langfranc didn't hold anything back – little point, with an ongoing investigation most of it would soon be out in the open – but most importantly, it was the only way to get across to Beaton the main details of why Jac thought he'd been set up.

'That's as may be,' Beaton said curtly. 'But until such time as the police adopt that stance, he's a fugitive. And so for now that's how this firm must deal with him.'

'I see.' Langfranc had expected little else. Beaton distancing the firm as quickly as possible. 'Are you saying also that you don't want me to continue representing Jac McElroy or his girlfriend?'

'That's exactly what I'm saying. That whole business of you knowing the gun was being hidden could get awkward. It's one thing knowing after the event, but *during* – the cry could come up of withholding. And without that – McElroy calling you in the process of that action – you've got no rationale for him running off. One of the main defence pillars collapses.'

'I understand. Okay.' Resignation in Langfranc's voice, but he held back from outright dissension; Beaton had a point. 'And what about Durrant? It's his BOP hearing tomorrow. Do you want me to go along?'

'I'm not sure yet what to do there. I need overnight to think on it some more.'

But Beaton had decided within the first minute of hearing the news: *more distance*. Although he didn't want the firm to in any way appear non-caring or negligent, so having the next morning prepared McElroy's dismissal letter and immediately notified the local media that due to the circumstances now surrounding Mr McElroy he was no longer with the firm, next on his list was Chief Warden Haveling. 'And given the sudden nature of those circumstances, we've unfortunately been left short on time to get someone else there for his BOP hearing later today.'

Haveling mentioned another possible option for the hearing, which Beaton, having engineered a few emergencies to fill Langfranc's diary for the day, duly relayed to Langfranc: 'Apparently, Durrant's got a good friend inside, Hector Rodriguez, who has basic paralegal experience and, more to the point, is fully conversant with the BOP procedure. Good chance he'll sit in with him.'

Langfranc wasn't happy, was sure there'd been some Beaton sleight-of-hand in the background – he hadn't become senior partner for nothing – but he reminded himself of that groan of disapproval, like the low rumbling of an approaching storm, when he'd told Beaton he'd been aware of McElroy disposing of his girlfriend's gun. While Beaton's pen was in dismissal-letter-signing flow, he didn't want to tempt fate.

Langfranc sighed resignedly. 'I suppose all the main arguments McElroy has already submitted in the petition before them. This Rodriguez *should* be able to handle it from there.'

But as Beaton agreed offhandedly, 'Yes, he should', and hung up, the words left a sour tang in Langfranc's mouth; he was getting almost as bad as Beaton. *Almost*, because while he might now and then spin the right rhetoric, he hadn't yet got to the stage of believing it himself.

Jac found it hard to stop shaking. Another car had passed him on the ramp, but a trailer-truck behind stopped.

He'd originally told the truck driver, half an eye fixed on the approaching helicopter light over the driver's shoulder, that he wanted to go to Gramercy – the first place to spring to mind on Highway 10 Westbound – then, when the driver mentioned stopping before that for gas and a quick coffee, Jac quickly amended: 'Well, on the way there. Small community between the Highway and the Great River Road. I'll point it out when we get closer.'

The truck driver – pushing forty, but trying to cling to youth with shoulder-length hair and an earring – obviously hadn't seen the news bulletin yet, but if they stopped in a busy roadside café, chances are someone there would have.

He had some Garth Brooks playing in the background, which after a moment with a 'Don't bother you none?', he turned up. Perhaps he'd had it up loud before, so hadn't noticed the sirens; though at such a busy junction, sirens wailing were perhaps nothing unusual.

At only one point, about six miles into the drive, did the driver eye him curiously – the T-shirt and the rain outside perhaps not correlating. 'Not the best night to be out?'

'Break-down,' Jac said. 'Tow-truck kept me hanging for forty minutes. But I didn't want to miss out totally on seeing this old friend. Haven't seen him for a while; since college, in fact.'

The truck driver nodded thoughtfully. The casual college-buddy dress, Jac flustered and wet from the rain, his uncertainty about where his 'old friend' lived. Jac hoped that the component parts slotted in.

But in the long gaps when they didn't talk at all, above Garth Brooks and the thrum of the truck's wheels on the road, Jac could still hear the thud-thud of the helicopter blades, pushing the images of the night through his mind . . . *Gerry with half his skull blown away* . . . '*You've shot him! You've shot him!*' . . . *Sirens wailing as he ran through the night* . . . '*You've got to give yourself up to the police, Jac*' . . . *The ram hitting the door* . . . *The helicopter light moving in* . . . '*Your new girlfriend* . . . *I'll bet you she hasn't told you what we did together* . . .'

'That coffee stop's about five miles up the road now.'

'*What?*' The thudding so heavy in his head that it took a second for the words to register. *Truck stop. Crowds of people.* Jac peered at the road ahead. He had to get dropped off before then. But they hadn't passed any houses or signs of life for a while. 'I . . . I think where I want is not far ahead now,' Jac said hopefully. 'This looks familiar.'

But as another two miles rolled by with nothing either side, Jac became desperate. *The TV on in the truck stop. People looking between the TV and himself, pointing*: '*It's him . . . it's him!*'

Finally, a few shacks and wood-frame bungalows appeared two hundred yards to his left.

'Yes, here . . . *here*!' A dead-and-alive place, but it was the best he was going to get. He couldn't afford to wait longer. Quick smile and 'Thanks' as he stepped down, a ''S'okay buddy' from the driver. But again that curious stare, Jac concerned that some things hadn't added up for the driver, and as soon as he got down the road he'd get on his cell-phone to the police.

Jac ran down the narrow road leading to the houses. Ditches either side, fields beyond. A small farming community.

The town, if it could be called that – half a dozen streets with forty or so small wood-frame bungalows – was deserted. The only person he saw was an old black man eyeing him with lazy curiosity from his front verandah as he went by. Jac slowed from a run to a rapid walk.

White man walking around in the dead of night in a small black farming community? Hands would be reaching to phone for the police as quickly here as at the truck stop; and as Jac got round the corner, already he could hear a siren approaching. Becoming stronger for a moment before drifting into the distance as it passed on Highway 10.

Jac eased his breath, swallowing back against his hammering nerves. This was ludicrous. Only an hour he'd been on the run, and already there was nowhere left for him to go. Truck stop. Small town. And as more people saw the news bulletin, it would get worse. Heading back to the city would be out of the question, as would contacting family or friends – by now almost certainly monitored. And the main reason he wanted to stay loose and free – trying to save Larry Durrant in the remaining days left – a million miles away. Impossible.

Jac shook his head. He had to face it. There was nowhere left for him to go. Nothing left that he could do.

'I'm sorry . . . sorry,' Jac mouthed softly towards the night sky, letting the raindrops hit his face for a second. Wash away the guilt. 'I did everything I could.'

Jac found a phone booth in the next street, but his body was still shaking as he approached it, the images still thudding through his mind – Larry Durrant's pleading face now among them: *Promise me, Counsellor . . . you won't just forget about me and leave me here to rot . . . because there's somebody I've been apart from already far too long . . . If I could just see his face, see that it wasn't me – I could turn and shout that out to her in the courtroom: It wasn't me, ma . . . it wasn't me . . . This is a dying man's drink, isn't it? You don't see much hope left . . .* Jac imagining that his last steps towards the phone booth were Larry Durrant's as he approached the execution chamber, and now there was nothing left to stop that.

Jac's hand shook wildly as he fed in the coins to call John Langfranc. But as the last dime slid in, Jac was struck with another thought.

32

Rodriguez thought he was doing fine. Until the woman on the left of the two men that made up the Board of Pardons panel started to speak.

Mid-forties, severe, hair in a small beehive, black-rimmed almond-shaped glasses which she perched on the front of her hairdo or end of her nose, peering unwaveringly at Rodriguez and Larry Durrant.

The questioning from the two men, one bearded in his mid-fifties, the other a clean-cut late thirties, had been mostly perfunctory, filling in the details: *When did you become more strictly religious, Mr Durrant? Five years into your term . . . any particular reason for the timing? Soon after your mother dying. Did you feel that might have been a factor, then? A catalyst for something that was already there, you say . . . is that how you'd like it termed in our report? Okay. And your correspondence degree in literature? How long did that take? Three years. That's a long haul and a lot of application. Very commendable.*

Larry answered most of the questions directly at first, but at that point Rodriguez took over more, as it became obvious that Larry was uncomfortable expanding too much about his personal achievements; private and guarded to a fault, even when his life depended on it.

Rodriguez had been nervous about speaking on behalf of Larry at first, especially with what was at stake: Larry's very life riding on how he handled things. But with Jac obviously not able to be there, what other choice was there? And faced with that Hobson's choice, he'd egged himself on: *'You can do it . . . can do it!'* Pacing up and down anxiously in his cell repeating set pieces and lines, and the same too in the waiting room for the six minutes that felt like a lifetime before they were called in; except then there was just pacing, the words seemed to have suddenly evaporated from his brain.

The amenable attitudes of the two men eased his nerves a fraction, the words starting to come back again, but Mrs Beehive worried him; that cool, unflinching stare each time he caught her eye. The only saving grace was that she hadn't spoken yet, and so Rodriguez was able to focus more on the two men.

Rodriguez waxed lyrical about Durrant's literary expertise and character in general and, as he'd done before with Jac, he'd brought with him a few books and prison magazines to illustrate Larry's writing and editing skills. A couple of approving nods from the BOP panel, but as Rodriguez used much the same line he had with Jac then, 'As you can see, he's a long way from the Larry Durrant he was when he first came to Libreville eleven years ago', he couldn't help thinking about the absent lawyer.

Bateson had hauled him and Larry into the TV room straight after breakfast, and he should have guessed from the gathering there, mostly his and Larry's clique along with Shavell and a handful of his die-hards – few prisoners without strong allegiances either way – that it wasn't for a run-of-the-mill Presidential or State Governor announcement, or a re-run of the last Saints game.

The item about Jac was first up as the bulletin shifted from national to local news. A wry smile from Bateson as Rodriguez looked around, a more open leer from Shavell, and the same numbed shock on Larry's face that hit Rodriguez in that instant, though with an added tinge of warped acceptance – as if Larry had seen so much, was so tired of it all with death now close, that nothing would really surprise him any more.

But the little show quickly backfired on Bateson as the news item fully unfolded. '. . . *police were apparently close to apprehending Mr McElroy late last night in the Mid-City area, but in the end that bid failed . . .*' BC on his feet, punching the air with one fist: 'Go, Jac . . . Go!' '. . . *and so he remains at* *large, with the police appealing to the public for fresh sightings and* *information on Mr McElroy, with the accompanying warning that* *he should not be approached directly*'. As Rodriguez got to his feet, joining the chorus of two or three that had quickly joined BC, Bateson, red-faced, hastily wound everything up, barking along with two other guards for them to clear the room.

'And heavy contributions to the prison magazine too, I see?'

Rodriguez brought his attention back to the bearded man, though the question was aimed equally at himself and Larry, who was nodding. The panel had been introduced at the outset of the meeting, but Rodriguez had promptly forgotten their names. They'd simply become Bearded-man, Clean-cut and Beehive.

'Yes . . . in fourteen of the sixteen editions, I believe,' Rodriguez said, doing the quick calculation: started four years ago, quarterly, only two editions that Larry hadn't contributed to. 'He's been one of the strongest voices and role-models for black inmates at Libreville.'

Another thoughtful nod from Bearded-man, one more quick note on his pad, Clean-cut following suit. But Beehive just kept staring at him imperiously, and finally she spoke:

'This new-found literary expertise is all very well, but I'm more concerned with how it has been put to use.' She puckered her mouth as if she'd encountered a sour taste as she turned the pages in the magazine before her, then held the position with one finger. She looked up again. 'Mr Durrant's article in issue nine of *Libre-View*.'

Rodriguez looked helplessly at the two magazines he'd brought along. Issue nine wasn't one of them. 'Right,' he said, a faint flush rising as his mind desperately scrambled for which article that might have been.

'In this edition he comments on the execution of Mary-Beth Fuller in Texas, and questions the Texas Governor's stance in not offering her a last minute reprieve, because, and

I quote, "Mary-Beth Fuller was clearly mad, yet the Eighth Amendment of the Constitution is equally clear in prohibiting execution of the insane . . ." ' Beehive looked up sharply above her glasses, her eyes shifting more directly to Durrant this time. 'You go on to say, Mr Durrant, that this is a subject uncomfortably close to home because of your own, and again I quote, "Poor state of mind and memory at the time of your arrest for the murder of Jessica Roche, which gave rise to your own good counsel questioning your own culpability." ' This time Beehive hadn't looked down for the quote, she'd just held the same steady stare, now alternating evenly between Durrant and Rodriguez.

'Yeah, I wrote that,' Larry said flatly, matter-of-factly. 'But I'm somewhat lost as to what exac–'

'I'm sure Mr Durrant wouldn't for a minute dream of detaching himself from that article,' Rodriguez cut in quickly, sensing Larry's belligerent tone heading for a confrontation. 'Just because it might now suit him to do so. He's understand-ably proud of everything he's written. But at the same time, it's only an opinion.'

'Yes, Mr Rodriguez.' Beehive exhaled heavily, as if mustering patience to deal with an errant schoolchild. 'But what concerns me about that *opinion* is the dilemma it now presents to this board. Two of the strongest factors we have to consider in recommending pardon is firstly that prisoners fully repent their crime, and secondly, and in hand with that, that they fully accept the judgement of the courts, justice system and our governor – upon whose mercy they now throw themselves. Yet here we have a prisoner who questions their very guilt – so how can we even get to the stage of acceptance and repentance?' Beehive shrugged. 'And on top is also questioning the judgement of our fair governor before he's even considered the issue.'

Durrant blinked slowly, a faint smile creasing his lips – acceptance or challenge, Rodriguez wasn't sure.

'I can see that,' Rodriguez said, eager to speak before Larry opened his mouth and possibly dug them in deeper. 'But I'm sure that . . .' Though as Rodriguez said it, he had no idea what he was sure of. His mouth was suddenly dry, his throat tight as Beehive stared at him curiously, expectantly. 'I . . . I'm sure that's not how Mr Durrant meant it.' All he could think of quickly.

The stare stayed steadily, evenly on Rodriguez, one eyebrow now raised imperiously, doubtingly, and it was obvious to everyone in the room that he was floundering, desperately treading water. A few basic legalese phrases strung together from first-year law books combined with some fast talk from the streets and being on the radio – who was he kidding? She'd probably ridden roughshod over some of the toughest lawyers in the state. But this might be Larry's very last chance; he couldn't just give up at the first obstacle. 'I can see how it might look,' he said, injecting more conviction. 'But that article's just one of many that Larry Durrant's written in *Libre-View.*' *Diversion*, thought Rodriguez. If he couldn't win on one front, shift to another. 'If we look at some others . . . this one here for instance in issue eleven that I've brought along, we see that–'

'Mr Rodriguez!' Beehive cut in sharply with a tired sigh. She wasn't about to be suckered in. 'Mr Durrant's literary expertise and comments in other areas are not in question. I brought up this particular article because it presents specific problems to this board in its recommendation for clemency.'

'I understand.' Rodriguez nodded, suitably humbled. A light buzzing now in his head, feeling slightly dizzy, disorientated. *Where else to head, what else to try?* And as that owlish, unwavering gaze cut through him, his cheeks burning and the room starting to sway uncertainly around him, he wished that he was anywhere than here at this moment.

'And so until such time as those issues are answered, if they can be, then I don't see the point in–'

Beehive broke off sharply and looked past Rodriguez's shoulder as the door opened behind them. '*Yes?*'

'I apologize profusely for the late intrusion. Darrell Ayliss, attorney at law.'

All eyes in the room were fixed on the man – late forties, overweight, oiled-down black hair greying at the sides, horn-rimmed glasses, a cream suit as if he'd just returned from Havana – as he stepped forward and handed cards to each of the BOP panel, then nodded briefly towards Durrant and Rodriguez.

'Because of the unfortunate turn of events with Mr McElroy, I was not informed of the situation until late in the day by my old colleague Michael Coultaine – who, as you are all probably aware, handled the original trial and appeal for Mr Durrant – and I got here as soon as I could.' Ayliss adjusted his glasses on the bridge of his nose and pushed a tight smile to all present. 'Now you were saying, Mrs . . . ?'

'Elleridge. Gloria Elleridge.'

'Mrs Elleridge. Your reputation precedes you. Heard much about your good work on the Board.' Ayliss's pronounced Southern accent had a smooth, lilting sing-song edge. The compliment raised a faint blush from Beehive. 'Now you just go right ahead.'

Someone else in on it? Carmen Malastra should have realized that from the outset: to prevent skimming, all employees, including the manager, were searched going in and out of his casinos, and were allowed no more than fifty bucks in their pockets. And Malastra regularly changed the security guards, in case they might get involved. So that meant to get any significant cash out of the Bay Tree regularly, Jouliern would have needed a courier.

The search for George Jouliern's likely money courier had gone well at first. From the video library of the Bay Tree Casino floor, Malastra built up a strong picture of who Jouliern had met with during the eighteen months to two years the scam had been running.

Jouliern was a popular man. Very popular. Very sociable.

A greeting for everyone, a few gracious words spoken before he'd touch their arm, smile and move on. But it was the occasions when more than a few words were spoken that drew Malastra's interest, or when a look of concern might cross Jouliern's face. Perhaps it might be someone he'd just sit next to nonchalantly, hardly paying them any attention; except that it would have to happen on a regular basis, and there'd be that moment when an envelope or small package would be passed between them, even if half-concealed beneath a table or left under a jacket draped over a bar-stool.

Malastra followed every inch of Jouliern's movements over that period, fast-forwarding, stopping, leaning closer to the screen when something caught his interest, zooming in, tracing one finger over Jouliern and the face next to him in the frame, wondering '*Could it be you?*' But the problem was there were too many faces, too many that Jouliern met with regularly and shared more than a few words with. Malastra had started off with forty or more possible suspects, but after days at the computer was finding it hard to narrow down beyond eighteen; no regular tell-tale envelopes passed from Jouliern that would immediately lift one of them from the pack.

Malastra became convinced that he wasn't going to be able to find Jouliern's courier, it was going to remain a mystery. He decided to pay a personal visit to the Bay Tree Casino floor, in case there was something he'd overlooked.

The new manager there, Tony Caccia, greeted him with a wide smile. 'Mr Malastra. So nice to see you here.'

'Yeah,' Malastra said curtly. He visited rarely, and usually went straight to the upstairs office without visiting the casino floor. He promptly turned his back on Caccia and went round the casino checking the angles of the video cameras, the manager following uncertainly from four paces behind. Having done a full circuit of the room, he turned back to Caccia. 'Any blind spots on the video cams that you're aware of?'

'No, don't think so. Why?'

Malastra looked at him sharply. 'If you're going to continue working for me, the first thing to get clear is never answer my questions with a question. Only Jewish businessmen and wily old Italians like myself do that. It's fucking annoying. Okay?'

'Okay. Sorry.'

Then only two days later, when he'd all but given up on it, Malastra saw the news item on Jac McElroy, lawyer to Larry Durrant, Jessica Roche's murderer of twelve years ago. But what piqued Malastra's interest was the victim's name, Gerald Strelloff. It rang a bell, and minutes later he found it on his computer. Strelloff had worked as a barman at the Bay Tree at the time of the scam, and the ex-girlfriend named in the news bulletin as part of the love triangle that led to the murder, Alaysha Reyner, still worked at one of his clubs, Pinkies.

Then Malastra recalled that Nel-M had phoned him when he'd first latched onto Jouliern's scam to apologize for Raoul Ferrer's hit. A coincidence, maybe, but it left Malastra with an uneasy feeling.

Maybe that's how Jouliern had done it? Instead of handing to the courier directly, he'd used the barman, Gerry Strelloff. Countless conversations between them every week, and numerous papers and envelopes with till receipts and stock re-order lists passed between them – the ideal cover.

But then Strelloff would also have been searched in and out of the casino, so would have needed someone else to pass on to. Malastra got back to his computer and started searching for the person Strelloff might have used.

Over the following forty-eight hours, Lieutenant Jerome Derminget's department fielded over twenty possible sightings of Jac McElroy. Seventy per cent of them could be discounted straightaway, and of the remaining thirty per cent they followed up, only one sounded like it might be bona fide: an elderly farm cooperative worker from a small settlement out by the Great River Road.

If McElroy had got a lift at the Morrison Interchange, as

they suspected, then the timing of the sighting coincided with when he might have been dropped off in that area.

But the man didn't phone in with the sighting until the next morning when he first saw a news report, and by then, understandably, McElroy had long gone from the area. Though what most worried Derminget was that McElroy seemed to have disappeared from every other area. From the other suspected sightings, a couple of close-but-no-cigars, the rest had been a mile off the mark.

Broughlan had been screaming for results, yet with each passing hour the chances of finding McElroy were looking slimmer. After twenty-four hours with no more firm sightings, despite McElroy's face appearing on every local news bulletin and in the newspapers, the first real concerns began to fester at the Eighth District station house. After forty-eight hours still with nothing, it was all but official: Jac McElroy had disappeared from the face of the earth. Had without doubt left the State, if not the country.

'He was incredible. Fuckin' awesome. The Zoro of how to cream the BOP with a few swift strokes.' Rodriguez mimed two elaborate sword strokes with one hand.

Rodriguez was holding court in the prison canteen the morning after the BOP hearing, and had the attention of everyone at his long table, with some heads also turned from the tables each side. 'First thing is he gets her to repeat her beef, which o' course straight-off gets her more shaky of her ground. Then, like he was doing her a favour, he cuts in halfway and says he knows and respects the point she's makin' and is glad she's raised it. "Only someone as astute as yourself, Mrs Elleridge, would pick up on the worrying sub-text of Mr Durrant's articles in the way you have."

'He's laying on the compliments like thick treacle to soften her up, and she's blushin' and so open to anything by now that she might as well have her panties down by her ankles. So then he gives her the first test jab, sayin' that he's sure that's not what Larry Durrant meant by that article. "What makes you say that?" she quizzes, knees twitchin' now, worried that she might have made a big mistake leaving herself so open. But it's too late; with a little teasin' smile, he rams home wit' the "Fuck you", says that if she noticed in the article, Durrant uses the third person throughout: he cites Texas statutes regarding Mary-Beth Fuller, and his own lawyer with culpability doubts in his own case. At no time does he express those opinions as his own.

'She starts splutterin' . . . "That's as may be . . ." realizin' now that she's gettin' fucked, but not sure how to stop it – and he rams home with the final killer stroke.' Rodriguez did another sword swipe in the air to accompany his hip thrust. " 'And that's supported too by what, from his files, Mr McElroy was faced with when he first saw Larry Durrant." "What was that?" she asks, wide open again – this girl jus' wouldn' learn.' Rodriguez smiled crookedly and shook his head. ' "The fact that at that point Durrant said he wanted to die – didn't want a plea made on his behalf."

'Mr Smooth-Southern-ass then looks at the panel long and hard, and says: "Now you can't get more accepting of guilt than that. You see, it's not Larry Durrant himself who's questioned his guilt or felt that his life might be worth pleading for – it's his lawyers: Mr Coultaine, Mr McElroy, and now myself. And if we've been wrong in doing that, then I humbly apologize." '

Rodriguez was in his element playing to his audience, laying on a thick southern accent for Ayliss and switching to high and squeaky for beehive Elleridge. Rodriguez punched a fist skyward as he finished. 'Fuckin' ace!'

Peretti was the first to show his support by slapping the flat of one hand against the table with a 'Yeah, yeah', which set off more table-slapping along with some 'Wuh-wuh' frat-boy monkey chants, Rodriguez taking a quick bow before he caught the quizzical glare from Elden on guard duty at the far end.

But as Rodriguez sat back down, the clamour as quickly dying, he knew that it was mainly bravado to fire everyone up, kid them, and himself, that there was still strong hope left. Drag them away from the reality: only eight days left now for Larry, and little hope.

'Okay. Give me the low-down.' Roche wheezed heavily into the phone, the panic of the past forty-eight hours and the nervous anticipation waiting for Nel-M's call back weighing like a rock in his chest. 'What have you been able to find out about him?'

'Darrell Christopher Ayliss. One of Mike Coultaine's old colleagues from way back. One of the best criminal lawyers in Mississippi at the time. We're talking almost twenty years back to seven years ago, late-nineties – before he went to Mexico.'

'Mexico?'

'Yeah, that's where he hightailed it to after his divorce. Messy business. On top of the half, his wife wanted a big chunk of his new partnership. He said, fuck it, in that case there is no partnership. Headed to Puerto Vallarta and started selling real estate and handling some conveyance for Americans buying there. He sent her maintenance, though not what she was claiming, plus presents and money for their daughter Christmas and birthdays. She apparently pursued him for the extra money for a while, then gave up the ghost when she moved to Oregon a few years back.'

'Is that why maybe he feels it's safe to come back here now?'

'Maybe. But if that's the case, it was a sudden decision. Like the minute that Coultaine got on the phone and said he needed help, Ayliss was on the next plane. Because from what I can find out, up until now he's been in Mexico.'

Roche chewed the information over for a moment, his breath falling more steadily. 'So he owes Coultaine a favour or two, or they're close enough for that?'

'Uh-huh. Ayliss was with Bowyer and Turnbull in Jackson before, then did a two-year stint with Payne, Beaton and Sawyer. That's where he and Coultaine first met – and when Ayliss went back to Jackson to start up a partnership, they kept in contact. And obviously they have since, too.'

'One of the best criminal lawyers at the time, you say?'

'From what I hear. Of those in the early nineties tipped to be the next F. Lee Bailey, Ayliss was a prime contender.' From Roche's more troubled breathing at the other end, that obviously wasn't what he wanted to hear. Nel-M forced a tentative chuckle. 'But after eight years selling condos in Mexico, he's probably as rusty as shit.'

Silence, just the steady rise and fall of Roche's laboured breathing. He wasn't in the mood to be humoured.

'And the psychiatrist?' Roche asked after a moment. 'Have you been able to find out if it's game-on again with him?'

'Bateson says, yeah, apparently so.'

'When?'

'Day after tomorrow.'

Roche exhaled tiredly. 'All that palaver with McElroy just to gain three days. Back where we started, and by the looks of it with a stronger lawyer to boot.'

Nel-M had half expected the taunt with it being his plan, but he was damned if he was going to apologize for it. Despite everything once again slipping sideways, it had without doubt been their best plan yet. 'Three days delay. That might be all we need at this stage. And the second session planned is for some reason two days later; before with McElroy it was scheduled straight the day after. So another day delay there too. You know, ticking away, ticking away.'

'You want to convince yourself so that you feel better about it, fine. But don't expect me to buy into it. If this psychiatrist cracks Durrant, whether it's a day or just an hour before his execution, we're screwed.'

Nel-M felt like reaching down the phone and squeezing the last feeble breaths out of Roche, but he had a point. 'Not exactly much we're gonna be able to do about it. As we've just seen, we get rid of the psychiatrist, they'll just get another one in.'

Nel-M could sense from Roche's breathing becoming heavier, more troubled, that this was the hardest part for him. Letting go. A lifetime of controlling, manipulating with his grubby little paws, it was completely alien to him admitting that, for once, he couldn't push and mould things exactly how and where he wanted.

'We might just have to ride this one out,' Nel-M added after a moment. 'And, of course, pray.'

But Roche was hardly listening, his thoughts cannoning frantically in rhythm with his fractured breathing. 'There must be something we can do . . . *something*?'

33

Darrell Ayliss was sweating profusely as he paced back through the seemingly endless, cavernous grey corridors of Libreville. He was a large man with an awkward gait, and the sweat poured off him.

Testament to just how hot it was in Libreville, or perhaps equally it was from Durrant's words still burning through his head from the session just finished with Greg Ormdern. Or the crushing reminder that had run through him like a red-hot pulse in time with the wall clock ticking down the minutes of the session: only six days left now to possibly save Durrant.

Ayliss inhaled deeply of the air outside just before he got in his rented Dodge Stratus, observed the 20 m.p.h. speed limit for the two miles of shale road back towards the guard post, then gunned it once clear the other side. He let out a slow, heavy breath, as if blowing off the steam of the prison and the session, and hit play on the tape recorder on his passenger seat.

Ormdern's voice drifted out, Durrant's more muted timbre interspersed, the tinny tone of the recorder almost matching how he'd initially heard it through the small speaker in the observation room with Pete Folley at his side, looking on through the glass screen as Ormdern questioned Durrant on a camp-bed set up in the adjoining interview room.

Ormdern had been adamant that there should be no possible distractions in the room, and the sound feed and glass screen at the same time gave Ayliss what he wanted: not only to be able to hear every word, but watch every nuance and beat of Durrant's expression. He wanted to *feel* the experience, not just hear it.

It had taken almost ten minutes to get Larry fully under,

then another few minutes for Ormdern to set mood and place, put Durrant in the moment: eighteenth of February, the Roche's Garden District residence.

'The night that everything went wrong with the robbery and Jessica Roche.'

Ormdern had said that he didn't want to use overtly leading words like kill or murder. 'There's part of Larry Durrant probably still in denial, most likely why he's never described actually pulling the trigger, and I don't want to inadvertently draw that out . . . put up his defences.'

'You've already broken in the house . . . and I want you to tell me what you see there in the rooms, before you're disturbed by Jessica Roche.'

'In . . . in what way? Which rooms?'

'Let's start with the library. You went there to rob the house, and that's where you found the safe, I understand.'

'Yeah, that's where I found it. That's where I was in fact when—'

'That's okay,' Ormdern cut in sharply. 'What happened with Jessica Roche has been covered many times already. It's going back before that, I'm interested in. *Before* . . .'

Ormdern dragged the word out, giving it a soothing quality. Larry's breathing had become agitated, irregular, and as Ormdern repeated himself, 'Before . . . *before* . . .' it gradually settled back down.

'That room . . . the library itself, for instance . . . what did it look like?'

'I don't know . . . it was dark. I didn't really pay attention.'

'Okay, *okay* . . . the safe, then? You'd have concentrated on that, because you were about to break it.'

'Yeah . . . *yeah*.' Larry swallowed, a long pause as he applied thought. 'Straightforward twist-tumbler lock, as I recall.'

'And the colour?'

'I don't know . . . grey or green, I think.' Another heavy pause. 'But it's difficult. As I say, it was dark, and I was disturbed pretty soon, before I'd really had a chance to—'

'That's okay, Larry . . . that's okay. You've done well.'
Now it was Ormdern's turn to pause. 'Anything else that
stood out in the house or that room, however small or inconsequential?'

Only the sound of Larry's steady breathing, a faint swallow.
Then he started mumbling something indiscernible, and
Ormdern lost him for a few moments at that point.

'Try and focus again, Larry . . . focus . . . *focus* . . .' repetitive, the voice fading softer each time, '. . . . that's it Larry . . .
that's it . . .' Gently closing in, Ormdern getting the images to
settle again. 'Tell me what you see?'

'Noth . . . nothing that stood out that much, really. Lot of
books in the room, obviously . . . along one side.'

Ayliss had to concentrate on the road for a moment. He
reached over and turned off the tape as he came off Highway
12 and negotiated the turn onto the Causeway. Lake Pontchartrain spread each side like a dark, moody blanket, the
only relief some faint moon glow one side and the reflected
lights of New Orleans in the distance. Ayliss didn't switch on
again until he was a few miles into the Causeway.

'Do you remember which side of the room they were?'

'Uh . . . uh. Right-hand side as you walk in, I believe. Oh,
and there . . . *there* . . .'

'Yeah?' Ormdern prompting as Larry paused heavily again.
'Go ahead, Larry. Tell me.'

'There was a large clock in the hallway, I seem to remember. One of those ornate grandfather clocks.'

Ayliss clenched a fist tight on the steering wheel. The sort
of detail that would seal Durrant's fate rather than save it. If
his memory of detail in the house had been scant, they could
have cast doubt on his recall of the murder itself, claimed that
it had somehow been suggested or even implanted. Those
few details could be enough to support that he was definitely
there – *unless* those descriptions didn't match what Ayliss
discovered at the old Roche residence.

'Okay. We've covered what you might have actually seen

in the house. But I want to deal now with what you might have actually *felt* while you were there. Your fear and anxiety with what happened with Jessica Roche has already been dealt with in depth . . . but I wondered if at any time you had the feeling that someone else apart from her was there at the time. Someone watching that you probably didn't see or know about . . . only *felt* their presence?'

I was there at the time.

Ayliss's hands clenched back tight on the wheel as he waited out the long silence on tape, recalling Larry's brow furrowing heavily. Finally:

'No . . . I . . . I can't say I did. Didn't in fact hear *any* sounds in the house.' Larry's breathing steady, measured, then, after a brief swallow, falling shorter again, uneven. 'Not even Jessica Roche upstairs – otherwise I'd have got out of there earlier. Only heard her footsteps approaching at the last minute *when –* '

'That's okay, Larry – you don't need to go there,' Ormdern cut in sharply. 'You've covered that more than enough in the past. Move on again to afterwards . . . *afterwards.*' That drawn out, soothing tone again. 'Afterwards . . . as you're leaving the Roche house. Apart from the woman walking her dog, do you recall anyone else that might have seen you?'

'No . . .' Brief silence. 'Not that I can recall.'

'At a neighbouring house, perhaps . . . in their garden or looking out from a window. Someone that you didn't notice before?'

Longer pause, then: 'No, sorry . . . nothing. I was running hard by then, my mind set on just getting away from there. Perhaps wouldn't have even noticed the woman with her dog if I hadn't looked back.'

'Right. I can understand that.' Flicking of paper as Ormdern checked back through the notes Ayliss had handed him before the session. 'I want to take you somewhere else now, Larry. Same week in 1992 – but a completely different place. The Bayou Brew bar and your regular pool game there with

your buddies: Nat Hadley, Ted Levereaux and Bill Saunders.'
A moment's pause as Ormdern let the new location and
people settle in Durrant's mind. 'Now, I want you to try and
recall, Larry – was your game that week before or after that
night at the Roche house?'

'Uh . . . uh . . . before, I think.'

Ayliss turned the tape off again for a moment as he came
off the Causeway, and didn't switch on again until after he'd
made the turn on to Earhart Boulevard.

'You *think*? Concentrate, Larry. It's important. Can you
place the day with any certainty?'

'Yeah . . . yeah. Before, I'm pretty sure.'

Think. Pretty sure. Too easily argued as reflecting uncertainty, Ayliss considered. Wouldn't get him past square one
with Governor Candaret.

'Okay, before, then. Do you remember how long – how
many days?'

'I don't know. A day or two before, maybe.'

Don't know. Maybe. More uncertainty. Heavy pause as
Ormdern consulted Ayliss's notes again, looking for the key
point mentioned that would help nail the day down: Bill
Saunders.

'Okay. Let's see if we can tie it down another way. What
and who did you see there? Were all your playing buddies
there that night?'

'Yeah.' Larry's tone offhand, Ayliss recalled him giving a
little shrug at that juncture. 'They were all there.'

As Ayliss turned onto Louisiana Avenue, he checked his
watch. Looked like he'd get there six or seven minutes earlier
than he'd said. He'd had to lay on the Southern charm thick
and heavy to get the new owners' agreement to look through
the house; though hardly surprising, given its past history.

'Are you sure about that? Particularly Bill Saunders. Was
he there that night?'

'Yeah, Bill was there.'

'Absolutely sure?'

'Yeah. A hundred per cent.'

This time Ayliss banged one fist against the steering wheel, rather than the air-punch when he'd first heard those words an hour ago in the observation room.

Ormdern had looked up at the clock at that point, only four minutes remaining, then had brought Larry back out, explaining to Ayliss afterwards that he didn't want to get deep into what else Larry might have seen in the Bayou Brew that night only to have to break his train of thought halfway through.

Ayliss slowed as he came to the first houses of the Garden District on Washington Avenue, taking the turn into Coliseum Street two blocks down.

At least they'd ended on a positive note. High chances that the pool game *was* that crucial Thursday night, because Bill Saunders had been there rather than running his daughter to dance lessons. Ayliss would know just how high once he'd spoken to Saunders.

Ayliss was counting numbers as he went along. He swung in and pulled to a stop as he came to the old Roche residence. A resplendent antebellum mansion with two-storey high Corinthian columns supporting a thirty-foot wide front portico.

Problem was, that coinciding pool game was at odds with the details Durrant had provided from the Roche house, *if* they'd been as he described: *grey or green safe with a twist-tumbler lock, grandfather clock, books along the right-hand side*. Because he couldn't have been both places that night: playing pool *and* killing Jessica Roche.

Everything hinged on what Ayliss found out now. And what the new owners, the Mortons, might remember: ten years now they'd been in the house. Roche had put it on the market straight after the trial, but it had taken eleven months to finally find a buyer.

Ayliss closed his eyes for a second to compose himself. If this fact-finding now went the wrong way, in an hour he could be phoning Ormdern to cancel the second session. Something along the lines: '*Those details Durrant gave match what I've been able to find out from the house itself. There's no other possible explanation: he was there that night. There's little point in us continuing, nor in fact do I even feel inclined – from a purely ethical point of view – to put in more time trying to save an obviously guilty man.*'

A light wind outside ruffled the trees. A timeless district like this, early December, probably wasn't that different to how it had been mid-February twelve years ago. Ayliss wondered just how much of the house inside might have also remained in a time warp.

He noticed a curtain moving on a downstairs window, the Mortons checking out if it was their expected visitor. With a resigned sigh, Ayliss got out the car and approached the house.

'Follow him. See where he goes and who he might meet with.'

Roche's predictable advice when he called back the next evening about Ayliss. Nel-M felt like ribbing, 'And how exactly should I go about that? You know, after a month of doing fuck all else with McElroy, I might need some guidance.' Not exactly that imaginative: simply swap one mark for another. But with the way those few words had been delivered, slowly and purposefully between pained breaths, as if they had real significance, Nel-M could tell that Roche was still in no mood for humour. So all he said was, 'Okay. I'll get right on it.'

Then, as if an afterthought, or Roche felt his instructions should be meted out separately in case Nel-M couldn't cope with more than one at a time: 'Oh, and get onto his ex-wife in Oregon, too. Tell her that her past dearly beloved is back in town, and so she might want to take the opportunity to slap the rest of that old maintenance order back on his ass.' Roche did actually manage a brief forced chuckle then, but it lapsed into a small cough as it caught an incoming breath the wrong way. 'Should keep him on his toes and hopefully his eye off the ball with Durrant, with his wife hot on his tail again. Might even hightail it straight back to Mexico, if we're lucky.'

'If we're lucky.' A bit more of a plan, but Nel-M played it low-key, didn't want to be too enthusiastic. She might just say that that was all history, she had no interest in chasing his sorry ass any more. 'I'll see if I can make contact with her.'

The next morning, Nel-M put a call through to Bateson and asked him to make a note of Darrell Ayliss's car-type and registration when he arrived at Libreville that evening for the session with Orndern. Then he started making calls to track down Melanie Ayliss's phone number in Oregon.

Bateson's return call came at 7.16 p.m., and thirty-five minutes later Nel-M left his apartment and drove out to just before the start of the Pontchartrain Causeway, made a hasty U-turn in a gap in the traffic and stopped at the first pull-in where he could watch cars coming off the Causeway.

He'd got there early, just in case, and had to wait over half an hour before Ayliss's steel-blue Dodge Stratus went past him. Nel-M let one more car pass, then pulled out and followed.

Earhart . . . then Louisiana . . . LaSalle. As soon as Ayliss took the turn onto Washington Avenue, Nel-M suspected where he was heading; confirmed as Ayliss slowed the other side of St Charles, looking out for Coliseum Street.

Nel-M had spent little time in the area since that night in 1992. Driven past it several times and through it on a few occasions out of necessity – but never stayed for any time there.

He kept straight on as Ayliss turned into Coliseum Street, then took the next turn on Chestnut and again on 2nd Street, effectively circling round the block; and, sure enough, as he nosed his car out enough to get a partial view, Ayliss was closing his car door and heading up the path towards the Roches' old house.

For the first twenty minutes of waiting, Nel-M stayed calm, tried not to think too much about what Ayliss might be doing in there. But as the minutes ticked by, his thoughts started to multiply: maybe some vital clue from the session with Durrant that Ayliss was checking out, or something Ayliss had picked up on that nobody had before; or perhaps he was just familiarizing himself with the crime scene. Standard practice.

The atmosphere of the street also began to close in on Nel-M then: its quietness and isolation from the city close by, the shadows heavier, deeper from the large mansions and more abundant tree cover. The reminders of that night drifting back: *Jessica Roche's eyes staring back pleadingly just before that final shot . . . the woman walking her dog holding his gaze for a second as he'd looked back.*

Nel-M's pulse was still raised a notch, his hands gently trembling on the steering wheel, when almost an hour later Ayliss left the house. He pulled out again to follow him.

St Charles, Jackson, Simon Bolivar . . . finally stopping at a hotel two blocks from the main railroad and Greyhound bus terminals. Again, Nel-M drifted past and then turned around and parked a block away where he had a clear sight of Ayliss's Dodge in the hotel's side parking lot.

Maybe Ayliss would head out later for dinner or another meeting, Nel-M considered, but after an hour of waiting – 10.43 p.m. by then – Nel-M began to think that Ayliss might be there for the night, had grabbed something to eat in the hotel. He left it another twenty minutes, then went into the hotel. He approached the reception desk.

'I've got a business colleague staying here, Darrell Ayliss, and I promised to drop off some papers for him tomorrow morning. But I don't want to miss him before he heads off, and he told me he was having an early night – so I don't want to disturb him now. But I wondered what time he might have an alarm call or breakfast ordered – might give me a clue as to when he'll be heading out.'

The desk clerk's brow furrowed. 'Mr Ayliss has already left, sir.'

'But his rental car's still in the parking lot.'

'I know, sir. He left the keys here for the car-rental company to pick up, and got in a cab forty minutes ago.'

Nel-M tried to recall the dozen or so cabs he'd seen pull up in that time, and the people he'd seen get in them. The only possibility had been a man shuffling in with a homburg hat pulled down. But it hadn't looked like Ayliss – no horn-rimmed glasses, no dark lank hair in sight, different jacket – which Nel-M supposed had been the idea.

A muscle twitched sharply in Nel-M's jaw. 'Thanks,' he said, and as soon as he was outside the hotel, he took out his cell-phone.

Perhaps Ayliss was moving around because of his ex-wife, or possibly Coultaine had whispered in his ear that – given what had happened to McElroy – it was advisable to remain shadowy and elusive.

Nel-M had phoned Melanie Ayliss's number earlier and been told, 'Mom won't be back till late this evening. Shopping and then sociology evening class.'

Nel-M hadn't planned to try her again until the next day – but if this was going to be the name of the game with Ayliss, Runaround City, the sooner his ex-wife was chasing his ass, the better. With two of them trying to find him, he wouldn't find it so easy to slip away.

Darrell Ayliss's cab took him deeper into the city – through the Warehouse District, CBD and French Quarter – to a smaller, more intimate hotel with a quaint Spanish courtyard and pool on the edge of Faubourg Marigny.

He glanced through the cab's back window a couple of times, nobody following that he could tell – but then he hadn't noticed anyone following earlier either. Just basic precautions: change his hotel and his rental car every day. Keep on the move.

He'd phoned to book the room under his name four hours back, and, as he checked in, the desk clerk informed him that his guest had already arrived. 'About half an hour ago.' The desk clerk handed him his key. 'Room twenty-nine. First floor.'

Ayliss nodded with a tight smile and, despite it being only one floor, took the elevator. He felt as awkward as hell moving around, felt as if all that clammy heat and stale sweat from Libreville was still trapped against his skin.

Noises from the en-suite as he walked in: running water. He'd knock the door in a minute, but meanwhile he couldn't wait any longer to get everything off. First his oversized jacket and shirt, then the padding strapped around his shoulders and waist that made him look seventy pounds heavier. He leant forward to shake and blink out the two brown contact lenses into his right palm, then finally, stripped to the waist standing in front of the dressing-table mirror, he started peeling off the skin-coloured prosthetic stuck tight to his cheeks and around his jaw.

The bathroom door opened, and, reflected in the mirror, he saw Alaysha Reyner leaning against the door frame in burgundy-red La Perla panties and matching bra. She smiled slyly.

'My, my, Mr McElroy. I swear I only recognize you with your clothes off.'

He felt an ache of longing as he looked at her, but as he remembered Gerry's words '. . . *I'll bet you she hasn't told you what we did together. Our dirty, sordid little secret . . .*' before he ran off into the night with her gun, it dissolved into something else in his stomach. Something sourer, more uncertain, but equally as painful.

34

As Jac had been about to phone John Langfranc that night out by the Great River Road, he'd suddenly thought of Morvaun Jaspar. He'd stood frozen in the same position for a couple of minutes, turning over in his mind whether the scenario that had just struck him might be at all possible. Yes, it would be one way of disappearing for a while and, yes, he might be able to get into Libreville with a good enough disguise. But some of the practicalities and worrying gaps in the plan he wouldn't be able to fill until he'd actually spoken with Morvaun.

Morvaun had seen the late news bulletin, ' 'Spect half of New Orleans has by now', and while his initial excitement over the idea outweighed his concerns, he reserved full judgement until they'd talked it over some more. 'First thing is t'get you picked up. Then we can sit over some hot coffee – an' maybe somethin' stronger – while we thrash out if this is actually gonna work, or is jus' the worst damn-fool plan since the Presiden' decided to go into Iraq.'

In the half-hour wait, despite hanging in the shadow of some trees until he saw Morvaun's car turn the corner, again Jac's nerves bubbled as if being pressure-cooked, worried that the man on the terrace – or someone else seeing him through a window – might have matched him to the news bulletin, and a squad car would get to him before Morvaun.

Though when he did show, Jac still had good reason to worry. Morvaun's car, a late fifties Plymouth Belvedere, two-tone pink and sky-blue with grandiose tail-fins that looked like they belonged on a Buck Rogers space-craft, couldn't have stood out more in the small community. If Morvaun had leant out of a side window with a loud hailer shouting

"Septuagenarian pimps' convention" or "James Brown's back in town!" – that would at least have half-explained the car's presence to them.

As the car coughed and jerked its way back up to Highway 10, with the occasional backfire, Morvaun half-turned towards Jac in the back seat.

'Now you keep down real low there, Jac. Outta sight. Don' wanna bring no untoward attention to ourselves.'

Jac swallowed back a muted chuckle.

Morvaun's driving was atrocious. Jac lost count of the number of horns blared at them as Morvaun pulled out when he shouldn't or drifted across lanes. As a car at a cross-street screeched and swerved around them, a narrow miss as Morvaun pulled out without apparently seeing them, Morvaun apologized.

'Sorry 'bout that, Jac. Haven't been drivin' this for a while.'

Jac looked around at the car. 'What, since nineteen fifty-eight?'

Morvaun chuckled. 'You wanna save what humour you got left fo' what the fuck I might make you look like later.' Then he shrugged lamely. 'Nah, eight months, perhaps. An' before that, jus' weekends now and then. 'Cause my eyesight ain't what it used t'be.'

Jac would never have guessed.

'. . . An' sounds like it needs a bit of a service now, too.'

Jac was convinced that, between Morvaun's erratic driving, the car's garish appearance and spluttering and gunshot-loud backfiring, they were bound to get stopped by a police car before they got back to Morvaun's place.

But somehow, miraculously, they made it, and over coffee and Kahlua – Morvaun didn't have brandy and whisky, only a wide array of exotic Caribbean and Pacific Island liquors – they got down to the serious business of not just if and how it might work, but most of all *who* Jac was going to be.

Jac quickly discounted implicating Langfranc, what with old-man Beaton no doubt now looking hawkishly over his shoulder, but Mike Coultaine was another matter: long-retired, no remaining allegiances, and a strong vested interest – having been thwarted both at trial and appeal – in saving Durrant's neck.

Coultaine was understanding of Jac's plight, but was non-committal at first, saying he'd phone back in an hour. But when he called back he not only had a name, Darrell Ayliss, but within minutes had e-mailed a j-peg to Morvaun's computer. Coultaine had spent most of that hour making arrangements, calling in old favours.

'Ayliss is ideal,' he explained, 'because he's been off the scene for a while – seven years – and there's hardly anyone in New Orleans that'll recognize him. Ex-wife's in Oregon, and the rest of his family in Mississippi.'

Morvaun agreed: ideal. Not only because of the lack of close friends and family in New Orleans, but the eight years since his last passport photo. 'Gives us a pile more leeway in how he might look now.'

Though to get the likeness as close as possible, Coultaine arranged the next day for Ayliss to e-mail Morvaun directly – along with scans of each page of his passport – details of his appearance now: hair colour, length, level of greyness, eye-colour, weight, type of clothes and glasses.

Coultaine had also covered their tracks by arranging for Ayliss to go to Cabo San Lucas for a week's fly-fishing. 'Some old favours owed between us – don't even ask the hows and whys. All you need to be assured of is that if anyone checks on Ayliss down in Vallarta, according to his staff he's simply away for the week. Where, they don't know – they weren't told.'

That evening, Morvaun went out to see Alaysha at Pinkies – the only way they could think of safely getting a message to her. Jac surmised that there wasn't nearly enough for the NOPD to hold her for any length of time, let alone charge her with an accomplice to murder rap.

As she leant close in the middle of a dance, Morvaun

whispered in one ear, 'Jac wants to see you. I know where he is.'

A beat's pause, then she resumed quickly in case Security thought that Ol' Man River had just made an inappropriate suggestion. And in the next couple of lean-ins, she got the rest of the details.

A rare treat for Morvaun, Jac reflected; hoping, that is, his heart held out. Part payment for helping out, along with 200 bucks Jac gave him towards a car service and a new paint-job.

'What, yo' don't like the pink and blue?'

Jac smiled dryly and shook his head, not sure if Morvaun was serious. Not sure of anything any more. Two-tone: more or less mirrored his life for the next week.

'You should have told me.'

'I tried, Jac. I tried.'

'When?'

'That same night Gerry came knocking on my door while you were there.'

Jac shook his head incredulously. 'What, when the knock came? Oh, that must be Gerry – I just remembered there's something I forgot to tell Jac. Or when he shouted through the door about your sordid little secret together?'

Alaysha's hands clenched in exasperation and the struggle for clarity. 'No, Jac . . . *before*. I tried – believe me. But you were too caught up in your own little story about that Archie Teale and your father dying.' As she saw him flinch, realizing how trivial she'd made it sound, she reached out and gently touched his arm. 'Sorry, Jac . . . I didn't mean it like that. But I *did* try to tell you then. Just felt like the right time, you know . . . pouring hearts out to each other time. Probably the first time between us that it had felt right to . . .' She cast her eyes down for a second, biting at her bottom lip, '. . . to share a secret like that.'

He nodded with a tight-lipped grimace, starting to understand. She needn't have come here, he reminded himself. She could have just stayed away. 'I know. I'm sorry too . . .' though he had to pause then to think what for. '. . . For being too hasty.'

All she'd said so far was that she and Gerry had conspired to rob someone that they shouldn't, and now it was coming back to haunt her – and he'd started putting her on the rack. 'You said rob someone that you *shouldn't* have. What, was it a defenceless old lady or friend or relative, maybe?'

'No.' Alaysha shook her head. 'I didn't mean *shouldn't* from a moral standpoint; it's because of the risk involved if we ever got found out. How much our necks would be on the line.' Alaysha looked down again briefly, swallowing. 'It was Carmen Malastra that we robbed. That's why we shouldn't have done it.'

Malastra. New Orleans' biggest, most-feared mobster. The name ran a shiver down most spines. 'Oh, I see.' All he could think of saying immediately, his head suddenly feeling hot and pressured.

Seeing the shock on Jac's face, she smiled awkwardly, shrugging. 'From a moral point of view, my slate's completely clean. In fact it was that that made me do it, in a moment of weakness, or madness, or both – my mother's illness.' She stroked absently at one thigh for a second. 'And, you see, that's why it felt right to tell you at that moment . . . when you were talking about your father.'

Jac just nodded, closing his eyes for a second in understanding, but didn't say anything. He could see that this was difficult for her to talk about, the right words elusive, hanging by slim threads between them, and if he spoke they might break, the chain of thought lost and her perhaps not able to get it back in quite the same way again. The shadows in her eyes shifted rapidly for a few seconds more before finally settling and focusing, and she started to explain.

Gerry had been telling her for a while about the Bay Tree's manager, George Jouliern, needing a courier for a scam he was planning, but she'd initially refused. Gerry had kept on about how much money it would mean to both of them, thirty to fifty thousand dollars each, depending how much of a skim Jouliern was able to get away with – but she'd had no interest or particular need for the money then, felt it was mainly to benefit Gerry, who'd got himself in deep with a twenty-grand debt to a local loan shark, Raoul Ferrer.

'Gerry kept piling on the pressure – "I gotta do something about Ferrer, otherwise he's gonna break my legs" – but still I said no; until, that is, I got news about my mother.' Her mother had been suffering with diabetes for years, but suddenly it had taken a chronic turn, 'Something called diabetic nephropathy. Suddenly it was life-threatening, she needed urgent, regular dialysis, the costs were sky-high and she didn't have medical insurance. And so, despite the risks involved – Gerry maintained there were little or none, Jouliern had it all too well planned – that thirty to fifty grand started to look like a godsend. My only chance of saving my mother's life. I finally agreed, said I'd do it.'

Jouliern skimmed from people at the tables who wanted extra chips without going to the chip-cashing booths. 'It happens a lot apparently if they're in the middle of a game or a roll and don't want the delay of cashing at the booths.

'So they'd be cashed at the table, and at the end of the night Jouliern had the responsibility of taking all the cash from the tables and tallying it with the chips provided. At that point, though, he'd pocket some of the cash and feed in chips from his own pocket – there was control of cash in the club, but not chips – and then the extra cash would be left in an envelope under the bar with Gerry.

'The only problem remaining then was that as part of that cash control at the Bay Tree, each employee, including Jouliern, was searched going in and out, and was allowed no more than fifty bucks in their pockets. So they needed a courier to get those money envelopes out . . . which is where yours truly came in.'

'What, you went every night?' The first question that Jac had asked.

'No, three nights a week. All I could manage. And Jouliern kept the skimming light too from the tables, so that the fluctuations wouldn't show.' Alaysha shrugged. 'That no-cash-out policy also gave Gerry some problems in paying Ferrer. Often, the only chance Ferrer would get to collect cash off Gerry was at night at the Bay Tree. So Gerry would put Ferrer's money in an envelope with his name on, and tell Security that it was to give to Ferrer later. First couple of times Security said, "Okay, we'll give it to him ourselves when he calls." But then when Ferrer complained about one of the payments being light, they said that Gerry could give it to him directly. "Just as long as you know that if he doesn't call by for it, it stays here with us when you leave. He'll have to pick it up later." That was the golden rule – *no* cash out of the Bay Tree – no matter the circumstances.'

Alaysha eased out a slow, heavy breath, as if glad she'd finally shared some of the burden. 'The whole thing went well, no hitches. And everyone was happy: Gerry paid off Ferrer, I saved my mom's life, and Jouliern . . . well, he never shared with us why he was doing it.' She pouted thoughtfully, which eased into a faint smile. 'Maybe half a million good reasons – because that's what he ended up getting away with.'

The shadows in her eyes deepened again then, and the smile twisted as she forced a brief, ironic chuckle. 'Bad choice of words – because in the end it doesn't look like he *got away* with anything.' The shadows sunk deeper still, hit something darker, more troubling. Raw fear, panic. 'You see, ten days or so ago I read in the paper about George Jouliern disappearing. And I thought – Malastra's found out about the skimming, and it's only a matter of time before the knock comes on my own door and I'm next to go "missing".' Her neck pulsed as she swallowed hard. She held one palm out. 'That's why I got the gun from my mom's. Not so much because of Gerry, but because I feared Malastra's men would be coming for me.'

Jac nodded slowly. He understood now why she'd done it, probably *too* well. If in those last months of his father's life there'd suddenly been a miracle cure, and at the same time someone had laid on a plate a clean, ingenious robbery to pay for it, with high chances of getting away with it, he'd have gone for it. No question.

He thought it'd be hard to beat his own nightmare dilemma; but hers, possibly on a Malastra hit-list, was equally as crushing. The mention of his father, though, reminded him: look to the positive. 'How long now since you read about Jouliern disappearing? Ten days or so? Then another four or five days before he'd have been officially reported as missing. At least two weeks. If that knock was going to come on your door, it would have probably happened by now. Chances are Jouliern didn't say anything about you – they just don't know.'

'Or they're still putting all the pieces together.'

He could see that his words did little to lift the crushing worry from her shoulders, her eyes haunted, looking for solutions that weren't there, her body trembling as she no doubt thought not just about her own neck, but how little Molly would possibly cope with her gone; Alaysha's mother now with not many years left to be able to take care of her. He reached one hand out and lightly touched her arm, tried to lift her out of her dark mood.

'Hey, come on . . . you know what I've said makes a lot more sense than any other scenario.' Her eyes lifted a bit, a faint, reluctant smile. 'But, you know, if you're still worried – just try and keep one step ahead. Stay at your mom's as much as possible, and when you're in town, maybe stay at my place. I know it's only next door – but you can look through the spy-hole and see if anyone suspect is calling at your door. Gives you that extra minute or two to get out or phone for the police, whatever.'

413

'Thanks, I appreciate it. And I'll probably take you up on that offer.' She forced a tame smile, then let out a fresh breath. 'But enough about me. What about you – the fugitive of the hour?' Her expression became more solemn again. 'How are you coping, Jac?'

'Oh, God.' Jac lifted his eyes heavenward for a second. 'Where to even start?' He tried to keep his explanation just to filling in the gaps in what Alaysha probably already knew from Langfranc or news bulletins, so that it wasn't too rambling. He raised the first full smile from Alaysha as he described walking through Libreville earlier that day disguised as Ayliss, already sweating because he was nervous, and with the unbearable heat of the prison and the extra padding and make-up, it literally pouring off of him. 'I feared the make-up would start running and half my face would come unstuck and start peeling off. I had to call Morvaun straight after: emergency pit-stop for face maintenance!' Alaysha was by now openly laughing – it was good to see her like that, Jac thought: the problems hanging over them for a moment forgotten. 'Morvaun in fact has to follow me round from hotel to hotel, giving me regular patch-ups.' He glanced at his watch. 'Next one is here tomorrow at seven a.m., before I head out. Meanwhile, you'll have to answer the door if room-service calls.'

She nodded, her smile fading as she became pensive again. 'And how did it go with Durrant?'

He sighed heavily before explaining, the images from just over an hour ago burning fresh through his mind: the sage-green safe with a twist lock, just as it had been twelve years ago; apparently it would have been too much upheaval to have it moved or changed. The new owners seemed to remember the bookshelves being on the right-hand side, though the library now was just another bedroom, and the grandfather clock would have obviously been moved along with Roche's other furniture and possessions, they pointed out. Though at that moment they suddenly recalled the sales brochure Roche's realtor had done at the time, which they'd kept – and there it was proud in the corner on the hallway shot: a full-length walnut-cased grandfather clock.

Jac shook his head. 'Everything . . . *everything* matched Larry's descriptions from the session. Not a single thing wrong. And it hit me in that moment, Alaysha, harder than ever . . . he *had* to have been there that night. And all this crap with pool buddies and other places he might have been . . . I'm wasting my time. Have been from day one.' Jac grimaced awkwardly. 'Only I didn't know it until now.' He bit at his bottom lip, but this time as he went to shake his head, it seemed to lock, leave him transfixed, staring into mid-space. 'And the thing is, I can't blame or even get annoyed with Larry for it – because he simply can't remember, doesn't know whether he was there and killed her or not.'

'It seems a shame to give up now . . . just when you're so close. Only six days left.'

Jac let out a half laugh, half defeated sigh. 'That's the thing, Alaysha. I should have given up long ago . . . back when you told me to after almost drowning in the lake.' Jac shrugged helplessly. 'Certainly before now – on the run from a murder rap, life in tatters, not able to contact even my own family. My only escape walking around like an overweight wax doll, worried that half my face might melt off at any moment and people will start pointing . . . it's him! *It's him!*' This time Jac's smile was forced, pained. Alaysha knew that she wasn't meant to join in.

Her eyes darted uncertainly for a second before she asked, 'But I thought you had some guy with dance lessons for his kid that would have meant Durrant was definitely playing pool that night?'

Jac nodded. 'Yeah, Bill Saunders. Though problems there, too. Larry remembered Saunders being there, which meant high chances that game *was* a Thursday night. But I called Saunders just before heading here, and he told me that once every month the dance teacher would change the day around.

Then also a couple of times a year she'd close the classes for her holidays – one of which was always at Carnival time. In February.' Jac grimaced. 'Like so much else with Larry, hardly have you grabbed hold of it – the next moment it's cruelly yanked away.'

Alaysha was thoughtful, the shadows back in her eyes, though from concern for him and Durrant this time rather than herself. 'But what if you find something that convinces you he was innocent *after* the six days, when it's too late – you'd never forgive yourself for giving up at the last moment. Especially with all you've been through.'

'I know what you're saying, Alaysha. But I'm tired, and I don't know what else there is to find out. And there's the real worry that I've been doing all this to try and free a guilty man.' As Jac exhaled, it felt as if that breath was taking his last strength with it. 'Every time I get up off from the canvas hoping that with the next punch I'll hit something to convince me that Larry wasn't there that night and didn't do it – another blow comes to tell me that he was, knocks me back down again. And this time, Alaysha, I don't know if I've got the strength to get back up.'

She reached out and gripped his arm then, lightly shaking, as if she might be able to inject some extra energy from herself into him. 'But it's only six days, Jac, and then you'll know for sure. And if you still haven't found anything and it looks as if Larry *was* there that night – at least then you'll be able to tell yourself that you tried everything. Did all that you could.'

Jac nodded and closed his eyes for a second in acceptance. He could see the sense in what Alaysha was saying, but the sudden turnaround made him question, 'What makes now so different to before – when you were urging me to give up, throw in the towel? Or is it just one of those perverse women-things: *always* take up an opposite stance?'

Alaysha could tell from Jac's sly smile that he was ribbing, but the effort of making it bore out what he was telling her: he was tired, defeated, had no strength left. 'Because *before*

Jac, you still had a long way to go – now you don't. Now there's only six days left to hang on.'

Six days. Said that like, it didn't sound long, but with the way Jac felt at that moment, it seemed like a lifetime. He'd felt tired and worn-down before the nightmare with Gerry and the gun. But running like a rabbit from the police and the role play with Ayliss, worried that at any minute, a few words wrong or bumping into someone who'd known Ayliss, the game would be up – the BOP hearing and walking back into Libreville had been particularly nerve-racking, draining – all of that had sapped his last reserves, so that now he felt he had nothing left to give.

Alaysha watched Jac crumble before her, saw his painfully conflicting emotions, wanting desperately to continue, but not sure any more how to, or whether he had an ounce of energy or resolve left to be able to . . . and that vulnerability, as before, made her realize how deeply she cared for him, *loved* him, made her suddenly want to soothe him, comfort him, protect him.

She leant in close then, putting one arm around him and gently rocking, 'Oh, Jac . . . *Jac*', starting to plant light kisses on his forehead and one cheek.

The softness and closeness of her made Jac melt. Jac, without knowing her thoughts, thinking how vulnerable *she* looked, still in her underwear, cross-legged before him, more concerned about his welfare than her own – even though a threat to her life might hang just around the corner for her. And in that moment, he didn't think he'd seen anyone so beautiful; not just outside, but inside too. Body and soul.

A couple of tentative kisses by his lips, and then their tongues were touching, teasing; then suddenly the kisses became deeper, more passionate, and they were tearing the remaining clothes off each other.

Jac remembered reading somewhere that in times of war, people made love more frequently and fervently. While the bombs dropped around them, in air-raid shelters or ditches or bedrooms that shook with nearby explosions, they fucked. Soldiers visited whores the night before they went to the front line, or lonely women took them in for the night because they seemed exciting or different or had a packet of cigarettes or some nylons to give them. And much of that desperate love-making was not only because it might be their last chance, but because in those few moments they were reaffirming that they were still alive, still vital; while so much around them was being robbed of life by bullets and bombs, they were indulging in the one act that represented continuance of life.

What was happening now was probably little different, Jac thought – though too urgent and feverish to be termed love-making. They fucked. They fucked on the floor, on the bed, up against the wall at one point – Alaysha's gasps and screams so loud that Jac thought the people in the next room would start banging and complaining.

They fucked with a heat and abandon they'd never known before, as if it might be their very last time; and perhaps, like the countless war-torn souls before them, that was because it might be. A bullet around the next corner for Alaysha, and a long-term jail cell awaiting Jac.

They fucked until all those dark shadows and worries finally lifted from them, and there was nothing left in this world that was important except the two of them staring breathlessly at each other only inches apart. Them. This moment.

35

'Okay . . . *okay*. You're there now, Larry . . . you're *there*.'
Ormdern's voice calming, yet with a nervous edge to it, as if
he was afraid of losing the delicate thread of thought that had
finally been established. 'Tell me what you see.'

It had taken Ormdern longer to get Larry under than last
time, and longer still to get his thoughts focused back again
on that vital pool game at the Bayou Brew twelve years ago.

Jac was more conscious now of time fast ticking away
against them and started to look anxiously at the clock as
Ormdern struggled in those opening moments: only four days
left now, and the heat and pressure now far higher with the
events of the last few days. Jac took the first sips of the coffee
that had been brought in for him and Pete Folley in paper
cups a minute ago.

'Bill . . . Bill Saunders is there. They're all there that night.'

As Ormdern realized that Larry was linking back to what
he'd covered last time, he gently moved Larry on. 'Okay,
Larry . . . they're all there. But I wondered if you could tell
me what any of them are doing, apart from playing pool . . .
anything that might tell you what day it is?' As Larry's brow
knitted, Ormdern added, 'Reading a newspaper, for instance
. . . something with a headline or date on it?'

Larry's head gently shook after a second. 'No . . . not that
I recall.'

'Or maybe even talking about the shooting of Jessica
Roche . . . because that would then definitely place that pool
game *after* she was killed.'

Longer pause this time, Larry's eyelids pulsing heavily. 'No
. . . nobody's talking about anything like that.'

The news had come through at midday from Governor

Candaret's office that Larry Durrant's plea for clemency had been refused.

Jac had phoned Candaret's office an hour later, and, laying on the smooth Southern Ayliss charm, had tried his utmost to sway Candaret, but he was adamant, immovable: 'I hear what you're saying loud and clear, Mr Ayliss, about Larry Durrant's state of mind and memory at the time, *and* about his good character and development since. But balanced against that, we've got the fact that he did finally admit that he committed the crime that night – and even if there were doubts raised about that recall, we have the irrefutable DNA evidence that puts him there at the time of Jessica Roche's murder. I appreciate the call, though, I really do . . . though I'm sure you can equally appreciate that this remains a particularly brutal and heinous crime that I cannot look upon lightly.'

With Aaron Harvey re-offending, the odds had always been against Candaret offering clemency, but now it was official. Now Jac knew with all certainty that this session – whatever Ormdern was able to drag out of Larry's fractured, shadowy memory from twelve years ago – was probably his very last chance.

'And the bar, Larry. Who was behind the bar that night?'

'Lorraine . . . Lorraine Gilliam and Mack Elliott.'

'Anybody else? Was Rob Harlenson there that night?'

'No . . . no. Don't see him there.'

Don't rather than didn't. Larry reliving being in the bar as he was twelve years ago, looking around the room.

Last chance. All the more poignant, meaningful now. Jac had taken Alaysha's advice to soldier on, and had gone back over all the old Durrant files and case notes for anything he might have missed, spread them out on the floor of his new hotel room the next morning – still switching hotel rooms and cars every day – along with the old crime scene photos.

The first thing that leapt out at him had been a long-shot of the library with Jessica Roche's body at the far end: bookshelves along the right-hand side and sage-green safe on the wall at the end. He went back to the case folders, quickly rifling through all the photos, and eighth print down, there it was: a shot of the hallway – presumably to show the two footprints with faint bloodied edges heading from the library – and at its end, larger than life, a full-length grandfather clock. That's how and why Larry could have recalled those details in the last session with Ormdern!

After the news from Candaret, he'd arranged to get to the prison half an hour early for a face-to-face with Larry. He slid the library photo across first, asking Larry if he'd seen it before.

'Yeah. At the time of police questioning, and at the trial.'

'Thought as much.' Standard police procedure to show the suspect the victim, gauge reaction. 'But this one they might not have troubled with at the time.' Jac slid across the hallway photo.

Larry paused for only a second. 'Yeah, that one too. They asked me if I recognized that shoe pattern.'

Jac had resisted punching the air; the sound was off between the interview and observation room, but Pete Folley was already behind the glass, looking on.

'. . . And what were the bar-staff doing, Larry?' Ormdern quizzed Durant now. 'Anything that was said or done that might pin down the day?'

'Don't know about the actual day, but . . . but a couple of guys turned up in carnival-type outfits. One had a chicken outfit, looked like he borrowed it from someone who'd been advertising a chicken restaurant . . . then just put it on for carnival. The other had a sequinned suit and whited-out face.'

'Did you know them or had you seen them before?'

'Didn't know them . . .' Larry thought for a moment, his brow knitting. 'And can't remember seeing them before.'

'And Lorraine Gilliam or Mack Elliott . . . did it look like they might have seen them before?'

Jac saw immediately where Ormdern was heading; if Larry couldn't pin down the day, maybe Lorraine Gilliam or Mack

Elliott could. Surely it wasn't every day that someone walked in the bar in a chicken outfit?

'No, didn't seem like it. Mack was giving them this look, you know . . . one he often gave to strangers: what the hell yo' doing in my bar? Got lost or something? And the outfits and the fact that they gotta bit rowdy didn't help. In the bars around Bourbon that time of year, nobody would raise an eyebrow . . . but the Brew was a long way off the main Carnival routes.'

'You said "rowdy". What, was there a disturbance?'

Jac clenched his coffee cup, took a quick sip. Something else that might help fix the day in Elliott or Gilliam's mind. Though no doubt the best hope was with Elliott; when he'd finally got hold of Lorraine Gilliam, she'd been vague about events back then. The session set-up was the same as last time, except that now the sound feed was two-way. If Jac spoke into the mike his end, it fed into Ormdern's earpiece, in case he picked up on anything vital that Ormdern missed; this was their last chance, so once the moment was gone it was gone for good.

'Not exactly a disturbance, no real trouble. Just that the guys were getting noisy and a touch outta control, and they started to annoy Mack 'cause he was trying to concentrate on something on the TV.' Larry's face eased into a slow smile. 'I remember Mack – having told the guys once to keep it down and they were still kicking up – warning the chicken guy to keep a lid on it "if yo' don' wanna end up like a Colonel Sanders chicken". "What's that?" the guy asks.' Larry's smile broadened. 'Mack gives him a quick flash of the Billy-club he kept below the bar for troublemakers, and says "Battered!"'

Ormdern nodded and smiled briefly. 'Anything, though, to fix the day or date? Anything mentioned? A Carnival party they were heading to . . . something at one of the nearby jazz clubs, maybe? Which might then also explain why they were in the area.'

Jac leant forward. A number of clubs held specific themed balls and party nights throughout Carnival; if one had been mentioned, it would pinpoint the night. A moment's concentration, Larry mumbling incoherently at one point, as if he was mentally sifting through their conversation, before he shook his head.

'No . . . no club or party mentioned . . . not that I can recall, at least.'

'Anything else happen that night . . . unusual or otherwise? Anything that might pin down the day?' The edge, the desperation in Ormdern's voice now evident. Larry's brow was knitted again, and, as it looked like his attempts at recall were trawling through fresh air, Ormdern added, '*Anything*. However small and inconsequential it might seem.'

Larry's expression slowly eased. 'Oh yeah . . . Nat. Nat Hadley. He was talking about his kid joining a Little League baseball team. Real proud, you know, running him there . . . watching the kid play.' Larry's smile was back again, though more wistful, with a tinge of sorrow. Lost years. 'Don't know if it helps much or not . . . but perhaps it stuck in my mind because I remember thinking at the time: I got all that to come.'

All that to come. Jac clenched a fist, his other on the coffee cup trembling as he closed his eyes. None of that for Larry had been to come: arrested only six months later, he'd seen nothing since but the inside of a jail cell, had hardly seen his kid. Someone else, different part-time fathers, had cared for Joshua, watched him grow, got his little hugs and kisses on the cheek, taken him to Little League.

And suddenly that thrumming was back in Jac's body, as it had been that last night with Larry, clinking brandy glasses together as the tears flowed; his own heartbeat in time with the throb of the prison boilers . . . *last chance* . . . *last chance* . . . the ticking of the clock on the wall joining that beat as he stared at it numbly, trying to think desperately of what to do next . . . *if* there was anything left to try. The clip-clop of his step from the many times he'd paced Libreville's endless corridors over the past six weeks, the final accompaniment a rhythmic banging from the cells as he walked along; as he'd headed in earlier that night, many of Larry's supporters had banged the cell bars with whatever metal objects they could lay their hands on – tin cups, bed-pans – willing Jac on . . . *save him . . . save him!*

'Were any days mentioned for the kid's games? Or perhaps who they were playing?'

Clutching at straws. It was becoming painful even to watch; the increasing edge in Ormdern's voice, the heavy pulsing behind Larry's eyelids as he searched desperately for that one fragment of detail from twelve years ago that might save his life now.

Finally: 'No, sorry . . . can't remember anything being said about dates or times for the kid's games. Just how proud Nat was, you know . . . being there for the kid. Supporting him.'

'I know.' A concluding tone, Ormdern looking back through his notes and last session's transcript for anything he might have missed asking about the Bayou Brew that night.

The silence suddenly heavy, stifling, only the sound of flicking pages through the speaker, merging, becoming one with the ticking of the clock and the pounding, thunderous roar in Jac's head . . . *last chance . . . last chance . . . save him . . . save him!*

Jac leapt up as the coffee splashed against one thigh. Unconsciously, he'd gripped the paper cup too tight, splitting it.

Ormdern looked up briefly, Jac's sudden gasp through his earpiece obviously startling him. He went back to his notes for another fifteen seconds or so, though with the silence the pause seemed interminable, before speaking again.

'I want to move on now, Larry . . . to when you first read or heard about Jessica Roche's murder . . . and first of all try and pinpoint that time in relation to the night we've just been talking about – when you were playing pool at the Bayou Brew.' Ormdern left a heavy pause to let the thought and the shift in time settle with Larry. 'Was it just the day after, two days . . . or maybe more?'

Jac was at the edge of his seat, breath held. Probably their last chance to be able to pinpoint the day.

It took a long time for Larry to focus his thoughts, the pulsing behind his eyelids becoming more rapid, frantic, the clock ticking on the wall probably seeming deafening to everyone in the room, not just Jac, in that forty second wait.

Larry gently moistened his top lip with his tongue as he spoke, his head lolling slightly. 'I . . . I don't know . . . A day or two, I think. Not long, anyway.'

'Please, Larry . . . *think.* Think hard. It's important. Which is it? Just a day, or *two* days?'

Jac clenched his hands anxiously as Larry sank back into thought. There'd been an anxious moment too in his pre-session with Larry when he'd slid across the photos, and shortly after had made a verbal slip: 'On our second meeting together, you mentioned . . .' Quickly realizing and correcting: 'I mean, on your second meeting with Jac McElroy . . .' But it was too late, Larry had picked up on it, staring at him intently in that moment, eyes boring past Ayliss's brown contact lenses, stripping away the prosthetic cheek and jaw bulking and the shoulder padding, as he uttered with a hushed, incredulous breath, 'It's you, Jac . . . isn't it? *It's you!*' And Jac, not saying anything, but giving his answer with a nervous look towards the glass screen and Folley; the sound link was off, but he worried in that moment that Larry's body language might give the game away or Folley might be able to lip-read. But Folley held the same nonchalant, slightly bored expression, hadn't picked up on anything, as Jac gently nodded his acqui-escence; and Larry at the same time had quickly killed his sly, disbelieving smile as he picked up on the signal not to give the game away to Folley.

Larry finally spoke. 'I . . . I'm sorry. I don't know . . . can't say with any certainty.'

Jac eased out a resigned breath. Ormdern had mentioned

that even if the memory of the murder had been suggested or somehow overlaid, its addition could create uncertainty in Larry's mind about the time gap from his pool game. But the end result was the same, Jac thought, feeling his stomach sink: last chance gone.

'Okay . . . okay. When you did actually hear or read about Jessica Roche's murder . . . exactly when or where was that? Morning or afternoon? On the TV or in a newspaper?'

'TV.' Larry answered almost immediately, then paused longer for thought before continuing. 'But there was no sound on . . . I couldn't hear what was being said. Only saw her face on the newsflash.'

'Why was that?'

'Because I didn't want to. I'd made sure to avoid all newspapers and early morning TV . . . but there she was suddenly, as I was passing a TV shop window.'

Jac's stomach fell again, as if a second, surprise trapdoor had suddenly opened. A completely different story to the one he'd got last time from Larry! Ormdern, too, looked perplexed, flicking back a page in his notes to double-check the earlier account.

'Are . . . are you sure about that? TV shop window rather than at home in the afternoon or early evening?'

'Yeah, sure.' Larry's brow knitted briefly with another thought. 'Okay . . . maybe early evening was the first time I actually *heard* it. But I remember clearly standing by that shop window seeing it for the first time.'

'And what time of day was that?'

'Mid, late morning, maybe.'

Jac stared back hard at Larry. Was Larry telling the truth now, or in his earlier account to Jac? Or was he clever enough to realize that his subconscious had suddenly produced a different story, so he'd slipped in a caveat . . . 'first time I actually *heard* it'. Maybe, with all of that reading, he was cleverer than *all* of them: knew and recalled perfectly well that he'd killed Jessica Roche, and now was just playing them all, getting them searching desperately through the haystack of his past for needles that he knew had never been there. Maybe, too, Larry had lied earlier about seeing those photos he'd slid across, realizing then that his subconscious had again given something away.

Just when Jac thought he knew Larry, was getting closer to him and the truth of what happened twelve years ago, he'd do another quick flip, become a conundrum again. A mystery.

Yet if Larry knew that his subconscious would give him away, why subject himself to this now? Was it just that with only days left to live, a random chance was better than no chance at all? One last laugh up his sleeve at them all desperately fluffing around him, trying to save his life. The attention he'd never got from his own family. But why then had he wanted to die when Jac first met him? Or was that the ultimate double-play: the last person you'd suspect of trying to fool you about their innocence was someone who'd already given up on being saved?

Perhaps, as Jac had suspected all along, Larry just didn't know. The memory loss had stayed with him, and he had no idea if he'd done it or not.

'And how did you feel, Larry, when you first saw her face on that TV through that shop window?' Though now the question seemed almost superfluous.

'I . . . I felt terrible, you know. Sick inside like you wouldn't believe.' Larry gently shook his head. 'That's . . . that's why I tried to avoid seeing it. Because I couldn't believe I'd done it . . . and once I'd seen it on the news, then it was suddenly real. Official. I *had* done it.'

And now Jac would have to tell Larry, as he'd promised to when the next day he got Ormdern's report: 'Sorry, Larry . . . looks like you *did* do it.' At least one consolation: when he was executed in a few days' time, in his last moments he wouldn't be left with that crushing sense of injustice that it was for something he hadn't done.

★

TV! The thought suddenly flared from the back of Jac's brain.

Sitting there watching the last minutes of the session tick away, that final thought about Larry's guilt just hadn't sat comfortably, and everything suddenly came flooding back – *Gasping for air as he fought back up through the dark lake . . . Running from the lights of the police helicopter . . . Walking back into Libreville disguised as Ayliss . . .* Surely all of that hadn't been for nothing. *Surely?* Could he possibly have read it all so wrong? Put his life on the line and . . .

And suddenly the thought had flashed like a supernova to the forefront: TV! If Mack Elliott had asked the chicken guy to pipe down because he couldn't hear what was on the TV, then whatever was on must have been important!

Jac leant over and shared the thought with Ormdern through the mike. Ormdern nodded slowly, Larry's eyelids gently pulsing as his mind questioned what was happening, why the sudden pause?

'Okay, Larry. Sorry. I want to take you back again to the Bayou Brew and the pool game. Specifically that moment you mentioned when Mack Elliott told off the chicken guy because he couldn't concentrate on what was on the TV.'

'Yeah . . . yeah.' The pulsing slowly settling as Larry got the memory back again.

'Now, what was it Mack Elliott was watching? Why was it so important that he had to tell the chicken guy to shut up?'

'I . . . I'm not sure.' The eyelid-pulsing increasing again. 'The TV's turned away from me . . . I can't see what he's watching.'

'And did he tell you? Something important perhaps that he wanted to watch that night?'

'No . . . no. He didn't mention anything.'

Slow sigh from Ormdern, the disappointment evident in his voice. 'Okay . . . from where you are, what can you *hear* coming over the TV?'

Marked pause from Larry as he applied more thought.

'Some cheering and clapping . . . a commentator's voice in between. A few shouts and jeers at some points.'

'What's the commentator saying?'

'I . . . I can't tell from where we are . . . it's too faint. Just a mumble. The cheering, clapping and shouting comes over stronger.'

'Okay. Cheering and clapping . . . some shouts. Any laughter?'

'No . . . no. Just the cheering and clapping.'

So obviously not a sitcom or even a variety or chat show, Jac thought. They would normally have some laughter.

'And how long did it go on for? How long was Mack Elliott watching?'

'Maybe twenty minutes or so . . . half hour, max.'

That ruled out a sporting fixture, too.

'And anything else you might recall about what Mack was watching then? Anything you might have heard or he mentioned?'

'No . . . that's it. Just remember some cheering and shouting . . . and him telling off the chicken guy.'

Already two minutes over the session time. Nothing else that Ormdern was going to find out. But if Larry couldn't remember what Mack Elliott was watching that night, maybe Mack himself could. Although it was twelve years ago, they now had some strong guideposts: cheering and shouting, guy in a chicken suit that he threatened with a Billy-club.

Having thanked Ormdern, 'I'll look forward to reading your final report tomorrow', Jac paced back through the endless corridors with that cauldron of conflicting thoughts from the session still burning through his head. He opened his car window and breathed deeply of the outside night air, trying to lose the heat and claustrophobia of the prison, and the second he was clear of the final guard-post, took out his cell-phone and dialled Mack Elliott's number.

Outside the prison gates, the crowd had swelled to eighty strong. One group, with long hair and long white flowing robes, as if they were a flock of angels or modern-day Messiahs, held up a large placard:

STAIRWAY TO HEAVEN
Go Larry, go...
Then you can get your own back on Candaret!
Don't let him in when he shows there!
...Though unlikely that's where he's headed.
The Devil claimed his soul years ago!

To one side they'd set up large speakers blasting the song out, the display no doubt inspired by Larry's strong religious beliefs.

'*Come on . . .*' Jac muttered impatiently as he sped away from the prison. *Last chance . . . last chance.*

But as Mack Elliott's line continued ringing emptily in Jac's ear, all that reached him was Robert Plant's voice sailing hauntingly on the night air, singing about the feeling he got when he looked to the west, his spirit crying for leaving.

36

'Have you heard from Jac at all?'

'No, not a thing,' Catherine McElroy said. The truth, but even if she had heard from her son, the last person she'd tell was her sister Camille. Family allegiances would hold for no more than twenty-four hours before Camille's 'Citizen's duty' wrestled advantage and she phoned the police.

'Terrible business . . . terrible,' Camille aired, though she was probably thinking more of the shock impact to her society set than to family, Catherine thought. 'It would probably be a lot better if the police *had* found him. At least then you'd know where he was, know that he was safe . . . and be able to see him and talk to him. Find out what happened.'

'Yes . . . I suppose so.' Some sense in that, Catherine supposed; but still she remained guarded, unsure whether Camille was just fishing to see whether she might know more than she was letting on.

'God knows what I'm going to say to Tobias Bromwell . . . *if* I ever speak to the man again. His number has come up twice now on my call minder, but I just don't have the stomach to phone him back. Don't know what to say. Too embarrassed.'

Now they were getting to it, Catherine thought; the condolences and niceties out of the way, now they were getting to what really made Camille's world turn. 'I understand,' Catherine said numbly. That's practically all she'd felt since hearing the news about Jac: *numb*.

'And you had absolutely no inkling of what was going on, what might be about to happen?'

'No, of course not.' The first edge to Catherine's voice; a ridiculous suggestion even by Camille's normal thick-skinned, lame-brained standards: '*Mum, I'm going out with a lap-dancer and we're planning to murder her ex-boyfriend.*'

'So you didn't even know about this other girlfriend? This . . . *this* lap-dancer?'

Catherine half-smiled to herself at Camille's difficulty in even saying the word. 'No, I didn't,' she said, hoping that Camille didn't read the half-lie. All she knew, from Alaysha directly while Jac had been in the hospital, was that she did some 'modelling'. Perhaps Alaysha didn't know what Jac might have already said, and they'd have both got around later to telling her more.

Camille sighed heavily. 'That's where it all starts to go wrong, don't you see? That initial deception. Two-timing poor Jennifer like that. And, for reasons that now become obvious, not telling *anyone* about this other girl.'

'*What*, you think one might lead to the other?' Normally, Catherine wouldn't have said anything, but she could feel her blood boil as Camille had continued: her society-circle embarrassment over Jac's two-timing and dating a lap-dancer put before the fact that he was being hunted like a rabbit by the police, might not even be still alive, with herself and Jean-Marie worried out of their minds. 'Like some sort of prelude: date a lap-dancer . . . next step murder.'

Only a split-second pause, but Catherine could practically hear Camille's flinch of surprise that she had dared to answer back. 'No, of course not. But you can bet your bottom dollar that this girl had more than a little to do with putting Jac up to it.' Camille snorted derisively. 'Types like that.'

'Like *what*, Camille?' Maybe Camille had been grating on her nerves for a while, but now, with everything with Jac, her patience levels were exhausted.

'Like, *you know* . . . I surely don't have to spell it out.' Again that reluctance to even say it, as if it would somehow soil her lips. 'But one thing's for sure: she's certainly an entirely different kettle of fish to a girl like Jennifer Bromwell.'

'She only takes her clothes off for money . . . no doubt to

put groceries on the table for her little girl. There's no sin in that.'

'*Please . . .* spare me.'

'And do you really think the likes of old-man Bromwell built up their fortunes by being squeaky clean? I hear he was involved in some messy low-rent housing early on. Complaints about rats, damp and unsanitary conditions, and strong-arm guys busting doors down and kicking whole families out in the dead of night when they complained too hard. Not exactly what he'd like to be quizzed about at one of your little dinner soirées.'

This time the surprise was clear at the other end; an audible gasp. 'Sometimes, Catherine, you're so . . . *so* French.'

Catherine wasn't sure whether the comment was due to her laissez-faire attitude about people taking their clothes off for money, or her socialist-slanted dig at Tobias Bromwell – but she decided to take it as a compliment. 'Thanks.'

'And while we're on the subject of low rents – don't forget whose house you're in!' Camille hung up abruptly.

Catherine took a fresh breath, feeling strangely invigorated. Camille might soon put in the thin edge of the wedge about her and Jean-Marie moving on, finding their own place – one more problem she didn't need now on top of all else – but all she knew was that at that moment, despite everything, she suddenly felt better. Freer.

'*And as . . . as I looked back, there was this woman. Don't know even what made me look back at that point, maybe the sense of her eyes on me . . . but there she was suddenly, this woman with her dog. Her eyes meeting mine for a second before I ran on.*'

'*How far away was she?*'

'*Maybe eighty yards the other way from the Roche house. A hundred or so from where I was then.*'

Jac stood twenty yards beyond the Roche house, where Larry would have been that night twelve years ago, and looked back to where he'd have seen the woman. Still dark,

433

with just the first tinge of dawn light, the light values wouldn't be far different to that night, Jac thought.

Jac rewound on his hand-held recorder and looked back towards the house.

'. . . *There were no lights on at the front, or the side – which is where I broke in. Maybe if I'd gone round the back, I'd have seen a light on . . . or maybe she'd gone to bed early and there'd a been no light on there either.*'

'*So you broke in at the side?*'

'*Yeah. Removed a glass pane and wired through on the frame so as not to break the alarm circuit. Two minutes, and I was in. Took a quick tour t'see where the best stuff was, and found a safe in the library that I reckoned I could break by drilling the lock without too much trouble. And I was just preparin' for that when I heard something behind me, and she . . . she was suddenly there. Like . . . like out of nowhere. Not there one minute . . . then the next. . .*'

Jac could see the side of the house from where he was, and closed his eyes for a second to picture the library from his visit two days ago, then shifted to how it would have been twelve years ago, Larry checking out the safe as Jessica Roche walked in behind him . . .

Something he was missing . . . *something* . . .

Jac eased out his breath after a moment, started to pace away.

I was there at the time.

He looked from side to side at the neighbouring houses and then along the street. If someone else had been there that night, then where . . . *where*? A neighbouring window or garden, or further away? Far enough not to have been noticed by the murderer.

Only three days left now. Jac shook his head. He hadn't slept well that night. He hadn't been able to get hold of Mack Elliott until almost 10 p.m., two hours after he'd checked into yet another hotel room, the photos from the murder scene again spread around him, word and sentence fragments from the session still bouncing through his head.

'You're as bad as that Jac,' Mack commented, 'the last guy handling everything for Larry . . . asking me to remember things from twelve years back.'

'I know. It ain't easy.' Jac laid on the Ayliss Southern drawl. 'But now there're a couple of notable things to hopefully remind you.' Jac set the scene with the chicken guy and his friend in a sequinned suit, pressing him to remember what might have been so important on the TV that Mack would have asked him to shut up; and at that moment – as now, staring emptily into the first dawn light of the street where twelve years ago the murder had taken place, searching for answers – everything seemed to freeze around Jac, hang suspended as he stood in the middle of a strange hotel room, cell-phone in hand, breath held, because he knew that probably Larry's very last chance depended on Mack's next words.

But with a long, tired exhalation, Mack Elliott said that he just couldn't remember what he might have been watching. 'Can't bring anythin' to mind clearly . . . I'm sorry. Too long back.'

'Will you keep thinking on it for me?' Jac reluctant to let possibly the last door close. 'Call me if you finally remember anything. Not long left now . . . only a few days.'

'I know.'

Jac wound forward again on the tape.

'And where did you run to then, Larry?'

'Back to where I'd parked my car . . . a few blocks away, on Carondelet Street.'

Jac looked around. Carondelet was to the north, a block beyond St Charles Avenue, which meant Larry would have taken the next right on 4th Street to get there. Jac headed that way as the tape continued, following the same route Larry had twelve years ago as he'd run in panic from the Roche house.

'And did you head straight home then?'

'Not straightaway. My mind was spinning with so many things.

435

I wanted to go for a drink somewhere, but I was afraid I might have some of her blood on me that people would notice. So in the end I just drove around for a while – maybe as long as fifty minutes – before I finally headed home.'

Jac could almost hear the prison clock again in time with his footsteps breaking the quiet of the Garden District dawn. *Tic-toc . . . clip-clop . . . not long left now . . .*

'And did you have the gun still with you?'

'When I left the house . . . yeah. But I dumped it in a trash can somewhere out in Metairie while I was driving around. And I noticed then that my jacket was clean. I kept that on . . .'

Click . . . Stop . . . rewind. Play again.

'I . . . I'd checked for a few nights beforehand . . . and there was no car either in the drive . . . or lights on that I could see. She . . . she wasn't meant to be there.'

'And where was . . .'

Stop. Silence again, only the sound of Jac's continuing footsteps. He thought about the mystery e-mailer's words. *I couldn't give my name or come forward before, because I'd have incriminated myself. And that still stands now. But I was there. . .*

Where . . . *where? Incriminated himself*? Or perhaps it *was* just a hoax or a friend of Larry's, another curve-ball along with Larry's differing accounts of when and where he'd first seen the news on Jessica Roche's murder.

Clip-clop . . . clip-clop . . . did do it . . . didn't do it . . .

Jac stopped as St Charles Avenue came into view ahead: more activity, gentle thrum of some early traffic. Now a block and a half away, nobody would have been able to see anyone leave the Roche house beyond where he was now.

He walked back again and stood for a moment by the Roche house, looking around one last time as he tried to picture Larry as he was that night, having murdered for the first time, breathless, panicked and running like a rabbit, the gun still with him, the woman walking her dog locking eyes with him for a second . . . and whether from the images spinning in his head, lack of sleep, or the exertion of walking

436

about with all the heavy padding from his disguise, Jac suddenly felt dizzy, the street and everything around him tilting into a lazy spin. *Last hopes tilting, slipping away . . .*

Jac snapped himself out of it, took a fresh breath. He got back into his car and grabbed a quick take-out coffee on his way back to his hotel. He sipped at it as he walked into his room, checking his watch: Ormdern's report should arrive in an hour or so; with so little time left now, Ormdern had promised to get it to him first thing.

Jac decided to use the time to go back over the tapes of Truelle's earlier sessions with Larry. He'd played most of them before, purely to get a feel for the lead-up to the crucial murder-admission session. Some segments now had more resonance, particularly when Larry started trying to remember old friends, some of them from those key pool games, but for the most part it was fairly mundane, day to day recall – Truelle's voice and Larry's answers after a while becoming little more than a drone, soporific, the last thing Jac needed after last night's fitful sleep. And so when something did suddenly hit him, so small that at first he almost missed it, it snapped him sharply alert again, made him sit up.

Jac quickly rewound to make sure he'd heard what he thought he'd heard.

Yes, it was there; no mistake. Then he started going back through the other tapes, listening to the same sections on each . . . and was halfway through the process when hotel reception rang through to his room to tell him that a package had been left for him by a Mr Ormdern.

'Yes . . . *thanks*. Could you send it up to me.'

Click, stop. Play. Click, stop. Play. Click, stop . . . four tapes left to try by the time the knock came at the door and a bell-boy handed him the envelope. Jac practically ripped it open, his adrenalin now on fire with what he'd just discovered, flicking though quickly to the main summary points in Ormdern's report:

Unfortunately, the incidental detail surrounding Larry Durrant's night at the Roche
house is inconclusive. While there isn't a
great depth of incidental detail – which
could then lean towards the memory somehow
being suggested or 'implanted' – conversely
the accuracy of what little he has recalled
could then support that the memory was real
and true.

Also, we have the problem I voiced when
you first raised this issue of possible
memory suggestion or 'implanting' before
these sessions with Larry Durrant. To suc-
cessfully do that, a full hour session,
possibly more, would have been required. But
from what you told me, the tapes are all
sequential and match every diary entry for
that period. And there were no extra-
curricular visits by Durrant outside of
those diarized.

Jac looked back towards the tape recorder. He thought he
knew how Truelle had done it, had got the sequence of tapes
to match the session diary entries. No gaps.

Ormdern's report concluded, '*I think your best chance rests
with hopefully getting corroborative alibis from the extra details
unearthed surrounding Larry Durrant's pool game that week.*

Two possible irons in the fire. The first he'd have to hit
Truelle with, *hard*. Pray that he could somehow break him.
Jac looked at his watch. If he phoned, Truelle would probably
do what he'd done last time: shuffle him off for a day or two.
No time left. It was time for an unannounced visit.

'Joshua, I want you to send an e-mail to your father.' Francine
kept her gaze level and constant, so that her son could be sure
that she was serious and it wasn't some kind of trick. 'In

Libreville. It's time. Probably in fact the last time you're gonna be able to do it. Say what you want to him.'

'I . . . I thought that you said –'

'I know what I said, Joshua.' She sighed heavily. This wasn't easy. She forced a tame smile. 'Take this as an early lesson that parents can be fickle too . . . and that time can change things.'

'But what about Frank? And the . . .' Joshua fumbled while he thought about how to cover up that he'd been continuing to send e-mails. Whether he'd get found out. Whether to say anything. '. . . the keyword. And what should I say?' Joshua's eyes lifted to meet his mother's.

'The keyword I know. Frank told me what it was, said that you'd *never* guess it. That is, if you've been looking?' She raised a sharp eyebrow and smiled dryly. 'As for what to say . . . well, I guess whatever you've been holdin' back on saying for the past month or so will do for a start.'

Joshua was sure from her look that she suspected he'd kept contact. He looked away again, nodding. 'Okay.'

'And . . . and to tell your father that we want to see him. Tomorrow, if possible. After that, they might not allow any visitors.'

She watched her request hit Joshua as if she'd jabbed him with a cattle prod. He didn't say anything, simply lifted those big eyes again to look at her directly. Perhaps to ask again if she was sure, or because *he* wasn't sure how he'd handle a face to face with his father at this stage. Or because it raised again the earlier question that she hadn't yet answered.

She shook her head. 'Don't worry about Frank. I'll square everything with him – you making contact *and* us going there tomorrow. If Frank can't understand why you should see your father for what might be the last time, then . . . *then* . . .' She looked away, chewing at her bottom lip, an image of past, happier times suddenly piercing her heart: Larry holding Josh up as a baby and singing to him in a silly coo-coo voice, and Josh looking back at him with those same big brown

439

eyes; *so loving, so trusting*. But in that instant the shadows crossing her eyes were probably read by her son as her being less sure about handling Frank than she'd made out, which was also true. 'You just leave Frank to me,' she said, trying to sound more confident, assured.

She gave Joshua the keyword, and heard his tapping on the computer just before she went back through the kitchen door at the end of the hallway.

She was glad the kitchen counter was close, otherwise she wouldn't have made it. She gripped tight at the counter-top as she felt her legs buckle, a white-hot scythe of sorrow and painful nostalgia that seemed to rip her stomach away and take everything below with it, racking sobs rising without warning from deep in her chest, as if they were her very last gasps.

She hadn't shed many tears for Larry over the years. The last had been when his mother died six years ago and it struck her then that he was all alone, nobody left to stand by him. But she hadn't cried like this since Larry had first been charged and locked in a police cell. Cried herself to sleep every night for a week, and the same again when he was finally sentenced. Cried and cried until it seemed all the love and hope had gone and she thought there was nothing left inside but bitterness and anger that he could have done this to her and Joshua. Deserted. Betrayed.

As last time, after receiving Bateson's call, Nel-M picked up on Darrell Ayliss's tail as he came off the Pontchartrain Causeway after Ormdern's second session with Durrant.

This time, though, Ayliss didn't switch hotels that night, was scheduled to book out the following day at midday, according to reception when Nel-M phoned to check. Nel-M didn't see the point in sleeping in his car through the night, watching and waiting. Besides, Melanie Ayliss wasn't scheduled to arrive until late morning the next day. The main event that was seriously going to shake Ayliss's cage, put him off his stride.

Initially uncertain when Nel-M had told her that her ex

440

was back in town – 'Maybe I've wasted enough time already on that loser – she'd then phoned back three hours later full of fire and pep and ready to go. She was booked on an early morning flight from Portland scheduled to arrive in New Orleans at 11.14 a.m. Nel-M told her to call him again immediately she arrived and he'd tell her precisely where her miserable scum of an ex was at that moment.

Yet having set everything up, Nel-M panicked when he arrived back at the hotel early the next morning: Ayliss's car was gone from the hotel parking lot! He phoned reception again, but they said that Mr Ayliss hadn't checked out yet. 'As far as we know, his luggage is still in his room.' Nel-M waited an anxious fifty minutes before Ayliss finally returned, Nel-M slipping down low in his car seat as he watched Ayliss pull back into the hotel parking lot.

Then the long wait, over two hours, before Ayliss headed out again, Nel-M anxious again because he hadn't yet received Melanie Ayliss's call: 11.42. More than enough time to have cleared check-out!

He thought Ayliss would be heading to a fresh hotel, but then felt his blood run cold as he followed him to Royal Street, watched him park and walk towards Truelle's office.

Each time Nel-M had spoken to Bateson, he'd asked him whether he thought anything ground-shaking had come out of the sessions. Neither Bateson nor any of his clique of guards had been present in the interview observation room, but he'd made sure to be standing close by as they all came out, observing expressions. 'They looked thoughtful, pensive rather than pleased with themselves . . . for sure nobody was punching the air or rushing to Haveling to tell him anything. So my read on it is *no*, they didn't hit on anything.'

So, maybe they were safe for now. Maybe. But that could all quickly change if Ayliss beat Truelle over the head with whatever Ormdern had unearthed at the sessions. Truelle, his nerves already strung-out tighter than piano-wire, wouldn't last long. He'd crack.

'For fuck's sake, come on ... *phone!*' Nel-M hissed, thumping his steering wheel; and finally, six minutes after Ayliss had gone inside Truelle's office, Melanie Ayliss's call came through. Flight had been delayed twenty minutes.

Nel-M gave her the address. 'And *hurry* ... I just don't know how long he'll be there.'

Nel-M gently closed his eyes as he hung up, praying that Truelle could hold out long enough for her to get there and put Ayliss off his stroke.

37

'Which part of *now* and *urgent* is it that you don't quite comprehend?'

'I'm sorry, Mr Ayliss . . . but I buzzed through for you: Mr Truelle is with a patient right now, and I can't see any slots in his diary for at least two days. I don't know what else –'

'It'll be too late by then,' Jac cut in. As he suspected, Truelle was giving him the run around. He glared towards the connecting door to Truelle's office, and his secretary Cynthia picked up late, *too late*, the decision he made in that instant. She was a step behind him as he burst into Truelle's office, swinging the door wide.

'I . . . I'm sorry, Mr Truelle,' she stammered in the background. 'I told him you were busy, but he –'

'What's the meaning of this?' Truelle exclaimed, his best mock outrage.

'What, you mean like the meaning of life, Mr Truelle?' Jac didn't bother with an introduction; Cynthia had already told him on the intercom that a certain Darrell Ayliss wanted to see him, '*Says he's the new lawyer just taken over representation of Lawrence Durrant.*' 'Or the meaning of death, as in what you did to Larry Durrant?'

Truelle looked towards his patient, a bemused middle-aged redhead, then back at Jac. 'You can't just barge in here in the middle of a session.' He reached for the phone. 'I'm calling the police.'

'Sure . . . *sure*. Go ahead. And when they arrive, I can tell them how you set up Larry Durrant.'

Truelle's hand hovered uncertainly by the phone, then he forced an equally uncertain smile towards his patient. 'I'm sorry about this, Mrs Venning. I think the only fair thing to do would be to credit you for the twenty-five minutes we've had today, and book you in again for a full session within the week.' Truelle pushed the smile again. 'So that you get the time we've had today free for the inconvenience.'

Mrs Venning got up with a faint smile, as if she was intrigued as to what might happen next and would have loved to hang around to hear it.

Truelle's gaze settled back icily on Jac as Cynthia ushered Mrs Venning out. 'Say what you've got to, then get out of my office.'

'Great bedside manner you've got there, Mr Truelle. But this little talk of ours today is going to run at *my* pace and dictate, not yours.' Jac's sly smile quickly faded as he returned the gaze with the same iciness. He watched Truelle's initial brash bravado quickly evaporate, his mouth setting tightly, anxiously. 'There's no doubt continued contact between you and whoever put you up to this – so you probably know already that I had a fresh psychiatrist see Larry Durrant these last few days.'

'I . . . I don't know what you're talking about.' The truth. Nel-M hadn't said anything, though he could easily see why not, fearful that the news might push him over the edge. Panic overload.

'Gregory Ormdern. You might remember him from the initial trial when he stood up for the defence.'

'Yes, I remember him.' Truelle blinked slowly, trying to remain calm, swallowing back against the fireball of nerves brewing in his stomach. 'But I fail to see what relevance Mr Ormdern now seeing Durrant might have.'

'The relevance, Mr Truelle, is all contained in Mr Ormdern's report on those two sessions with Durrant.' Jac patted the envelope from Ormdern as he laid it on the desk. Truelle continued to blink slowly, as if this was all tiresome and uninteresting, but Jac could read the terror behind his nonplussed façade. Jac might as well have laid a dagger there. 'You see, all along there were only two ways this cat could have been skinned. Either Larry Durrant was telling the truth and his memory of that night was real, or, if not, it had to have somehow been suggested. "Implanted" – I believe that's the trade expression.' Jac paused and smiled tightly. 'And the only person in a position to do that would have been yourself, Mr Truelle.'

'That's ridiculous,' Truelle said, a hint of vehemence to lift it beyond stock defence.

Jac rolled on as if Truelle hadn't spoken. 'And the main test as to whether that account might have been "implanted" is the amount of incidental detail recalled outside of the murder itself.' Jac patted the file and smiled again. 'And guess what Greg Ormdern discovered?' Jac watched Truelle's face redden, but it quickly transformed to bluster.

'As I said, ridiculous . . . *ridiculous*!' Truelle leant forward, gesturing with one hand as if to throw the report back across the desk. 'And I strongly resent your implication.'

Jac had fully expected Truelle's professional hackles to rise. What else could he do? And perhaps, as Jac, he'd have backed off and, if hit with more of the same, pretty soon packed up his tent and headed off. But as Ayliss, a world-weary criminal lawyer, he felt he could bluff it out. In fact, it was *expected* of him; anything less wouldn't have been true to Ayliss's character.

Just the other night he'd commented to Alaysha that that was one advantage of being Ayliss to compensate for all the padding and discomfort: he was like Jac's alter-ego, the heavyweight criminal lawyer that Jac hoped to be in five or ten years' time. And so under the guise of Ayliss, he was able to get away with all the things he might not get away with as Jac.

Jac eased his best syrupy Ayliss smile with Southern drawl to match. 'Now come on, Mr Truelle. You and I both know the truth of what's going on here. And if you don't, now we've got Mr Ormdern's report to tell us.'

Truelle looked at the envelope reluctantly, as if unwilling

to accept its existence. He felt his stomach sinking deeper with every double-time pulse-beat, and wished the floor would open up. *Detail?* He'd embellished with quite a bit of detail, he thought, even covering elements after the event that he thought the police would question Durrant about. '*The first thing you saw about the murder was in a TV shop window late the next day . . . You'd made sure to avoid all newspapers and early morning TV . . . but then there she was suddenly . . .*' That hadn't even come up in police questioning, but it was there nevertheless, embedded in Durrant's subconscious. *No*, he'd added more than enough detail.

'You're wrong or misguided, or simply not telling the truth. I implanted no false memory in Mr Durrant, and I don't believe for a minute that Mr Ormdern's report suggests that I did.' Truelle briefly challenged Ayliss's smile as best he could with his own.

Jac didn't flinch for a second, his steady gaze boring straight through Truelle. Unmoved, unimpressed. Again, he spoke as if Truelle hadn't said anything. 'So, we've covered incidental detail – or rather lack of it.' He nodded towards the file. 'But the part of the equation that was always missing was opportunity. *When* might you have been able to implant all of this in Durrant's mind? The esteemed Mr Ormdern reckons you'd have needed at least an hour-long session, maybe more, for all that mental conditioning. But the problem was that all of the sessions were sequential with diary entries to match. No gaps.'

Truelle adopted again his best nonplussed poker face, blinking slowly, the writhing snakes of nerves in his stomach coiling tighter. It was like watching an impending car crash. Knowing that you wouldn't like what you saw, that it would turn your stomach, but remaining transfixed all the same in case the cars miraculously missed each other at the last second, or just to see how dramatic and gory it might be.

'And then I discovered this . . .' Jac took the cassette player from his pocket and pressed play. Truelle's voice with the date and time of the session, then two faint clicks straight after, which Jac ensured Truelle heard by turning up the volume. 'That's it right there, you see. Those two faint clicks.' Jac quickly slotted in another tape and ran the same segment with Truelle announcing the date and time, again turning the volume up for the two clicks. 'And again *there* . . . and the same on five other tapes. And the background noises too are different to the session where Larry describes the murder . . . and on which there's only *one* click.'

'I . . . I did the introductions afterwards rather than before on those. It happens a lot.'

Jac twisted his mouth as if he'd tasted something sour. 'On its own, that story might wash. But, combined with Ormdern's findings about lack of incidental detail, it answers *how* you did it. The sessions were mostly two a week, and you used one of the later sessions in your diary, just before Larry's murder confession, to mentally condition him. Then you shifted all the other session tapes forward to cover it by putting in new intro dates and times. The gap was then shifted back five or six weeks, *before* the month of tapes with diary entries to match requested at trial. The gap wouldn't have shown.'

'You've got quite a vivid imagination there, Mr Ayliss, I must say.' Truelle pushed a tame smile, but inside the writhing tension in his stomach had wormed its way through every vein and nerve-end. He pressed his hand firmer on the desktop to kill any visible trembling. 'But if you *really* felt you had something with all of this, you'd be at the DA's office right now with it, not sitting here with me.'

'That's where I'm headed next. I came here first to see what you had to say, purely as a courtesy. You see, if you turn State's evidence, you could probably cut a deal that would keep you clean and clear, or at least doing easy time – six months, a year tops.' Jac held one hand out. 'If not, you're probably looking at five years.'

Five years? Truelle swallowed anxiously. Though that was

447

nothing to what he faced from Nel-M: thrown off a high building after a tango, or, if he was lucky, quick and painless: two bullets in a back-street parking lot, like Raoul Ferrer.

Jac watched intently every small tic and nuance of Truelle's expression. *Everything in the balance*; the final gauntlet down, the tension crackled like raw electricity between them. Jac knew that he didn't have enough to go to the DA or Candaret. Everything depended on how Truelle responded to the bluff, which way he jumped now.

Truelle let out a sudden snort, half-laughter, half-derision. 'Do you really think I'd do something like this? Conspire to frame an innocent man?' Truelle leant forward, his voice firming with each word. 'If so, you're deluded, Mr Ayliss. Because I'd never, *ever* have agreed to something like that.' The second truth to pass between them: he never would have gone along with the scheme if he'd believed Durrant had been innocent.

Jac flinched fleetingly at the fresh conviction in Truelle's voice, but hopefully covered well, feeling in that instant as if they were two poker players bluffing the hell out of each other. The game to see who crumbled and folded first. He kept his stare level and even on Truelle, laying on thick the Ayliss drawl.

'Yes, I do believe that's exactly what you did. Because I believe this man actually committed the murder.' Jac took from Ormdern's envelope one of the photos Stratton had taken of Nelson Malley and slid it towards Truelle. 'Do you know this man?'

'No . . . no, I don't.'

Truelle had hardly glanced at the photo. 'Are you sure?' Jac pressed, sensing a niche of uncertainty again.

'Yes, I'm . . . *look*, Mr Ayliss.' Truelle's red-faced bluster resurfaced. He pushed Malley's photo back across the desk-top. 'Forget this man, *and* any others you might wish to put in the frame. The DNA evidence puts Durrant at the murder scene. He was *there* that night, and he killed Jessica Roche. Get used to it.'

Truelle pushed his words home hard, clinging to his belief in them: *DNA!* The final raft of moral justification he'd held on to all along. He was doing nothing wrong, because in the end Durrant *had* done it. Roche and Nel-M had been telling the truth all along: he *was* guilty.

But with each word and accusation of Ayliss's, he'd found himself drifting further and further into a sea of doubt, with that raft all that was left to cling to. No, no, no . . . *no!* Durrant *did* do it! He killed her! And if Ayliss did finally prise his grip from that raft, there'd be nothing to hold on to . . . *sailing free into the night air as Nel-M let him loose from his dance grip.*

'I hear what you're saying,' Jac said, and even if Truelle did finally break now, Candaret might say exactly the same when he laid it all before him: '*This is all very well, Mr Ayliss, but the DNA evidence puts Durrant there. There's no other possible explanation: he killed Jessica Roche.*' Jac took a fresh breath. 'But if they can set Durrant up so perfectly with everything you've helped them with – then I'm sure they also worked out how to set up the DNA evidence. Only nobody's worked out how yet.'

Further adrift . . . Truelle clinging so hard, his nails dug painfully into one thigh. He stood up abruptly. 'I'd like you to leave now, Mr Ayliss. I believe we've discussed everything we have to.' Get Ayliss clear of his office before he fell apart completely.

'I know it's hard to face.' Jac grimaced tautly. 'But deep down you know the truth of what's happened here, Mr Truelle. And you're probably the *only* person left now that might be able to save Larry Durrant.'

Last few fingers wrenched loose . . . *sailing free.* Truelle didn't respond directly or even look at Ayliss, simply buzzed on his intercom. 'Mr Ayliss is leaving now, Cynthia.' And put the hand quickly back on his desktop, bracing as he felt himself sway slightly, as if he'd been drinking.

Jac wrote down his Ayliss cell-phone number and slid it across. 'And remember, be careful where you call from with anything too juicy or incriminating. Your phones might well be bugged.' He slipped Malley's photo into the envelope and looked back from the doorway as Cynthia held the door open. 'It's not going to simply go away, or be any easier to face in front of the DA. Especially with five years hanging over your head.' Jac smiled tightly and waved the envelope. 'Twenty-four hours – again, purely as a courtesy. Then I go to him with all this.'

Nel-M had been tapping his fingers so incessantly against the steering wheel, he could feel them starting to go numb. Where the fuck was she? Already twenty-five minutes Ayliss had been in there, and still no sign of her.

He had her number from her last call, and called it back.

'Hi again,' Melanie Ayliss said. 'I shouldn't really be talking on this now.'

'Why's that?'

'You know, while I'm driving.'

'I thought you'd be jumping in a cab?'

'I'd already booked this from back in Portland . . . didn't take long to get the paperwork done.'

Nel-M closed his eyes. No wonder Ayliss had fucking divorced her! He felt like screaming, *I thought I told you it was urgent!* . . . but no point in alienating her. He took a fresh breath. 'He's still here – but maybe not for much longer. Where are you now?'

'On Simon Bolivar . . . just crossed Melpomene.'

Six or seven minutes, thought Nel-M. No more.

'Okay. See you soon.'

But just as it hit the six minute mark, he saw Ayliss head out of Truelle's office towards his car. Nel-M phoned again, a couple of rings before it answered, Ayliss already back at his car, getting in.

'He's just leaving!' Nel-M's voice sharp with immediacy.

'But I'm right there.'

'Where?'

'On Canal Street . . . just turning into Royal.'

'What car have you got?'

'Uuuh . . . Blue Chevy Metro.'

Ayliss starting up, looking around, pulling out.

And Nel-M spotted her then: blue Metro, brown-haired woman at the wheel with a cell-phone in her hand.

'He's just pulled out!' Nel-M screamed. 'Grey Buick Century . . . heading your way.'

'What? Where . . . *where?*'

The woman frantically scanned the road ahead as she assimilated the information, Ayliss's car twenty-five yards away at that point, starting to pick up speed.

And at only ten yards away, she finally spotted him, her eyes locking fully on the car and Ayliss inside as they came alongside. Her eyes went wide for a second, and then she did something foolish – although nothing would have surprised Nel-M about her by that stage. She braked. *Hard.*

The car behind, a Dodge Dakota, didn't have a chance, crushing most of the back of the Metro into a concertina. Nel-M closed his eyes and cringed; and when he opened them again, it wasn't pretty. Though she still looked alive. *Just.*

Ayliss had kept going, might not have even noticed the conflagration twenty yards behind him. Quick decision to make: head into Truelle's office and pull out fingernails until he found out what had happened, or keep tailing Ayliss? The sound of a distant siren made his mind up: there'd be a scene here now, police cars arriving at any second. He could catch up with Truelle later and, besides, he'd need Ayliss's whereabouts for when his ex got out of the hospital.

Nel-M swung out to follow Ayliss, but at that moment the man driving ahead decided to stop to assist the accident victims, his car blocking the road.

'Out the fucking way!' Nel-M screamed, his head out of the window. 'You fucking numb-brained mor–' Nel-M's voice trailed off as he saw a squad car ahead turn into the road.

Nel-M looked over his shoulder, one arm across the passenger seat as he did a hasty three-point turn, praying that he was able to get around the block quick enough not to lose Ayliss.

The perfect set-up.

Over a couple of shots of Jim Beam, which rapidly became three, four, five and more, Leonard Truelle pondered whether Darrell Ayliss's claim might be right.

In the very beginning, he'd had strong doubts, but he'd had little choice then: Raoul Ferrer's hefty street debt one side, which they offered to clear, his drink problem and the threat of exposure and getting struck off, the other; then the final sweetener on top: $250,000. On one side crushing problems, on the other all the decks cleared and a hefty chunk of cash on top.

But when they'd still sensed some reluctance from him, they'd started piling it on about Durrant being guilty in any case. Adelay Roche had put feelers out on the criminal network, and Durrant's name was the main one to come back as having killed his wife. But the coma and selective memory situation had conveniently blotted it out. The police couldn't even apply standard question and interrogation tactics in such a situation, and in any case simply didn't have enough evidence to haul him in.

Truelle had offered to get the information out of Durrant conventionally, but they'd said no. Too risky. If he'd blotted out the recall, or his memory of it was sketchy, the police still wouldn't have enough to nail him. And with taped sessions, they couldn't later go back and add or embellish; then it *would* look suspicious, as if the memory had been falsely embedded.

No, *all* the details had to be there, so there was no possible error or come-back. That's what they were paying for: over $400,000 with Ferrer's debt.

He should have pulled out right then, but the money and all his problems cleared at the same time was just too tempting. And so he'd gone along with it, used the next session to condition Durrant: '*You went to a house that night on Coliseum Street, Lawrence . . . large antebellum mansion in the Garden District with grand white columns on its front portico. You know the type. It was a planned house robbery, Lawrence, and you felt guilty about it because you'd promised your wife not to commit any more robberies. And unfortunately, while you were there a woman was still in the house that you didn't know about . . . and it all went wrong . . . terribly wrong . . .*'

A masterful mix of what he'd been fed from Roche and Nel-M, along with what he knew himself about Durrant's background.

He shifted the previous session tapes to cover, and the next session dropped the right prompts to tease it all back out of Durrant's memory as the tape ran. Then two days later he phoned the police.

Telling himself all along that he could pull back from the brink later, when he had Ferrer off his back and had worked out how to cover for his drink problem so that he didn't get struck off and . . . *and then*, as the police investigation gathered steam, the DNA evidence on Durrant came in!

Eighty per cent of that doubt and guilt suddenly lifted from his shoulders. They'd been telling the truth all along! Durrant *was* guilty.

And that's pretty much how the years since had rolled on: guilty about what he'd done, but consoling himself all along that the end justified the means . . . though always with that twenty per cent of nagging doubt. That percentage swung back and forth at times: higher with the first news of Durrant's execution date, thirty or forty per cent, maybe even . . .

Truelle suddenly jolted in his seat. Nel-M!

He relaxed again as he managed to focus through the haze of the five Jim Beams swimming around in his head – just a black man of similar height and build. Truelle knocked back the rest of his drink, lifted a hand towards the barman for another.

A minute after Ayliss had left his office, there'd been an

almighty bang outside, and as he looked down at the accident he saw the police car swing in and Nel-M backing up and doing a three-point turn. Nel-M had been watching outside as Ayliss paid him a visit!

He told Cynthia to cancel the rest of his day's appointments, he had something urgent to attend to. 'And if anyone calls for me, *anyone* . . . you don't know where I've gone.'

He hastily left the office, past the policemen surveying the accident, heading for a bar or *anywhere* that Nel-M might not find him. For that reason, he avoided Ben's or any of his regular haunts, went deep into the CBD before he felt he was on safe enough ground, a sprawling Irish-flavoured tavern on Julia Street.

Thirty per cent . . . forty per cent . . . that doubt fluctuating wildly along with his own mood swings and shattered nerves, reaching more for the bottle each time it raised a notch.

But now this smooth-tongued Southern lawyer, Ayliss, had rocketed that doubt into the stratosphere. He seemed to be right about everything else – had pretty well worked it all out – then why not the DNA as well?

Truelle noticed that his hand was still shaking as he raised his fresh glass. Six stiff ones and he was still shaking like Jell-O in an earthquake. He doubted that he'd get calm and level this time, no matter how much he drank.

Some squeaky violin music scratched at the back of his brain. While a good bar in which to hide away, lots of dark corners – and better still as it started to fill with an after-office crowd – as it had become busier, they'd also turned up the frantic-fiddler *Riverdance* music.

But he still needed to kill more time. Okay, he'd sat it out beyond office hours, but now that his office was closed, Nel-M would probably be waiting at his apartment for him. He wouldn't be able to go back there either!

Stay here and be driven mad by frantic Irish fiddlers? Or risk all out there with Nel-M: thrown from a rooftop or a quick bullet through the brain?

With the aid of three more Jim Beams, he managed to brave it out at the Irish bar for almost another two hours, smiling like an idiot and tapping his feet to the music at one point, as the drink finally made his senses swim and sway.

Then he went to a nearby restaurant, picking at a Chicken Royale, his stomach still too jumpy to swallow much. Though he did manage to wash down the five mouthfuls with a full-bodied bottle of Côte de Beaune.

He finished off the evening with four lingering night-cap brandies between two bars on Maple Street, by which time, spilling himself into a taxi at almost 1 p.m. – hopefully Nel-M would have given up waiting for him by then – everything was drifting and sailing around him so wonderfully that he hardly cared if Nel-M put a bullet through his head. He'd hardly feel it, and such a great moment to go out on: the lights of the city spinning and sparkling all around him like he'd never seen before. Everything so beeyootiful . . . *so fucking beeeyoootiful* . . .

Though he did snap to, sharpen his senses a bit as the taxi approached his apartment. If Nel-M's car was anywhere nearby, he'd simply tell the driver to head-on, spend that night in a hotel. But it was nowhere to be seen.

He eased out a breath of relief as he told the driver to stop, paid, staggered out, and, taking the stairs two and three at a time, opened his door and slammed it behind him as quickly, sliding back the three dead-bolts; then leant against the door for almost a full two minutes, breathless, eyes closed, the city lights still spinning all around him.

He went to the window. No sign of Nel-M's car or anything else suspect. But still he didn't put any lights on, except for a small back bathroom light which wouldn't show through to the front.

He noticed the red light on his answer-phone flashing as he went back into the lounge. He played the message.

'*Hi, Lenny . . . Chris here. Chris Tullington. You know I mentioned you coming up here one Christmas. Well, me and Brenda and little Giles — or not so little any more — we're heading inland to Vernon for Christmas. It's the ideal Christmas setting — fir trees, lots of snow and skiing and big log fires. You'd love it! We'd be real happy to see you, if you could make it. Give us a call here in Vancouver, if you think you'd be able to. We're heading off there on the eighteenth for ten days.'*

Fir trees. Skiing. Warm Christmas fires and old friends. Yeah, he'd love to be able to make it, but it felt a million miles from where he was at that moment.

He looked anxiously towards the front door. If the bell rang, he simply wouldn't answer it, just phone the police straightaway, say he had an intruder at the door.

Surely Nel-M wouldn't be able to shoot or hack his way through all the dead-bolts before the police arrived? He wouldn't even risk looking through the spy-hole if it rang, in case Nel-M tried to shoot him through the door. He'd immediately shut and lock every connecting door and barricade himself in a back bedroom.

And that's where he lay as he finally put his head down to sleep, though with all the connecting doors open so that he could listen out for even the slightest sound from the corridor outside; and he was still in the same position over two hours later, eyes darting rapidly as he listened out for those small sounds that hadn't yet come, the barrage of nerves again gripping him as the effects of the drink started to wear off, spinning city lights battling against dark demons, until his conscious mind finally gave up caring and he fell asleep.

38

Fuck, fuck, fuck, fuck . . . *fuck* . . . *fuck*!

When Nel-M got round the block, Ayliss was nowhere to be seen. He trawled as far as ten blocks up and four or five each side before finally giving up with the thump of his palm against the steering wheel . . . *fuck*!

Twenty minutes already gone, he went to a coffee bar and gripped a steaming cappuccino so hard that he thought the cup might shatter, his eyes fixed steadily, stonily ahead, until he'd killed a further half hour and was sure all the police and ambulances would have cleared from in front of Truelle's building.

But when he got back there, Truelle's secretary said that he wasn't in. He barged through to Truelle's office in case she was lying, then asked where he was and what time she expected him back.

'Don't know . . . he didn't say. For either.'

Faint ring of truth about it, but it wouldn't get him anywhere pulling out *her* fingernails. Truelle wouldn't get back any quicker. He'd just have to sit it out.

Another flat-handed bash of the steering wheel as he got back into his car . . . *fuck*! Two more as an hour rolled past and Truelle still hadn't returned, three each at the two and three hour marks, and then finally, as it got close to office closing time and Truelle still wasn't back, a machine-gun roll of them as Nel-M felt his nerves finally snapping.

He daren't even phone Roche or answer his call if he rang. If he told Roche he'd lost *both* Ayliss and Truelle and that Ayliss's wife had ended up in hospital, the resultant incredulous gasping fit would send Roche into seizure; one good result from the afternoon, perhaps, but not the one he was after.

He waited another hour in case Truelle was late getting

back to his office, left with another flat-handed *fuck*, one more as he arrived in front of Truelle's apartment building and saw no light on at his window, and was halfway through another couple at the one hour mark with Truelle still not back, when his cell-phone rang. Vic Farrelia.

A slow smile crept across Nel-M's face as Farrelia related the call that had just come in on Truelle's line. Truelle's second, so far elusive, insurance policy: Chris Tullington, wife Brenda; Vancouver, Canada. Shouldn't be too hard to track down. Now they had them both: full house.

Nel-M checked his watch. Both would have to be taken out at the same time, no question, and if possible that very night. But which one did he take himself and which did he leave to Tommy Garrard, who'd so effectively taken care of Dr Thallerey? Vancouver or upstate New York? Not much to choose between them travelling-time-wise.

He called Roche to tell him the good news and see if he had any preferences. Leave him with that last bit of power and decision-making he so coveted.

Every joint and muscle of Melanie Ayliss's body seemed to scream and ache as she made her way up the steps of the Eighth District station house and approached its front desk at just after 10 p.m.

'I have a complaint to lodge.'

'Oh, *really*?' A bright-eyed young sergeant called Brennan quickly killed his faint smile and the surprise in his voice as he realized his sarcasm had been lost on the sour-faced woman before him. Rule fifty-eight of the police manual: never joke with heavily bruised women in neck-braces. He lowered his voice an octave; feigned gravity. 'And what would that be ma'am?'

'I had an accident earlier . . .'

'*Oh*?'

She looked at him sharply, unsure whether he was still kidding or not. 'And part of the reason for it was that I'd just been told that my ex-husband – who in fact I haven't seen for the past seven years – was on a certain street. But when I looked at who I thought was my ex-husband, it wasn't him.'

'And this ... *this* caused the accident?' It was hard for Brennan to keep the incredulous tone out of his voice, but he kept his face serious, slightly furrowed. Striving to understand.

'Yes ... *yes*. Because when I saw that it wasn't him, I braked.' Melanie Ayliss was striving equally hard to emphasize, make her point. 'And the car behind went straight into me.'

It was taking every bit of Brennan's willpower to keep a straight face. Any of the phrases rolling through his head at that moment – '*Fancy that?*' or '*Why on earth would they do a fool thing like that?*' – would have sent him into raptures of laughter, rolling on the floor.

'The main point I'm trying to make,' she said, her voice getting testy for the first time, 'is that someone is driving round impersonating my ex-husband.'

'Oh, right. I see.' Brennan was glad she'd extracted the main point from all of this; it might have taken him a while. 'So this man doesn't *look* like your ex-husband, but is nevertheless passing himself off as him?'

'No, no. It *does* look like him – well, a close-enough resemblance. But it wasn't him.'

Brennan blinked slowly. 'Oh, right. You actually spoke to him?'

'No, *no*. I didn't.' Testiness quickly verging into annoyance at this wet-behind-the-ears desk sergeant still grasping the wrong end of the stick. Or was he purposely being obstructive? 'Just that two-second look before ... before the car behind went into me.'

This was getting harder by the minute. Brennan ran one hand through his hair, sighing. 'And you haven't seen him, you say, for seven years?'

'That's right.' She went to nod, only then realizing that she couldn't with the neck-brace.

'Yet you're sure it wasn't him . . . even though you say it actually *looked* like him and you were only able to eyeball him for a couple of seconds?'

'Yes, *yes* . . . a hundred per cent *sure*.' Her voice practically a hiss, her eyes narrowing. Having spent two hours unconscious and the rest of the day being scanned, probed, stitched, strapped, and jabbed with a succession of needles, the last thing she needed was another prick. 'Believe you me, when you've been married to someone for twelve years, you know it's not them in the first millisecond, let alone two seconds. Even after seven years.'

'Oh . . . okay.' Brennan wasn't about to argue with that.

Her eyes flickered briefly to one side. 'Also, there . . . there was no recognition on his face when he saw me.'

What, he didn't suddenly slam on his brakes as well? But from the glint in this woman's eyes, her patience worn, Brennan knew that he'd be taking his life in his hands to show even the trace of a smile. He'd be joining her in wearing a neck-brace. 'And any idea, ma'm, why this other person might be impersonating your husband?' Brennan made sure, too, to keep any further doubt out of his voice; his best formal procedural.

'No, uuuh . . . not really.' One thing she hadn't thought about. She smiled tightly. 'Hopefully that's something you'll be able to tell me . . . *when* you've caught up with him.'

Spinning city lights . . . spinning all around.

Floating. The sensation pleasant. But suddenly Truelle sensed that something was wrong. The lights were spinning rapidly towards him . . . and now that horrible, gut-wrenching sensation of falling . . . *falling!* Nel-M had taken off his hood just before throwing him from the building! . . . *falling . . . falling . . .*

Truelle's eyes snapped open and he sat bolt upright at the jolt of hitting the ground, his breath short, heart pounding like a jack-hammer. And there was a woman's voice in the background, coming from the lounge – '. . . when you get this message, Lenny . . . if you could call me . . .' – leaving a message on his answer-phone. He jumped out of bed, legs unsteady, everything still spinning slightly around him, ran towards it. 'Strangely enough, when . . . when Alan spoke to you a couple of weeks back and got that letter of yours, he talked about us all getting together again and –'

'Hello . . . Maggie. I'm *here*. It's Lenny . . . what is it?' He could tell from her voice that she was distraught, almost as breathless as he was at that moment, sniffling slightly. Then he felt his legs almost give way completely, still *falling*, as she related the horror of what had happened earlier that night: Alan shot dead. Her and the kids were out at the time, she'd gone to pick their son up from a Scouts' evening and had taken their daughter along for the ride. The police, putting it all together, believe that the alarm on Alan's car in the drive-way was set off to get him outside, then he was taken inside by his assailant and some papers rifled through in his office before he was shot.

'I . . . I found him when I came back with the kids.' Fresh breath to fight back the tears. 'But the crazy thing is, there doesn't seem to be anything of value taken.'

Falling . . . 'Oh, Maggie . . . *Maggie*. I'm so sorry.'

'Something like this, it's . . . it's *unbelievable*.' She forced an ironic snort through her shaky voice and sniffles. 'That's why we moved upstate, because we thought it would be safer.'

'I know . . . I know.' *Falling* . . . the breath grunting out of him as his legs finally gave way, sinking to his knees as he clung to the telephone table with his other hand.

'I started my calls at six, not long after the police left. Relatives, friends . . . and I called you, Lenny, not only because you're a good old friend of mine and Alan's, but because I wondered what you wanted done now with that envelope you sent – *if* I can find where Alan put it.'

'*Oh?*' Not daring to tell this mother of two – this *widow* – that it probably wasn't there any longer and that her husband had very likely been killed because of it. Truelle looked towards the clock for the first time: 8.08 a.m.

She forced an awkward, tremulous chuckle. 'I remember him smiling about it at the time, because you'd given instructions of what to do if anything happened to you . . . but not what to do if anything happened to *him.*'

'Well, I . . . I hadn't really thought about that.' He swallowed hard, closed his eyes. City lights still spinning in his head, along with an image of Alan being shot and Maggie screaming and spilling tears over his prone body when she found him, her two children shaking and fearful in the background. 'And I . . . I can't really think clearly about it now.' He took a fresh breath. 'And you . . . you've got other things to worry about right now.'

'I know.' Sniffling, the tears close again.

'There . . . there's no urgency. I'll give you a call in a few days time when I've thought about it and things have settled down more your end.' He sighed heavily. 'And again, Maggie, I'm sorry . . . *so sorry*. If there's anything I can do over these coming days, *anything* . . . don't hesitate to contact me.'

Truelle found it difficult to stand up again after they signed off, still gripping to the table as if it was that last raft or the edge of a high building. Oh God . . . *Oh God*!

But why *now*? If they'd known of Alan's whereabouts all along, then why not just after he'd first sent the envelope? Or maybe it was just a terrible coincidence. People got shot in upstate New York too. Or was it because of Ayliss visiting him yesterday and him then going AWOL. Nel-M fearing the worst and not able to catch up with him, so . . .

Truelle got up then, in fact leapt back a full two paces from the phone as if it had given him a high-voltage shock, staring back at it accusingly as he recalled the message that had come in the night before from Chris Tullington in Vancouver.

'*Be careful where you call from with anything too juicy or incriminating. Your phones might well be bugged.*' McElroy too had warned him earlier, but he'd already had his lines checked and cleared! Office *and* home.

He'd also spoken to Chris two weeks back when he'd first sent the envelopes. He racked his brain for what might have been said then, shaking his head after a moment; it hardly mattered now. If for whatever reason everything was going down *now*, Chris was in danger, and himself: if his line was bugged, they'd now know he was back at his apartment. Nel-M could be on his way already.

He shrank back another pace from the phone, then rushed over to the window, looking out. No Nel-M in sight, nothing else that looked out of place or worrying. He grabbed his keys, a handful of coins from a side-drawer, and leapt break-neck down the apartment building steps. He gave the street a furtive each-way scan, then ran round the corner, finally settling on a kiosk three blocks away, in case Nel-M mean-while pulled up by his place.

His hand shook wildly as he anxiously fed in the coins and dialled Chris's number.

'Hello.' A woman's voice, but it didn't sound like Chris's wife Brenda.

'Is . . . is Chris there?'

'I'm afraid not.' The tone subdued, grave. 'I'm afraid some-thing's happened. Who is it calling?'

Truelle's stomach plummeted. *Something's happened!* 'It's, Len . . . uuuh, a friend. What's happened?'

'I'm a RCMP liaison officer, Jackie Melkin. And I'm sorry to have to report that there was a serious incident earlier this morning involving Mr Tullington, a homicide, and his wife's not able to speak to anyone – because she was injured too in the incident. You say you're a friend of the Tullingtons . . . *Len*, was it? Could I have your full name, please, sir? I have strict instructions to make a list of all callers.'

'I . . . *uuuh*, it . . . it doesn't matter.' He hung up abruptly. Not sure where the conversation would head, or if he'd even be *able* to talk any more. His writhing nerves had tightened

463

around his chest and throat like a vice, so that he could hardly breathe ¬ all that came out was a strangled, breathless gasp as he clenched his eyes shut and banged one fist repeatedly against the kiosk glass. *No, no, no . . . no . . . no!*

But you had your lines cleared of bugs! You had them cleared!

He could no longer be sure of that until he'd made one more call; but he didn't have time now. He had to get away. As far away as possible!

He made a quick stop at a deli for a take-out coffee to clear the dust from his throat and his head-throb from last night, sharpen his senses – though fear and adrenalin seemed to have already done half of that job for him. And running on that high-octane mix of fear, adrenalin, caffeine and night-before Jim Beams and brandies, within seven minutes he had everything he needed from his apartment packed in a suitcase and was heading back down the stairs.

A final anxious scan of the road outside, having already checked every other minute while packing, then he scampered a block round the corner and hailed a cab to an internet café in Metairie where he'd make the rest of his travel arrangements.

Cuba! The remotest-placed friend he could think of – probably the *only* one of his old friends who hadn't yet been shot. Not a million miles away, but with US travel restrictions a nightmare to get to: he'd be travelling half the day with stop-offs at Atlanta, Miami and Nassau to get there. Then a six hour drive from Havana.

The arrangements made, he suddenly thought of something he'd forgotten. He couldn't leave it in his office, yet he couldn't risk going back there, either. He checked his watch. 8.46 a.m. He called Cynthia's cell-phone – he'd need to tell her he'd be away for a few days in any case – and instructed her where to find what he needed and the mailbox in Cuba to send it to.

'DHL . . . immediately you get to the office. And don't for God's sake tell *anyone* where I've gone.'

Anyone? She told him about Nel-M's visit the day before.

'Big black guy, eyes like a dead frog's. Seemed to be the day for people barging into your office.'

'Him in particular don't tell.'

But Cynthia knew that something was seriously wrong, probably from the breathless, rapid-staccato way he spat everything out, as if afraid a minute later it would be too late; and as the questions started to come, he cut her short.

'I can't tell you, Cynthia. I *can't*.' *I might have set up an innocent man, and everyone who gets near to knowing about it ends up dead!* The stale drink, caffeine and sour bile were like a bubbling quagmire surging up through his lungs. *Hard to breathe!* The throbbing in his head and his body's trembling were so heavy that it felt as if a limb might fall off at any second. 'I just need to get away for a few days, that's all. Just DHL that package straightaway and don't tell *anyone* where I've gone – you'll be okay. And Cynthia: be especially careful what you say on the office line. It might be bugged.'

He hung up quickly before any more questions came, and dialled straight out to his friend in Cuba as he went outside and hailed a cab to the airport.

'Yeah . . . *yeah*, Brent . . . on my way right now.'

'Be great to see you, old buddy. Been a long time . . . lot of catching up to do. Four-shot *Mojito* session, at least . . .'

Never any doubt. But if he hadn't been able to stay with Brent, he'd have simply booked a nearby hotel. As his taxi headed towards the airport, he made his last call; the one that had troubled him more and more the past hour.

'Bell South.'

Truelle explained about the engineers' visits he'd booked three weeks back to clear suspected bugs from his home and office telephones.

Brief flurry of keyboard taps. 'Yes . . . I've got them here. Both booked at the same time on the fourteenth of last month.'

Truelle's hopes raised; then, with a few more taps at her end, quickly sank again as she looked at the next entry.

'And then both cancelled again the following day.'

'That's . . . that's not possible,' Truelle spluttered. '*I* didn't cancel them, and two different engineers called at the times arranged, *both* wearing Bell uniforms.'

'I'm sorry, sir. If those visits actually happened – then we don't have any record of them here on our computer. The last recorded entry we have is for the two cancellations. And no new times set for alternative visits.'

No point in arguing further with the girl; he now knew the truth of what had happened. How they'd done it.

'Thanks.' *Falling* . . . sinking deeper into the abyss, his voice little more than a hollow, detached echo rising up through it.

The two engineers had put the bugs *in* rather than taken them out! From then on, they'd listened in to every word. And when Chris had left the message with his details, he'd signed his own and Alan's death-warrant.

Truelle shut his eyes as he felt the first tears of the day sting them. Maybe Ayliss was right: if they were clever enough to set all of that up, perhaps they'd set up the DNA evidence as well. And in two days' time, he'd have Durrant's death also on his conscience.

Truelle kept his eyes shut, the tears rolling gently down his cheeks as the taxi sped to the airport. But at least the battle inside his head was over: there were no longer any spinning city lights, only dark demons.

Melanie Ayliss's enquiry landed on the desk of Joe Rayleigh, a portly, six-three black detective with a constant scowl. He glanced briefly at its opening page as it arrived. He had a stack of murder, rape, missing persons and armed robbery files on his desk; impersonation wasn't exactly a priority. The only thing to give it a curious edge was that it concerned Larry Durrant's new lawyer, Darrell Ayliss.

Rayleigh glanced at his watch. Not much he could do about it that night. But at 9.20 the next morning, he called the two places where he thought he might get a contact number or the current whereabouts of Darrell Ayliss.

At Libreville prison, Warden Haveling's secretary said that it was likely either Warden Haveling or his assistant Mr Folley had a number for Mr Ayliss. But Folley had been on night duty and wouldn't be in until midday, and Warden Haveling was tied up in a meeting until 10.30 a.m. 'But I'll get Warden Haveling to call you back the minute he comes out of his meeting.'

Rayleigh left his number and made his second call to Payne, Beaton and Sawyer, the law firm that previously represented Durrant, and was put through to a John Langfranc.

'No, unfortunately I don't have Mr Ayliss's number,' Lang-franc commented. 'But I know someone who very likely has: Mike Coultaine. He used to work for us and apparently has kept in contact with Darrell Ayliss since. In fact, I understand that it was Mike Coultaine who recommended Ayliss to the Durrant case now.' The small bit of scuttlebutt he'd found out when he'd called Rodriguez to find out how the BOP hearing had gone.

Rayleigh took Coultaine's number, and dialled it the second he hung up on Langfranc.

'Yeah. I know how to get in touch with Darrell Ayliss,' Coultaine said. 'In fact I met up with him just a few days ago. What's this all about? Something to do with the Durrant case?'

'No, no. Some query to do with his ex-wife.' Rayleigh was thinking more about the first part of what Coultaine had said. 'You mentioned you met up with him. What did he look like?'

'Like . . . like Darrell Ayliss.' It was obvious from Coul-taine's tone that he found the question odd. 'Why?'

Rayleigh sensed that he was about to make a serious horse's ass out of himself unless he explained a bit more. He told Coultaine about Melanie Ayliss's brief encounter with some-one she'd expected to be her ex-husband in a car the day before. 'And although it was only for a couple of seconds and she hasn't seen her husband for seven years, she's got it in her head that the man she saw wasn't *him*. So, I have to ask you, sir – do you know Darrell Ayliss well? Well enough, when you met him a few days back, to know whether it was him or not?'

Coultaine exhaled heavily. 'I shared an office with Darrell Ayliss for three full years, with him no more than a few yards from me. And, unlike his ex, I've had the benefit of seeing him far more recently. I've visited him in Mexico twice now, the last time just fourteen months back. It was him. There's no question about it.'

'Right. Thanks for that, sir.' Rayleigh chuckled awkwardly. 'You know, we get these things in . . . we gotta chase them up.'

'I understand.' Fresh breath from Coultaine. 'But I think you'll find this is more to do with Melanie Ayliss's old maintenance battle with her ex-husband. She's trying craftily to make use of police resources to track him down.'

'Yeah, yeah . . . could be.' Sounded about right. But he loved it when they were cleared up quickly. 'Thanks again.' The second he rang off, he threw the folder onto the 'Case closed' pile.

And at Coultaine's end, as soon as he hung up, he called Jac.

39

The phone was on its fourth ring before Bob Stratton finally picked up and Jac worried for a moment that he wasn't there. He put on the drawl and introduced himself as Darrell Ayliss, said that he'd seen Stratton's name in the file he'd taken over from Jac McElroy.

'He's noted here that you're good at finding people – *with* an exclamation mark. And that's exactly what I'm after.'

I was there at the time . . . I'd have incriminated myself . . .

The thought had struck Jac in the early hours of the morning, woke him sharply at 5.40 a.m. – not that he was sleeping that well in any case, different hotel beds every night and the turmoil of thoughts in his head – *another crime going down at the same time!* That's why he hadn't been able to come forward; fear of self-incrimination.

Maybe he was clutching at straws – maybe it was just an old friend or hoaxer – but with still no reply to his last e-mail and only forty-eight hours now remaining, that was all there was left to do: squeeze every last drop out of the few remaining possibilities.

He explained his thinking to Stratton. 'Probably not in the Roche house itself – too much of a coincidence – or even immediate neighbours. But somewhere within, say, fifty or a hundred yards . . . close enough that this person would have got a reasonable look at the murderer leaving the Roche house that night. Enough to say that it wasn't Larry Durrant.'

'And you say you've got some photos and a description of this mystery e-mailer?'

'Yeah. From a girl in the internet café, I . . . I see from McElroy's file.' Having to be careful every second what he said. 'Though the photos don't give that much, they're only partial cam-shots with at most thirty per cent facial profile, and the description – black, stocky, five-ten, maybe six foot, late thirties, early forties – could fit ten or twenty per cent of the city's black population.'

'Okay.' Stratton was thoughtful for a second. 'But if I get fresh photos of a few live-ones in front of this girl, something might strike a chord.'

'Yeah, possibility,' Jac agreed. 'Except don't forget we're looking for someone that was active twelve years ago. If they're not active now, mug-shots are going to be thin on the ground.'

'True.' Stratton took a fresh breath. 'But that's going to be stage two. The first thing'll be to find out if another crime did go down nearby twelve years ago. Then we'll have a start point to know if it's even worth looking further. And also what type of crime and connected mug-shots we're looking for.'

Nel-M tried to grab some sleep on his twenty-minute-delayed 6.45 a.m. flight from Vancouver, but the images still surging through his head were making it difficult.

If only everything his end of things had gone as smoothly as Garrard's. *If only*.

He'd spoken to Tommy Garrard two hours ago and it apparently had gone like clockwork: car in the drive, alarm set off twice, husband comes out, no other family there at the time, into the house to get the envelope, two quick shots, and away again.

'Nobody saw me. But just in case, like you suggested, I wore a mask at the time.'

But with Nel-M's target, there'd been no car in the drive-way, and he'd had to bang a side-passage trashcan to hope-fully get the man of the house out to investigate. Three sharp bangs at two-minute intervals, Nel-M starting to worry that he'd bring the neighbours out as well, before a heavy-set guy finally emerged – wielding a baseball bat and moving surprisingly fast for his size, perhaps not realizing Nel-M had a gun until it was too late. Nel-M floored him with a leg shot, then had to drag the stumbling, bleeding body back through the house with his wife and son, no more than eleven, looking on – swinging his gun towards the wife for a second as she made a move towards the phone – to get the envelope from a bedroom drawer. He'd made sure to ask about the envelope while they were still outside, out of earshot of his family, then clamped a hand across his mouth as they moved inside, knowing that if the man did mention it, he'd have to shoot them too.

But as he levelled his gun to finish the job halfway back down the hallway, his wife screamed and lunged for him then – only a split-second to turn his gun from the head-shot to put one in her leg to take her down. Then he stood over them both for a second, breath falling rapid and short, as he pondered whether to finish her too.

He'd also used a mask from a joke shop – so what else would her and her son have seen other than a bit of dark skin and some salt-and-pepper curls either side of an Ozzy Osborne mask? Then at that moment she groaned heavily with pain from her leg wound, made him worry that she'd disturb neighbours; but as he raised his gun, he caught the look in her son's eyes, questioning, pleading. What was he going to do – shoot the kid as well? As Joe Pesci once said, *'You could be out there half the fucking night.'*

He waggled the gun at them threateningly as he backed away along the hallway and out the front door, then turned and ran off into the night.

But now, as he tried to sleep on the flight, that boy's eyes were with him again, strangely haunting . . . reminding him of that night twelve years ago with Jessica Roche, that woman walking her dog staring at him. Only once before had he left a witness alive, and look where that had led.

Jac sat anxiously outside Truelle's office building, his earlier telephone conversation with Cynthia still rattling through his mind.

'When do you expect him back?'

'I don't know. He didn't say.'

'Do you know where he's gone?'

'Didn't tell me that either.'

'What about the patients he has today?'

Cynthia sighed tiredly. 'That, if you don't mind me saying, is none of your business.'

Jac sensed he was getting the run-around, that something was wrong – but if he pushed harder and she revealed anything sensitive, anyone listening in on Truelle's line would hear it at the same time, and so he'd signed off then, 'I'll try him again later', deciding in that moment on another unannounced visit.

He'd originally planned to wait outside and observe for thirty or forty minutes, then barge in and let loose with all guns – on Truelle if he was there, on steel-blonde Cynthia if he wasn't. But then Mike Coultaine's call about Melanie Ayliss had come through just as he was leaving his hotel, and suddenly he felt vulnerable sitting in the open in the street. It was bad enough posing as Ayliss, padded out like a WeightWatchers reject, feeling as if he was in a constant pressure-cooker, worried that half his face might suddenly melt and slide off – but now he had this crazy ex on his tail, telling the police or anyone who'd listen that the man running around town as Darrell Ayliss wasn't her husband!

After only fifteen minutes, his nerves were worn, spending as much time looking round at the street for anyone who might be looking at him as at Truelle's entrance and window.

Still no sign of Truelle, only a couple of people he didn't recognize, perhaps going to other offices in the building, and a DHL messenger heading in and then out again two minutes later. Jac managed to last only another three minutes.

A short gasp from steely Cynthia as he burst in, then a cool, imperious eyebrow raised. 'What do you want? I told you earlier he's not here . . . and he still isn't.'

'Save it!' Jac snapped. He went through to Truelle's office to check, then glared back at her. She held the same cool stare; she was getting used to this by now. He moved towards her desk, leant on the edge of it. 'So, let's try again. What time do you expect Mr Truelle back?'

'I don't know.'

Jac sighed tiredly. A re-run of their telephone conversation forty minutes ago. He asked where Truelle had gone and she said she didn't know that either. Jac closed his eyes for a second, the sigh heavier now – *severely* pissed off. He leant over a fraction, more intimidating.

'We could spend the next half hour with me asking variations on those same questions, with you continuing to be uncooperative – but the only problem with that is, I don't have much time. I've got a man on Death Row because of Truelle, and the clock's ticking fast against him. That's why, when I was here yesterday, I gave Mr Truelle a deadline.' Jac glanced at his watch. 'Now at that deadline, only half an hour from now, if Truelle isn't in the DA's office ready and willing to talk, then the DA is going to have him arrested. And if he's not here to arrest, then he's going to have *you* arrested instead and charged with obstruction of justice.' A bluff, but he doubted Truelle had told her enough for her to know that; he'd probably simply instructed, *don't say anything.* She stared back at him, hardly a flicker or flinch. Mrs Cool-steel-blonde. 'And you'll end up having to answer these same questions after a night in a jail cell and with a year's sentence hanging over your head.' Jac eased the syrupy Ayliss smile. 'Only I don't have time to wait for you to languish in jail for a day – I need the answer to those questions *now*!' He slapped one hand against the desk for emphasis; in the quiet of the office, it was like a rifle-shot.

She didn't move or flinch, all it raised from her was a slow blink. Defiant: *you're not going to break me.* She returned the smile smugly.

Jac reached for his back-up ammunition, took the photo of Nelson Malley out of his briefcase and slid it across her desk, asking, 'Do you know this man?'

'No . . . no, I don't.'

Jac knew that she was lying; the flinch in her eyes, the first so far, screamed *Yes!* And, like Truelle, she'd hardly looked at the photo, as if afraid to fully confront it.

'He's going to come round here, too . . . asking you the same questions. But he's not going to be nearly as nice as me. He's going to have his hands round your throat and a gun in your face sooner than you can blink.' Another faint flinch, her blinking a beat quicker. 'And he's not going to think twice about pulling the trigger.'

A faint swallow, Cynthia looking down rapidly, not wishing Jac to see that he'd struck a chord.

And as Jac looked down too, he noticed the open appointment diary before her, her arms on it, guarding. From upside down, he thought he could make out the word '*Rearranged*' and then another time written alongside on a few entries. He grabbed for the book to turn it his way, but she held onto it tight, and he had to twist and wrench hard, finally shoving her back with one forearm to wrestle it free.

He could now see more *Rearrangeds* with fresh times alongside, with some on the next page as he flicked over. Seven in all rearranged over the next three days, and she was probably working on the rest as he'd walked in.

'So, now at least we know how long he's going to be away – at least the three remaining days of this week. And with all those appointments rearranged for the end of next week and some the week after, maybe as long as a week.' Jac raised an inquisitive eyebrow, but she just glared back at him, red-faced and slightly breathless from the brief tussle. 'So now all that's left to find out is *where* he's gone?'

'I don't know, he . . . he didn't tell me.'

But Jac could see that she was more hesitant, less sure of her ground; perhaps uncertain now, after their brief tussle, just how far he'd go to get the information. He gave the diary one more quick scan, an entry to one side hitting his peripheral vision, but not at that instant seeming relevant. He laid the diary back in front of Cynthia, leaning over again at the same time.

'Come on, Cynthia . . . I don't have time for any more of your fooling around.' *Three days.* Larry would be dead by then! 'I need to know where, *where*?'

She looked down awkwardly again, not wanting Jac to see what was in her eyes; or perhaps, in that instant, seeing in Jac's eyes everything he'd been through: *almost drowning in the lake, being framed for murder and hunted by the police, representing a man who he was sure was innocent now only a day and a half away from execution.* Dawning on her then that having gone through all of that, he wasn't simply, after a few trite fob-offs, going to walk away.

And as Jac looked down again, he noticed that Cynthia seemed to be more concerned with covering that side entry – that's what she'd been covering before! From where he was, he'd been able to see the rearranged appointments. Shielding them hadn't been as vital.

He yanked back at the appointment book, shoved her arm away from covering the entry, and read fully what before had only half registered:

Apartado 417, Sancti Spiritus, Cuba.
DHL: 8422016CS.

Jac stabbed the entry with one finger, glaring back at Cynthia. 'That's where he's gone, isn't it?'

Cynthia, red-faced, shook her head. 'I . . . I don't know.'

Jac slammed one hand on the desk again, another rifle-shot, and this time Cynthia did flinch. 'Yes, you fucking do! Because I saw the DHL man come in and out just ten minutes before I came up here!' Cynthia chewed at her bottom lip, clinging by her fingertips to her last shred of resolve. One last push. 'And if my man on Death Row, who I truly believe is innocent, should die because of you – then God help you. I'll push the DA with everything I've got for the maximum for obstruction. Two years in the hardest possible women's prison! And as tough as you think you are, Cynthia, you won't make it.' Jac leant closer still, so close that hopefully she'd feel the syrup from Ayliss's sly smile drip on her, his voice lowering to a hiss. 'You *won't* fucking make it.' Cynthia chewed harder at her lip, crumbling inch by inch before him. Jac tapped Malley's photo. 'And if this man catches up with your boss before me, then God help him too – because he'll be dead long before my man on Death Row . . . and all your efforts today will–'

'Okay . . . *okay!*' Breathless exhalation as that last inch went, her resolve finally snapped. 'That *is* where he's gone.' She looked up at him anxiously. She shook her head. 'But I didn't tell you, okay? I promised I wouldn't.'

'Do you have any other information?'

'No . . . *no.*' She shook her head again. 'That's it. And I only had that because he asked me to send something there.'

This time Jac sensed she was telling the truth. 'And what was that?'

'A cassette tape. He told me where to find it in his office.'

'Okay.' Jac nodded thoughtfully. *Tape?* Perhaps the tape that had got bumped when Truelle shifted all the sessions. Jac wrote down the Cuba mailbox number and gave Cynthia one last look at Malley's photos before he slid it back into his case. 'And do yourself a favour, Cynthia. If this man calls asking for your boss – and for sure he will – make sure you're not here. As I say, he won't be nearly as nice as me. And in the end, I wasn't really nice at all.'

Carmen Malastra visited the Bay Tree Casino floor once more to confirm everything that he'd put together on screen from studying cam videos the past weeks. Filling in the final shades: the envelopes passed from Jouliern to Strelloff, him stashing them below the bar – easily covered as part of the bar float until the final tally was done at the end of the evening – and then Strelloff in turn passing the envelopes onto the courier.

476

Malastra walked the areas that he'd seen on video, looking back thoughtfully towards the cameras, wondering how many more envelopes might have been passed that he hadn't picked up on. The hand-over at times obscured by activity on the casino floor, people milling about.

This time Caccia didn't follow him round like an obedient puppy, sensed after the first few paces that he'd rather be alone. 'I'll leave you to it, Mr Malastra. If you need anything . . . anything at all, I'll be at the end of the bar.'

Malastra's steps retraced Jouliern's and Strelloff's movements on those nights: from the tables where Jouliern took the money, half of it pocketed and chips substituted to match before he passed everything onto the cashier's booth; then, an hour before closing, passing all the skimmed money in an envelope to Strelloff behind the bar, and finally Strelloff passing it to the courier at the end of the evening. Not every night, though; they were restricted by how often the courier could call. Two or three times a week by the looks of it; and, with the association, not at all suspicious that they would be there that often.

Malastra leant against the bar and looked back towards the two main cameras covering it. He hadn't managed to pick up every envelope handover, but enough to piece together the pattern.

With a curt nod to Caccia, Malastra went back to his office and computer. After forty minutes of checking angles again and running through the dozen or so sequences where the images were clearest, he freeze-framed and printed off what he thought were the best shots, then picked up the phone and summoned Bye-bye.

'This is who we're looking for,' he said as Bye-bye approached, passing across two photos. 'That'll then end this whole Jouliern saga. I want it done quick and so smooth and clean it'll be like an oyster sliding down Pavarotti's throat.' He looked up sharply at Bye-bye. 'Understand?'

Bye-bye nodded, studying the two photos. 'Yeah, sure.'

'And be careful on this one, don't get complacent. With Jouliern gone, they might have guessed we'll be coming for them. So they could well be looking out or have made some safeguards. Be prepared for that.'

40

Larry couldn't take his eyes off Joshua. Not, he liked to think, because it was the last time he'd see the boy; but because he hadn't seen him now for eleven months, and the boy had changed so much in that time.

He looked a good two inches taller, his voice a shade deeper, the look in his eye more thoughtful. Larry thought he could see the first shadow of the man that Joshua would become: kind, thoughtful, caring, but hopefully nobody's fool. And maybe much of that had come about, that transformation starting so early, because he'd had to shoulder so much more than other boys of his age. The taunts, the different surrogate fathers, careful what he said between and about his real father and them in case it looked like favouritism; difficult, if not impossible, Larry thought, to get that balance right from what he'd read in Josh's e-mails.

Or maybe that was all just wishful thinking, Larry projecting his thoughts because he knew now that he wouldn't actually see how Josh turned out.

'Come here!' Trying to project too every ounce of love he'd missed giving the boy these past long years, and now the years to come, as he hugged him tight. Not wishing to smother Josh or make him feel too awkward, so letting him go sooner than he'd have liked; he could have stayed hugging Josh all day.

Francine looking on, her eyes glassy with emotion, her voice breaking slightly, 'Oh, Larry . . . *Larry*', as she took Josh's place and they embraced; though this time it was more her hugging Larry, patting his back a couple of times as if he were the child that needed consoling.

Then silence for a moment. Tense, uneasy silence. He'd

covered most of the day-to-day, regular stuff by e-mail with Josh over the past few months – though Franny wasn't to know that – and he and Franny hadn't spoken for so long now, they hardly knew what to say to each other any more: casual, light stuff seemed too trivial given what he was facing, and the heavier stuff which might remind him of that or, worse still, tackled it directly, seemed just as bad. So they just sat there for a moment, in that silent gap in the middle.

They'd been allowed a cell near Haveling's office for their final meeting so that they weren't forced to just clasp fingers through the holes in a glass screen, and had semi-privacy: the back of a guard's head was just visible through the door's open inspection hatch.

'I appreciate you coming here today,' Larry said finally. 'I understand from Josh's e-mail it wasn't that easy. You had to lay it on the line with Frank.'

She nodded. 'Yeah. Had to tell him straight-out: that's it, we're going . . . no point in arguing. It might be our–' She broke off then, bit at her lip, realizing the minefield this conversation was going to be, but no other word that she could think of that wouldn't sound pathetic or contrived. 'Our *last* chance to see you.' Her eyes glistening heavier, she closed them for a second, as if in apology for having said it.

'That's okay.' Larry reached out and touched her shoulder. 'Whatever the reasoning, I'm just glad to see you both here now.'

She nodded, and after a second finally thought of a subject that was weighty and worthy enough for discussion, Joshua's schooling, talking about how well he was doing. 'Straight As in most of his subjects, a couple of Bs, and nothing . . . *nothing* below that. We both got good reason to be proud of him there, Larry.'

Joshua beamed awkwardly, flushing slightly.

Larry nodded, looking away from the boy, back to Francine. 'Yeah, you've done a good job with him there, Franny. Even though often it hasn't been easy.' Last chance for him to tell Franny how proud he was of her, keeping a stable home wrapped around Joshua, despite the odds.

Larry talked directly with Joshua for a moment about school, asking him which subjects he preferred, even though he already half-knew from their e-mails back and forth: preferred English and History to Maths and Science. Liked languages too, particularly French. Preferred Tolkien to Rowling, though of recent he'd turned more to some of the older classics: Dumas, Dickens, *Lord of the Flies* and *Tom Sawyer*. 'Fantasy is, okay, but they tell me a bit more about how *real* life is. Or *was*.'

'That's good . . . that's good.' Larry nodded sagely. Practically retelling his own words when he'd first recommended the books in e-mails months back. Josh's way of telling him that he'd taken the advice and was reading them. Telling him before it was too late.

That trivia barrier broken without them hardly realizing it, Francine talked about her work in the shoe shop, that if she could find another job with the same friendly hours that paid better, she'd take it like a shot. Larry appreciating that in fact it wasn't that trivial, because the hours were linked to her being able to meet Josh from school. *Sacrifice*. Larry deciding then to lighten things by telling her about Roddy's last Crosby routine, Franny holding one hand by her mouth as she laughed, as if she shouldn't be laughing in a place like this, and especially not at this time; an anxious glance towards the guard outside through the open viewing hatch, worried what he would think. But Larry thinking, it was so good to see her laughing. *So good*. Hardly in fact able to remember the last time he'd seen her smile or laugh; brief, fragmented flashes of their wedding day and Joshua being born making the years since seem all the more lost, *wasted*.

Larry hastily pushed the thought away. 'Though I told Roddy straight that it wasn't half as funny as seeing him struggle to save the day in front of that crab-faced woman at the BOP hearing. He was back-paddling faster than a duck facing ten Chinese chefs . . . until that Ayliss guy turned up to save his neck. Or mine, as it so happens.' Larry shook his head, grimacing. 'If I'd miss anything from this place, then it'd be Roddy. And maybe the library a bit, too.'

Ayliss. Saving neck. But as much as they'd all desperately tip-toed around the subject, talking about anything but, suddenly it was back before them. Larry's death. Only thirty-two hours away now. The shadow of it hanging so close that it was stifling, suffocating. *Inescapable.* With the mention of Ayliss, Franny's eyes darting rapidly as if unwilling to accept the inevitability of that shadow, she leapt for what she saw as a possible escape route.

'I heard that new lawyer of yours, Ayliss, on a radio phone-in a few days back after Candaret turned down your pardon . . . and he said he wasn't giving up yet. Not by a long shot. Said that he truly believed you were innocent and in fact had someone visiting the prison over the next few days that would hopefully, once and for all, prove it.'

'Yeah.' Larry nodded, smiling dryly. Jac hamming it up as Ayliss, trying to get a doubt bandwagon rolling. Never say die. 'A psychiatrist.' Larry explained about Ormdern's two sessions and what they'd hoped to find either with his old pool game or lack of detail recalled about the Roche house. He shook his head as he finished. 'But in the end, they didn't hit on anything. Not enough, anyway.' He shrugged. 'Though apparently Ayliss is still out there, chasing down, from what he tells me, "some vital final leads uncovered from the sessions".'

Francine reached out and gently clasped one of his hands. 'So there's still *some* hope left. Still someone out there fighting for you.'

He clasped back at her hand, realizing in that moment that, like her smile and laugh, she'd touched him more in this past half hour than she had in eleven years. He grimaced tightly. 'Franny, I don't think it's right to fool ourselves that he'll suddenly pull a rabbit out the hat. He's probably saying all

482

that just to make me feel good, keep my hopes up. Candaret said no, and in the end those sessions didn't dig up anything. I might just have to accept that that's it.'

'But surely, Larry, if he's still out there trying, then –'

Larry squeezed tighter at her hand. 'It's okay, Franny . . . it's *okay*. I've accepted it. Because, you know, at . . .' He looked down awkwardly, the right words suddenly elusive. 'At some stage . . . I've got to. It's just not right clinging on till the last moment with false hope, when I should be trying to make peace with–' He was about to say 'my God', but changed tack at the last second; it de-personalized too much from Fran and Josh. 'With myself in my own mind. And that inner peace is real important to me right now, so I can say the things to you and Josh that need to be said.' He kept hold of her hand, though more gently now. 'I want to thank you first off for bringing Josh up straight and true when, like I said before, God knows often it couldn't have been easy with me not there through all the years. And I don't even have to ask you to promise me to keep doing that good job, because I know you will. And to say that . . . that I *always* loved you . . . even though I often had a strange way of showing it back then.' Francine, eyes glistening heavier with tears, shaking her head as if to say, *No, no . . . you don't need to say this to me now,* or perhaps feeling awkward at hearing it, not wishing it to be the last thing she heard from him, remembered him by; and him eager to get the words out before his resolve went, say what he should have said years ago, but never did because he was too blind or proud or foolish or stubborn, knowing that if he didn't say it now, he never would. 'And I . . . I probably never did stop loving you. And to say that . . . *that* . . .' But as hard as it had been to say everything so far, this was by far the hardest. 'I'm . . . I'm sorry. *So sorry* for having done what I did. Let you and Josh down.'

Francine crumbled then, the tears flowing freely down her cheeks. Joshua's eyes too were glassy, both of them still clinging to that hope mentioned of Ayliss still trying to save him, not wanting to accept what was happening, not wanting to hear from Larry what sounded now like a goodbye speech, their pleading eyes screaming at him, '*You might have accepted what's happening, found peace with yourself, but we haven't. We haven't!*' And as much as one part of Larry was glad that he'd said what he had – in fact what he should have said eleven or twelve years ago – another part of him cursed ever having met Jac McElroy. For filling him with hope, caring again.

Before that, he'd had it all pretty well worked out: his family had all but given up on him, so in turn him giving up on them and what little there was left in this life for him wasn't that difficult. Seemed almost the next natural progressive step, as did turning to God. Though he did truly believe, it wasn't just a second option, a crutch because God was the only person left in this world who he felt hadn't deserted him.

But one effect it had, though it hadn't dawned on him until later, was that when he turned more to God and away from worldly life, love and caring – most of it already stripped from him in any case – when he made that final turn away, nobody really noticed. As if he was already a shadow, and so that final slipping away was barely visible. And at that moment he also half-died, and the daily grind and horrors and isolation of Libreville over the years steadily chipped away at that other half until there was practically nothing left.

At that final low moment, the only consolation was that death – the shadow of execution hanging over him – no longer held any threat, because there was so little of life left for him. So little would be taken.

But then this Jac McElroy had come along, talking about family and caring and hope, about *life*; and as he finally let himself be drawn into that, started to care once more, he'd become afraid of death again. Because there was suddenly much more of life, more that seemed worthwhile, that would be taken away. He wanted nothing more now than to see his son grow tall, go to college, get a girlfriend, avoid all the mistakes he'd made . . . rather than just have to imagine it all happening; but the last thing he wanted at this moment was his son to see that, see his fear of dying, the longing in his eyes.

And minutes later, as they said their final tearful goodbyes, and Larry hugged them tighter than ever before, while he felt his heart soar as they said they loved him too, Josh adding that he'd never forget him – '*You'll always be my pa*', as if the others since had only *half* filled that role – Larry couldn't bear to see the pain and unwillingness to accept his death in their eyes.

And so part of him wished it had been like before: him already half-forgotten, just a shadow, and then he could have just quietly slipped away without anyone hardly noticing. Not caused them any pain or trouble.

'So there she is in this neck-brace, her face like she's gone five rounds with Tyson, and she says: I've been in an accident. *Really?* I say.'

Two vice detectives and another sergeant smiled as Brennan started with the story in the Eighth District canteen. This sounded like it was going to be good.

'But she's as sour-faced as a turkey's ass, this one. I got more chance of raising a smile from a funeral director.'

The smiles lapsed into chuckles as Brennan got to the reason for her accident: slamming on her car brakes because she'd just seen her ex-husband of seven years, and then convinced that it wasn't him. 'And when I suggested to her that maybe, with her only seeing him for two seconds, she might have been mistaken – she looks ready to kill. Starts giving me a lecture about when you've been married to someone for a while, you recognize them in the first millisecond, and anyway, she says, there was no recognition on his face when he saw me. *What*, he didn't slam on his brakes too? I'm about to say . . .' More chuckling, Brennan in his element as he hammered up the story, saying by that stage he was worried for his own safety if he showed even the trace of a smile, starting to get lockjaw from holding it in check. 'And at one point she goes to nod, but can't with the neck-brace . . .' Full-blown guffaws now. Brennan held out one palm. 'Then it started to get even more interesting, because it turns out her ex is no less than Darrell Ayliss, Larry Durrant's new lawyer . . .'

At the table behind them, Lieutenant Pyrford had only been half-listening to the story as he sipped at a coffee. He was waiting for robbery reports on four downtown stores for a suspect held over at the Fifth District, and had been told they'd be fifteen minutes or so. But as Darrell Ayliss and Durrant were mentioned, he looked over. And as the penny at the back of his brain dropped fully, he leant across and interrupted the conversation.

'Excuse me . . . you said that this ex-wife of Ayliss's claimed that the man she saw wasn't her husband?'

'That's right.'

'Pretty close look-alike – but not him?'

'Yeah . . . yeah.' Brennan slightly bemused by Pyrford's sudden interest. 'That's about it.'

That single penny becoming a jackpot cascade as the rest of it fell into place. *McElroy. Morvaun Jaspar. Ayliss.* 'Do you know who's heading up the Jac McElroy investigation here?'

'Lieutenant Derminget,' one of the vice detectives answered.

'Do you have a number?'

'Yeah.' The detective flipped open his cell-phone, scrolled down, read it out.

Pyrford dialled and drifted out of the canteen into the corridor as it answered – background traffic noise – and explained his thinking to Derminget. 'It's just that with McElroy having represented Jaspar, Jaspar's past strong form with disguises . . . and now Ayliss's ex-wife claiming that it isn't him. I might be putting two and two together and coming up with six – but it would certainly explain why McElroy's suddenly disappeared off the face of the earth.'

'*Yeah* . . . it certainly would.' No sightings or trace of

486

McElroy now for a full week. Broughlan had chewed his ass so hard, he hardly had anything left to sit on. And as Ayliss, Derminget reflected, McElroy would have been able to continue representing Durrant. 'Thanks for that.'

'Do you want us to haul Jaspar in again, see what we can find out?'

'No. Not at this stage. I don't want him alerted until I've worked out the best way to handle this. I'll call you back if I need some help there. And again, thanks.'

By the time Derminget got back to his car, he'd worked out how to play everything: he didn't want to alert Ayliss/McElroy either. He'd made that mistake once already. That ruled out politely asking Ayliss in under some spurious guise related to Durrant – he'd get suspicious – *or* putting out TV or news bulletins: if he saw them before the public pointed the finger, he'd go to ground again. The other problem was that they didn't have a photo of the real Ayliss, and those available would probably be from seven years ago.

Derminget started up, but as he looked round to pull out, the thought suddenly hit him. He got Libreville's number from 411, then phoned them and asked whether they might have some good security cam shots of lawyer Darrell Ayliss who'd recently visited them. 'As close and clear as possible.' He gave them the Eighth District e-mail to send them to, stressing the urgency. Then he phoned into Central Dispatch to put out an APB on Ayliss. 'Photos should be with you shortly.'

Hopefully they'd get Ayliss under arrest before he knew they were even looking for him; before he knew what hit him. Then, if they'd made a big mistake, they could apologize later.

Fuck, *fuck . . . fuck*!

Nel-M was back to bashing his steering wheel as he returned to his car, having checked Truelle's office and discovered that nobody was there, not even his secretary.

He drove over to Truelle's Faubourg Marigny apartment, but Truelle wasn't there either.

Fuck . . . *fuck*! Two more steering wheel bashes, one leaving Truelle's apartment, the other arriving back at his office. Still nobody there.

After the messy drama in Vancouver, he'd been hoping for an easy ride with this one: get Truelle out of his office on some ruse, two quick shots in a side alley, and done. *Finito*.

Years now he'd been looking forward to putting a bullet through Truelle's head with impunity. No possible comebacks. And now that moment was finally here, Truelle was nowhere to be found. Sensing that everything was suddenly closing in on him, Truelle had no doubt decided to disappear until after Durrant's death.

Truelle's secretary obviously knew where he was; that's why she'd hightailed it too. Didn't want to stay front-line, facing all the flak.

Nel-M took out his cell-phone and called Vic Farrelia.

'Truelle's secretary, Cynthia? Do you have anything on tape with her full name or the district she lives in, so I could maybe track down her address?

'I can do better than that,' Farrelia said. 'I picked up her full address somewhere, I'm sure. She gave it one day to a friend she hadn't seen for a while. Give me a minute or two, I'll try and find it.'

Twelve minutes after Farrelia's return call, Nel-M was knocking on Cynthia's second floor apartment door in Bywater.

'Who is it?' she called out.

Nel-M didn't answer. Then, hearing her move close to the door the other side, probably looking through the spyhole, he barged hard against it.

'Western . . .' Another hard barge . . . 'Fucking . . . Union!' The lock gave way on the last barge; obviously she didn't have Truelle's heavy dead-bolts.

Cynthia was wide-eyed, shrieking with each barge and

backing a step away, then turned to run as Nel-M finally burst through. He slammed the door behind him and caught up with her at the end of her hallway, clamping one hand over her mouth to stifle her shrieks. Breathless, sweat beads popped on his forehead, he listened out for a second for whether anyone had heard: doors opening across the corridor, footsteps coming along to investigate. But there was nothing, no movement.

Half lifting Cynthia, her shrieks and groans heavily muffled by the hand across her mouth, he bundled her into a back bedroom, shut the door.

'Okay,' he said, taking his gun out. 'We can do this one of a few ways. Either you tell me straight out where your boss Truelle has gone – or after we've played breaking fingers or Russian roulette.'

She shook her head, lips pressed stubbornly tight as she looked anxiously between him and the gun; hoping, praying that it was a bluff.

Nel-M reached out and grabbed one of her arms, placing her hand in his, her wrist gripped tight, but his touch against her hands and fingers curiously light, soothing. He arched an eyebrow. 'Are you sure you wanna go through this? Be a lot easier just to tell me?'

She shook her head again, though less certainly this time. She writhed and tried to wrench her hand from his grip, but he was too firm, too strong. He gripped tighter and, pushing hard back on her index finger, snapped the bone as if it was a twig.

Her howling scream was quickly muffled by his hand back over her mouth. 'Okay, let's try again. Where's Truelle gone?'

But again that wide-eyed defiant stare, tears rolling down her cheeks now from the pain and from fear. He broke one more finger, her still defiant, Nel-M deciding then that she was making too much noise and it was hard for him to cover quickly with his hand over her mouth.

He tipped the bullets out of his gun, holding one up as he put it back in, then, just before sliding the barrel into her mouth, asked her again where Truelle was. Still that wide-eyed, fuck-you stare, though scrunching tight at the last second as the empty click came, her whole body shuddering. To Nel-M's amazement, she managed to brave out one more empty click before her resolve finally snapped and with a breathless, 'Okay . . . *okay*', she agreed to tell him.

She'd brought the appointment book with her in case someone broke into the office to read it. He shuffled her through to the lounge, one arm clamped tight around her, as she got the book and pointed out the Cuba mailbox address.

Nel-M wrote it down. 'And that's all you have?'

'Yeah. That's it.'

The truth, he sensed. 'And have you given this to anyone else?' She started to shake her head, but as his eyes narrowed, reading her hesitancy, *untruth*, he moved his gun towards her again.

She changed to a hasty nod. 'Yeah . . . yeah. A lawyer. *Ayliss* . . . I believe that was his name.'

'How long ago?'

She shrugged. 'Four, maybe five hours.'

Nel-M nodded thoughtfully, absently sliding the bullets back into his gun. *Cuba, four or five hours jump on him?*

Cynthia's eyes were fixed on his gun, her breath catching slightly. 'There . . . there weren't any bullets in your gun all along.'

'I know. I palmed it.' Nel-M smiled slyly as he slid in the last two bullets. 'When you were a little girl, didn't you just love surprises?'

Yanking her hair back, Nel-M put the gun barrel back in her mouth and pulled the trigger.

'Yep, I managed to dig up something,' Stratton said. 'Mercedes 300SL lifted from a driveway on 4th Street, just two houses in from Coliseum, while a couple were away on holiday. They apparently already had a Jaguar and a Caddy in the garage, that's why the car was out.'

'Sounds promising.' Jac had decided to use his time waiting for flight-boarding to make his follow-up calls. He'd tried Mack Elliott's number to see if he'd recalled anything yet – no answer – then he'd called Stratton. 'And it happened the same night as Jessica Roche's murder?'

'That's the thing that can't be said for sure. The couple, the Lapointes, were away for ten days, and from the police report the neighbours were vague on when the car went missing. Closest it can be nailed down to is two days before the night of the murder or three days after. But there's at least a *chance* it went down that same night.' Stratton sucked in his breath. 'Thing is, that's the only recorded crime close by that could have been that night. It's either that, or nothing.'

Fourth Street? From Jac's pacing the district a few nights back, that's where he'd worked out the murderer would have probably cut through to get back to his car. 'Yeah, okay. Certainly it's close enough for someone there to have seen the murderer leaving the Roches' house. Anything else yet on it?'

Jac looked up as his flight was called. *Echoing PA, clamour of other voices swirling around.* He'd checked in for his flight as late as possible, was nervous being too long among crowds, knowing that Melanie Ayliss was on the prowl for him.

'Still waiting on a list of possible MO matches from that time. Then fast-forwarding to those still active now before I can get some mug-shots in front of the staff at that internet café.'

'Yeah, right.' Jac got up and headed towards the gate. Echoing footsteps among the voices, *walking through Libreville* . . . legs shaky, nerves biting as he viewed the passport officers ahead. First time Ayliss's passport had been put to the test. 'And timing?' *That clock-hand ticking hour-by-hour heavier in his head.* Only thirty hours left, and half of that would now be eaten up getting to Truelle in Cuba.

'Hopefully, I'll get everything I want before the day's out. And if that internet café's still open, get the photos in front of them tonight. But if not, it's going to have to wait till first light tomorrow morning.'

'Okay.' Six people ahead in the queue, Jac's stomach doing a quick turn as one of the passport officers ahead, surveying who was approaching, eyed him for the first time. *Melanie Ayliss's eyes locking on him.* A rock had sunk through his stomach as Coultaine had told him about her notifying the police. Coultaine said he was sure that he'd put their minds to rest on that front, but what if he hadn't? 'I'll be plane-hopping pretty much till the early hours, anyway. But I might get a chance to contact you between connections late tonight.'

'Sure, if you can. Where are you going?'

'Nassau, Bahamas.' Because of US travel restrictions, Jac had been warned not to mention his destination was Cuba until he was actually in Nassau. The officers ahead were close enough to hear him now: the queue down to three, passing quickly through . . . *two.*

'Nice.'

'Wish it was. Like everything else right now – another last-ditch shot at saving Larry Durrant's life.' That officer ahead locking eyes on him again, Jac worried that with all the Ayliss padding he was sweating more than he should, looked more nervous than he should. Or perhaps part of his face had finally melted. Something in the officer's eyes. *Something.* Jac swallowed hard. *Forged passport, Melanie Ayliss's police alert, travelling to Cuba when you shouldn't, face melting off* . . . take your pick on what might be wrong! *One.* 'I'd . . . I'd better go now.'

'Yeah, speak to you later. Good luck.'

'Thanks. You too.'

The usual offhand reciprocation; but as Jac handed over his passport and saw again that look in the officer's eyes, and he was then asked to step to one side as his passport was passed to a colleague behind to check on his computer – he was in little doubt which one of them needed luck the most at that moment.

41

Torvald Engelson, Tor or TDO to the other Libreville guards and inmates, liked to think of himself as a good and caring 'death custodian'. Since the changeover from the electric chair to lethal injection in 1991, the final lethal dose was given by expert medical practitioners from outside, different ones each time, administered in a separate adjoining room to where it would finally feed through to Larry Durrant, strapped down to a gurney. And even with those six straps holding him down, each one would be secured by a different guard from the 'execution team'. At each stage, responsibility for Durrant's death was shifted as much as possible away from any single person.

In that same spirit, throughout the whole process Torvald himself would never touch Larry directly – except perhaps to lay a comforting hand on his shoulder the night before and say 'goodbye' – but it was Torvald's responsibility to make all the preparations, make sure everything ran without hitch: arrange the practitioners, a medical examination of Durrant two hours before that, select the 'execution team', check-list of those who wished to be present in the viewing room, timing to go through to the 'night-before' cell, priest, last meal . . .

Torvald had all of that turning through his head as he paced, clipboard and folder in hand, towards Larry's cell.

At forty-one, a 'striking' rather than conventionally good-looking man, with a shock of dark blond hair and green eyes inherited from a Norwegian father, who forty years back had decided to fish in the warmer waters of the Gulf of Mexico, and pale mahogany skin-tone from an African-American mother – when he'd asked inmates why the nickname TDO, 'The Dark One', they'd answered that he had the darkest skin you could imagine for a blond-haired man. But Torvald suspected it was because of his work not only as death custodian, but also as one of the main guards in the prison hospice. They thought he had a fascination with death.

Not true, Torvald knew in his heart; in fact, quite the opposite. He did it because he cared; at times, probably too much. Horror stories abounded of the old electric chair malfunctioning and half-frying prisoners before they finally died; and with injections, prisoners with so many track marks that the IV for the poison feed couldn't be inserted properly, or the necessary medical checks weren't made and they reacted badly, their body contorting so wildly they had to be sat on by two or three guards.

Not on his watch. Prisoners had been stripped of all dignity in life, he was going to ensure it was at least there for them in death; and with that same philosophy, his work in the hospice had become a natural follow-on.

But the problem with all of that caring was that in the final hours, by necessity, Torvald would find himself drawn closer to the prisoners – then so quickly they'd be gone! Torvald had never quite got used to that wrench and the void it left. Though he'd never complained to the prison psychiatrist at the bi-annual counselling sessions established to ensure prison guards' continuing stability; always feared that if he said anything, that duty might be taken away from him.

To him, the prisoners' mental well-being in those final hours was more important than his own.

The guard on duty, Warrell, let Torvald through the last gate to Durrant's cell-row. The clock on the wall behind read 5.38 p.m. Warrell then accompanied him for the final fifteen paces.

Closeness. Caring. The only problem with Larry Durrant was that over the past few years he'd become something of a favourite of Torvald's; he held a soft spot for him aside from the extra closeness that, by necessity, the death process would bring.

It had only happened a couple of times before, when he'd allowed himself to get *that* close, and both times it had ripped his heart out.

Torvald closed his eyes for a second, solemn acceptance, as he nodded for Warrell to open Durrant's cell door. This wasn't going to be easy.

'Four or five hours ahead, you reckon?'

'Yeah. But if Ayliss got the flight I think he did, we might have shaved some back. He had a longer wait than me for the next flight there.'

At the other end of the line, the steady cadence of Roche's breathing measuring options. Though for once Nel-M found it strangely soothing, like the gentle fall of surf. He could easily drift off to it: he hadn't slept much on the flight from Vancouver, and no doubt more fitful hours lay ahead. He checked his watch: thirty-five minutes till boarding.

'And getting a gun there?'

'No problem. Dollars talk loud down there. Within a half hour I'll have found a guy in a Havana back street to sell me one, along with his sister thrown in as part of the deal.'

'Okay.' The breathing settling, accepting. 'But we might have to face that if this Ayliss gets to Truelle first, he could break him before you even get there. It might be time to put our contingency plans into play.'

'Suppose so.' If they didn't play those cards now, they never would.

'Which means you and I have each got a call to make.'

Derminget's APB announcement had gone out almost three hours after Jac went through the check-out at New Orleans Airport.

The passport officer there, Paul Styman, had found his eye drawn to Ayliss because of his crumpled cream suit and perspiring, anxious appearance – but he'd have nevertheless quickly waved him through; until, that is, he looked at his passport and flight destination. Seven years in Mexico, now heading to Nassau.

Styman decided to have his colleague check him against a list of suspected drug runners, just in case.

Nothing came up. He waved Ayliss through, and an hour after that he handed over his shift.

But when he returned eight hours later, within fifteen minutes he spotted the APB alert on screen when he leant over to check something else.

'This is the guy we checked out early afternoon,' he said to his colleague, still on from the earlier shift. 'How long has this been through?'

His partner shrugged. 'Five hours or so.'

'And didn't you recognize him?'

His partner shrugged again. He wasn't sure he'd even looked at the man or the passport photo, had probably just tapped in the name for a match. And he'd done eighteen or twenty name checks since.

Styman looked at the contact details: Lieutenant Derminget. Eighth District. He called the number and explained what had happened.

'*Nassau*?' Derminget confirmed. 'Nine or ten hours ago, you say?'

'Yeah. But I remember it was a pretty roundabout route on the ticket. Stop-offs in Atlanta *and* Miami. He might not have arrived yet.'

'Thanks.' Derminget called out to one of his team to get through to Miami International while he phoned Nassau.

Both airports said that they'd get back directly with information.

Derminget tapped his fingers anxiously against one thigh as he paced up and down a tight four-yard run, waiting. As the hours of the day had ticked by without anything happening, no news or sightings of Ayliss, he'd feared he was in for another long haul. McElroy somehow alerted and gone to ground again.

Miami phoned back after nine minutes, Nassau after fourteen.

But with Miami informing them that Ayliss's flight to Nassau had left over three hours ago, they knew that he'd have probably long since passed through Nassau customs. They weren't holding their breath when Nassau's call came through.

'Yeah, yeah,' Derminget said almost disinterestedly. 'Pretty much what we'd already guessed from the call we just had from Miami.' Derminget checked his watch. Not that large an island. He'd just have to get the Bahamian police to try and track Ayliss down.

'But then we have him catching a later flight to Havana with Cubana Airlines. Left not that long ago, by the looks of it.'

'How long ago? *How long?*' Derminget realizing that he was practically shouting as half the squad room looked over. The past week of McElroy giving him the run-around with Broughlan snapping at his heels had worn his nerves thin.

'Just over forty minutes ago.'

'And what's the flight time from Nassau to Cuba?'

'Uuuh . . .' Sound of keyboard tapping. 'An hour and a half.'

'Thanks.' Fucking yes . . . *yes*! It looked like they were still in time to have Ayliss stopped at Havana customs.

Derminget called across the squad room for someone who might have good Spanish.

Priest? 'Yeah. As long as it's Father Kennard and not that asshole Chaplain Foster. I think that Stephen King line – the important thing is whether God believes in *you* – went straight over his head.'

Torvald smiled as he got back to the rest of his check-list. *Haveling holding his hand at the last minute?* No. Larry could get to God on his own, thanks, didn't need Haveling's help. *Last meal?* Beef Po-Boy. Reminded him of his childhood and good ol' days in the Ninth. *Family and friends to be present at the execution, observing?*

'No . . . None. That's why my family came today.' Fran and Josh had trouble enough accepting his death, let alone watching it. 'And Roddy and Sal and the rest here, I'll say my goodbyes to tonight.'

'Okay. But before ten, Larry – because that's when you have to go through to the night-before cell. And if you want a shower, last chance is tonight, too. There's a sink in tomorrow's cell, but no access back to the showers or anything else this side.'

Larry nodded pensively. It was almost as if as soon as he went through that last gate at the end, he'd already died. No access back to the rest of the world. But perhaps that was just a natural continuance of his life for the past eleven years: gradually diminishing as he was shuffled from one box to another, access denied to family and friends, love and *life*, until there was only one box left.

Torvald felt his chest tighten as he watched the emotions on Larry's face. Another part of his duty as death custodian: observe how the prisoner was coping with the situation. Last hours counsellor.

He'd started the meeting with a shrug and an apology. 'Sorry about this, Larry. Few things to go through . . . some of them maybe seeming stupid.' They knew each other too well to try and hide behind bullshit or formality. 'But, you know, it's gotta be done.'

'That's okay, Tor. Glad it's you rather than some of those other oafs out there.'

Oafs. Torvald shared with Larry the guards he'd nominated for the execution team, Larry appreciative that he'd been careful to avoid any of Bateson's clique. 'Thanks.'

But from then on, Torvald had gone through the rest of his check-list mechanically to help shield his emotions; and he noticed too that Larry answered quickly, offhand, even when talking about his family visiting, whom he hadn't seen for a while.

And he wondered whether Larry too was trying to distance himself from what was happening, and was treating him coolly because, despite their past closeness, Larry now saw Torvald as part of the machinery of his death.

But it wasn't that. It wasn't that at all.

Because as much as Larry knew how the life had been crushed out of him these past long years, so that now there was only a faint vestige left – he'd also seen it crushing his wife and son that day. The years for it to take its toll on him, he'd seen oppressing them in only a few minutes as they faced what was happening to him the next day, that terrible weight slumping their shoulders. And at the last second, as they realized he might see the last hope dying in their eyes, they made sure to avert them, wouldn't look at him directly.

And he could see it happening now too with Torvald Engelson. This guard with whom he'd exchanged more thoughts than any other guard over the years – had recommended books on Norse and Viking history and *Beowulf* when he'd wanted to learn about his Norwegian roots, and fifteen months back had shared with him how he'd coped with his mother dying when Torvald lost his father – could hardly look him in the eye any more, his shoulders too slumped with what was about to happen to Larry, even though, as death custodian, that process should have long ago stopped fazing him.

But Larry didn't, *couldn't* blame them; he blamed the system. The death-penalty machinery that crushed relentlessly all in its path.

In murder cases, premeditation was a vital factor; Larry should know more than most, because it was one thing argued as missing in his own case to try and spare him the death penalty. The final element that transformed random violence to callous calculation.

If a murderer admitted in court that they'd told their victim they were going to kill them at a specific time on a certain day, then left them in a cell to contemplate their impending death – the jury would consider it one of the most chilling, calculating murder accounts they'd ever heard.

And the victim, unwilling to accept their fate, would scream and claw at the cell walls. The family too, if told of that impending fate, would wail and scream and protest.

But prisoners on Death Row didn't. Their shoulders simply slumped, the light of hope faded from their eyes, and they accepted.

Because it was the system.

The weight of it pressing inch by inch down on them. Accept. Accept. *Accept.* Until they caved in totally in defeat, no hope left for them to cling to.

And as ten minutes later Torvald finished his briefing and the cell door slammed back behind him, Larry had never felt so cold and alone, the impact jarring icily through him, making him shiver. His eyes filled, a single tear rolling out; that too feeling lonely and cold as it trickled down one cheek. *Alone.*

At the last minute, Torvald had reached out and touched Larry's arm. 'If there's anything you need over these next hours, Larry . . . just ask.' And at that second, he did finally meet Larry's eyes, and Larry saw what he'd suspected: that last light of hope had gone from them.

Because as much as at times he'd given up on himself, there'd always been that light and hope and warmth from others; he could see it in their eyes. And now that was finally gone, there was nothing left. No hope. Nothing left to save him.

Within three hours, Bob Stratton had a list of likely MO mug-shots for the 4th Street grand-auto theft of twelve years ago, and an hour and a half after that had received an update with current mug-shots of those still active now.

Sixteen photos. But only five looked like they might have a chance of matching the partial cam-shots and the description Ayliss had given him. Stratton looked at his watch: 6.34 p.m. If he was quick and downtown traffic was kind, he just might be able to get them in front of the staff at the internet café before they closed at 7 p.m.

He got there with four minutes to spare, but there was some calling out as to who might have been working the day in question, before a light bulb of recognition came on in the eyes of a blonde-with-a-green-stripe wiping down the espresso machine. Tracy.

'Yeah . . . yeah, I remember,' Tracy said. 'Lawyer guy that phoned in a panic and ran in a couple of weeks back, just missed the guy. Gave him a cam-video to take away.'

'That's the one.' Stratton had decided to show her all sixteen mug-shots in sets of four at a time, and laid the cam photos to one side as a reminder. 'Now, out of these . . . anyone that looks like the guy that was here that day?'

One photo in set two, though she couldn't be sure; but then she twisted her mouth in the same way over another photo in set three. 'Uuuh, again, I can't be a hundred per cent sure.'

Stratton put the two photos side by side. 'Strongest bet – if you were forced to choose?'

She pointed to one, but then seconds later became unsure and her finger wavered over the other. 'I'm sorry . . . on this one his hair just isn't right, too wild, too much of an Afro – but the rest, hmmm? Maybe his hair's changed since this photo.' Tracy tilted her head, as if to get a better angle. 'If they were both smiling, I'd know for sure.'

'Why's that?'

'He's got a big gap between his front teeth.'

Stratton could just imagine how that advice would go down with police departments: ensuring there's no smiling on mug-shots might make perps look more severe and menacing, more like *criminals*, but you miss out on valuable dental recognition.

Stratton nodded with a no-teeth smile. In the end, not

enough to choose between them; he'd just have to chase up both. 'Thanks.'

And as soon as Stratton got back in his car, he called his contact again, Jack Harris of Fourth District, and got addresses for both names.

'Last known for Roland Cole is Mid-City . . . and Steve Thelwood, along the coast at Long Beach.'

Stratton wrote down the addresses. 'Great. Thanks, Jack.' Then he tried Ayliss's number to bring him up to date, but it didn't answer. Still plane-hopping, no doubt.

When he got to the address in Mid-City, Roland Cole wasn't there and the new apartment tenant didn't know of his whereabouts. 'I been here seven months now, and you're not the first person called askin' for him,' a Biggie Smalls look-alike in jogging pants and a vest informed him. 'Easy to see now why he left no forwardin'.'

Stratton headed along the coast to Long Beach.

There were times when head-guard Glenn Bateson liked to stamp his authority on Libreville; that sense of power over the life and death of its inmates would hit him strongly, make his head almost swim with it, and he'd in turn mark his presence by making his boot-step heavier, more purposeful, along its corridors.

He could practically feel that step shuddering through prisoners from thirty or forty paces away, getting more intense with each stride, so that when he finally came alongside their cells, they could barely look at him, a scant fearful glance that said, '*I'm not really here. You didn't see me.*'

He felt that way now; that sense of power over life and death stronger than he could remember in a long while, as he paced towards the cell of Tally Shavell. But his step wasn't heavy now, in fact it was far lighter than normal, because he didn't want to bring attention to where he was heading.

No scant or uneasy look as Shavell greeted him, those cold, soulless dark eyes stayed on him steadily, unwavering. Equal ground; equal control over life and death at Libreville. The only emotion Shavell showed was the faint lifting of one eyebrow as Bateson explained what he wanted.

'I know.' Bateson thought he hadn't heard right at first and had asked Nel-M to repeat himself above the background activity and voices. Somewhere busy. 'Hit me as strange too, given the timing.'

Shavell kept the eyebrow raised. 'And for doin' this good deed?'

'Thirty grand. In cash to a named account, or translated into disposable goods in here.' Bateson smiled crookedly; he was on the same, and they'd probably each make another thirty big ones from the pills or powder sold on. 'If you know what I mean?'

Shavell's eyes shifted from Bateson as he started planning things out in his mind, with no acknowledgement as Bateson left his cell.

42

When the call came through to Havana's Jose Marti airport, it was taken first of all by a young officer named Ruiz.

Quickly realizing that he was out of his depth, he handed over to his Captain, Sebastian Moragues, who'd started looking over inquisitively as he'd repeated segments for clarification.

New Orleans. Suspected false identity. Cubana flight from Nassau. Moragues' inquisitive frown deepened as the request was repeated.

'So, let me get this clear. This Mr Ayliss arriving soon – you suspect that it might be someone else posing as him? False identity?'

'Yes, that's right.'

'And do you have an official arrest warrant your end for that?'

Brief pause, conferring the other end. 'No . . . no we don't. It's just a suspicion at this stage. Though a very strong one.'

'And based just on this *suspicion* . . . you want us to stop and detain him?' Moragues was old school Castro, and for them the unwritten rule book was clear: no favours for Americans, because they've done none for us the past forty years. So unless it posed a threat to Cuban national security or involved drug-trafficking, which Cuba was keen to keep itself free of, Moragues was going to take a lot of convincing. And with not even the right paperwork in place their end? *Madre de Putas!*

Heavier conferring at the other end, Moragues shaking his head with a wry smile towards Ruiz. *Americanos!*

In New Orleans, Derminget had become increasingly frustrated with the three-way conversation. A young sergeant, Tony Salva, had stepped up to the plate for the call. His family had left Puerto Rico when he was fifteen, and his Spanish, he'd explained to Derminget, was still *'seventy per cent there'*.

'You tell that stiff-head in Cuba,' Derminget barked at Salva, one hand stabbing for emphasis, 'that the guy we believe is posing as Ayliss is actually wanted for murder. And that, we do have a fucking warrant for!'

'I see. Murder. That *is* more serious,' Moragues commented as the translation came over, his smile still there from hearing Derminget's agitation in the background. 'But this suspected connection between these two men. Have you taken *that* before a judge with some sort of proof to get an arrest warrant?'

Heavier background shouting from the other end, almost screaming at one point. Moragues held the receiver a few inches away from his ear, shrugging towards Ruiz before he brought it back again for the translation.

'No . . . we haven't got that particular warrant yet.'

'Then I would kindly suggest that when you *do* have that . . . that would be the time to be troubling us here in Havana. Otherwise we could both find ourselves in an unfortunate mess if it turns out to be a false detention.' Not good for tourism: complaints about foreign nationals being unnecessarily detained at Havana airport!

The background commotion hit fever pitch this time, with a fair few expletives – the only words in fact that Moragues understood. His smile widened. He couldn't wait for the translation.

'My . . . my boss hears what you say. But he's still insistent that you stop Mr Ayliss when he arrives at Havana airport in half an hour's time. In fact – as one recognized police authority to another – he demands it.'

'He does now, does he?' Moragues gently licked his top lip. 'Well, you tell your *Jefe* from me that he can take his *demand* and, along with the trade embargoes of the past forty years and the exploding cigar the CIA sent to our dear Fidel – stick it in his *culo!*'

At the other end, Derminget's nerves had all but snapped; and as he saw Salva's face redden as he listened to something more lengthy, he started screaming, 'What's he saying! *What's he fucking saying?'*

Salva looked up finally as he reached to put the phone down. 'He says he doesn't think he can help.'

Last shower . . . *last time he'd feel water against his body.* It felt strange, unreal; the same as it did accepting that seeing Fran and Josh earlier that day had been for the last time. And tomorrow, last meal, last time food would touch his lips, *then . . .*

Even though he'd had eleven long years to get used to it happening, now the time was finally here, it felt odd, surreal; and so now the only way he could accept it was to numb himself to it, switch off a part of himself. Like one of those machines or computers on sleep-mode. Brain half-switched off, body . . . *soul.*

But as part of him switched off, another suddenly became more attuned. He could hear things in the prison he hadn't heard before: beyond the steady background thrum of its boilers, a faint clicking as pipes contracted; distant voices through the ceiling grille, echoing along the ventilation shaft from guards or prisoners talking; and earlier that night, a steady breeze rustling through the trees outside, and, as it drifted a certain way, some music carrying on it. He'd been told that the protesters beyond the gates were playing music, but hadn't heard it until that moment.

And now as he felt the water running down his skin, memories that he thought had long ago faded: bathing Joshua as a baby, feeling the water slide like velvet against his soft skin, Josh's eyes bright and dancing as he looked back up at him, giggling . . . Fran and himself on the beach one day when they'd gone along the coast to Gulfport, the year before Josh was born, Fran splashing him as she ran in the shallows, and him splashing her back, her looking so bright-eyed and beautiful . . . *so beautiful . . .*

The images now so real that he fancied he could still taste the salt in the water as some of it splashed on his face . . . before realizing that it was his own tears as they'd touched his lips.

I was only dreaming . . .

He'd faded out the foreground, there was just the background left; maybe what he should have done all along in Libreville. Faded out the heavy clump of the guards' boots along the walkways, their shouts and taunts, the night-time weeping of other prisoners, the cacophony of voices now in the showers . . . faded it all out until there was nothing left but him and Fran and Josh together again, smiling and hugging each other as if the eleven years in between hadn't really happened . . . *just a dream . . .*

Larry jolted sharply, as if he had suddenly awoken. *Cacophony of voices!* They *had* faded, it wasn't just in his head. It was suddenly quieter in the showers. *Roddy!*

Larry leapt out and looked towards Roddy. Since the attack three weeks back, he'd made sure to shower at the same time as Roddy every night. He'd said his last goodbyes to Sal, Roddy, BC and Theo just before, then had headed to the showers with Roddy. Last night of protection, BC saying he'd cover Roddy's back as best he could after Larry was gone.

And so Larry was slightly confused as he saw Tally Shavell emerge through the steam, with Jay-T moving in a few paces behind himself, and Silass to one side. Why didn't they just wait a day when Roddy would be more vulnerable?

Then, as he saw the focus and intent in their eyes and their angle of movement, he realized that they were moving in on himself! Though it didn't compute quickly enough given the odd timing, Jay-T taking the last two steps to grip him from behind as the shiv appeared in Tally's hand and he lunged for Larry.

Larry swung back in reflex with an elbow at Jay-T, twisting his body away at the same time. He managed to shift his abdomen eight inches, but still the shiv caught him on one side, slicing through the soft flesh just above his hip-bone.

Tally pulled back and thrust swiftly again for mid-stomach, but Larry's second elbow swing caught Jay-T directly in the wind-pipe, and he managed to jerk free and completely side-step Tally's second lunge as Jay-T fell away, choking. Tally went then for a scything sweep, Larry jumping back clear of it and shifting round so that Silass couldn't get to him easily, would have had to move through Tally's path. Roddy had sidled around the back of them, and now, seeing that Larry was more in control, darted off to alert the guards.

Tally's eyes gleamed wildly, his breath falling short. Larry had the measure of him now, and he could see from Tally's eyes that a part of him knew it too – though still fighting against it through a fireball mist of adrenalin and hatred – and as Tally lunged again, Larry side-stepped easily and gripped his knife-arm, snapping it at the joint against his thigh.

Larry snatched the shiv and had Tally twisted around in a forearm neck grip, the shiv blade tight at his throat, before Silass could move in. He backed away a step and pressed the blade hard against Tally's skin, drawing a teardrop of blood. Silass and Jay-T glared back challengingly, but held back.

Flurry of boot-steps in the background, Warrell and another two guards appearing, Roddy just behind them. Warrell held one hand up towards him.

'Don't do it, Larry!'

'Why not? I'm dying tomorrow – I've got fuck-all to lose.' The alarm bell started jangling then, more guards starting to appear behind Warrell.

'Because . . .' Warrell was lost for a second for an answer. 'Because, what's the point?'

Larry glared back defiantly. 'The point is, getting rid of this slimy fuck once and for all! After I've gone tomorrow, how long do you think Roddy's going to last with Tally still alive?' He jabbed the shiv tighter against Tally's neck, drawing another teardrop of blood. 'I'd be doing not only Roddy a favour, but everyone else around here. One last good deed before I go!'

'With that busted arm . . . he's not going to be able to do much for a while in any case,' Warrell said.

'He's still got *one* good arm.' And, impulse reaction, Larry jammed the shiv into Tally's good arm by his biceps, grinding it around and feeling it tear through muscle, Tally roaring with the pain. Then, as Silass and one of the guards moved half a step closer, he pulled it out and put it tight again to Tally's throat.

At that moment, he could think of nothing better than slitting Tally's throat, rid Libreville of him once and for all, but then, as if reading his thoughts, a voice came from the back of the circle of guards.

'This ain't you, Larry. Don't do it. You're *not* a killer.' Torvald Engelson.

Larry's eyes fixed on Torvald as he came to the forefront to stand by Warrell. 'Don't pride yourself, Tor. You don't know me *that* well. And that's not what the State of Louisiana and the judge said.'

Torvald closed his eyes for a second in submission. 'I didn't know you then, Larry, so I can't say what happened. But I think I know you well enough now: you're *not* a killer. And if you do this now, you might not get where you want to tomorrow.' Torvald closed his eyes again fleetingly, hating himself for playing the religious card now on Larry, but not knowing what else to do. 'Like you said to me the other day – a question of whether God believes in *you*, Larry. Whether *he's* going to accept and understand if you do this now.'

Larry felt himself split like never before in that instant: between what his gut and instinct told him was right, and his heart and conscience said was wrong. Larry felt himself start shaking, his eyes filling as he thought again of the warm reverie of only minutes ago, and him standing here now, cold and shivering, blood streaming down him as he held a shiv to another man's throat.

'I don't know what to think any more, Tor. Long ago given up on what's right and wrong in here. I . . .' But his body language said then what his words were unable to finish. His grip weakened on Tally's neck.

Sensing his indecision, the guards moved in. And as the last of Larry's resolve went and the shiv slipped from his grasp and fell to the floor, they grabbed him and carried him away, Larry nodding towards Torvald with tight-lipped acceptance; Larry not even sure whether it was in thanks, or simply acknowledgement that Torvald knew him better than most.

Killer? Not killer? Twelve long years Larry had been asking himself that same question, along with a few other people that had got to know him along the way; and now, in his final hours, the question was still being asked.

Alaysha found that whenever she was back at her own apartment or Jac's next door, every small sound on the corridor outside made the hairs stand up on the back of her neck.

For that reason, she'd spent as much time as she could at her mother's place, and when she did need to be back home would grab what she needed from her own apartment, then go quickly next door to Jac's. *With* Molly some nights, without when she was working and needed an hour or so to get ready at her own place, Molly already dropped off with Alaysha's mom.

The first night she'd done that, she'd spent half an hour sorting out her clothes and putting on make-up at her own place – but then a sound outside on the corridor had made her skin bristle. When she looked through the spy-hole, it was nothing, visitors to another apartment three doors down; but it suddenly made her more aware of what would have happened if it *had* been something. She moved her main clothes and her make-up bag permanently next door to Jac's.

Secrets. She hadn't told her mother about robbing Malastra. Didn't want her to shoulder any burden of guilt over what the money had been for. *It was for your dialysis and treatment,*

Mom. I know it might have been foolish, but we're talking about your life here!

The only person that knew was Jac. And he wasn't here for her to talk to any more, tell him that with each passing hour her nerves were mounting, jumping out of her skin at the smallest sound outside. She'd been hoping to see him the next night, but there was a message on her answer-phone when she'd grabbed a couple of things before coming to his place to do her make-up for work.

'Alaysha. Adam here. I can't make our meeting tomorrow night, I'm afraid. I've had to leave the country unexpectedly. In fact, I'm on my way right now. Something to do with that big deal I mentioned. I'll call you as soon as I get back.'

Adam. The name he'd chosen, his father's, in case the police were listening in on her line, Jac changing his accent yet again from his own or Ayliss's. *Big deal*: Durrant. A lot of echoing and noise in the background, sounded as if he was actually phoning from the airport.

They'd arranged to meet at nine o'clock, three hours after Durrant's scheduled execution. It would all be over by then; Jac would have been able to share with her how everything had gone. One way or the other. Tears on her shoulder, or cracking a bottle of champagne together.

Alaysha focused in the mirror as she started applying her eyeliner. Some life they were living: her boyfriend like a chameleon, on the run for murder, and her sneaking around from one place to another, anywhere but—

Her nerves suddenly leapt, her eyeliner pencil dog-legging off a quarter-inch, as she heard her doorbell ring next door. She hadn't even heard anyone come along the corridor! She padded silently in her stockinged-feet to the door, looking to the side through the spy-hole: a messenger. FedEx, complete with buff uniform.

He rang the bell again, and at that moment Mrs Orwin's door opened behind him. He pointed to Alaysha's door, saying something about 'special delivery', though Alaysha couldn't see a package in his hand, and then her heart froze as Mrs Orwin's bony finger lifted and pointed to Jac's apartment.

She'd noticed Mrs Orwin peering out a couple of times the night before as she'd gone between one apartment and the other, perhaps eager to alert the police in case that 'killer McElroy' returned, and obviously she'd done the same tonight.

The messenger nodded his thanks and approached Jac's door – Alaysha shrinking back a step as the doorbell rang, her heart beating hard and fast. Memories of that black kid with a message, Gerry at her door a second later. *The gunshot. Jac running through the night from the police.*

She swallowed hard. But that was a street boy; this is a recognized messenger, in a uniform! Get a grip.

He rang the bell again, then four seconds later knocked.

Alaysha moved forward again, risking another glance through the spy-hole: the messenger looking down at his feet for a second, Mrs Orwin still behind him, frowning slightly; an 'I'm sure she was there' expression on her face.

Then finally, deciding he'd waited long enough, he wrote something on a card and slipped it through the mailbox. And as Alaysha saw it come through, saw the official FedEx logo on its top, she thought: it must be real! Maybe even an urgent message from Jac. And what could possibly happen with Mrs Orwin still looking on?

She quickly slid back the latch and opened the door, caught the messenger as he was only a pace away. He turned back and smiled.

'Mrs Reyner?'

'Yes.' Alaysha watched Mrs Orwin pull back behind her door, close it again. And of all the times she'd found her neighbour's spying annoying, now she felt like screaming: '*No, no! Stay here looking until at least this messenger has gone. Be as nosy as you fucking like!*'

'*Alaysha* Reyner?'

'Yes.'

'I have something for you.'

And as the messenger reached his hand towards her and she saw what he held, her breath caught in her throat, and she knew then that she'd made a mistake opening the door. A big mistake.

As Larry Durrant's death approached, its tentacles reached out like an octopus.

There'd been a steady build up over the past weeks, but now in the last twenty-four hours, those tentacles carrying news of his fate spread deeper and wider than ever before: the night-before vigil was on every news channel, there were evening debates pro and con death penalty, more again on breakfast TV, Durrant's last meal, how he'd spend his last minutes, medical details of how he'd be executed, background to the recently failed clemency plea to the Governor, details of the murder twelve years ago, drama with his last lawyer, his new lawyer Darrell Ayliss apparently no longer available for comment . . .

Louisiana and half the States beyond, who knew little about Larry Durrant's life, got to know every last detail of his impending death, as if they were a modern-day Roman amphitheatre crowd blood-lust hungry for it.

Those tentacles reached people they never had before, and some felt deeply touched and saddened by Larry Durrant's plight, became more anti-death penalty, while others simply munched their popcorn faster, *Come on, get on with it. Give it to the fucker!*

But those tentacles gripped tightest around those who knew Larry Durrant. Francine Durrant changed channels or turned off the TV every time it came on, couldn't watch it any more. Mike Coultaine found himself tapping his fingers anxiously on tables and counter tops, increasingly looking towards the phone, praying that Jac had managed to run the gauntlet through customs and would be in Cuba by now, that any minute the phone would ring with good news. And

Mack Elliott stared absently out of the window at Henny's onto a bright winter's day, street bustling with life, as he bit into a Debris Po-Boy and tried desperately to remember what he'd seen on TV twelve years ago.

And as those news broadcasts talked more and more about *time* – time of last meal, time for the final medical examination, time Durrant would walk to the death chamber, time of execution – those tentacles pulled everyone's eyes repeatedly to the clock; half the state, two million people or more, watching the hours and minutes tick down to his death.

Roland Cole was no exception. Over the past two hours, his eyes had lifted twenty times or more to the clock in the Algiers fish warehouse where he and a colleague were busily shifting that day's shipments onto the right pallets.

'What's wrong wit' you?' the colleague said. 'Yo' got a hot date tonight or somethin' – can't wait to leave today?'

'No, it's not that.' Cole's hand went to his stomach where his mounting anxiety had settled like a bucket of eels writhing in acid. 'Somethin' I ate last night – it's half killing me.' With a meek smile, he rushed to the washroom at the back again; his fourth visit that morning.

'You timin' to make sure you don' shit yo'self?' his friend shouted after him, chuckling.

Cole closed his eyes and shuddered as he sat on the toilet.

Stealing away the time alone was the main thing. Time alone with his own thoughts, but most of all away from TV, news broadcasts and clocks.

Durrant's face had been on news broadcasts twice the night before, but even though Cole had made sure not to turn on breakfast news and had rushed past every newsstand on the way in, that image was still with him practically everywhere he looked: around the warehouse, at his friend . . . *at the clock!*

Not me, not me . . . *not me! I'm not the man you saw that night!*

A thousand times he'd replayed that night in his head: hot-wiring the Mercedes in the driveway as he saw a man run round the corner from Coliseum Street: six-foot, stocky, skin-colour and tone not much different to his own, breathless and jaded as he stared back momentarily. Cole sunk down even lower beneath the dashboard, praying that he hadn't been seen. And four minutes later, when he was sure the guy was long-gone, he started up the Mercedes and drove off.

Then when Durrant was first arrested, he saw from the news that it wasn't the man he'd seen that night. He read as much as he could about the background to the case, but there was no possible doubt: the other eyewitness had only seen *one* man leaving the scene, and the timing matched exactly with the guy he'd seen run past. It wasn't Durrant!

But the problem was, he couldn't see a way of coming forward without also holding his hands up to the grand-theft auto. Five to seven years, maybe more if they linked the MO back to other luxury auto-thefts over the past few years.

Cole managed finally to push it to the back of his mind; but then when Durrant's execution date was set, it was back at the forefront, with a vengeance! And so he sent the e-mails; as far as he felt he could go without putting his own head in the noose.

Cole shook his head, a shiver running through him as he felt his stomach cramp and tighten again. Surely they couldn't go through with killing Durrant? He'd told them in those e-mails that it wasn't him! What the fuck more did they want: five to seven years of his own life?

43

Atlanta customs, Miami, Nassau . . . *Havana*.

A re-run each time of Jac's ordeal going through the pass-port check at New Orleans, perspiring, his stomach doing somersaults, praying that they didn't notice his hand shaking as he handed over his passport.

But it was worse after the call from Mike Coultaine. Far worse.

Jac had landed at Atlanta an hour and fifty minutes before-hand, had just twenty minutes before boarding for the next leg to Miami, when Coultaine's call came through. Bad news, Jac. *Bad news*.

Coultaine explained that while he believed he'd success-fully quelled the suspicions of the officer that had called, he thought it worth keeping an eye on. Just in case. And so he'd called an old police contact who owed him a few favours, said that he'd just had a strange call from a certain Joe Rayleigh of Eighth District regarding Darrell Ayliss, an old lawyer buddy of his. Probably nothing, but could he contact him on the QT if anything came up on police radar about it.

'And he just called a few minutes ago, Jac. There's an APB been put out for Ayliss. Carrying false identity, false impersonation and fraud.'

'Oh, *Jesus!*' Jac closed his eyes momentarily, glad that he was sitting when the news came.

'But what's odd is the "approach with caution" note. Bit extreme for the crimes mentioned . . . until, that is, my friend told me the contact name on the APB: Lieutenant Derminget! And it all suddenly fell into place and made sense.'

Jac only half-heard Coultaine go on to say that it looked like Derminget had somehow worked it all out: *McElroy,*

Ayliss . . . the disguise. 'Don't know how, but he obviously has.' The echoing terminal activity and pounding pulse in Jac's head half-drowned it out.

That pounding heavier still, legs shaky and uncertain, as fifteen minutes later he rose to go through passport control.

And then that same ordeal at Miami, Nassau and finally Havana. Not knowing how he managed to face each one, feeling almost physically sick after passing through each time, his nerves mounting again in flight as he steeled himself to face the next one. So by the time he went through the last check-out at Havana, he was exhausted, emotionally drained.

Part of him felt like jumping in the air or doing a quick fandango in relief and excitement, but his body had hardly the strength left to put one foot in front of the other. His step heavy, laboured, eyes bleary and unfocused from lack of sleep as he headed away from customs – before the guards, no doubt with their eyes still on his back, changed their minds – and sought the car-rental desks.

Closed! Jac shuffled over to the café area at the end, one of the few things open, and on the second try found a waiter with good enough English.

'They open at seven o'clock, senor.'

Jac looked at the clock on the café wall: 6.23 a.m. His friendly waiter said there wouldn't be other car-rental companies open yet in the city, most in fact wouldn't open until 9 a.m., and the train to Sancti Spiritus took eight and a half hours. With already fourteen hours eaten up getting to Cuba, Jac hated to lose even one more minute of what little time Durrant had left – but with little other option, he ordered a coffee and waited, meanwhile checking his phone messages. He'd switched his cell-phone off immediately after Coultaine's call and hadn't used it since, worried that with the APB out, the police might be able to zone-track where he was. He risked turning it on now briefly. Only one call: Bob Stratton. New Orleans was one hour behind: 5.31 a.m. He'd call him back in a couple of hours.

Jac finished his coffee and ordered another, his body suddenly craving more caffeine to combat his over-tiredness, kick some life back into it.

Realizing, as he finally got on the road at 7.09 a.m., squinting at road-signs as he sped across a dawn-lit Havana, that he'd have risked falling asleep on the drive without the caffeine. And, having chosen the car-rental company's most powerful option, an Audi A6, hoping that he could make up the time. The caffeine didn't help his already wire-taut nerves, his stomach jittery and his hands trembling on the steering wheel, but at least he was alert.

Cienfuegos . . . Trinidad . . . Sancti Spiritus . . . Jac's route was by now indelibly implanted on his mind. As Jac swung on to Highway A1 and he saw the first sign for Cienfuegos, he put his foot down hard. Six and a half hours driving time, they said. Maybe he could cut that to six or even five and a half hours.

The car-rental companies were already open when Nel-M landed, but he lost time through having to buy a gun in Havana's old town, an old Browning 9mm, before he could get on the road again.

He was just under four hours behind Ayliss as he hit the start of the A1 highway towards Cienfuegos.

With the call from Glenn Bateson while he was at Miami International waiting for his flight to Nassau – '*It didn't work. My guy only managed to injure him . . . and not that seriously*' – everything hinged more than ever on catching up with Truelle as soon as possible.

If Bateson's man had been successful, it would have stopped Ayliss dead in his tracks, he'd have probably just slumped his head on his steering wheel in the middle of Cuba as soon as he heard the news. With Durrant already dead, what would have been the point in continuing?

But right now Truelle was like a powder-keg, and if Ayliss had enough time to light the right match, Nel-M had little doubt that he'd explode and tell all. And if so, Nel-M doubted that Roche's one remaining contingency plan could contain that explosion.

He glanced at the gun on his passenger seat. As so often had happened in his long association with Roche, while Roche troubled himself with fringe details, the core of every problem was left for him to deal with; just as with Roche's wife twelve years ago that had started it all. Nothing had really changed.

Mack Elliott had drifted out of the Ninth Ward into Bywater because there was a bar on North Rampart that had one of the largest screens around, always tuned to sports, usually football. He'd missed the big Saints game the night before, but there was an early afternoon highlights re-run that he knew they'd have on.

And that's where he was, cold Beck's in hand, watching the over-sized screen among a lively throng shouting support or derision with the ebb and flow of the Saints' performance, when the thought suddenly hit him. *Highlights!* That's what he'd been watching that night!

It hadn't been a full game, because the Saints had been playing away in Philadelphia and there was some charity telethon on – but he'd been keen to watch the condensed highlights when they'd come on later. That's why he'd told the chicken guy to pipe-down!

Mack left his half-finished beer on the counter, went out the back to a pay-phone, got the number of the *Times-Picayune* from 411, and asked to be put through.

'Do you have a sporting archives section, perhaps?'

'We've got a general archives section, sir – which would include sport. They should be able to help.'

The girl that looked up the information used a keyword search on the *Times-Picayune* data-bank, but she could just as easily have found it on the internet. 'Here it is . . . Saints v. Philadelphia Eagles game. Eighteenth of February 1992.'

'Thanks.' Mack banged a fist on the wall by the phone, closing his eyes for a second. It *was* that same night! Larry *couldn't* have been at the Roche house.

He took the piece of paper from his pocket, Darrell Ayliss's number, and dialled . . . but it rang unobtainable, a service provider message telling him to try again later. He tried again, just in case, but it did the same.

He started to panic, beads of sweat popping on his forehead as he checked the time: less than four hours left. He had to get the message through somehow!

He got hold of 411 again and asked to be put through to Libreville prison.

But the woman that answered said that Warden Haveling wasn't available because of final preparations that day with Lawrence Durrant '. . . and his assistant Mr Folley is right now handling a media conference call regarding the same. But I . . .'

'It's actually about Larry Durrant that I'm phonin' now!'

'Yes, sir, and I . . . I have someone that I believe can still help.'

Some top-dog guard or other, Mack didn't catch the name. But when after the transfer his voice answered, Mack ran too quickly at first, had to calm himself to get the information across clearly.

Mack Elliott. Bayou Brew bar of twelve years ago with Larry Durrant. Sessions with Darrell Ayliss and Greg Ormdern to try and find out what happened that night. 'But I wasn't able to remember what I was watchin' until just now – and I just checked it out a minute ago with the *Times-Picayune.* That game *was* the same night that Larry Durrant was mean'a be at the Roche house. He couldn't have been there! It *wasn't* him!'

'I understand, sir . . . and I'm glad you've come through to us now with this information.'

'You gotta stop the execution! Larry *didn't* do it! Get hold of the Warden or Governor or whatever it takes to stop it.' Mack realized he was speaking too excitably again, almost garbling. He took a fresh breath to calm himself, his voice lower, more purposeful. 'You'll make sure t'do that? Get hold of the powers that be to stop this now wit' Larry?'

'Don't worry. As soon as I get off the phone, I'll pass your message directly to Warden Haveling. Get him to phone the Governor or whatever he needs to do to action it.'

'Thanks . . . and thank God too that I remembered before it was too late.'

'Yeah. Thank God you did.'

And as soon as he hung up his end, Glenn Bateson screwed up the piece of paper he'd written on and threw it in the bin a yard away.

'Good to speak to you, Governor Candaret. Been a while.'

'You too, Mr Roche. Always good to speak to the more illustrious among my constituents. Especially if they still support and vote for me.'

'Oh, I do, Governor Candaret. I do. More than you can imagine.'

'That's good to hear.' Both of them were old hats at this, thought Candaret. Both of them knowing that these smooth introductory gambits often meant almost the opposite of what was said. From the heart, Roche would have been more likely to say, '*You're a slimy, jumped-up toad whose station in life has risen far above your God-given ability*', and, in truth, Candaret would probably have said much the same about Roche. But that would have got neither of them what they wanted from this conversation now, which brought Candaret sharply back to wondering what Roche *did* want by calling him now, the very day of Larry Durrant's execution. He kept prodding with the niceties, as if he was keeping a rattlesnake at bay with a long stick. 'Good indeed to hear. And what, pray, might I be able to do for you today, Mr Roche? Or is this just a social call?'

'The latter, mostly. Though if I'd called earlier, it might have seemed otherwise.' Roche swallowed, getting his breathing even. Getting the right words in place. 'You see, if I'd called you *before* you made your recent clemency decision, it might have looked as if I was trying to pressure you to do the right thing regarding the murderer of my dear wife. But now that you've actually made that decision, I felt it only right to thank you for what I consider to be a good and true decision and not shirking from your duty. Making this call now when there's no longer danger of it being misread – it can finally be taken in the spirit it's intended. No more, no less than an honest thank you.'

'I . . . I appreciate the sentiment. And thank you too – for not earlier bringing any undue pressure to bear. That was very thoughtful.' Still prodding, though more gently now. Maybe Roche wasn't as bad as he thought; maybe a heart did actually beat beneath that stone-dwarf shell.

'And indeed there's another reason, partly tied into that, why I didn't call until now.'

'Oh?'

'I wondered if the names Amberley, Cleveton, Rossville and Leighgrove strike a bell with you?'

'Yes, I . . . I seem to remember a couple of them from my campaign fund list.' Candaret felt the first nervous twinge in his stomach at where this might be heading. He'd recognized the names far more than he'd made out. Four corporations that, between them, comprised almost half his Presidential campaign fund for the following year.

'Obviously, I've had to go to some lengths to shield my name from being behind those corporations, for two reasons: firstly, the regulatory issues and awkward questions raised by too much funding coming from *one* source, and secondly, because of what I've already mentioned – you might have felt I was putting inadvertent pressure on you to make the right decision regarding my wife's murderer.'

'I . . . I understand.' Though Candaret wasn't sure any more that he did. He felt that twinge in his stomach bite deeper as he thought about what would happen if a journalist or Senate committee now uncovered the source of his funding; but, again, if Roche was now raising it as some sort of background threat or pressure, why hadn't he done that earlier?

'And that's also why I didn't tell you about my involvement in that funding until now. So that you wouldn't misread it and see it as somehow connected with Durrant, feel unduly pressured. You could accept it with the good and honest grace with which it is intended: you have a good friend out there who would like nothing more than to see you in the White House.'

'Why . . . why, thank you. I . . . I don't know what to say.' The first truth to pass Candaret's lips since they'd started talking. He didn't. His thoughts were still in turmoil with Roche's revelation, in particular the timing.

And after a minute more of mutual fawning and treacly niceties as they said their goodbyes, in contrast to Candaret's still bemused expression as he hung up, Roche beamed broadly.

He'd got exactly what he wanted from the conversation. Even if Ayliss did manage to crack Truelle and phoned at the eleventh hour, it was going to take a hell of a lot now to convince Candaret. Kiss goodbye to the White House and a truckload of regulatory problems one side; an elaborate, hard-to-believe story the other. No contest.

Don't pick up any hitch-hikers. Watch out for potholes. Street-lighting is poor or non-existent. And there's a lack of signposts – particularly beyond Havana.

It was the same road all the way, but at a couple of angled junctions where the continuation was ambiguous, car-rental cautions one and four became at odds, because as soon as Jac stopped to clarify directions, he was asked for a lift. With only one in thirty owning a car and infrequent buses, it seemed that half of Cuba was waiting at street-corners and junctions for the next passing car to catch a lift.

'*Perdón, no posible . . . problema urgente.*' One hand lifted apologetically as he sped away. And at the one stop he made thirty kilometres before Cienfuegos – to use the toilet and for a hastily grabbed coffee, Coke and ham roll – two dusty workmen looking for a lift took a step back when he had to be more insistent, shouting at them that a man could die unless he hurried. His bastardized Spanish scream of '*Muerte . . . muerte!*' making them worry for a second that he was threatening to kill them.

When he'd earlier tried Bob Stratton – twice at ten minute intervals – and there was no signal or dialling tone on his cell-phone, he realized that there were patches of poor reception on the open road. He finally got hold of him as he approached Cienfuegos, but it was mixed news: while Stratton had managed to get the internet café girl to pick out two possibles, one wasn't at his last known address and the other, as soon as he opened his door in Long Beach, Stratton knew wasn't the same man as on the internet cam.

'So the only option left is to try and track down the first guy gone AWOL from his last known – Roland Cole. If I can find a credit card linked to Cole's last address, then trace it to a new address, I might get lucky. But, you know, with only the few hours we got left now.'

'I know.' Crystal clear: tall order, don't hold your breath. 'Phone me if you get a break, or I'll phone you. I'm suffering some connectivity problems here.'

Palms, sugar-cane, towering tobacco plants with fronds as high as two-storey houses – the scenery was spectacular, but most of it sped by in a patchwork blur as Jac's speedo needle crept over 130 k.p.h. on every clear, flat stretch where he could get away with it, one eye peeled for traffic police.

But as the miles rolled by, Jac felt the waves of tiredness come back. As if the caffeine could only keep him going for so long – his hands shaking increasingly on the steering wheel, combined with the high-speed vibrations of the car on the often rough road surface, starting to set off tremors through his entire body. That shaking, along with the wild adrenalin rush of the past days and hours, all that was keeping him going – and when that fever-pitch hit overload and he finally burnt out, the rest would come crashing back in: the tension, the lack of sleep, the emotional drain, the dog-tired exhaustion – mental and physical – the feeling at times that he could hardly make it another yard, let alone hundreds of miles.

And as the caffeine and his body's nervous tension lost their last grip, he'd fall asleep. The snap of a finger, blink of an eye as he sped along.

Twice already he'd pulled himself sharply back awake, a shudder running through him as he realized that sleep had grabbed him for a second, maybe two; and as it mugged him for a third time, forty-five kilometres before Trinidad, he was suddenly reminded of caution two, *potholes*, with a bang.

As Jac's eyes snapped sharply open, he thought for a second that he'd swerved into a ditch or side-shoulder – but then he saw the truck coming straight towards him. The pothole had jolted him into the oncoming lane! Jac swung sharply back again, braking, the truck also braking then and missing him by only a couple of yards, its horn blaring hard as it swept past.

Jac kept going – the truck had slowed to almost a stop as Jac looked in his mirror – and a mile further on, when it was safely out of sight, he pulled over, closing his eyes as he waited for his wild trembling to settle. Madness! *Madness!*

But it was hardly any better after almost two minutes of slow, deep breaths, and Jac feared that if he kept his eyes closed any longer, he might fall asleep. And so he pulled out again, turned the radio up loud so that hopefully Perez Prado and Benny Moré could keep him awake, grabbed a coffee at the first stop seven kilometres up the road, then stopped again 80k beyond Trinidad for another to keep him going.

Fuelled by that mix of caffeine, mambo-rhythms and adrenalin-starved exhaustion, his eyes red-rimmed, nerves ragged, he finally ran up the steps of the Sancti Spiritus post office at 12.53 p.m.

*

The man he approached at the counter ahead had limited English, but when Jac showed him the mailbox number, he pointed to a side counter. 'Amparo . . . she do *apartados de correo*.'

Thankfully, Amparo's English was far better, but as Jac explained what he wanted, she started to frown.

'I'm sorry, senor. I'm not allowed to give out the addresses of people holding boxes – *apartados*. It's against regulations.'

'But, *please*. This is very important. I'm an American lawyer,' Jac slid Ayliss's card across the counter, 'and a man's life depends on this information. It's vital that I locate the holder of this mailbox urgently.'

'I understand, senor. But it really is difficult . . . *impossible* for me to give that information.' Amparo inclined her head in apology as she said it. A striking woman in her late forties, with soft brown eyes and the first tinge of salt in her black hair, Jac could imagine that twenty years ago she'd been stunning.

Plan two. But as Jac turned his palm on the counter to reveal two fifty-dollar bills, he knew instantly it was a mistake. Her eyes hardened again; she looked genuinely offended.

'That . . . that won't do any good. The *regulations* are very strict.' This time as she said it, her eyes glanced to one side, as if unseen eyes might be watching them.

Jac closed his eyes for a second. *Oh God!* For it all to end here with soft-eyed Amparo.

'There is *one* thing I could suggest,' Amparo said, a more hopeful tone as she flicked a page in a leather-bound register to one side. 'I notice there's a package arrived for that *apartado* today – which means the postman will put a notification through their door tomorrow. If you want to leave a message here, I can make sure they get it when they pick up the package in a day or two.'

'That'll be too late,' Jac said with a heavy sigh, his eyes closing fleetingly again. *Plan three.* He could still feel all the bubbling tension of the long drive, and his hand shook heavily as he unfolded the newspaper clipping from his pocket and spread it before her. 'You see this man here – Larry Durrant! He's going to die tonight at six o'clock, unless I can speak first to the man who has this mailbox.' Jac prodded the article with one finger, his voice rising. 'You see the day for him dying here . . . *la fecha*. It's today! And *that* . . . that's me mentioned there – Darrell Ayliss.' Jac took Ayliss's passport out and turned it towards her, as if her doubting him might be part of the problem. 'You see now why it's vital I contact this man, and why I . . . I don't have much time left. Because after six o'clock tonight, it'll be . . . be too–'

The emotions suddenly rose in Jac's throat, choked off the rest of his words. He hadn't planned this part of it, even though, as the tears welled in his eyes and started running down his cheeks, his breaking down had softened Amparo more than anything else so far; she looked close to relenting.

As he'd mentioned *time* and looked towards the clock, he'd suddenly had an image of Larry looking at the clock by the death chamber at that moment, wondering what had happened to him, whether Jac was just another in a long line of people to desert him, let him down; until now, in his dying hours, there was finally nobody left. Forty hours since he'd last spoken to Larry, when he'd told him he was chasing down some final, vital leads . . . *and now!*

'I'm sorry, señor. So sorry.' Amparo reached one hand across the counter to touch his arm. 'If I could help – I truly would.'

And looking back at Amparo at that moment, her eyes glistening with emotion, he believed her. She would. *If she could.*

'That's okay. I . . . I understand.' And, embarrassed by his tears and worried that if he stayed a second longer, he'd break down completely, Jac turned and walked away, his step echoing emptily on the marble floor of the *correo . . . footsteps through Libreville . . . Larry's last steps towards the death chamber, with now nothing left to stop him dying . . .*

He should have turned his back and walked away on day

one, left Larry as he was then, at peace and ready to go to his God, instead of filling his head with false hope and empty promises.

The tears streamed down Jac's face as he walked away, his shoulders slumping more with each step. All over. *All over.* Apart from Stratton's snowball in hell – *more false hope* – nothing left to do.

Jac wiped at his tears with the back of one hand, and, the catharsis already half spent as he reached the steps of the Sancti Spiritus *correo* and took a fresh breath of the air outside, all that was left was to take a leaf out of his father's book, *look on the bright side*, consoling himself that he'd done everything he could, *everything*; far, far more than anyone else would have. And now at least he'd be able to sleep . . . no doubt for three days solid. Find a small local hotel and–

The touch against his arm made him jump. *Amparo!*

She handed him a piece of paper, still glancing around for those unseen eyes. 'This is the holder of that *apartado*. On the coast near Tunas de Zaza.'

Jac looked at it: Brent Calbrey, Villa Delarcos. 'How far?'

'Forty, forty-five minutes drive. Six kilometres from Punto Ladrillo heading to San Pedro. You can't miss it. Big white villa with four or five holiday casitas in its grounds.'

What had changed Amparo's mind? – the tears and his deflated slump as he'd walked away, or being able to give him the message away from prying eyes – Jac didn't know, and at that moment he didn't care. He leant over, giving her a big hug.

'Amparo, you're beautiful. *Guapa . . . guapa!*'

Amparo smiled awkwardly, a couple of people approaching the *correo* also smiling, probably thinking they were two long lost lovers with the embrace and their eyes glassy. But as they parted, Amparo's eyes had shifted from soft to thoughtful, faintly troubled. She touched his arm.

'And, señor. Good luck. *Suerte.*'

*

When Nel-M approached the Sancti Spiritus *correo* counter almost four hours later, Amparo wasn't as helpful.

Nel-M suspected that Ayliss might well have played the Death Row card, so he kept to a similar story, saying that he was connected with the DA's office seeking urgent information before the execution that night. But Amparo just kept repeating something about *regulations*, didn't budge, despite him at one point showing her $500 in his cupped palm.

One consolation, Nel-M thought: it looked doubtful that Ayliss would have got anything either – but when he'd asked Amparo if anyone had called earlier asking for the same information, she'd shaken her head, *No*, despite the flicker of recognition in her face he thought he'd seen when he'd first mentioned Durrant and Death Row.

As Nel-M headed down the steps of the Sancti Spiritus *correo*, he had much the same feeling, *nothing left to do*, that Jac had had in that same spot four hours earlier – but then that nagging doubt pinched again, and he looked back thoughtfully. He wondered whether, however much he'd tried to shield it, Amparo had sensed how frantic he was. Certainly, that's how he *felt*: the nightmare in Vancouver, the runaround with Truelle and the long flight to Cuba, now the breakneck drive to Sancti Spiritus; the three-day fly-kill holiday from hell. But, aware of that, he thought he'd covered with his best warm and gracious smile, the cool and collected DA official trying to get information, rather than the patience-long-gone, bubbling-acid-nerves hit-man.

Nel-M's eyes shifted to a bar across the road. One way he might get to know.

A dead-and-alive town, Sancti Spiritus's ramshackle buildings looked like they'd been slowly crumbling since the fifties, with a hotchpotch of blue and pink shutters that tried, but failed, to offer some relief. Apart from the post office, the bar's blue shutters appeared to be the only ones in the street to have received a recent lick of paint.

Over a beer, Nel-M talked to the barman, and – after a lot

of finger-pointing and juggling between the barman's basic English and the few Spanish words that Nel-M was able to translate – he got some idea of who'd visited the post office earlier that day.

Americanos, nuevo coches, Nel-M quickly picked up were the key words. He'd noticed that there were very few new cars on the road apart from his own. The barman explained that nearly all new cars were rental cars for tourists or taxis; the rest of Cuba either didn't have a car or relied on old relics, most of them left over from the Batista days.

Nel-M nodded and sipped at his beer. That explained the Buddy Holly time-warp when it came to cars. But that also meant, as with his own BMW series-5 now parked in front, Ayliss's car would have been one of the few new ones to have pulled up outside the post office earlier.

Nel-M stood up from his bar stool as he described Ayliss. 'Big man . . . quite fat. *Gordo*. Black hair oiled back.' Nel-M swept one hand over his own hair. He didn't know the Spanish for cream suit, so tugged at his own light-grey jacket and said, '*Blanco* . . . white suit. New car. *Nuevo coche*. Four hours ago . . . *cuatro horas!*'

And finally there was a gleam of recognition in the barman's eyes. '*Si* . . . *si*. Car like yours. *Muy similar*.' He pointed to Nel-M's car outside, then frowned as he tried to remember the make. He took a beer mat and drew a few interlocking circles.

Audi! That would at least narrow it down, Nel-M thought. But as the barman continued, with something about the man in the white suit hugging a woman, Nel-M began to think that maybe it wasn't Ayliss after all. As he looked towards where the barman was gesticulating, Nel-M suddenly jolted, his expression as if he'd seen a ghost. He held one hand up towards the barman. No need for further explanation.

Nel-M squinted sharper as a man across the road took the last step and entered the post office. *Truelle!*

Nel-M kept the same hand held in the air as he moved

closer to the window, as if he was a conductor holding an orchestra in silence; a pregnant, expectant pause as they waited for it to come down again for the crescendo finale.

And a minute later, as he saw Truelle emerge holding a padded buff envelope, walk thirty yards down the road and get in a white classic Corvette, that hand did finally come down, as with an, 'Old friend . . . *amigo!*' he rushed out to his car to follow.

When Jac arrived at the door of Villa Delarcos at just before 2 p.m., Brent Calbrey, a tall gaunt man in his early sixties with a heavy tan and wavy grey hair, informed him that he'd just missed 'Lenny'.

'By about half an hour. He's headed into town.'

'Sancti Spiritus?'

'Yeah. Few things he wanted to pick up. Things he likes that I didn't already have in the fridge. Oh, and he said he was also going to the post office.'

'Oh, right.' *Post office.* Jac looked back down the road. 'I . . . I probably passed him on my way up. What's he driving?'

'My car.' Calbrey smiled tightly. 'White Corvette . . .'71 classic.'

Jac couldn't remember if he'd passed one or not. There were a lot of old American cars on the roads. 'Do you know when he'll be back?'

'A couple of hours, he said.' Calbrey raised an eyebrow. 'Can I give him a message?'

'No, it's okay . . . I'll try and catch him later.' Jac didn't want to leave a name, possibly frighten Truelle off. He turned away.

'Old friend?'

'Yeah, old friend,' Jac said over his shoulder, smiling wanly.

And, as he was a few paces away, Calbrey called after him, explaining that 'Lenny' might return direct to the casita rather than the main house itself. 'Its entrance is forty yards along.'

Jac looked towards where Calbrey pointed and saw the white Moorish-style bungalow, a smaller version of the main house, on a small promontory with panoramic views over the sea lapping fifteen yards its other side. Everything was white, Jac thought: the villa and casitas, Calbrey's Bermudas and cheese-cloth top, the Corvette. Jac nodded his thanks and, as he got back into his car, looked anxiously at his watch.

He couldn't just sit there for two hours, knowing that meanwhile Larry's life was ticking away. He started up, heading back to Sancti Spiritus. But halfway there, his foot suddenly eased from the pedal. *Two hours?* Hardly would he have arrived there before Truelle was heading back out to the villa. And if Truelle heard that meanwhile someone had called for him, he might rush off again, go to ground.

No, the only safe thing was to wait there and watch. At the next side road, he did a hasty three-point turn, headed back; and, eighty yards along from the bungalow, with a clear view of it and the main house, he parked and waited. Watching hawkishly every car that approached and passed, though there weren't many: seven in the past hour.

But as an hour became an hour and a half – *two hours* – he found himself looking repeatedly at his watch, tapping his fingers anxiously on the steering wheel in rhythm with his pulse and mounting tension, the constant tremor in his body becoming heavier.

Waves of tiredness were again swilling over him as he watched the unchanging scene ahead punctuated by the occasional car. Three times he'd shaken himself back awake as he felt himself close to the brink.

He put the radio on again as a precaution; though he'd have thought that with the tension running through him and his constant finger-tapping, that alone would have kept him awake.

But that rhythm after a while formed its own soporific monotony, along with the long spells of static vista, the occasional passing car, the hum and click of cicadas, the surf lapping gently fifty yards away; and as that rhythm finally combined with the music from the radio, became one medley, it dragged him gently towards what, for the past twenty-four hours, he'd been staving off with raw tension and adrenalin, caffeine, mambo and salsa. A deep, satisfying sleep.

44

Last meal.

Lockdowns one . . . two. Breakfast, lunch, supper, exercise hour . . . final lockdown. Life at Libreville. Except it had been no life; just various regimented stages towards death, Larry now realized.

And now there were only a few stages left: medical examination, last eighteen paces to the death-chamber, strap-down and final injection.

He'd already had an extra-curricular examination from the infirmary medic who'd put fourteen stitches in his shiv wound the night before. Flesh wound, nothing internal damaged. But Torvald had asked the medic down to check it again two hours ago, just to be sure.

Larry only ate half of his last meal. Not only because he didn't feel like it, but because in the end it didn't bring back old days in the Ninth; it just reminded him all the more that he was here at Libreville, with cooks who didn't have the slightest idea how to make a good Po' Boy. Libreville had steadily eroded most of his good memories over the years; he didn't want to spoil more with his last meal.

The night before when he'd said his last goodbyes, Roddy had started to tell him a joke, but had broken down halfway through; and as they'd hugged, Larry had muttered in his ear: '*You know that Ayliss . . . it's actually Jac.*' Thinking, as he gave a quick, hushed explanation and saw Roddy's incredulous expression, that all the years Roddy had told him jokes, the last surprise and punchline had been his.

'Has he called yet?' Roddy had asked.

'No, not yet. He's apparently still chasing down some last minute things.' Larry shrugged. 'You know what he's like . . . never say die.'

'He *will* call. I know it.'

'Maybe.' Larry shrugged again, his eyes shifting uncomfortably to one side. 'But, you know, it's not right for me to keep clinging onto hope till the last hour, when–'

Rodriguez clasped one of his hands in both of his, shaking gently. 'I meant either way, Larry. *Either* way.'

And at that moment, Roddy was one of the few people left who could still look him in the eye. The guards called out 'Dead Man Walking' as they escorted him along, but their eyes had already said it: '*You're already dead, I can hardly bear to look at you.*' Torvald, Fran and Josh the day before, the two guards outside his open-bar 'last-night' cell – in case he attempted suicide – the guard that had brought him his last meal; none of them could meet his eye.

The only other person who had been able to had been Father Kennard that morning when, after having prayed with him, he asked, 'Do you want to deal at all with what you did all those years ago, Larry? Ask God's forgiveness?'

And it was Larry then who was looking away uneasily, unable to meet Kennard's eye. 'I ... I don't think I can, Father. When even now, I can't rightly say whether I killed her or not.'

'I understand.' Father Kennard nodded thoughtfully, pursing his lips. 'But I had to ask, Larry.'

Either way. Larry wondered if that was why Jac hadn't yet called. Because, as with everyone else who could no longer look him in the eye, he couldn't bear to give him bad news.

Larry had tried to avoid looking at the clock too frequently, expectantly, that morning. But after his last meal, he began to look at the clock increasingly: two o'clock, two-thirty, three ... By the time it got to 4 p.m. and Torvald came to his cell to tell him that it was time for his final medical examination, Larry knew then that Jac wouldn't call.

Jac couldn't face telling him what Larry could already see in everyone's eyes: he was already a dead man.

*

Bob Stratton finally got the breakthrough he'd been frantically chasing for half the day at 2.14 p.m.

Roland Cole had ditched his two credit cards shortly after he left his last address; both of them left hanging with big bills and no forwarding address, no possible link-on. Cole had covered his tracks well.

But Stratton decided to check new credit card applications over the past ten months, when Cole might have applied for a new one; and out of eight R. Coles processed in that period in Louisiana, he hit gold with an exact birth-date match: *Roland T. Cole, Verret Street, Algiers.*

Stratton leapt into his car; twenty-five minutes drive, he made it in nineteen.

First-floor apartment of a rundown, chipped-paint, three-storey block with its front doors accessed by outside planked walkways.

Stratton rang the bell, then knocked after five seconds. No answer. He rang and knocked again, still nothing, and was about to try a third time when the neighbour's door opened.

'I don' think you'll find him there.' A bleary-eyed man in a T-shirt, squinting as if he'd just awoken from an afternoon nap. 'He left half an hour back carrying a holdall. Lot of banging of drawers an' that before he went.' The man scratched his chest absently. 'That's why I looked out when his door slammed – thought for a minute he might have been ransacked.'

'Oh, right. Do you know where he works?'

'Yeah. Three blocks away.' He pointed with a hooked finger, a slight shrug as if he didn't see the importance. 'Opelousas Packing.'

'No idea where he might have gone, I suppose?'

'No, none at all.'

And Cole's work colleague at Opelousas had no idea either. He'd left work an hour ago complaining of a bad stomach.

'An' 's far as I know he was headin' for home and bed and stayin' there.'

As Stratton got back in his car, his nerves still racing from the rush, he took out his cell-phone to call Ayliss.

At 2.30 p.m., Roland Cole jumped on a Greyhound bus bound for Miami via Pensacola, Tallahassee and Tampa.

Durrant's face *everywhere*, he couldn't stand it any more: warehouse walls, work colleagues, a man in the local café at lunchtime who reminded him of Durrant . . . the clock there too didn't help and a film of sweat broke out on Cole's forehead. And when the café owner flipped channels on the corner TV from a daytime soap to the news, Cole stood up sharply as Durrant's face loomed out at him.

'Man, I can't take any more o' this,' he said to his friend. He rubbed at his stomach and looked with disdain at the barely eaten burger on his plate. 'I gotta get home before I die. Tell Max for me, would ya?'

The Greyhound bus was ideal. No TV, no newspapers, no clock; and, as the miles rolled by, no New Orleans either. Out of sight, out of mind, the continued thrum of its wheels on the road would hopefully, finally, push the images of Durrant from his mind.

So he tucked himself away at the back of the Greyhound where nobody would notice him and, more importantly, he wouldn't notice them – more faces that might remind him of Durrant – and waited for that moment to come. Like Rizzo in the last scene of *Midnight Cowboy*, he thought as he closed his eyes.

And after a while curled up at the back of the bus, as if in support of that image, he found that he was trembling; although, unlike Rizzo, in his case it was from the tension still writhing in his stomach and the shame of what he'd done, rather than pneumonia.

★

Truelle called a halt after three brandies.

Cuban measures were generous, a third of a balloon, and the road to the villa was new to him; he didn't want to risk wrapping Brent's prize Corvette round a lamppost.

He'd phoned Cynthia for the DHL reference number soon after she'd sent the package, then when he'd phoned to track its progress that morning was told that it was scheduled to be delivered to the Sancti Spiritus *correo* before midday. He didn't want to leave the package there any length of time, and, while Brent's *casita* fridge was generously stocked, there were a few essential favourites he wanted to pick up: Earl Grey tea, anchovy-stuffed olives and salted almonds. He decided to pick them up first, then head to the post office; he didn't want to risk leaving the package in his car.

The Earl Grey tea proved impossible to get, he gave up after the third store visited, and the place where he bought the salted almonds told him of a shop halfway across town where they might have the olives. When Truelle got there, half of it was a deli with shelves jammed ceiling high with produce from Spain and Latin America, the other half a café where he ordered a coffee and brandy while he perused what else they had, ending up also buying some salami and spicy chorizo.

As he knocked back the last of his brandy, he tried his office number again; still no answer. Then Cynthia's home number; the same. He'd tried both numbers earlier to find out if anyone had called by the office after he'd left, but with the same result. Maybe with little for Cynthia to be there for, she'd decided to take a break at the same time too.

When he'd first arrived at Brent's after the long journey, Brent had given him an anxious sideways glance as he opened up the casita for him. 'You okay, buddy? Something troubling you?'

'No, fine . . . *fine*. Just overwork. Burning the midnight oil on too many patient histories.'

He no doubt looked at that moment how he felt, a total

wreck, but he hadn't got half his own mind around what had happened, let alone to explain it to someone else: *I did something with a patient twelve years ago that I shouldn't have, and as I became worried about the people I'd done it for, I took out a couple of insurance policies — but when I phoned the other day, both of those policy holders had been killed, and now . . .*

Truelle ordered another brandy. He couldn't get Maggie Steiner's voice out of his head, cracking pitifully as she told him that Alan was dead. Then that Vancouver policewoman telling him about Chris and Brenda, *that* . . . Put the phone down. Shut it out of your head. Have another drink. Push it away, push it away . . . *push it away . . .*

He knocked back the brandy in three quick slugs, raised his hand for another. The shopkeeper eyed him with concern as he poured.

'Are you okay, señor?'

Again, 'Fine . . . fine. *Bueno. Muy bueno.*' Just don't get too close to me, that's all. *Everyone who gets close to me gets killed.*

Half the world asking if he was okay. The stewardess too on his last leg from Nassau to Havana. For the first legs of the flight, he'd kept to soft drinks, his stomach still churning from a volatile acid–bile mix of last night's drinks and wire-edge tension. But by the time he came to the last leg, his hands were shaking so heavily that he felt he just had to have a drink to get them steady and try to dull the nightmare images burning hour by hour stronger through his head . . . *push them away . . . push them away . . .*

He knocked back a quick malt whisky at Nassau airport, ordered another as soon as he was airborne, and as he took his third in-flight whisky from the stewardess, his eyes bleary and red-rimmed, hand shaking on the glass, she asked if he was okay.

Fine. *Fine.* And even if people didn't ask, it was there in their eyes. That look of concern. On the faces of the people as he now stepped outside the shop, squinting and swaying slightly as the bright sunshine again hit him. On the face of the woman at the post office as he handed across the note from Brent and collected his package. A young couple heading into the *correo* as he went back down its steps, unsure whether to side-step him or help him down.

Truelle closed his eyes as he got back into Brent's car, taking slow, deep breaths to try and get his nerves calm. And, as he opened them again and started up, he checked his watch: *four more hours*. Then perhaps finally it would all be over, the nightmare of the past twelve years ended. Maybe then at last it would all be fine, fine. *Bueno, bueno*.

Jac was sitting with Larry having a brandy, both of them looking anxiously at the clock. As Jac passed across Larry's glass, Larry said:

'Tell my mother, Jac. Tell her it wasn't me, before it's too late.'

'But I can't see her, Larry.' Jac, looking over Larry's shoulder, suddenly realizing that this time they were in the courtroom. He couldn't see anything, in fact; it was just mist and shadow beyond Larry. Vague shapes, none of them clear.

'But she's *there*, Jac. I know it. I can feel her eyes boring into the back of my right shoulder. Tell her, Jac, please . . . *please*, before it's too late.'

'I . . . I can't see anything any more, Larry.' Jac perplexed why it had all suddenly become misty. 'There's nothing there but hazy shadows. I've . . . I've become like you, Larry. Can't see anything clearly any more.'

'*Please*, Jac . . . don't do this!' Tears streaming down his face as he clasped Jac's hand. 'Please don't let me die without her knowing that it wasn't me!'

Ringing in his pocket.

The tears welling too in Jac's eyes as he clasped back. 'But now that I can't see anything clearly, Larry . . . what do I even tell her? If *you'd* been able to see things clearly, you'd have been able to tell her yourself long before now, before . . .'

Telephone! As the dream fell away, Jac shuddered awake and answered the call.

Bob Stratton's voice competing against Justo Betancourt on the radio. Jac reached out and turned it down, blinking heavily, fading afternoon light, approaching dusk. As Jac looked at his watch, 5.52 p.m., he jolted to suddenly, fearing in that second that's why Stratton was calling: *only an hour till Durrant's execution!*

Then he remembered the one-hour time difference, his caught breath and his pulse settling back as Stratton told him about his efforts with Roland Cole. Close, *very close*, but in the end no cigar.

'And don't look like he's planning to return any time soon. Not in the next few hours, at least. That's it.'

'Yeah, looks like it.' Soft, resigned exhalation. 'Thanks. You tried your best.'

That's it. Jac, surveying again the white villa, *casita* and road ahead, now knowing with certainty that his very last chance rested with Truelle.

Almost two hours asleep? Still no sign of a white Corvette. But what if Truelle had returned in the meantime and headed off again? If he'd seen the Audi up the road and had come close enough to see him inside asleep – no doubt the first thing he'd have done!

The sleep had taken some of the edge off Jac's jaded nerves, but as the minutes dragged with the last of the day's light fast dying, they started to intensify again, Jac's fingers tapping steadily once more on the steering wheel. Where *was* Truelle? Maybe he should give Calbrey another knock; even if Calbrey lied, he might see something tell-tale in his face, some clue as to –

Car approaching two hundred yards away, side-lights on. And as it came thirty yards closer, Jac could see it clearly: *white Corvette!* His finger-tapping changed to an anxious clutch.

And for a moment, no more than a fleeting shadow, Jac thought he could see another car a hundred yards behind it.

But as he squinted harder, he could no longer see it. Either it had pulled in somewhere, been swallowed up with the fast-fading light, or it was just a trick of his eyes.

Jac watched Truelle park the Corvette and get out carrying a briefcase and a shopping bag.

Calbrey came to greet him and they talked for a couple of minutes. Truelle looked around anxiously at one point, then with a tight smile and half-wave, Truelle headed across the lawn to the casita.

Jac watched the lights come on inside and outside the casita, illuminating a terrace area with table and umbrella on the promontory.

As much as Jac couldn't wait to pounce on Truelle and get his hands – verbal and proverbial – around his neck, he could see Calbrey watering some potted plants at the casita-side of the main villa. Confronting Truelle would without doubt be better without any interference, but *fuck it*, if Calbrey didn't head in soon . . .

Jac's finger-tapping increased, almost double-time to his pulse and the cicadas and crickets, and he managed to hold out only another ninety seconds before his hand was reaching for the door handle and, *wait*, Calbrey seemed to be putting away his hose and calling out something towards the casita.

Jac watched their brief exchange, Calbrey going inside the main villa as Truelle headed – briefcase in one hand, drink in the other – towards the table on the end of the promontory.

Jac waited only twenty seconds for Truelle to get settled at the table, then, checking his watch, 6.12 p.m., got out of his car.

45

Grab him by the throat and scream at him; hit him; speak gently and appeal to his better nature; shout and threaten and appeal to his worst: all the different ways of handling Truelle had spun wildly through Jac's head over the past hours, so much, *too much*, depending on it. Now, as he walked across the casita lawn towards the promontory, they were still spinning, nothing decided, words and fragments of sentences jumbling around until finally they all merged together and became little more than a buzz. A buzz that progressively became stronger with the blood-rush to his head, competing with the hum and click of cicadas as he got closer to the table and Truelle.

The promontory was no more than twenty feet above the sea, but it was enough to give a panorama: clear sea one side, a string of islands and cays, a mile offshore, the other. Truelle had taken a seat at the table, then angled his chair to face the sunset view. He didn't become aware of Jac, still in his Ayliss disguise, until he was only a few yards away.

Truelle jolted with a sharp breath, his eyes darting anxiously to one side and past Jac, as if for a second escape might be an option before realizing the futility, *rugby-tackled after a few yards*, and his eyes settled back. Or perhaps he was hoping that Calbrey might come out and save him?

'How . . . *how* did you find me?'

'Cynthia. And a friendly woman at the Sancti Spiritus post office.' Jac shrugged. 'But don't blame Cynthia. She only told me because I convinced her that if I didn't get to you, then Malley would. And he'd kill you.' With all the Ayliss padding, Jac was hot from the rapid walk from his car, his breath falling short. The buzzing was subsiding, only his rapid pulse-beat beneath . . . *ticking down the seconds left for Larry*. Jac smiled tightly. 'In the end she had your best interests at heart.'

'I . . . I phoned her, home and office. There was no answer. I was beginning to–'

'When I left her,' Jac held one hand up, placating, 'I told her not to hang around the office waiting for Malley to turn up there. She obviously took my advice.'

Truelle nodded thoughtfully, but then his eyes clouded again, looked unsettled as Jac took a seat and placed the small cassette recorder from his pocket on the table between them.

Jac took a fresh breath. 'Now, we could sit here for the next half hour with me piling on the pressure about the DA and how if you let Durrant die I'm going to make sure he adds on an Accomplice to Murder rap – ten to fifteen of the hardest time you can imagine – but, you know, the problem is I don't have the time any more. I got to call Governor Candaret right away and get him to phone Libreville prison and stop Durrant's execution.' Jac's Ayliss drawl heavy, he leant over menacingly and laid one hand on Truelle's thigh, feeling the jerk of discomfort and the underlying tremble. As Jac clenched hard against it, he could feel the pulse at his own temples, the buzzing in his head stronger again for a moment. 'And having flown for half a day and driven across half of fucking Cuba . . . I don't have the patience left, either.' Jac glared hard at Truelle, and, giving his thigh one last warning grip, lifted his hand towards the recorder. Truelle's eyes fixed on it as if it was a loaded gun. 'So I'm just going to press record here while you tell me, chapter and verse, everything that happened twelve years ago.'

'I . . . I can't.' Truelle shook his head, staying Jac's finger an inch above the button. He closed his eyes as if in submission as a small shudder ran through him. Opening them again, he smiled meekly. 'Like you said before . . . he'll kill me.'

'Malley?'

'Yeah. Nel-M, as he's known. He's killed two others . . . *that* I know of. *Both* good friends.' Truelle closed his eyes fleetingly again, *shutting out the images*, and then looked to one side, as if consulting someone unseen as to whether to finally say anything. He took a fresh breath. 'Not long after this all started twelve years ago, I began to get concerned and so took out a couple of insurance policies—'

Jac's hand went to press record, but Truelle held a hand up, staying it again; clear indication that if Jac did, he'd immediately clam up.

'They . . . they were accounts of what happened with Durrant twelve years ago left in sealed envelopes with a couple of friends – *only* to be opened in the event of something happening to me. I changed those policy holders not long ago, but then found out early yesterday that . . . *that* . . .' Truelle closed his eyes again. *Catharsis.* What he'd always advised patients to do, unburden, share the weight that was too much to carry alone; but he'd never imagined that it would be to this sly and gushing Southern lawyer that he'd just met. And now not even able to say the word that would help him start accepting it, healing. Dead. Dead. *Dead.* 'Both of them. One, I spoke to his wife and she told me . . . the other a police officer answered.' Truelle swallowed, exhaled gently. 'That's why I jumped on the first plane here to Cuba.'

'Thought you might be next?' Observing Truelle's doleful nod, his eyes red-rimmed and fearful, that thinking made perfect sense; but as Jac considered it more deeply, an incredulous leer rose. '*What*? You think that if you just sit it out here in Cuba for a few hours until Durrant's dead – after that, everything's going to be fine?'

Truelle shook his head. He didn't know. He didn't know anything any more.

Jac saw Truelle start to crack, rode it. '*Afterwards*, it's going to be just as bad – probably even worse.' Jac leant over and held one hand towards Truelle, a few inches short of a direct prod. 'After Durrant's gone, you'll be the *only* one left to know what they've done. You think for one minute they're going to leave you alive?'

Another head-shake, Truelle scrunching his eyes shut. *Push it away . . . push it away . . .*

'In fact, if you asked me to put money on it, I'd say that not only is Malley going to kill you after Durrant's gone, but he's going to do it quick. *Real* quick.' Jac grimaced tautly. 'Everything done and dusted at the same time.'

'I . . . I don't know.' The words shuddered out on Truelle's fractured breath. But maybe a part of him *had* known all along. That gap between what the subconscious knew and conscious mind wouldn't accept; basic Jungian theory. And he'd tried to bridge that gap by either shutting it out of his mind or with drink, but had never really succeeded. And what now? More bottles stacked under his sink, more bodies of close friends? Maybe Nel-M putting a quick bullet through his head would be for the best. *Quick release.* The thoughts raged inside him along with his strung-out nerves and acid-bile stomach, the ghostly images of his dead friends now stabbing his brain – finally spilling over with a spluttering exhalation. 'I would never, *ever* have gone along with it, if I thought–' Truelle broke off then, suddenly realizing he'd let the genie out of the bottle, but looking at it strangely, as if someone else had done it without asking his permission. 'Thought for a minute that Durrant was innocent.'

'*What*? You went along with it *only* because you believed he was guilty?' When Truelle had said it the other day in his office, Jac thought it had been just a ruse, a fob-off.

'Yeah. Roche and Nel-M – though I never actually saw Roche over the whole thing, Nel-M was always the go-between – they claimed that, from word on the street, Durrant was the main name to come back as his wife's murderer, but his accident and coma had conveniently blotted it all out. The police couldn't even apply basic questioning and interrogation. Wasn't even worth hauling him in.' Truelle shrugged. 'And when the DNA evidence came in, I was convinced they were telling the truth.'

Jac nodded pensively. The buzzing had faded again; only

his steady pulse-beat now in rhythm with the cicadas. He checked his watch. Just over one and a half hours left to get the call in to Candaret. 'And at which stage did you become *not* so convinced?'

'I don't know.' Truelle's eyes shifted, sifting through the past. 'I've always had *some* doubts, I suppose. And those have become stronger recently. Though I'm still far from sure – *either* way.' Truelle shut his eyes again for a second, *final closure*, then looked across directly. 'It's important, though, that you understand I wouldn't have done this if I'd truly thought Durrant was innocent.'

Jac wasn't sure what Truelle wanted: absolution, or simply understanding. Jac nodded. 'I understand.' Jac was quick to reassure that, with him now cooperating, he'd push the DA for the lightest possible sentence, 'And also get him to offer a good WPP – if you think you'll need it.'

Truelle nodded, but as Jac went to press record, Truelle stopped him again with a gentle grip on his arm.

'One last thing. What I say now is no doubt going to save Durrant's neck, get him off. But what if that DNA's right and he *is* guilty?'

Jac looked thoughtfully ahead for a moment. The last of the sun was dipping into the sea, crimson–blue dappling every wave.

'I do strongly believe that Durrant is innocent. Though in the end, as with you, I can't be a *hundred* per cent sure.' *DNA*: the one factor that had made Jac doubt more than a few times over the past weeks. 'But that can't be your concern right now. You've got to say what happened, finally do the right thing *and* clear your own conscience. And whatever Larry Durrant has done is then between him and *his* conscience. And Governor Candaret.'

The second that Nel-M saw Ayliss's Audi, he knew that he'd have to move quickly, couldn't risk leaving him together with Truelle for any length of time.

As soon as he saw Ayliss get out of his car and head across, he pulled his own car out from behind a tree where he'd tucked it when he'd first spotted the Audi, and edged a hundred yards closer. Then got out, deciding to do the rest on foot.

He gripped the Browning in one pocket as he went; the small plastic water bottle he'd picked up at Cienfuegos, now empty, makeshift silencer, was in the other.

The two figures by a table at the end of a promontory as he got closer, Ayliss taking a seat. A lot of talking, gesticulating and head-shaking, Nel-M concerned how long he could risk leaving it, but nervous about moving in yet; it was still light enough for them to see him approach. And as they did, one of them would probably rush to the main villa to alert Truelle's friend, with him then on the phone to the police. A nightmare before he'd started.

If he waited just eight or ten minutes more, it would be completely dark. He could move in without either of them seeing him. Until it was too late.

Nel-M waited on the setting sun.

'Most of the details came back out from Durrant pretty much how I'd fed them to him. Some were weaker, some stronger or even embellished with how, from his own psyche, he thought he'd have reacted. And some small details *never* did come out . . . unless maybe it was in police questioning that wasn't shown at trial.'

Jac nodded pensively. Maybe that explained some of the extra details and reactions from Larry in Ormdern's sessions. *Maybe.* Halfway through, Jac had taken out his cell-phone and put it next to the tape recorder in preparation to call Candaret.

Eleven minutes it had taken Truelle to pour out his soul, tell all. Eleven minutes to end twelve years of hell for Larry Durrant. The sun setting, the last light fading over the coast-line of Cuba as the first light of hope finally hit Larry Durrant, Jac thought ruefully.

Another minute for Truelle to wrap up the background, incidental details, and he'd call Candaret. As Truelle saw his eyes go to the phone, he lifted a hand up, as if he'd suddenly remembered something.

'Oh, and when you phone, apart from what you've now got on tape,' Truelle took a step to one side, reaching for his briefcase, 'there's something else that will—'

Truelle froze then, as if he'd been struck with an arrow. As he'd stood up, part of his field of vision had swung wider, and he stood transfixed, looking past Jac's shoulder.

Jac swung round sharply and stood up, the faint tread of footsteps reaching him in that same instant. *Malley . . . Nel-M!*

Nel-M smiled tautly as he moved closer, his gun at waist level trained on them.

'My, this is cosy. Very cosy indeed.' He moved a step closer, bringing their awkward triangle in tight to only three yards between them. 'So, what have you been telling him, Lenny?'

Truelle didn't answer. Jac saw him swallow, and was sure it was quiet enough to hear it if it wasn't for the buzzing back in his head.

Nel-M's eyes shifted to the recorder on the table, cassette still turning. 'Looks like I got here just in time. Would you?'

Nel-M indicated with his gun, but as Jac reached towards the recorder, Nel-M took a plastic bottle from his pocket, and with a 'On second thoughts – let me do that for you', shot through it.

Inches from his fingertips, Jac watched the recorder shatter, pieces flying as it spun off the table.

Jac's heart dived, eyes squeezing tight, *Last chance gone to save Larry . . .* Nel-M's figure bleary through salt tears as he opened them again, tilting gently . . . or maybe Jac was swaying, his legs suddenly uncertain as he took a step towards Nel-M.

Nel-M prodded the air with his gun, took half a step back to maintain the distance between them. 'Now let's not try and be brave.'

Then silence. Their triangle tenser now, eyes darting, measuring options. What few were left. Jac's pulse-beat was suddenly heavier at his temples, the thrum of the cicadas louder.

Jac noticed Truelle's eyes shift for a half-second towards the main villa, perhaps hoping that Calbrey might have heard the shot and come out. But it had been little more than a dull thud, and as Jac checked fleetingly too, Calbrey was still inside, French windows closed.

Nel-M followed their gaze for an instant; it was obviously something he'd thought of too. He wasn't going to hang around out here long.

Something, Jac thought desperately, surely *something* he could do. *If he could get Truelle out of this, then he could get him to speak to Candaret directly and . . .*

Then, as if answering his last two thoughts, Nel-M suddenly shot Truelle in the stomach, bringing him to his knees.

'No, no . . . *no!*' Jac's screams rose from deep within, impromptu, the buzzing in his head now so loud that he could barely hear them.

Nel-M's gun moved briefly towards him, as if he was unsure for a second who to kill first. *He who makes the most noise gets it.*

But then as the gun shifted quickly back to Truelle, levelling at his head, in that final second all Jac could think of was that last head shot in the police report . . . *Jessica Roche's sprawled body in the photos, meeting Larry for the first time . . . sharing a brandy with him that night . . . and Larry now, looking at the death-chamber clock, waiting for him to call . . .*

With a grunting wheeze, as if the last air was being pushed out of him, Jac suddenly propelled himself towards Nel-M.

Nel-M, distracted fleetingly by the sudden movement and noise, squeezed off the shot anyway. But in the beat's pause, Truelle started to move – the shot hitting him in the shoulder.

Then Nel-M's gun was swinging swiftly towards Jac.

Jac hit Nel-M full in the chest before the gun had completed its arc, the breath shunting out of him heavily as they stumbled back.

Nel-M's gun was swinging back towards him again, Jac gripping his arm before the barrel could point at him, wrestling, still falling back – and then suddenly the ground seemed to fall away beneath Jac's legs, them both spinning, tumbling through a small bush, and then into the air . . . *falling* . . .

In that final, blind-fury second, Jac hadn't paid any attention to how close to the promontory edge they were, or how far his momentum with all the Ayliss padding would carry them . . .

They hit the water quickly, no more than two seconds, the breath bursting out of Jac as something hit hard against his right shoulder, rock or coral a few feet beneath – then they were spluttering back up through the water, still grappling, Jac struggling to focus again on Nel-M.

Faint moonlight finally picked Nel-M out, dapples swilling back and forth, Nel-M's features twisted, distorted through the few inches of water between them as he tried to push Jac deeper under.

Gun! Jac choking, spluttering, trying desperately to see whether Nel-M still had it in his hand.

Writhing hard, pushing back – Jac managed to gasp two seconds of air before Nel-M thrust him back under, grappling at his neck and face.

Then suddenly Nel-M froze, his face wide-eyed as it swam in and out of focus in the water between them; Jac realizing in that instant that Ayliss's facial prosthetics had come away in Nel-M's hands, and Jac McElroy was suddenly staring up at him from beneath.

But Jac was still desperately trying to focus on Nel-M's gun hand, see if he still had it; and as he saw the wavering shadow of Nel-M's right arm move towards him and heard the shot, then another quickly after – saw and felt the warmth of his own blood swilling all around him in the water – he knew that Nel-M had.

And in those final seconds, as Jac saw Nel-M's face slowly fade as the water between them became deeper, darker, suddenly he was back in the lake again, sinking down through its dark depths; though this time he knew there was nothing to save him.

'It's time now, Larry.'

'I know.' Larry nodded dolefully.

The cell bolt slid back, the door opened, and Larry got up and joined Torvald and the six guards outside.

They walked three each side of him, Torvald slightly ahead, as they went along, their footsteps echoing starkly, emptily.

Gone from their eyes.

In the end, to be able to cope in the final moments, Larry had taken a leaf out of their book. If he'd already gone from their eyes, then all that remained was to shed the last vestiges of himself in his own mind.

He'd already considered it a good idea not to think about Josh and Fran, so that he didn't end up a quivering, blubbering wreck at the last moment.

And so, having rid himself of every good and warm past memory of Fran and Josh, all that remained was to cast off the rest: holding his hands up high after his first big boxing win, the pride in his mother's face – still there even when he fell into bad ways, her refusing to accept it – Roddy's sly smile as he told a joke or funny story, Sal in the library, BC in the muscle yard, passages from his favourite books . . . *sharing a brandy with Jac McElroy that night.* It didn't take long, wasn't too difficult, because there weren't that many good memories left. Libreville had eroded most of them already over the years.

Footsteps echoing emptily. And as he took the last few steps towards the death chamber, of all the years that he'd heard his own footsteps echoing like a ghost's through Libreville, only now was it finally in step with, fully mirroring, how he felt. *Empty.* Devoid of all memories, all feelings, all emotions.

Hands gently guiding him, laying him on the gurney. Hands of strong guards that could have pushed, but sensed in that moment that they didn't need to.

Larry looked through the glass towards the observation room as he was strapped down: Warden Haveling, Father Kennard, the prison psychiatrist, one of the medic team, a *Times-Picayune* journalist who'd visited him the day before and Larry had agreed to have there.

And as the last strap was secured, Larry smiled gently towards his audience – they probably thought that he'd finally snapped, gone mad, or that he'd made some sort of inner peace in his mind and was looking forward to going to God . . . *Ascension Day*.

But the thought that had hit Larry in that moment was how he'd robbed them, cheated them. They'd put on this big event, this circus – Governor's final thumbs down, scores of protesters and media trucks outside the prison gates, on every news channel with analysis and cross-analysis, pro and con death-penalty debates – to kill Larry Durrant.

But he'd robbed them of that privilege without them knowing it. The past long years at Libreville had already taken half the life out of him, and in the past hours he'd managed to strip and erode what was left. In the end, they weren't killing Larry Durrant at all. They were killing just a shell.

46

Black. Everything black.

But gradually some grey started to wash through, as if a gentle light was trying to seep in, soften the edges. Make the darkness not so absolute.

While the grey was softer, there was also some pain attached to it, and so the black felt warmer, more welcoming. He wanted to go back to it, where he'd been a minute ago. No pain.

A steady *beep . . . beep . . . beep* now too as more of the blackness swilled away and became grey, like an alarm going off. Prompting him gently, incessantly . . . wake up . . . wake up . . . *wake up*. But Jac thought: I'm dead. And surely that's the one advantage of being dead . . . not having to wake up to annoying alarms any more when you don't want to.

Beep . . . beep . . . beep . . . beep . . .

As the grey too started to swill away, get whited out, Jac opened his eyes and focused: a monitoring machine at his side steadily beeping, a nurse by the end of his bed checking a clipboard chart, looking up at him as his eyes flickered open.

'Ah, you are with us again?'

Jac looked down at himself, blinking, still trying to make sense of everything. '*But . . .* but I was shot?'

The nurse shook her head. 'No, señor, not you. You have a cracked shoulder joint, which was also dislocated, and a lot of water had to be drained from your lungs. It was the other man with you, *el hombre negre*. He was shot twice from behind.'

The blood warm and swilling all around him, maybe even too the last impetus of the bullets hitting Jac as they'd come straight through Nel-M. But it not computing in that instant that it could possibly have been Nel-M shot. Nobody there to shoot him? '*Who* . . . who shot him?'

The nurse shrugged. 'The police don't know. They are still investigating.'

But then the rest hit Jac, what he'd been there for in those final minutes, and he tried to sit up. *Larry!* His eyes shifted to the clock on the wall, 1.47 a.m., 11.47 p.m. in New Orleans, the tears welling, stinging his eyes. *Almost five hours since Larry had been executed!* And this time his father's die-hard tenet, *look on the bright side*, didn't, *couldn't* help; no bright side possible. The tears flowed freely, the nurse looking at him with concern.

'You shouldn't cry, señor. You're alive. You made it.'

'I know,' Jac said, wiping at the tears with the back of one hand. But that's half the problem, don't you see? he wanted to scream at her. *I feel ashamed to be alive.* Getting the proof to save Durrant and still letting him die made it all the more painful. *Unbearable.* 'It's . . . it's not me,' Jac explained. 'It's my friend.'

The nurse lifted her eyes hopefully. 'But your friend – he's made it too, señor. He was hurt much worse than you with a stomach wound, *muy malo* . . . but they've already operated and the surgeon thinks he'll pull through.'

Jac could see from a name-tag that she was called Carmita Terra. He shook his head as he realized she was talking about Truelle. 'No, not him – another friend. In New Orleans.'

'Oh.' She looked blank for a second, then, seeing how distraught he was, tears once again welling, she gave a tight-lipped grimace, her eyes softening. 'I am sorry to hear about your other friend, señor. So sorry.'

In those last minutes, Larry had stopped looking at the clock.

But everyone else started watching it all the more then; and as the final minute approached, their eyes were riveted to it. They could hardly shift them for one second to look at anything else.

None more so than Warden Haveling as he watched the second hand start on its final sixty-second sweep.

And everything suddenly fell deathly silent. Not only in the observation room looking onto the death chamber, but in the prison beyond, inmates looking up from their bunks with heavy, expectant eyes; the protesters outside, having stopped playing their music twenty minutes ago – even the mutter of their voices at that instant died as they looked on at the prison gates, breath vapours pluming gently on the cool night air; and half of New Orleans, too, hands halted mid-air with coffee cups or beers as live newscasts took them to reporters outside the prison gates in those final seconds.

Though two more people didn't look at the clock then. Josh Durrant, bedroom door shut, face down on his bed as he started sobbing. And Francine, TV off, refusing to acknowledge the time, tried to distract herself by preparing dinner, but her hands felt like lead, hardly able to move or pick up the right things; until, in the end, she wasn't able to move at all, her eyes gently closing as they filled, feeling those final seconds tick inside her with her laden heartbeat.

All of that silent expectation weighed heavily on Warden Haveling's shoulders as he watched the second hand make that final sweep; the silence so heavy that you could actually hear the clock ticking, making the seconds seem to pass more agonizingly, before finally, the last few seconds ticking down with the slow deliberation of full-swing axe-blows, Haveling gave a small, solemn nod towards Torvald Engelson.

Engelson acknowledged with equal solemnity, half-closing his eyes for a second, and then he lifted one hand towards the two medics.

They started feeding through the sodium thiopental.

Carmita's eyebrows furrowed at something Jac had said the moment before.

'*New Orleo*, señor? There have been some calls from there for you. Mickel something?' She looked towards the corridor outside. 'Your other friend in white brought your phone with him in case you needed to call anyone.'

Mike Coultaine. Calbrey. Jac nodded. 'Yes, I . . . I might need to make some calls.' But he was thinking more of calling Alaysha, telling her that he was all right and pouring out his soul, before hearing all the bad news from Coultaine. He wasn't sure he could face that news right now. But when Carmita returned with his phone a minute later and he tried Alaysha's number, there was no answer.

He scrolled down and looked at the time of Coultaine's calls: one forty minutes before Durrant's execution, no doubt to press for what was happening his end, *Not much time left now* . . . then two more since, one twenty minutes after and the other just over an hour ago to find out what had happened. Though Coultaine probably already half knew if he'd spoken to the hospital staff or Calbrey. With a tired sigh, Jac pressed to dial Coultaine back.

It answered after the first ring.

'Mike . . . it's Ayliss, uh . . . Jac.'

'Jac . . . *Jac*! Thank God! You're back in the land of the living!'

'Yeah . . . yeah.' Jac's voice subdued, not really wanting to share Coultaine's exuberance at him still being alive at that moment. He exhaled heavily. 'I'm sorry, Mike . . . I *tried*. And the damnest thing is, I had the proof right there in my hand at the last moment! Truelle had–'

'Jac . . . *Jac*! *Stop*! That's why I've been calling . . . there's still time!'

'*What*?' Jac sat up sharply, sudden lance of pain in his shoulder. 'What do you mean – *still time*?'

'Durrant got an injury the night before, which was stitched. But as the first of the knock-out feed came through and he strained against the straps, one of the stitches burst and the wound started bleeding. Head of the execution team, guy called Engelson, stopped it right there. It was re-stitched, medics then had to check and re-check him, the media here meanwhile having a field-day . . . and finally it was re-scheduled.'

'*When*?' Dizzy from sitting up so sharply, the room swam in and out of focus for a second.

'Midnight. Just over an hour from now.'

Jac's eyes darted frantically. The tape had been shattered, ruined! His eyes fixed back on the nurse. *Truelle*!

'Gotta go now, Mike. Got some fast shuffling to do.' And the second he hung up, he asked the nurse, 'My friend shot in the stomach – where is he? And how long before he comes round?'

'I . . . uh.' Momentarily flustered as to which question to answer first. 'Just around the corner, next *vestíbulo*. Not far. And a while.' She held one palm out. 'Though I can't say exactly how long. Only his doctor can answer that.'

'You'll need to give me a hand with these. I have to get up.'

'Señor, you're not meant to . . . *por favor*!'

But with Jac already half-up, seeing that he was going to rip all the tubes off in any case, she quickly attended. Detached the monitor links and IV and saline feeds.

'You'll have to show me where,' he said over his shoulder, already breaking into a run, Carmita struggling to keep up a few steps behind.

Jac felt the pain knifing through his shoulder sharper with each stride, the corridor tilting and shifting at one point, Jac bracing with a hand against one wall, afraid that he might be passing out again.

'His operation was only completed twenty minutes ago,' Dr Delgado, Truelle's surgeon, informed Jac when Carmita located him a minute later. 'So, at least another five or six hours before he comes round.'

Jac's stomach dived. 'Any possibility of sooner?'

Delgado shrugged. 'Three and a half, four hours perhaps. But you'd be lucky to get more than a few words out of him then – he'd still be very groggy.'

Jac cradled his head in one hand, rubbing at his temples, the buzzing back suddenly, the corridor swaying again and tilting away for a moment . . . *all options sliding away with it.* And towards its end he could see Brent Calbrey sitting, elbows on knees, hands steepled thoughtfully against his chin.

Friends . . . insurance policies! Truelle said that he'd left details of the whole thing in envelopes with them.

Jac went towards Calbrey and asked him. 'Left with close friends, apparently. Any idea who they might be?'

Calbrey shrugged. 'No, sorry. He didn't mention anything. I didn't know many of his friends Stateside.'

'*Both* killed recently,' Jac prompted. But Calbrey's expression remained vague. 'Are you sure he didn't say anything . . . *anything*?' The clinging desperation in Jac's voice echoing off the corridor walls as Calbrey shook his head.

Jac felt himself swaying uncertainly, the grey edges threatening to drag him back under. And in that moment it struck him that maybe it was better if they did, or if he hadn't woken up in the first place. To get *two* shots at saving Durrant, and still fail. The cruellest fate of all.

He asked Calbrey the time, 12.07 a.m., fifty-three minutes left now, but it hardly mattered, there was nothing left to –

Briefcase! As Calbrey checked his watch, Jac recognized it from Truelle reaching for it earlier '. . . *apart from what you've now got on tape, there's something else that will* . . .' Jac confirmed with Calbrey that it was Truelle's briefcase.

'Yes, I . . . I brought it with me because it's got his papers – including his blood group on a donor card.'

But Calbrey became hesitant when Jac pressed that there was probably something in it he needed urgently, and Jac's patience snapped. '*Look*! I don't have the time to fucking argue with you – I've got a man's life to save! You can sort it out with Truelle later whether or not you were meant to let me have it.'

Calbrey handed the briefcase over with a palms out, hey,

I'm not the enemy. It was me who fished you out of the sea, for Christ's sake.

Jac opened the briefcase, saw the buff envelope addressed to Truelle at the Sancti Spiritus *apartado* – ripped it open with trembling hands.

Cassette tape, nothing else inside as Jac tipped the envelope up. *Anthony Redmort* written on one side of the tape, no other wording. Jac began to worry that it was nothing to do with Durrant, just another patient's history.

Jac asked Carmita if there was a tape recorder somewhere in the hospital, and within three minutes she'd got one from another floor.

As Jac pressed play, Truelle's voice from twelve years ago – conditioning Durrant with all the details of the robbery and murder of Jessica Roche – echoed eerily along the corridors of the Sancti Spiritus hospital, Jac's voice crashing in after the first few sentences as he punched the air: 'Yes, yes . . . *oh, fucking yes!*'

Pain rocketed through his shoulder, even though he'd used his good arm, but he hardly cared at that moment. He dialled Candaret's number straightaway.

'Governor Candaret . . . Jaa . . . Darrell Ayliss. Larry Durrant's attorney. Earlier today, I received a full confession from Leonard Truelle, Larry Durrant's psychiatrist of twelve years ago, that he falsely conditioned Durrant in regard to the murder of Jessica Roche. All of this a conspiracy led by Mr Roche with a certain Nelson Malley doing his bidding – who in fact was probably the real murderer. And now a tape which categorically supports this, which I think you'd want to hear . . .' Jac played almost a full minute of the tape over the phone before bringing the receiver back to his ear. 'I've got the entire tape right here, Governor, but I think that's probably enough there to have given you the flavour.'

'I don't know, Mr Ayliss.' Candaret sighed, Roche's call still fresh in his mind. White House drifting out of reach. 'You call me now at the eleventh hour with a completely fresh account of the murder, supported by some tape from years ago played to me over the phone. It's not exactly conclusive.'

'The tape I've got here,' Jac's voice strained, breath staccato with exasperation, 'goes on for almost an hour – Truelle giving *every* possible detail of Jessica Roche's murder for Durrant to repeat at his next session. You can't get more conclusive than that.'

'I hear what you're saying, Mr Ayliss. But the problem I have with that is one of–'

'Governor Candaret,' Jac cut in, exhaling tiredly. 'I don't have the time now to fool around. And more to the point, nor does Larry Durrant.' Jac's patience was gone. Long gone from hit men, almost being drowned twice, police hunting him like a rabbit on a false murder rap. 'If you don't phone Libreville prison right away and stop Larry Durrant's execution – then when I get back to New Orleans, I'm going to make sure to get on every TV and radio show I can and play this tape. And when I do, I'm going to make it clear, *crystal clear*, that I played this same tape to you now in front of two good witnesses –' Jac nodded at his end, smiling tightly towards Carmita and Calbrey – 'and you *still* let Durrant's execution go ahead.'

Candaret's sigh was heavier this time, almost a groan. It looked like the White House was sliding out of reach now either way, but it would do so a lot quicker dragged through the media over Durrant than by Roche meddling in the background. He clarified a few details about the set-up between Roche, Truelle and Malley, then asked: 'And tell me, Mr Ayliss – did Mr Roche know earlier today that something on this front might be happening?'

'Yes, he did. In fact, he sent Malley to try to kill Truelle before he could talk.'

'I see.' Now Candaret understood that earlier call from Roche. There were a few things he hated, and being manipulated was one of them. He was a politician; that was *his* job.

'As . . . as soon as I get off the phone now,' Jac said, 'I've got to call the NOPD to pick up Roche. Not only for this now, with Durrant and the attempt on Truelle, but two other murders that I know of.'

'That's okay, Mr Ayliss.' His sigh now calmer, more satisfied. 'That's actually a call I'd like to have the pleasure of making myself. *After* I've called Warden Haveling to stop Larry Durrant's execution.'

Bye-bye waited until he'd reached Cienfuegos before he made the call.

'It's all done.'

'Clean? No hitches?'

'Some small last-minute complications, but I got aroun' them. Nobody saw me.'

'That's good to hear. See you soon. Give my regards to Fidel.'

Small complications? One thing you learnt working for Malastra over the years: play everything down so as not to raise the old lizard's blood pressure too high. As soon as he'd phoned Malastra from New Orleans airport to tell him that Nel-M was booked on a flight to Nassau, everything had been a mad rush: a suitcase dropped off for him complete with clothes, passport and a plastic Glock 17 that would pass undetected through airport X-rays. Then he'd had to call again from Nassau airport.

'He's heading onto Cuba.'

'I told you. I told you.' Malastra convinced that Nel-M somehow knew that they were on to him and was fleeing. 'Keep with him. Finish it.'

There'd been a brief opportunity when Nel-M had been sitting in his car looking on at the villa with the white Corvette – but then somebody came out of a house two up from where Bye-bye was parked to put out the garbage, and, the moment gone, he decided to wait until it was dark. Not long to go, nobody would see him then.

But as soon as it got dark, Nel-M was on the move.

Bye-bye followed and watched the tableau of figures on the promontory, hoping to get Nel-M as he came back his way. But when Nel-M tumbled over the edge with the other man, Bye-bye ran in. The third man was on the ground, looked like he'd blacked out or was already dead from his two shots. Bye-bye hoped for a minute that Nel-M might have got mangled on rocks or had drowned, save him the trouble; but looking down at them, he saw that Nel-M seemed to be on top of the other man, pushing him deeper under. He squeezed off two quick shots and ran back to his car.

In his office, Carmen Malastra smiled ruefully as he started deleting the whole sorry saga from his computer, the last to go the cam photos of Gerry Strelloff handing the envelopes to Raoul Ferrer.

They thought they'd worked it all out so well: Jouliern skimming off the tables, handing the money to Strelloff, then Strelloff handing to Ferrer. The rule was *only* casino employees checked; but even if there had been a spot check of Ferrer one night, he was a street loan-shark, he'd be expected to be carrying a lot of cash.

But Malastra didn't believe in coincidences, and that's where they'd slipped up, made their big mistake: the hit on Ferrer, with Nel-M even having the bare-faced cheek to call and apologize with some feeble excuse about Ferrer ripping-off Roche, and a sweetener pay-off to boot. That's Malastra thrown off the scent, Nel-M no doubt thought. Then Gerry Strelloff killed as well – *too much* of a coincidence – with someone else in the frame so that it didn't link back directly to Nel-M.

From that moment Malastra was on to it, and as he looked back through the video-cam footage of the casino floor and saw the envelopes being passed between Strelloff and Ferrer, he knew. He knew without any remaining shadow of doubt: Nel-M had been in on it with Jouliern from the start – he should have guessed earlier that it was a bit rich for Jouliern's blood to plan on his own – and Nel-M's part of it had been to get rid of the couriers in the middle so that there was no possible trace back.

But in the end, that's *exactly* what had alerted him: they'd tried to be too thorough, too clever. *Divine justice*, Malastra thought as he made the last delete key-tap.

When Alaysha had seen George Jouliern's name on the back of the envelope that the messenger held out, her heart leapt into her throat. A note from the grave: '*They know. They know it all. And they're coming to get you.*' Or maybe the messenger would now hand her a second note from Malastra: '*We found this letter addressed to you from George Jouliern. Just go quietly with the messenger, no fuss, into the car parked outside.*'

But the messenger simply smiled as he took her signature for George Jouliern's letter, and walked away.

Her hands still trembled faintly now as she read the letter again. How many read-throughs for it to finally sink home that it was all over? She was safe.

If you're reading this, then it means I'm no longer around and Malastra has probably put together the pieces of our little scam.

But with you trying to save your mother, out of all of us you were probably the only one to have noble, unselfish reasons for doing what you did, and that touched me. I knew too that you were only roped into all of this by Gerry. All in all, I thought it would be unfair if Malastra's hammer came down on you as well. So I took the precaution of erasing all the video-cam shots where you're passed the envelopes. Hopefully I've been successful in burying everything. Good luck with your mom.

Alaysha's eyes filled, and she closed them as a faint shudder ran through her. Hopefully, finally, shaking off the last of the nightmare. Jac too would be so pleased, so relieved to hear; but at that moment, it looked like he had more than enough on his plate.

The ups and downs and last-minute dramas of the Durrant case had filled every news channel throughout the day.

And when she did finally speak to Jac close to midnight and he told her breathlessly, 'I made it! That's it . . . it's official! They've stopped the execution!', it was as if the last of his nightmare was falling away from him too. Falling away with each excitable, faltering breath. He was quick to reassure that he was fine, just minor injuries, then, hardly pausing for breath, he told her the rest: the Sancti Spiritus post office, Truelle and Nel-M, the hospital, the delayed execution, the tape from Truelle's briefcase that finally saved the day. 'And then when I get hold of Candaret with just forty minutes to spare, he starts arguing the toss. I think that's the first time I've told a State Governor exactly what I thought of them.'

'Oh, Jac . . . *Jac*. That's great, *fantastic*! You must be ecstatic . . . not to mention exhausted.'

'Yeah . . . yeah.'

But at that moment, as Jac finally paused for breath, realizing that he'd talked non-stop for almost twenty minutes – or perhaps suddenly remembering that he still had one nightmare to sort out, his own false murder rap – and he asked how *she* was, Alaysha didn't mention anything, simply said she was okay.

'Fine . . . everything just fine here with me and Molly.'

This was *his* day. There'd be time enough for her to tell Jac when they were together face to face. Hopefully a lot of time.

47

Two Christmases.

It took eight days to clear up Jac's problems with his own false murder rap.

The first breakthrough came when Nel-M's rental-car was seen on a cam around the corner on St Joseph Street a minute after the murder. Then the timing of the calls on his cell-phone to Strelloff, and finally when the police searched Nel-M's apartment, they found a jacket with blood-spots that matched Strelloff's and fibres from the same jacket on the hallway outside Alaysha's apartment. The charges against Jac were dropped.

By then it was 16 December, and Jac was told that it might take yet another five days to sort out the immigration issues, *both* ends, caused by flying into Cuba falsely as Darrell Ayliss, and flying out again as Jac McElroy. Diplomatic machinations between the USA and Cuba were slow. So Jac phoned Alaysha and asked if she and Molly would like to spend Christmas in Cuba.

'There's this great beach near Havana – Playa Paraiso. Pure white sand, crystal clear Caribbean waters . . .'

Alaysha arrived with Molly four days later. And between playing on the beach with Molly in the day and sipping rum punches, candlelight lobster dinners, dancing the samba and making love at night, they'd get occasional calls from Mike Coultaine with updates on Roche. About right, Jac thought wistfully: their heaven while hearing about Roche's hell.

The first main detail to come out was about the DNA evidence, Roche apparently almost gloating over the ingenuity of the set-up. After his wife's death, he'd contacted Dr

Thallerey and asked him to send back her blood and ovary samples, '*Something to remember her by. I've even kept a lock of her hair . . .*' But he did so *after* Lieutenant Coyne had questioned Thallerey, so no suspicions were raised. Then Nel-M broke into Durrant's apartment and placed some spots of Jessica Roche's blood on one of his jackets.

'That's why Dr Thallerey was killed,' Coultaine explained. 'When they heard over your tapped line that you were planning to visit Thallerey, Roche feared that that detail might come out, and you'd put all the pieces together.'

The motive, though, behind killing his wife, Roche was more reluctant to talk about, and took another five days of police questioning to finally come out. Jessica Roche had suddenly become a keen 'green' and ecologist, and discovered a false report he'd had made by a marine survey company regarding water quality by one of his plants. She'd pushed him to become more green and make the necessary changes at the plant, and, when he dug in his heels, she threatened to blow the whistle.

'Roche said that he could have bitten the bullet over that one plant and made the changes – but he'd apparently been doing the same thing for the past eight years with false water-reporting at *all* his plants. And that's what he feared coming out.'

Far from the noblest of motives, Jac thought, but as Coultaine went on to explain, the resultant shares collapse from the news would have ruined Roche. Not to mention the five-year jail term for fraud.

Larry spent that first Christmas out of Libreville with Mack Elliott, though he had a full day with Franny and Joshua at a top downtown hotel, the Royal Sonesta, on Boxing Day. Turkey and all the trimmings, champagne and the best cigars, all courtesy of Governor Candaret's office. Gracious gesture, but also a great photo-opportunity with strong media points scored for Candaret's next year Presidential bid, Jac thought. He was becoming cynical.

It was a trait he found useful handling Larry's compensation claim against the State of Louisiana over the following months. Five hundred thousand dollars was offered, two million dollars was demanded, and they'd probably settle somewhere in-between on the courtroom steps.

The Durrant case was big news. The biggest. Criminologists and legal experts had started busily debating the ingenuity of the set-up against Durrant, and no doubt would for many years to come, and with talk from the police about Roche hyperventilating so hard under questioning that he almost collapsed a couple of times, the *Times-Picayune* came out with a story headline that had half of New Orleans smiling: '**A Breathless Set-up by a Breathless Man**'.

Torvald Engelson had played up the dramatics of saving Durrant at the first execution attempt, describing that last-second blood-drop as 'like an angel's teardrop', which, combined with Larry's heavy religious leanings, became another headline: '**Angel's Teardrop Saves the Man that Planned to go to Heaven**.'

And with all the hoopla, Jac was suddenly in demand. Beaton was keen to have him back, and there were offers too from three other firms, when Mike Coultaine called with a proposition. He admitted that he'd only retired early because he found old-man Beaton such a pain-in-the-ass, but he would love nothing more than to return and keep his hand in, say, three days a week. 'And it just so happens that Dale Keller, one of the best lawyers it's ever been my privilege to know – apart from Darrell Ayliss, of course – is also looking to hang up his own shingle.'

Jac liked the idea, it turned out that John Langfranc was also keen to jump ship – probably his only chance of ever becoming a full partner – taking far more loyal clients with him than Beaton had anticipated or was happy about. Two months after Christmas, Keller, McElroy, Coultaine & Langfranc was founded. Larry Durrant's compensation claim was one of their first main cases.

Durrant's case also opened the floodgates for other possibly false or questionable imprisonments. In the months that followed, they took on four more cases from Libreville's Death Row, one of which was that of Hector 'Roddy' Rodriguez. Jac launched a fresh appeal, arguing that while the day's delay before Rodriguez visited his victim looked like premeditation – it was not to murder, since Rodriguez had only gone there to warn the man off; it was his victim's violent reaction to that visit that led to the murder. Jac was seeking a reduction to manslaughter and a 'time-served' sentence. Chances were high.

There'd also been some re-shuffling at Libreville: Haveling was still there, but Bateson and two more of his clique had been suspended pending enquiries, while Tally Shavell had been transferred to Wetumpka Penitentiary in Alabama, where apparently they had an even harder-assed prison fixer. The bets were that if Shavell didn't keep his head down low there, he wouldn't last more than six months.

Alaysha stopped lap-dancing five months later, when, having turned more of her attention to interior decoration, her client list finally started to grow. She also started to become franker about telling people that she used to lap dance, stopped trying to cover up or being embarrassed by it.

'And now?' they'd ask.

'The same. Except now it's just for an audience of one.' A saucy glance at Jac as she joked.

Jac's mother had also broken out more on her own, finally getting her work visa and with her past art expertise landing a job at a gallery on Chartres Street two days a week, which within three months became full-time. She and Jean-Marie moved out of Aunt Camille's place in Hammond and into their own place in Bywater, only a mile from Jac and Alaysha.

With Jac busy with the new company, he and Alaysha had stayed as neighbours, constantly in and out of each other's apartments, and while they'd talked about getting a place together, they didn't finally start house-hunting until late summer – just as *Katrina* hit.

The hurricane completely transformed the city. Some districts, like the Ninth Ward, were totally flattened, and when they were re-built would never be the same again. The most vital criterion for New Orleans house-hunters would for ever now be 'find a place on high ground'.

Everything from the new firm was shifted in box files to a makeshift office in Baton Rouge, and when they finally returned six weeks later, the city still looking like a war-zone and the smell of damp seeping through their newly painted walls, Coultaine commented, 'Oh well, just think of all the compensation and re-building claims.' Jac shook his head and smiled wryly. As bad as his father: *always look on the bright side*.

Larry's compensation was finally settled soon after they moved back into New Orleans: $1,500,000.

Larry had been seeing Joshua regularly every other weekend and some weekdays too, and whether from that pressure or other problems between Francine and Frank – apparently things had become increasingly tense between them – they finally split up just a month before *Katrina* hit.

Larry and Francine started seeing each other tentatively again then: occasional dinners out, or often she'd cook dinner for them all when Larry came round to see Joshua. When the compensation paperwork was being completed, Larry remarked to Jac how scared he was by the whole process. 'So afraid of making the same mistakes as last time. It's . . . it's like starting out all over again.'

You *and* the city, Jac thought, but when he told Alaysha, she thought it was cute, touching. 'Almost like they're teenagers on their first dates all over again.'

Jac and Alaysha started looking at houses again in late November, and finally found a place on the West Bank at Algiers Point – a period bungalow with great river views from its front terrace – to move into just a week before Christmas.

Their first Christmas with family – Jean-Marie, his mother and Alaysha's – since the nightmare of a year ago.

It was a mad rush. They were still unpacking boxes from their apartments as they put the last decorations on the Christmas tree. And as Jac opened one of their Christmas cards, he suddenly paused, his eyes starting to fill.

It was from Larry.

Jac, thanks for everything! Josh told me that he'd never seen snow before, so I thought it was a good idea to bring him and Fran up here to Aspen.
Merry Christmas!

But it was the small Polaroid inside that had brought a lump to Jac's throat: Larry with an arm around Franny and Josh each side, the three of them by a snow-laden fir tree as they smiled at the camera.

Hands trembling as the emotions gripped him, Jac passed the photo to Alaysha. 'Isn't that . . . that picture worth a thousand—'

Alaysha, hearing the tremor in his voice, simply touched one finger against his lips, seeing in his eyes in that moment all the softness and vulnerability that had first drawn her to him; and as she looked at the photo and felt the tears softly sting her eyes too, she started planting gentle kisses where a second ago her finger had been. 'Yes, it is, Jac . . . yes it is.'

And Jac, feeling those kisses, was reminded of all the times in the dead of night when he'd suddenly find himself back in the dark water, struggling to make it to the surface, *breathe again* . . . and Alaysha would lay the same kisses on one cheek as she shook him gently back awake, 'Are you okay, Jac . . . *are you okay?*'

The dreams were less frequent now, the stark, chilling memories fading with each passing month – until finally, hopefully, they'd be like Larry Durrant's memory of being at the Roche house that night all those years ago.

Someone else's memory, not even his.

He just wanted a decent book to read ...

Not too much to ask, is it? It was in 1935 when Allen Lane, Managing Director of Bodley Head Publishers, stood on a platform at Exeter railway station looking for something good to read on his journey back to London. His choice was limited to popular magazines and poor-quality paperbacks – the same choice faced every day by the vast majority of readers, few of whom could afford hardbacks. Lane's disappointment and subsequent anger at the range of books generally available led him to found a company – and change the world.

'We believed in the existence in this country of a vast reading public for intelligent books at a low price, and staked everything on it'
Sir Allen Lane, 1902–1970, founder of Penguin Books

The quality paperback had arrived – and not just in bookshops. Lane was adamant that his Penguins should appear in chain stores and tobacconists, and should cost no more than a packet of cigarettes.

Reading habits (and cigarette prices) have changed since 1935, but Penguin still believes in publishing the best books for everybody to enjoy. We still believe that good design costs no more than bad design, and we still believe that quality books published passionately and responsibly make the world a better place.

So wherever you see the little bird – whether it's on a piece of prize-winning literary fiction or a celebrity autobiography, political tour de force or historical masterpiece, a serial-killer thriller, reference book, world classic or a piece of pure escapism – you can bet that it represents the very best that the genre has to offer.

Whatever you like to read – trust Penguin.

read more
www.penguin.co.uk